A Song Twice Over

by the same author

The Clouded Hills
Flint and Roses
The Sleeping Sword
Days of Grace
A Winter's Child

A Song Twice Over

BRENDA JAGGER

William Morrow and Company, Inc.
New York

Library of Congress Cataloging-in-Publication Data

Jagger, Brenda, 1936–
A song twice over.

I. Title.
PR6060.A425S66   1986   823'.914   85-15586
ISBN 0-688-06169-9

Printed in the United States of America

2 3 4 5 6 7 8 9 10

BOOK DESIGN BY JAYE ZIMET

A Song Twice Over

1

*T*hat a woman with a child in her arms and little more than the price of a train ticket in her pocket is in need of a man to help her must be quite certain. Therefore Cara Adeane, sailing from hunger in Ireland to no great certainty of eating her fill in Liverpool, could not long delay in making her choice.

She had come aboard the ship in darkness, endured an unspeakable, overcrowded night on a hard plank bench, her child sleeping—or perhaps simply shocked to silence—in the folds of her skirt. But now, on this new morning of sun-streaked cloud and salt breezes, having somehow managed to smooth her hair, to freshen her cheeks and even fluff out the feather in her bonnet, she had found herself a place on the open deck, a vantage point on a bale of sacking where she sat with great composure, looking as if she had slept all night in a feather bed.

She was nineteen years old, traveling alone with two carpetbags, a heavy, three-year-old child, a parasol and now, with Liverpool only an hour or so away, was in a considerable hurry to make the acquaintance of someone who might be willing to carry them ashore.

A man; as young and well-muscled and obliging as possible. And although there were a great many of them crowding the deck all around her she could tell, at a glance, that they would not do, being diggers of ditches and cultivators of potato patches from the far western shores, sailing—on this vessel of dubious antiquity, its belly sagging far beneath the waterline with its dead weight of grain, its live weight of cattle and pigs—to swell the ranks of their fifty thousand fellow-countrymen who annually crossed the water to England at this season.

For this year of 1840 was no particular year of famine, no lean year as years went—there being no fat years in Ireland—but simply the summer time, the hungry time when, with the old potatoes running out and the new crop not yet in, it seemed better to any lusty lad who was able, to dig English canals and build English railways than sit idle-handed and empty-bellied at home.

But none of these cheerful and, in many cases, handsome laboring men could hope to be of service to Miss Cara Adeane, herself city-bred, city-wise; no barefoot, shawl-wrapped country girl from a mud cabin but a young woman of a certain, hard-earned experience in the world, who wore real kid boots on her feet and a proper straw hat on her head like a lady.

Though she was not a lady of course, and saw little point in pretending, her father being the black sheep of a Dublin family of small shopkeepers and schoolmasters, her mother a Frenchwoman, a skilled embroideress, who had once earned her living as a maid: Cara's own status in the world remaining serenely *un*married despite the solemn, sleepy infant curled up at her side.

She was not ashamed of her son. Such a thing had never crossed her mind, her present need being not to apologize for him but to convey him—and her carpetbags and parasol—with as little effort as she could contrive from this ship to a train which would take her to Manchester; another train, or perhaps two if the line remained unfinished, to Leeds; and then—with luck—by wagon to the smaller Pennine town of Frizingley, ten miles away from any railway track, where her parents awaited.

A natural state of affairs in her experience, for the pattern of her life had always consisted of following the trail blazed by her father, whimsical, beguiling Kieron Adeane, self-styled doctor of law or philosophy or music or whatever else might promise him a passing advantage, for whom the grass on the other side of the mountain was always infinitely more enticing, and whose habit it had always been to rush off alone to "establish himself" at the end of each fresh rainbow, before sending for his family to join him.

He had "sent for them" from the four green corners of Ireland; time and time again from Dublin; twice before from England. He had "sent for them" from Scotland and even from France. As a child Cara had been taken to him by a mother who never seemed fully alive unless she was by his side. As a grown woman—for so she had considered herself these several years past—she had sometimes resisted his blandishments, taking a road of her own until freedom, quite suddenly, had fallen flat, rebellion turned stale, and hastily packing her bags, she had run to him.

As she was doing now. As she supposed she always would. Sometimes to her advantage. Usually not. Although she tended to believe, with her father, that no experience could be wholly bad if one could learn at least—well—a smattering of something or other from it. And the many roads she had traveled with her father had taught her much.

There had been Edinburgh, for instance, her father involved in some chemical enterprise, some hair restorer or youth restorer guaranteed to make him rich, while Cara, in a dark brown cavern of a shop, had acquired the art of pinning sumptuous velvets and brocades around well-corseted, middle-aged posteriors; and the even more essential art of flattery, so inseparable from the dressmaking trade.

There had been a sour back room in Manchester—departure from Scotland having become urgent when the hair restorer had produced little but sore patches and spots—where, in a windowless, nauseous space, she had stitched fine cambric shirts for gentlemen until her fingers bled. She had learned endurance from that. Not patience precisely, but the art of biding her time. And holding her temper.

There had been the fresh green breezes of Kilkenny soon after, her father having invented, or purchased the invention, of a new brand of pony-nut, Cara feeling herself almost on holiday in a graceful Georgian mansion where, in her trim parlormaid's apron and cap, she had answered the door, dusted the china, and acquired not only a great many cast-off skirts and bodices and silk stockings, but a store of secondhand gentility.

There had been milliners' shops and silk mercers' shops of many descriptions, both in Ireland and in France, where she had worked her twelve hours every day behind the counter and slept under it—as befits an apprentice—every night. There had been a common lodging-house once—in fact twice—where she had boiled soup in greasy vats for seamen and dockers and shared her wages with her father, in need of money to pay for his defense when his pony-nuts had been accused of causing somebody's mare to die of the colic, and with her mother, whose nerves, that year, had been somewhat in decline.

Hard times, she supposed, although she had never seen much sense in brooding. Particularly when her father, after all, had escaped conviction and the transportation to Australia which had threatened. Her mother's nervous collapse had not taken place, or at least not so totally as she had been warned to expect. And Cara had given up her own drudgery in the lodging-house kitchen and gone to work for a fanmaker.

One did what one could and usually—as her father always told her—enough could be salvaged to begin again. And always, in the background of her life, shimmering with all the colors of her father's brightest and most distant rainbow, was the promise of "money from America"; the legacy from her father's sister, Miss Teresa Adeane, who kept a bakery in mythical New York and who had no one except her brother—said Kieron Adeane—to whom she could possibly wish to leave it. And, in the meantime, who knew which bright morning would bring a letter begging them all to set sail at once and join her? Enclosing the passage-money, of course, and a little something left over for new coats and shoes for Cara, so as not to disgrace "dear Aunt Teresa" before her friends.

As a child Cara had dreamed of it sometimes quite feverishly, believing it would happen tomorrow, and then, when she understood that even to her father it was little more than a comforting fable—a shred of hope being better at times than no hope at all—she had put it to the back of her mind. For this Aunt Teresa of America had most bitterly resented the "throwing away," as she had once savagely phrased it, of her clever brother on a French lady's maid and therefore could hardly wish to share the rich, full life of her bakery with a mongrel niece she had never seen and a sister-in-law whose existence she had never brought herself to acknowledge.

The "money from America" would remain a dream. So said Odette Adeane, Cara's patient, soft-voiced mother. And since she rarely spoke out on any subject with conviction, her husband—whose current series of lectures on the evils of tight-laced corsetry and the consequent advisability of purchasing his new brand of smelling salts did not seem to be drawing the crowds—had paused in the addressing of another affectionate missive to his "dearest sister Teresa" and decided, at the toss of a verbal coin, to try his luck in England once again, in a certain West Yorkshire town where a friend, "a capital fellow, the kind one can stake one's life on," had spoken to him of work.

Not an offer, of course. Not directly. But if work of the right caliber existed, with prospects, opportunities, high expectations of advancement, then who better than Kieron Adeane to seize them?

He packed his bags that very day.

"I'll make you a queen in England, Odette my love," he vowed, hand on heart, to his wife.

"Yes, Kieron. I know."

They both were compelled to believe it. Kieron Adeane because, without this faith in himself, what had he? Odette because, after these twenty precarious years, she was still in love.

"I'll go forward, my darling, and send for you." Four months later he had done so. And now, four months after that, he had sent ship-money and train-money and wagon-money to Cara, urging her to forsake the mounting and painting of fans and to join her loved ones, his invitation sparkling with good spirits and good luck.

He had secured a managerial situation in a textile factory, he wrote to her, where, in view of the number of Irish immigrants employed, his services were fast becoming invaluable, his standing in the thriving Irish community very high.

(A clerk, translated Cara, reading expertly between his lines, adding and subtracting his ledgers for twelve cramped hours a day and making a little extra composing letters home to Ireland, sent by men who could not write to families who could not read.)

While Odette too, the letter went on, had found excellent employment with a local milliner, a spinster lady of an age to see in Odette the daughter she had always wanted, and who seemed, moreover, most touchingly to appreciate such advice on certain practical matters, as Kieron himself had been glad to offer. An elderly woman alone, after all . . . ? Who knew? Great things might be expected in the fullness of time.

(A few years of servitude and spite, translated Kieron's daughter, dancing attendance on an old woman's whims and fancies just to find an unsuspected cousin or nephew at the funeral holding out a legitimately greedy hand.)

There had been "expectations" such as these before. And it seemed to Cara—the letter still held speculatively between her fingers—that fan-painting was not really such an arduous trade. Yet—and somehow she could not stop herself from reading the letter twice over—her mother and father appeared to be well-lodged in this northern town of Frizingley, this monstrously expanding industrial miracle, as much the creation of industrial machinery as the steam engines and power looms which caused it to keep on doubling and redoubling its size. A town where gold could be found in plenty among the engine grease and grime, where one could sense it—as *she* could sense her father's excited desire for it—glinting through the ever present pall of factory smoke, illuminated by the sudden flare of molten iron from a foundry, its prevailing harmony being the hissing and belching of industrially harnessed steam.

Not a pretty place. But the Adeanes had good beds there—she had her mother's word for that—good coal fires, good bread, shop-bought meat pies, *opportunity*. And what a pleasure, wrote Odette, to see, through all the smoke and dust, so many fine carriages and high-stepping horses, so many finely dressed ladies in high-plumed hats. How *advantageous*, wrote Kieron Adeane to *his* daughter, to place oneself in such close proximity to the rich.

He had "sent for her" once again.

"We are comfortably settled, my little love." Well—possibly. But it had taken the feel of his money in her hand to convince her; and then not entirely.

"Your mother misses you—and frets herself cruelly for our little Liam."

Yes, of that much she was quite certain. And she needed no more than the evidence of her own eyes to know how much the child Liam was fretting for his *grand'maman* Odette.

And so since it was, after all, the summer time, the hungry time, with fans not much in demand anymore and employment for a lone woman and child precarious at any season, she had packed her bags, her skills, her little son and set sail once again across the water.

Her expectations were not immense. But adequate. Realistic. A good bed. A meat pudding. Her mother's gently flowing affection which both she and Liam had been sorely missing. That much—surely? And beyond it, not riches, no fabled "money from America" or anywhere else, but, nevertheless, a view of herself to which her circumstances did not entitle her, a conviction that Fate had never really intended her to be poor. Had Fate blundered then? Her father had always believed so. She believed it too.

Yet, for the moment, here she was on the deck of a creaking cargo boat, sitting on a bale of sacking about whose inner contents she did not wish to inquire, her child, exhausted by the journey, hardly stirring beside her, silent, lethargic, unwilling to support his own weight on his own two legs since there was nowhere *he* particularly wished to go.

She had developed her own manner of never quite explaining his existence in the world.

"A bonny boy," some woman or other seemed always to be remarking, the inevitable question already half spoken.

"Yes," she would reply demurely smiling. "Thank you."

"And his father? Is he . . . *gone?*"

And with all the patiently controlled sorrow of a young widow—and there were many of those in Ireland—she would cast down her eyes and release a faint, resigned sigh.

"Oh yes—gone. So young, too. Oh dear . . . I try to *accept*—isn't that right? . . . do the best I can?"

Not the truth, of course, but not entirely a lie since her lover had indeed "gone," although no farther than his home in Donegal and then to America, parting from her before either of them had realized her condition. And if it struck her later that he ought to have taken the possibility into consideration then, in all fairness, so, she concluded, ought she.

"I'll send for you, Cara."

His words had been very familiar.

And when she had understood, from his letters, that the "New Life" he had dreamed of had nothing particularly new about it after all; that, just as in Donegal, he could barely keep himself in buttermilk and potatoes, much less scrape together the wherewithal to maintain a pregnant bride, it had seemed pointless even to mention it. What, after all, could he have done had he known, except worry and feel ashamed of himself? And she had chosen to spare him that.

Her own mother, Odette, had looked after her, welcoming the baby, Liam, like a rare jewel. Kieron, her father, had sat with her through her long labor, telling her tales of Kings and Empires and high adventure, telling her she was beautiful. She needed no others. She had been sixteen then. She was nineteen now and had taken care ever since to preserve her virtue as the only means she knew of avoiding unwed motherhood again. For if once might be judged unfortunate and could be accommodated, twice must surely be seen as slatternly or dull-witted. And she was neither.

When she thought of her lover now, it was none too clearly and without rancor. She *knew* she had loved him but could no longer quite remember the feeling. Nor was she consciously aware of any unusual degree of tenderness for her child. Did she make professions of love, after all, for her own shoulder-blades or her elbows? Hardly. But she took good care, just the same, that they were well nourished and warm, and would make short work of anyone who threatened them with harm. Her solemn black-eyed Liam seemed as naturally a part of her as that. And he had his pretty *grand'maman* Odette, more often than not to croon to him and cosset him, to dote on him so exclusively that when he spoke at all, which was seldom, his accent was wholly, delightfully French.

Yet it was really on his account that she stood in such urgent need of a man's help in Liverpool.

Without Liam she could have gone ashore as freely as any of the country lads around her, as hardy and fit for work as they, to be seen by the port authority as another pair of hands for the loom or the plow, capable of fending for herself without recourse to charity. But a lone woman with a child in her arms might be required to convince some official person somewhere along the hard road to Frizingley that she was truly expected there, rather than simply making one among the two or three million Irish who came close to starvation every summer, fair harvest or foul; a growing multitude for whom no work existed, and who knew that if they could somehow scuttle aboard a ship for England, then the English Poor Law—before shipping them back again—would be quite likely to give them a hot dinner.

And since Cara was not entirely convinced that the trains her father had mentioned really did run from Liverpool to Manchester and then to Leeds, nor by any means certain that, once in Leeds, she would actually find, at the address he had given, a carter willing to take her to Frizingley on the terms he professed to have arranged, she felt her need of a traveling companion to be great.

A man, young enough and presentable enough to match a woman in kid boots and a straw traveling bonnet with silk ribbons, strong enough to carry her two shabbily bulging yet infinitely precious carpetbags ashore while she managed her son, so that anyone who might be watching—Poor Law Guardian, brothel keeper, sweatshop man— might see them as a couple and not trouble her. A man, best of all, who might have reasons of his own for wishing to avoid official scrutiny and so might be persuaded not only to put her on her train but to accompany her some part of her way. And if he expected to be amorously rewarded then she would make promises and break them with a clear conscience, it being her firmly held opinion—since the birth of Liam—that men, having nothing to lose from sexual encounters, ought only to ask such favors at their peril from women who most certainly did.

A man; not a gentleman, of course, since one did not encounter members of that particular species on the deck of a cargo boat, lounging among the baggage, but someone *likely*, who looked as if he might belong to her. Or she to him. Although she was not in the habit of regarding the relationship of man to woman in quite that fashion. And her practiced eye had already seen him, last night as she came on board, leaning against the deck-rail above her, watching while she negotiated the shaky gangplank with her carpetbags and her son, sure of her balance—precarious pathways being much as usual in her experience—her mind busy with her current necessities, her senses wary.

A man. She had looked up and there he was, young and lean and straight as an arrow, no bulk about him but a taut, whipcord strength promising toughness and the kind of well-paced, well-disciplined stamina she understood; a dark, clever face, a cool stare following her with an insolence and speculation to which she was no stranger; following her again this morning as she had picked her way across the deck—looking for *him* although he could not know it—positioning himself neither too close to her nor too far.

"Good morning," she had said crisply in passing, to let him know that he had stared long enough, speaking English words with only the merest hint of Ireland, a whisper of France, on her tongue. He had smiled, raised his hat, a little shabby she'd noticed—like her own—but at least a proper curly-brimmed beaver, not a common corduroy cap, and sweeping past him, managing despite the carpetbags and the stranglehold of Liam to make her skirts glide and sway with the weight of the half-dozen stiffened petticoats beneath them, she had installed herself on this bale of something reasonably soft and odorless and remained there, waiting for him.

He did not come at once. Others, indeed, came before him and were rejected calmly, pleasantly, in accordance with her policy of offending no one, since who knew what she might need before the day's end? She had seen his interest and unless someone else should arouse more of it . . . ? The brim of her pale straw bonnet shading her eyes from the brilliance of summer sky and sea, she glanced swiftly around the deck, encountering no one among the women to challenge her. Just an unlettered country girl here and there and a

few sad little wraiths of women, widows every one, draping themselves like empty shrouds over fretful children who, unlike her own
drowsy, dreamy Liam, persisted, despite the perfect sailing weather,
in whining and feeling sick.

The young man in the beaver could have no use for these.

"Good morning," he said a half hour later, his voice as neutral as
her own, a traveling man whose accent, too slight to be easily identified, would strike no false notes anywhere, and whose keen eyes,
accustomed like hers to planning his route ahead while, at the same
moment, guarding his back, had already measured her shabby, styl-
ishly cut woollen dress against his own faintly threadbare but fashionable broadcloth coat and narrow trousers, the flamboyance of his
scarlet neckcloth against the vanity—and the weight—of her flaring
petticoats. And it seemed to him that a woman who would so over-
burden herself in these cramped and dangerous conditions for her
pride's sake, was not to be despised.

Nor to be easily handled either. But if anyone watched for him, as
they might, in Liverpool, they would be looking for a man alone,
moving fast and light without baggage, not a man with a sleepy,
heavy child, two carpetbags, a woman with long black hair and sea-
blue eyes. And in any case he was a young man in whom passion of
many kinds was quickly stirred, impulsive by nature, taking risks for
the pleasure they gave him; and from the moment he had first caught
sight of her on the quayside dragging her burdens as if she rather
pitied all those who did not possess them, he had understood two
things. He would approach her because she could be of use to him and,
even had it been otherwise, he would have approached her anyway.

"My name is Daniel Carey."

"Cara Adeane."

"Where are you bound?"

"Frizingley in Yorkshire."

"I'm going to Leeds."

And they smiled at the same moment with the same satisfaction,
the same self-congratulatory pleasure in having chosen right.

They were traveling in the same direction.

"And is there no one to meet you in Liverpool, at all?"

"No one."

"You'll be needing help then, I'm thinking."

She smiled and nodded, making a helpless gesture at her bulging
carpetbags with long-fingered, brown-skinned hands which had no

real helplessness in them whatsoever. No wedding ring either, he was quick to notice, although he felt no urge to condemn her for that, his own inclinations being far from domestic, his tolerance for the sins of the flesh extremely broad.

"Then if you will allow me to assist you . . . ?"

Of course she would. What else might she allow? For another half hour her bright, bold eyes smiled and seemed to make promises in direct contrast to the careful pitch of her voice as softly, demurely, she offered the picture of herself she wished him to see. And when he leaned a little closer, hearing only the unspoken promises, she inquired suddenly but just as demurely, "Is it no baggage you have, then?"

"None to speak of."

She smiled at him. "Daniel Carey, how does that happen? What can you be running away from? *Home?*"

He returned her smile, his dark, shrewd eyes meeting her shrewd, blue ones and holding them a moment in a kind of acknowledgment. A recognition. He was twenty-three years old and "home" had been very long ago, an impression, merely, at this distance, from which he could gain nothing now by remembering.

"Home" had ended suddenly, very savagely, forcing him overnight, as one forced hot-house plants, from a serious, studious child to a disciplined, tempered man, and he knew that this girl did not really care what—if anything—he might be running from now. What mattered to her was the convenience of his protection on her way to Leeds. What mattered to him was getting there, and then the next place. The one after.

They were two coins disturbingly alike on one side, dangerously dissimilar on the other. He was a young man who believed in grand designs and complex ideals of truth and freedom. While Cara Adeane, on that golden summer morning, believed in nothing but herself.

"Have you made the crossing before?" he asked her.

"That I have. Twice before. And you?"

"I come and go."

Yes. She had understood that much about him at once. And she supposed that the authorities—who did not care for *too* much talk of freedom when they remembered what it had led to in France—while not snapping at his heels precisely, had already started to be *curious* about him, just beginning to take notice of his "comings and goings" and the identity of his friends.

Not a wicked man. Not a criminal. Just someone—and the Adeanes had always known plenty of those—who wanted something that others did not wish to have. The opening of English ports to cheap foreign corn perhaps to make the price of bread more reasonable. Or the right of the common man to vote at election time. Even a secret ballot so that he could use his vote against his landlord if he chose, or against his employer without fear of losing his cottage or his job. None of these things being greatly to the taste of landlords and employers like the Duke of Wellington or my lords Melbourne and Palmerston and the rest of the Queen's ministers who seemed forever alarmed that the revolution of the common man, which had begun so bloodily and not really so very long ago, in France, might spread with its tumbrils and guillotines and its Rights of that dangerous common Man, to London Town.

And to which particular brand of Liberty, Equality or Fraternity, she wondered, might Daniel Carey subscribe? For she knew every one of them by heart, having heard them expressed heatedly, poetically, violently, evangelically, in every lodging-house and workshop and servants' hall she had ever frequented, while she had listened, smiled, agreed with each and every solution and put her faith in none. So that she felt no concern—why should she?—about the exact cause for which Daniel Carey chose to risk himself, as she supposed he did, or to go hungry for, as it seemed he sometimes must by the pared-down, fine-drawn look of him. He was just a man, after all, who would take advantage of her if he could. Unless she put a stop to it. Or seized her own advantage first.

Yet his lean, dark face had an oddly slanting smile of a kind she had never seen before, a sudden, entirely *different* smile at which she had to stop herself from looking, while his eyes—flecked with brown and amber like an agate stone—kept on looking openly at her, seeing her too clearly for either her comfort or her vanity, so that she found herself bending her neck to show him the heavy black gleam of her hair, displaying her hands, too broad and brown and capable for good-breeding but which had never yet cut peat or dug potatoes and did not intend ever to try. Wanting his admiration. Knowing, quite soon and with a deeply felt satisfaction, that it was hers.

"And what do you do in the world, Daniel Carey?"

"Oh—what I can. I am a schoolmaster sometimes."

That could hardly impress her when her father had half a dozen brothers—dry as dust, he called them—who did the same.

"And have you been to France?"

"I have."

That was better. Indeed, it was the highest proof of sophistication, in her eyes, that he could offer. Although—since poor schoolmasters did not go to France for a whim or a fancy—it also marked him as someone who had found it expedient to leave his own country for a while, a political exile in Paris as she had been a financial one, who had concerned himself far more with the rights and wrongs of his fellow men than with the embroidered satins and osprey feathers which *she* had found so enchanting.

"What did you do there?"

"I looked about me."

"And what do you do now?"

He gave her a slight bow and his faintly slanting smile.

"Oh—shall we say—yes, let's say that I escort beautiful strangers on their way to Leeds."

She neither expected nor wanted him to say more. And it sufficed, in any case, for her to label him as a dangerous acquaintance who could disappear to suit his own need at the very moment when she might need him the most. And it was in her mind, therefore, from the start, that it would be foolish—most foolish—ever to need him *too* much at all.

Handsome, of course. And exhilarating—if she had the leisure, one day, to be exhilarated in that particular fashion. A challenge to the mind and the senses. But so was her father. And she could see little difference between the dreams of Kieron Adeane, professor of grandiose schemes, creator of false and fascinating rainbows, and the dreams of another kind which she had detected in Daniel. The result, in both cases could be the same. Cheap lodgings, darned linen, a gnawing, never-ending anxiety about the payment of a doctor's bill, a pawnticket, the rent. And although her mother had settled patiently and sweetly for a lifetime hovering on the fringes of such disaster, Cara already knew that she could not.

Stirring against her side her son, Liam, opened eyes as dark and velvet-textured as the heart of a violet and, finding the sea too vast for his contemplation, the sky too distant and nothing else to interest him on the crowded deck—crowds being his natural habitat—burrowed down into the folds of his mother's skirt and fell asleep again. Or at least appeared to sleep. She was never sure. For he had been very quiet since Odette, his adored *grand'maman*, had sailed for England, leaving him behind. Too quiet? Had she allowed herself to dwell on it she may well have thought so. But she had had enough to do, surely, with finding the means to feed him and clothe him, running all over Dublin tracking down work wherever it could be found, and in her fatigue and flurry she had not encouraged her son to prattle. Had she even told him, in any way he could understand, that now—at last—she was taking him to Odette? Glancing down at him, feeling the sharp tug of almost anguished affection she often felt for him but rarely managed to express, she hoped so.

"A fine child," said Daniel Carey, meaning it, for he had once been a silent, secretive boy himself, observing the world minutely, critically even then, basking in the adoration of a mother as handsome as this one, although softer, sweeter; a saddened woman—her image fading now in his recollections—who often reminded him how overwork in the cause of the mass of suffering, downtrodden humanity had killed his lawyer father. A woman meticulous in the discharging of her social and charitable obligations, who had taken him driving in a carriage piled high with lilac silk cushions, delivering invitations to reform meetings to her friends and blankets to the poor, until a soldier, faced with the sudden menace of an angry crowd during a famine year—did it matter which?—had fired wide as they drove by and put an end to her.

But it was a long time now since he had dreamed of red stains on lilac upholstery; and on his hands.

He had gone to France, to spend the rest of his boyhood with an uncle, the editor of a radical journal living abroad to escape the prison sentence imposed for his refusal to pay the stamp duty on his publication which would have made it too expensive—as the government had intended—for the working man to read. A good man, or so Daniel supposed, but one whose burning concerns for the welfare of mankind *en masse* left him no time even to notice whether or not his own small nephew had been adequately washed or warmed or fed.

Not that Daniel had ever minded that, since it had hardened him and made him resolute. And now, his uncle bankrupt, disillusioned and dead, he lived as he pleased or as best he could on a small private income which had come to him from his mother and would have been just sufficient had he not been so ready to give it away, not carelessly nor even generously but merely to avoid the weight of possessing it, money having no interest to him beyond traveling expenses, the freedom to move, to learn to "look around."

And in any case if he wished to understand poverty he must first endure it—his uncle had taught him that; not only the carefree, bohemian insolvency of his student days, when to be short of money had seemed part of the fun, but the constant, grinding hardship of men who, born to poverty, would very likely die of it. As his father had died, worn out from paying other men's bills and rarely charging for his own professional services as a lawyer. As his uncle had died. As Daniel himself did not intend to die, having equipped himself for his chosen life of endurance by the simple process of learning to endure, by a stripping away of unnecessary flesh and unnecessary emotions, a reduction of appetite, tempering himself like steel to a sinewy hardness of nerve and muscle, a sharp, sometimes cold strength of mind, so that he would be fit to do whatever he might one day be asked to do, not for any one nation or creed or power—his vision sweeping infinitely further than that—but for his fellow men.

Attitudes hardly likely to match the vanities—he was well aware—of this self-possessed, self-polished girl sitting on a heap of dusty sacking as if it were an imperial throne and who, when the position of the sun and a certain hollow ache in her own body reminded her of hunger, simply unwrapped a parcel of bread and bacon which Daniel could not bring himself to share when so many others around him had eaten nothing that day, very little the day before, and had no guarantee about tomorrow. It would be his pride to fast with them. But Cara, unabashed, shrugged half-amused, half-scornful shoulders at his refusal, broke her bread and fed crumbs to her child as to a sparrow and shreds of apple to quench his thirst, with no apparent concern for the hollow stares of a dozen other children, or the native dignity with which the knot of famished men and women close behind her turned their heads away.

Had she *looked* at them, of course—really looked and fully considered—then something would have pierced her, she knew it well, the same pang of remorse and uneasy tenderness she often felt on catching a sudden, unguarded glimpse of Liam. Therefore—because nothing could be gained by it, *because it could make no difference*—it was no more than sound sense not to look at all. She had worked hard—well, hadn't she?—for this half loaf of indifferent bread, these few wizened apples, this knob of salt bacon, and what was the good of dividing it a hundred ways, as she supposed Daniel Carey would like to see her do, so that no one's appetite would be satisfied?

She thought him foolhardy; and fascinating.

He thought her insensitive. And magnificent.

He wanted her badly now and knew it, with none of the quizzical, fleeting passion he usually felt for the women he wanted but with a sharp, almost painful desire not just to have her but to *take* her. And keep her? Hardly that. Nonsense even to think of it, since he had not the least inclination to alter his wandering, uncertain life and was too much a gentleman—despite his rejection of such things—to ask any woman to share it. No. Certainly not to keep her. Yet he could not keep his eyes away from her. It was as simple as that. Nor she from him—which seemed far from simple to her. Desire creating a mood of languor between them, an intensity of listening, watching, feeling, which it took the approach of Liverpool to break.

"Here we are." The sudden tumult around her seemed to take her by surprise, as if she had woken suddenly from sleep. Liverpool. She had never greeted the end of any journey so reluctantly. And she knew that it was not wise.

"Dear God," he said. "These dark gray cities. I always forget the look of them."

And there was an old woman among his fellow passengers, from a mud cabin somewhere in the far west of Mayo or Donegal who believed—as someone may even have told her—that her few shillings passage-money and these few miles of coldly swelling sea had brought her to the golden land they called New York. And if there should be no one to meet her in Liverpool—as Daniel Carey well knew, though the old lady of course did not—then she might be picked up for vagrancy tomorrow or the day after and, as a cheaper alternative to keeping her in one of the new English workhouses, could find herself being shipped quietly back again to Mayo or Donegal.

So too might the hollow-cheeked woman standing nearby her, a widow by the look of her whose half dozen children would make it half a dozen times harder for her to find work or lodgings, and a hundred times more willing to offer her labor for the pittance fast becoming known as "Irish wages."

So too might those other women, pressing against the splintering deck-rail in shrill excitement that held a high note of anguish, small-boned, wild-eyed children peering like weasels from every fold of their skirts.

So too might the furtive band of squatters, silent, alert, ragged beyond the comprehension of thriving, up-and-coming Liverpool, whose citizens had never been reduced, like these, to living in open ditches beneath a shelter of branches in the good weather, digging themselves holes to survive the winter, making the journey now because some landlord had given them the passage-money to have them off his land and off his conscience.

"Poor devils," said Daniel Carey, sitting Cara's child on his shoulder and picking up her carpetbags, waiting his moment before hazarding himself, and her, among the fearful confusion on the dockside below, a kaleidoscope of human pieces carelessly shaken, heedlessly thrown down, somber-colored specks that were men and women huddling, settling a moment, starting off again in yet another wrong direction, falling. And not always picking themselves up again. The lucky few had relatives to meet them with wheelbarrows into which whole lifetimes of bags and boxes, a baby, a dazed old grandmother, were hastily bundled. The "squatters," in the manner of those accustomed to concealing themselves underground, had melted away as if they had never been. But the widow with her six children had simply walked six feet of hard-paved English ground and then, not knowing which way to turn and suddenly realizing the futility of turning anywhere, had sat down cross-legged on a paving-stone, her children about her, waiting in silent, well-mannered desperation for what would happen next. No longer even curious to wonder if it might be worse than what had happened before.

And what else but despair had brought her here in the first place? Daniel Carey had no need to ask her story. Her husband had died, judging by the ages of the children, about a year ago. And with him had gone the cottage and the couple of acres, repossessed by a landlord who did not care for the complications of a lone woman and infant children on his land. For there would have been no lease, no security of tenure, just a "tenancy at will," the "will" in question belonging to the landlord who might evict as and when he chose. And therefore, while she still had a few possessions that would fetch a few coppers, he had evicted at once. As he had evicted the squatters. Although that had been a long time ago.

"Poor devils," said Daniel Carey once more and then, his eyes narrowing, their expression hard and bitter, he shrugged and said "Ah well—it's better—fed we are and better-dressed than they. So I reckon we'll get by."

"We'll get by," murmured Cara Adeane somewhat to herself, walking down the gangplank empty-handed, unencumbered, gracefully swinging her parasol. "Because we have better sense."

She had expected him to leave her in Leeds. So had he. Yet when, late in the afternoon, they had located the alley her father had named, opening on to a littered courtyard behind Boar Lane, with the carter just about to set off on his Wednesday delivery of cheap dress goods to the milliners of Keighley and Bradford and Frizingley, he had said his goodbyes, wished her luck and then surprised her, although not himself—so much of his life being dictated by impulse in that way—by leaping into the already moving cart beside her.

"I may as well see you to your father's door. It's not far. And it doesn't look like rain."

Did she want his company now? Regretfully she admitted she did, although nothing obliged her to tell him so.

"I thought you had friends in Leeds."

"That I do."

"Will they not be waiting?"

"Hardly. I'm to visit the editor of the Leeds *Northern Star*. But there's no call for hurry—since he's in prison for printing treason."

And leaning back against the bales of printed calico and housemaid's cotton he raised an amused eyebrow and smiled at her.

"What treason?"

"Oh—" and he sounded very far from alarmed about it. "Much as usual. That working men should have the vote. That members of parliament should be paid salaries so that men like me could get ourselves elected and keep our own bodies and souls together without being in the pay of my lord duke or my lord millmaster—and having to dance to his tune. You know the kind of thing."

"I do."

"And you don't care?"

"What difference could it be making to me?"

"It might. If I get elected who knows if I wouldn't make it law that all girls with black hair and blue eyes had to wear silk dresses? But for now I'll just see you on your way to Frizingley—satisfy myself that's *really* where you're going—and then I'll persuade this good gentleman carter to give me a lift back to Leeds again. I expect he'll be glad of the company on his homeward trail."

But he had not climbed into the peddler's wagon to air his views on electoral reform. He did not know why he was here, except that he had not yet had his fill of looking at her, which had seemed reason enough when he had chased the cart down the alley a moment ago and vaulted over the tail-board. Reason enough now. Why explore it? Particularly since that strange languor they had experienced on the crossing had come back again, warmer and sweeter and deeper—much deeper—than before, hushing them, lulling them, filling their entire, complicated, busy minds with the one simple, all-absorbing pleasure of *looking*, listening to the sound of the other's breathing, taking in the odors—like no other odors anywhere—of hair and skin, so that the rough, jolting miles and the scowling, dark gray mill villages blending one into the other on the road through Leeds to Bradford and then to Frizingley passed very nearly unnoticed.

The cart stopped.

"Oh . . . Are we here?" Once again, as on the approach to Liverpool, she spoke with a slow-dragging reluctance, oddly fearful of the answer.

"What a vile place." And now it was Daniel who spoke resentfully, sullenly, as he retrieved her bags and her child from the cart-tail and set them on a sodden patch of unpaved ground.

Vile? Blinking rapidly, clearing her eyes of Daniel Carey and the bemused trance he had created, she looked for the first time at this place to which her father's letters had brought her. Not a pretty place, he had called it. And she saw that in that, at least, he was to be trusted.

She stood in a mean, dark street in the decaying center of an old town, a pleasant enough place once, perhaps, before the belching chimney stacks of newly created industries had blackened it; even a quiet place before the demands of the factories for labor had caused workers' cottages to spring up like acres of ragged mushrooms around every mill-yard. While here, in the street to which her father had directed her, the tall, narrow houses, standing on what had once been a picturesque location with their backs to an old shipping canal—nauseous and gaseous now with industrial waste and human sewage—had lost their status as "residences" and become lodging-houses crammed far beyond their brim.

"What a pest-hole," he said, angrily, as if he held her to blame for it. "Is it better here you'd be than in a mud cabin in Tipperary?"

Yes. Although she could not tell him so. Because where could one mud cabin in Tipperary lead to except another? What could one aspire to in Tipperary? Whereas here, through the gloom and grime and the low, gray cloud—did it never lighten?—there would be ordinary men and women somewhere, not just lords and ladies as seemed always to be the case in Ireland, who wore fine clothes and drove fine carriages. She had her mother's word for that.

Nevertheless, a vile place, the light—such as it was—just fading, a hint of dampness in the heavy air, a crowd of indifferent passers-by, slouching heads down into the coming rain, who had seen too many arrivals and departures to pay much heed to yet another Irish girl with her glib chatter coming, as so many came and went, to a town already bursting at its seams with an alien population.

"Well," she said briskly. "Here we are." And it was not a moment for promises and declarations, with the bags to be rescued from the hooves of the carter's heavy horses, the child to be prevented from falling in the gutter, a sense of impending family reunion, a chance that Odette might glimpse her grandson from a window and come rushing out to claim her; excluding Daniel. Not the moment. But would there ever be another? And it was then, for the first time, that he put a hand on her, his hard fingers touching fire into her skin, his mind already groping for words of love although his tongue could not yet employ them. So that he spoke to her instead—to hold her attention—in a manner he knew she would expect and understand.

"You owe me, Cara," he said.

She did not intend to deny it. For the journey had been difficult and without him she could so easily have been left behind in Liverpool, where there had been only one train that day with third-class accommodation and ten people from every place on those sparse wooden benches. No roof either, just open wagons packed to bursting and Liam no longer sleepy and silent but screaming, terrified not so much by the scramble on the station platform but by its ferocity. As she had been scared herself—she knew it. For she was not always brave and calm and, with that frantic multitude struggling around her ready to kill and be killed for their right to board that train, she had lost her head thoroughly, seizing hold of Liam so fiercely in her dread of seeing him trampled underfoot that she had come near to suffocating him, until Daniel Carey had opened a way for her, less by brute force than by a steely and most effective determination.

And once inside the train she had sat for a long time gasping for breath, fanning herself with her hand, her nerve broken, covering her ears to Liam's whining, unable to bear it, unable to stop it, so that Daniel had taken the boy on his knee and pointed out to him, by way of distraction, the silk-hatted gentlemen "riding outside" on the roofs of the first-class carriages up ahead, as "sporting gentlemen" had always been wont to travel on the box of a stagecoach.

So his sweet-faced grandmother Odette would have spoken to him.

But then—as Cara swiftly reminded herself—so too would her father, the charming but entirely bogus *Dr.* Adeane.

Manchester had been easier, the third-class carriage, although open-sided, having a roof, which had proved a blessing with the rain coming on. But there had been a long delay, made bearable—*enjoyable* had she cared to tell the truth—by Daniel Carey's wit, the clean bench he had found her to sit on, the sponge cakes he had bought her, with what might have been the last of his money for all she knew, not from a street trader but from a proper baker's shop.

She had been—what? Moved by the gift? Ridiculously so. What remained in her mind was that they were the best cakes she had ever eaten. What remained in her mind, far too clearly, was that she had been happy sitting there, on a station bench, eating them. And sensations of happiness were rare with her. What her mind also retained was an anxiety—equally rare—about how much, if anything at all, he really did have left in his pocket, whether or not and how soon he could get more, whether or not she could risk offending him by offering to share the very little she had left in hers. Or whether or not she should contrive to give him the whole of it in some manner he could not refuse.

And this impulse of generosity to a stranger was the rarest thing of all.

Yet in Leeds he had been no stranger, striding ahead with Liam on his shoulder, teasing her because she could not keep pace with him, so that she had quickened her stride, taken up his challenge, arrived at the peddler's yard laughing and breathless. And regretful.

"I may as well come the rest of the way."

How her heart had leapt.

But what was the good of it?

And now here was his hand on her shoulder, a caress which bit her to the bone, the whole of his lean, disciplined body an inch away from her; his slanting questioning smile.

"You owe me, Cara."

Yes. Of course she did. She acknowledged the debt fully and freely, with a surging gratitude of which she had not believed herself capable. Although she would not pay it. Naturally not. How could she take the risk, especially now when it had suddenly become not just the fear of another pregnancy to ruin her but the greater fear that she might go gladly to her ruin, with this man.

And so she would do what she had learned to do on such occasions. Promise and smile. Smile and delay. Break her word without shame, having too much to lose for guilt.

"Yes. I owe you. I know."

"When can I see you?"

"Tomorrow," she said. It would always be tomorrow. If he came she would have a dozen excuses. *If* he came. To her own great surprise she suddenly threw her arms tight around him and kissed him, briefly, just a swift pressure of her closed mouth against his, but fiercely nevertheless, willing him not to come back and make her lie to him, willing him not to want her—while, at the same time, it seemed unbearable that she dare not want him.

"Go to your mother," he told her roughly. Gently.

Reaching out, making the familiar grabbing gestures which, from long practice, would automatically connect her hands to her carpetbags and her son, she turned her head, her eyes stinging with tears, and ran.

She found the house at the steepest and narrowest part of the street called St. Jude's and knocked on the door, registering only—and without too much surprise—that it was not the private dwelling her father had appeared to promise but a lodging of perhaps the middling variety, with not much more to offer, she supposed, than the airless back room she had just vacated in Dublin. But she would have that out with him later, her present need, like Liam's, being to see her mother, who would not strengthen her nor even advise her—being somewhat dangerously certain that those she loved must always be right—but who would simply offer so warm a welcome that the joy of it alone would be a balm.

Perhaps it might even make Liam chatter again.

"Sure and we'll see *grand'maman* Odette in a minute," she told him, realizing by the way he continued to droop and drag so listlessly at her skirts that he did not believe her.

"Liam . . . ?" And once again she felt that tug of anxiety, hastily suppressed, since the parting from Odette, which had brought on all his brooding, was over now. She had told him, often enough, that it soon would be. Had he no faith at all in her? Well—he'd soon see. But when the door opened it was not Odette who stood there, but a woman as old and gray as granite, a tall and upright sentinel guarding her property against the intruder, and inquiring, with a heavily raised eyebrow, by what right this bold young woman, clutching her carpet-bags and her whimpering infant, presumed to enter it.

"What can I do for you?" The deep voice with its broad vowels of the industrial West Riding clearly did not expect it to be very much. "I'm Cara Adeane."

"Aye?"

What more could the woman need to know but that? And why had Odette not suddenly come running up behind her, laughing and crying both together, taking them both in the breathless, loving embrace which had always made the cuts and bruises of childhood—hers *and* Liam's—seem better, the pain less, the broken bone or the broken heart certain to mend? Fiercely she wanted her mother and was quite ready now to be sharp-spoken about it.

"I'm Cara Adeane."

"Aye. So you said. I'm Sairellen Thackray. What does that tell you?" Cara bit her lip, knowing she had been told to mend her manners. And although she was by no means intimidated by the reprimand, she could see nothing to be gained at this stage by giving battle. This grim woman held the key to her mother's whereabouts and if charm was required to obtain it from her, then charm it would be.

"I do beg your pardon, Mrs. Thackray."

The woman nodded, her manner signifying "Aye, lass—it's as well you do."

"But I believe my mother and father are expecting me . . . ?"

"Indeed."

Cara's mouth had gone dry. "Mr. and Mrs. Kieron Adeane? *Doctor* Adeane? They *are* here . . . ?"

Of course they were. Even her father would not do this to her. She refused to believe it. But if he had . . . ? Suddenly the gray town

29

at her back menaced her as a gamekeeper's trap menaces the running fox, alien streets swarming with furtive or ferocious hands ready to seize her and hunt her down—unless she went to earth or somehow kept on moving—as surely and savagely as a pack of hounds.

And there was Liam.

The woman spoke again, her voice harsh and unwilling.

"Well, it's like this, my lass . . ." And perhaps, rather than wishing to be unkind, she simply saw no point in offering sympathy in a case—like this one? Dear God?—where no practical help could be given.

"Yes?" Cara's mouth was parched now and her throat aching.

"Your mother's out—don't ask me where. Why should I know her business? And your father's gone."

Gone? The word had only one meaning for her at that moment. And it was unthinkable.

"No," she said and repeated it so that Liam, hearing her panic—and since Odette was not there after all—wrapped himself around her legs and began to whine again.

She did not hear him, her whole mind on her father. All her life he had been footloose, spendthrift, unreliable. Wonderful. All her life he had been *there*. She had quarreled with him many a time, told him to take himself off and good riddance. She had loved him. No man—when he was being kind—had ever been kinder. Or more amusing. More *alive*. She knew already that she would never stop missing him.

"Steady, lass. He's not dead, if that's what you're thinking . . . ?"

Of course he wasn't. Thank God. But then—where the devil . . . ?

The answer came quickly, gruffly, wanting the whole sorry business over and done.

"He took himself off, lass—last Tuesday morning. To America."

And as there had been grief, so now there was anger, and a familiar desire to break something, coupled with a new and strange desire to laugh, so that it was in a state as near hysteria as she had ever been that she first entered the house of Sairellen Thackray; aware, through all the turmoil in her head, that the words, "You'd best come inside," had been spoken grudgingly, out of no concern either for her or Liam but because the indomitable Mrs. Thackray did not care to entertain the neighbors to any spectacle of grief or anger or betrayal on *her* doorstep.

The kitchen was small and steamy and very hot; and, in terms of the back-breaking effort involved, painfully clean, the stone floor meticulously scoured, the walls washed white, the big cast-iron range gleaming with black lead. A good housewife, Sairellen Thackray, that much was certain, a woman who bleached and scrubbed her kitchen table and carried her rag rugs out into the backyard every morning to be shaken and beaten free of dust. A woman whose bed linen, hanging now to dry around the fire, gave off a bracing odor of strong soap and lye, an impression of strong hands scrubbing and wringing, never ceasing until the job was done, a strong, straight back adapted by nature for the carrying of burdens.

Heavy burdens. And she had always had plenty of them to carry. Her own. Not Cara's.

"Sit down then," she said and Cara, still feeling dry and sick, sat obediently on a hard wooden chair by that spotless wooden table, paying no heed either to Liam or to the young man sitting quietly in the chimney corner, his shoulders hunched over a book, her mind given wholly to whatever Sairellen Thackray chose to say.

And since she was not, in fact, unkind by nature but simply economical and realistic, it would not be the whole story.

There had been a letter from America. That, at least, seemed straightforward.

"You have an aunt, I hear, in New York. In a fair way of business, according to what your father told me. She sent for him to join her. Wanted his advice, she said—*he* said—in extending her property. Made up her mind to it very sudden, it seems. So did he. As I understand it he's to send for your mother—and you, very likely—when he's able."

Cara closed her eyes.

"What else?" she said.

A great deal, if the indomitable Sairellen should decide to tell it. But having watched Odette Adeane sink into grief like a woman sliding into deep water, she was not certain how much this girl—Kieron's child by her face and figure but perhaps Odette's in spirit—could endure. And the girl could not afford to collapse. The matter was as simple as that. As Sairellen could not afford to look after her if she did.

Sairellen Thackray was not generous with her affections, reserving them as she reserved her physical stamina, her occasional treasures of fresh eggs and butter, the benefit of her sound advice, strictly for the few she called her own. But, if she had allowed it, she could have grown fond of Odette Adeane, a woman whose disposition was so sweet and loving that she not only saw the best but usually managed to bring it out in everybody. Yet her selfless acceptance of her husband's abandonment—because what else could one call it?—her heart-rending efforts to conceal her distress so as not to distress him; the way she had kept on insisting so cheerfully that she could manage very well alone, right up to the moment of his departure; the way she had broken down immediately after it, had all irritated Sairellen. Noble, perhaps. But if so, then Sairellen had no patience with nobility, knowing that in Odette's place she would have been far more likely to have brained him with a sledgehammer and taken whatever he had in his pockets for herself. And for her children. The man was a scoundrel. Anyone who did not happen to adore him—as not a few unaccountably did—could see that. And now here was his daughter who might be just as ready to make excuses for him, and to pine for him, as Odette.

A handsome girl, there was no denying, although that had always had its disadvantages in Sairellen's experience, leading, as it did, to the kind of temptation which, in young Miss Adeane's case, had evidently not been resisted. A flighty girl, then, by the look of her and not much given to honest toil either, if she took after her father. And Sairellen was ready to dismiss Cara entirely—being unwilling to waste her time on those who could not help themselves—had not the sea-blue eyes suddenly turned green in their anger, like a cat.

"I see." And the young voice was curt, sarcastic, offended. "I expect my aunt only sent enough passage-money for one."

"I expect so." Sairellen looked better pleased.

"I expect so too. She never liked my mother. But she sent him a single ticket once before and we spent it on taffeta for summer dresses. Why should he be after taking it now?" Sairellen shook her head.

"All right. You don't know. But you can tell me *when* she sent it, can you not? And how long after that did he write to me? Do you know that?"

"I do." And the dates were supplied accurately, in full knowledge of their implications.

"I see," repeated Cara, closing her eyes again, seeing inwardly, as clearly as Odette and Sairellen had seen, in their different fashions, how adroitly her father, in the very act of grasping his own opportunity, had still managed to save his conscience. For who could really accuse him of abandoning his wife in a strange city when he had first taken the precaution of summoning their daughter to look after her?

"I'll send for you, my darling. I'll make you a queen in America."

Not even his loving, trusting Odette had believed him. She had not blamed him either. And Sairellen had marveled, not for the first time, at the depth of devotion that could be aroused in a good woman by a feckless man.

"God keep him," Kieron Adeane's abandoned wife had said, with sorrowful, selfless tears which meant "He couldn't help himself. It was his last chance. How could I stand in his way?" pouring beneath her closed eyelids. "God keep him."

"If I ever see him again," said Kieron Adeane's daughter, her blue-green eyes snapping open once more, "I'll more than likely strangle him."

"Aye." Sairellen Thackray answered her and then, without speaking another word, got up and set a mug of hot tea in front of her and relieved her of her child, putting him down on the hearth-rug beside a basket overflowing with kittens of which, in the complex depths of his misery—his contemplation of yet another strange new world without Odette—he took no notice.

"So you'll strangle him, will you?"

Cara's hands, clenching themselves into fists and then uncurling to show their long fingers, their square, serviceable palms, looked quite capable of it.

"That I will."

"*If* you see him again. How do you rate your chance of that, young lady?"

"Unlikely."

Sairellen nodded, made the brief, sardonic grimace that was her smile and sat down at the other side of the table as grudging in her respect as she had been in her initial welcome—or lack of it. And, once again, it was not unkindness, just the simple good sense of survival. She had no place, in her home or in her heart, for Cara. And it would be as well—in fact it would be kinder—to say so now, and have done.

"That's right, lass. Unlikely. Happen your mother thinks the same, although she's not saying. So I'll tell you the rest now, while your temper's high and you're better able to stand it. According to his lights he left your mother provided for."

"Yes. That he did. He provided her with me. And what I want to know is why he didn't just send her back to Dublin?"

"There is a reason, lass, if you'll let me come to it." Sairellen, who was not of a talkative disposition, who used speech to convey orders or information rather than engage in conversation, did not like to be interrupted. "He waited until he had your letter, saying you were coming over. Then he left your mother with a decent roof over her head—mine—and in decent employment, so she could keep it there. He left her some money too, as much as he had, I reckon. Told her to buy a new bonnet. That was ten days ago. The money went first. Then the job. That's where she is now, unless I'm much mistaken—pleading to be taken back again. And unless she is—or finds something else . . . I expect you'll know where I'm leading."

Too well. In meticulous, miserable detail. But first, before getting down to that, there must be other avenues to explore?

"There was a milliner," said Cara sharply. "A Miss Baker? My father wrote to me about her—said she had given my mother a job and was—a friend?"

"Aye. There's a Miss Baker." Sairellen sounded unimpressed. "She turned your mother off, without a character and with wages owing to her—by your mother's reckoning. Last Thursday."

"She did *what?*" Cara was shocked, enraged, could hardly believe it. For her mother was the most gifted embroideress in Dublin. In Paris. Anywhere. Conscientious. Attentive to customers. A soothing influence in the most volatile of work-rooms. A marvel of tact. Honest in the extreme. Miss Ernestine Baker—unless she happened to be half-witted—should have been glad, *grateful*, to employ her, anxious not to lose her rather than wishing to turn her off.

"I dare say," said Sairellen, her eyes glinting with a sharp, faintly bitter humor. "But it was this way, lass. Your mother fell into a daze once your father'd gone. Sat here, at this table, staring at the wall and missing her work. Two days she did that, leaving Miss Baker up to her eyes in straw bonnet shapes and osprey feathers. And when she did go back, it seems Miss Baker caught her crying into the hatboxes . . ."

"That's not a reason to refuse her a reference. Not if she was fond of her . . ."

"Who told you that?"

And when Cara hesitated, fearing the worst and—where trouble was concerned—not expecting to be disappointed, Sairellen shook her head and smiled. "Nay lass, it was not your mother the woman was fond of."

"I see." That too had happened before. "Do you know her?"

"Ernestine Baker? Well enough. A spinster woman who looks like the taste of vinegar but . . . Well, spinsters have natural feelings too, under the surface, sometimes, that don't improve with keeping. And Ernestine Baker must be past forty-five. I dare say it was a shock to her. Jealousy, I mean."

Cara shook her head, not denying it, and then—because time was pressing—reverted to her practical needs.

"What happened to the money my father left her? She wouldn't just spend it."

"No. She didn't give it to me in advance rent, either."

"Well then?" The word "rent" was always ominous. When spoken in that fashion, with that sardonic lift of the eyebrow, that grim smile, Cara knew it to be very grave indeed. But before coming to grips with it, before making her promises and smiling her smiles in true Adeane fashion—"If you could just give me until the end of the week, Mrs. Thackray, then I feel certain . . . And, in the meantime, if I can be of any service about the house . . . ?"—before that, she had to know the whole truth. The worst.

"Your father left a debt."

"Yes?" Her mouth had turned so dry now that it felt cracked, her tongue swollen as from a long, desert thirst. But there were debts and debts, some enforceable, others not. And since it was never easy to extract payment from a helpless woman, she could make it her business, whenever circumstances required it, to be very helpless indeed.

"There is a man here," said Sairellen, speaking slowly, "who lends money—among the other things he does. He is landlord of the Fleece, the inn down in the square. Among the other things he is. And the other things he owns. Well—I'll just tell you this. Your father owed him fifty pounds. A fortune to me—and you. Nothing to Christie Goldsborough. Nothing at all—except that he'd take the same steps to get it back as he'd take for five thousand. To amuse himself, I reckon. Or else he'll lend an amount he knows can never be paid, and let the debt stand. That way—and it may have been like that with your father—he can have those who owe him at his beck and call. So your father had to leave quietly, hadn't he?—which is why he couldn't send your mother back to Ireland."

"And this man took the money my father left behind?"

Sairellen nodded, watching Cara's hands clenching into fists again and then uncoiling, flexing their long, supple strength.

"So there's somebody else you want to strangle now, is there, lass?"

Yes. First her father. Then the milliner, Miss Baker. Then the landlord of the Fleece. But she could wait for that. Only one thing now remained for her to know. Perhaps the most important of all.

"There's work here, isn't there?"

"What work are you fit for?"

"Anything."

Sairellen smiled, having received the answer she had expected. The answer she would have given herself, since she, too, had spent her life turning a hand to anything that offered, her memory extending far beyond the coming of the steam engine and its raucous progeny of power-driven machinery, to a different world—forty years ago in time, a thousand in spirit—when Frizingley had consisted of little more than an old parish church, a few coaching inns, a handful of quiet, grassy streets built from the same gray Pennine stone as the surrounding hills. While the hills themselves, and the tough-grained, gruff-spoken breed of men who inhabited them, had had everything they required for the slow—but where was the hurry?—domestic manufacture of cloth. Moorland sheep in plenty with good fleeces on their backs. Fast-flowing moorland streams to wash the raw wool and turn a water-wheel. Patient, industrious women to sit all day at their cottage doorways spinning yarn for their menfolk to weave by hand on the upstairs loom, at that steady, laborious rate—but, there again, where was the hurry?—of one piece of cloth a week. A whole sturdy family to cart the finished goods down to the Piece Hall in Frizingley to sell at the Thursday market. A whole family to work all together in their own houseplace, like beavers, in the hope of cramming seven days work into six, or even five, and declaring the remainder a holiday.

And not a whisper or a curl of factory smoke above the valley. Not a face in Frizingley or for miles around that one had not grown up with, except for the merchants on market day, the excitement of a peddler—a foreigner from Lancashire or Cheshire sometimes—or a wandering Methodist preacher delivering his sermon in a field, along the canal bank, or in a coal yard.

And the canal had run sweet and clean in those days, carrying the products of Frizingley's cottage industries to Leeds in leisurely fashion. For, when all was said and done, why hurry when one day, one year, one generation scarcely differed from another?

Sairellen's father had woven heavy worsted since his boyhood from yarn spun first by his mother, then his wife, then by Sairellen and his sisters, several "spinsters" being needed to keep one weaver occupied. And when the daily quota of spinning was done they had rushed out into the open air to the adjoining meadow—as thick now with streets of workers' cottages as it had been thick, then, with daisies—to tend the milk cow and the bacon pig, or had run off to pick blackberries on the moor or mushrooms on Frizingley Green.

A hard, simple life. No paradise, Sairellen thought, as some now liked to call it, but with its measure of dignity and independence. Not that anything was to be gained by looking back now that power-driven machinery had so effectively put an end to it. The mechanical spinning-frame, to begin with, producing its eighty threads at a time instead of one, which had killed the domestic spinning-wheel; and then, when the weavers had finally stopped complaining about waiting for yarn and were up to their eyes in it at last and reveling, had come the power-loom to sound *their* death-knell too.

Steam-driven looms to keep pace with these monster supplies of machine-spun yarn, and factories to house them in.

No decent Yorkshireman—or so many said—would submit to the tyranny of the millmaster, the infamous opening and closing of the factory gates with a captive work-force locked inside like cattle, no longer pacing themselves to natural rhythms but to the hands of the factory clock, the cold heart of its engine. And so, of those who vowed it to be intolerable, many came close to starving in their cottages and breaking up their precious handlooms for firewood, or went on the tramp to look for work elsewhere; or otherwise disappeared.

Not that the millmasters had had much use for them in any case, the new looms being so light that women—and children, who were much cheaper and far less trouble—could handle them. And so they had sent to the poorhouses of the south for cartloads of nameless, orphaned "pauper brats" as young as five years old who had slept, after their daily toil, on heaps of wool-waste in a corner of a factory shed; and were still here now, some of them—the survivors—living in the mean back-to-back cottages which had sprung up so thick and fast on Sairellen's childhood meadow, sending their own undersized children into the mill.

Sairellen's father, a man of stern morality, had vowed he would rather see his daughters dead than weaving by steam, locked up every morning in the heat and grime and promiscuity of the sheds, at the beck and call and mercy of overlookers and engineers, *men* about whose virtue there could be no guarantee. But they had gone, one by one, just the same, Sairellen herself as a young wife of seventeen, a widow at nineteen and the mother of two children; her second husband, Radical Jack Thackray, claiming her a year later.

After which her troubles had begun in earnest, Jack's mind being given to such wide-ranging political freedoms as were explained to him in the unstamped and therefore outlawed radical press, the right of the common man to vote having so much importance to him that he had died for it, twenty-one years ago this August—she still faithfully kept the anniversary—cut down by the saber of a British soldier on the battleground of St. Peter's Fields in Manchester, when swords had been drawn to disperse a peaceful crowd—in a holiday frame of mind almost, she remembered—assembled to demand a mild enough alteration in the method by which parliament was then elected.

It had taken her a long time to recover from that. But recovery—with bairns to be fed and rent to pay—had been essential, her grief a private matter, her gratitude for the money presented to her by a group of radical journalists in her husband's memory, being dignified but not carried to excess.

She had used it to take the lease on this house and had run it ever since as a lodging for decent working men, four to a room and one small, slope-ceilinged attic she would occasionally let—on a very temporary basis—to a married couple. Hard beds and somewhat narrow, but clean. Tea and oatmeal every morning. Barley broth from the cast-iron pot on the kitchen range every night. Bacon on Sundays. An occasional leg of pork if one of her acquaintances killed a pig. Eggs from the hen-run at the end of her backyard and, from time to time, a chicken which had foolishly ceased to lay. A well-ordered house in which Kieron Adeane had been a mistake and in which there was no room at all for a handsome and regrettably fertile young woman like his daughter.

Once again it was not unkindness. Just hard and simple common sense. For what could the girl do in a house full of single men but cause trouble? And now, with workers pouring into Frizingley from all directions, train-loads and cart-loads discharging daily, whole gangs turning up on the tramp ready for anything and prepared to cut up rough unless they got it, the town's population swollen from the few hundred quiet families of Sairellen's childhood memory to thirty thousand badly-housed, underpaid strangers, what chance did this pert young woman really have of any decent employment? What millmaster would waste time and money to train her when he could have his pick from the crowd of skilled weavers and spinners assembled at his gate every morning? What millmaster's wife would take her in as a parlormaid with that gleaming mane of Spanish black hair and those sea-blue Irish eyes? And what else remained—when hunger really gnawed and no other door would open—but the brothel on the corner. On every corner. And the workhouse for Odette.

The circumstances of Sairellen's life had not permitted her to be tender-hearted but, just the same, she did not wish to see that happen to Odette. And, since she believed it to be inevitable, it would be well to stand back.

"I'll put it to you very plain," she said. "Your mother's room is paid for until Friday next. After that, if she finds work, then she's welcome to stay. But I have no accommodation at any time for single women, or for children. You will understand."

Cara nodded and smiled—stiff-lipped but a smile of sorts nevertheless.

"Yes. I understand. It's turning me out into the street, you are."

"I am. I reckon there must be two hours of daylight yet."

The young man, still sitting by the chimney corner, so motionless, so absorbed in his reading that Cara had barely noticed him, looked up from his book.

"Mother . . . ?" he said, just the one word, not quite asking a question nor issuing a warning, something in between, so that Sairellen turned to him and smiled, not in the least surprised, it seemed, at his intervention.

Sairellen Thackray had borne thirteen children and lost twelve, most of them in infancy of the cholera or the measles, a daughter in childbirth, two sons as a result of industrial injury, another from injury of a different kind received at a protest against women and three-year-old children working down the mines, leaving her with Luke, her last born, the child of her middle-age, now a man—twenty-six years old—of whom she had always been proud.

Not that she had ever felt the need to tell him so, having merely grunted her approval when, as a little lad, he'd tramped off regularly if not religiously to Sunday school to learn to read and write—skills she herself had never had the chance to acquire—and, later on, to the Mechanics Institute where he still spent his time poring over volumes of history and old maps. She'd done little more than grunt when he'd been promoted to overlooker at Braithwaite's mill either. She just made sure that there was always a hot dinner waiting for him, a clean shirt, kept the lodgers out of his way as much as she could, took not a penny more of his wages than she absolutely required. Left him in peace with his books and rarely asked questions about his other pursuits, either amorous, political or social, having implicit trust in his sense and decency.

She supposed he was not handsome, although *that* was of no importance, being tall and craggy and loosely put together like herself, with a thatch of coarse fair hair, steady gray eyes, an overcrowded face of large, heavy features, a finely developed conscience which—since his life had been marginally easier than hers—made him rather more easily put upon.

And she had known from the start that he would object to the putting out of doors of a young woman and child.

Well, perhaps she objected to it herself. What decent person would not? But, as she had told Luke many a time, Frizingley was full of stray dogs—whimpering little lost puppies like Liam; bright-eyed, vagrant cats like his young mother ready to charm themselves a place at any fireside; sad and dignified creatures like Odette, not wishing to be any trouble—all of them able to touch the heart. And since, with the best will in the world, one could not take them in—since one had to face the brutal fact that there was simply not enough to go around—far better to send them off at once. Better—for one's own peace of mind—never to raise false hopes. Better for them.

She had told Luke that too, but felt nothing but her habitual grunt of pride in him when he stood up to her, not aggressively as he could well have done considering his height and the rough work he was used to, but with easy good-humor.

"I reckon you'll want them to stay overnight, mother."

"Why should I want that, Luke?"

She enjoyed these confrontations. Perhaps because no one else, these days, ever confronted her.

"Because Odette is a good woman. And she's been counting the hours until they got here."

"I've nowhere to put them, Luke. Odette knows that." He smiled. "Aye. But you'll have been keeping it from her—to surprise her I reckon—that the little lad could sleep in her bed tonight. And that we could manage a chair by the kitchen fire for his mother."

Had she found a champion? Cara, her turquoise eyes agleam, would have rushed to thank him had not his mother prevented it, placing herself between them, *her* eyes as shrewd and watchful as ever, in no mind to expose her son—a man with natural inclinations after all— to the obvious temptations of a female in distress.

Not that he required gratitude, returning with an expression of quiet amusement to his chair, stretching out long legs toward the fender where Liam still sat in stunned silence by the basket of kittens, while Cara began, very ably, to defend herself.

Just a chair for the night, no need to keep the fire going. She wouldn't dream of accepting such luxury and would be gone in the morning, first thing.

"Aye. I reckon you will," said Sairellen. And if, in the meantime, Mrs. Thackray would be so kind as to give her the address of Miss Ernestine Baker, the milliner, she would run along there this very minute to meet her mother and perhaps say a word or two of her own about the wages which, if Odette said were owing, then assuredly must be. She wouldn't be long.

"What about the bairn?" inquired Sairellen.

"Oh—" Cara's blue-green eyes were widely, innocently open, her mouth curving in an angelic smile. "It seems a shame to move him— doesn't it?—poor little thing, quiet as a mouse—and I'll only be half an hour . . ."

Sairellen sighed.

But a moment later Cara was running down the street called St. Jude's, her mind obliterated of all anxieties but the need to find her mother, taking one thing at a time as seemed best to her at crisis points like these, when every problem was urgent, terrible, and to tackle too many at once would overwhelm her.

One thing at a time. First her mother, to be rescued from the spite of Miss Ernestine Baker, to be consoled, defended, reunited with Liam. Then Miss Baker herself, either money to be extracted from her or, if she *could* be charmed, then charmed into taking on Cara in her mother's place she must be. Then—and her heart sank at the thought of it—the sinister landlord of the Fleece, to ascertain to what portion of her wages—once she had them—he felt entitled. Then the long, slow, often humiliating rounds of anybody who might give her work. Anybody. Except the brothel keepers who would not be slow to offer, the elderly, comfortable women one saw in every railway station, every coaching inn, every town square when the daylight was fading, looking for girls to suit one sexual purpose or another.

She had never even remotely considered that. She did not consider it now and was therefore ready to defend herself when she felt a man's hand on her arm; until she saw that it was Daniel Carey.

"Oh dear God." And it was a lament, full of grief for what they could have been to one another, anger at the knowledge that they could not. He heard only the anger.

"What are *you* doing here?"

She was in the most desperate situation of her life, as near the brink of total disaster as she had ever been. How could she pause now in her mad rush to salvage whatever *could* be salvaged—if anything at all—how could she possibly add to the sum total of her disaster by allowing herself to fall in love?

Not now. *Please*—let it be later. When it would be resolved, one way or another, and she would have time to think only of herself. And torn badly, most distressfully by a conflict of racing emotions— a burst of sheer, pure joy at the sight of him, an urgent need to send him away, terror that he might not come back—the tears in her throat causing her to clench her jaw as if in temper, making her voice cool— although he could not know that—she rapped out, "Wouldn't the peddler take you back on his cart?"

"Oh yes. I got on, right enough. And off again." There had been no sense to it. He knew that. No certainty even, of seeing her again that day. He had simply, suddenly, and most urgently desired to be *here*. And so, once again, he had vaulted over the tail-board of the wagon, already a mile on its homeward track, and had come back to the street called St. Jude's with no specific intentions, his aim now extending no further than to draw her into the narrow passage between two darkened warehouses and then into his arms.

"I had to see you, Cara. Now. I couldn't risk going back to Leeds and then tomorrow finding you gone. I couldn't wait."

Nothing had ever equaled the ferocity of her gladness. He was all she wanted. For the brief moment in which she allowed herself to rejoice in him, to live *as* herself *for* herself wholly and fully, she knew that there could be nothing more wonderful anywhere in the world than the love and passion and folly vibrating from his body, his mind, to hers.

And then it was the folly, after all, which really counted. The folly she had sworn never to commit again. And how could she give in to it now? How could she?

She could not.

But, choked by her tears and frustrations, she could not tell him so. Nor could he—as unused to love as Cara, although quite comfortable with passion—understand her muttered fears as she began to resist, pushing him away with one hand and holding him with the other, refusing his kisses and then abandoning herself to them almost, never quite, entirely; increasing his fever.

"Cara—come with me . . ."

"Where?" She was scandalized.

"Just with me—away. Anywhere."

He had forgotten her parents and her child, forgotten the business which had brought him to Leeds. All he saw was Cara Adeane, who did not resemble in any way the kind of girl he had expected to love. And yet it seemed that he loved her. Unwisely. Far too suddenly to be able to cope with it, to go beyond the astonishment, the unease, and convert it to tenderness.

He had been tender, sometimes, with other women in a light-hearted, highly enjoyable fashion, had teased and cajoled and usually had his way. What seemed to matter now was that she should not escape him. And the only way he could be sure of her was physically to possess her. After which—calm in the knowledge that she was his—he would soon learn how to tell her what was in his heart.

And caught up in the heat of his own new emotions, he was angry with her for not understanding this, angry with himself for his sudden inability to communicate.

A moment more and they were bitterly quarreling.

"You don't think I can look after you," he accused her. No, of course she did not.

"You don't trust me." It surprised her, even in her condition of near hysteria, that he could think she might. Men did not exist to be trusted. Nor were they put on the earth to look after women. She was very sure of that. They could be loved, of course. They *were* loved.

"You won't see me again," he told her.

"Well—I won't die of that." But as he turned away white with anger, and strode off down the street, she felt that he had killed her already.

She had not told him of her plight. Once he had turned the corner she would have no way of finding him. And who knew where she might be herself tomorrow?

"Daniel . . ." But it was only a whisper with no hope of reaching him, spoken only to comfort herself as she leaned for a moment, feeling sick and shaken and totally desolate, against the stone wall.

And then, slowly, deliberately, she tidied her hair, smoothed her skirts, straightened—almost an inch at a time—her suddenly aching back.

One thing at a time. And she must steady herself now, compose herself, in order to achieve it. First her mother. Then Miss Baker. Then the landlord of the Fleece. Then somebody, somewhere—Please God—to employ her.

But the name in her mind was Daniel.

3

Gemma Dallam would always remember the first time the Irish girl came to call as the day on which she made up her mind to marry Tristan Gage, her mother's godson.

Not an easy decision. Nor—above all—in the least romantic. But, as the threads came together in her mind, oddly natural.

She must marry someone. She and her mother, for rather different reasons, were both agreed on that. And since she was plain, rich and, at twenty-two no longer in the first bloom of youth, being of a practical disposition and quick wit, short of stature but high in her financial expectations—a combination which made it unlikely that she would ever be courted for love—then surely, among the several who had offered, it would be better to take shallow, charming, undemanding Tristan than a man of greater substance who would exercise the right, with which marriage empowered him, to demand a very great deal.

Better Tristan, who was poor and who, having no home of his own, would be glad to remain here in the ancient, inconvenient but—to Gemma—uniquely beautiful manor house her father had purchased with the profits of his weaving sheds, rather than Ben Braithwaite, young autocrat of Braithwaite & Son, worsted manufacturer, who had inherited a tall dark house to go with his mill, complete with Braithwaite family traditions, a tribe of Braithwaite relatives to be entertained, Braithwaite interests to be first and foremost considered; even the vague malice of a widowed mother.

Better Tristan, who took little in life very seriously beyond the set of his lace cravat, the cut and quality of his jacket, than Uriah Colclough, master of Frizingley Ironworks and *Non*conformist lay preacher who would require *her* to conform, nevertheless, and most strictly, to the very letter of his moral principles.

45

Tristan, who saw her fortune only in moderate terms of thorough-bred hunters and good living and would think it ill-bred to question her own expenditure, rather than Jacob Lord of Lord's Brewery, who was over-meticulous with money, or the heir to a certain local baronet who, while making her Lady Lark of Moorby Hall, would also use her last penny to keep his crumbling ancestral home intact and to purchase for his half-dozen noble brothers a seat in Parliament, a commission in a crack regiment, a sugar plantation in Antigua, appointments in the Foreign Service and in the English Church.

Tristan, who did not love her but would be polite about it, who, like a cat of high and indolent pedigree would require nothing from her but a silk cushion to recline on, a prettily served quota of fresh cream, rather than all those other men who had wanted her to be a *wife*, to be the "angel" in her husband's home, the source of his pleasure and procreation, his freshly laundered shirts and hot dinners; to submit herself absolutely to his protection and authority, having no desires beyond his gratification and no opinions beyond those he might choose to give her; to yield sweetly and innocently to his religious beliefs and his sexual whims and fancies; to relinquish everything she owned or might inherit into his grasp, becoming herself *his* possession entirely. So that he might, with truth, be able to say "My wife and I are one. And *I* am he."

As Gemma's mother—and most happily—had chosen to belong to her father.

But Tristan Gage was too light in weight and heart *and* aspirations for that, too much the grasshopper flitting through a lifetime of summer meadows to trouble himself—or her—with such cumbersome thoughts as possession or conjugal authority; and had no particular opinions on anything which mattered to Gemma for her to echo.

Tristan, then, who would never do anything of note in the world but grace it with his charming presence. But who would allow her space in which to breathe. And grow.

She was standing in her father's garden among the late roses, gathering full-blown petals for potpourri as the thought struck her. Tristan. Of course. To marry him seemed suddenly not only the best but the obvious solution. And it was as she laid her flat, straw gardening basket down and went into the house to find him and tell him so, that she was waylaid by her mother's iron-gray housekeeper, Mrs. Drubb, with the information that "a person" had called, asking to see "the ladies."

"A *person*, Mrs. Drubb?" And perhaps it was curiosity alone which led her to the small parlor behind the kitchen where callers who could not be shown into the drawing-room were entertained. For Mrs. Drubb made short work, as a rule, of those she judged unworthy of Dallam attention, so that Gemma was interested to find out why this one appeared to have evaded her net.

"A sewing-woman, Miss Gemma."

"Good Heavens—why should I want to see one of those? Is my mother not at home?"

"She is. But I'd not care to trouble her with a stranger."

A difficult stranger, perhaps? Fearsome indeed if she had managed to intimidate Mrs. Drubb. Or else exceedingly pitiful if she had succeeded in touching *that* crabbed old heart. She must take at least a peep.

"What kind of woman, Mrs. Drubb?"

"Talkative, miss ... *Very*."

Had she *wheedled* her way in, then, past this cynical and unyielding guardian of her mother's privacy? How very surprising. Clever, too. Yet the first thing she noticed about the "person" standing beside a battered carpetbag and an old wooden hatbox with what looked like French words painted on it, was something which would not have counted with Mrs. Drubb at all. Her beauty. Not "ladylike" beauty, of course. Not the fine porcelain complexion and soulful eyes, the dainty figure and discreet attractions which Gemma's mother called "fashionable," but a gypsy boldness of coloring and carriage, a dazzling contrast of ebony hair, amber skin and long, incredibly turquoise eyes. Too much beauty, perhaps—and too obvious—which any woman of breeding would have toned down to a becoming subtlety so as not to make herself *too* disturbing, *too* much stared at in the street.

Or so Gemma knew her mother would have considered. The kind of girl one did not employ as a parlormaid if one valued the peace of mind of one's grooms and footmen. Or the virtue of one's younger sons. But Gemma, who had made up her mind long ago that, having no beauty of her own, she would not be churlish about it, came forward with a brisk but pleasant greeting.

"I am Miss Dallam. What may I do for you?"

"My name is Adeane, Miss Dallam—Cara Adeane, Dressmaker and Milliner, newly arrived in this area ..."

"From where? Are you Irish?" To Gemma's mother *that* would not be a recommendation. Nor to Mrs. Drubb either.

"From Paris, Miss Dallam—from the rue Saint Honoré. The establishment of Madame Juliette Récamier, a milliner of great talent, who passed on so much of her knowledge to me—so many of her designs. May I show you?"

"Madame *Récamier*, did you say?"

Gemma, smiling, did not believe a word of it. But Cara, smiling back at her, had already lifted the lid of her hatbox, nimbly undone the complicated fastenings of her carpetbag, and began to fill the room with a rainbow swirl of fabric and color, a white silk shawl intricately embroidered with white and silver flowers, another with blue forget-me-nots, which she threw carelessly but oh so becomingly across the back of a chair; quilted silk petticoats and starched muslin ones all differently flounced and frilled and trimmed with lace of a quality and design to which Cara referred with enormous reverence and no regard for the truth whatsoever as "Chantilly," "Valenciennes," "Point de Venise"—"One can always tell *quality. Don't* you think?"

"I dare say," murmured Gemma, to whom lace was only, and somewhat tediously, *lace.*

And then the hats. A natural straw ruched with pink silk inside the brim and covered with pink silk roses without. A demure cottage bonnet with bows and a lace frill. A dashing wide-brimmed confection of black velvet ribbons and white feathers.

"Just samples, you understand, of the work I do—the stitches— the *style*—which is what really matters. Something a little out of the ordinary. Only a small selection, of course. As much as I can carry. But anything else you might require, I should be only too happy— from lace-edged nightcaps to ballgowns—a trousseau?"

Gemma smiled again, understanding the rapid professional assessment this other girl—this girl from a different universe of experience to her own, surely?—had made of her. Rich. Not much to look at. Over twenty. Therefore certain to be thinking of marriage. True enough, she conceded, wondering what assessment she could make, in her turn, of Miss Cara Adeane, once one got beyond the beauty? Bold, certainly. And glib. Neither too scrupulous nor too honest, for which Gemma—having been told that honesty, among the lower orders, must needs operate at a correspondingly lower level—did not feel able to blame her. Younger perhaps than she looked and sounded.

A strumpet, her father would have said, his face stern as befitted his rank of industrialist and paterfamilias, but with that glint of humor in his eye which only Gemma—never her mother—understood. While her mother would have been likely to treat this girl with the outward show of superiority, the inner timidity and suspicion one might accord to some exotic jungle animal, expecting it to be tame enough but never *quite* certain.

And what did Gemma herself really know of the streets of Frizingley—the natural habitat of "persons" such as these—beyond the observations made from an open landau in summer whenever her mother, who was nervous of crowds and noises and the way the hot air might stir up a riotous populace or a crop of infectious diseases, could be persuaded to visit the shops. Or from an occasional visit to her father's mill when she would be shown over the counting houses and the pattern rooms, never the weaving sheds.

She was twenty-two years old, well-read and exceedingly well-mannered, capable of handling servants, keeping household account books, issuing accurate commands for the restocking of food cupboards and linen cupboards, organizing dinner and appropriate entertainment for any number of guests. She knew French, Italian, Latin and German, had a working knowledge of mathematics, and—although her mother had begged her never to refer to this in "company"—was acquainted with the aims of Her Majesty's present government and the names and dispositions of Her ministers. She had her own views on import tariffs, knew exactly why the Corn Laws should be abolished, and even more than even her father realized about the state of Frizingley's textile trade. Yet had never once been outside the shelter of her father's garden walls alone, without the chaperonage of at least a maid, a coachman and her old governess, as befitted a young lady of rank and fortune whose delicacy and whose reputation must at all times be protected.

A rule not to be relaxed until her marriage, when—like her dowry—she would pass from her father's control to her husband's.

And what restrictions would Tristan be likely to impose? Would he even remember, at the end of any day, to ask or care just how she had spent it? Doubting it, she smiled at Cara Adeane, wondering if a girl like this, accustomed to roaming wherever she pleased, could understand the reasons why Miss Dallam of Frizingley Hall was indeed contemplating marriage? Not for security or companionship or affection—since she had always had these things in plenty—but quite simply to be rid of the gentle, well-meaning hand on her elbow hurrying her away from anything at which it might be thought improper for her to look; to be free of the earnest, kindly voice murmuring its warnings about the many vital prohibitions—not understanding politics, not eating cheese, never disagreeing with the gentlemen, dearest. *So* simple—which Society imposed on its ladies.

No. This beautiful girl with her living to earn, her eyes drinking in the luxury with which Gemma was surrounded, would not easily understand that. Just as Gemma, as she readily conceded, understood little about the earning of livings, such pursuits being inappropriate to her in a world which did not permit paid employment to its gentlewomen. No. Her task in life was to live on the fruits of other people's labor and she was honest enough to admit that she could not really know how she might feel without the absolute security of her father, John-William Dallam, and his weaving mill, behind her.

Freedom might seem precarious then. Freedom to go hungry, as she supposed this girl had often done; would do again, perhaps, unless she sold some of these shawls and bonnets.

"We always go to Miss Baker in Market Street," she said now, not unkindly but not wishing to arouse false hopes, since she doubted if her mother would wish to buy. While Gemma herself, as the "daughter of the house," no matter how cherished, lacked the authority to order goods without permission.

That too would alter on her wedding day.

"Ah to be sure—Miss Ernestine Baker," the lilting Irish voice sounded faintly amused although wishing to be good-natured about it, the sparkling sea-blue eyes issuing an invitation to poke a little gentle fun at that excellent but—goodness—that *dreary* lady. "I know her well. The poor soul. How hard she tries—to keep pace, I mean. But with fashion sweeping along these days, and ladies everywhere running so fast after it . . . And her eyesight, of course. It saddens me whenever I think of it. But, at her age, what else can one expect? And fine needlework, you know, gets along much better if the seamstress can actually *see*. Not that Miss Baker sews her own seams . . . Heavens, no. One can get little charity-school girls with eyes like sparrowhawks to do that. But when it comes to embroidery and cutting and design—to the *flair* . . . Well—you can't rely on charity-school girls for that. At least *I* wouldn't care to."

"I suppose not." Gemma, who knew Miss Baker's eyes to be as keen as ever, having been fitted by her very recently for an evening gown, felt, nevertheless, much inclined for laughter, as beguiled by the melodious voice, the graceful gestures, the teasing brilliance of the blue-green eyes as even hard-hearted Mrs. Drubb had been.

"How long have you been in Frizingley?"

"Three months, madam."

Three hard months, perhaps, thought Gemma, toiling on foot from one cold door to another, dragging the weight of that carpetbag and the cumbersome wooden hatbox with its worn leather strap and its newly painted lettering "Miss Cara Adeane. Dressmaker and Milliner." Months without much profit either, for Gemma had detected no anxiety as to falling trade in Miss Ernestine Baker, no hint of any unwelcome competition, when she had called, only a few days ago, with suggested patterns for Mrs. Dallam's winter wardrobe.

And somehow, without knowing *how* she knew it, she realized that behind her sparkle the girl was tired, weary to the bone in a way Gemma's over-protected body had never been weary. Was she hungry too? Or thirsty? Very probably. But there were inflexible rules about the offering of refreshments, all-powerful decrees of Etiquette from which she had been trained never to deviate. One served tea to one's social equals in the drawing-room. One might offer a charitable loaf of bread to a beggar at one's gate. One took soup to the "deserving poor" in their cottages or, in her mother's case, waited in one's carriage looking apprehensive while one's coachman carried in the lukewarm nourishment packed in hay. One knew that the servants sometimes gave a jug of ale to a tradesman on a hot afternoon at the kitchen door, and not even Gemma's mother made a fuss about it. But one gave nothing to visitors such as this but ten minutes of one's time, at the most, and a pleasant dismissal. One simply did not encourage them. Her mother's policy on the matter was clear enough, and it was certainly not the business of an unmarried "daughter at home" to change it.

How it would horrify her mother, and Mrs. Drubb, should she lose her head sufficiently to offer the girl a chair, and a drink. But then, since she had already decided to accept the proposal Tristan Gage had made her, in his diffident, charming manner, two days ago—"You know, my dear, that I'll just be holding my breath, don't you, until I have your reply"—why not use her own judgment again, in this.

How irksome—truly—that she even felt the need to hesitate.

"Perhaps you would care to wait a while, Miss Adeane," she said calmly, "while I go and tell my mother what you have to offer? Do sit down. Those bags must be so heavy. And I will have them bring you some tea."

She had broken a social commandment. She waited a moment, listening as if for the shattering of glass, and when none occurred went off with a quiet smile to find first Tristan Gage and then her mother.

Amabel Dallam, much-loved wife of the industrialist John-William Dallam, had been aware all morning that something exciting was about to take place. She had sensed it at once on waking, something which happened to her fairly often, for she was highly sensitive, even "fey" she liked to think, and when something was in the air it had small chance of escaping her notice. So she had been telling everyone who would listen ever since breakfast-time, her maid, her house-keeper Mrs. Drubb, Tristan Gage himself and his sister, Linnet, both of them her godchildren, who had been guests in her house for so long that she could hardly bear to part with them. And if her dear daughter, Gemma, *should* decide to accept Tristan's very obliging pro-posal, then perhaps she wouldn't have to.

Amabel Dallam was a woman of a "certain" age—a little over forty—with the kind of porcelain prettiness—pale, delicately chiseled features, fine, fair hair, a frail breathlessness of figure which had sur-vived the passing of girlishness to give her an air of endearing frag-ility.

She was also a happy woman and, in accordance with her own values, a successful one, being the possessor of everything she had ever wanted in life. Except a son, of course—all her pregnancies ex-cept the first having come to nothing—although, should her daughter prove so inclined, the lack could be remedied in Tristan. Not that anyone would dream of forcing her, nor of exerting even the slightest pressure, as anyone could tell by the number of "eligibles" dear Gemma had already turned down. Good Heavens, no. One simply took the obvious precaution of putting suitable—and *only* suitable—young men in her way. No more than that. But what—wondered Gemma's fond mother—could she find amiss with Tristan Gage?

Amabel herself had married at the earliest moment she possibly could, straight from the schoolroom in fact, just sixteen years old, the outright winner of the matrimonial race that season, the envy of all her older sisters and cousins, her own heart almost bursting with pride as she'd gone to the altar with John-William Dallam, twenty years her senior, of course—as her father had been that much older than her mother—since gentlemen did not marry until they could afford to support a wife in a proper manner. And John-William Dallam had wished to embark upon the state of matrimony as he had done everything else. With considerable style. And perhaps as much because of the difference in their ages as the dependent quality of her character, she had always found it perfectly natural that he should lead; and she should follow.

She had continued to adore him, had placed her life in his square-palmed, slightly roughened hands with perfect confidence. If John-William said it would be all right, then it would be. Her creed consisted, quite simply, of that. And how relaxed and easy and *gracious* her life had been, how free from all anxiety, since there had never been the least need to worry about anything so long as John-William was there. How safe. How untroubled by the need to make decisions, having decided, once and for all, on her wedding day, to trust him. Not only to submit to his guidance but to thrive upon it.

Nor had she ever been unduly burdened with the toils and tediums of housekeeping, since her husband, having made his fortune *before* their marriage, had naturally chosen to advertise his success to the world not only by the purchase of a large house but by the employment of maids and cooks and the admirable Mrs. Drubb to make him comfortable in it. It had always been a matter of pride to him that he could afford to keep his wife as an ornament in his best parlor. It had always been *her* pleasure to decorate. And if she regarded him emotionally as a father rather than a lover she was supremely content to be his much-loved, over-protected child.

Certainly there *was* a whole wide world stretching beyond her husband's ornate and very solid front door. Of course she knew that, could even smell it all too clearly sometimes whenever she was obliged to drive through Market Street in the summer, a wisp of cambric soaked in lavender water held to her nose. But she counted it her good fortune never to have been obliged to venture too far. She had everything she desired in her home, in *him*, and whenever he became a little *too* autocratic, as all gentlemen sometimes did—one knew that—then she had her own pretty ways of coaxing him back, without a cross word spoken, to good humor.

She was not clever, of course, and would say as much to anyone who cared to know, freely admitting that numbers were a mystery to her and anything but the very lightest of novels beyond her grasp.

Why not? Since everyone knew that gentlemen did not care for clever women. Sweetness and prettiness were what counted, and Amabel Dallam was pretty in everything, from her dainty frilled and berib-boned dresses to the crystallized fruits she nibbled in place of lunch-eon; from her violet-scented writing paper and her violet-colored ink to the silk-upholstered landau in which she drove out, shaded by a fringed parasol, to deliver her letters; from the lace butterfly caps which sat like gossamer on her honey-gold ringlets to her butterfly hands, hovering all day about a piece of fine embroidery, at which no one ever saw her take a stitch.

Pretty too, not only in her genuine helplessness in all practical matters but in her gratitude to the many who undertook them in her place, so that her servants grew protective toward her and usually stayed with her longer than they had ever intended. Pretty in her impulsive generosity, the ease with which her sympathy could be stirred and her purse strings opened: easily-put-upon, in fact, had not her husband watched over her so carefully.

In short, a contented woman, finding herself in the one situation to which she was ideally suited, conforming as naturally to the rules of Etiquette as if they had been written on her behalf, her own ex-perience of marriage, which was, indeed, the only career open to a woman of good birth and good manners, so very pleasant that it puzzled her to see her only daughter still single, by her own choice, at twenty-two.

That Amabel loved her daughter was beyond question. Nor did she even remember, now, her faint whisper of regret that this pre-cious only child had grown to resemble her sensible, serviceable father instead of her pretty mother. Gemma was Gemma and, therefore, perfect. Adorable. And if, when she had chosen her daughter's name, the "gems" in her mind had been delicate seed pearls, elegantly spar-kling diamonds, rather than the square-cut amethyst in a heavy gold setting which Gemma had become, then she had forgotten that too. Not that the dear child was large or clumsy, simply rather more dig-nified in her build, "stronger" than present Fashion liked to see, hav-ing inherited John-William's squareness instead of Amabel's fashionably sloping shoulders, John-William's capable hands and feet, designed for standing firmly on the ground; a fitting occupation for him, of course, but something not really to be encouraged in a young lady.

She had his brown eyes too, instead of Amabel's cloudy blue, set beneath well-marked eyebrows which had been known to come together—like his—in a frown, his rather olive complexion, straight brown hair that was neither dark enough to be called brunette nor light enough to lay claim to blonde. And, moreover, when it became apparent that Nature had not blessed her, she had lacked the necessary vanity to attempt improvements. Nor Amabel the resolution to force her.

Amabel herself, at her own mother's insistence, had worn tight-laced whalebone stays day *and* night from the age of thirteen until her marriage, when sleeping in corsets had become inappropriate. But when Gemma, in her turn, had wept at the discomfort, Amabel had wept with her, allowing the laces to be loosened so that her daughter's waist had grown with the rest of her, to a full twenty-four inches, which made her bosom, by contrast, seem smaller than Dame Fashion decreed.

Yet her smile—her mother insisted—was lovely, her temperament generous and loyal, her accomplishments numerous—*too* many, perhaps, in a girl destined by rank and wealth to idleness—and Amabel, who was loyal too, had once spoken sharply—for her—to Mrs. Braithwaite of Braithwaite & Son, worsted manufacturers, for describing Gemma as "sturdy." *And* Lady Lark of Moorby Hall for calling her "studious."

Sturdy and studious. Amabel still trembled at the memory of it. But these calumnies had taken place *after* Gemma's rejection of Ben Braithwaite and Felix Lark in marriage, so what else had it been but spite? And when Gemma had gone on to reject Uriah Colclough of the iron foundry and Jacob Lord of Lord's Brewery, she had consoled herself with the thought that none of them had been quite good enough. Gemma, after all, could marry absolutely anybody she wanted. Gemma's mother choosing to close her mind, a little, to the fact that, so far as Frizingley was concerned, her choices were running out.

And then Tristan Gage had burst upon their horizon, taking Amabel's breath away, no matter the effect he may have had on Gemma's, so that she had at once detected the happy sound of wedding bells. And what a romantic bridegroom he would be. Not rich, alas, like the Braithwaites and Colcloughs, and with no title to bestow like Felix Lark, but well-born just the same, and with that air of "the great world" about him, of "London" as opposed to "provincial" society, so alluring to a woman like Amabel who had never quite dared to venture into it.

His mother had been the dearest friend of her childhood, a fascinating, *fashionable* creature even at fourteen, who had married romantically—whereas Amabel had simply married *well*—becoming the wife of the younger son of a baronet who had expected to inherit one of the family's various titles, from which only the frail life of a cousin or an ageing uncle had separated him. But Fate, alas for her dear friend Laura Gage, had not so decreed. The young cousin had survived to become *Sir* this or the other. The decrepit uncle had married on his death bed and lingered to produce a son. Nor had Fortune smiled over-warmly in the matter of investments, appointments, games of chance.

Yet nevertheless, for all her troubles, Mrs. Laura Gage had lived what had always seemed to Amabel to be a thrilling life in such places as Belgravia, Knightsbridge, Cheltenham, Bath, returning North once or twice a year to see her family and her "sweet Amabel" from whom, in the most discreet and delightful manner, she would occasionally borrow a little money and show herself most grateful when Amabel tactfully converted her usual Christmas and birthday presents to the Gage children into cash.

Amabel had invited them both to stay with her when their father died—Linnet, an enchantingly pretty girl of fourteen, Tristan a year younger—and had written affectionately to Linnet ever after, completely unaware that she had seen in this slender, fair-haired, wholly feminine creature, the reflection of herself which she missed in Gemma.

Linnet was destined to become a great beauty and the bride of a titled gentleman. Both her mother, Mrs. Gage, and her godmother, Mrs. Dallam, had been quite sure of that, although an engagement entered into at the age of nineteen had come to nothing, while several other suitors had been unable to proceed for the lack of a dowry. Poor dear Linnet. She was twenty-four now, as lovely in the correct pale-porcelain fashion as her doting Aunt Amabel had expected, dainty and delicious and thoroughly worn-out—although she would never admit it—from nursing her mother in her final illness, in circumstances of genteel poverty which made Amabel shudder.

Quite naturally she had rushed to the rescue, inviting the poor orphan at once to Frizingley, where she had proved so agreeable a companion, so full of charm and wit and "London" manners—*so* like her mother—that Amabel had fallen happily and completely under her spell.

And then the long summer recess of the House of Commons had brought an adult and fascinating Tristan from Westminster, where he had been eking out a living—wasting himself, said his sister—as sec-retary to some minor political gentleman; a young and very non-chalant Adonis, tall and fair with the thoroughbred slenderness and elegance of a greyhound, making light of his troubles and no secret at all of his appreciation of his dear Aunt Amabel's excellent dinners.

Was it too much to hope that Gemma might be charmed by him too? And surely, if this turned out to be what Gemma wanted, her father would not withhold consent, being well able to afford a luxury of this kind for his daughter, and having taken no steps to dictate her choice of a husband other than making absolutely certain that she met no one to whom one might seriously object.

From the day of his arrival Amabel had prayed for it. Gemma and Tristan. Linnet. The new house she had set her heart on in the still unspoiled countryside around Frizingley so that she might be spared the alarms and odors of the town. Just those few little miracles, oh Lord, and she would be forever content. Tristan and Gemma. And as they came into the drawing-room, her serious, brown-haired, "sturdy" daughter and carefree, gold and ivory Tristan, not hand in hand pre-cisely but looking as if they ought to be or perhaps *had* been, her heart began at once to flutter, her small hand to reach out excitedly to Linnet.

But Linnet Gage, for whom her brother's marriage to Gemma—or rather to Gemma's dowry and expectations and the goodwill of her mother—was of the most vital importance, neglected, for the first time, to make a dash for her "dear aunt's" smelling bottle, leaving her to get on with her palpitations while she glided toward the—surely by now?—*engaged* couple, graceful even in her moments of agitation, only her voice betraying her by its sharpness as she called out "Tristan?"

"Yes," he said quickly, putting her out of her misery at once, knowing all too well what this marriage would mean to her. A secure home at last. An established role in Frizingley society which, although depressingly provincial and limited was better, as both brother and sister had agreed, than hanging on to the fringes of London as their mother had done, keeping up her pretenses until they had killed her, and fooling no one in the end. Above all a chance for Linnet to find, among these rough and ready northern millionaires, a husband for herself. And since Tristan Gage greatly admired his sister and, in his amiable, rather lazy fashion, had long been in the habit of following her advice—more often than not—it seemed to him that any one of these Braithwaites and Colcloughs should be downright grateful to get her.

"Yes, Linnet—Aunt Amabel—aren't I the luckiest fellow alive.... She said yes, don't you know."

And then, having pressed her cool, pale cheek fervently against her brother's, and bestowed a brief kiss upon Gemma, making a great show of bending down—"Darling, we are to be sisters"—Linnet was all concern for her dear aunt's emotions, supplying in swift succession, her smelling bottle, her cambric handkerchief, her violet-scented writing paper so that a note could be instantly dispatched to her husband at the mill.

"My darling girl, I am so very glad." Gemma was embraced over and over again by her mother, whose bliss grew larger every time she spoke of it. "Dear Laura's son. All I wish is that you be as happy together as I am, with your father."

And smiling, Gemma accepted her mother's happiness—and her father's—knowing it to be real yet saddened by her own inability to feel at ease with it. She loved her father, admired his hard-headed, hard-wearing qualities, respected his integrity and—more often than not—his judgment. Yet she knew that to become the childlike, doll-like wife of such a man would seem no better to her than a gradual suffocation in honey and velvet. She loved her mother. Yet only, she realized, as the child, the doll to be petted and played with, the cooing dove to whom her strong, sure father hurried home each evening with such perfect content. And although she was glad with all her heart that their form of marriage did content them, she had known, for a long time, that for her it had all the makings of a trap.

"You will be happy, won't you, love?" For a moment Amabel, understanding happiness only as she had learned it from her husband, looked anxious.

"Yes, mother. Very happy."

And responding at once to her daughter's stronger character, her far more natural authority, Amabel's frown was gone.

"Then we must have champagne at once—do tell Mrs. Drubb. And oh—my darlings—do you think a *Christmas* wedding? Lovely—how lovely, with holly in the church and white velvet, and Christmas roses. The very best time of year."

And a midsummer grandchild perhaps, for her to smother in lace and swansdown and affection; to provide her with yet another reason for persuading her husband to buy her the house of her dreams on a green hillside miles and miles out of this smoky, hideous old town. Clean air for the child? John-William would surely listen to that.

"Invitations," she said. "Guest lists. The trousseau. Bridesmaids. The *complications*. Good Heavens."

"Dear Aunt Amabel," murmured Linnet. "I am here to help you."

And they sat down together, their scented heads very close, infinitely confidential, to begin their preparations, leaving Tristan smiling vaguely out of the window, feeling himself somewhat surplus to their requirements but not liking to appear ungracious by hurrying away to take his horse to the blacksmith, the destination for which he had been heading when Gemma had intercepted him. "We must go and tell mother," she'd said. Here he was. And now, with the sort of composure he was used to in Linnet, it was Gemma, with a frank, straightforward smile he thought both friendly and reasonable, who gave him leave to go.

"You were taking your horse to be shod, weren't you, Tristan? Shouldn't you be on your way?"

"Oh—I say—is that all right? You don't mind?"

"Not at all."

He smiled back at her gratefully, charmingly, knowing that practically any other girl—certainly Linnet—would have expected him to dance attendance for the rest of the day. And if Gemma had wanted that, then he would have done it, and with a good heart too, for although he knew himself to be a fortune-hunter and would cheerfully admit as much to any of his college friends or hunting friends— since what else was a fellow to do when the family coffers were empty, if he wasn't precisely a genius and wanted to keep up his standards?—he believed, nevertheless, that one had to be as decent as one could about it. After all, the girl—any girl—was entitled to a proper return on her money. And whatever Gemma wanted from him—and he wasn't fool enough to think it was due entirely to his good looks—then she must have it. He was a gentleman and a sportsman after all, and there was such a thing as fair play.

"Do hurry, Tristan. Our blacksmith is a mighty man and hates to be kept waiting."

He gave her another quite dazzling smile and left, whistling merrily enough to convince anyone who happened to meet him that he was a young man in love. Although Gemma herself had been grateful to him, half an hour before, when she had accepted his proposal, for not forcing upon her a display of emotion she knew he did not feel.

Not a few of Frizingley's young ladies would envy her. Her mother was still blissfully, volubly, in her seventh heaven. Her father, when he returned from the mill, would talk terms and settlements and, before giving his formal consent, would feel obliged to bring up the subject of Tristan's career, making it plain that a secretarial position with an obscure MP could not impress him. But Gemma knew that when all was settled to his liking about her trust fund and the allowances he proposed to make her as a married woman, she would soon persuade him to buy her mother the country home she wanted, and give this house to her.

Certainly he would never wish to dispose of it in any other fashion, for the purchase of this strange, dark house with its low ceilings and tiny mullioned windowpanes, the ancient seat of the Goldsborough family, lords of the manor of Frizingley for long generations, had been one of the crowning glories of his career. And he had never lost the deep glow of satisfaction afforded him on the day that he, John-William Dallam of no pedigree whatsoever and precious little education, had brought his wife to be mistress of the Goldsboroughs' by then long-empty home at Frizingley Hall.

Not that she had ever liked it much, or so she now imagined, the history and nobility which so appealed to her husband—and to Gemma—being no compensation in Amabel's eyes for the proximity of Frizingley itself. For the house, once set apart from the town on a slope of woodland and green meadows, had been an early victim to industrial expansion, the Goldsboroughs not realizing perhaps, or not caring, when iron ore was discovered on their land, that the sale of the mineral rights to the first Mr. Colclough entitled him to build a foundry which in turn required workers who, in *their* turn, required row upon mean little row of cottages to live in, mean little shops in which to spend their wages, ale-houses in such quantity—since men who work all day with hot iron are famous for their thirst—that the first Mr. Lord had come along to open his brewery, with more cottages, more clatter, more carts creaking up and down the hill, more heavy horses. More urchins collecting the manure for sale and paddling in the sewage channels. More mongrel dogs. More fleas. So that the Goldsboroughs, appalled at the desecration of their fields, the felling of their trees, the invasion of their lordly privacy, and having lost what little remained of their money by then in any case, had sold all they had left to sell—the manor—to Mr. John-William Dallam, of Dallam's mill.

The Goldsboroughs had dispersed, married money where they could, taken refuge in the army, gone off to manage sugar plantations and tea plantations in hot Colonial places; in some cases—one heard—had gone to jail. And now all that was left of them was the faintly sinister, probably disreputable *Captain* Goldsborough—a claim fully substantiated by his sun-dried military look—who, turning up some years ago from nowhere he seemed much inclined to mention, had taken possession of the derelict city properties still attached to the Goldsborough inheritance, establishing himself at the Fleece. A gentleman by education, no one ever doubted, although he had made Amabel very nervous on the two or three times she had met him, entirely dispelling her first romantic notion that, as the last of the Goldsboroughs, he would make a fitting husband for Gemma.

"*Not* a marrying man," John-William had said and she dated her dislike of the manor from the time of Captain Goldsborough's arrival, mainly because she had to date it from somewhere, although, in fact, she had been unhappy with these heavy beams and creaking floorboards ever since the Braithwaites had built their imitation Gothic castle, and the Colcloughs and the Lords had moved to high, spacious houses with wrought-iron balconies and a great deal of ornamental stonework a mile or so out of town.

And then, of course, she had become acquainted with the Larks of rural "Queen Anne" Moorby Hall.

But Gemma, intimidated neither by Captain Goldsborough in the flesh nor the portraits of his ancestors still hanging in the upstairs gallery, had always loved these dim, quiet rooms, cool and serene with age and full of unexpected light and shadow, the garden, rich with ancient trees and crumbling stone pathways, thickly enclosed by an ivy-clad wall, as hushed as a cloister on one side, a raucous city street on the other whose teeming life was a source of stimulation rather than offense to her.

She loved it. As a married woman she could—with a little contriving—live here as its mistress, ordering her life according to her own judgment. Yes. There seemed no doubt that if she handled matters correctly her life as a fully adult woman could now—*at last*—begin.

"Petticoats," she heard her mother say. "And chemises. At least four dozen of each, wouldn't you think? Oh dear. I wonder how Miss Baker will ever cope with it? What with the bridesmaids' dresses and the evening gowns, and something decent to go away in. And then all our guests will be ordering new things for themselves, I dare say.

Such a heap of work for the poor woman—Easter bonnet time and Christmas rolled into one. I shall have nightmares, I do assure you, in case she lets me down."

"There are plenty of other milliners," murmured Linnet. "Manchester, perhaps? Or London?"

Yes. Why not a trip to London for the trousseau? Linnet, with an eye to a trousseau of her own, would enjoy that and would certainly benefit, in the silk mercers' shops, from the overflow of Amabel's generous heart. But Gemma, her mind on her own well-charted future, feeling that she was more than halfway to taking the reins into her own hands, suddenly remembered the Irish girl, still waiting, she supposed, with her heavy bag and her bravely painted hatbox, her sparkling chatter of French and Venetian lace, the failing eyesight of her rival Miss Baker, and her own triumphs in the fabled rue Saint Honoré.

"Oh mother—by the way," she said, speaking briskly so that Linnet might hear her authority. "A young woman has called to see me —quite a talented dressmaker, I'd say, by the things she showed me. She's waiting in the back parlor. And since we're talking of petticoats, I'll just fetch her."

And hurrying along the passage—not quite the mistress of the house as yet but, there again, no longer *quite* its unmarried, dependent daughter—she opened the parlor door and said pleasantly, "Miss Adeane, I have just become engaged to be married. You may congratulate me."

"That I do, Miss Dallam."

At once Cara's eyes were swiftly, expertly measuring her, clothing her in bridal brocades and satins, a going-away dress for a winter honeymoon, feathered bonnets, embroidered, lace-topped gloves.

"You'll be needing a trousseau then? A big one?"

"I do believe so. Would you come into the drawing-room to discuss your part of it?"

Cara's smile, banishing all traces of exhaustion, was dazzling. "With pleasure, *madam*." And to her surprise, the smile with which plain, sturdy, serious Miss Dallam answered her held a hint of mischief, the unremarkable brown eyes a most becoming twinkle.

"Good. But I wouldn't mention your Madame Récamier. It may cause confusion. And as to the lace you showed me earlier, my mother won't know the difference between Chantilly and Point de Venise. But my fiancé's sister is there, and one has the distinct feeling that she will."

4

*L*innet Gage did not take kindly to Gemma's "Protégée" as she at once chose to call her, although her objections were no more than soft-voiced little hints as to the unreliability of strangers, addressed carefully to Amabel. "One can't help wondering where girls like that come from. Or, indeed, just *where* they go."

And had Amabel been slightly less enchanted by her new status as the mother of a bride she would have heard, drifting on the cool air behind Linnet's voice, the suggestion of squalid city tenements, immodesty, strong drink and—above all—the dread, ever present in Amabel, of disease conveyed in the hem of a dress, the sole of a shoe, the point of an embroidery needle as it pressed typhoid or cholera or the pox into the lace insertions of her only daughter's wedding lingerie; the four dozen petticoats, nightgowns, chemises and "everything"—Amabel knowing no word she cared for to describe that *other* undergarment—she had ordered as a trial from a girl Linnet had instinctively mistrusted because she was beautiful and because Gemma, rather than Linnet herself, had recommended her.

But, leaving the cloistered manor garden and hurrying back through the rows of brewery houses and foundry houses to the street called St. Jude's, her carpetbag and her hatbox feeling light with triumph in her hands, Cara remained untroubled by Miss Linnet Gage's hostility. She had sensed it, certainly, for it was her business to be aware of such things, forewarned and then forearmed, always careful, always guarding her back, which had been aching rather more than she liked these last few days. Nor did she underestimate the influence a penniless, clever woman like Linnet might come to have in a rich household, particularly over a woman such as Mrs. Dallam who could surely be influenced by anybody. But, miraculously and for reasons she had no time to question, Miss Gemma Dallam, the young bride soon to be a young matron with her own household staff to clothe, her own money to spend, had taken a fancy to her. And what mattered was that after these three weary months of finding nothing but a bonnet here and there to be cheaply remodeled, an old evening gown to be laboriously unpicked and made over in the latest fashion, she was going home with some real work to do.

Not by her own hands alone, of course. In fact, thinking of the quality of the needlework which would be required to impress Mrs. Dallam and pass the scrutiny of Miss Linnet Gage, perhaps not by her hands at all. But by Odette's, her mother's; a far finer craftswoman than Cara herself ever hoped to be. Although she had taken good care at the Dallams', not to mention that.

For if Odette had grown stronger—*looked* stronger, at any rate—since the night of Cara's arrival in Frizingley, she was still far too quiet, too reticent, too "dreamy" to make the right impression of flair and self-assurance on a customer.

Cara had found her mother soon after leaving Daniel that night in a state very much as she had expected, grieving inwardly and hopelessly, without tears, as Cara had seen the widow-woman grieving in Liverpool, sitting down on the ground to wait, with blank despair, to be comforted or condemned, to be locked up in official custody or left at liberty to starve; not much caring about either.

So too had been the face of Odette Adeane: beyond anxiety, quite ready to place her patient neck into the noose with dignity—the only coin she had left—and even a certain measure of relief, until Cara had hugged her and shaken her, reminded her of Liam, of how her grandson—and her daughter—loved her and needed her.

"Mother, I love you. *Maman, je t'aime. J'ai besoin de toi.* So does Liam."

Smiling wanly Odette had acknowledged her daughter's words to be true. And even then she had been reluctant to push aside the veil of damp air in which she seemed to have been moving since her husband's departure, a veil so heavy that although its dragging pressure had wearied her and slowed her down, it had also prevented her—as she stood very quiet and cold on its other side—from seeing anything too clearly, from feeling anything too sharp.

"He has gone such a long way, Cara—this time."

"Yes, mother." And Cara's hot words of blame and accusation had faded on her tongue, not worth the dissipation of her energy. He

64

would not come back. Her mother knew that. Nor, while he remained dependent on his sister, would he be likely to send for her. She knew that too. And if Miss Teresa Adeane of New York made life sufficiently agreeable, then he might in his middle years entirely lose his appetite for chasing rainbows. In which case—as his daughter at least could grimly acknowledge—he would put those shimmering colors out of his mind altogether. And forget.

He would make a new life for himself without them.

So must they.

"He was tired," Odette had whispered. "And he was afraid."

"I'm not afraid, mother."

But, as they had stood close together in the gathering twilight of an alien city, her courage had been a lie. It often was.

She *had* been afraid. Only a fool, she thought, would have been otherwise.

"I don't think—Cara—that there is anything we can do."

But Cara's youth, her vanity, her quite ruthless appetite for the nineteen years already lived and at least a hundred more to come, would have none of that.

"There's always something to be done."

Odette, retreating again behind her veil—her shroud—had smiled gently, pityingly, and shaken her head. No. Her money had gone. Her employment had been terminated in such a manner that no one else would employ her. Unjustly? Of course. But what of that? There was money owing. A debt which never *could* be paid. And she too was tired. Not afraid precisely. In fact, and most oddly, not afraid at all. What would happen would happen. Perhaps she would just sit down somewhere and wait for it.

Taking her roughly by the elbow Cara had hurried her at once and with all the speed she could muster to the Thackrays, pushed her through the door to be claimed and held fast by Liam and then, before Sairellen could stop her, had dashed off again down the cobbled street straight into the clamorous heart of Frizingley, to find Miss Ernestine Baker, dressmaker and milliner, whose arid, virginal heart had been aroused—most likely, she thought, by accident—to love and cruelty by Kieron Adeane.

And there, in the dark, discreet shop with its odors of thread and fabric she had stood with meekly bowed head, offering herself as a new victim to appease Miss Baker's jealous ire; her bewildered outrage that she could have entertained such sentiments about an Irish wastrel in the first place and that he—when he had deigned to notice them—had spurned her. Had preferred, in fact, his sad little foreign drab, Odette.

"I have considerable experience in the dressmaking trade," Cara had murmured, meaning "You have abused my mother until it bored you. Now—if you like—you can abuse me." It was almost a promise. Odette had not understood Miss Baker's need to punish. Cara did not consciously understand it either. She simply knew that jealous old cats require to scratch and that this one might scratch as hard as she pleased if it opened the door to employment.

"What experience?"

And Cara had not spoken of Paris, neither Miss Baker's restrained appearance nor the discreet quality of her merchandise having much in common with the rue Saint Honoré, but of her apprenticeship in the more serious-minded city of Edinburgh, her work as a skilled journeywoman in Dublin.

"It has long been my view," replied Miss Baker, "that persons of Celtic origin are not reliable. An opinion not unshared, believe me, in this locality where you will find many doors completely barred to—*Celts*."

But Cara had merely breathed, "I am sure you are right," her voice promising to be humble, to do penance for her father's sins in any manner Miss Baker liked, for as long, that is, as she continued to pay living wages.

And Miss Ernestine Baker, immaculate spinster of the parish of Frizingley, had been tempted.

"Our hours of work in this establishment," she had said, tight-lipped, straight-backed, quite certain that this flibbertigibbet would never stand it, "are twelve daily, from six in the morning until the same hour at night, including Saturdays. That is, of course, when conditions of work are normal. During periods of increased business— Easter, for example, when all my ladies are requiring new bonnets, or a ball at the Assembly Rooms to which all my ladies are naturally invited—then my women are required to remain at their work until it is finished. Simply that. Eighteen hours. Twenty. For as long as the busy period lasts."

"Of course, Miss Baker." As much would be asked of her any-where else. And she had too much sense even to imagine that Miss Baker would pay overtime.

"Very well." Miss Baker drew back her thin lips, exposing prominent, well-regimented teeth in a satisfied smile. "Let me give an example—Adeane—of the effort which will often be required of you. Last winter, shortly before the festive season, my orders for ball gowns and dinner gowns were such that my women, apprentices included, had no time even to change their clothes for seven full days and nights. They remained here, in the workroom, for the whole of that time, taking turns to rest on the mattress I provided, not even leaving their work for meals which I had served to them at their work-tables. I even had their meat cut up for them by the good woman who cooks for me, to save delay. Such—you see—is my reputation for excellence in my trade, that the ladies of Frizingley and hereabouts refuse to go elsewhere."

"You are to be congratulated, Miss Baker."

"Yes. I am. And furthermore, I require my women to be of good behavior and good character. Milliners, who often leave their place of employment at a late hour to walk home alone in the dark, inevitably find themselves accosted from time to time by men—one assumes of the lower sort. As a result of which the trade has acquired a reputation for moral laxity which I do not tolerate in anyone in *my* employ. It has even been alleged, perhaps with good reason in some quarters, that needlewomen, in the off-season, are much inclined to supplement their incomes by—well, shall we say by according their favors to men for money? You take my meaning?"

"I do."

"Then also take note of the fact that I do not expect seasonal fluctuations of trade to affect the moral standards of *my* women. I had a competitor—once—whose business never recovered after the loose behavior of her girls during the slump of 1831 came to light. Ladies do not care to be pinned and fitted into their dresses by hands which are morally unclean. It is not only the indecency they mind, but the possibility of disease."

"Of course, Miss Baker."

"I repeat. No breath of scandal. Nor do I expect you to put yourself forward in front of customers nor to pass comment of any kind unless specifically invited by *me* to do so. In which case you will simply agree with whatever opinion I happen to have been expressing. Otherwise keep your mouth full of pins when called upon to assist with a fitting, and your eyes on your work."

"Yes, Miss Baker."

The wages would suffice to pay for Odette's board and lodging—

hopefully Liam's—with Sairellen Thackray. But there remained the matter of a lodging for herself. And the specter of her father's debt for which, not the law of England perhaps, but the personal legal code of the landlord of the Fleece Tavern might oblige her to be responsible.

She had still a long, hard way to go.

Liam had shared Odette's bed that first night. Happily, Cara supposed. Although she had had no time to ask him. No energy either, as she had attempted to ease herself into the wooden chair which was all Sairellen had seen fit to offer her, the kitchen grown chilly without its daytime steams and odors of drying laundry and simmering broth. But Luke Thackray, without any expression of concern or sympathy —just getting on quietly and competently with what he thought to be right—had brought her a pillow and a blanket and had made up the fire, in his unhurried manner, with enough coal to last the night.

"Aye, that's right, lad," his mother had told him with heavy sarcasm. "Don't stint. Just pile it on. There's plenty more coal in the pit, I reckon. So I wouldn't want you to worry about what's left in my cellar."

But it was no more than the gruff-textured, sharp-edged quality of their affection and instead of reminding her—as he certainly could have done—that, having paid his fair share for the coal he was entitled to his share of the use of it, he merely grinned up at her and went on constructing, with his engineer's precision, a pyramid of fuel designed to burn slowly and steadily and evenly throughout the night.

Such a man was Luke Thackray, who had brought her a mug of hot tea at half past four the next morning, an even more welcome jug of hot water and a shallow metal basin so that she could wash and tidy herself for her first appearance in the workroom of Miss Ernestine Baker. And even Sairellen, with her inbred understanding that a family which fails to feed its workers loses its livelihood, had broken her rule about waifs and strays and offered Cara a slice of the bread and pork-dripping she was putting up for Luke to eat in the mill at breakfast time.

He would come home, of course, at noon for his bacon and potato pie and his barley broth, the fuel a working man needed as much as those infernal machines of theirs needed their steam. What could Cara Adeane find, throughout the next twelve captive hours, to still her hunger? And roughly, abruptly, before she thought better of it,

Sairellen had thrust into her hand another slice of bread and lard tied up in a clean red and white spotted handkerchief. A proper mill worker's bundle.

"Not dainty enough for Miss Baker, I reckon. But if it stops you from swooning into the hatboxes—like your mother..."

And smiling a "thank you kindly" she had known better than to say out loud, Cara had gone off into the damp Frizingley air of a quarter past five o'clock, Luke Thackray beside her, his own spotted calico bundle under his arm, to join the slow-moving ant-stream of workers hurrying three and four abreast to the mill, some of them— the less fleet-footed—fearing to be late and locked out already. For the mill-gates of Mr. Ben Braithwaite and Mr. John-William Dallam were closed tight shut five minutes after the warning hooter at half past five, to be opened again only at eight o'clock breakfast time. And who, in this crowd, could afford the fine for late arrival and the loss of two and a half hours pay?

They were women mostly, shawl-wrapped against the cold, and anonymous, their feet in wooden clogs strident on the cobbles. And children. A little older than they used to be since "The Act"—seven years ago now—had forbidden the masters to employ children under nine years old; although Cara had noticed plenty that morning who looked no more than a frail, bleary-eyed six or seven. For who but a mother could be expected to remember just when a child was born? And, with many an overlooker being happy to take a mother's word, they were still coming in droves to the factories, pasty and puny for the most part, marked with the crooked spines and bandy legs, the stunted growth that came from forcing soft young bones to hard work and long hours too soon. Although the hours were fewer now, since "The Act." No more than forty-eight a week for children from nine to thirteen, rising, at eighteen, to a mere sixty-eight.

Sairellen Thackray had known far worse than that in her day. So had Cara. So had Odette, having spent even more time than her daughter in the one-room workshops of the sweated trades where none of "The Act's" new factory inspectors came to call. Nor would have gained admittance had they done so.

Children were put to work by their parents who needed the money. It had been ever thus. And if John-William Dallam's clever daughter, Gemma, disliked the sight of these wizened, visibly ageing babies tottering through his mill-gates every morning then—as he had once sharply reminded her—she would do well to follow her mother's example by declining to look. Whereas Cara had looked so often that her vision was often blurred, busy with other matters, obscured.

But a child had stumbled against her that first morning and watching her set him to rights, Luke Thackray had said "You'd not care to take your own little lad to the mill this morning? Or put him down a mine?"

"I would not."

"Nor I. It is a vile practice. An abomination." Yet he had spoken the emotional words quietly, no agitation even remotely visible on his craggy, overcrowded face.

"Yes. I suppose it is." She saw not the remotest possibility of anything being done to change it.

"Have you heard of Richard Oastler?"

No. She had not. And unless he had a silk mercer's shop in which to employ her, or was about to set up business as a fan maker, what could she wish to know?

"Oastler of Huddersfield? They call him the Factory King."

A rich man then? Powerful? Her interest had rekindled. But no.

"He is the leader of the Ten Hours' Movement. Have you heard of that? A ten hour working day, not just for children but for everybody."

"The Act" again? But Luke had shaken his head.

"If the Act had gone far enough you'd not see these little sleep-walkers now, would you? They'd be still in their beds, or getting ready for school, which is where they *ought* to be going. And I wouldn't have to keep my eyes open all day to make sure they don't fall asleep at their work. One of my own brothers, years back, lost an arm from nodding off over a loom. And if the lasses get their hair caught in the machinery, then like as not, it scalps them. I make them pin their hair up but not everybody bothers. And twelve hours a day—at nine years old—with happen a three mile walk to get there and a three mile walk back . . . Well—they get sleepy on that, the little 'uns. And, in a factory, sleepy bairns can mean dead bairns—often enough. That's why so many of the overlookers use a strap. Better a few clouts on the backside than arms and legs going round the shaft. Oastler was determined to put a stop to it. Still is."

"And you follow him—this Oastler?"

Looking down at her Luke Thackray gave her his steady smile, his pale eyes filled with a quiet, shrewd, wholly clement humor.

"Aye. Although Ben Braithwaite would very likely sack me if he knew it. I walked ninety miles behind Oastler once. Me and a few thousand others—Ten Hours' Men, and women, from all over the West Riding. Eight years back when we were fighting for "The Act"—or for what we thought an act of parliament ought to be. He'd called a mass meeting in the Castle Yard at York and we marched every step of the way—to get justice for the factory children—Oastler with us. And he still had the strength to stand up and talk to us for about five hours when we got there, and attend the dance we gave in Huddersfield when we got back. Four days on the road in all it took us. To get ourselves cheated by that fiddling little Act. We'd asked for ten hours a day for women and children, knowing that it wouldn't pay them to keep the engines running just for the men—so it would be ten hours all round. They gave us twelve hours for the very young, which means no respite at all for the rest of us, since all the masters do is employ the bairns in relays, which means they can keep the mills open day and night. It wasn't enough. And Oastler said so. He's in prison now."

A sudden, sharp memory had stung her then, very hard, of Daniel Carey lounging on the peddler's cart among the bales of calico, telling her that the man he had come to Leeds to see was in prison too. For printing dangerous opinions about "one man, one vote" and the payment of salaries to MPs.

"For treason?" she said. Was it treason to interfere with the working hours of factories? To plug the source of cheap labor which had made so many fortunes in Frizingley and elsewhere? It sounded highly likely. But, once again, Luke Thackray had given her his unhurried grin.

"No. For debt. He put all his savings into the Short-Time Movement. And borrowed more. So that made it easy, I reckon, for anybody who happened to want him out of the way. They sent him to the Fleet Debtors' prison in London just a few days ago."

And Luke, noticing the flicker of sarcasm in her eye that said, "Oh yes. Another idealist, this Factory King. Another who wants to save the world and can't look after himself," had not told her that he had made over one tenth of his income as an overlooker at Braithwaite's mill—where small children were employed in droves, the smaller the better—not to church or chapel as many did, but toward the support of Richard Oastler's wife and family and the eventual repayment of his debt.

Instead, reaching the end of Market Square where he had to take the left hand turning and she the right, he had said, very calmly, "Don't worry about your little lad. My mother won't turn him out. She walked those ninety miles to York with Oastler too, to save the factory brats. So she'll not send yours to the workhouse, if she can help it."

"You mean if *I* can help it."

He had smiled again, not touching her although it had seemed to her that, without any physical contact whatsoever, he had somehow given her a handclasp of friendship and encouragement.

"Aye. So I reckon."

And thanking him, liking him—enormously relieved that he had not spoiled the ease of their relations with all the amorous nonsense she had so often to contend with—she had run off to Miss Ernestine Baker's, to spend her twelve hours double-hemming the cambric frills on another girl's trousseau and thinking about Daniel Carey, indulging herself, when Miss Baker's rule of total silence became hard to bear, with her few but infinitely precious memories of him.

She supposed she had fallen in love with him, not the pleasant, flirtatious loving she had known with Liam's father which, for all its awkward consequences, had left her a certain taste of sweetness, a faint murmur of laughter, but in the deep and dangerous manner of her mother, Odette. And if *that* was what it was then, having seen its effects at such close quarters, she must guard herself against it. Bending low over her work in case a flicker of all she was feeling might show in her face and be thus revealed to Miss Baker's watchful, waiting eyes, she acknowledged, fully and finally, that, left to herself, she would be ready to walk barefoot through the world with Daniel, to endure abandonment in tedious, troublesome places—as her mother had always done—and then go running joyfully to meet him at his call. Like Odette. Considering herself, in those moments of passionate reunion, the most fortunate of women. How terrible. If he called to her now she would lay down these empty lengths of cambric and leap through that window over there, if necessary, to get to him. Floating. Flying. Transformed by love. Exalted. Or she knew she would like to. Had there been no one else but herself to consider. But there was Odette. And Liam. And a part of herself, moreover, which still fought hard against him, seeing his love as tyranny, bondage. And not all of her wished to be bound. Very little of her wished to spend her life in the pursuit of grand ideals—no better than her father's rainbows—which would neither warm her in winter nor even thank her any too kindly for her self-sacrifice. *Very* little of her could feel any enthusiasm for that. None of her, in fact.

Yet she had been told often enough, by Odette, that true love comes only once. And having seen its intensity in her mother, having felt it now in her own far from trusting heart, she felt much inclined to believe it. Very well. If this was true love then it frightened her. It enchanted her too, of course, made her feel weak and foolish and aglow with a most ridiculous happiness when there was absolutely nothing to be pleased about at all. But mainly she was afraid. Of him. Of herself. Of what this wild and beautiful intoxication could do if she really let it take hold of her. If she allowed herself to need it and take the risk of becoming a wraith in a damp veil of misery without it. Like Odette.

Far better never to see him again. Far safer and saner to content herself with the lesser emotions of liking, growing fond, the negative pleasures of *not* agonizing, *not* burning, *not* longing. Not exalting either, of course, but never sinking into the pit. Always in control. Bending a little lower she began to pray in the vague direction of any saint or angel who happened to be listening. "Please help me. 'Tis more often I can manage on my own than not. But you can't be expecting me to be strong about everything. Now can you? Well— how's this? If I don't trouble you about looking after Liam and my mother and about how to pay my rent can you just be helping me not to lose my head—or worse—over *him*?"

And that evening, released from bondage of a more familiar sort, with Miss Baker's parting instructions to conduct herself becomingly in the street, to walk close to the wall like a nun, ignoring the lascivious glances of men, above all to go straight home and to bed in order to equip herself for tomorrow's labors, she had murmured, "Yes, Miss Baker," and gone instead to make her arrangements with the landlord of the Fleece.

She had expected a raucous pot-house full of navvies and whores and local bullies like the Rose and Crown on the opposite side of St. Jude's Square; or a sinister, pitch-dark cavern like the Dog and Gun—both these hostelries rumored to belong to Captain Goldsborough—where stolen goods were thought to change hands in the furtive shadows, and unstamped radical newspapers were certainly read. Or the Beehive on the other corner of St. Jude's, where they still matched fighting-cocks illegally on moonlit nights in the inn yard and held bare-knuckle prizefights sometimes—in which a young lad, not long ago, had been killed. One of the other journeywomen at Miss Baker's, who seemed intimately acquainted with a sporting gentleman, had told Cara all about it during their short midday break. And she had been surprised—pleasantly, for a moment—with the low-ceilinged, oak-paneled bar-parlor of the Fleece, the wood black and rich with age, impregnated to its core with the odors of beer and spirits and tobacco which had caused her to blink for a moment in the gloom and then almost to gasp at her good fortune as her eyes focused on the man coming around the bar to meet her. No sinister usurer after all but a huge, amiable-looking man with the massive build and the scarred, knocked-about face of an ageing prizefighter who had perhaps not gained *too* many prizes. An Irishman too. What luck. A man whose eyes, sunk beneath their puffy, battered lids, looked at her with the kind of longing-to-touch with which she was all too familiar, yet whose cordial strong-man's gentleness—the faint deference of a man who knew himself to be ugly—did not threaten her. A man who liked women and who could therefore be *managed*.

"I'm Cara Adeane. Kieron Adeane's daughter."

"I'm Ned O'Mara."

Her heart sank instantly, coldly. Of course, she should have known.

"The captain's away," he told her. "Don't ask me where. He comes and goes. He said if you come along and you was looking for work I was to give you some. We always need a barmaid. Ha' you done that afore?" She had.

"All right then. I suppose he reckons that if you're not earnin' then you can't be payin' him. And he'll settle with you, as it suits him, when he gets back."

So be it. "I can come just after six o'clock."

"Until midnight? Fourpence an hour and whatever the customers like to give you."

It was riches. And when a man was taking pleasure in being generous and had that particular half-foolish look in his eye it was a time to ask for more.

"And my dinner?"

He had shrugged. "There's always food here."

She would need it. Twelve respectable hours with Miss Baker. Six more she would be advised to keep quiet about here at the Fleece. Fourpence an hour. And tips. And the incredible bonus of meat pies and suet puddings standing untended in the inn kitchen, finding their way into her never-quite-satisfied stomach and into her pocket for

Liam. A mouthful, here and there, filched from the corner of a beef-steak or a mutton chop. Deep custard tarts rich with eggs and vanilla which crumbled easily—if one knew how to go about it—and so could not be served to customers. A jug of ale at suppertime which was safer than drinking water in these pestilential cities and would help to keep her strong. And a drop to take home for Odette, to put her to sleep and do her good. Nourishment. So that she could use her precious fourpences for other things.

"I suppose you know that the Fleece is no place for a decent woman?" Sairellen Thackray had told her, with no real condemnation in her hard eye, since decency—as they both knew—had rarely counted for much against the essential keeping together of body and soul.

"I know, Mrs. Thackray."

"Aye. I reckoned you would."

And Sairellen had made no more than a token protest when Luke had taken Cara across the street, where the back-to-back cottages began, and showed her the empty two-roomed hovel—one up, one down—from which a family of twelve had recently been evicted for arrears of a not particularly modest rent, and sent to the warehouse.

The place had been a pigsty, of course, reeking with the stagnant memory of half a dozen incontinent children and as many cats, the floorboards moist and rotting, unpainted walls streaked with grime, the outer door off its hinges, the inner doors having been chopped up long ago for firewood. And not much chance that the landlord would offer to replace them. But the landlord in question was—as almost always, it seemed, in that area—Captain Goldsborough of the Fleece. And, in the Captain's absence, Ned O'Mara had let her have the cottage without an increase in rent. There was no indoor water supply anywhere in St. Jude's, of course, except the taverns, and find-ing no stand-pipe turned on after three o'clock in the afternoon, she had begged buckets of hot water from Sairellen's fireside boiler which Luke had carried in tireless relays across the street, working beside her in an easy silence at an hour of the night which Sairellen not only considered immoral but dangerous, since it kept him from taking his hard-earned rest in bed.

"That's right, lad. Stay up all night, and then we shall all be split-ting our sides tomorrow when we hear about the overlooker—not the bairns—falling into the machines. Dead tired. Or—as I expect somebody'll be saying—dead drunk. Dead, at any rate. Like your brother Mark. And your brother Tim. But don't let that stop you."

75

"I reckon not, mother."

And calmly he continued to repair the windowframes and the outer door while Cara and Odette had scrubbed and mopped and Odette, at least, had wept with fatigue into the pails of dirty water.

"Charity begins at home," Sairellen had reminded him grimly. "And even at home there's only so much to go around."

And she had fixed Cara with a sharp, scathing stare which had warned her loud and clear, "I've got your measure, my lass. He's a good man. And if you think all you have to do is flash those bright eyes to get the best of him, for as long as he's useful to you, then think again. Because *I* won't stand for it. He walked ninety miles for Richard Oastler with my blessing. But, mark my words, I'll make sure he doesn't walk an extra yard for you."

But when Cara returned from the Fleece the following night, her head and her back, her whole over-strung body aching from her twelve cramped hours of needlework, her pert, brightly-smiling, footsore duty behind the bar counter, Sairellen and such of Sairellen's neighbors who owed her a favor had scoured the two rooms from top to bottom, made up the cracks in the plaster, blocked the mouse-holes, painted walls and windowframes, black-leaded the hearth, given her the bare, bleached framework of a home.

She begged a mattress from the lumber room at the Fleece and a pair of old barrels to stand outside her door to collect rainwater—often much cleaner than the cloudy stand-pipe brew—so that she could wash her hair whenever she wanted, and her son. Slowly, week by week, she had bought unredeemed chairs and rugs, pots and pans, odds and ends, from the pawnshops which stood so conveniently on every corner, running from one place of work to another like a fox with the pack at her heels, while Odette, from her store of fabrics and trimmings collected in better days, had begun to fashion the dainty garments of silk and lace, the marvels of embroidery, the dashing feathered hats which she was too timid to sell.

A life. The wolf still at the door perhaps but not by any means across the threshold. The rent paid. Bread in the stone jar above the sink. Odette's potato soup with whatever could be gleaned from the Fleece kitchens simmering on their own hearth in their own iron pot. Liam talking again, mainly to Odette and in French, clinging to her more than he should, perhaps, and getting himself laughed at by the neighboring children who, left to their own devices while their mothers went to the mill, could be very rough. As she herself had once been. Not Liam. And it seemed foolish to complain about that.

A life. And not such a bad one when she remembered other lives, in other places. Nothing in pawn. Nothing owing; except the specter of her father's debt which, in Captain Goldsborough's continued absence, she had pushed to a comfortable corner of her mind. To be dealt with later, perhaps never. No news from her father, but her own heart hardened toward him far beyond grief, her mother finding consolation—surely?—in Liam. A good friend in Luke—when he could spare the time from his lectures at the Mechanics Institute, his reading, his Sunday walking in the hills, his mother. A steady man, the only one she had ever known, who did not seem to desire her or, if he did, chose not to make it a burden. A friend of sorts in Ned O'Mara, who seemed content, at present, to do her small services for which he had not asked—as yet—to be rewarded. A killing fatigue, of course, from time to time. But she was being paid reasonably well for it.

A life. So that when Daniel Carey had suddenly reappeared in Frizingley, rising up from the pavement before her, as lean and angry and beautiful as she remembered, she had been able to toss her head at him and tell him tales of triumph about her sweet little new house, her wonderful situation with dear Miss Baker who treated her like a daughter, covering up her employment at the Fleece with bright chatter of "friends to visit," "friends coming to call," "Life is such a merry whirl in the evenings in this friendly little town."

But he had watched her, made his inquiries, and had stepped out of the shadows again, blocking her path, demanding explanations, laying a furious hand on her arm which she had just as furiously shaken off, telling him he had no right—none—go away; his answering snarl of accusation, which had branded her a liar, a cheat, far worse than that, causing her to strike out at him, wanting to hurt him, and badly; his violence answering hers until somehow what was burning inside them had assumed a different identity and they had found themselves pressed close together against the wall of Miss Baker's infinitely discreet shop, shaking in each others arms, hurting each other now with love and, at the same time, presenting to Miss Baker the very spectacle of Cara's debauchery she had been waiting for.

Like father like daughter. Very well. Now—since the father had eluded her with such villainous cunning—let the daughter be punished. For she had offered money to Kieron Adeane and, even in the dire predicament in which he had been struggling, he had refused it. Not even his fear of Christie Goldsborough had been able to bind him to her. Therefore *somebody* would have to pay for her humiliation.

"You are a slattern," she had declared joyfully the next morning, having assembled her entire workroom to witness Cara's dismissal and disgrace. "And, as such, I am—naturally—unable to give you a recommendation. Which means—Adeane—that you will find no further employment in Frizingley."

"Ah well, Miss Baker." And Cara, having nothing more to lose, had grown flippant and hard. "Sure and at least I won't die a virgin."

And the next morning she had painted the brave slogan "Cara Adeane. Dressmaker and Milliner." on Odette's old hatbox and, the paint barely dry, begun the patient, persuasive, often mortifying business of knocking on doors.

Her personal treasures, her earrings and silver bracelets had gone to the pawnshop forever, her best skirt and bodice reposing there for usually a day or two each week until some generous or drunken reveler at the Fleece gave her a tip large enough to get them out. Luke had offered to lend her money which she had gladly accepted. She had thrown in Daniel's face the few coins he had managed to scrape together and told him to take them—and himself—to the devil. She put in more hours at the Fleece and stole rather more pies.

She suffered such exhaustion, and such fear, that she became brittle and light-headed sometimes, could hear her own voice chattering like a demented starling about "Madam would look exquisite in blue satin —a marvel in lavender—just a touch of blonde lace at the throat"— while her own throat grew tight with panic, her skin crawled, every hair on the back of her neck rising in disgust and horror whenever she passed the new workhouse they were building on the hill beyond the top of St. Jude's Street.

All that would be needed—she was constantly and fully aware of it—was for her to slip on these wet cobbles and break a leg, catch a chill or a fever, become pregnant with another child, be unable, for the few weeks it took to heal from her malady, to pay her rent, and those workhouse doors would open wide. And although the Poor Law commissioners insisted that the workhouse was not a prison, *how*—once her furniture and her clothes and Odette's clothes had been sold by the Poor Law officer to pay for her accommodation by the state; once her son had been whisked away from her into the children's ward to be glimpsed, perhaps, but not spoken to, only in the distance; once she and her mother had been dressed and degraded in that coarse workhouse clothing, kept weak and obedient by that thin workhouse gruel; caught syphilis or typhoid or madness from the other paupers whose beds would only be inches away from theirs—once all that had happened, how did one find the strength to walk out and face the world again? Or, at least, how could she persuade a Board of Workhouse Guardians to release, into *her* custody, Liam and Odette.

Thinking of it—and she thought of it far too often—she shuddered. As she shuddered whenever the woman with the long, damp red hair, lounging in the doorway of her shuttered house at the end of St. Jude's Passage, her plump body wrapped in a fringed green shawl, called out, "Good day to you, Cara Adeane."

It was no surprise to her that the brothel keeper should know her name. Nor had that other woman, well-dressed, almost genteel, who had come gliding up to her in Market Square surprised her. "My dear, I just had to come and say how very charming you are looking today. And that I have a friend—among many—who is simply burning for love of you. Oh yes—five guineas he will pay to quench his thirst. Just fancy."

Such offers had been coming her way since she had turned thirteen. But surely the trousseau of Miss Gemma Dallam, if it led to all the things she intended, might put a stop to that. She could not stay at the Fleece much longer if she wished to guard so much as a shred of her reputation, especially since Ned O'Mara could not be kept forever at bay. And if she succeeded in pleasing Miss Gemma Dallam—who had probably never suffered much from the unwelcome attentions of men, never really suffered at all—then, if she spoke to her friends and they to theirs, then surely . . . ? *Surely* there was room in Frizingley for another milliner? A younger, more fashionable woman with style enough to suit these rich, pampered, impossibly innocent girls who had so much money, so little experience in the arts of self-defense, who could be so easily persuaded—by her—to buy whatever she told them was in fashion? Why not? Luck changed. Kieron Adeane's daughter had every reason to know it. And today—well, look at it—the rain had stopped and she had not, as she had feared, ruined her best—her only—boots and the hem of the one good dress out of pawn. The sun was shining. She had been served tea at Goldsborough Manor, won an order for four dozen of "everything" from Miss

Dallam, who could easily afford four dozen more. She had even managed to persuade Miss Dallam's mother, considerably against the judgment of that handsome but tricky Miss Gage, to allow her to do part of the work in her own "workroom" rather than in the Dallams' back parlor. Forgetting to mention, of course, that the airy, businesslike premises she had led Mrs. Dallam to imagine were situated in the evil heart of St. Jude's. Absolutely giving no inkling that it was because the fancy embroidery was rather beyond her and she needed Odette. Later, of course, if things went well, she'd produce her mother with a flourish as the best embroideress from the most famous establishment in the rue Saint Honoré. Odette would know the name. But, to begin with, it was essential that her customers should have full confidence in Miss Cara Adeane herself. Yes. Luck changed. If things could get worse, then they could get better too. Much better.

The sun was still shining as she hurried down to the Fleece, the memory of the flowered china she had drunk from at the Manor still pleasing her, although the tea itself had been too weak for her liking. But never mind that. She could forgive them their poor tea if they would be willing to make her, not rich she supposed, but no longer obliged to worry so much, no longer forced to put up with things which, quite simply, didn't suit her. Being touched by men, for instance, tonight in the bar parlor, who evidently believed in their right to touch her; although she did not. Being at the beck and call of anybody who had a few coppers more in his pocket than she had in hers; which seemed to be just about everybody she knew.

Was it too much to ask? Very likely. But, as she entered St. Jude's Square and crossed over from the Rose and Crown to the Fleece she had decided to ask it anyway. And moreover—having been too busy all day for frivolities—she realized why the day had seemed so propitious. It was her twentieth birthday.

 5

*R*eaching the Fleece, famished as always, she went in through the kitchen door, her mind full of pies and tarts and then, even through the tantalizing odor of roast chicken—a leg for Liam, a wing for Odette if she could manage it—became conscious of something taut and tricky and vaguely unpleasant in the air.

Nor, considering the keenness of her appetite and the frank dishonesty of her intentions, was she pleased to see Ned O'Mara standing by the ovens looking gloomy and giving orders for somebody's dinner.

"Hello, Ned. It's my birthday." She flashed him a saucy, barmaid's smile and a glint of her sea-blue eyes, hoping he might give her a glass of wine or a shilling, hoping he wouldn't want to kiss her in exchange. But his pummeled, prizefighter's face looked out of sorts and out of humor, a man coming down with a cold or a fever, until she realized his ailment was quite simply the condition—unusual with him—of being cold sober.

Had he been mildly, merrily drunk then for the past three months? She supposed so. Had that been the cause of the easy atmosphere, the food and drink so readily to hand, the mattress and the barrels and the copper saucepan he had given her?

She bit her lip.

"The captain's back" he said.

"Oh." She had feared as much. "Does he want to see me?"

"Christ no. Not until he remembers. He's in the bar parlor drinkin' brandy. Him and his doxy and his doxy's husband. You'd best be stayin' in the taproom out of his way."

But it was a Thursday night when the mill hands had been paid, the end of the month too with the navvies from the railway line they were slowly cutting between Frizingley and Leeds, erupting into town with four weeks' wages in their pockets. And no great certainty of even being alive next pay day, considering the explosives they were always tossing about. There was to be a dog-fight too, she heard, at midnight, with bets already flying, tempers rising, as somebody began to extol, somebody else to belittle, the fighting spirit of the brown bull dog—more bull than dog, they were saying—belonging to the landlord of the Rose and Crown. Cara wrinkled her nose. She hoped she would miss that. But the taproom, already in ferment, needed Ned, ex-champion of the bareknuckle ring and the other, coarser-grained barmaid, to keep order, especially when Cara was wearing her last good dress which must be kept as fresh as possible to pass Dallam scrutiny tomorrow. And since she could hardly avoid Captain Goldsborough forever, she went through to the bar parlor, the gentlemen's bar, and took her accustomed place behind the counter, her palms sweating and her hands shaking a little, but her head very high.

The low, smoke-blackened, age-blackened room was quiet, only a dozen or so men, all familiar to her, drinking spirits in pairs at separate tables, and a trio of strangers in the best chairs by the hearth, a bottle of brandy and three ornate glasses—Captain Goldsborough's private store, she supposed—set out before them. A plump, pink-cheeked gentleman, very crimped and curled, very drunk, who—according to the other barmaid—must be Mr. Adolphus Moon, the sugar millionaire, come home from the West Indies to buy up the whole village of Far Flatley, eight miles away, where he was planning to live in style. A woman with an alabaster skin and pale gold hair who must be his French wife, Mrs. Marie Moon, a well-known actress in her day, the other barmaid had said, and more besides. Much more, in fact. A woman of sin and scandal and subtle sophistications, who had known other men before, and evidently since, her husband; and who would be certain to set the dovecotes of Far Flatley—and of Frizingley if it came to that—sadly aflutter.

Two expensive, faintly exotic strangers traveling from London, she supposed, or even all the way from Antigua or Martinique in the company of Captain Goldsborough, enjoying his hospitality, Mr. Adolphus Moon considerably too well if his drunken torpor was anything to go by, his wife, the glorious, scandalous Marie, ignoring her husband entirely as she leaned forward intently, rapturously it seemed, her whole beautiful, expertly alluring body flowing toward the man sitting far back in the chimney corner. Captain Goldsborough him-self, although Cara could see nothing of him but a dark, broad shape, long legs booted and spurred, stretched out at their ease on the fourth chair, to which a dog was fastened by a short chain.

And for a moment it was the dog which held her attention, a squat, heavy-jowled, black and white animal, ugly as the devil, its body shaved smooth and its ears docked in what she knew to be the proper "sporting trim." A fighting dog with no ear-flaps and no tufts of hair for its opponent to seize hold of, a brute fed on raw butcher's meat to sharpen its appetite for blood, with malice in its heart and a jaw like a man-trap which had been trained—by Captain Goldsborough, she supposed—to bite deep and never to let go once it did.

When a dog like that took hold they would have to clog its nostrils with flour and half choke it before it would unclench those murderous teeth. She shivered, remembering the havoc those curs could create when, their fighting days over, they were turned loose more often than not, to scavenge in the street. And feeling her eyes on him the animal stirred and snorted a brief warning, so that she turned away, pity making her unkind. Damned dog. She hoped that his opponent, when he came, would be big as a house and lion-savage. And then— for all she cared—they could go inside to the boarded dog-pen behind the stables and get it over, tearing each other to pieces while the men yelled and took bets and lost the money for which some of them had worked all week; and the dogs lost an eye, a leg, a life. It was Thurs-day, after all, when most men had money. It happened everywhere. And she found this type of combat easier to bear than the screaming of the cocks she could sometimes hear from the Beehive or the rat-ting-matches they were forever holding at the Dog and Gun, ratting dogs being such tiny, frail-boned terriers, with such pretty faces, that it never failed to turn her stomach whenever she saw the hampers of sewer-rats and barn-rats arriving, to be killed in the ratting-arena, for sport.

At least this dog was hideous as well as savage. And it was as she glared at it again that she heard the blonde woman, Mrs. Moon, begin to speak to the captain in rapid French, not troubling to lower her voice, since her husband was lying with his head on the table, very evidently asleep, and it did not occur to her that anyone else, in the bar parlor of a provincial tavern, might have the gift of tongues.

"Christie." And her voice was throaty, husky, an actress's voice intending to fascinate. "Shall we go away again?"

"Marie, we have just come back," he said and although Cara could still not see him, the first words she heard him speak were in perfect, easy French, her mother's tongue.

"I shall never forget it. Is it really over? It can't be?" Marie Moon was the wife of a rich man. She was a beautiful woman. Accustomed, in either of these guises, to getting her way.

"Every road has its end, Marie." He sounded tired, thought Cara, of exploring this one.

"But you don't *want* it to be over." It was not a question. And swiftly Mrs. Moon began to outline the ways and means by which they could continue to commit adultery.

"Why not?" he said.

"Darling—don't you remember—Martinique?" And, her rich voice rising to the occasion, she began to remind him.

"I remember." Cara supposed it could not have been more than a few weeks ago.

"And does it excite you?"

"It does. Please go on."

She obeyed him, laughing. He prompted her. "Marie, my love, don't stop. Don't, above all, be shy."

She was very far from that, her wonderful voice regaling Cara's embarrassed but exceedingly interested ears with tales of passion a thousand years beyond either her experience or her imaginings. Not that she was much given to *imagining* the sins of the flesh, being far more concerned with putting a stop to those that were forever being thrust upon her attention. But, just the same, what an actress the woman was. What a charmer. And what a *tart*. Yet, although she supposed that these were whores' tricks that Mrs. Moon was describing they had a refinement and sophistication which seemed to have little to do with the blowsy, red-headed madam in St. Jude's Passage.

Cara had never considered the sexual act to be a fit subject for conversation, much less believed that it could be presented in this witty, downright informative fashion. Shocking, of course. But goodness—how entertaining. Good Lord, did people really go to such lengths just to . . . ? Evidently they did. What a—yes, what a *lark*. Not that she had the least inclination to follow suit. Lord no. Like so many other things this was for the rich who had the leisure to get bored and the energy to invent fresh enjoyments. Rich women, in particular, for whom pleasures of this exotic variety did not inevitably

---

84

end, it seemed, in the choice between pregnancy and a half-guinea abortion. Provided, of course, that one could find the half-guinea.

Marie Moon paused, more for effect than breath, it seemed to Cara and then, as a throbbing finale, made her grand declaration in a voice that would have filled an auditorium.

"Christie, you know I adore you."

"I know it amuses you to think so." He sounded almost disappointed.

"You may believe me. *Do* believe me."

"My dear—" and once again his voice held that provocative note of disappointment. "Is that wise?"

She laughed. "I hope not. How dull if it were." But, for all her laughter, he had not given her the answer she had expected, had not spoken of flinging caution to the winds, of risking *all*, although of course she would not have cared to go quite so far as that.

"Yes. As you say. How dull."

He emerged suddenly from the shadows as if something had propelled him, pushed the empty brandy bottle aside and called out to Cara "You there—bring me another one of these."

"Certainly, sir."

And so engrossed had she been in their conversation that she was halfway across the room before she realized that he had spoken to her, and she had answered, in French.

Had he engineered the situation deliberately to embarrass Mrs. Moon, using Cara as his tool? Very likely. For it never once crossed her mind that his use of French to her had been accidental. Guessing who she was and knowing the nationality of her mother—seeing, no doubt, how avidly she had been eavesdropping—he had encouraged the other woman to talk and then snared them both in a cynical, dangerous trap. Dangerous to Cara. For he had made a fool of Mrs. Moon and, by her outraged expression, had made for Cara the very thing she took pains never to make for herself. An enemy.

"Why, Christie?" the lovely woman said, hurt and angry and full of the bewilderment of a true beauty whom no man had ever before treated less than carefully. "You knew this girl could understand, didn't you?"

"I thought it likely."

"And did that amuse you? Do *I* amuse you?"

He clicked his tongue, as if gently chiding her. "Alas—no."

She shook her pale blonde head, still not quite believing it, opening her slightly painted mouth to speak some immortal lines of depth and passion which would throb in his mind forever and, in her shock, producing nothing but the merest commonplace.

"Christie—I have given you everything."

"Thank you *so* much, Marie."

She got to her feet looking tragic and beautiful and horribly wronged. An actress, after all, of some distinction, Cara remembered they had been saying in the other bar.

"I could kill you, Christie."

That seemed to please him better.

"Yes. So you could."

Speculatively, almost lazily, his eyes went to the empty brandy bottle on the table between them and then to the woman's white, frantic hands which could so easily have picked it up and smashed it across his head.

"Yes, Marie. You *could* kill me—or try to . . . ?" Was it a challenge? Had he instructed her—or taunted her—by his glance at the bottle as to how it could be done? If she had the speed, the strength, the resolution? If she really wished to do him harm? Would he even— until perhaps the final instant—bother to defend himself?

"Well, Marie?"

For a moment she stood motionless, ghastly, her own eyes fixed on the bottle and held there, staring with horror and fascination at the violence he seemed to be inviting and to which almost—*almost*. And then, blinking fiercely, she released her breath in a long, hollow sigh.

"This is a vile place," she said. "I shall leave it." Through a haze of brandy and indolence her husband woke for an instant, smiled, and nodded his head.

Captain Goldsborough did not even turn to see her go. He looked, instead, at Cara. She looked at him. He was squarely, strongly built, and as swarthy as a Spaniard. In his early thirties, Cara supposed, black hair growing low in the nape of a powerful neck, his eyes like pitch. Not handsome with the lean, arrow-straight beauty of Daniel Carey, which was the only beauty her heart could recognize. Heavier than Daniel in bulk and in feature. Coarser, she thought. But a man who made the hairs on her arms and her neck rise, her skin tighten like a cat's with the knowledge that *here* she must be very wary.

She put the new bottle on the table, her stomach knotted and uneasy, her skirts—and her ankles—too close to that damnable, hideous dog. Yet her instinct told her that if they sensed her fear, both man and dog alike would use it, enjoy it, play with it. And smiling, playing the barmaid—for what else was she? what else could she do?—she tried hard to grow angry, believing temper, although it might get her into trouble, to be at least more dignified than panic.

"So you're Ned O'Mara's new fancy, are you?" His voice, speaking English, had the lazy drawl of a drawing-room gentleman.

"No, sir. Not that I've noticed."

"You have a look of your father, Cara Adeane."

"Thank you, sir."

"Have I paid you a compliment?" The tilt of his heavy eyebrow indicated that, in her place, he would not be too sure of it.

"I take it so."

"Then you're fond of your father?"

No longer. But she did not choose to tell him so.

"That I am."

"Good. And is there not a little matter to be discussed, concerning him?"

"Whenever you like, sir."

"Precisely."

She had been dismissed, yet something in the movement of her skirts, or in her tight-clenched apprehension, disturbed the dog, bringing it upright and snarling on short, bandy legs, still attached by his chain to the captain's chair-leg, but blocking her way.

"My champion doesn't seem to like you, Miss Adeane."

"No."

"Perhaps you don't care for him either?"

And as the man and the dog fused together in her mind, both equally detestable and ugly and vicious, she shook her head.

"I can't afford to get bitten, Captain Goldsborough, I have my work to do."

"Then do it, Miss Adeane."

He was watching her, she suddenly realized, as speculatively as he had watched Mrs. Moon a moment ago, his eyes *interested*—no more— as she had contemplated the act of violence he had himself suggested, and then scornful when—predictably, it seemed—she had decided against it. And now, recognizing Cara's fear of the animal, he had maneuvered her into a corner from which she must either beg him to release her: or not.

"Certainly, sir," she said and, closing her eyes, walked blindly straight ahead, feeling the dog's warm, snuffling breath through her skirts, the skin of her back stone cold and cringing long after she had passed out of range of the fangs.

Very well. He had had his amusement. Would he leave her alone now? For tonight at least, she hoped so.

They took torches and lanterns out to the backyard at midnight, the sporting elite of Frizingley with money in their pockets or stuck into the band around their hats, navvies from the railway encampment on the moor above Frizingley Green swaggering in their corduroys and gaudy spotted neckcloths among foundry workers and loom tuners and colliery lads, a few sporting gentlemen and gentlemen "traveling" in the textile trade, and a sprinkling of masters' sons, a fifteen-year-old Braithwaite whose mother believed him to be spending the night with a friend from the Grammar School; the slightly older black sheep of the Methodistical Colcloughs of the foundry who did not allow strong drink of any kind to pass their lips; a young Mr. Lord of the brewery whose father could not object to drink but would have been seriously displeased, nevertheless, to see him squandering hard-earned guineas—earned by someone else, that is—on the ability of Captain Goldsborough's black and white dog to maul and mangle the brown bull dog from the Rose and Crown.

There were few women present. Just the red-haired madam from St. Jude's Passage who seemed well acquainted with the landlords of both taverns; a thin, excited young girl pressing herself against Master Braithwaite of the Grammar School, prepared to relieve him of his virginity if it could not be avoided, certainly of his wallet; a frantic woman, her head concealed in a blanket shawl, looking for her husband before he gambled *all* his wages; and Cara.

"He says you're to stay," Ned O'Mara told her. "He has a word to say to you after. If he wins you'll be all right."

"Will he win?"

"Likely so. A good dog he's got. Not that he cares. I reckon he only does it to watch the lads losin' money. To see how they take it—or not . . ."

And so she stood by the window in the bar parlor looking carefully at nothing as the human seconds led their gladiators past her and out into the tumultuous, torch-lit yard to be cheered and jeered and wagered upon as Ned himself had been in his prizefighting days; the ugly bandy-legged black and white bull dog and the brown, smooth-haired killer from the Rose and Crown. Damned dogs, she thought. Mad dogs, deliberately maddened by these stupid men so they could throw their money away and call it sport.

Had they no homes to go to? No children? She knew, all too well, that most of them had.

"Have you seen a man in a brown checked cap and a red shirt?" The frantic housewife had rushed up to her, almost wringing her hands in anguish. But the yard was full of checked caps and gaudy, Sunday-best shirts, full of pay-packets that were needed—every bit as much as this one—to buy shoes for undernourished children and pay the rent. To get this poor woman's boots out of the pawnshop, very likely, since her feet were in clogs, the hem of her skirt badly worn.

Cara shook her head, closing her eyes again. But she could not close her ears to the hoarse yelling, the guffaws of mindless laughter, and then the avid hush, the greedy silence of the Roman arena as the snarling started. Not much at first, no more than one could hear at any street corner any day of the week until the seconds went to work, whipping it up to mutilation and murder, setting the crowd howling and swaying, one voice, one movement, one pair of savage eyes looking for blood and money, one pair of nostrils savoring it. One single, unsound thrill reaching its crescendo—*Get him, boy. Kill him. Hang on there, lad. Mangle him.*—and then dying down like the sighing tail-end of a high wind leaving a mutter of sick excitement as the seconds went in to prise loose, if they could, the winner's teeth from his opponent's throat.

Damned dogs. The woman in the shawl went away, downcast and probably weeping, her husband's wages gone now, one way or another, beyond her recall, leaving Cara alone in the bar parlor as the crowd dispersed, the winners to celebrate, the losers to console themselves with an extra drink, on credit if the landlord should be so kind, or—if not—to start a fight. And there would be cards, of course, now. And dominoes.

No one came into this smaller, quieter bar now that the Moons and the rest of the carriage trade had gone. Could it be that Captain Goldsborough—winner or loser she had no notion—had forgotten her? Ought she quite simply to take the custard tarts and the pieces of chicken she had managed to conceal behind the bar, wrapped up in Sairellen Thackray's clean calico handkerchief, and make her way home before these men spilled out into the streets and became troublesome? A whole grimy rabbit-warren of alleyways lay between the Fleece and the comparative safety of her door, and if any of these brawny men took it into their heads to come after her, then her only hope would be in speed.

Perhaps he *had* forgotten her? Certainly, when he entered the bar a moment later, his attention seemed wholly on the basket, carried in by the cellarman and placed by the small parlor fire, in which the black and white dog lay shivering and bleeding.

"You lost then," she said, quickly turning her head away, the palms of her hands feeling damp again, her skin cold. She had forced herself to face this animal's menace. But she could not—absolutely would not—look at the poor ugly brute in its misery.

Captain Goldsborough smiled.

"The dog lost, Miss Adeane. Not I. He has had his day. As all dogs tend to do. Whereas I have gained substantially. From a bet, placed somewhat late in the proceedings, I admit, but just in time to be legal, nevertheless. On his opponent." She did not feel in any way moved to congratulate him.

"You asked me to wait, Captain Goldsborough."

"Did I?"

She nodded, feeling cold again and strained.

"The money . . . ?"

"Oh yes—a little matter of fifty pounds owing by your father."

"Hardly *fifty*." And it was desperation which gave her the courage to interrupt him, "Since you have had twenty back from my mother . . ."

But slowly, still smiling, he shook his head.

"I fear not—since your father borrowed a further twenty, presumably to leave with your mother when he went off to his promised land. Fifty."

Damn him. Her father? Yes. Undoubtedly. May he know no peace, no joy. May the bakery of his sister Teresa turn to dust and ashes in his hands. And damn this thick-set bully in whose power he had left her. *And* that foul dog whimpering its pain on the hearth-rug, its bandy legs a mangled ruin, one of its cropped ears torn off.

"So—Miss Adeane?"

He had taken off his jacket, she noticed, his shirt unbuttoned almost to the waist and showing far more of his bulky, hairy chest than she thought decent—far more than Daniel Carey or Luke Thackray would ever show—his skin so swarthy against the fine, white cambric that only the gold earrings were missing, she thought, to make him a gypsy. Or a pirate; although she had never seen one. No gentleman, at any rate, despite the perfect French, the drawling, well-bred English, and the beautifully-made, carelessly-worn shirt which had cost him a pretty penny, as she had good reason to know.

"So—Miss Adeane. A little straight talking, perhaps. Are you up to it?"

"I am." And if only that dog would stop twitching and whining, so that her eyes kept straying to it as it cowered there in its blood, trying to lick its wounds and making them worse, without even the sense to lie still—clogging up her mind with nonsense about bandages and hot water and *pity* when she needed all her wits about her. Damned dog.

"Tell me, then—how much knowledge do you have of the law, as it concerns yourself?"

"Not much."

"I thought not. Then consider this. Does it seem likely to you that any English court of justice would hold you—a female under the age of twenty-one—responsible for a debt contracted by your father?"

She considered, feeling herself once again to be a specimen—just that—pinned down for observation by those pitch-black eyes. And then, with no hope of getting away with anything at all, swallowed hard.

"No. It doesn't seem likely."

"And what conclusion do you draw from that?"

"None that comforts me."

He smiled, a flash of white teeth—a great many of them, it seemed to her, and very bright—against his dark skin.

"Good girl. So much for the law of England. Now shall we turn our attention to the law as it is understood in the quarter of this city known as Jude's?—roughly from Market Square to St. Jude's Street and all the little nooks and crannies in between. What do you think about that?"

"I think," and she was in no doubt whatsoever, "that it is as *you* decide it will be."

He smiled again.

"Then, do you owe me fifty pounds, Miss Adeane? Or do you not?"

Once again, and very strongly, came the sensation of being pinned down for scrutiny, dissected, maneuvered. Played with.

"That is for you to say," she told him, giving him the humble answer, the *right* answer, yet biting each word off at its conclusion like embroidery thread.

"Yes. So let us say you owe me nothing."

She did not believe him. And in her amazement, in the quick stirring of hope—could he mean it? Dear God, let him mean it—and the small voice of reason whispering to her that of course he didn't, it was a trick, she was suddenly helpless, floundering. Exactly, she supposed, as he had intended.

"Why?" Another woman had used that same, startled word to him, earlier on.

"Because it pleases me."

She shook her head. Yes, possibly it did please him. But hardly for reasons she would be likely to appreciate. What could they be? And how much more, in the long term, would they cost her?

"Well then—because I have won a great deal of money tonight and am feeling generous. Does that sound better?"

He was laughing at her. Well, if *that* was what he wanted then he was welcome to it. She could stand his mockery without flinching. Or could she? And once again the whimpering of the dog cut her ears, making her wince.

"Don't you trust me, Cara Adeane?"

He sounded as if he expected an answer and, shaking her head, she made a wide gesture of confusion, apology, appeal, anything he chose to call it. *Trust* him? She would rather put her bare hand into a snake pit.

"Then I must make a gesture of goodwill, I think, to put your mind at rest. Shall I do that?"

And she sensed, very clearly and with a seething resentment, that she was giving him pleasure, entertainment; proving rather more of a diversion than he had perhaps expected. More amusing, even, than Marie Moon.

"Of course. I have it. It is your birthday today. I heard someone mention it. My dear—the very thing. Let me make you a gift."

And, the mirth in his dark, heavy-textured face proving too much for her, inviting her to look about her for something hard and sharp to hit him with—as he had invited Mrs. Moon—he bent down to the basket, picked up the injured dog and, before she could step away or hide her hands behind her back, had put it in her arms.

"Happy Birthday, Miss Adeane."

And for a horrified moment she stood and faced him, clutching the suffering body, loathing it yet already trying to give it ease, her skin crawling with disgust, and pity, as she cradled the ugly, wounded, by no means abundantly grateful head against her chest where it continued to whine and shiver and to bleed—copiously, abominably—down the bodice of her last good dress.

*D*aniel Carey had intended his present business in Yorkshire to last three weeks, a month at most. A visit to the newspaper editor, Feargus O'Connor, imprisoned at York, a few days in the Leeds office of the *Northern Star*, discussing with any of O'Connor's men who remained what might be salvaged of the movement they had christened Chartism.

Very little, perhaps, since the leaders seemed either to be in prison like O'Connor, or embroiled in the bitter conflict which already threatened to split the newborn creed asunder; the "moral force" men of Birmingham who believed they could obtain their People's Charter by means of petitions, mass meetings, rational discussion, and the "physical force" men of the North who thought it might best be obtained by a little judicious brandishing of pike and gun.

And there had been a great many pikes manufactured in Yorkshire and Lancashire this last year or two, on the anvils of radical blacksmiths who could knock a lethal weapon together as fast as they could shoe a horse, particularly when the middle-class intellectuals and artisans of the "moral force" brigade had failed to persuade anybody at all with their speeches and petitions leaving it to the men of the North, led by Peter Bussey of Bradford and Feargus O'Connor of Leeds, to take stronger steps.

Not that they had been noticeably more effective either, it seemed to Daniel. At the National Chartist Conference called by the "physical force" men in Heckmondwike last November he had heard a great deal of talk about pikes and guns, had seen a great deal of drilling, afterward, on the moors on winter nights with makeshift weapons for those who had them and walking sticks, pickaxes, broom handles, for those who had not; had even listened to the call, by some, for the overthrow of the government and the setting up of a Republic, as working men with home-made pikes like these had done in France.

But Heckmondwike, for all the oratory and fervor, had led to nothing but some disorganized rioting here and there, for which the leaders had been sentenced to death and then, to avoid the dangerous creation of martyrs, locked up or transported to Australia instead: Peter Bussey having hidden himself behind his own flour sacks when he heard the call to arms, to avoid leading his Bradford Chartists to war.

Yet the cause had been just and, despite the muddle and the police informers and the betrayal, it remained so, Daniel himself having spent that winter moving quietly about the counties and cities of England and Ireland, conveying messages from one Chartist leader to another.

For nothing, it seemed. Yet the great Charter still existed. And what did it ask for that could not lay claim to be called democracy? A vote for every man in England, whether he owned property or not. The abolition of the property qualification for MPs so that any man could stand for election. A salary to be paid to him should he be elected so that he need not be beholden—and thus have his arm twisted—by a paymaster. Above all the end of the system by which every man who had a vote was forced to declare publicly how he had used it. *That* was the People's Charter. And if it would take revolution to achieve it—the noble lords of Her Majesty's Government being understandably unwilling to share their privileges—then Daniel was ready.

He had no overriding interest—like Luke Thackray—in what seemed to him the narrow issues of factory reform, of ten hour days or the exact ages at which children might be sent to labor. Such abuses would be cured automatically by the reform of the system as a whole. And his concern was with democracy on a grander scale, international, universal, the Rights of Man—from which followed, naturally, the Rights of Woman and Child—to freedom, justice and opportunity. He had therefore made the journey to Leeds to meet the hotheaded, emotional proprietor of the *Northern Star* and had met Cara Adeane instead.

And, contrary to his normal practice with the women he encountered on his travels and with whom he shared what it had seemed right and pleasant to call love, he had been unable to forget her.

July, August and September had kept him chained, furiously some-times and resentfully, in the neighborhood of Frizingley, looking for her, quarreling with her more often than not when he found her, giving her advice at which she laughed and tossed her head, hating the life she led and growing illogical, unreasonable, with the hatred. And the jealousy. Wanting to guard her and keep her, as a husband his wife, when he *knew* he would never have a secure home to offer. Wanting her to need him, to lean on him, when he *knew* he could offer her no guarantees, no certainty even as to his whereabouts be-yond tomorrow. Wanting her to be sweet and yielding and gentle in his arms when he *knew* that without her toughness she could not survive.

Quite simply wanting her.

And now Autumn was crisping the air, finding him still jealous and irresolute, unable either to leave her or to stay with her. Seeing quite well that she too could neither leave nor live with him.

He understood her fears. He also understood himself. The only decent thing to do then—surely—would be to leave her in peace? Of course. But what had decency to do with this hungering and burning, this terrible conviction that without her he would never be wholly alive, wholly enthusiastic, never be *whole* again? He walked out alone one October morning to try and come to terms with it, needing air and solitude, striding sure-footed over the rough ground without really seeing it, the town well below him beneath its dense cloud, a thin blue sky above him which gave him no ease. Could he change? Could he take employment as a schoolmaster again, instead of the random journalism by which he now eked out a living, and settle down? Could he give up the broad view, the grand vision, for a blinkered security which, even as a supposition, appalled him.

If he loved her then he could. He could not. But he *did* love her. He wanted his own way of life. And Cara. She wanted him just as he was. But differently. There was no solution. Sitting down on a rock he attempted to face it, to compose himself sufficiently to go to her calmly and say goodbye. Calm above all. For there must be no quarrel at the end. His last memory of her must be a good one, something he would bury deep, perhaps, but which would always be there, he supposed, rising to the surface to plague him whenever he tried to fall in love in his old free and easy fashion, with somebody else.

Because of course there would be other women. He might never feel like this again. Indeed, no man in his right mind could possibly wish to do so. But he was too much of a realist to imagine that he would hunger for her, in this intense and painful fashion, forever more. No. He wouldn't do that. Nor would she. He'd learn, eventually, to make do with second-rate emotions and be content with him. And that, perhaps, was the saddest part of all.

Sad. But, from his vantage point on the moorland outcropping of rock, he began the hurtful process of making up his mind to it. For the world, after all, was full of women who were not Cara and he'd learn to enjoy them again. He'd have to. There was even one now coming along the stony little track below him, near enough for him to examine her in detail, too far away for her to be incommoded by his stare. Younger than he'd first thought, although not handsome in any way he understood, sturdy enough to cut peat and dig potatoes in Tipperary, although all dressed up like a lady in a dark purple mantle with shoulder-capes, a gray fur muff, a bonnet with a gray feather, accompanied by a stout old gentleman who—since the girl was really not the stuff a rich man's mistress would be made of—must be her father.

Daniel, from his perch just beyond their view, watched them idly because there was nothing else to look at, feeling no great stirring of interest in this prosperous Frizingley couple out for their moorland constitutional, the young lady for the good of her figure and her complexion, he supposed, the old man for his health, to balance the effects of his four square meals a day, no doubt, his vintage port and brandy; although limping a little, Daniel noticed, as if the gout were troubling him.

A large man, heavy by any standards, particularly those of Daniel Carey, who had pared his own whipcord body down to the hard muscle and bone. A clumsy man, too, stumbling over the tiny, scattered stones, straying off the path into the tufted, spiky grasses and blundering there a moment in city-soft confusion, calling out to his daughter, who had plowed solidly ahead. Clumsy: until Daniel saw the agonized line of the bent back, the hand clutching the chest, the horror on the girl's face as she turned and ran back to him.

And although he felt no particular inclination to help them, although he was bitter with his own pain and had no pity to spare, or to *waste* on such as these, he made a grimace of annoyance—Lord, this was *all* he needed—and then, with a wry smile, a shrug, slid down from the rock and easily, swiftly, descended the slope toward them.

Bending over her father as he crouched, groaning and sweating on the damp ground, Gemma Dallam, who prayed only at the conventional hours of Sunday morning service and Evensong, could think of nothing to do but close her eyes in a request for Divine Assistance. For although she had been brought up to believe that all women were born with an inbred ability to nurse the sick she had never believed it, having had occasion to wince, herself, many a time, at the ministrations of so many medical amateurs. Therefore, being convinced that good intentions alone could never be enough, she prayed, "Please help me to do the right thing." And when she opened her eyes the young man was there, straight and direct as an arrow, asking her cheerfully, "Is the gentleman not feeling well?"

"No. Oh please—can you . . . ?"

"That I can." She didn't know what she was asking but he, very evidently, had handled sick and heavy men before. Easily. Without panic. Without much effort either although he was neither tall nor broad nor obviously strong.

"Here, let me be taking him. There's no sense in trying to hold him up, the weight he is. He'll be better on the ground. That way there's nowhere else for him to fall. And if that's a muff you have there, then it might go well behind his head."

John-William Dallam's half-conscious, desperately struggling body—because *he* wasn't ready to die yet. And not here, God dammit—was large and unwieldy yet the young man laid him neatly on the ground, undid the starched linen at his neck and his waistcoat buttons, arranged him so that he looked almost to be resting rather than agonizing. If one could imagine John-William Dallam taking his ease on the bare ground. Help had come: although it made no real difference to the pinched, blue look around her father's lips, the sinking of those high-colored, well-fleshed cheeks of his into mottled hollows, the grunting and laboring of his breath.

"Thank you so much." She was thinking a little more clearly now, her panic subsiding, but not entirely. For if her father was dying, as he might well be, then she was about to lose not simply a parent but the person upon whom her cloistered world totally depended. The architect and foundation stone of that world. And her mother's. A loving tyrant perhaps. And that potent blend of love and tyranny had, since her birth, built padded walls of warmth and certainty around her a mile thick. And the shock of their removal, she realized, would leave her—despite the independence of her spirit—feeling exposed and bewildered and cold.

"We left our carriage about a mile down the road. Could we—is it possible to get him there?"

He got to his feet, smiling. "If I were Hercules, miss, then it might be. But since I can't carry him on my shoulder, why don't you sit yourself down with him and be keeping him company while I fetch your coach and horses?"

He set off, not running but walking fast, almost jauntily she thought; a mile of stony track to the place where they had left Williams with the victoria and then a mile back in the carriage. How long could it take him? How much time did they really have? She sat down to wait in the tufted grass, making the kind of foolish, female noises one made to frightened children—"It's going to be all right, father. There's no need to worry."—to which he irritably responded by closing his eyes, having regained enough consciousness now to understand that he had no strength to waste in arguing with his daughter. No. He must keep very still now and very quiet, carefully guarding what vital forces he had left for the grim business of keeping his soul—to which he'd never before given much consideration—and his body in the same place, where they belonged.

In Frizingley he was a man of power, a master of other men, of machines, and a great deal of money. Here, on this sparsely covered moorland hillside with the rain coming on, he was just an old man with a pain in his chest and a dizziness in his head, who might die here with no more consideration than a tramp without a penny in his pocket.

Very well. He accepted that. But if death wanted him, then there'd be a struggle. No doubt about it. And if it turned out that he had to meet his end here, alone with the girl, then all he hoped was that the shock of it wouldn't addle her brain and turn her silly. A sensible lass, Gemma, as lasses went. But one never knew with women. His wife Amabel, for instance, would have run amok by now, screaming and carrying on and very likely twisting her ankle on a stone or falling over one of these ledges and breaking her neck. Sweet, helpless Amabel. How he loved those qualities in her. Amabel, his luxury. His indulgence. What joy she'd given him. And what a gracious pampered, privileged life he'd given *her*. Amabel, as young at heart now as on the day he'd married her. *Twenty* years younger than he was, dammit. One day—if not today—she'd have to learn to live without him. Could she do it? Groaning, squeezing his eyes tight shut, he knew she couldn't.

"It won't be long now, father," said Gemma, just to remind him that something was being done, that she was there. "The young man seemed pleased to help. He could be Irish, I think."

Inwardly John-William Dallam groaned again and bit his lip. Irish? Whatever was the girl prattling on about? Of course he was Irish. He'd heard *that* turn of speech often enough in loom gates and navvy camps and road gangs—even in the discreet arms of a certain bold and black-eyed woman before Amabel—to recognize the hint of it on a man's tongue. He knew the Irish all right. He'd even imported whole families of them, piecemeal, from Mayo and Donegal, in his younger days, when he'd needed the kind of muscle to get his factory started that one didn't find too often in local men bred to the weaver's trade. He'd just written to the parish priest of some unpronounceable village and placed his order. Simple as that. Four families. Ten families. Passage paid. And even then it had worked out cheaper, paying "Irish wages." Although they'd been scoundrels, every one. Like that handsome young devil who'd just gone off striding down the track—fit as an overstrung fiddle, damn him—and who most likely wouldn't bother to come back. Why should he? Particularly since the girl had forgotten to mention that she'd make it worth his while. No. He'd just go merrily on his way, whistling his damnable Irish jig, feeling young, *being* young, with all his life before him. Damn him to hell.

A lad in his twenties. Acutely, with an agony far more piercing than the pain in his heart, John-William Dallam could remember another lad like that, striding out into his future. Taking it by the scruff of its neck and squeezing out of it his ambitions, his dreams, his pleasures. No longer. And feeling the incredible spurting of tears—since when had *he* ever cried before—he turned his head away and concealed it, as best he could in the collar of his coat, thinking it unseemly that any woman, especially his daughter, should see him cry.

"Yes. I expect he's Irish. Although he didn't look like a workman. Rather shabby, but well-spoken, I thought and polite. He didn't sound like a navvy."

There she was, running on again. Talking and saying nothing. Like her mother. And how the devil did she know what a navvy sounded like when he'd taken good care never to let one get within a yard of her? Good God, what did she know about anything? Not much, he supposed. Which was perfectly right and proper so long as he was there to know it for her. She was a good girl. He loved her, dammit. If she'd been a boy he'd have been proud of her. But she wasn't a boy. And what he regretted now, with all that remained of his heart and the taste of ashes on his tongue, was his own softness in not forcing her to marry Ben Braithwaite when he'd had the chance. Not that he was particularly fond of young Ben—*old* Ben's eldest lad— who had a queer temper sometimes and a mean streak like his father. But he had a good, hard head on his shoulders, knew how to keep his house in order and how to look after his women. Like John-William Dallam. And now, because he'd been fool enough to think himself immortal, it looked as if he might be leaving Gemma, and Amabel, and the mill, to Tristan Gage, who had no real harm in him but was a silly, posing fellow just the same, all very well in a lady's drawing-room making Amabel laugh, and looking very good on horseback or in evening-dress, which, John-William supposed, must have attracted Gemma. (Just like a woman.) But not much good for anything else.

Well, thank God he'd found a good mill manager who could blind the likes of Tristan Gage with science any day of the week *and* tied up ample funds for Gemma in such a way that unless she took to wild speculation, which seemed unlikely, she'd never run out of money.

Not so Amabel.

And abruptly realizing what had always lurked in his mind as an obscure dread, that Amabel, if he died, would have her butterfly hands on large sums of money for the first time in her life, a despairing panic seized him. Somebody would have to look after Amabel. Somebody would have to steer her away from all the beguiling vultures in doves' and peacocks' clothing who would come flocking around her the moment he was gone. Ben Braithwaite, of course, being part vulture himself, would have done the job to perfection. Not Tristan. Did Gemma have it in her? Suddenly he believed so. And if he survived he'd show her the way to do it, re-arrange his affairs a little to give her the means.

"Not long now, father."

There she went again, telling him comforting lies as if he'd been a child—like he'd always treated her—when she must know as well as he did that even if young Master Paddy O'Riley or whatever his name might be managed to deliver her message to the coachman that they'd never get that finely-sprung, over-priced victoria—Amabel's favorite carriage—down this steep and narrow track. At best they'd have to leave it on the strip of flat land just below and carry him down the slope like a sack of flour. Well, they'd need Irish muscle for that, since Williams, the coachman, a handloom weaver in his youth, had the bandy legs and narrow shoulders associated with the cramped, airless conditions of the textile trade.

The girl must have understood that.

She had. But her instinct still told her not only to keep him company but to keep him calm. Nor did she doubt for a moment that the young Irishman would return.

"It won't be long."

It seemed an eternity, her father hunched in his silent agony, the sharp moorland air growing cold and damp, unless it was the grief and fear which chilled her. But she remained as outwardly composed as if he had done no more than turn his ankle. And when the carriage came she had already measured the slope of the land, the ungainly, angry bulk of her father.

So had Daniel Carey. And, having once had a coachman of his own, no matter how long ago, he stood on no ceremony with Williams.

"Here—take his feet. I'll take his shoulders. Then you go first—and go steady. You'll have to hold the horses, miss."

She slid down through the rough grasses, feeling clumsy and inadequate, and held the restive animals steady, her head averted while the two men labored to get her father to the carriage, Williams doing his share of grunting and groaning, the Irishman seeming scarcely out of breath.

They lifted him inside, wrapped a rug around him.

"There we are, miss. You can go away home, now."

"Will you ride with us to Frizingley?"

Was she offering him a lift to town or begging the further security of his company? She hardly knew. But, still smiling, still cheerfully serene, as if to run a mile over stony ground and pick up a sixteen-stone man at the end of it was a mere trifle to him, he shook his head.

"You'll be all right now. Put him straight to bed and call the doctor. You'll know what to do."

"Yes, of course. Thank you."

Was there no more to be said? She couldn't believe it. Yet, unless *she* detained him she was in no doubt that he would simply disappear over the ridge whence he had come, whistling and smiling, and she would never even know his name. Not that it mattered, of course. But he *had* been kind.

"I am Miss Dallam of Frizingley Hall." Lord—how pretentious that sounded, how very much the lady of the manor being gracious to her social inferiors. She had never meant that.

"Good day to you, then, Miss Dallam of Frizingley Hall."

And realizing that he had deliberately increased the Irishness of his voice, she blushed.

"What I mean . . . I am so very grateful to you. If you would like to call—later on—to inquire as to my father's progress—then—then please do so." Floundering, coming lamely to a halt, she knew she had turned crimson now with her embarrassment. What on earth, she wondered, was making her so inept? And exactly what was she saying? Come to the kitchen door, my good man, to collect a guinea for your trouble? Good Heavens. Most certainly she did not mean that.

But Daniel Carey continued to smile, his manner changing so visibly into the jaunty young Irish vagabond, the Paddy O'Riley of her father's imaginings, that she could have wept for shame.

"Well now, Miss Dallam, and so I might at that, one of these fine days when I chance to be passing . . ."

She knew he never would. "I won't forget your kindness." She was speaking the truth.

"To be sure, and think nothing of it at all. Just get your father safe home."

"Yes, indeed."

And with her father still hunched in his pain, still breathing what might be his last on the seat behind her, was it really the moment to concern herself with whether or not she had offended a stranger?

There followed an anxious afternoon and evening, a doctor for John-William, a nurse for Amabel, who, having suffered an attack of her own at the first sight of his, lay shivering on her bed, the specter of widowhood leering at her from its foot, Linnet Gage being splendid, making sure that afterward, whatever the outcome, somebody would be sure to say, "Whatever would we have done without Linnet?," rustling from one sickroom door to the other, thinking of everything, somewhat to the annoyance of the housekeeper, Mrs. Drubb, who had usually thought of it, whatever it was, already. And when it became apparent that John-William would live, Linnet stood beside Gemma, to support her in her emotions, while the doctor explained that it had been a warning, no more, but one which should be heeded nevertheless. His hours at the mill should be considerably shortened. Fresh air and moderate exercise were to be recommended.

"How wise," murmured Linnet, smiling as she tiptoed to Amabel's bedside to whisper the glad tidings and tell her that the doctor had as good as recommended a move to the country.

By morning the crisis was over, Amabel, still pale and tearful, had been installed on a chaise-longue by her husband's bed, while Linnet, her private thoughts running with some excitement on the prospect of country houses and Sir Felix Lark, who had been looking at her lately in a way she recognized, now found the time to direct her brother's behavior toward Gemma. The girl had had a shock. She needed affection, a manly shoulder, the support of a manly arm. Never more than now. For although her engagement to Tristan had been already announced with fitting celebrations, a death—should one occur—would necessarily delay the wedding. And since Aunt Amabel would certainly wear her widow's weeds for the full two years and keep Gemma in black as long as she was able, Tristan might have to woo his bride all over again, or to make very sure of her now, if he wished to keep her. No doubt about it. Not that Gemma, being such a plain little thing, was in any way flirtatious. But, with John-William out of the way, other men, the downright "undesirables" he had kept firmly out of his daughter's sight, would surely come flocking. And Linnet, whom no stern father had ever protected, had good reason to know the dangers of that.

"Let her lean on you, darling," she now told her brother. "Just as hard as she likes. And, of course, if you felt inclined to take a little advantage—you know, whatever men do when they find themselves alone with a girl who happens to be *leaning*—then I'm sure no one could blame you. And most girls would appreciate a kiss or two at a time like this. It might take her mind off her miseries."

It would also fix Tristan irrevocably in Gemma's affections, Linnet felt sure of that. For a girl who did not kiss lightly, who may never even have kissed before, would see a kiss as something quite tremendous, something that would bind her very fast.

"Just *comfort* her, Tristan."

He grinned and kissed his sister, instead, on her cool cheek.

"Are you a schemer, my darling?"

"I do what circumstances force me to do, Tristan. For both of us."

Yes, he knew that. Had she succeeded in getting any of those old men to marry her, the ones who'd been ogling her and pawing her and making her skin crawl throughout every London season since she'd turned fifteen, she'd have gone through with it happily, gritted her teeth and done whatever the old codger might have asked her, to provide a home for herself and her brother. And now that things had turned out this way and he was the one who'd got the chance of a good match, then he'd just have to stir himself. For her. His sexual experiences had been adequate—even plentiful—for a man of his age and class but his emotions had never been touched by anyone—so far—but Linnet.

Not that he had ever put it into words or found it in the least unnatural. A fellow was supposed to love his sister, after all, and since he and Linnet had had to rely on one another more than most, it stood to reason that they should want to look after each other. Since who else would? And she was a splendid girl, who deserved the best. If he could pave her way to one of these rough and ready millionaires then he'd be the happiest man alive. And she'd make herself the leading light of Frizingley, no doubt about it, since there was nobody here to hold a candle to her. Yes, she'd show them all a thing or two—or half a dozen. A triumph he'd be overjoyed to see.

So he'd start right now by making a little love to Gemma, nothing that would offend or frighten her but enough to convince a virginal young lady of narrow upbringing that she had made a physical commitment. And he'd be as charming and gentle about it as he could, a pleasant experience for both of them if he could manage it, both now and later when, as her husband, he'd have the right to do anything he liked.

Not that his desires, physical or otherwise, were in any way unusual. Peace of mind, mainly. The comfortable, rather graceful life of his childhood before money and his father's temper had both grown so damnably short. And if Gemma could give him that delightful time back again, then he'd do his level best to make sure she never regretted it. Good old Gemma. A pity, of course, that she hadn't the looks of that glorious Irish creature he kept seeing about the house with her sewing. No chance at all that Linnet would ever send him to make love to *her*. And if it ever happened—her or somebody like her—then he'd take good care that Gemma never got to know.

So now he would go and kiss her, pretend to lose his head a little, proceed just as far as she would allow—not far, he suspected—so that she would be aware, no matter what became of John-William, that she already had not just a fiancé, but a lover.

"Where is she?" he said.

She had gone into the garden to escape, not him precisely, not Linnet, nor the pair of elderly, ailing lovers holding hands in the sickroom upstairs; rather a blending of all these things, which she found oppressive. And so she had gone to walk among the October leaves already scattered about the pruned, ready-for-winter garden where, to her considerable astonishment, she saw the young Irishman of yesterday coming toward her.

She did not know his name.

"Good morning," she called out, meaning "Good Heavens." And then, thank God she had met him here, on his way to the house, to avoid all that terrible business of the tradesman's entrance or the front door, the servants eyeing him askance, not knowing what to make of him, offending him once more.

If he *had* been offended. Just amused, perhaps. Or scornful. That seemed rather more likely.

"Good morning, Miss Dallam. How is your father?" His voice, to her intense relief, had shed that mocking imitation of an Irish tinker, no Paddy O'Riley this morning but himself—whoever he was—a young man of some education, she was sure of it, despite the shabbiness and thinness of his green jacket, the collar turned up, just a little in tinker fashion, against the bite of the wind. Had he no overcoat? She supposed not.

"My father is much better, thank you."

She realized, with some amusement, that he did not wish to know any more about her father than that. And, far from being offended by his lack of interest, his relegation of the august John-William Dallam to the store of tedious matters which have to be mentioned and then forgotten, she found it—what? Yes. Refreshing. Honest. Ben Braithwaite and Uriah Colclough would feel exactly the same when they came to call, except that *they* would pull grave faces, and pretend.

"Good. I think you lost this."

And opening his hand he held out the small amethyst and diamond cat she had worn on the shoulder of her cape yesterday.

"It was near the slope where you were sitting."

He had picked it up with a flicker of irritation. Dear God, hadn't he done enough by rescuing the father without having to go off now delivering the daughter her jewelry? He had no wish and saw no point to meeting either of them again. And if the brooch had been less valuable he'd have been much inclined to forget the Dallam girl altogether—who had jewels in plenty, he supposed—and give this one to Cara, who might never get another chance to own an amethyst and a few little diamonds in her life. A parting present.

But the brooch was obviously worth a fortune. Enquiries might be made about it which could lead Cara into trouble if she tried to sell it, or pawn it, as he supposed she would. And so here he was with the amethyst cat in his hand, standing in a wind-raked garden with this little brown cob of a girl who all too clearly had no idea what to make of him.

"My name is Daniel Carey," he said, taking pity on her confused proprieties. "I am a schoolmaster sometimes—a journalist sometimes. Sometimes I make translations from the French."

Perhaps now that he had established himself as an educated man, not a digger of ditches who might suddenly use a rough word or beg a shilling, she would be more at ease with him.

She was.

"Mr. Carey—indeed I *do* thank you, once again. I should have been sorry to lose my little cat. I believe I have had him since I was fifteen."

Ten years ago, he wondered? Perhaps less, for although her sturdy little figure in her dark, rather severely cut wool dress, her voluminous cashmere shawl, looked quite matronly, her cheeks were smooth and young without being in any way girlish, her brown eyes thoughtful and quiet, her hand, when it took the jewel from him, small and square and sensible, *capable* even in an untried, untested manner; completely unblemished.

"Will you come into the house, Mr. Carey, and take some refreshment?"

Perhaps it was daring of her to ask him. He had not moved in these polite, class-conscious, self-conscious circles for so long that he could hardly remember. Yet the house must certainly contain a silk-and-lace dragon of a mother, a hawk-eyed governess, a stiff-necked brother, perhaps, to question his intentions or imagine he had come to claim a reward. And since he had no intentions, no claims and could not be bothered with social posturings and pretensions at any time, he shook his head.

"I wish you would."

She seemed to mean it.

"Why? Is it gloomy in there?"

She smiled, and although it did not transform her face nor endow it with any more beauty than Nature had intended, the smile itself was frank, intelligent, open, not at all displeasing.

"Well, they are all at sixes and sevens a little. My mother collapsed when she saw my father . . ."

"Poor lady. I expect she thought it obligatory."

Incredibly Gemma could not suppress a peal of laughter, of which she was instantly, although not wholly, ashamed. How could she? Had he questioned her mother's sincerity? Insulted her? But his eyes were alight with an amusement she could not believe to be unkind. No. Of course he had not insulted Amabel. He had simply, tolerantly, *understood*. Had spoken aloud, in fact, the thought which had been in Gemma's own mind all the time. Because Amabel *had* considered her collapse obligatory, an absolutely essential display of affection between husband and wife. She had, of course, been deeply shocked and grievously alarmed. But Gemma knew—and Daniel Carey knew—that she would have fainted anyway.

"My parents are much attached," she said rather stiffly although her smooth, oval face still retained the quiet harmony of her smile.

"Then they'll be busy enjoying each other's company, which makes it dull for you . . ."

"A little."

Was the expression in her eyes hopeful? He thought so. Good Lord, then she must *really* be lonely. But the last thing he wanted was to sit on a rigid straight-backed sofa drinking weak tea from paper-thin china and making small talk—*very* small he imagined—with her tedious relations. He didn't want to disappoint her either.

"This garden is rather unusual, isn't it?" he said, by way of compromise.

"Oh yes." It was an invitation to show him the old trees, the rosebeds planted by some long-ago Goldsborough, the sun dial, the sunken Italian garden with its empty fountains and sooty stone cherubs, looking so incongruous in this cold climate, to which she at once responded.

"Do you care for gardens, Miss Dallam?"

"I care for this one. And for the house. My mother thinks it small and inconvenient and poorly situated. She longs for rooms a mile high and a marble hall with a great turning staircase in the middle, lit by half a dozen chandeliers. But I think this house has—well—*character*."

"Charm," he said. And to stifle what felt suspiciously and incredibly like the beginning of a blush—*she* who never blushed—she said quickly, "What part of Ireland are you from, Mr. Carey?"

"Ballina in County Mayo. Do you know it?"

She shook her head.

"Nor I, if it comes to that—since it must be a dozen years since I went away."

"Are your family still there?"

He smiled at her, intending to make a simple negative reply, or even to say "Yes, indeed," since to agree was quicker and required no further explanation. Why tell her what had really happened to the Careys of Ballina when it had already *happened*, when he had coped with it and felt not the least need for anybody's pity. Why hers? Intelligent she may be. More so, in fact, than she had been encouraged, in this cloistered atmosphere, to show. Lonely too—which, since she could rarely ever have been physically alone, must imply a lack of understanding in those around her. But how much might *she* be expected to understand? Could she, with her quiet, sheltered eyes, endure even a glimpse of reality?

Yet, nevertheless, to his surprise, he said, "I have no family. My father died in prison of a fever, when I was five. My mother was killed by a stray bullet during a food riot, six years later."

How would she take it? He braced himself for the gasp of horror, the gush of consolation, already inwardly wincing. But when she turned to look at him her face was composed and compassionate, offering him no more sympathy than he could tolerate.

"I'm sorry. I think—perhaps—you don't often talk about it, do you?"

How had she known that?

"No. People don't like tragedy. It makes them feel awkward."

"Yes, of course. One feels so sorry without knowing how to express it. And the questions one would like to ask . . ."

"Ask me the first thing in your head. Come now—the very first."

"Why was your father in prison?"

"That's easy. He didn't like the land policy in Ireland. Do you know what it is?"

"Not really."

Ben Braithwaite or Uriah Colclough would have looked wise, looked *down*, and murmured, "No need to bother your pretty little head over it." John-William Dallam would have grunted, or thundered, according to his humor, a warning that it was no fit topic for a lady. Tristan may not have understood the ins and outs of it himself and would not have cared in any case. But Daniel Carey, easily, courteously, began at once to inform her, finding it perfectly natural, she thought, to speak to a woman as if she were a man.

"Our land policy is based on the supreme power of the landlord and the total helplessness of the tenant. Evictions at will. No security of tenure, you see. No lease. So when the landlord wants his land back he takes it. He also takes, without compensation, any and all improvements the tenant may have made. And since, more often than not, there was nothing on the land but green grass when he took it, that means everything—the cabin he built for himself to live in, the shed for his livestock. Everything. So, you see, the Irish peasant who relies entirely on his plot of land to grow his potatoes to feed his family, has no guarantee of staying on that plot for so much as a full year. I suppose it doesn't help, either, that most of the landlords happen to be English. But—whatever the ramifications of that—the tenant lives in the kind of insecurity that doesn't encourage him to be thrifty. Nor too loyal either, since he may never have set eyes on the man who actually owns his farm. Just a stranger from over the water who wants nothing from his Irish estates but his rent money and employs an agent—who naturally wants *his* percentage—to get it. No tolerance, therefore, no leeway if the harvest is bad. Just the rent money—or out. Unless the plot is wanted for the landlord's whim or fancy, or just for somebody who can pay a little more. In which case he's out anyway.

"And since the landlords have calculated that they can squeeze more profit per acre if they divide the estates up into dozens, or hundreds, of tiny holdings, then no single tenant ever has enough land to do more than live—pretty meagerly—from one harvest to the next. Everything he grows he eats or sells for rent money. No chance of ever putting anything aside for a rainy day. That's why a man who loses his land can be reduced—very quickly and easily—to digging himself a squat-hole in a ditch. That's why we come over here in our thousands and make ourselves unpopular working for what you call Irish wages. Often enough it's either that or dying of hunger in the ditches. Many do. My father saw the injustice and said so. He was a lawyer and so he knew how to be very eloquent about it and annoyed a lot of people. Landlords mainly. I don't know what were the exact charges against him but *that* was the reason. And our family had a bad reputation in any case. My grandfather was involved in the rising of 1798. They hanged him on Ballina bridge."

She was, of course, appalled. It was the most shocking thing that she had ever heard. Yet this, after all, was a *real* conversation and, from the safe distance of her mother's drawing-room, she had always known reality to be shocking.

She rallied.

"1798? That was forty-two years ago. You can't have known him."

"Certainly not. I'm twenty-three."

"I'm twenty-two."

No lady *ever* revealed her age. No gentleman would ever dream of inquiring. It was "not done," could not *be* done without causing serious embarrassment and offense. Yet how easily and naturally they had just broken one of Society's strictest taboos. With no ominous rumblings of protest in the firmament, no indication whatsoever that the sky was about to turn faint with the shock, and fall.

"I know little of Ireland," she said. "Only what the English know."

"Which is?"

She smiled at him, her quiet eyes suddenly aglow, for she knew, in fact, rather more about the male preserve of politics than she ought to know, more, indeed, than she had realized herself until it came flowing into her instantly alert and excited head. Would he listen to her? Would he *hear?*

"Oh," she said, "that whenever invasion has threatened us you have invited our enemies into your country so that they could attack us through our back door. As you did with the Spanish Armada in the days of Good Queen Bess."

He smiled too. "So we did. We felt closer, you see, to the Catholic king of Spain than to your Protestant Elizabeth."

"I do see." He *had* heard her. And now she heard her own voice going smoothly on, speaking rational words as easily as one who is permitted to be rational every day of her life. Easily and naturally and with a joy that might have risen to her head had it not been set so firmly on her shoulders. He—an educated man—was taking her seriously. And the greatest miracle of all was that it began to seem right and proper to her that he should.

"But was it fair, Mr. Carey, to let the Spanish Inquisition loose on us—as you tried to do—and have us burned at the stake as heretics?"

"Oh—fair enough, I think, since your Good Queen Bess was not very good to *us*, you know—sending her pikemen to take our land

and then giving it away as birthday presents, or whatever, to her court favorites—because we wouldn't join her in the Protestant Fold."

"Well—" and she was gravely, humorously considering, "perhaps it was too much to ask that you should join us, but you could hardly expect *us* to stand tamely by while you helped the Spanish Jesuits to conquer *our* country."

"And you didn't, did you?" His eyes were teasing, yet as tolerant as her own. "You made a conquered nation out of us instead. Elizabeth brought us to our knees and then, at stated intervals, your Oliver Cromwell and your William of Orange finished us off."

"Did they?" But they were both aware that she already knew the answer. Daniel without any particular surprise, Gemma with jubilation.

"Oh yes—in true Puritan fashion. No Catholic allowed to vote or sit in the Irish parliament or hold any other kind of office either in government or in the army or navy. No Catholic allowed to buy land. No Catholic father allowed to leave his estate to his eldest son unless that son became a Protestant. Otherwise the land to be divided up among all the children so that soon no Catholic owned any sizeable piece of land at all."

"I suppose *that* happened because when we threw out our Stuart kings you raised an army to support them, intending to overthrow William of Orange, the new king we had just chosen to govern us."

"Yes. *Protestant* William of Orange."

Cheerfully, she was quite ready for him. "Yes. And the *Catholic* Stuarts who had every intention of forcing their Catholicism on us, a Protestant country."

Serenely, he nodded. "So they had."

"And in 1798, when England was in grave danger from the armies of Revolutionary France, you let the French into Ireland, to stab us in the back again."

He nodded. They both smiled.

"We are a conquered nation, Miss Dallam. You allow us nowhere but the back to aim for. We are not even a nation at all since the legal Act of Union between your country and mine in 1801. Some said the loss of our national identity would be compensated for by a share of English trade. What happened was that England has used us as a dumping ground for surplus English goods. Some said that the loss of our own parliament would give us a greater voice in yours. I have yet to hear it. Mainly it was said that the Union would bring the discrimination against Catholics to an end. But your statesman Robert Peel got himself into very hot water, only eleven years ago, when he allowed Catholics to become MPs."

She thought for a moment, deeply, seriously, with a greater awareness of herself as she actually was, as she *wished* to be, than ever before in her life.

"How very sad. It seems that whatever is good for my country has always been bad for yours. And that in order to defend ourselves we have always been obliged to wound one another. How dreadful."

"So it is."

"Are you a Catholic, Mr. Carey?"

That too was something one did not ask. *Ever.*

"Yes. But I think I am also a little of everything else. Are you a Protestant?"

"Yes. It suits me—which is not to say that it must suit everybody."

"What enlightened people we are, Miss Dallam. What a pity we are just two, and not a multitude."

Enlightened? She hoped so. She had grown accustomed to thinking of her views as inconvenient, to be concealed both from her father, who would feel it his duty to put a stop to them, and from her mother, who would worry that she might be considered odd. Enlightenment was quite another matter.

"And what do you plan to do with your life, Miss Dallam?"

He knew, as he spoke, that it was a foolish question, when he was well aware of how carefully her life must have been mapped out for her by others. What choice *could* she have?

"I am to be married in December," she told him quietly.

Of course. Girls like this were born to be married. What other alternative existed except the sorry captivity of middle-class spinsterhood which seemed unlikely in her case.

"I wish you very happy."

He meant it. Graciously, she inclined her head.

"What do you plan to do, Mr. Carey?"

Suddenly, for Daniel, the world seemed very wide, the wind, from that vast, pale, October sky, very fresh.

"Oh—I may go to France. In a day or two. Or even Italy."

Anywhere. Smiling, he filled his lungs with the clean, cold air, rejoicing in his own blessed if often far from luxurious liberty, neither his exaltation nor the shabbiness of his coat escaping the notice of Tristan Gage as he hurried along the path to retrieve his fiancée.

Good Lord, Linnet was right, as usual. The "undesirables" were massing already. Not that Tristan blamed any man for having a damned good try at any and every opportunity as and when it offered. By no means. And this fellow talking to Gemma now, despite the poor quality of his coat, had a fair measure of cut and dash about him. In other circumstances Tristan would have been the first to wish him good luck. And even now he saw no point in delivering what would amount to "Sorry, old chap, she's spoken for," other than in a perfectly pleasant manner.

But he'd have to make himself clearly understood, just the same, since he couldn't help but notice, as he waved and called out and came striding up to join them, that Gemma was not wholly pleased at his interruption.

Who *was* the fellow? Thank God for Linnet.

"Oh, Tristan . . ." and although not priding himself on his sensitivity he knew her welcome to be a shade or two less warm than she was pretending. "This is Mr. Daniel Carey—the gentleman who helped me with father yesterday. Mr. Carey, this is Mr. Tristan Gage, my fiancé."

The Irish knight-errant. Of course. Come to improve on the excellent impression Fate had helped him to make on the moor yesterday. Tristan, who would have done exactly the same, was extremely affable, exceedingly proprietorial, in his thanks.

"Lucky you were nearby, old chap. Can't thank you enough for looking after them."

"Think nothing of it."

So this was the fiancé. Handsome. *Very* handsome, in fact. A real gold-and-ivory drawing-room Adonis with a shallow smile and amethyst eyes which judged all men by their bank-balances and all women by their dowries. This plain, sturdy little cob of a girl was worth a dozen of him.

Did she know it? Struck by the conviction that she knew it very well he felt himself suddenly awash with remorse and pity. She knew it and therefore it followed that this was the best she could do. She had made up her mind that with *this* she would have to be content, for what amounted to the rest of her precious, unrepeatable life.

And if such a girl, with all her rich and powerful relations, had to settle for this mediocre destiny, then what would happen to Cara, who had no one to protect her? How long could she go on alone? With the taste of what he recognized as poison on his tongue, he acknowledged that it could not be long. What further exploitation awaited her? What old or what powerful man, crouched somewhere nearby like a spider in his web biding his time and knowing it would come? Dear God, it was hard enough sometimes to be a man. But to be a woman. Could there be a more pitiful fate than that?

He shuddered.

"Are you cold, Mr. Carey?"

At once she was solicitous, still open and friendly yet already retreating through that drawing-room wall.

"I believe I am. I must be on my way now, Miss Dallam."

"Yes. Of course."

The amethyst cat still lay in the palm of her hand and although she longed to give it to him as a keepsake, a token, she knew better—with Tristan looking on—than to make the attempt. And he would forget her in any case. She knew that. Just as clearly as she knew that she would always remember him. How foolish. And how very unlike her when she had no trouble at all in forgetting the faces of Braithwaites and Colcloughs and Larks the moment they were out of sight.

"Good luck, Mr. Carey."

She had a strong impression that he would need it, his way of life being precarious and hard, perhaps, beyond her understanding. She would like to hear, some day, in some roundabout fashion, that he had succeeded. That he had done whatever it was that mattered to him most.

"Goodbye, Miss Dallam."

Yes. That was the right word to use. Goodbye. She echoed it and watched him very intently for a moment as he walked away from her toward the garden gate, so that when she turned to Tristan her eyes were full of a hard, dark, arrow-straight, wholly male beauty which made the blue and gold of him seem garish, and then insipid.

"A very pleasant fellow," he said. And his voice, after the low, harmonious lilt of Daniel Carey, sounded flat and loud, abominably self-assured.

"Yes. I think so."

Had the scoundrel touched her heart? Tristan thought it rather looked like it, and so much the better since it meant that she had a heart that could be touched, and passions, therefore, which might be aroused.

"Gemma?"

"Yes, Tristan?"

"Everything *will* be all right, you know."

Gradually, word by word, his voice—it seemed to Gemma—was returning to the familiar accent with which she was comfortable; with which she could cope. Slowly, as her eyes emptied of Daniel, he was becoming handsome again, elegant, familiar. Beautiful, shallow, unloved and unloving Tristan, who neither confused nor threatened her.

Much better so.

She had made up her mind to it.

And what harm could it do to remember, from time to time, a young man who would not remember her and could not know that she had had, with him, the first real conversation of her life?

7

*N*o one could take to the black and white dog. Sairellen Thackray, on sight, had named him cur, trouble-maker and thief. Luke, who often came over in the evenings to read his books in the Adeanes' chimney corner, which was far quieter than his mother's, gave fair warning that a nature so warped by the fighting-pen and the heavy diet of blood that went with it, could never be tamed. Liam observed the animal sidelong, as it lay snorting and snuffling on an old blanket by the hearth, and kept well away. Even Odette, disposed by nature to seeking out the best in every living thing, could find no good in him.

"My poor child, whatever are you thinking of now?" she had inquired with a gesture approaching despair when Cara had almost fallen through the door bearing her grisly birthday gift. And indeed, Cara herself often wondered why she had not simply dumped the animal in the first alley she came to and left him there to heal, or to die, alone. A fate by no means uncommon to fighting-dogs who had had their day.

Yet, instead, she had staggered through that maze of treacherous streets and up the whole, steep length of St. Jude's with the beast in her arms, buckling at her knees with the weight of him, cursing him—and his master—every time she stumbled on the cobbles, a pain in her chest and pure despair in her heart every time she thought of the blood, all over her pale blue bodice and her white lace collar, which would probably not come off.

It had not done so.

Nor—while she set about the dismal process of soaping and soaking her ruined garments—had the dog shown the least sign of remorse or gratitude, having done his level best to bite Odette as she bathed his injured legs, snapping at her hands whenever they came near him, only the pain it caused him to move his head preventing him from doing her serious harm. And when Cara, who had spent what remained of the night making a new bodice for her dress from two old ones, brought him a saucer of water, having nothing else to give him, he had bared his teeth at her and, with a spiteful jerk of his muzzle, had spilled her offering disdainfully all over the hearth-rug.

Damned dog.

"You can't afford to feed him," Luke had told her, with sweet reason. "He needs meat and, when he's better, if he doesn't get it he'll kill for it. He'll raid everybody's hen-runs and rabbit hutches and cause you trouble."

Luke was right. She knew that. He usually was. Damned dog.

"I expect he'll die," she said. "Let's hope so."

Yet that same evening she begged a marrow bone from Ned O'Mara which, as Sairellen Thackray acidly pointed out to her, would have made broth for every one of the eleven undernourished children in the house next door, and tossed it within reach of the dog's scornful jaw.

"Go on then, foul creature—eat it."

Eventually he had condescended to do so, growling ominously, until the marrow was scraped clean, if anyone came within a yard of him; unless their intention was clearly to make up the fire. The following night he accepted, with crushing condescension and grossly bad manners, the scrapings from every plate Cara had been able to lay hands on at the Fleece, supplemented by some scraps of raw shin beef she had snatched at the last minute and simply hoped no one would miss.

So it went on.

"He'll keep the mice down," she told Odette. "And you might feel safer with him here at night when I'm at work. If he lives."

He lived. Mainly on the rag rug in front of the fire snoring and snuffling somnolently at the coals, heaving deep, jerky sighs, sleeping a great deal and whining occasionally in his dreams; although he woke up fast enough if anyone seemed to threaten his territory or lay hands—except to fill it—on his dish. Squat, ugly, evil-tempered, totally unlovable. Fit for nothing but to limp outside to foul the gutter—which was already foul enough—two or three times a day. Or, if the sun happened to be shining, to lay himself down with a thud and a ruttling sigh between Cara's two precious rainwater barrels where, in fact, the wickedness of his temper proved quite useful whenever the woman next door, a slattern for whom it was too much trouble to wait at the standpipe for water and carry it home like everybody else, sent one of her brood with a water-jug, to steal.

Before the dog came, the water barrels had been a source of open conflict, the next-door children, a pack of sore-eyed weasels, dipping in sly hands whenever Cara was not looking, leaving off the lids so that the soot and everybody's stray cat could get in, throwing in noxious things themselves, sometimes, to pay her back whenever she had boxed one of their ears too soundly; a rusty horseshoe, a handful of nails, once a never-to-be-forgotten load of frog-spawn so that Odette, who never liked to be hard on anybody, had almost had a fit. Dreadful children. No wonder Liam ducked his head and closed his eyes whenever he saw them coming, refusing absolutely to play with them. And although Cara made no bones about slapping them or pinching them or pulling their hair whenever she caught them near her barrels, the dog saved her the trouble of all that.

They feared him. Their father, when he came to complain that the dog had bitten a hole in his son's trousers and reduced several of his daughters' pinafores to rags, feared him too, being an undersized weasel of a man himself, ferocious only when drunk.

"Your children have always been in rags," Cara told him, standing tall, her hands on her hips.

"That is hardly their fault," Luke told *her* when the little weasel-man slunk away.

"*I'm* not in rags, Luke Thackray."

"You haven't got eleven children, Cara."

"No. I make very sure of that."

He smiled, his quiet tolerance making her just a little ashamed; a feeling which soon faded once she had reminded herself of all the many good uses to which she put her water. To wash herself, for instance, and her child, to wash her clothes, and his. To scrub her floorboards so that they never stank of urine and worse, like the house next door. To soak her bedding so that it never crawled with bed-bugs, just as her son's head never crawled with lice like those abominable little Rattries who hung about all day, scratching and picking their fleas, rubbing their sore eyes, grinning at her and showing their little blackened stubs of teeth; stealing her water. Although for what purpose they required it she could not imagine.

"Mrs. Rattrie doesn't have your good judgment, Cara," Luke said quietly. "Nor your energy."

No. She agreed wholeheartedly with that. For, while the next-door Mrs. Rattrie lay on her mattress all day recovering from the birth of one baby or just about to produce another, *she* was out and about, working, coping, stirring herself. And what temptations could ever have come the way of this washed-out weasel-woman that could be compared with the invitations to sin and indolence—and eventual maternity—which were offered daily to Cara? No. The woman was a slattern. Her husband either half asleep or dead drunk. Her children withered in the bud. Not one of them at work and at least five of them over ten years old. Two of them well into their teens. A family worth no one's trouble.

Yet Luke Thackray took the trouble, during the sharp days of October and November when Cara's dog first began its grudging defense of her property, to show the eldest of the Rattrie daughters—carrying water being classed as work for women—how to manage the stand-pipe. And when Mr. Rattrie, maddened as he often was by cheap gin, threw his wife and children out of the house one frosty night in their underwear—or what passed for it—and barricaded himself inside, it was Luke again, without making much fuss about it, who brought a shawl for pregnant Mrs. Rattrie as she stood shivering and whimpering in the street. Luke who broke down the not particularly solid Rattrie door, dragged the man out and deposited him, with a certain wry humor, in the horse-trough at the end of St. Jude's Passage.

"That's Luke," Sairellen told Cara flatly. "Don't think you're the only one he's ready to fetch and carry for—Miss Adeane, Dressmaker and Milliner. And keep that dog of yours away from my clean doorstep. He'll get pepper in his eyes if I catch him loitering there."

Sairellen, Cara concluded, felt safer with the Rattries, who would neither question her authority nor be likely to entice her son. Yet did Cara herself entice him to any warmer thoughts than friendship? She was never quite certain. Arriving home at the odd hours her employment forced upon her, she would often find him there, sometimes reading in the chimney corner while Odette sat tranquilly embroidering the Dallam trousseau; sometimes reading aloud to Liam, who would not talk to him or answer his questions other than with a swift ducking of the head to signify yes or no, but who, at least, did not shy away from him and cling to Odette as he was still prone to do.

But sometimes Luke would be alone, both Odette and Liam in bed, the dog—she had no name for him, just Dog. Damned Dog, more often than not—snoring on the hearth-rug, the fire carefully banked up for the night. And at such times, always a little out of breath from that perilous walk home, either satisfied with her day or devastated by it—emotions which any man could use to his advantage—she felt no awkwardness with Luke, was simply and wholeheartedly pleased to be safe home, to feel the warmth of her own fire; and to see him sitting there, quietly beside it.

Occasionally, whenever the town was more raucous than usual, when the navvies from the railway camp had drawn a substantial bonus or there were soldiers passing through, he would come down to the Fleece to meet her, or rather to the iron gate of St. Jude's churchyard just beyond the square, where she would see his pipe glowing its signal to her in the dark. And when she saw that dull gleam, caught the scent of his pipe tobacco on the air, she would feel instantly secure, not simply because of his protection against the designs of strangers, but because Luke himself did not threaten her.

Nevertheless—every now and again—she found it wise to ask herself just how she would feel should he suddenly take her in his arms, something men tended to do sooner rather than later in all her previous experience. With Luke she could not imagine it. Not that she doubted for one moment his masculinity. It was just that, in a world where the desires of men had always stalked her, where over-heated hands were always grabbing her and clutching her and trying to undress her—where men so often wished to satisfy their bodies by the use of hers, without responsibility—she did not think so poorly of Luke. He would not touch her unless he knew—as Daniel had known—that she was longing to be touched. And if the longing never came then he would settle, without a word of reproach, for the friendship they already had.

Friendship. How strange. She had never before considered it even as a possibility between a man and a woman. Not surprising, perhaps, when the men she knew rarely took the trouble or felt the need to look beyond the gleaming fall of her hair, the brilliant turquoise eyes, the lithe, sensuous body which, although it had had one lover and borne one child, had no real knowledge, as yet, of sensuality. Perhaps—she thought dimly, still groping for an explanation—it made no real difference to Luke whether she was beautiful or not. Perhaps what mattered to him was the smaller, often fearful, frequently wrongheaded, usually well-meaning girl who lived inside her skin, very well concealed, more often than not, by the boldness of her smile, the deliberately nonchalant swaying of her hips.

He would never take advantage of a girl like that. Of any girl. And, in the meantime, while she still attempted to wrench Daniel Carey out of her heart, she had Luke's undemanding companionship, his decency and good humor, his quietness on the many occasions when, very noisily, she lost her head; his large, unhurried hands not exploring the nape of her neck and her backbone as poor Ned O'Mara was always trying to do, but mending the lock on her coal-place door so that no thieving Rattrie could help himself to a furtive shovel of her precious winter coal; replacing a pane of glass which a Rattrie stone had splintered; offering her a handclasp, from time to time, not of lust but of reassurance.

She knew that Odette, her own romantic mother, would have liked her to marry him. She knew that *his* shrewd, hard-headed mother would rather see her dead than as her son's wife.

On the whole she thought Sairellen was probably right.

Her days were still immensely long. She awoke at first light, made up the fire to warm her rainwater and, no matter how chill the morning, how glacial their little downstairs room, went through what she believed to be the essential toilette of a lady, standing naked before the hearth with only the thin wool rug between her bare feet and the splintered floorboards, to wash her hair and as much of her body as she could manage without freezing, before either Odette or Liam were up; only the dog looking on, grunting his displeasure at her intrusion—since this was *his* rug now, after all, *his* fireside—his small, sardonic eye informing her that *he* knew she was no lady, whatever she might pretend to Mrs. Amabel Dallam. Just a barmaid from the Fleece, that vicious little eye kept on reminding her, with no more chance of rising above it than a crippled fighting-dog. Also from the Fleece. And the rightful property, whenever he chose to reclaim it, of the Fleece's owner. Or whenever he chose to call in the debt which she did not really believe to be canceled.

He would want something from her one day. Not her body, like poor Ned, who had reached the stage of trembling now and turning pale whenever he managed to lay a hand on her. No. Not that, since Captain Goldsborough had women enough around him who knew far more about catering to the finer points of his appetite than she did. She felt in no danger from him there. Why should he demean himself with a barmaid, after all, when he still—albeit surprisingly—had the celebrated actress Mrs. Marie Moon from Martinique and Paris. Not to mention the red-headed woman in a black riding-habit and a man's tall hat who appeared like a thunderbolt sometimes in the afternoons, when her husband thought her out hunting, Cara supposed; and an assortment of others, not all of them beautiful, some of them positively strange, but with an air of quality or style about them, coming to spend a night or two in the huge four-poster bed in his private rooms—the "seraglio" they called it—at the head of the back stairs.

In his place Cara would not have demeaned herself with a barmaid either.

But eventually he would want something and she would very likely find herself summoned to his rooms—the "seraglio," the harem, the lair—not for sex like Mrs. Marie Moon and the lady of the riding-habit, but for instructions, as she watched so many others, both men and women, climb that back staircase every day.

She had no idea what he asked of them, no notion at all of what aims or ambitions he might wish to foster, or what—if anything—mattered to him in life. Yet she was in no doubt at all as to the sources of his power. The possession of two things. Property. And information.

For when the Goldsboroughs, of whom he seemed to be the last—she could only say Amen to that—had sold their manor and their land they had *not* sold their ramshackle dwelling-house and warehouses and their tumbledown squares of old taverns and shops—perhaps none of it quite so ramshackle then—leaving their final heir in possession of what had once been the very heart of Frizingley.

Everybody, therefore—or very nearly—in the decaying cobweb of streets and squares and alleys loosely called St. Jude's paid him rent, or owed him rent, being, in consequence, very much at his disposal. No shopkeeper or tradesman could afford to forfeit his goodwill, since he owned their business premises and the homes of their customers. No dubious tavern, and there were several, could keep its secrets from him for the same reasons, so that he would know the names and faces of the men who attended the radical meetings in the back room of the Dog and Gun, the Chartists, the Ten Hours' Men, the Owenites, the Anti-Poor Law Leaguers, who would be certain, of course, to lose their jobs should Ben Braithwaite or Uriah Colclough or John-William Dallam ever come to hear of it.

He would know, too, who brought illegal gaming cocks to the Beehive and about the discreet back door of that tavern, shrouded with ivy, where men were admitted who had stolen goods for sale. He would know what happened to those goods when the thieves had been paid off and gone, who bought them, who remodeled them, who melted them down. He would know which pawnbrokers were honest and which were not. He would know, since assignations of this type usually took place in a room laughingly known as the "bridal chamber" at the Rose and Crown, which women deceived their husbands, whether it was for love or for money, with whom, and for how much. He would know who was in debt and how steeply, since usually the debt would be to him. He would know, so well, which debts could never be paid and must therefore be settled, to suit his whim, in some other fashion.

And so when he smiled and said, "There is a little something you can do for me . . ." it was done. Always. One way or another. Sometimes, waking abruptly and startled in the night, a sick, cold dread would come over her that one day his queer humor might find it amusing to try and give her to Ned.

It was a part of her life she took great care to conceal from the Dallams. Appearing at Frizingley Hall bright and early throughout October and November, never staying long enough to make it obvious that she had no other work but always on hand to seize any scrap of opportunity which might come her way, she was Miss Adeane, Dressmaker and Milliner, to the life; always—and at a cost in effort none of the Dallams could even imagine—immaculate in her pale blue wool dress, refurbished now with tiny royal-blue satin bows from neck to hem, and a dark blue cloak made from the unworn bits joined together of a pair of old plush tablecloths she had inveigled from Ned O'Mara.

She had gloves too with embroidered tops done by her mother, her old cream kid boots dyed black to hide the scuff marks at the toes, her freshly washed hair elaborately coiled and ringleted, not a stain upon her anywhere, not an odor of anything but the lavender and violets and rose-petals she gathered surreptitiously from *anybody's* garden she happened to pass, and which Odette brewed into perfume in the cellar. Miss Adeane, bright as a button, neat as a new pin, as she cheerfully responded to Amabel Dallam's bubbling enthusiasm for her daughter's wedding. Diverting it, whenever she could, in her own direction.

It was to be at the end of December, as near as possible to Christmas yet not later, certainly not in January, Amabel being unwilling to forfeit, by a day or two, the distinction of marrying Gemma in this year of 1840 when the Queen—a year younger than Gemma—had gone so blissfully to the altar with her Albert. And if Gemma should further follow the example of the Queen, who, married in February, was expecting her first child for November, then Amabel would be well-satisfied.

A honeymoon baby. What a pity one could not use the term "love child" which, Amabel knew, meant something rather different. Perhaps Miss Adeane, who had done such exquisite embroidery on the wedding chemises, would be interested in the layette? Most definitely Miss Adeane would. Although the wedding-dress, white satin like the Queen's, with masses of lace and orange blossoms, had been ordered, of course, safely and securely and considerably to Linnet Gage's satisfaction, from Miss Ernestine Baker, who was *always* called upon for wedding dresses. In fact Amabel knew of no one in Frizingley—who was *anyone*, that is—who had not gone to her. And no one who had been dissatisfied.

"What a wonderful woman she must be," murmured Cara. "One wonders, with so many bridal gowns to churn out in a season, how she manages so that they do not all look alike."

Perhaps they did. A little.

"Heavens," Cara smiled, knowing she had sown the seed. "How clever of her to remember everything. Even to stitching the little sachets of sugar in the hem. She does do that, of course . . . ? Doesn't she?"

"My dear . . . ? *Sugar* in the hem?"

"Why yes. A symbol of the sweetness of the married life to come."

Amabel was charmed.

"But, Mrs. Dallam, we *always* did that in the rue Saint Honoré. For good luck."

What else did they do there, Amabel was bound to wonder, what other elegant and thoroughly delightful innovations which had not yet arrived in Miss Baker's establishment in Market Square? What fun it would have been at the reception, murmuring that little snippet about the sugar to Lizzie Braithwaite and Maria Colclough and Ethel Lord. A pretty trifle, of course. But Amabel's life was made up of such things. And now the wedding dress was finished, hanging in guarded splendor in a locked wardrobe upstairs, a fairytale creation—

if, perhaps, bearing just a whisper of resemblance to the fairytale creation Maria Colclough's daughter had worn—and which, she was dimly aware, had aroused her admiration a shade more warmly than Gemma's.

"What a dream! Sheer bliss," had enthused Amabel when the dress had been delivered, seeing *herself*—and perhaps Linnet—in those fluted tulle frills, that May-blossom of lace with which the white satin foundation had been covered.

"Very nice, mother," Gemma had said.

Oh dear. Would Gemma have preferred something a little less . . . ? *Girlish* was the word which came into her mind. Dainty. *Pretty*. Would Miss Adeane, who was not dainty either, have had other ideas on how to dress Amabel's dear but often so difficult daughter? *Was* there another way?

Amabel, who had been so radiantly happy lately, with her husband well on the road to recovery and her daughter bringing her the very son-in-law she had most wanted, was suddenly troubled and perplexed. She had simply desired to make Gemma beautiful on her wedding day, to hear the gasps of admiration, the sentimental sighing echoing around the church as her daughter entered it. Would Miss Ernestine Baker's dress produce that gasp, those sighs? Or would Gemma be just another Frizingley bride going to the altar in the same tulle frills as Maria Colclough's daughter, although rather more of them, the same wreath of orange blossom as Queen Victoria, perhaps, but which young Amanda Braithwaite had also worn when she became Mrs. Jacob Lord?

Having produced the impression she desired, Cara bowed her head over the nightgowns she had just delivered, unfolding them slightly to show the elaborate pin-tucking, the delicate white on white of the embroidery, no two alike, nothing to resemble them anywhere in Frizingley she was quite certain—since Miss Baker would never have taken so much trouble with undergarments which did not *show*.

Miss Baker would have considered it uneconomical to expend so much time and ingenuity on a petticoat or a chemise. Unnecessary even, with orders for a wedding gown and bridesmaids' dresses on her hands. But Cara and Odette had put everything they knew into the work, everything they could imagine. Four dozen of "everything," one hundred and ninety-two garments altogether, each one different, Cara doing the cutting and plain sewing, Odette working at the embroidery all day with Liam at her skirts and continuing, when she had put him to bed, by candlelight and firelight until her eyes burned and a blind headache forced her to stop.

Even so, Cara had calculated that when the order was completed, their profit would be six times more than they would have earned doing the same work for Miss Baker at her rate of twopence an hour. And if they could achieve that much, laboring in cramped, poorly lit conditions, on these fiddling undergarments which ate up more time and trouble and embroidery thread than an evening gown, what could be done with good light and good orders for *real* clothing. Day wear which required cut and style. Evening wear which demanded a little more daring than could ever be found in Miss Baker. Feathered and ribboned hats—Cara's own speciality—which she could put together much more quickly and profitably than these cobweb-fine chemises.

The prospect excited her. Opened doors and windows in her mind leading outward and upward, offering her at the very least—and it was a great deal—a *future*. Another rainbow? As her father had so often glimpsed it? Did she resemble him then in other things besides the dark hair and bright blue eyes? But when had he ever worked so consistently, miserably hard as she was doing now? Another rainbow? Perhaps. But her father, in the moment of running toward it, would already have filled his eyes and his mind with a tantalizing glimpse of the one beyond. And so would allow both to pass him by.

Recognizing that flaw in him, she set herself to resist it. Never to deviate. To persevere. Yet she had a great deal against her, not least the renewed animosity of Miss Ernestine Baker, who, despite Cara's precautions, was not long in discovering her connection with the Dallams of Frizingley Hall.

And it was Linnet Gage, for reasons of her own, a little exercise in power, a tiny flexing of her claws, just to test how far she could go, who let Miss Baker know, one morning in late November when Miss Baker had been shown into Amabel's dainty little private parlor to answer some inquiry about the bridesmaids' dresses.

"Miss Baker," said Linnet pleasantly, as the woman was on the point of leaving, not really knowing what she might discover, simply aiming a shot in the dark. "What is your opinion of the work of this new dressmaker from France we keep hearing of? Miss Cara Adeane? I assume you must be acquainted?"

And seeing the shock on Miss Baker's thin face, the angry flush which mottled it, Linnet opened her blue eyes very wide, very innocently, and smiled.

"Good Heavens—Mrs. Dallam—how is it that you have been importuned by such a creature?"

The story was revealed. Miss Baker, in her turn, had a great deal to say, apologizing, as she said it, for the need to lay such indelicate information before a woman of Mrs. Amabel Dallam's sensibility, and two as yet unmarried young ladies.

"These are not matters which one would readily discuss . . ." Yet she discussed them nevertheless in some detail, from the perfidious disposition of Mr. Kieron Adeane, who, to escape his creditors, had abandoned his foreign and therefore necessarily suspicious wife, down to the loose moral character of Miss Adeane herself, of which Miss Baker, despite the virginal ears of two of her listeners, did not shirk from producing the evidence. She had *seen* with her own, presumably virginal, eyes. Therefore, she *knew*. The girl was . . . Perhaps there was no need to use the ugly word. No need either to point out the dangers, the downright health hazard of her acquaintance?

Miss Baker departed, clothed in her own virtue and self-righteousness.

"Oh dear," said Amabel, relinquishing with some regret that entertaining notion of sugar in little pink and white sachets stitched into a hem. What else might accompany them? Good Heavens. She shuddered, worrying desperately now about all those chemises. If one had them washed, perhaps, very thoroughly, several times before wearing? So pretty. But, Goodness, it was *safety* that counted. And Amabel had started to feel very safe, all over again now, with Miss Ernestine Baker.

"Oh dear," echoed Linnet, her mouth drooping down a little at the corners, sadly and sweetly, but her light eyes shining. "One feels, perhaps, that one has seen the last of Miss Adeane? It would be wise, I think, dear Aunt Amabel, to ask your stout-hearted Mrs. Drubb, perhaps, when she calls again, to tell her so."

And there was no doubt at all that Amabel would have gladly agreed had not Gemma suddenly spoken, her voice, coming from the window-seat where she had been glancing at the pages of the *Ladies' Magazine*, startling Linnet into light, perhaps slightly nervous, laughter.

"Do you think so, Linnet? I don't see why."

"My dear—you heard what the woman said."

"Yes, Linnet. I did."

"Can you doubt it?"

The dressmaker, Cara Adeane, was of little importance in herself to Linnet Gage; what mattered to her—the *only* thing which mattered to her—being her own position and the position of her brother for which, against the drawbacks of a criminally extravagant father and a self-indulgent, weak-willed mother, she had always had to fight. And if the exposure of Miss Adeane as a wanton and a slattern could strengthen her influence with Amabel Dallam, could reinforce in Amabel the feeling that Linnet was ever vigilant, ever solicitous, that with Linnet at her side she would always be safe, then she would expose the girl thoroughly, cruelly, making as much capital out of it—for herself and Tristan—as she could. For who knew what either of them may need as time went by? And it was Linnet's opinion that Amabel Dallam, for all her fads and fancies—perhaps because of them—might well live, and thus have favors to bestow, for a hundred years to come.

"I am so sorry," she said now to Gemma in her light, Mayfair voice. "I realize the girl was your discovery, but any of us can be deceived ..."

What an excellent opportunity to let dear Aunt Amabel know that although Gemma had been taken in, she—Linnet—had not.

"Oh yes indeed," said Amabel almost obediently. "I am sure the girl was most plausible—likeable ... No one could blame you, Gemma."

"I should think not." Getting up from the window-seat and coming into the center of the room, looking very small and brown beside Linnet's silvery fairness, Gemma was smiling. "What a storm in a teacup, mother."

"Oh darling—hardly ..."

"Yes, mother—most decidedly. And I am sure Linnet thinks so too—or will come to that conclusion when she has had a moment to reflect. Won't you, Linnet?"

"Gemma—really—I think ..."

What *did* she think? Was Gemma challenging her? It rather looked like it. And if so would it be wise to provoke a confrontation now, before the marriage contract was safely signed and sealed? Perhaps not. It was her intention to remain on good terms with Gemma if she could, certainly until she had established herself rather more securely in Frizingley. It might be unwise, therefore, to antagonize her on an issue which could be of little real significance to either of them, just now. Later, of course, when Gemma was married to Tristan and owed him the obedience of a wife, there would be no need for either of the Gages to tread so carefully.

Linnet smiled again, very sweetly.

Gemma, her eyes on Amabel, smiled too.

"What have we really heard against her, mother? We can hardly blame her for what her father has done. Can we, now?"

Amabel, bending as always to a stronger will, looked endearing and very helpless as she shook her head.

"I suppose not . . ."

"And if she is working hard to support her mother, as Miss Baker tried *not* to tell us, then perhaps we ought to admire her, rather than condemn her, for it. Don't you agree?"

"Oh dear, I suppose I do. But darling—the *other* matter . . . ?"

Gemma's smile now was frank and open, far too certain of itself for Linnet's peace of mind.

"Well, mother, Miss Adeane is very handsome, you know?"

"Yes, isn't she. I *do* think so. A little like a gypsy of course, which is not quite the thing for people like us, but *quite* lovely . . ."

"In which case, why be surprised that she has a lover? And neither you nor I nor Miss Baker can have any real notion as to his intentions. When Miss Baker saw them together he may have been asking for her hand in honorable matrimony, you know. And anyway, perhaps Miss Baker is not the *best* judge . . . Do admit, mamma, that it must have been a very long time, if ever, since a handsome young man made an attempt on *her* honor."

"*Gemma.*" But Amabel, who had never heard her daughter make such a shocking, yet nevertheless entertaining, remark before, burst into a peal of laughter; the kind of merriment women shared in whispers on the corner of a sofa, their heads close together. The kind of faintly malicious, vastly diverting gossip of which she had always been fond and which she had missed, until now, in Gemma.

Well, then. She had been right after all. Love and marriage had been all her darling daughter needed to make her so refreshingly just like everybody else. Instantly, luminously, Amabel brightened.

"So you see, mother, *I* think Miss Baker may have rather misjudged the situation. Don't you?"

It rather looked like it. Poor old Miss Ernestine. Worried about the competition too, perhaps. Amabel knew her darling John-William would have come to *that* conclusion at once. Yet a slight wrinkle of doubt still remained. What did Linnet think?

She asked her, and it was Gemma who replied.

"Oh, Linnet thinks as I do, mother. I expect she saw through Miss Baker right away. Didn't you, Linnet?"

Gemma was not wholly concerned with Miss Cara Adeane either, although she did not care to see an injustice done. But, since she was marrying Tristan in order to free herself from petty restrictions such as these, it seemed an appropriate moment to nip Linnet's interference in the bud. She had always known that Tristan's sister would be a problem. So it was perhaps as well to start as one meant to go on, by claiming the right to choose one's own dressmaker. Paid for, after all—John-William Dallam's daughter felt bound to add—by one's own money.

"Poor Miss Baker," murmured Linnet, choosing discretion as her best weapon, for the moment. "Jealousy can be a terrible thing."

And the next morning, when Cara arrived with the very last of her chemises, she was shown, to her astonished delight, a length of brown satin, heavy and rich, quite plain until the light caught it, deepening its sheen to a burnished copper.

"I have had this for ages," Gemma told her. "It was a gift from an aunt who thought it came from China. Perhaps it does, for I have never seen anything like it before. My mother thinks it far too dark and plain for an evening dress but I rather like it. Could you do something with it for me?"

At once, before the golden moment had any chance at all of slipping away, before anybody else could dash it to the ground casually or maliciously, by saying "Oh no, darling, not *that*," as Mrs. Dallam seemed about to do, Cara produced the pencil and paper she always had about her and began rapidly to sketch.

"Something like this, Miss Dallam?"

She might not be the best needlewoman in the trade, she knew that, and, when it came to embroidery and fine sewing, would never hold a candle to her mother, but she could translate brown Chinese satin or any other kind of satin—in seconds—into a design to suit not only the shape and size but the *nature* of anybody who asked her, giving this one an uncluttered elegance, even a little severity, to please Miss Dallam, yet narrowing the waist, curving the silhouette, drawing the garment on a taller, slimmer version of Miss Dallam, to please Miss Dallam's mother.

"Yes, Miss Adeane. I should like that very much."

"Oh, darling." Amabel sounded doubtful. "You will surely have some trimming—scallops of blonde lace, perhaps, all over the skirt? That would be nice. And a great swirl of it around the shoulders?"

Gemma shook her head.

"Darling."

Amabel bent anxiously over the drawing, and Cara, catching Gemma's eye, held it a moment, signifying "Leave it to me."

"A little embroidery," she said. "Just a little. Very discreet. Something in the nature of a gold fleur-de-lys."

"Yes," said Gemma. "Gold embroidery, mother. You'll like that."

Miss Adeane, from her miraculous carpetbag, produced tape, scissors, a length of plain linen which was soon cut into Miss Dallam's personal pattern against Miss Dallam's firm, well-rounded little body, and then stowed away in the bag again with the gleaming Chinese satin.

"Would it not be wise," murmured Linnet Gage, by no means defeated, "to have the work done *here* rather than—wherever it is Miss Adeane does her work? I am sure Miss Adeane would oblige..."

Her thin voice trailed off into thin air, leaving its faint warning of damage, dirt, even theft. For Miss Baker after all, may have been right. And if Miss Adeane was a wanton then might she not also be a thief? And while cambric for the fashioning of chemises was one thing, costly brown satin from China must surely be another?

Miss Adeane appeared to have become rather deaf.

So did Miss Dallam.

"Perhaps you would be ready to come and give me a fitting on Friday afternoon?"

Miss Adeane agreed that she would, hurrying back to St. Jude's with a shout of triumph in her heart, to find that Odette and Liam had gone out and that Daniel Carey was waiting for her.

She had not seen him for a month. They had said goodbye already. What now? Why say it all over again? But her pulses had started their racing, her heart its pounding at the first sight of him, her stomach lurching, as it always did, clean over and then, for hours afterward, refusing to be still.

"For the love of God—what do you want, Daniel Carey?" But already her mind was full of him, her triumph shrinking, slipping between her fingers like that future of silk and satin and feathered bonnets she had been dreaming about so eagerly an hour ago. Miss Cara Adeane. Dressmaker and Milliner. She might even attain that future. Faced now with the future upon which she dare not hazard herself, the other seemed suddenly quite possible. And would she be any better off than Miss Ernestine Baker, at the end of it, without Daniel?

"Your mother let me in," he said. "And then she took Liam out to the park. Or so she said. I suppose she knew I was wanting to talk to you."

"Talk, then." There was no point in being sweet and understanding and breaking her heart all over again about it.

"I'm away to London tonight and then to France."

"You told me that last month, so you did."

"I know. But I have my ticket now. And since it's about all I do have until the end of the month I shall have to use it."

"I suppose so."

"I've given up my lodging in Leeds, as well. I have a friend in London who'll put me up until I get myself sorted out. A fine man . . ."

"Yes. The world's full of them. What has *he* been in prison for?"

He smiled. "Selling untaxed newspapers. And handing out broadsheet ballads about the Charter. But he *is* a fine man."

"I'll take your word."

"Goodbye, Cara."

She turned her back on him, praying that he would not touch her, her throat so tight now with tears that it seemed to be closing, her chest feeling as if frantic hands were hammering it from the inside, bursting it—in several raw, sore places—wide open.

"Cara, you can't go on . . ."

They had been through all this before.

"Yes I can."

"Cara . . ."

They had said it all. Gone over it, through it, around it, beyond it, and ended, every time, trapped in the same corner, backed up against the same blank wall.

She turned around again to face him.

"Goodbye."

It was almost a command. He understood the reason. They had decided to part. Part, then. Do it and have done with it. Since all they were achieving, by these repeated farewells, was to inflict the same wounds over and over.

"If I leave you an address . . . ?"

"No," she said. "I won't write to you. Don't be writing to me either. I won't be here much longer in any case. Things are looking up. And if they go on like this I shall need something bigger and lighter. Much bigger, to take a real sewing table . . ."

"Cara . . ."

"Just go, will you."

"Yes. I will."

"I don't care, you know."

"Why should you? I'm not much of a catch. Just a poor schoolmaster who can't afford to keep you in the style to which you've never been accustomed . . ."

"If you were even a schoolmaster. When did you last teach anybody anything except how to get locked up . . ."

"Don't quarrel with me, Cara. Not now."

"You say that every time."

"I know."

She could force no more words through her aching throat. Nor he. Go then—and be damned. God bless you. Come back to me.

"Oh Christ," he said. "You're the most glorious creature God ever made, Cara. I swear it."

"No. You are." And she went forward as if some irresistible force, slowly gathering behind her back, had suddenly erupted and hurled her against him.

His body had been expecting her.

"Come to me, Cara."

She was here. And his. If he could take her *now*, overpowered as she was by her emotion, and take her *quickly*, before she started to reason and to be afraid again, then he thought he would be able to keep her. She might be angry afterward and certainly she'd be terrified in case he'd made her pregnant, but she'd get over that. And once she'd given herself to him, she'd stay with him, one way or another. She'd be his woman, which was all he wanted. Faithful to him, even if they would have to be apart sometimes, as he'd be faithful to her, although he knew she'd take more than a little convincing about that. He loved her. And it was love, just as much as that damned dog by the hearth suddenly growling and rising its hackles, which made him hesitate.

Had he simply desired her he would have taken both her and the consequences then and there, booted that evil-looking brute of a dog aside, and made love to her, gloried in her, possessed her once and for all, on the hearth-rug. But the dog rose shakily on its bandy legs and bared its teeth. And his desire had too much love in it, too much natural chivalry, to take what he knew to be advantage of a vulnerable moment. Loving her, he wanted that moment to be perfect, to be hers as well as his. And since whatever happened he would have to take the London train, could he really expose her—a woman who had one child and so could surely have another—to the risk of her own fertility? Only if he knew her to be ready to take that risk herself.

He knew she was not. Knew, indeed, that she feared it more than anything else in her life.

Yet, even then, he could neither leave her nor cope with the weight of his frustrations, and the blurred, cumbersome feeling growing inside him, which, when some of the numbness wore away, he knew would be misery.

"Come with me, Cara." It was a last and desperate chance. "Come now—while we can . . ." She was shaking, crying as if every teardrop scalded her.

"Come where?"

"Anywhere." That too he had said before. "Just come with me. Cara . . . God knows how much time there is left in the world for any of us."

"Not much," she said. "Not much, if I have to walk barefoot through my share of it, following you—waiting for you—being left behind by you—with a tribe of children trailing after me."

"Cara . . ."

"And see you hanged at the end of it, like as not."

She was shaking again. Horribly.

"I'd rather die now, Daniel Carey, believe me. So I would—now—this minute—than go through all that. Like my mother."

Because if he treated her as her father had treated Odette, she knew she would not bear it so patiently, would not bless him on the day he finally left her, as Odette had done, but would go after him with a knife to hunt him down. One fatal blow to his heart. The second to her own. Since, all too probably, she would love him still.

She did not see him leave. She turned her back again, her shoulders heaving, her eyes blind with tears. And when she calmed herself sufficiently to face him he had gone.

Thank God, at least, for that. Much better so. Or, at least it would be when she managed to dry up these damnable tears.

She was still crying, quietly but persistently, when her mother returned.

"I'm perfectly all right," she said.

"So I see."

"Wonderful news, mother. Just look at this glorious satin . . ." She told her tale of triumph.

"Wonderful news," said Odette.

"So we should make a start now. I've already cut the pattern. Shall I cut the dress while you do a sample of a fleur-de-lys? Have we any gold thread?"

"Yes. Gold thread we have. Sorrow we have too, it seems to me."

"I'm all right, mother."

And she sat down, took out her scissors, wiped the backs of her hands against her eyes, found her pins and linen pattern.

Shed her tears.

"I'm all right, mother."

"Yes, my darling."

It would have helped, she thought, if Odette had pretended to believe her. It would have helped, perhaps, had she not known that Odette, in her place, would have given up everything and anything—had, in fact, already several times done so—for love.

8

By Friday morning the brown satin dress was ready to be fitted, its rare, coppery sheen catching even the perpetual sooty twilight of St. Jude's as Cara folded it in layers of clean muslin and stowed it carefully away in her bag. She had cut the skirt wide, the neck low into a broad band falling away from Miss Dallam's perfectly presentable shoulders into huge, puffed sleeves which finished above the elbow, giving a curving softness to Miss Dallam's square-cut silhouette which, in turn, would have a narrowing effect upon her waist. The embroidery, a pattern of golden lily-flowers dotted here and there, each one at a fair distance from the other, would be confined to the shoulder band and to a broad sash fastening at the back in as large a bow as Miss Dallam would tolerate, its ends falling to the hem of her skirt.

Miss Dallam's mother would, at first glance, think it Quaker-plain. But Miss Dallam would not only feel at ease with it but would look well in it too. Far better at any rate, than in the diaphanous sweet-pea tinted frills in which her mother and Miss Ernestine Baker seemed intent on smothering her.

Not that Cara had anything against tulle frills. Far from it. On Miss Linnet Gage, for instance, one could create a positive sea-foam of gauzy draperies dotted with lace bows and silk rosebuds to the extent of one's imaginings. On Mrs. Marie Moon one could write a fresh drama every morning in black lace, sequined taffeta, white watered-silk with one huge splash of crimson at the waist. On every woman Cara had ever seen one could do something to enhance what Nature had given, or cover up what had been left out. She loved clothes. She understood them too. She knew how to dress other women and how to dress herself. And when Mrs. Amabel Dallam remembered to pay her for all those wedding chemises she might just take a few shillings to a certain bazaar in Leeds where she'd heard good dress-lengths were to be had at bargain prices and make *herself* a new dress for Christmas.

That, at least, would be something to look forward to, a new dream, albeit a small one, a poor one, to spread wanly into the corners of her mind and try to fill them; now that the real dreams had gone.

But a dream—God dammit—nonetheless.

She wished to arrive at Frizingley Hall that day around two o'clock, a convenient hour when, with luncheon just over, Mrs. Amabel Dallam would be lying on her bed recovering from the exertions of ordering and then pecking at her food, Miss Linnet Gage reading aloud to her, perhaps, as an aid to the digestive processes of one lady, the nest-building of the other, so that Cara might give Miss Gemma Dallam her fitting alone. And, further wishing to appear brisk and fresh, as if she had simply alighted at the manor gates from her carriage, she allowed herself plenty of time for the familiar trudge down the cobbled hill of St. Jude's Street to the flat plain of St. Jude's Square and Market Square in the valley below and then up the other side, past the brewery and the iron foundry, through the maze of brewers' and iron-workers' cottages, to the manor, the skyline beyond it dominated by the squat, square bulk and the huge, foully belching chimney-stack of Dallam's mill.

She was as much a part of this murky landscape now as if she had been born here, every step of the way between Miss Gemma Dallam's cloistered corner and her own—in spirit a universe apart—being so familiar to her that it seemed she had always known them, or had known them before, in another place, a dozen other places; another life. A wheel designed just to go on turning, never stopping, so that for a hundred years with a hundred more to follow, she had been coming out of this cottage doorway, carrying her carpetbag, filling her lungs with this damp, sooty air which had started to make Liam cough, reminding herself—as one simply *had* to do—to be thankful for such mercies as came her way, however small. Thankful that this was the *top* of St. Jude's Street, for instance—with the immaculate Thackrays on one side of it, the abominable Rattries on the other—and not the bottom end, where the factory smoke collected, hung low, never lifted, spreading a deep, damp gloom in which old men coughed and spat blood, and women—old before their time—bred babies like rabbits, who died like flies.

Not that the Rattries were doing much better, three of the youngest—Cara did not know which—having died the week before of measles, Sairellen Thackray thought, or some such childish ailment involving a rash and a cough. No doctor having been called, even had they been able to find one willing to attend, since one glance would have been more than enough to convince any practitioner of medicine that his fee could not be paid. And no other care taken either, except for the broth Sairellen had sent round, and the collection she had organized afterward to pay an undertaker and avoid the consequences of a pauper's grave.

Cara had not seen much sense to it. Or so she had said. The Rattries were destined for the workhouse anyway, sooner or later. Everybody knew that. So why not sooner? Why not now, by leaving them to admit, to the Poor Law Officer, that they had no money to bury their children? At least that way the remaining infants would be deloused, taught to read and write, fed, and Mrs. Rattrie, by being separated from her husband—since paupers were not allowed to breed —would have been spared the trouble of having any more. But when Luke Thackray came round with his cap, she'd put a penny or two in it just the same, like everybody else, knowing, as they all did, that Disaster, which had struck the Rattries today, might strike any of them tomorrow.

She'd tacked a few scraps of old cotton into a baby-gown too and sent it round next door for the new Rattrie baby, born very inconveniently, as it turned out, the day after the funeral, her fit of generosity entirely misplaced, since the child had only lived a few hours and the gown—upon which Odette had worked a few hasty stiches of embroidery—had ended up in the pawnshop—Cara had seen it herself in the window—to help pay, she supposed, for yet another infantile disposal.

Ah well. Never mind. The Rattries would remain abominable, the father drunk, the mother vacant, such children as survived a damned nuisance. Just like all the other children who swarmed in their rat-packs all day and half the night in the nooks and crannies of St. Jude's. Turned out into the street, most of them, every morning— Cara knew well—while their mothers went to the mill, a ragged band of infant desperadoes, all under the magic age of nine when they too could be put out to labor. Little pests until then though, scuffling and squabbling, paddling their bare feet in the sewage channels, hanging about the shop doorways for warmth and anything else they could manage to lay a hand on before the baker or the pork butcher, both mighty men, sallied forth and scattered them like a flock of starlings. Little boys of seven, bandy-legged as old men expertly running for cover, little girls of five or six remembering, more often than not, to pick up the new baby and last year's baby, to grab the two-year-old, the three-year-old before they ran off too.

Cara nodded and smiled at the pork butcher as she passed him by, being fond of the pies he would sometimes sell off at half price before closing his shop on a Saturday night. She smiled at the baker too, rather warmly, not for the sake of Saturday's bread bought cheap on Mondays but because his wife detested the Irish in general and that "bold, brazen strumpet from the top of St. Jude's" very much in particular. And because her bag was light, with only Miss Gemma Dallam's brown Chinese satin in it, and her hopes as high as she ever allowed them to be, she smiled at everybody else who came her way, the fishmonger, the old-clothes dealer pushing his cart with its flea-ridden bundles; the organ-grinder whose emaciated monkey, cowering sadly on his shoulder, always caused her a stab of pain.

She smiled at the decent, hard-working housewives like Sairellen Thackray—too busy to smile back at her—who were scouring their doorsteps with pumice stone and polishing their door-knockers; waging war to the death—their own, quite likely—against soot from the mill chimneys which attacked their washing lines; against foul air and foul water which attacked the bodies of their children; against bad housing, bad weather, a spell of bad trade when a reduction in a husband's wages could cause their whole, grimly constructed edifice to crumble.

She smiled at the slatterns too—why not?—most of them living a little lower down the street, who, for one reason or another, had lost all taste for building edifices of any description, hanging on by the skin of such teeth as they had left, to a precarious existence of borrowing today to pay what one owed from yesterday and hoping that tomorrow would somehow take care of itself. Inadequate women, some of them, both by nature and by inclination. Others who had coped well enough to begin with on those scanty mill wages, who had even picked themselves up and patched things together, the *first* time that demon of bad trade had halved their weekly pay; the *first* time there had been sickness and doctors' bills to eat up anything they had been able to put by during the good times—never much; the *first* time a husband had suffered injury at the mill or the foundry, which meant no weekly pay-packet at all. Nothing, if the injury persisted, but whatever a man's mates might collect for him by passing around a hat. The first time. Sometimes even the second. Rarely the third; when gin might seem a cheaper and faster way of easing pain than any other.

Nevertheless Cara smiled at them that morning, as she smiled at the frail, clerical-looking gentleman who was both their savior and their torment, the pawnbroker who held his court on one corner of St. Jude's Passage, the other corner housing the red-headed madam of the fringed shawl who did not emerge from behind her green shutters so early in the day. Two establishments of furtive commerce which marked the end of the part of St. Jude's Street which even tried to be respectable. The place where even the barest sketch of family life ended and vagrancy began.

Entering St. Jude's Passage—her most direct approach to St. Jude's Square and the old market place which would lead her to Miss Dallam's side of Frizingley—Cara was at once hemmed in by tall houses as sinister and insubstantial as shadows, tottering almost beneath a weight of sheer dilapidation and the load of displaced humanity they carried. Lodging-houses these, not of the ruthlessly spotless kind kept by Sairellen Thackray but terrifying places—even to Cara—where men and women slept twenty or thirty together on whatever mattresses or bundles of rags had been thrown down on the rotting floor, tramps, drunkards, lechers, syphilitics, crude young whores, wan little virgins turned out of charity-schools who would not be virgins in the morning, packed side by side in the dark and in a horrible proximity which made Cara shudder.

A terrible place, St. Jude's Passage. Dark kitchens where men could purchase an hour or two on a chair by the fire and a tin mug of bacon grease and hot water. Cellars sprouting fungus from every dripping crevice, where those who could not even afford a place on an upstairs mattress paid a penny to sleep standing up like horses, leaning against a rope which would be simply untied the next morning when the landlord considered they had slept long enough. Narrow staircases, infested with mouse droppings, where those who had no money whatsoever huddled on the steps for shelter, coming like wraiths in the night when they were less likely to be turned away, and drifting off again in the early morning. Except for the few who tended, from time to time, to inconvenience the landlord by dying there, passing so imperceptibly that it sometimes went unnoticed for an hour or two, from a state which had not really been living at all.

For it was in St. Jude's Passage that such corpses as were picked up in Frizingley—whether they had been reported missing or not—were usually found. Children, quite often, who were classed brutally but realistically as orphans and rarely identified. New-born infants, of course, more than somewhat. And, every now and again, their young mothers, since at least three old ladies in the neighborhood of the Passage were well-known for their services to girls in trouble. An occasional man or woman who had been stabbed or beaten or strangled but who, far more often than not, had simply gone without food for a week or two, and given up.

Irish men—and women—not a few of them, but Cara had been long enough in Frizingley to know that the Irish had no monopoly on starvation, that good, solid Englishmen, handloom weavers, for instance, on the tramp for work and farm laborers from the south who had lost their farms due to land enclosures, could do it just as easily. For although there *was* work here, there had never been enough to supply the desperate horde which had applied for it, choking this ancient heart of the town to death with its demands for air and space and water, overwhelming its sanitary resources, clogging its sewage channels, fouling its canal, draining its reservoirs. A fragile, breakable, disposable population, with no more than a toe-hold on life when trade was good and employment more plentiful; flicked off life's surface, almost without being noticed, when it was not.

And with so many work-hungry applicants to choose from, the millmasters had never felt obliged to pay very much.

A dreadful place, this Passage. The stuff of which Cara's worst nightmares were woven, night-images of herself crushed beneath twenty alien, naked bodies on one of these lodging house mattresses, struggling to get up because she had to find Liam and Odette, who would surely suffocate beneath all this bare, sweating flesh, without her. Dreams which turned her cold even now, when she was wide awake and full of her day-time urgencies, hurrying to make herself pleasant and useful and *necessary*, if she could, to Miss Gemma Dallam, who knew nothing, as yet, of nakedness. One could be quite sure of *that*.

Hurry then, and leave this damnable place behind. Not that she was afraid of it. Disgusted, and contemptuous of it, certainly. Because *she* had never sunk so low, and never would. Cautious of it, of course, as one had to be in any den of thieves where pickpockets and cut-purses abounded. Good. St. Jude's Square lay before her, level and familiar, flanked by its old taverns and the graceful iron railings of St.

Jude's churchyard where Luke still often waited for her; the square crowded and ebullient today with the stalls for the Friday market, with traders and dealers and peddlers of fancy braids and buttons, fans, feathers, bright little birds in cages, beads, sequins, secondhand dresses that could be unpicked and made over, secondhand bonnets that could be remodeled, old belts that sometimes had decent buckles, sugar sticks the color of rubies and emeralds that would be a treat for Liam.

And it was as she hesitated, thinking of Liam, touched as so often, and usually at the wrong moment, by the silence and sadness of him which so troubled her, wondering if a sugar stick would lighten it, that she felt herself suddenly surrounded not by the usual ebb and flow of the market day crowd but by something much more purposeful. Something which she, brought up in a crowded street, could not fail to recognize.

Her pockets, as she well knew, had nothing in them but the stray penny she was thinking of spending on Liam. Her bag! Instantly her hands tightened their grip. Her resolution tightening to match, so that they would have to cut her wrists, she thought, to make her let go. And since they could hardly do that in so public a place, these ragged youths half her size who were pressing around her, she was not really afraid. She'd just box a few ears, knock a few heads together like she did with the Rattries, and chase them off. Little vermin. Little weasels.

That was still the thought in her mind as she struck the ground, not knowing how she came to be there, as one never knows, having suffered a blow aimed from behind which came at her like a thunderbolt, felled her in the presence of a hundred indifferent spectators and left her prostrate, struggling as in those terrible lodging-house dreams, to get up, to breathe, while the weasel-pack fell on top of her, shrieking with laughter. Just another rowdy street game, a half dozen ragamuffins playing rough-and-ready with a woman who was probably a drunken whore, on market day. Very likely. Who cared?

No one. A strength that was not of her body but rooted in absolute desperation got her to her feet, rising with the urchins still clinging to her and then shaking them off as the she-bears, once chained in this square for sport, had shaken off the baiting dogs. She knew her bag was gone. She had not seen the thief nor which direction he had taken. She saw only a half-dozen dirty, twelve-year-old faces grinning at her, a half-dozen skinny little bodies beginning to disperse, to lose themselves in the alleys where they would be indistinguishable from dozens more. She heard a madwoman howling—herself—but on market day, in St. Jude's, with the taverns serving gin and strong beer from five o'clock in the morning, who was likely to be disturbed by a little howling? And madwomen, women in despair, in panic, at the end of their tether, were a common enough sight any day of the week.

Her only slight hope was to catch one of them, any one, and when she had him . . . ? What? Time enough to think of that when it happened. Time now to run, to fix her eyes on that tow-headed lad with the green scarf around his stringy, chicken's neck and never lose sight of him, no matter who got in her way, to catch him and crucify him if necessary to find out where her bag had gone.

Little bastard. She was going to kill him and enjoy it. She could taste blood now on her lips where her own teeth had bitten them, could see blood flecking her vision, hear it pounding in her ears as she ran, propelled by the first hot rush of her panic so that when she collided with the rough corner of a market stall she did not feel it; when she stumbled again and scrambled to her feet she was unaware of her grazed hands and knees; heedless of brewers' drays, the hooves of heavy horses; the outrage of the passers-by she pushed aside; the woman with the heavy market basket she knocked over.

She did not even realize her hair had come down and that she had lost her hat until she found herself leaning against a wall somewhere on the other side of St. Jude's Passage, her lungs bursting, her temples and her pulses hammering out their distress, her whole appearance wild and disheveled and attracting not the least attention in that place which—no matter what might have befallen her—had seen it all before.

She knew, although she did not know for quite how long, she had been running aimlessly. The boy was gone. She had refused to believe it at first, her mind so full of him that her eyes kept on seeing him, playing tricks on her, raising false and cruel hopes. But her eyes were empty now. He had gone. And with him had gone Miss Gemma Dallam's brown Chinese satin and every shred of hope Cara had cherished for the future.

Everything.

And so perhaps the time had come just to sit down somewhere on the ground and wait. Just that. Hands folded, head bent, to make it easier for the axe, when it fell.

"All right, are you, love?"

A man, smelling strongly of spirits put a hand on the wall behind her head and leaned over her. No. She would never be all right again. But, pushing him aside, she gathered her cloak around her, made so bravely from those two old plush tablecloths, and began to walk downhill—the direction she happened to be facing—until she came to St. Jude's churchyard where she sat on a gravestone, her head in her hands, and shivered.

No one came near her. She expected no one. For why should people involve themselves with a stranger when the one thing that everybody had in plenty was trouble? And what real help could anyone give her? With a calm she knew to be unnatural it struck her that her life was probably at an end. Yes. Very likely. And those six little gutter-weasels and their heftier accomplice who had pushed her over would never realize, when they sold Miss Gemma Dallam's valuable satin for a shilling or two, just what they had done to her.

"Would it not be wise," she heard Miss Linnet Gage's light voice saying, "to have the work done *here* . . . ?"

Miss Linnet Gage, who disliked Cara, had already hinted at her dishonesty. Was it prudent, she had really been suggesting, to put temptation in Cara's way? Miss Linnet Gage, therefore, would not believe and would not wish to believe Cara's story. And if *she* did not, then why should Amabel Dallam, who bent with every prevailing breeze? Or Gemma Dallam, who had her wedding day on her mind? Or John-William Dallam, who was known, in St. Jude's Street, as a hard master who believed in keeping his operatives strictly in what *he* considered to be their place. Properly subservient.

They would not hate her, if she tried to sob out what would sound to them like a typical housemaid's melodrama. They would simply raise disdainful eyebrows and say what else could one expect of the lower orders; the Irish? At the very best they would dismiss her, as Miss Ernestine Baker had done, with an icy reminder that she must never expect to work in Frizingley again. And since they certainly would not pay her for the work she had already done on the trousseau, where else could she go? But at worst, and far more likely, they would simply hand her over to a magistrate as a thief. A necessary precaution—she heard a voice she imagined to be John-William Dallam's *say* the words—to discourage others of her kind from following her criminal example.

Of course. For she had learned long ago of the mistrust and fear these upper-class households felt for "her kind" with whom they were surrounded. Maidservants who had access to storecupboards and the family silver. Cooks who were being constantly accused of purloining cream and chickens, butlers of watering the claret. Tradesmen who might overcharge or who might tamper with locks and window-catches to let burglars in. Dressmakers who might prefer to sell a valuable piece of material rather than settle for the modest profit of making it into a dress.

A short-sighted profit. But such things *did* happen. Feather-headed serving girls who could not possibly hope to go unsuspected *did* steal from their mistresses. Milliners' assistants *did* take feathers and fancy buttons from their workrooms and told amazing tales when they were apprehended wearing them in their Sunday hats. An Irish dressmaker from nowhere, called Cara Adeane, might well try to make off with Miss Dallam's satin. John-William Dallam would give her credit for no more sense than that. Particularly when it was discovered—as it would be—that she was the mother of a bastard child, the daughter of a man who had left Frizingley heavily in debt, and had already been dismissed by Miss Ernestine Baker for her loose behavior in a public street.

She could not defend herself against them. What magistrate would listen to her lame excuses, in any case, if John-William Dallam named her a thief, and Miss Ernestine Baker testified that she was a slattern?

They would take her to York castle, she supposed, and lock her up. For how long? She knew of a woman in Dublin who, for the theft of a few pounds, had gone to prison for five years. With hard labor. Or they might put her on a prison ship to Australia, as they'd done with two girls from St. Jude's a couple of months ago, because—on those farms where the transported convicts worked all chained together—there was a shortage of women.

And if either of these things happened to her, then Odette and Liam would be separated and taken away to the workhouse, Odette with her heart in pieces and her nerves in tatters, Liam retreating so far into that anxious silence of his that nothing would ever bring him out again.

A length of brown satin would have killed him. And Odette.

Leaning forward, still shivering, wanting to be sick yet unable to raise anything from her empty stomach but an acrid bile which made her retch again, she attempted to find a chink somewhere in the blank wall, growing granite upon unyielding granite, around her.

Finding none.

Her education had been sketchy, vague in the extreme, but she understood the law as she had always seen it in operation around her. John-William Dallam's law, according to which, had she committed an offense against "the person"—provided the person in question had been one of her own kind—then her sentence might well have been light; a leniency by no means extended to offenses against "property" which must be strenuously, mercilessly put down. So that a knife in Mr. Rattrie's feckless ribs would have cost her less in penal servitude, if she had not actually killed him, than Miss Gemma Dallam's satin. The Dallams and Braithwaites and Colcloughs and the rest feeling in no way threatened by skirmishes between one resident of St. Jude's and another, yet closing ranks in a punitive fury when it concerned no matter how small a portion of their worldly goods.

She continued to lean against the gravestone, sick and shaking, her teeth chattering, her stomach as knotted and tormented as it had been in childbirth. It did not occur to her to ask the police for assistance. There were two constables now in Frizingley, she'd heard, since Sir Robert Peel had created his "peelers" or his "bobbies" as everybody was calling them, just a few years ago. But nobody liked them. Nobody had wanted to be regularly policed as people were abroad, preferring to leave it to the magistrates to swear in special constables as they'd always done in times of civil disturbance, or use the troops. Cara had seen neither member of Frizingley's force herself; nor was she in the least surprised that two men armed only with truncheons should shirk from attempting to enforce their will upon St. Jude's. Exactly what duties they *did* perform she was uncertain but in matters of law and order it was Christie Goldsborough, and only Christie Goldsborough, who sat in judgment here.

There was no doubt at all about that.

And even then it took a few more strangled moments before she could force her numbed brain to function with anything more coherent than a scream of anguish. But something was becoming clear to her, *something* was emerging. And, clenching her teeth and her jaw, digging strong, pointed nails into the soft undersides of her arms, she slowly gathered herself, through pain and concentration, into some semblance of order. Stolen goods required a rapid disposal. To be taken, in fact, for the perusal of certain pawnbrokers in St. Jude's Street, or to the back door of either the Beehive or the Dog and Gun. And Christie Goldsborough, who owned those pawnshops and those taverns, could find out if he so wished just where her satin had gone.

He could recover it.

She jumped to her feet, her brain no longer numb and resigned to her destruction but awash, all over again, with hope and a new blaze of panic. She could be saved. Therefore she was no longer willing to be destroyed. She *would* not be destroyed. Christie Goldsborough could save her. She could think of no reason why he should take the trouble nor of anything he seemed to want from her with which to persuade him. Yet, if he would, he could. With his assistance she could return to that blessed, wondrous world of—when had it been?—an hour ago, before disaster had fallen upon her, when she had been blissfully on her way to pin Miss Dallam into the dress that would make both their reputations in Frizingley for elegance. That earthly paradise, only sixty minutes gone, when Liam had still had the chance of growing up to be a man, Odette of growing old. Before the prison doors had opened, or she had been stuffed into the hold of that ghastly convict ship, to spend her life scrubbing and cleaning and whoring for rough and dangerous men.

Captain Goldsborough—*please.*

Blindly she moved forward, panic crashing now through every barrier she had managed, through her twenty precarious years, to erect against it, flooding her whole mind, sweeping away her sense of reason and reality, so that she could already feel the coarse fustian of prison clothing and workhouse clothing against her body as she ran, could feel her skin crawl from every one of prison's basic indignities, her stomach heave with revulsion. And terror. No—she didn't want to be locked away to die, yet as she rushed across the square she escaped death by inches from a dog-cart without noticing it, the magnet that was Christie Goldsborough drawing her in a straight line, through brick walls if need be, to get at him.

And what to say to him when she did? She had not the faintest notion. Yet, when she found him, more or less alone in the bar parlor although she was aware of Ned O'Mara somewhere nearby, she couldn't stop talking, words rushing out of her, spilling one over the other, over and over: "Please, please, oh please, you can help me if you want to, I know you can, and I'll go mad you see if they take my little boy away, because he's not—not just as he should be— more delicate than he should be. He cries in his sleep—God dammit—for my mother and if they take her away too then he'll just turn his face to the wall and fade away. And if I'm on a prison ship at the other end of the world—because that's where they send women, isn't it? I mean young women, strong enough to breed like the cows every spring time and dig the fields in between—isn't that what they want in Australia, for all those men? And I can't—I can't—for a length of brown satin I didn't even steal. I can't. I won't. *Do* something..."

She knew she was hysterical yet could do nothing to calm herself, could hear her own voice rising higher and higher, going on and on, and could do nothing to make it stop. She knew that Christie Goldsborough was looking at her strangely and that other people, somewhere in the room—pushing into the doorway to see what was going on—were looking at her too. What of it? She had always lived in a crowd, other people's dramas and her own played out through a thin wall for the benefit of anyone who chose to listen. What could that matter now?

Her voice went on.

It seemed that he was about to slap her and she leaned forward to take it, accepting it as the thing one did for hysteria. That or a jug of cold water full in the face. Either. She didn't care. He took her by the shoulders and kissed her instead, a real kiss with his tongue and his teeth and a strong aftertaste of brandy.

That silenced her. Instantly.

"Oh Christ—" she said, limp suddenly, as if that one contact had drained her of her vital energy, preparing her, weakening her, for what was to come.

"Oh Christ..."

"You want Christ to help you now, do you?"

"No," she whispered. "You." And although other people were certainly present they seemed to have faded to some other level of reality, very far removed from herself and this bulky, swarthy man who was letting her know, without a word, not only that he *had* her, but that should he now refuse to open the trap and let her in she would plead with him to do so. On her knees, if he required it.

"You flatter me, Miss Adeane."

"You can get it back, can't you? The satin?"

"I do believe I might."

"Oh—please say you can."

"I have said so. Nothing goes on in St. Jude's that I don't know about—should I choose to inquire."

"And will you?"

"Will *you*, Miss Adeane?"

He kissed her again, several pairs of eyes watching differently as he received her submission. Ned O'Mara frozen behind the bar. The other two barmaids, all agog, who would talk about nothing else for the rest of the day.

"I didn't know you wanted me," she said with total sincerity. Perhaps she would have come sooner if she had. For, no matter how distasteful this was, one did not die of it.

He smiled, that flash of large, white teeth against his dark, slightly oily skin she had always disliked and which now, quite suddenly, turned her stomach queasy.

"Ah well, I won't pretend to be precisely on fire for you, my dear, like poor Ned over there and one or two others. But they can't have you, can they? Whereas I—for a length of brown satin—do believe I can. Tell me . . . ?"

Yes. For a length of brown satin, for her life, and Odette's, and Liam's, he could.

She bowed her head.

He nodded.

"Very well. Then go upstairs, while I set the necessary wheels in motion, and wait for me."

She went, moving like a sleepwalker past Ned O'Mara, who might even be in love with her, past the ginger-haired barmaid who would have been happy to settle for Ned and therefore hated her, past the mousy-haired barmaid who had a good man of her own and could therefore afford to pity her. She mounted the stairs, entered the captain's sitting-room with its Turkey carpets and leather chairs, sat down, hands folded, mind folded, heart scarcely beating, by the fire to wait for him. And when he came she went, in passive silence, to his bedroom, took off her clothes at his direction, lay down on his bed, her arms above her head, her body outstretched and unresisting, and closed her eyes.

It was of vital importance that she should not *think* of him. This was an ordeal which, like all others, would eventually end and although she had made up her mind to suffer it, nothing obliged her to accord it so much as one shred of thought; or memory. Whores did this, after all, a dozen times a day and would not recognize the man should they meet him in the street an hour later. For as long as this lasted she was a whore. But the shame was *his*, not hers. And nothing he did could force her to look at him. Even if he now commanded her, as he was undressing, to open her eyes she would not *see* his powerful, barrel-chested body as it came at her. Feel it, yes.

Endure it. But that was all. And when he had done with her, she could wipe him from her mind, obliterate him. In her own private fashion, destroy him.

"Miss Adeane," he murmured, somewhere above her, "if this pose of the sacrificial victim is intended to impress me, I ought to warn you that it does not."

He was laughing at her, of course, as he laughed at everybody. She had expected that. But what else? What more did he want from her? She put an arm across her eyes and opened them beneath it, seeing him in such a way that he could never be certain whether she had looked or not, naked and hairy and black as she might have imagined, thick-set and arrogant and very ready—that much at least was certain—to take her without any further preamble.

Let him take her then, and have done.

He took her, or began to, in the direct, unsentimental manner in which she had always understood men took their whores, hurting her slightly not from any particular roughness on his part but because her body had turned dry with protest, resisting him as her supple mind did not.

He grunted something she did not catch. Why should she even listen? She could not avoid his penetration. She had agreed to that and named her fee. But what more could he reasonably expect of her? Did a bitch do more than submit when she was mounted by a strange dog in the street, held down by his teeth in the loose flesh of her neck to keep her still and ensure his better satisfaction? What else was this? She closed her eyes again, wondering how long, and then opened them wide, staring in disbelief as he withdrew from her, his act far from complete, got up and with the purest gesture of impatience she had ever seen, threw an Oriental robe of some kind in garish, tribal colors, around his shoulders.

She sat up, puzzled. She had had only one lover so far, a very young man who had taught her little more than caution. And she was uncertain now whether she was getting off lightly, or had been rejected.

"Dear Miss Adeane," and once again she saw that unpleasant gleam of white teeth against his dark face. "*Most* kind of you. But I think I shall decline. Vices I have, but commerce with marble statues—or unfrocked nuns perhaps—is not among them."

She stared at him again, not moving, not really knowing what to do. He told her.

"Miss Adeane, you have my leave to go."

He had dismissed her, then. That much was clear. Very well. Very good, in fact. Wonderful. Unless . . . ?

"My satin?" she said.

And now she was staring to the full capacity of her vision and her mind, reading him, sensing him, willing him—for God's sake, for *God's* sake—not to make further sport of her now. Of her, perhaps, and Ned O'Mara both together. He had sent her, with Ned and the barmaids and Heaven knew how many others watching, to wait for him in his bed. So far as they were all concerned he had had his way with her. Indeed, so he had, for she had stripped meekly for his observation and had allowed him to do everything else he had wanted. And how were they to know that he had not wanted very much? Or was that to be his real pleasure? Did he mean to let Ned know that he had not found her up to scratch and then, after so much humiliation, deliver her over to the Dallams?

Something seemed to open or to expand in her brain, releasing a cold voice which she had never heard there before, telling her that if he cheated her she might just as well kill him. Why not? And then she could go off to Australia with a real crime on her conscience.

Not that it would trouble her overmuch with guilt.

"My satin?"

And she was already looking around the room for the gun or the knife that he would surely have about him somewhere.

"Satin?" he yawned, showing her those wolf's teeth again. "I think not. You haven't kept your part of the bargain, have you? Why should I?"

Whatever it was that had expanded in her head snapped now, very distinctly, convincing her that no gun would do. Not even the more intimate destruction of a knife. And so she threw herself at him, leaping for his throat, a tall, strong, totally desperate girl with nothing whatsoever to lose, who would have been hard for any man to handle, even a man as powerful and totally unchivalrous as Christie Goldsborough, had he not been ready for her. And had he not been perfectly willing, of course, to hit a woman every bit as hard as he would have struck a man.

And even then she managed to land one blow on the side of his head, to get her teeth, albeit briefly and not very deep, into his shoulder, to kick him a time or two although her bare feet fell short, each time, of a vital spot.

152

"That is rather better," he told her.

"I'll kill you!" she shrieked back at him.

"I doubt it."

She tried, not caring how much pain it cost her.

"I hate you!" She meant it, a fierce spike of hatred which seemed to impale her. She said it again, spitting a cat's venom, a snake's venom at him, menacing him with claws and teeth and a most glorious savagery, her eyes out of focus perhaps but glittering like jewels, her supple, slender, long-legged body having lost all consciousness of its nakedness, her firm, high, amber-skinned breasts rising in their fury; doubly enticing.

"Hate me," he invited, his eyes on those breasts. "You might even earn your satin with it. That's what a *clever* girl would do."

The surface of her mind rejected his meaning. At that level it was still murder she desired. But beneath it she understood, accepted, found it far easier to hate him, when he fought her back to the bed, than to ignore him; the bitings and scratchings of anger coming near enough to passion so that when he entered her again she found it possible, in her loathing, her detestation, her bitter resentment, to wrap her own strong, hard limbs about him in a grip designed to wound and crush him but which could also excite.

"Dear Miss Adeane—that is really much improved."

And when something odd began to happen in her own body, a sensation she wished to call ugly because she had never felt it before and did not wish to feel it now with him, she released her temper again, thrashing about quite wildly beneath him to hurt herself and make the treacherous feeling go away.

It went. Thank God, at least, for that. She would never have forgiven herself for feeling it, nor him for becoming aware of it. He might work off his lust on her body and she could despise him for that. But if any part of any one of these female organs hidden away inside her dared to enjoy it, then she would have to despise herself.

Fortunately it had not come to that. And now what she had to do was maintain her temper at white heat until he had pumped his pleasure into her so that she would not lose her nerve—and possibly her satin—by cringing away from him at that vital last moment—vital for him, fatal perhaps for her—and pleading with him not to make her pregnant.

Better not even to think of it. Just go on hating him, ill-wishing him until his body reached its natural conclusion. On a groan and a sigh as men are supposed to attain their pleasure and then—as she remembered from her one other experience—there came his reluctance to move away from her, her panic urgency to be free of him while there might still be a chance that no damage had been done. And the anger which had sustained her now evaporated, slipped out of her and away, leaving her defeated, used, worn out, unutterably forlorn. As ready to lie down and die as she had ever been.

So that was that. He had had what all men wanted, exactly as he had wanted it. And she would be pregnant now, of course, no doubt about it, which was better than being in a convict ship bound for Australia, where somebody would have made her pregnant in any case. Better than that. So she would tell herself when she was sick and retching and dizzy, in a week or two, as she'd been with Liam. Except that this man, unlike Liam's young father, could afford to give her the money for a clean abortion. Surely he'd be willing to do that much for her? And what choice would she have? What had choice to do with women, anyway? Men chose. Women simply did the best they could. Men took—whatever there was to be taken. *This* was what happened to women.

"The satin," she said.

He got up, flung the strange, savage robe around his shoulders again and went into the other room where she heard him shouting through the door, "Is that little matter sorted out yet, at the Dog and Gun?" She was aware of Ned O'Mara on the landing, mumbling a reply, probably hating them both, and then her carpetbag landing heavily, miraculously, on the bed beside her, thrown by an arm in a garish, foreign sleeve.

"Your property, madam. All present and correct, with not a stain on it anywhere. Although no doubt you'll want to check."

Indeed she did, for having sacrificed herself for this damnable dress material it was no more than common sense to make certain that no part of it had been damaged or soiled, that she could go to Miss Dallam presently, when she found the strength to get up out of this bed and tidy her hair and her cuts and bruises, as if absolutely nothing had occurred.

Yes. The satin was perfect, had not even been removed from its muslin wrappers. Perfect. She could go now about her business. The clock had been turned back. She could be as she had been before.

So she told herself. Although only a damned fool would believe it. And she had never been that.

Closing her bag with a defiant snap she lay down again, very suddenly, against the disordered pillows, a heavy odor of musk and cigar smoke in her nostrils, a great weight of weariness coming near to sweeping her away. Had she ever been so tired in her life before? She doubted it. Had she ever felt so brittle and so cold? Or so terrified of what she knew she could no longer hold back?

She had just given her body—so long and so carefully guarded—for a length of brown satin. Three days ago she had refused her final chance of giving it for love. And now, before she had to get up again, to go downstairs and face the mockery and malice which awaited her, before she had to compose herself and complete her walk up the hill to see bridal, virginal Miss Dallam, she closed her eyes and thought, with pure agony in her mind, and in her heart, and in her soul, of Daniel.

Gemma Dallam was married on a perfect December morning of silver frost and bright, crystal-clear sunshine. The bride herself remaining calm throughout, her mother, who had prayed so ardently for this day, finding herself utterly overcome by it; having slept not a wink, of course, the night before and melting into tears—of anxiety, of joy, of overwrought nerves—the moment she got out of bed; unable, no matter how hard she tried, to do her own soft, fair hair to her satisfaction and suffering a sudden and quite dreadful conviction that the powder-blue taffeta she had ordered from Miss Ernestine Baker was somehow not right.

"There *is* something the matter with it," she told her maid, her eyes swimming with tears again. Was the dress too plain? But when she quickly added a white lace fichu and a long, lacy shawn, the effect reminded her of nothing so much as the icing on her daughter's wedding cake.

Panic overcame her. What could she do? Her wardrobes of course, were bulging with dresses but, apart from the evening gowns she had had made especially for Christmas, they had all been worn at least once before. And how could she go to her only daughter's wedding in an outfit that *somebody* in that church would surely recognize?

All too clearly she could not.

"Please fetch Miss Gage," she whispered, her lower lip trembling. "Or Mrs. Drubb." But Linnet Gage, as chief bridesmaid, was already much occupied. Mrs. Drubb with a wedding-breakfast for a hundred guests to organize had more than enough to do. Even Amabel could not go so far as to trouble Gemma.

John-William?

He came, amiable, assured, and planted himself in her doorway to inquire what all the fuss was about.

"John-William, I look a frump."

"What—*you*, Amabel? Never. Put your bonnet on."

She did so. Very pretty. The same blue as her taffeta gown, the deep brim lined with tiny, ruched frills on the underside, a huge bow at the back with waist-length streamers stitched with tiny blue and white beads. And then there was the blue velvet pelisse to go over the dress, with its white fur lining and deep fur hem, and a glorious white fur muff on which that clever Miss Adeane had stitched, at the last moment and quite behind Miss Baker's back, a truly enormous blue velvet bow.

"Amabel, there'll be nobody in Frizingley to touch you," said John-William Dallam, sitting down rather heavily, since he had run upstairs a little too quickly at her call and did not want her to see how easily, these days, he could lose his breath.

But she was examining her own reflection far too anxiously to notice.

"Oh John-William dear, do you *really* think so?"

She brightened. Glowed. Even simpered, thought her exasperated maid. And indeed when she reached the parish church she received a moment of instant gratification at the sight of her dear friend Lizzie Braithwaite looking far from her best in a regal but positively strident magenta. But then, dear Lizzie, for all the money—and it was reputed to be in millions—that her late husband had left her, had never known how to dress; nor did any of the tribe of Braithwaites sitting around her, who had clearly chosen whatever had turned out to be the most expensive and put it on their large, angular bodies just anyhow. The Braithwaites were like that. Except for Ben, of course, the eldest son, who had acquired a little polish somewhere and was even quite stylish today, Amabel thought, in his brocade waistcoat with a rather splendid diamond pin in his cravat.

Which was more than she could say for Uriah Colclough, a spare, already balding man in his mid-thirties who, having been torn all his life between a religious vocation and a natural Colclough desire to make money, lived like an industrialist but dressed like a vicar.

Yet Amabel said a very pleasant good morning to his mother, her dear friend Maria, who had been most gratifyingly keen to marry this ecclesiastical son of hers to Gemma. And if Gemma had chosen, at the end of the day, to bestow her well-dowered hand upon a penniless stranger then Amabel had no apologies to make for it, since the Queen had done the very same; her German Albert, although a prince and full of education and charm, not having two farthings to call his own.

And the Dallams were not expecting the Nation to pay for Tristan.

The church was very full and although Amabel could not speak to everyone on her progress to the front pew, she paused before taking her seat and smiled sweetly, generally, at the congregation, hoping that no one would feel left out. Particularly those dear, good people at the back who, although asked to attend the service, could not be invited to the reception.

People she had known forever, many of them, and had not seen for ages. How very touching. Gemma's first nanny. Various music masters and dancing-teachers. Miss Ernestine Baker and Miss Cara Adeane, who had managed to sit well away from each other, she noticed. Senior clerks from the mill and their wives, looking very self-conscious. Had it been a mistake to include them? Anxiously she hoped not, although she had had one or two uneasy moments about certain other guests who were not simply here to witness the ceremony like the gentlemen from the mill and the dressmakers, but would have to be entertained to champagne and bride-cake and all the other delicacies Mrs. Drubb had prepared for them afterward, at Frizingley Hall.

Naturally one had wished to invite Mr. Adolphus Moon, who had just purchased a delightful house with extensive grounds near the village of Far Flatley, where Amabel herself would dearly love to build. Thereby making Mr. Moon her neighbor. A gentleman of wealth and distinction, most anxious to be agreeable, and forever entertaining large parties of distinguished friends from London. A highly desirable acquaintance, in fact. Yet how could one possibly become acquainted with his wife, Marie, a woman who had been on the stage and who, it was known, had lived with him in adultery *while waiting to be divorced!*

Horror upon horrors. Amabel had never exchanged a word with an actress in her life and had never even set eyes before on a divorced woman. And although the adultery had taken place abroad and several years ago, the Moons having hidden themselves away in Martinique—Amabel was not quite sure where that was—to give the scandal a chance to die down, what *was* one to do?

John-William had come across Mr. Moon several times in Leeds and Manchester, had found him to be a decent fellow, and received a strong impression that for the sake of his children—offspring of his first wife long deceased—he would be glad to get back into Society again.

One could not fail to understand that. One would even be delighted to give him a helping hand.

But Mrs. Moon, with those taints of actress, adulteress, divorcée branded so plainly upon her, could not be received by anyone. Nor could visits be paid to her. And should Mr. Moon ever be encountered by chance in his wife's company, then he could not be acknowledged either, other than by a glance of mild regret when no one was looking.

A procedure which anyone with any pretensions to correct behavior would perfectly understand.

Could Mr. Moon, then, be invited to the wedding without his wife, Amabel had wondered? Certainly. Linnet had been most positive about it. Such things were often done, as a woman of Mrs. Moon's experience would know very well, being altogether *au fait* with the social niceties. She would even be glad—thought Linnet—for her husband's sake and for his children, a woman's love containing, after all, so strong an element of self-sacrifice. Surely dear Aunt Amabel must agree with that?

Well, yes. She supposed she must. But would Mr. Moon consent to come alone? Would she—in Mrs. Moon's place—be just a little saddened if he did? Yet she was pleased, nevertheless, to see him sitting halfway down the church, resplendent in silver gray and the very fanciest of brocade waistcoats imaginable. And more pleased than ever when Captain Goldsborough, arriving rather late as somehow one had expected, went to sit beside him and keep him company. *So* kind.

There had been no hesitation of course with regard to the captain, who, despite *rumors* and only rumors about his taste for low company—which she supposed any military man might possess—was a Goldsborough of Frizingley with nothing really known against him but his preference for living in a tavern. That too, perhaps, a throwback from his regimental days. And when Amabel had discovered his close relationship to such ancient and noble families as the Larks of Moorby Hall and the Covington-Pyms, she had written out his invitation card at once.

The gentry were allowed to be a little eccentric. Everybody knew that. It was because they had been rich and important for so long, generation after generation, rather than just since the invention of the power loom and the spinning frame, like her John-William. And although some of them were a lot less well-off than they had been, they still seemed to get away with most things, feeling not the least need to prove themselves, she supposed, like herself and Lizzie Braithwaite, and Maria Colclough, and Ethel Lord.

Not that she was in quite so much awe of the Larks since Sir Felix had failed to marry Gemma. For—while Sir Felix had nothing much wrong with him except a wild look in his eye sometimes and a tendency to go off in fits of what Gemma had called "unstable" laughter—she had heard certain tales of moral laxity about his brothers and uncles and even one or two of his sisters, which had done nothing for her peace of mind. And she was bound to confess that the Larks had always made her nervous, that she had always dreaded her visits to their crumbling, chaotic, downright shabby ancestral home, with dogs leaping out at one from every chair and all those things they kept on shooting—pheasant, partridge, grouse, poor little scrawny things—hanging up to rot simply everywhere.

Quite ghastly.

No indeed, one never knew quite what to expect from the gentry. She had resigned herself to that. Yet they were here today in gratifying numbers, a double row of Larks looking very bronzed and weathered from striding over those ancestral acres, which men like her husband and Lizzie Braithwaite's husband could never possess; and their cousin, Colonel Covington-Pym, Master of Foxhounds, with his rather glorious, highly intimidating wife, a tall, red-haired woman who could be seen in Frizingley sometimes wearing a black riding-habit so tight that she must have been stitched into it—Linnet said— and mounted on a colossus of a horse very nearly the same color as her hair.

Amabel had spoken to Mrs. Covington-Pym only once and had been completely unable to follow the lady's conversation. But the Colonel and John-William were both Justices of the Peace, often serving on the same Bench together, and although she had so far shirked inviting them to dine—the prospect of being alone with the Colonel's lady frankly terrifying her—she was delighted to see them here today, feeling that their presence lent great distinction. And perhaps with Linnet at her side she might pluck up courage, one of these days, to pay them a call.

She smiled once again, and very warmly, at the back of Tristan's pale gold head and then at his truly Grecian profile as he turned to look up the aisle hoping—she supposed—to catch a glimpse of his bride. Was Gemma late? Amabel, who never knew even approximately what time it was, looked puzzled for a moment, waiting for someone to tell her. But John-William—who *always* knew to the very minute—was engaged in the happy task of bringing his daughter to church to be married. Linnet, who wore such a pretty little diamond watch pinned to her bosom, ought to be in the carriage ahead of them with such of the Dallam cousins and Amabel's sisters' children who had claimed the right to be bridesmaids.

Surely nothing had gone wrong? The morning was cold and very frosty. Had a horse slipped on those treacherous Frizingley cobbles— something she always dreaded—and broken a leg? Had a horse bolted? Something she dreaded even more. Oh dear. Oh—Good Heavens. One lived surrounded by dangers. She could feel them, quite acutely sometimes, pressing in on her, always from the outside. She could feel them now—dangers everywhere—gathering all around the churchyard wall, biding their time until a door should open, just a crack, and let them in. John-William. Would someone please send for him?

There was a flaring of organ music and he came, filling the aisle in his progress, a square, brown man with his square, brown daughter beside him, looking very small in her white satin covered by that additional weight of lace frills and bows and lover's-knots of satin ribbon. A beautiful dress. Was Gemma simply not tall enough for it? Was her waist just a shade too stiff for so massive a skirt? Biting her lip Amabel reproached herself thoroughly and sincerely for not having forced her to wear those whalebone stays all night when she had been growing up.

Yet the orange blossom sat prettily on Gemma's head, her hair looking soft and glossy against it. Her back was very straight, the line of her little nose and chin just glimpsed beneath her veil looking pensive and sweet, as a bride should. Not studious at all. *Not* plain.

Lovely. Gemma's mother gave a sigh of deep satisfaction and love.

And then, walking behind her at a rather greater distance than might have been thought usual, came Linnet Gage in a dress that fell from her tiny waist as gracefully and naturally as a waterfall, each diaphanous tulle frill overlapping the other with perfect simplicity, her face as delicate and beautiful as rare porcelain, her blue eyes clouded by a dream of remote but tantalizing sweetness, which also touched the corners of her lips, raising them very slightly in a smile of which every man present must have wished to know the secret. She wore her hair low on the nape of her neck, its weight giving fragility to the long, slender throat, the chignon itself gleaming like spun silver.

She looked exquisite, breakable, so desirable that not a few lustier members of the congregation, whose minds should have been on holier things, found themselves in a sudden, quite ferocious state somewhere between arousal and bewitchment, which could bring any man to his knees.

She looked almost angelic, untouchable. Yet with a frail woman's tenderness that could surely be touched by the man clever enough to find the way.

She moved slowly, so slowly indeed that for a moment she was alone in the center of the aisle, a swan gliding on still water—abandoned there, waiting to be rescued—creating such emotion in several manly breasts that not everyone noticed that the bride and groom had already reached the altar, waiting the approach of their chief bridesmaid before they could be joined together.

Gemma, in this her last moment of being Miss Dallam, did not notice the stir Linnet was creating and would not have minded if she had. She knew that the fussy, frilly bridal gown did not suit her but had accepted it, as she had accepted so much else in her life, for her mother's sake. In everything concerning the trappings of the ceremony this was Amabel's day, not hers, and she willingly made a gift of it to her mother in sincere, if perhaps slightly exasperated affection. Amabel, looking so delightful in her blue taffeta, who had made up her daughter's love-story as she went along, with not the faintest suspicion in her heart that Gemma was marrying for convenience. And were she now to inform her of it, Gemma knew that her mother, once the shock had abated and the smelling-bottle been put away, would only murmur "My darling, I know you will grow to love him."

Gemma did not think so. Smiling at her father, who probably did not think so either if he would permit himself to be honest about it, she placidly allowed him to give her hand to Tristan, who looked down at her very intently, his face noble and moved and marvelously beautiful in the jeweled light from the stained glass window. A perfect bridegroom. Was that even a tear in his eye? She believed so. And, oddly enough, there was a tightness in her own throat as they exchanged their promises of loving and cherishing and, in her case, of obedience.

She smiled at him and then, once again, at her father from whose authority these vows released her. "Dear father, thank you so much," her smile said—for he had loved and cherished her most tenderly, claiming her obedience as his right, his due. She had given it with affection, but would have been forced—by custom, by law, and by John-William's iron will—to give it anyway. Now, with her smile, she withdrew it. Now her duty was to her husband, who must guide her and guard her and speak out for her on all occasions. And she had no doubt that Tristan would listen when she explained to him what it was she wished him to say on her behalf, or in which direction she wished him to urge her to go. As her father would never do.

"I pronounce you man and wife." The organ flared again, the young husband bending to kiss his wife lightly on the corner of her mouth. She belonged to him. So said the Church. So said the State. But, to all practical intents and purposes, particularly in matters of finance, Tristan himself had merely joined the favored band who belonged to John-William Dallam. Or so John-William Dallam's lawyers had made clear to him when he had signed the marriage-contract a week ago, telling him what his allowance was to be, what it was meant to cover, by how much he could overdraw, to whom he would be answerable if his affairs fell into disarray, making it all sound more like an application for employment than a romance.

Not that he had minded in the least, for if he had a daughter as rich as Gemma and a fellow like Tristan Gage were to come along he'd take all the necessary steps himself to see that she could never be cheated. But there was no need to worry in his case. He wasn't greedy and there was more than enough for everyone to have his share. Enough to satisfy a dozen fellows like him. And Gemma was surely the most agreeable girl a man could wish for. A good sort and no mistake. Sometimes he could hardly believe his luck. And if she wasn't very pretty...! And she wasn't. Well—perhaps white was simply not her color. He had no intention of getting himself into a stew about that. A man couldn't have everything. One had to add a dash of realism and a great big dollop of gratitude to a situation like this. And anyway, he didn't suppose for a moment that there could be another girl in the world as lovely as Linnet.

As they all squeezed into the vestry he told her so. "What a witch you are, my darling." An opinion endorsed by not a few others who whispered among themselves—some of them when Amabel was not listening, others when she very obviously was—that Linnet Gage had stolen the show. Ben Braithwaite, lusty, thirty years old, his own master and master of a sizeable fortune since his father died two years ago, certainly thought so. Uriah Colclough, who had seen an angel just like her once when he had been fasting on some religious occasion, thought so too. And when the bridal party came out into the church porch and stood blinking and smiling in the winter daylight, Sir Felix Lark, his wild eyes excessively unstable, was instantly at Linnet's elbow, topping the suave invitations of Mr. Adolphus Moon to meet his artistic friends with offers to mount her for the Far Flatley hunt.

Even Captain Goldsborough, looking rather dangerous and disreputable the ladies were all saying—fascinating in fact—in a long, dark driving-cape with a black fur lining, had a word or two to whisper in Linnet's ear, although he did rather more whispering, Gemma noticed, to the Amazonian Mrs. Covington-Pym of whom her mother was so terribly afraid. What a strange man. What a strange wedding-gift he had given her too, when he came up to the manor the other afternoon, making her feel like a tenant in her own home; which, of course, had once been his.

Yes. A very odd present. A large sculpture, primitive in nature and in texture, African she thought, although she had not cared to ask him, fearing he might expand rather more than she had bargained for on the origins of what she suspected to be a goddess of fertility. And a most disturbing one at that; too disturbing by a long chalk to display on one's sideboard to embarrass one's guests.

A strange man indeed, disdaining now to join the wedding party escorting her and her bridegroom to their carriage but going off on his own down one of the narrow churchyard pathways, toward the dressmaker Miss Adeane.

What could he want with her? Now *that*, Gemma decided, was a foolish question. Miss Adeane was beautiful. And a girl who looked like that must be forever finding herself pursued by men. Men of the predatory kind, that is, like Captain Goldsborough. And Ben Braithwaite too she rather suspected. Not Tristan though, who might like to flirt a little and might not run too fast should he be himself pursued but who was certainly no beast of prey. And she had no doubt that Miss Adeane could take care of herself.

Smiling at her brand-new husband she slid her hand into his, taking him somewhat by surprise although he responded instantly and correctly by giving her short, brown fingers a squeeze and then, realizing he could do rather better, raising them to his lips. Thus presenting a most romantic picture as they were driven smartly away to their wedding-breakfast amid a flurry of good wishes and a merry ringing of bells.

Cara had attended the Dallam wedding mainly to annoy Miss Ernestine Baker and, having thoroughly annoyed her, had suddenly lost heart and walked off among the gravestones to contemplate what she was coming to recognize as the end of another rainbow. Another vision almost but never quite within her grasp. Another crock of gold that had turned out to be precious metal all right; but for somebody else. And winter coming on.

She had tried. Never harder. And when the satin had been recovered and she had found—after a painful, dry-mouthed fortnight of dosing herself with cheap gin and jumping down the cellar steps whenever Odette was not looking—that she was, miraculously, not pregnant, she had believed her luck to be on the turn.

But the Dallam trousseau had brought her no further orders but the brown satin dress which, since it had not been worn yet in Frizingley or anywhere else, had given no one the opportunity to inquire the name of its maker. And could she hold on until someone did? She was beginning to doubt it. She had the money Mrs. Dallam had paid her for the petticoats and chemises. Riches: until she had given Luke the money she owed him, paid a month's rent in advance, redeemed a few things from the pawnshop, bought extra coal for the cold weather, taken Liam to a doctor because something had to be done about his cough; looked down the bleak distance of the weeks ahead with no work promised. Nothing for certain but the dark weather and the bitter cold. January and February when even rich women like Mrs. Dallam and the new Mrs. Gage would not be thinking overmuch of new clothes. Nothing much to hope for, in fact, until Easter-bonnet time. And how could she last until then? Particularly now that Ned O'Mara had turned against her, watching her like a hawk so that her source of pies and tarts and bones for her dog had come to an end. Poor Ned, cruel with his jealousy, who had already made it clear to her that as soon as Captain Goldsborough went away again—as he surely would—to see to his interests in Antigua and Martinique, then she would have to give Ned exactly what he wanted. Or go. So she would go. And since Ned would also be empowered to put up her rent and see to it that she was refused employment at the Beehive or the Dog and Gun, just where she would go had become a constant, gnawing ache never leaving the back of her mind.

So much worse, so much more perilous, because of the winter.

She still had no doubt that she could succeed in Frizingley. That she could really become that elegant, well-nourished creature Miss Cara Adeane, Dressmaker and Milliner. The brave legend she had painted on her hatbox. But not through January and February. Not until Easter. Perhaps only barely by then, until she managed to get something behind her, the reserve, the "something put by for a rainy day" which neither she nor anyone else in her hand-to-mouth world could ever quite hold together.

And the trouble was that she was tired. Aching sometimes with weariness, bruised with it, yet unable to sleep. Spending far too many nights staring wide-eyed into the dark, growing hungry for rest, and irritable, so that this morning she had even spoken sharply to Odette.

Not that she was sorry, even now, for what she had said. She had meant every word of it. But she did regret making her mother cry. Would it not have been kinder had she pretended to be glad—since it was Christmas time, after all—when Odette had come rushing to show her that letter from her father? A few cheerful lines from a man who appeared to have nothing on his conscience, to a family he assumed to be still affectionately his. He was in good health. Cara had not been in the least surprised to hear it. He had taken over the management of his sister's bakery. That too came as no surprise. He sent his fondest love. Would she not send him hers, her mother wanted to know? No. She would not. He might go to hell and rot there for all she cared. Her mother had her full permission to tell him so, for reasons she had bitterly and eloquently specified. She had slammed the door as she set out for the Dallam wedding, leaving Odette in tears. And because Odette had been crying, Liam had been crying too.

And now, having walked all the way across Frizingley in her thin pale blue dress and her dark blue tablecloth cloak she would have to walk back again—and fast—before she froze to death where she stood. For if that sudden drift of snow in the air a few minutes ago had seemed romantic to the young bride—or the bride's mother—it had not in any way pleased Cara. Hot spiced wine and log fires for Mrs. Dallam and Mrs. Tristan Gage, perhaps. But for Cara and Liam and

Odette, it meant sleeping downstairs all together by the fire with the dog and even then not really keeping warm; chipping ice from the water barrels every morning with blistered fingers; doing something about the worn soles of her boots. Liam's cough.

Ah well. Roll on, Easter-bonnet time. And it was then that she saw Christie Goldsborough coming toward her along the path, his spectacular, fur-lined driving-cape swinging loose around his shoulders, *his* feet encased in the finest quality leather, his carriage—a shiny, high-perch sporting phaeton—waiting for him just there, in the road beyond the church wall, whenever he had a mind to take the reins in his gloved hands and go dashing off to drink champagne and eat bride-cake at Frizingley Hall.

And what would Gemma Dallam—Gemma Gage—think of that, she wondered, if she knew the price he had made another woman pay to recover her brown satin?

He had had little to say to her since then, having turned his attention to the red-headed horsewoman she had today identified, from the servants' gossip at the back of the church, as Mrs. Covington-Pym. She wondered what he could have to say to her now, not expecting it to be pleasant. Not much caring. Since what *had* been pleasant lately? What *had* turned out even halfway right?

"Miss Adeane, you are looking unwell."

Was she? She realized that she was feeling it too, frozen to the marrow in this bitter East wind which kept whipping her cloak off her shoulders as contemptuously as if it had been made of pocket-handkerchieves instead of tablecloths, her stomach hollow and aching, her head feeling light and aching a little too. But that was only because she had eaten nothing since last night and had been so furious this morning about her father's gall in writing that damnably cheerful letter. Nothing worse than that. Just lack of food and bad temper coming together, which never did her any good.

"I'm quite all right, thank you. Just cold."

"You are not expecting a child by any chance, are you?"

She opened her eyes wide and amazed, and then lowered them as she made a rapid calculation. Since he had troubled to inquire, then he might be willing to help. Should she tell him yes, he had made her pregnant, and see if he would give her a guinea or two to put it right? That way she could buy a little warmth and cheer for Christmas and how would he ever know that she had lied?

"No. I'm cold, that's all."

She felt him watching her and, ill at ease beneath his scrutiny, said quickly, "Everybody seems to be going off to the wedding-breakfast. Shouldn't you?"

He gave her the gleaming smile she detested.

"Are you dismissing me, Miss Adeane?"

"They won't be liking it if you're late."

She'd be there in good time herself, given half a chance, to eat their game pies and their plum cakes and drink their wine, to stand by their log fires to warm herself. Oh God—it was going to be a terrible winter. She could feel it coming. Ice and snow and killing damp, sore chests and feet and hands, the stand-pipe frozen over, coal and candles coming to an end, no water, no heat, no money, from now until March at the soonest.

And Liam's cough.

"I won't be late," he said and it took her a moment to remember that they were speaking of Miss Dallam's wedding-breakfast. "I drive rather faster than these upright commercial gentlemen. Because they tend to worry, you see, about spoiling their Sunday suits and their dignity. They can't risk a roll in the gutter, can they now, with all their factory-hands looking on? So they go sure and steady. I don't. And perhaps I know a short-cut or two to Frizingley Hall, which ought not to surprise you . . ."

"Oh?" She was barely listening to him. She was just cold. *Cold.* She just wanted to go home and had started to worry about the hour it would take her to get there, the sorry state of her boots, the snow coming on.

"I was born there, Miss Adeane. They are all very much aware of *that.*"

"Oh," she said again, not much caring. And then, remembering it would be unwise to cross him, added quickly, "I don't know where I was born."

She had never given much thought to it either. She very much doubted that when she got home, if she ever did, she would think it worth asking her mother.

"In your case," he said, setting a well-shod foot casually upon a gravestone, his warm and wonderful fur cloak eddying snugly around it, "it can hardly matter."

"No. I suppose not. Any old scrap-heap would do."

He laughed. "My dear young lady, why so bitter? Did the fairies take your cradle to the wrong address? Ought it to have been a palace?"

She shrugged. If palaces were well-heated, yes. *I'll make you a queen in England, Odette my love.* She heard her father's voice somewhere in her aching head speaking those words, making his wild promises. Breaking every one. Had he even married her mother, she wondered, other than by common law, by simply announcing their intention of being together? Like the Rattries, she supposed, who would never have had the money for a marriage license or to put in the vicar's collecting plate. Nor have seen the sense to it if they had.

Marriages then, like palaces and warm fires and good soles on one's shoes, were just refinements for the rich. Captain Goldsborough, wrapped in his thick, black fur, and with a little time to while away until the road should be clear of wedding-carriages, appeared to be telling her so.

"Marriage is only a device, after all," he said, "by which property can be inherited. A man only starts to worry about the virginity of his bride or the virtue of his wife when he wants to breed an heir. And if he has nothing to leave behind—no counting houses full of money like these pompous millmasters, or no land, no *name* like those of us who are rather less common—then why take the trouble?"

She didn't really know about that. But one thing had caught her attention.

"Common? Do you think the millmasters *common?*"

He looked very much amused. "I have met no species commoner. Nor so clumsy. The only thing that distinguishes the Dallams from the vulgar, upstart herd of Braithwaites and Colcloughs and the rest is that John-William Dallam had the imagination to buy the manor and leave it relatively unscathed. Although his wife's chintz chair-covers bring on a certain nausea whenever I am obliged to call."

"She hates it there." Cara realized she had enjoyed telling him that. "She wants to move to the country. To Far Flatley, wherever that is . . ."

He threw back his head and laughed, very heartily. The landlord of an unsavory city tavern. The owner of every thieves' kitchen in St. Jude's. Goldsborough of Frizingley Hall. Contemptuous, in all his guises, of the pretensions of these new-made millionaires.

"It is Lark country. Covington-Pym country. Your little Miss Dallam will never survive it. The exquisite Miss Linnet Gage may do better. Her father was a cousin of the Cheshire Bartram-Hyndes, she tells me."

"Do you know *her?*" Instinctively Cara bristled, knowing her enemies, ready to defend herself.

"Only slightly. The lady is looking for a husband and she has been about the world sufficiently to know that I am not one of those. And, in any case, the Bartram-Hynde side of her nature, which might have made her interesting, has been somewhat watered down, one finds, by her mother—a cotton-spinner's daughter with social ambitions, I believe, from some dreary middle-class suburb somewhere or other. Miss Gage wishes to be respectable."

"Is that wrong?"

"Dull. And timid. As all these posturing middle-class women are timid. So terrified of doing the wrong thing that they do nothing at all—except bleat like sheep about their petty rules and regulations and their morality. A sorry crew, Miss Adeane. Setting up their own gods in their own mealy-mouthed image. Thrift and Economy. How very thrilling. One wonders how many symphonies were ever composed or how many masterpieces created with that. And those castrated accents of theirs, making sure one knows exactly what everything has cost. Working five-year-old children to death in their mines and mills and breeding their own daughters to swoon at the sight of an injured sparrow. Believing, as fervently as they *say* they believe in their Almighty, that money can make up for anything, even bad taste and bad manners."

"It can." If she believed in anything at all then it was that.

"To you, perhaps, Cara."

"Then why do you attend their weddings?"

"For my amusement. To see the efforts they make to be ladies and gentlemen and the constant strain it puts them under. To see how far I can go with them, sometimes. To watch them pretending not to know all the things about me which I take not the least trouble to conceal. Things they won't admit so that they can keep on asking me to dinner—because my name is Goldsborough. And they would like to buy a name to go with the millions. Felix Lark has put his up for sale, after all. The first young lady ready to pay off the mortgages on his land can be Lady Lark tomorrow."

"You haven't got any land left, though—have you?" But her spite—for such it was—did not dismay him.

"Oh yes—my dear—I have. There are a great many acres in St. Jude's and thereabouts. Growing a very adequate crop, in their fashion, I do assure you."

"Rents, you mean? So you don't despise money, really—do you?"

And she had no way of knowing how hungrily her eyes had fastened upon his fur.

"By no means. When used with style and not exclusively to breed one fortune from another in a bank vault, as these people do. Money is for decorating life, Cara—one way or another. For acquiring pleasures. And powers. And not being ashamed of them. For opening doors and not giving a damn about what anybody else has to say to it. But these people use theirs to make strait-jackets to strangle each other. Marie Moon did well to stay away."

"Was she invited?"

"I am sure she was not. Could our good Christian Mrs. Dallam possibly expose her daughter, and her friends' daughters, to a woman like Marie, who has shown herself on a public stage for money, and lived with one man while married to another? One quite sees that she could not. Although Adolphus Moon, of course, is another matter. He is a drunkard and a profligate and has certain amorous peculiarities which even Marie—and sometimes the law—finds hard to tolerate. But all our tender young ladies can be exposed to him quite happily because he has never been *caught*. At least, not precisely in the act of anything Mrs. Dallam would not care to know about. Or anything he has not been able to hush up. So Adolphus Moon can be received. So can Audrey Covington-Pym, who is the most accomplished whore of my acquaintance. Because *she* has not been caught either, or not so blatantly that one has had to stop pretending to look the other way. And Audrey has never been on the stage, or left her husband, or made a false move in public in any direction."

"I am sure Mrs. Dallam doesn't know all that."

"I am sure *Mr.* Dallam does. And Miss Linnet Gage, who would marry Adolphus Moon herself, like a shot, if she got the chance. *And* put up with him, as well—like poor Marie."

"*Poor* Marie?"

"Money again, Miss Adeane? I don't doubt he pays her well. Which brings me to what I really have to say to you . . . You *are* cold, aren't you?"

She believed she was ready to expire with it. The churchyard had emptied, the wedding-carriages had rolled away, taking their fragile gaiety with them to another world, so far as Cara was concerned. Here, in *her* world, an icy wind was gathering force and malice, preparing to freeze the path beneath her feet, aim fierce arrows of hail and sleet at her cringing back, bury her—unless she could drag herself up St. Jude's Hill fast enough—in snow.

"Yes. I'm cold."

At that moment it was *all* she was. Cold, and terrified of growing colder, so that when he opened his arms and put them around her, his musk-scented cloak coming with them, ample enough to cover them both, all she felt was the salvation of his warmth, his hard, hot body supporting her as she shook and shivered against him, that blessed, beautiful fur enclosing her as in a nest, muffling her from the killing storm.

A nest, of course, that had a huge, probably wholly malevolent, black-browed spider at the center of it, King Spider himself warming her up for his dinner, she supposed. But the cold had numbed her senses and all her ingenuity and she could think of nothing at all to do about that.

If she was going to be devoured, well then . . . She was going to be devoured. She closed her eyes.

"So—Cara Adeane. Would you care to spend Christmas with me?"

What on earth was he saying? Why her? Surely he had women enough?

"Ah yes." And his breath too was warm against her cheek and down the back of her neck, making her spine tingle. "But my mistresses go home to their husbands for Christmas, and although I *could* stay at the Covington-Pyms and ride out with the hunt on Boxing Day morning, and call round at the Moons on my way back to cheer up poor Marie . . . I think not. Variety, you see . . . So—Miss Adeane? What do you say to Christmas underneath a warm fur blanket with as much to eat and drink and as many logs on the fire as you like? And anything else I decide to give you—or teach you. And there *are* things you really ought to learn, you know."

She didn't know. Or care. She felt his hands on her back and her waist and could not manage to care about that either. Last time it had been for a length of dress material. This time it would be to stop herself from freezing, or starving, to death.

Only one thing had to be settled.

"I have my little boy and my mother to think of."

"I know." She had expected he would. "I see no difficulty. Your mother looks after your son, doesn't she? Perhaps a little money would make *her* festive season easier to endure. A cellar full of coal. A roast goose. And—shall we say—anything else you can steal in ten minutes from my kitchen and carry home? You'll enjoy that."

It struck her—thinking of Marie Moon and Audrey Covington-Pym—that if she was going to sell herself, and it seemed she was, then it would be as well not to come too cheap.

"My little boy has nothing to wear for the cold weather."

"Of course."

"And it's a decent doctor he needs for his cough."

"You may instruct him to send his bill to me."

"All right."

She had agreed to it. She was a whore then? Sairellen Thackray had always said she had the makings of it, would come to it one day. So the day had come, and she was accepting it very calmly. Why not? She had seen it happen to others many a time. No one in St. Jude's could blame her. No one had ever stood on the edge of that abyss where she had been teetering for so long, that held hunger and cold, sickness that could not be treated for lack of a shilling, children one could afford neither to raise nor to bury, would have a harsh word to say. No one who had ever struggled in the mire as she had, could fail to understand.

It was not what she had wanted. He was not what she had wanted. But he would not keep her long. And in the meantime, since he had spoken of things she ought to learn, she would see if he could tell her just what it was that women like Marie Moon and Audrey Covington-Pym did to stop themselves from bearing child after child after child.

That would be worth knowing.

"Poor little Adeane," he said kissing her ear and her neck. "Women don't survive alone, I'm afraid. It entertained me watching you try. Shall I help you to try again?"

"How?" She was growing warmer now, and more alert.

"We might work out a formula—if the next few days go well, that is. If you continue to entertain me. What do you want out of life, Adeane?"

She sighed. How could *he* understand.

"Peace of mind."

"Oh *that*." She had known he would treat it with contempt. "You mean money in your bank, don't you. I can show you how to manage that. What else?"

She screwed up her eyes, feeling suddenly fierce.

"Not being at everybody's beck and call."

She felt his mouth smile against her forehead.

"Well, so long as you remain at mine, I think the rest could be managed. Nothing else? Nothing beyond coal and candles and cough medicine—in this your one and only lifetime?"

A fur cloak, she thought, like this one. Even a ride back to St. Jude's in his phaeton would be something to begin with. But she doubted he would offer either.

She was quite right.

"Very well then, Miss Adeane. I had better go now and pay my respects to the petty bourgeoisie. I shall see you tonight. In my seraglio. At eight o'clock, shall I? To make our arrangements?"

The wind, as he moved away from her, was like a knife.

"Yes," she said. "Unless I freeze solid on my way back."

He smiled, adjusting his cloak, drawing on his gloves.

"Yes, the wind does have a raw edge to it, I must admit. May I advise you to hurry home as fast as you can."

She walked with him to his carriage, the reckless high-perch phaeton she had seen often enough outside the Fleece, his horse held now by a wizened little urchin quite blue with cold, to whom he tossed a coin.

He mounted, settled his eddying fur comfortably around him, the reins loosely in his hands, the horse skittish—feeling the cold too perhaps—and ready to be off.

He looked down at her, smiling.

She looked up, clutching her inadequate plush tablecloths, the supple line of her body begging him for a ride.

"Until this evening then, Cara."

"Yes."

"Hurry home, now—we can't have you catching a chill."

"I won't do that."

"Of course not—if you walk briskly, as I told you."

He drew in his reins, raised his driving whip.

"You haven't thought of anything else you'd like me to give you— by any chance?"

"Yes." And she had gritted her teeth to stop them from chattering.

———

"Yes, I have." A ride to town? That, surely, was what he was expecting. Please Captain Goldsborough—I'm so small and poor and *cold*. And when she had said it—when she had put so pathetic a value on herself—he would still drive off and leave her standing there, with those steep, chilly miles to go. To the devil with that.

Many things were becoming clearer to her now.

"I'll have Miss Ernestine Baker's dress shop," she said.

Shortly before the second anniversary of her wedding Mrs. Tristan Gage suffered a miscarriage which kept her in bed for several cosseted days surrounded by every possible luxury and attention, including the embarrassed affection of her husband, who had rather more idea how mares and hound bitches might feel at such moments than women, and the deep concern of her mother, who throughout her own twenty-six years of marriage had herself miscarried eight times.

And Gemma had not the heart to tell either of them how much they wearied her.

"My dear, it is God's will," Amabel kept on saying because that was the thing her own mother and her dear old nanny—both gone now—had always said to her.

"You're looking simply splendid, Gemma. Isn't she looking splendid, Aunt Amabel?" Tristan kept on saying because that—surely—was what any woman must want to hear.

"Oh, a little pale perhaps," murmured Amabel, because paleness seemed essential to the occasion, although with dear nut-brown Gemma it was rather hard to tell. And she had looked so well since her marriage, so calm and composed and so . . . Well, not matronly, at any rate, as wicked Lizzie Braithwaite had suggested. *Noble* was the word which sprang to Amabel's mind. Regal, even. Although Queen Victoria, who had married just two years ago like Gemma, had produced the Princess Royal ten months after the wedding service, the Prince of Wales eleven months after that, and was thought on excellent authority, to be expecting again. And Victoria was even shorter in stature and a whole year younger than Gemma. Amabel, although hovering on the brink of tears, tried valiantly, in her own fashion, not to mind. Or not too much. For she had actually been engaged in the very pleasant task of deciding which room in her new house at Far Flatley might best be converted into a nursery when a messenger had come from Frizingley with the awful news.

And Amabel could not stop herself from thinking that this dreadful, dirty town must surely be to blame, that if Gemma had been less stubborn about remaining here, in this dark old manor, standing cheek-by-jowl with the brewery and the foundry and those hundreds and hundreds of unwashed, unlettered people who worked in them, then this tragedy would not have occurred.

Oh yes—*naturally*—a young wife needed a home of her own. A young couple in the first blissful days of their union needed to be alone together. Not that Gemma had actually said as much, although Amabel's tender heart had at once understood. But John-William had bought so much land at Far Flatley from Colonel Covington-Pym, a whole bank of his river and several fields beyond, that there would have been ample room to build Gemma and Tristan a dear little nest. Although Almsmead, the house they *had* built, was big enough, she felt quite certain, for half a dozen pairs of newly married turtle-doves to lose themselves in delicious privacy whenever they chose. *She* would have been the last person in the world to interfere with that.

And Almsmead was her own dream come true, a medieval castle in pale, newly-quarried stone on the outside, spacious and high-ceilinged and fitted with every modern gadgetry within. Bigger, wider, grander in all its dimensions than the houses the Colcloughs and the Lords had built, since John-William had cleverly engaged the same architect and told him to produce something similar but much more splendid. And the dear, good man had designed Almsmead, in the center of a green field; had surrounded it with a rose-garden; given her apple trees and a lily-pond; a trellised, covered walk down to the river with its clear, clean water in which she could see smooth pebbles and little silvery fishes instead of the slime and gas bubbles and dead cats one saw—if one had the stomach to look—in Frizingley's canal.

There were no rows upon rows of mean, *diseased* little cottages now to press upon her and worry her. As they *had* worried her. Enormously. No longer that terrible clattering of clogs in the street to wake her every morning and start her thinking about all those poor people and those ragged little children hurrying to the mill. Nor those dreadful factory hooters, Mr. Colclough's from the foundry, Mr. Lord's answering it, her husband's from the top of the hill, Ben

Braithwaite's intruding as stridently as his mother's purple taffeta dresses from the other side of town, each one of them blasting out its five minute warning as to the pains and penalties of being late.

She could sleep now in peace and with her windows open to sweet air and silence, nothing to disturb her in the mornings but birdsong and the lowing of Colonel Covington-Pym's cattle, the barking of a dog that would most certainly be a pedigreed animal bred for the retrieving of partridge and pheasant, as far removed from the yapping mongrel-packs of Frizingley as could be. And when her maids had got her dressed and done her hair and she had breakfasted by her tall windows overlooking her manicured rose-garden and a green, daisy-starred meadow, she had nothing to alarm her throughout the day but the possibility of a visit from the formidable Mrs. Covington-Pym or the awkwardness, as she took her carriage-exercise, of encountering the wife of her dear friend Mr. Adolphus Moon who had made himself so very agreeable. Particularly to Linnet.

The house, of course, had been long in the building. John-William insisting on having everything just so, Amabel herself taking time and immense delight in her choice of furnishings, living a dozen delightful dramas every day over Aubusson rugs and inlaid cabinets, the recklessness of silk damask on newly plastered walls, the sheer extravagances of crystal and china which Linnet—the dear child—had encouraged her to commit.

For years she had cherished Almsmead in her imagination. For ten months she had watched it grow, had chosen the textures and colors of her own personality in which to clothe it. For almost six months now she had known the joy of waking every morning in a brand-new feather bed like a fluted, pale pink shell in which no other woman had ever slumbered.

It was the most exciting time of her life. The happiest. Or would have been had Gemma not insisted on remaining in the very center of so much decay and corruption and "horridness," in Frizingley.

She had spoken to her about it, not sharply, of course—she could never do that—but with disappointment to which Gemma had calmly replied, "Mother, I told you all along that I didn't want to live in the country."

"Oh yes, dear." Amabel's chin had quivered. "But I just never believed you. How *could* I?"

How indeed, when Almsmead was so much better in every way than this creaking old hall and the Goldsboroughs' possibly valuable but, in her view, horribly antique furniture which had come with it, held together, she often thought, by little more than the beeswax with which it was polished. And these tiny, mullioned windows in their deep embrasures which let in the light so strangely, shadows like dark brown varnish suddenly filtered through by thin beams of light which might be any color from silver to amber. And the sickening clamor of street noises beyond the cloister wall, the sickening odor of those who made them. Amabel had worried that Tristan would not like it.

"Gemma dear, he has a right to be considered and I believe he is a fresh-air man—the Gages and the Bartram-Hyndes have all been brought up to that. And at Almsmead we have everything that a gentleman could possibly require, hunting and shooting and fishing and maypole dancing and cricket on the village green . . . ?"

"Yes, mamma. I am sure Tristan will enjoy all that."

"But darling—how can he? If you stay here?"

"Mother, he may come and go as he pleases. I do not keep him tied to my apron strings."

And Amabel, who never could feel quite safe unless John-William was somewhere in the house or, at most, at the mill where a note might easily reach him, had been scandalized.

"Gemma my love—oh dear—how can I say this without giving offense? It is just that gentlemen are . . . Well, it does not *do*, you see, to be too much apart."

And in Amabel's experience it had always been the wife who complained of it, Ethel Lord, for instance, fretting herself into a decline, or very nearly, when her husband had taken to spending so much time in Leeds; Maria Colclough turning to religion because her man emerged so rarely from his counting house; even strident Lizzie Braithwaite complaining that she had been neglected for the sake of the business.

Yet Gemma had shown nothing but good-humor when Tristan had subscribed to the Far Flatley hunt and stabled a tall bay mare and a chestnut gelding at Almsmead. She had even bought him a hunting dog as a present, a sleek, golden, sweet-tempered animal from which he at once became inseparable. And since the dog also resided at Almsmead—Frizingley very clearly being no place for one of his pedigree—so too, for most of the time, it seemed, did Tristan. While Gemma—still perfectly good-tempered—remained at the old manor, seeing no one of greater significance, so far as her mother could make out, than the spinster lady who ran the mill school, and the mill manager.

Excellent people, of course, particularly that good Mr. Ephraim Cook who was so clever about taking care of the business so that John-William could take his rest. But hardly fit company—an employee, after all, and his rather blunt, not very pretty wife—for Gemma.

Yet Gemma had shown no more than a polite interest in Almsmead while Linnet, who was very dear but not Gemma, after all, had positively thrown herself into all the excitements of housebuilding and furnishing, taking to Far Flatley as if she had been born there. Particularly after her unfortunate experience with Ben Braithwaite.

Dear Linnet. Amabel smiled at her now as she sat by Gemma's bedside tranquilly embroidering a cambric handkerchief, patient and beautiful as an angel and so terribly wronged.

That Ben Braithwaite had most ardently desired her was beyond question. All Frizingley knew it, even his mother who had grown so incensed about Linnet's poverty that she would have poisoned her if she could. Harsh words had been exchanged, in strident Braithwaite voices, between Lizzie and her eldest son. Amabel, for the first time in her life, had felt in less than perfect harmony with her John-William when he had declared that Linnet, on the small dowry he was prepared to give her, was aiming too high. Would he give more? "No," he'd said flatly in a manner which meant he would not change his mind. "If the lad takes her then he must take her for passion and hope it stays hot."

It had burned a whole year long, and the half of another, the image of Linnet gliding down the aisle behind Gemma like a lovely, abandoned swan so engraved on Ben Braithwaite's memory that he would have no peace, no rest—he'd vowed—until he had possessed her. He was his own master. He could afford her, God dammit. He'd *have* her then. He told her so. And grew frenzied enough, more than once, to attempt to take her, a half-rape, half-seduction, to which she appeared to submit and then, at the last moment, eluded him; leaving him more famished and furious and consumed by passion than ever.

A whole year long of hungering and thirsting, and the half of another. Yet last week he had married Magda Tannenbaum, daughter of Sigmund Tannenbaum of Bradford and Hamburg, a wool merchant of legendary wealth, enormous possessions, and no son to inherit the lion's share of them.

Linnet had attended the wedding, of course, looking exquisite in dove-gray velvet with a swansdown hat and muff, her face calm and remote, betraying not the least flicker of anything which anyone could call unbecoming, even when she saw the bride, thin as a stick and hideously sallow, led to the altar dripping pearls and diamonds and a London-made gown with a train half a cathedral-aisle long.

Amabel, torn between sympathy for Linnet who had loved and lost and this poor little jeweled bride who was unlikely to be loved at all, had suffered a severe headache that day. Linnet—who could doubt it?—had endured untold agonies beneath her cool, just a shade too persistent smile, finding a little consolation, perhaps, but hardly so much as she had pretended, in the renewed attentions of Uriah Colclough.

Gemma had winced slightly—Amabel could never forget it—as they left the church and, later that day, had started to lose her baby. A day of celebration and a day of tragedy, one superimposed upon the other, so that Amabel, who did not even wish to be rational, found it easy to believe that Ben Braithwaite had broken not only Linnet's heart, but Gemma's.

"Never mind, my darlings," she said now, bathing them both in her overflowing affections, Gemma propped up on her pillows looking polite and pleasant—surely that could not be right?—Linnet still remote and very tranquil. "Never mind."

"About what, mother?"

And since she could not say, "About horrid Ben Braithwaite for wasting two years of Linnet's youth and having his dreary wedding on a day when Gemma would have been better off staying in bed," she chirruped brightly, "Everything, darlings—because this is what I want us to be. Just as soon as you are better"—and she meant both of them—"we'll get out the carriage and go down to that sweet little shop of Miss Adeane's to buy bonnets and shawls and order new dresses. And then we'll just run across the street to Miss Baker's and order some more, so that the dear old thing will not feel left out. Shall we do that?"

She meant well. Very well indeed.

"Yes, mamma" said Gemma.

"Oh yes, Aunt Amabel—do let's," said Linnet.

"Can I come too?" asked Tristan, playing his part.

"To make eyes at Miss Adeane?" inquired Gemma, playing hers.

"Oh, absolutely not, my darling. Since it is Miss Ernestine Baker who has my heart."

"Incorrigible flirt," teased his sister.

"Heartbreaker," teased his wife.

"Really, girls—how can you?" protested Amabel, dimpling with smiles.

So that when John-William Dallam came into the room it was to find his womenfolk as he most liked to see them, cheerful, comfortable, and under his roof safely and securely together.

He knew his arrival would disperse the party, being well aware that his presence made both his son-in-law and pretty Miss Linnet frankly nervous.

"I think I'd best step outside a moment and see to the dogs," said Tristan. "I left them in the stable."

"Dogs? What's this?" said Linnet. "Have you found a friend for Goldie?"

"I have. That pure white bitch Adolphus Moon could never handle."

"But, darling—what fun. How wonderful."

"Why not go and see?" murmured Gemma.

They went, wreathed in love and kisses for their dear Gemma yet tiptoeing slightly as people do when making an escape.

Mrs. Drubb came in with offers of tea.

"Why not take it downstairs, mamma?" whispered Gemma. "I believe Mrs. Drubb has things to say to you."

She went, leaving John-William Dallam alone, as he wished to be, with his daughter. Had Gemma sent them all away, then? He believed she had. Clever girl, his Gemma. What a clever man she would have made. What a useful, reliable, clear-headed *son*. And what a trick Fate had played on him by putting the very qualities he had wanted to see in that son in a daughter. There'd have been no need for Ephraim Cook then to manage the business when he was gone; an upright, Nonconformist—Mr. Cook—the kind who never allowed a drop of alcohol, or a smile, to pass his lips and whose well-trained conscience would never allow him to cheat Gemma nor to waste a penny of her money, no matter how hard Tristan tried.

A good man, Ephraim Cook, with a good, strait-laced, sensible wife, a man who'd keep the looms turning and the profits coming in long after John-William himself was in his grave. No imagination though. None of that extra quality, whatever it was, which had got the business going in the first place, which had ensured John-William success in those early rough-and-ready days of colossal risks and colossal returns, when so many had failed. The drive—perhaps that was what he ought to call it?—which Gemma may well have inherited in abundance. If she'd been a man.

"Are you happy, lass?" he wanted to say to her. But one could never speak so directly to a woman. At least he couldn't. And so he muttered, "Are they treating you all right?"

"Of course, father."

"Aye—but if there's anything you want that *they* can't get you . . . ?"

He would see to it at once. She knew that. Yet it gave him pleasure to tell her so.

"You're not feeling so poorly then—as you were?"

"Oh no. I feel quite well. I'd like to get up. I'm sure I could. But they won't have it."

Her father looked shocked.

"I should think not, my lass. You just stay where you are." *His* wife, who had miscarried he was no longer sure how many times, had stayed in bed two or three weeks without setting her foot to the floor on every occasion, and had then spent a week or so more, he remembered, on a sofa in the drawing-room looking not merely untouchable but as if even a heavy footstep across the hall might shatter her into pieces like spun glass.

He felt a twinge of unease even now at the memory. Poor Amabel. He had wanted a son and had made her suffer for it. Not that she had even thought of complaining. Yet the sight of his daughter going the same way seriously displeased him. He had no intention—absolutely none—of letting any man make *her* suffer. And what need had Tristan Gage for a son and heir in any case when he had nothing to leave him? What need had he, John-William Dallam, for a grandson, he thought grimly, when he would be dead and gone, by the look of things, long before he could teach the little chap how to run the mill?

No. Let Ephraim Cook keep the business in order for Amabel and Gemma, and whoever came after them must take care of themselves. As he'd had to do. For he was no landed gentleman like the Larks and the Covington-Pyms who'd go to any lengths to pass on their noble names. Names, indeed. Dallams were ten a penny in the backstreets of Frizingley. Always had been. It made no difference to him. And if young master Tristan, with his fancy education and his airs and graces had any such notions about founding a dynasty then *he*— common or garden John-William Dallam—would soon put a stop to it.

———

"It's not the whole world, you know, Gemma," he said gruffly, ". . . having a family, I mean. Some do. Some don't. Some *can't*. And that's that."

It was the most intimate thing he had ever said to her. An acknowledgment of her womanhood coupled with his offer, at all times, to protect it. "If that fancy lad doesn't suit you," he was really telling her, "then we'll get rid of him. Church wedding, marriage settlement, your mother's godson or not, he can have his marching orders whenever you say the word."

She held out her hand to him and smiled.

"I'm absolutely all right father—really."

He hoped so. He was even ready to believe her. Although he couldn't understand it. And if he'd come across any other married woman who kept on buying her husband horses and dogs and fishing tackle and pointing him toward the open countryside while she stayed in town, then he'd have known exactly what to think. But not Gemma. His daughter had no taste for flirtation and social high-jinks like Miss Linnet Gage, he was sure of that. Although just what she *had* done with all her unencumbered time since he'd moved the rest of them to Almsmead, other than take an excessive interest in the mill-school he'd had to build to keep on the right side of that damned, interfering Factory Act, he was uncertain.

She'd moved the furniture around at the manor, he'd noticed, and got rid of Amabel's chintz chair covers by the look of it. Thus annoying Mrs. Drubb and convincing her that she would be better off at Almsmead looking after Amabel. Had Gemma got rid of Mrs. Drubb too? Well, in the old days, two years ago, when she'd been his Gemma, she'd have had no choice but to pack her trunks and live under the roof he provided, wherever he chose to provide it. No question then of her remaining here, as a single woman, alone. No question now, married or not, had it been apparent to those who might gossip about it, that she *was* alone. But with her husband constantly coming and going between this house and the other and looking so damned pleased with himself, pretending not to understand when John-William had tackled him about it looking odd, then what—without causing a mighty rumpus—could he do?

And John-William, still distressingly short of breath, still tired out far too easily by any undue exertion, was not in the mood for domestic strife.

It had been bad enough, this year that was just ending, without that. The worst year for strikes and lock-outs and bitterness between masters and men that he could remember since the power-looms had been brought in under armed guard twenty years ago and the Luddites had started swinging their hammers. But he'd been in his prime then, a match for any King Lud who'd taken it into his weak head to break into the Dallam weaving sheds, in the dead of night, and start smashing *his* machines to bits. As several had tried and been hanged for it. Hungry lads from the bottom of St. Jude's. One of them called Dallam. Yes. He'd been in his vigorous prime then, all right. As Ben Braithwaite was now. And that arrogant devil Christie Goldsborough who'd caused the trouble, so far as Frizingley was concerned at any rate, by egging Ben on to cut the wages at Braithwaite's mill.

Not that it was the first time they'd been cut. Not that John-William himself hadn't done his share of cutting and laying-off, as the state of trade required it. And nobody's order books had been full this summer.

And what did Goldsborough care about that? What did he care about getting rid of the Corn Laws either—which was what the whole argument had been about—since they'd been created in the first place for the benefit of his land-owning friends?

But he'd sat there listening, with that sneering smile of his, drinking Ben's claret as if he was doing the Braithwaites a great favor, while Ben, who'd had his share of claret too, lamented the fall of the Whig government, which might have done something for the manufacturing classes, and the election of the land-owning Tories, that bunch of country squires like the Larks, who would not. The Corn Laws had to go, Ben had been saying, hammering his mother's carved mahogany table. John-William had been saying the same thing himself when Ben Braithwaite had still been in his cradle. A squire's trick, the Corn Laws, banning the import of cheap foreign grain—which would have meant cheap bread in the cities—so that the squires, who grew the stuff on those ancestral lands of theirs could charge as much as they liked for it. And since an expensive loaf caused havoc in St. Jude's and trouble in everybody's weaving sheds, with demands for higher wages keeping profits down at a time when trade was far from good—when it would probably never rise again to the level of those early, heady days when the machines first came in—then Ben Braithwaite and his dinner guests had reason for their anxiety.

Except Christie Goldsborough, who'd sat watching them, as supercilious as if he found their accents comical or difficult to understand which, when one remembered what he must be accustomed to hearing in St. Jude's, he certainly did not. And then, leaning back in his chair, *lounging* as all the gentry seemed to do, as if they were permanently half asleep and just about to put their spurred and booted feet on the table, he'd said, "If the new government won't play your way then you'll have to stir it up a little, won't you?"

"How's that?" Ben Braithwaite, who could never stand being told what to do, particularly by the landlord of a common tavern, even if he did have a diamond on his swarthy hand and his name was Goldsborough, had spoken sharply.

"I'll tell you." And Goldsborough's voice had been like velvet. "Don't avoid trouble. Cause it. If your employees are hungry then make them hungrier. Don't worry about them coming out on strike. See to it that they do. After all, if your order books are as empty as you say they are, then how can you lose? So long as they're on strike you can keep their wages, can't you? And if they get very famished and very desperate and enough of their mates come out to join them, then how can Sir Robert Peel and his Tories fail to listen when you tell him it's all because of the Corn Laws? If the trouble spreads far enough and he thinks he can buy peace with a cheap loaf of bread, then I should think he will. Wouldn't you?"

It had sounded very plausible through the claret and the brandy and the smoke of Ben Braithwaite's excellent cigars. Less so the next morning when, his stomach seriously disordered and his head aching, John-William had started to wonder why a man like Goldsborough, who was "gentry" through and through despite his odd goings-on at the Fleece, should be making revolutionary suggestions as to how the "squires government" might be brought down.

Not that John-William was particularly opposed to revolution if he thought he had a chance of winning. He'd threatened to withdraw his money from the Bank of England in 1832 like all the other manufacturers of his acquaintance, and to withhold his taxes, in a bid to force the government's hand so that the new industrial cities could elect their own MPs. Giving the vote, in effect, not only to men like Goldsborough who had always had it as a birthright, but to men like himself and Ben Braithwaite's father who had come up the hard way. And remembering how furiously the Larks and the Covington-Pyms— and no doubt Goldsborough himself—had opposed the opening of parliament to the new and much despised middle-classes, he wondered afresh why the captain should now be murmuring against his own kin.

Or was he? Might he not be playing a far deeper game although not a new one, since it would not be the first time that the man who hatched the plot and encouraged others most ardently to join it, should be the very one to turn his fellow conspirators over to the magistrates? For money. Or for his own twisted amusement. Both, John-William had concluded, in the case of Goldsborough.

But, by that same morning, Ben Braithwaite had started to believe that he had thought of the cut in wages all by himself. Uriah Colclough, unable to see beyond his pious nose-end, had at once cut his to match. So too did many others, on both sides of the Pennines, not all of them obeying the mischievous hints of Captain Goldsborough, of course—since even he could not have been in so many places all at once—but intent on stirring up trouble nevertheless. A commodity never difficult to find, in John-William's experience, particularly now when the Chartist leaders, who had been locked up after the troubles of 1839, were all out of prison again; except for that Sheffield lad, of course, who'd died at twenty-seven, from the hard labor he'd been put to at Northallerton jail.

John-William, who knew that he would have been a Chartist himself had he remained a poor man, felt sorry about that death. But he was not a poor man and had been naturally and sensibly alarmed to hear of the 50,000 disgruntled people who had attended the "martyr's" funeral in Sheffield, which had given the Chartists something to build on. *Something*—he wasn't sure just what—which had caused the entire North to rise like yeast in sudden and furious ferment, the whole of industrial Lancashire and Yorkshire seething with militant men and women—*highly* militant, those women—on the march, carrying banners and loaves of bread on the end of sticks, singing hymns and psalms and chanting that it was no longer a matter of wages. Although most of them were being paid so little that employment had become a farce, an irrelevance. Nor even a matter of starvation. Although many of them had starved in the past and were therefore well equipped to recognize starvation now that they had met it again.

No. It had become less simple and at the same time less complicated than that. They were on strike for the Charter which, in its six points, would give them the power to redress their own wrongs. They were on strike for the right to vote, to elect men like themselves to positions of authority—as the gentry and the millmasters now did—who would make laws not only to suit the needs of squires and of the middle-classes—but of the common man.

They were on strike for the Charter and only for the Charter, a multitude of them, coming like the tributaries of a great river, from everywhere. Pouring across the Pennines from Lancashire to be joined by eager exalted crowds from Bradford, Halifax, Barnoldswick, Huddersfield, Frizingley, some of them carrying sticks and flails and homemade pikes, most of them empty-handed and full-hearted, singing their Chartist hymns of freedom and justice and brotherhood and stopping every mill they passed on their way by the simple process of removing the plug from the boiler, letting off the mill-dam, and drawing the workers into their ranks with the irresistible attraction of a ragged, hundred-handed Pied Piper.

In one day's march thirty-eight mills had had their plugs drawn in Dewsbury, the masters standing amazed in their empty sheds while the workers streamed out to join what to some had become a Crusade, to others a Pilgrimage; an opportunity for revenge; an exciting chance for a holiday. Every mill in Hebden Bridge had been shut down. Leeds and Cleckheaton had been cordoned off by troops to stop the crowds from getting in. Halifax and Frizingley had been invaded from all directions, the streets sprouting Chartist placards like weeds from every chink in the cobbles, demanding what John-William himself had once demanded. Democracy. Dignity. His right to govern himself by his own vote, which he had fought for and wrestled from the grip of the landed gentry himself only ten years ago.

Well, they hadn't got their Charter. Not this time at any rate. They'd got themselves arrested, in dozens, and sentenced to terms of hard labor and transportation to Australia, as always happened. But most of them had come back to work reasonably cap-in-hand, preferring to be half-starved on half-pay than to starve altogether on none. That always happened too. Although quite a few had subsequently been dismissed, both Braithwaite and Colclough having had their spies in the Chartist ranks, men who had sung those Chartist hymns about freedom and justice the loudest as they had been memorizing names and faces to sell afterward to Uriah and Ben. As Christie Goldsborough, the sardonic, black-skinned devil, had no doubt whispered Ben's name, and Uriah's, and John-William's own, into some haughty, landowning, Corn-Law-loving ear. Thus swelling the crowd of bitter, hungry men forever hanging around St. Jude's with time on their hands to plot their treasons. Thus adding to the number of women and children already in the workhouse, already overburdening the rates.

And the Corn Laws had not been repealed.

Would they ever be? Would it even matter, if this rabble of which he had himself once been a part managed to get their vote and fill the House of Commons with men who would pass Factory Acts galore, including that damnable Ten Hours' Bill of Richard Oastler's, so that no man would be able to control his own affairs? And small good it would do any of them. Because there had never been enough of anything to go around, and never would be. John-William had always known that. Dog ate dog. And man ate man. Not just in the alleys of St. Jude's, where John-William had taken good care never to be devoured himself, but everywhere. And when these poor fools won their vote what would it really mean to them but the right to choose their own oppressors?

John-William had not cut his wages this time, and no one had thanked him for it. They'd taken the plug out of his boiler just the same and let off his mill-dam without a thought for what it was going to cost him—and *them*, he'd see to that—in the long run. And now, to set the seal on this disastrous year, the member of parliament for Frizingley, old Charlie Bowen, who had been John-William's man and Ben Braithwaite's man and knew exactly what he had to do to earn the money they paid him, had fallen off his horse—the damned fool—and broken his neck. Which meant all the hullabaloo of a by-election, with a new man of their own to find, and the Larks and the Covington-Pyms trying to get their own man in. And a Chartist candidate too, he'd heard, if one could believe the insolence, bringing his Chartist banners and his hymns to Frizingley again; with not a hope of winning, of course, since the men who would like to elect him had no votes to do it with. But—since those men were numbered in thousands—with every opportunity in the world for rekindling those ugly sparks of revolution.

Thank God he had taken Amabel safely away to Almsmead.

Leaning back in his chair John-William was unaware of the sleep which abruptly overcame him, an old man's sleep from which he would wake presently with a start and in great confusion. But Gemma saw it and smiling at him, her affection undiminished, closed her own eyes gratefully. Not to sleep but simply to think, freely and unobserved, without the burden of her mother's solicitude, the obligation not only to look cheerful but to go on repeating how well she felt so that Amabel—always unnerved by silence—should not weary her further by growing alarmed.

She was, of course, quite well in the sense of feeling no actual grief or pain. She was, in fact, *all right*: not unhappy, not dissatisfied, not anything in any way so definite as that. She was very much as she had expected to be, having found in her marriage nothing to surprise her nor to cause her the least distress. Tristan had been—well, *Tristan*. Amiable, agreeable, never making a fuss, trained as carefully—by Linnet, she supposed—in the arts of correct behavior as he himself had trained his dogs. A charming if somewhat absent-minded companion. Undemanding as a lover, she was beginning to realize, but so beautiful, of course, that few women could have objected to his touch.

She did not object to it. She had not known what to expect from this side of marriage, since there was no literature available to her on the subject and her mother had told her nothing. Nor would it have been possible to ask, nor even to rely on any information which might have been forthcoming, since Amabel, who always retired to bed for the duration of her own "monthly curse" had said nothing more to the point than, "Darling, I must beg of you never to speak of this to anyone," when Gemma at the age of fourteen had first seen evidence of hers. While Mrs. Drubb, with no more explanation than that she was a woman now and had better keep well away from men, had then scolded her for upsetting her mother.

She had taken to her marriage-bed, therefore, a certain natural innocence and all the ignorance considered essential to her station, of which Tristan had relieved her as gently and pleasantly as he had been able, his passion lacking the intensity which might, on those honeymoon nights, have alarmed her; being, instead, a light-hearted master, full of the nonchalant reflections of the man himself. A gentleman, in fact, of sporting rather than truly amorous inclinations who would never dream of forcing his attentions on anyone but was always absolutely delighted to oblige.

"Gemma, you must be the most agreeable girl in the world—a rattling good sort." Those were the words he spoke to her as she lay in his arms in the vulnerable moments following his pleasure when only a lout—in his opinion—would turn away from a woman without a word and go to sleep. In her opinion too, although she had no idea how other men behaved, nor any way of measuring the depth of Tristan's desire for her; whether it came easily and naturally to him, as any stallion would mount any mare, or whether it required a degree of effort he chose to conceal.

Certainly there had been times when he had started to caress her and then, with a certain boyish sweetness, had turned lovemaking into conversation, letting the moment pass. But more often than not, whenever they were under the same roof together, he shared her bed and, now that her initial awkwardness had abated—for she had never seen a naked human being of either sex before and had always been discouraged from looking too closely at herself—he made love to her with a straightforward vigor she found attractive.

Perhaps he did not touch her very deeply but he did not shock her either, her body moving easily, without apprehension, beneath his; her mind remaining open to the possibility of sensation, observing his pleasure with affection—glad that he should have it—yet wondering more and more frequently if a similar capacity for such joyful sensuality lay concealed somewhere within herself.

Other women, who now spoke to her freely as a married woman among married women, certainly thought not.

"You will find 'all that' very wearisome, my dear," Amabel had murmured, blushing like a girl, on her return from the honeymoon. "But *do* bear it patiently. It is so important to the gentlemen. And when you have a dear little baby to show for it then I expect you will think it worthwhile."

And she knew now that the worst accusation to be leveled against such women as Marie Moon was that they found "all that" much more than simply worthwhile.

They enjoyed it. The wantons. Like men.

Her own mother contemplated such depravity with sorrow, convinced that it could do the poor creatures no good. Her mother's friends Lizzie Braithwaite and Maria Colclough and Ethel Lord were incensed by it, having used the act of sex all their wedded lives as something to bargain with, employing their very contempt for it as a punishment regularly meted out to husbands who lusted after the nasty performance far too much. And if one started to lust after it oneself, as much as the men—and let them see that one lusted—then what weapon had one left? So said Lizzie and Maria and Ethel, whose marriages had always been conducted along the lines of a pitched battle.

"*Do* bear it patiently," Amabel had continued to urge. "They do not mean any harm, you know. It comes quite naturally to *them*."

Gemma was beginning to believe, contrary to all her expectations and her mother's teaching, that it might also come naturally to her.

"What a rattling good sort you are, Gemma—absolutely first class." Yes, that was all very pleasant. Very much, in fact, according to plan and she had no wish to complain. He had done everything she had asked of him. He had taken to life at Almsmead with all the enthusiasms she had hoped for. He had joined her, with all the whimsical mischief of a schoolboy, in her small conspiracy against her father with regard to the manor. He had never questioned either her motives or her decisions, allowing her a most aristocratic freedom of movement far beyond anything her middle-class upbringing in general and her life with her father in particular had encouraged her to expect. And if the only deep emotion she had ever seen in him had been on the day of Ben Braithwaite's engagement to Magda Tannenbaum, then she felt no right and no reason to be astonished at that.

He had taken his sister to town that morning, to Miss Baker's and Miss Adeane's where all the gossip would be flowing free and strong, and bought her a new hat and gloves and a flask of the perfume Miss Adeane kept hidden discreetly away for customers who wished it to be believed that they smelled naturally of lavender or roses. Two exquisite thoroughbreds, she supposed they had looked, chatting to one another in their high-pitched, well-bred, "London" voices, filling each shop in turn with their faintly tittering laughter, making Frizingley aware—whatever it chose to whisper behind their backs—that the dynastic alliance of one "trading" and therefore "common" fortune with another could mean nothing at all to them.

And that night when Linnet, face to face with her own reflection in her solitary looking-glass and the stark realization of how much it *had* really meant to her, had been unable to sleep, Tristan had walked with her for hours in the manor garden, Gemma watching them from her bedroom window as they paced beneath the chestnut trees, engrossed, almost entwined, like turning to like, intent wholly and exclusively upon one another.

So had she once walked and talked herself in that same garden—or so it now seemed to her—with the young Irishman who had recovered the amethyst and diamond cat which she still wore, very often on her collar and which she had longed—very badly, she remembered—to give him as a keepsake. She had been unable to do so. Tristan's arrival had prevented her and she would never have found the right words to accompany the gift in any case. It would have appeared to be charity and she could not have borne that. Yet, whenever she pinned the brooch to her dress, she remembered him, pleasantly, wishing him well, not in the least distressed by the absolute conviction that he would never once think of her.

He had been going to France, she recalled. Or Italy. Anywhere in the wide world which happened to call his name. And she hoped he had answered freely, fortuitously, and had found his heart's desire at the end of the road.

Whatever it had been.

While as for herself, surely she already possessed as much as it would be sensible for her to desire? And she had always set great store by common sense.

She had the manor and with it a great many pleasures which were negative perhaps but no less welcome for that. No need to gossip every afternoon away at Amabel's tea-table with Amabel's friends. No need to accept every one of the invitations which kept on being delivered because of Amabel's fear of giving offense. No need to be constantly laying down her book in case Mrs. Braithwaite should catch her reading and name her "studious" again. No Mrs. Drubb, or not for much longer. No need to go to bed when Amabel went because she did not like to keep the servants sitting up and had had nightmares, ever since Gemma's birth, about accidents with bedtime candles. No need to explain one's reasons for suddenly looking out of the window. The sheer, exhilarating wickedness of going out, if she had a mind for it, in the rain. The socially useless companionship of Mrs. Ephraim Cook, the mill-manager's wife, a plain-faced, plain-spoken woman, who had aroused Gemma's interest in the mill-school and the somewhat ineffective spinster lady who ran it.

The school, of course, had existed for some years now, ever since the Factory Act, which her father could not mention without turning purple, had thought it advisable for factory children to be given some education, feeling that an hour or two a week per child, perhaps, or reading, writing and arithmetic, would not go amiss. Like the Braithwaites and the Colcloughs her father had not agreed with that. But being steeped, like them, in the philosophy that if one did a job at all one might as well do it splendidly—or at least a good deal better than the Braithwaites—he had built a very decent stone school with a walled yard and a tiny house attached for the use of the teacher, where anyone who paid him rent for his mill-cottages or any of his other employees who resided elsewhere might send their children—to suit the convenience of the teacher—free of charge. Not that many came in any sort of regular basis, much preferring the excitement of the streets to the acquisition of learning for which even the teacher herself, who had known far better days, considered they would have little use.

Mrs. Ephraim Cook did not agree with her, believing that every child should learn to read as firmly as she believed they should wash behind their ears every morning and not relieve themselves, like dogs, in the street. While Gemma, who had never thought very much about it, her own education having come to her just as easily and plentifully as soap and hot water and extremely private sanitary arrangements, had found it something to think about *now*, when any new thought would have been welcome. Something useful. Something which could interest her without being thought so eccentric or so socially damaging that it would upset her mother.

Something to do. Particularly now when there was, after all, to be no baby.

Better luck next time, everyone had said.

Yet it occurred to her now, as she lay quietly on her pillows, listening to the fire crackling in the winter chimney and her father peacefully snoring beside it, that such a time may never come. She had wanted her child. Badly, in fact. More, far more, than she had cared to show. Yet her body had rejected it so soon, with a firmness which had seemed quite final. Almost as if her body did not find it natural to bear a child.

"Nonsense," the doctor had muttered gruffly when she had attempted to explain her fears to him. "You ladies have strange notions at times like these. Well known for it. You'll be laughing, Mrs. Gage, at the very idea—this time next year, perhaps. Or the year after."

She had not believed him. She did not trust him either, considering him to be little more than a teller of comforting lies, her mother's doctor oozing reassurance from every pore. Yet she had smiled obediently, taken her tonic, eaten her nourishing broth, allowed him to earn his fee.

"Yes, doctor."

But her own body told her a different story which, lying here for the long days of rest which had been prescribed for her, she had heard clearly enough through the bird-twitter of Linnet and her mother, and Tristan's determined joviality.

Perhaps she would never have a child. Perhaps—in fact most certainly—it would be sensible to face the possibility. She faced it, therefore. Wept over it a little whenever her mother was safely out of the way. And then found her thoughts, which desperately needed a new direction, turning slowly toward the mill-school.

No child of her own. But there were other children. Ragged urchins, of course, sitting on those school benches on the occasions of her visits. Cleaned up for her inspection she supposed and even then many of them very far from tidy. But intelligence could not possibly be reserved for the washed and monied classes. Far from it, indeed, when one remembered Felix Lark, who would have been thought half-witted had he not been a baronet, or Amanda Braithwaite, who, no matter what her mother said, had never really learned to read.

Certainly in that plain, square classroom there would be bright, quick minds behind not a few of those dirty faces, and budding abilities, *potential,* which she—with so much leisure and ease and money— could surely discover? Some clever little girl full of hope and fun and joy of living as Cara Adeane, the Irish dressmaker, must once have been. And what would one have made of Miss Adeane, Gemma wondered, had her talents been properly nurtured from the start?

Any one of a dozen useful, exciting, challenging things. Just as there might well be a dozen little Cara Adeanes waiting up there.

Something to do. It was what she most urgently craved for.

"Father—?" His moment of waking was often the best one, sometimes the only one, in which to approach him with any certainty of success.

"What? . . . what is . . . ? I wasn't asleep . . . Just resting my eyes . . ."

She was content to let him believe it.

"Father, there is something I would like *so* much . . ." And she had spoken deliberately with the voice of Amabel.

Still half asleep he smiled indulgently, scenting a victory, since he had wanted to be generous all day and had been feeling mildly irritated with her for not giving him the opportunity. So now, after all, there *was* something she had set her heart on. He just hoped it would be difficult to come by and very expensive.

"I would like full responsibility for the running of the mill-school."

What had the girl got into her head now?

"Although I'm not sure you can do it, father . . ."

What was that? He could do as he liked with his own property, couldn't he? Who challenged him?

"Mrs. Ephraim Cook has taken it under her wing, father . . ."

The manager's wife? He'd make short work of *her*.

"And I would so enjoy turning it into the best school of its kind in Frizingley. In the West Riding even. Because if a job's worth doing, then it's worth doing well, father. Very well. That's what you've always told me, haven't you?"

"Aye, lass." And John-William closed his eyes again, squeezing them tight shut to force back the painful, incredible start of tears.

What a damn shame, he thought, what a tragedy that she was a woman instead of what she *ought* to have been. A useful, sensible, hard-headed man.

11

Daniel Carey returned to Frizingley as its Chartist Candidate entirely by chance, the gentleman who had originally been selected to fight the by-election having taken up a longish residence in jail on charges of plug-drawing and helping to demolish a workhouse near Rochdale.

A substitute had been required, therefore, in haste—and Daniel, who had never reached France or Italy after all but had spent the last two years at the London office of the Chartist *Northern Star*, had seemed as good a choice as any. Better than some, in fact, since he had once had West Riding connections and, as young political agitators went, possessed a relatively unblemished reputation, with not so much as a single term of imprisonment, as yet, to be used against him at the hustings.

A pleasant, very nearly a respectable, young man, it seemed, which was far more than could be said for the fellow they had put up for Bradford in 1841, an Irishman of the wilder variety who had served his apprenticeship to the political trade in such select establishments as Northallerton House of Correction and the castle jails of Lancaster and York.

Yet the disreputable William Martin had won an enormous following in "Worstedopolis," culminating in a mighty show of hands at the hustings which had left no one in any doubt that, had those hands possessed a vote apiece, he would have been elected overwhelmingly as a Bradford MP.

Could Daniel Carey do the same in Frizingley? Better even? Could he ruffle the smugness of manufacturing Whigs and land-owning Tories alike by reminding them of what hands such as these had done in France? Of the Liberty and Equality too long denied which had been so bloodily taken? Very likely he could. And so they had sent him North, not to win, of course, perhaps not even to poll a single vote, but to lay the Charter once again before the people, to let them know what *could* be done in a land where every man had his vote and the freedom to use it without intimidation, as he and he alone thought best.

To Daniel it was a battle worth fighting, an opportunity to be of service which he had long desired. And if he would have preferred it not to be Frizingley, to be, in fact, anywhere else but there, he managed to quell his initial misgivings by the grim reminder that he would be unlikely to know anyone in St. Jude's now. No one at all. Two years had passed. A long time by any standards. Longer than ever by his—and hers.

She would not be there.

And even if he did find her, what more had he to offer her than before? *What*, indeed, might he discover except ills that he still could not remedy, and wounds—both hers and his—that still could not be healed?

Better then—far better—not to look. Safer to close his eyes and his mind to her and give his entire concentration to the matter in hand; a resolution to which he firmly held, even when, after a tumultuous welcome at Brighouse—the nearest railway station to Frizingley—he was escorted, with an appropriate accompaniment of banners and Chartist hymns, to a lodging-house at the top of St. Jude's street where the landlady, Mrs. Sairellen Thackray, had offered to accommodate him free of charge.

He had expected to stay at the Dog and Gun, a tavern well known for its radical associations, where unstamped, illegal newspapers had always been laid out openly on the bar-counter for the perusal of anyone so inclined. But, when certain pressures had been brought to bear upon the landlord—Daniel had not been told why or from where—the redoubtable Mrs. Thackray had come forward at once to make her contribution to the cause.

A good woman, someone had explained to him on the road from Brighouse, the widow of Radical Jack Thackray, something of a local hero, who had been cut down by a saber at St. Peter's Fields in Manchester, asking for rather less in the way of electoral reform than Daniel himself was demanding now. A woman who was afraid of nothing and who would feed him, starch his linen, give him peace and quiet in which to compose his speeches, until the campaign should be over. And it was not until Mrs. Thackray's tall, craggy, fair-haired son had shouldered his luggage and led him to the top of St. Jude's Street that he had realized his peril.

Yet—just the same—she would not be there. And he had not come here as a lover, in any case. He had embarked on a serious and very likely dangerous undertaking which, until its conclusion, must precede anything and everything in his life. He was the Chartist Candidate for Frizingley. That was what he meant to Mrs. Sairellen Thackray as she served him the first of her good dinners of boiled beef and potatoes and onions toward which the town's Chartists had all made their contributions. That was what he meant to Luke Thackray, her son, who was to sleep in the kitchen so that the "candidate" might have the privacy of his tiny but spotless room. And so it was as the "candidate" that he spoke to them, his accent so neutral by now that he could have come from anywhere and everywhere, his green broadcloth jacket still shabby but worn as jauntily as if it had been lined with ermine, his lean, dark face handsome enough to please the women and hard enough to reassure the men.

Young, of course. Or so he seemed to Sairellen Thackray, who preferred her leaders to have the mature dignity of a Richard Oastler, whom she had followed on foot those ninety miles to York and back when they had been campaigning for the ten hour working day. But Richard Oastler was still in his debtor's prison, more than a thousand pounds short of the repayment of his debt, despite the money which Luke and thousands like him kept on collecting, week after week, from their wages. Nor had the ten hour day yet come to pass. And so when Luke had brought home a copy of the People's Charter and read it aloud to her she had listened; considered; believed.

"If we could all vote, mother, then we'd get our way. And if this candidate they're sending should be more interested in Home Rule for Ireland than our Ten Hours' Bill then what of it? With the Charter we could have both."

So be it. Although, despite her principles and her ingrained reluctance to compromise, she could not suppress a pang of gratitude even now—as she dished up her broth and herb dumplings for the candidate—that an attack of the low fever, caught as usual from terrible, tormented Mrs. Rattrie, who this time had died of it, had kept Luke in bed during that wild week last summer when the plugs had been drawn from Braithwaite's boiler and all Luke's brave young friends who had got into the habit of gathering to smoke their pipes and set the world to rights of an evening in her hen-run, had gone marching off to join their "brothers" from across the Pennines. And thence to Halifax where they had entered the town in their thousands, led by the women, Sairellen had been pleased to hear, walking four and five abreast, empty-handed and bare-headed as she had herself once walked to York, singing the psalm she too had sung on that day.

> "Make a joyful noise unto the Lord, all ye lands.
> Serve the Lord with gladness,
> Come before His presence with singing.
> We are His people and the sheep of His pasture."

And like sheep they had eventually been ridden down by soldiers as her husband had been ridden down at Peterloo, the crowd dispersed and then hunted over the open fields like running hares, so that of Luke's companions one had crawled into a hedge with a leg that might have been mangled in a bear-trap and had bled to death there; two or three others had taken refuge in haystacks and barns; two had been arrested and sentenced to hard labor. While those who had gone back to Braithwaite's mill had been picked out of the crowd by wild little Oliver Rattrie, the eldest Rattrie boy—nineteen or twenty she supposed he'd be by now—the twisted, crook-shouldered lad who had done more talking of pikes and pistols and bloody revolution than anybody else at the meetings in her backyard. A betrayal which had secured their dismissal from Mr. Ben Braithwaite himself, who had branded them as troublemakers with no hope of employment anywhere in Frizingley again.

Not that it had done Oliver Rattrie any good, since he'd been caught the day after by those same Chartist women who had marched into Halifax singing the One Hundredth Psalm; sheep no longer but howling Furies who had seized him, puny little thing that he was, and thrown him in the canal where, in his struggle to keep himself from drowning, he had lost every last shilling of the blood-money in his pockets. Unless it was true, as he'd alleged, that the women had robbed him before tossing him in the stinking water.

Perhaps they had. With husbands in prison, or disabled, or thrown out of work by Oliver's treachery, who could blame them? But when he had had the effrontery to go whining to the constable, attempting to get back the money for which he had, after all, sold his twisted little soul, no one in St. Jude's Street could remember seeing or hearing anything about the accident at all.

Sairellen herself had met the constable on her doorstep and kept him there, her arms folded across her impassive chest, her eyes like chips of granite. Oliver Rattrie? Had he fallen into the canal? Well— and what of it? He'd have been drunk, she supposed. Like his father. In *her* opinion anybody with any sense would let the matter rest there.

There it had rested.

But Sairellen knew all too well that had Luke not been delirious with fever that day he would surely have marched to Halifax; not with a pitchfork or a flail or a home-made pike in his hands, since he had never been a "physical force" man but *there*, just the same. A voice for moderation and good order—like many others—but his head as bare as the rest when the bricks started to fly, his body as vulnerable to saber cuts as his father's, his countenance indistinguishable to those young and possibly nervous soldiers from the real "physical force" brigade they were supposed to be looking for, who had raised everybody's temperatures by ambushing and stoning a military escort at Salterhebble.

And if Oliver had betrayed him, as he had betrayed all the others, what would she have been able to do for the Chartist candidate then?

Was it even safe to be helping him now? But she would be a sheep indeed to be ruled only by that.

"You'll take some treacle tart," she told Daniel, the set of her pugnacious jaw warning him that she was not asking a question so much as issuing a command.

"So I will." He gave her a slanting, quite roguish smile, cleverly designed to appeal to her both as a woman and a mother. A charmer, she thought, although she had long passed the season for such things. And a wanderer, a political vagabond as she would permit no son of hers to become. And Irishman too, which was not, in her eyes, the best of recommendations. What would he be likely to know or care of children worked half to death in English factories?

"You'll be after Home Rule for your own country, I expect," she said.

"I'll be after justice and freedom for everybody, Mrs. Thackray."

"Aye. I reckon you will." She had heard those words too many times before to be impressed by them. "My husband died at Peterloo for that, my lad. Twenty-four years ago."

Had it really been so long? Sometimes it seemed another lifetime. Sometimes no farther than yesterday. But Luke, she remembered, had been four years old, tall for his age but thin as a stick and pale with excitement, that day, at the journey to Manchester, the speeches, the exalted, psalm-singing atmosphere of the crowds. Was he outgrowing his strength, she'd wondered, as her other children had done, her vague fears of wasting fevers and rickety limbs vanishing to be replaced by incredulous horror as the soldiers on their tall horses had begun to charge. Why had she brought him here? She ought to have known there would be trouble. She *had* known it. There had simply been nowhere to leave him. And Jack, her husband, had had some high-flown notion of dedicating the lad to the cause. In blood, it seemed. "Damn you, Jack Thackray," she'd screamed. "Now you've killed us all." Even now, in the night, she was sometimes startled from sleep by the sound of those words; that scream.

She had thrown Luke to the ground, herself on top of him, and when the yelling and the thudding and the terrible, high-pitched howling of collective terror had been over, when the cavalry had charged through the crowd like a scythe through a cornfield and silence—such a silence—had fallen, she had opened her eyes and seen blood everywhere, in her hair and her hands, all over the stupefied, half-suffocated child. Jack's blood. Jack, who had thrown himself across them both and had died in her arms, an hour later, without speaking a word.

Radical Jack Thackray. Her last words to him had been a curse yet she had felt him at her side on the day she had marched to York with Richard Oastler. It was for him that she had raised Luke to be the man he was. It was for him that now she was entertaining this arrow-straight, dark-eyed young scoundrel who would be likely to repay her by seducing her daughter, she thought, if she still had one, and who would probably forget everything he'd ever heard about hunger in St. Jude's, or in County Kildare for that matter, should he ever find himself well-fed in Westminster.

Handsome young rascal with hands that had never lifted anything heavier than a pen by the look of them. She would prefer to put her trust in a plainer, simpler, hard-handed man. Like Luke.

"You'll like your tea strong." Once again she had given him an order.

"I would."

And then, giving no sign of either self-disgust or self-betrayal, although he was feeling both in full measure, he very casually mentioned, "I knew an Irish family once who lived nearby. Just across the street from here, I think—although after so long I may well be mistaken. A mother and daughter and her daughter's little boy?"

He found, to his immense distress, that he could not persuade his tongue to pronounce "Adeane," much less the simple, lovely name of "Cara."

Sairellen felt no such restriction.

"You'll be meaning the Adeanes." It did not surprise her. She had judged him, all along, as one of their kind.

"Yes. That was the name. They will have moved on by now—surely...?"

And having asked the question it now occurred to him that with this woman's shrewd, sharp eyes upon him, he may be unable to bear the answer.

"Aye, you'd think they'd have moved on, wouldn't you? Folks like that. But no. You'd be wrong."

"They're here?" He would have given a great deal to have sounded less incredulous.

"They are. Odette and the bairn still across the street just where they used to be."

"And—Miss Adeane?" He still could not trust himself to say "Cara."

"Come up in the world. Or so the world calls it. She has a shop in Market Square. Miss Cara Adeane. Dressmaker and Milliner. Like she always said she'd be."

"Yes." He said very quietly. "I see."

Clearly, in fact. Beyond all possibility of error. For she could not have risen so far on her own. He *knew* that. It was a condition of life in St. Jude's. A condition of life everywhere, to one degree or another, for a woman. And he would just have to learn, and quickly, to be glad of it. To accept that whatever she had done or promised or performed to maintain her position in Market Square, then her choice could only have been *that* or the workhouse. Or the brothel. Or to become the pregnant drudge of a working man.

No choice at all.

"Are they—*well*, Mrs. Thackray?" He knew she was watching him very keenly.

"Marvelously well, I'd say. Never better."

"And Miss Adeane lives over her shop, does she?"

"Aye. She finds it more convenient, I reckon—for her visitors."

"Mother." Luke Thackray's warning served only to increase the sarcasm in his mother's face.

"I'm telling no secrets, Luke lad. You'll not be denying that every-body knows for certain?"

He put down his knife and fork tidily, his rough-hewn, over-crowded face completely calm.

"No. But I won't be judging either, mother."

"Then I reckon it's high time you did. Where Miss Cara Adeane's concerned, at any rate."

He shook his head, unperturbed it seemed, not in the least put out yet altogether immovable, a man whose quiet strength struck Daniel suddenly as impressive, a steadily burning, dogged persistence which would be likely to endure far longer than his own vivid bursts of fire.

"She does the best she can, mother. And, considering the alterna-tives, *I'm* not much inclined to blame her."

"I've never seen her crying over her lot, Luke my lad—whatever we might choose to call it. Nor hanging her head with shame."

He looked up at her, with a sudden, whole-hearted grin. "No mother. I reckon you never will."

No more was said. Having finished his dinner the candidate retired to the spick and span little room no bigger than a cubbyhole they had placed at his disposal and, when he had put his thoughts and his speeches in good order, stepped out for a breath of air, a short stroll which led him—as he had known it would—to the newly painted door of Odette Adeane.

His memory of her had been indistinct, a little Frenchwoman speaking only in soft whispers, so frail and quiet and hesitant that she had seemed almost transparent beside Cara, hardly there at all. An old woman, anxious and harassed half to death, wearing some colorless kind of garment which had seemed to hang on her, fitting where it touched. Shabby, he'd thought, and plain, so that he was taken aback by the neatly-rounded woman who answered his knock, a most presentable person in a dark, well-cut woollen dress with what looked like a gold brooch at the neck, her smooth oval face miracu-lously ironed of the creases he remembered, her mouth smiling the serene welcome of a woman who has no reason to expect trouble from a knock at her door, a woman who eats well and sleeps well and can settle all her bills. A contented woman, subject to no alarm. Until she recognized him.

"It is Mr. Carey, isn't it?"

"Yes, Mrs. Adeane. May I speak to you?"

"Of course." For when had Odette ever resisted an appeal? "Do come in. Please do. Please be at ease."

Although she was not at ease herself and did not expect to be until she had told him all the painful things he would surely wish to know. Until she had wounded him, perhaps. And then carried the news to Cara.

He no longer recognized the room into which she bade him enter, a bare place once furnished with the haphazard gleanings of pawnshops and charity, now beautified beyond anything in St. Jude's by rugs and armchairs and a chintz-covered sofa, heavy red plush curtains at the window, a table with a fringed, red plush tablecloth to match, pictures on the walls, china ornaments, a good fire burning, something savory and appetizing in the coal oven beside it.

The wages of sin, he supposed, trying to be glad, for Cara's sake, that they appeared to be so good.

No dog, he noticed, but Cara's son, the silent child who had always made him feel so ill at ease, still sitting by the hearth as if he had grown there from a morose three-year-old into a clean and tidy, almost dandified five. A handsome child, Cara's bold image, it seemed, with Odette's timid spirit, apparently engrossed in a book—or was he?—from which he did not lift his eyes.

"Daniel," said Odette, already faltering. "She is not here, you know."

"I know. I have come from the Thackrays."

"Oh yes . . . ?" Her face was blank.

"I am here for the by-election, Mrs. Adeane. I shall be here for a little while. As the Chartist candidate. I thought you would have been gone, all three, long ago."

"And so we would, had she not . . ."

"*I know.* Is she—*well*, Mrs. Adeane?"

"Oh yes. *Yes.* I am sure she is. She has the shop, you see. Nothing grand, as yet. Quite small, indeed—and there is still Miss Ernestine Baker across the street, making all the trouble she can. But Cara is so clever and she works so hard. She never stops working. It is all she thinks of. I supervise the workroom for her and keep the girls in order as best I can . . ."

"Yes—to be sure."

She smiled at him a little wildly, not knowing what to say except that it seemed best to keep on talking.

"Yes indeed, because dressmakers can be very excitable, you know.

205

Someone must keep them calm or the scissors soon start to fly. One wonders that murder is so seldom done. And I do the fine embroideries. And teach others, which I find very pleasant... I live here, with the child because... Well, it is not suitable for a child, is it, to be too much in a workroom among so many foolish women? He goes to school now, of course. She insists upon that. And then he comes home with me. She finds it convenient to live above the shop... Naturally one cannot leave business premises unattended. But the accommodation there is too small for the three of us..."

He was unprepared for the pain the room gave him, the fierce memory of the last time he had been here, when only that impulse of chivalry, or folly, had prevented him from taking her, as he could have done, from making her his own instead of handing her over to whoever had got her now. From forcing her, by an act of love, to follow him through the world, not barefoot as she'd accused him but in no great luxury, instead of "obliging" the man who had given her her chance. Was she happier this way? Through clenched teeth he hoped so. He had no right to do other than wish her well.

Yet it scorched him that he had been unable to give her that chance himself. Unable to give her anything but the bitter regret which struck out at him afresh, raising a sting of tears behind his eyes, an abominable tightness in his chest.

He must get out of this house and out of these memories as quickly as he could.

"I am so sorry," whispered Odette.

He could not answer her quite at once. It took a moment. And then, rapidly, he said, "I understand. I do realize... Mrs. Adeane, there is someone—of course—who helped her—a man..."

"Oh yes. I *am* so sorry."

"No. Please. Please don't distress yourself."

"My dear boy, it is *you* who are suffering..."

"Yes." Why hide it? She had seen it in any case and she was not Sairellen Thackray, who would look down her granite nose at him and sneer. This gentle little lady would sit down and suffer at his side.

He could not bear that.

"But I must bear it," he said. "It is my own fault. And I have no right—none—to criticize. No rights of any kind. I want—I would be happy if you could tell her..."

"Oh yes—anything..."

"Just *that*. That I could not ever blame her. For anything. Could you tell her so in a manner she would tolerate?"

Odette shook her head and smiled sadly. "I will try."

"And should she wish to see me . . . ?"

Her narrow, fluid hands came apart in a wide, pitying gesture which said "My poor boy. I do not think so."

"I cannot suppose she will. But I cannot hide my presence from her either, Mrs. Adeane. I am here to make speeches and take part in processions. She will be bound to hear of me. Of course, why should she care? I cannot imagine she does."

Odette had nothing to say to that.

"But . . ."

"Yes, Daniel?"

He drew himself up very straight. "If she would like me to call on her, then I will gladly do so. If not then I will do everything possible to keep out of her way. It is entirely for her to decide. Whatever is best for her."

He meant it. He had given her nothing so far. Indeed, he had left her only in the full knowledge that he never could give her the things she wanted. He was ready, therefore, to submit to her wishes now whatever they may be. To make any sacrifice. At least he could give her that.

Odette had not meant to return to the shop in Market Square that evening, yet nevertheless, having given Liam his dinner and left him—happily for him—sketching railway engines with Luke Thackray, she did so, finding her daughter in the room at the back of the shop which served her as both office and sitting-room, going through the day's accounts.

Miss Cara Adeane. Dressmaker and Milliner. A handsome, elegant woman, thought her mother, although a *woman* of course, in no way a girl; twenty-two years old yet looking at least five years older, her gleaming hair drawn back into an intricate chignon which made her cheekbones higher and caused her brilliant turquoise eyes to slant upward a little at their corners like the eyes of a sleek and haughty cat; her figure the most perfect in Frizingley, in Odette's opinion—and she had measured most of them—a tiny, supple waist, high, firm breasts, long legs, a thoroughbred arch to her back, the shoulders of a queenly Amazon.

A regal temper too, these days, imperious and unpredictable, working herself too hard, of course, and expecting the same of others, so that Odette spoke very carefully to her now as she described her interview with Daniel Carey.

But the storm did not come. It was not in Odette's nature to inflict pain without suffering it herself. Yet Cara listened to her now, looking remote, polite, her ledger still open before her, her pen in her hand, waiting, as if it had been a matter of a badly-cut bodice or a late delivery of thread, for the explanations to come to an end. And when they did she said calmly, "It's all right, mother."

"Darling—how can it be?"

"It just *is*. So there's no need to talk about it again. And if you do happen to see him just tell him ... to get on with what he has to do, and so will I. Which reminds me, I had Mrs. Maria Colclough here today, just after you left. How about that? One of Miss Ernestine Baker's best customers asking *me* to make suggestions for her youngest daughter's wedding gown. And nervous as a cat about it too, in case Miss Ernestine had seen her slipping in here—as she probably had. I've made some sketches. So if you can do some samples of embroidery—by tomorrow afternoon—then I'll call on her. Because if we can get the Colclough wedding, mother ..."

She pushed forward the sheet of paper on which she had developed, through several experimental stages, a gown intended to give Miss Rachel Colclough something between the allure of a white satin lily and the piety of a nun. The Colcloughs, as a family, being very religious but also very vain, requiring value which could be *seen* as value for every penny they spent yet without any blatant ostentation.

"So we want a very simple embroidery pattern, mother. Some kind of biblical flower, if such a thing exists. You'll know—and *they'll* know—it's holy, if no one else does. But worked in tiny, tiny seed pearls, if I can persuade them to run to that. I expect I can. We have some pearl beads in the workroom so—since you're here—you might like to take them home and make a start tonight? I daren't put off seeing Mrs. Colclough later than tomorrow afternoon because she's bound to have asked Ernestine Baker for sketches days before she plucked up enough courage to ask me. So I have to get over there quick and talk her out of whatever Baker has put forward, before they can finalize. I don't want fobbing off with a couple of extra evening-gowns for the honeymoon this time. So—now that I've got the wedding dress right, I'm going to sit up late and do my designs for the bridesmaids—make them look like lilies-of-the-valley to Rachel's arum lily if I can. *And* the going-away outfit. If I can deliver all that by tomorrow it ought to impress her, particularly if Baker has got no further than her everlasting tulle frills."

But when Odette had taken the pearl beads and a few scraps of white satin and gone away, half-reassured, half-saddened by the apparently cool frame of her daughter's mind, the pencil soon fell from Cara's hand, a fit of restlessness driving her from her desk to the empty shop, upstairs to the workroom and then back to her desk again. She would eventually set to work on her sketches, having deliberately made much of them to Odette so as to give herself no choice in the matter. Her mother, who would certainly sit up late herself over those pearl beads, would expect to see Cara's ideas for the whole of the Colclough wedding procession tomorrow, including a hat of suitably discreet extravagance for the mother of the bride. Otherwise she would know that Cara had allowed her memories of Daniel Carey to distract her from what had become her way of life.

Her *chosen* way; chosen not entirely by herself but near enough, as close, she supposed, as she would ever come to it. And since she could not turn aside from it now, then what was to be gained by stirring up pain where there had been no pain? No joy either, of course, but a relatively inoffensive hollow space to which she had grown accustomed and had no desire to refill.

So she would do the sketches. And more than that, she would recover every drop of the excitement she had been feeling about the Colclough wedding, until Daniel—through Odette—had taken it away from her. Well—she would just get it back again. In a little while. She would go over every dirty little trick she intended to play on Miss Ernestine Baker, too. Would rehearse, with glee, every word of the honeyed malice she meant to pour into Maria Colclough's sharp but not incorruptible ear. Yes, she would do it all. Before the night was through. But, just now, she needed a moment. Just *time*, which could not always be counted on to heal, but which would certainly pass. At least one could rely on that. And sitting down in the red velvet armchair of which she was so proud, her dog snoring and snuffling his habitual evil-temper from the fur hearth-rug at her feet, she allowed the elegant arch of her back to admit its fatigue, her cheeks to acknowledge the ache of another full day of false smiles; allowed her eyes, which had missed nothing since early that morning, to close.

The shop was not large, for Christie Goldsborough had not showered her with ease and plenty or anything like it, his generosity being concerned far more with his own entertainment than with her peace of mind. And since what entertained him most was her determination to drag herself out of the mire, he had given her no more than the bare essentials with which to do it, along with his permission to be as determined as she liked.

So had she been. Determined. Hard. Frantic, sometimes. Occasionally strained almost—never *quite*—to her limits. For if she failed in this then there would never be another chance. If she fell down now she would never get up again. She was constantly aware of that. And so she must neither fall nor fail.

He had given her a small amount of capital which—no matter what else she gave him—would certainly have to be repaid, and her choice of the premises he had had available for rent. And needing good light above all things in her workroom she had chosen this building in Market Square, despite its derelict condition, for the height of the upstairs windows which, by letting in so much natural illumination, would—she had calculated—save not only lamp oil and candles but her needlewomen's eyesight. She had needed, too, a decent frontage, a decent or at least not a downright disreputable location where no lady would care to hazard her carriage, and this tall house on the very edge of the square, just before it became St. Jude's—which would not have done at all—had seemed to have not certainties—since who would ask that?—but possibilities. Something to work on. A start.

It had been filthy, of course, having been used as a cheap squatting place for peddlers and tinkers—she preferred not to dwell on how casually Christie Goldsborough had evicted them all—and she had scrubbed out the ordure of their occupation herself, several times over, before hiring a scrubwoman to keep the rooms as clean and fragrant as she had left them.

She had painted her workroom walls a tranquil apple green—a color guaranteed to induce calm, according to Odette—installed tables high enough to avoid the twisting of the spine one endured at every other workroom in her experience, including Miss Baker's; provided footstools which, by giving additional comfort to an embroideress would also enable her to remain at her work rather longer. She had divided the second upstairs room into an ironing-room, thus isolating the heat and steam of goffering and pressing which was famous for giving seamstresses the headache, and had kept her stock of fabrics and trimmings out of sight—largely because she had lacked enough to make a display—thus giving her premises an uncluttered look of which she quickly took advantage by laying out pattern books and fashion magazines, cultivating, rather by chance, a leisurely and—as it turned out—a pleasant atmosphere.

She had repaired her shop-front extensively, or rather had persuaded others to do it for her at a bargain price, causing Miss Baker to pinch her lips and raise pained eyebrows when the woodwork, painted a most frivolous pale blue—the color of happiness—had acquired its gracefully curving lettering—in gold—spelling out the name of Cara Adeane.

She had pale blue hatboxes too, with that same gold lettering, for the hats Miss Baker declared she would never sell, pale blue walls in the shop itself with little blue velvet chairs on which no self-respecting customers, in Miss Baker's opinion, would ever sit. While her shop-window, polished with lemon juice every morning so that even Miss Baker, from her far more advantageous position on the top side of Market Square—as far away as possible from St. Jude's—could not avoid its gleam, was soon filled by bonnets on plaster heads that were actually painted like real faces—a practice which Miss Baker, without knowing why, felt to be thoroughly immoral—and with shawls, fans, embroidered gloves, lace caps and collars, the exquisite little snippets of temptation which might entice someone inside to order a gown.

She had taken immense pains with her window; changing it constantly—having little else to do in those early days—so that the eye of young Mrs. Magda Braithwaite, for instance, which had been attracted by a cream silk gown displayed with a high-crowned cream straw hat, would find it replaced by a Mary Stuart bonnet with blue velvet ribbons when she passed by the next day. She would therefore be obliged to step inside if she wished to see the cream straw hat again, finding—if she did so—just the very shawl, in cream silk deeply fringed in a dark brown, which exactly matched the feather curled around the hat.

Eventually Mrs. Magda Braithwaite came. And came again. Although Mrs. Lizzie Braithwaite, her mother-in-law, remained loyal to Miss Baker. Mrs. Amabel Dallam and Mrs. Tristan Gage came too, and bought generously, although Cara knew that Miss Linnet Gage, who often made her own dresses, steered them toward Miss Baker's whenever she could. Young Mrs. Jacob Lord, who had been Miss Amanda Braithwaite, still went where her mother took her and bought what her mother told her to buy, although Mrs. Ethel Lord, Amanda's mother-in-law—perhaps in defiance of Mrs. Braithwaite—had been one of Cara's first customers.

Although only for small things, only for the extra gown or mantle, the extra half-dozen petticoats Mrs. Lord thought it would be as well to have when she had ordered the bulk of her season's wardrobe from Miss Baker. Only the bonnet which she happened to see in passing, or those wicked lace garters—Mrs. Lord being of a frivolous turn of mind—that sweet little beaded reticule, that lace-edged Spanish parasol.

Like the rest of them, playing safe and sound and giving their large orders, their real work, to Ernestine Baker. Until today, when she had been approached to do sketches for the Colclough wedding.

She would begin to crow with triumph about that. Quite soon. When this uneasy moment, full of Daniel, had safely passed. And then—she was quite sure of it—she would start to feel her excitement mounting to that spurt of honest, joyful exultation she always felt whenever one of her ruses, no matter how small, came to bear its fruit. When she'd run that supplier to earth, for instance, who dealt in those beaded reticules and Spanish parasols and persuaded him to sell to no one in Frizingley but herself. When she'd found the vague yet altogether biddable woman who made facial preparations from lemons and cucumbers to freshen the skin and herbal washes to lighten or darken the hair, which she'd put into fancy bottles and now sold discreetly, along with the little pots of rouge and powder and Odette's floral perfumes which she could always produce, without any husband being the wiser, from her bottom drawer. When two of Miss Baker's journeywomen had come knocking on her door to beg employment, which she would have given them had it meant the sacrifice of her own daily bread. When Lady Lark sailed through her door one day like an arrogant and exceedingly shabby galleon, looking for cut-price splendor for a hunt ball, which Miss Baker seemed unable to supply. When Mrs. Audrey Covington-Pym, declining to enter the shop, had called her outside to show her wares at the Covington-Pym carriage step, and she had sent Odette, who had managed, nevertheless, to take an order for a riding-habit. When Mrs. Marie Moon—yet another of the Goldsborough stable of women—had draped herself languidly against the counter, blinking with absent-minded myopia as every length of silk and satin Cara possessed had been displayed—casually, of course, as if there had been at least a hundred more—

choosing, at length, two evening gowns, one black, one white, one to be paid for, she'd murmured to Cara, by her husband, the other by "our mutual military friend."

"Colonel Covington-Pym?" Cara had inquired sweetly. "Or Captain Goldsborough?"

But Marie Moon, who was basically good-natured and often slightly drunk, had shrugged without rancor and wandered away, while Christie Goldsborough had been sufficiently amused by the episode not to question Cara's bill for the black dress which, by covering the bodice with jet beads, she had managed to make at least twenty per cent higher than the bill for the white dress which she sent to Adolphus Moon.

Marie, of course, had looked exquisite in them both. And exquisite without them. The captain had assured her of that, although he was very well aware that his continuing relationship with Mrs. Moon caused not the least concern to Cara.

Why should it? No doubt he had both of them as and when he chose. Certainly Cara had never refused him, nor even considered it. When she received a note telling her to join him at the Fleece or anywhere else he named, she went. Without delay. Which was why she had kept the cottage in St. Jude's for Liam and Odette and lived here with no other company but that damned dog, who would surely live forever, snoring all day by the fire and waddling upstairs to the workroom every now and then to snap at the journeywomen's fingers as they fed him scraps.

Ugly-tempered brute. Like his master. Although she had learned a great deal from Christie. Some things which she had been most eager to know and others which often lay heavily upon her, making her feel brittle and weary and at least a hundred. Ancient in sin, that is, if not in wisdom. He had taught her how to calculate her profits, what to pay and what to charge, and she had lapped up his instruction like a greedy kitten at a cream pot. He had removed her fear of pregnancy by showing her how to set up an inner barrier of sponges soaked in vinegar—like Marie Moon and Audrey Covington-Pym and Queen Cleopatra of Egypt too she shouldn't wonder—a procedure so simple and which had been going on for so long that she often wondered why she had never thought of it for herself. He had taught her about wine and food, how to choose it and present it and savor it. He had taught her about appetite of another kind, how to arouse his occasionally jaded sensuality, how to please him in ways she most certainly would *never* have thought of; whore's tricks, she supposed, although she had come to terms, of necessity, with that side of herself.

And in one thing only had she ever resisted him. She would give him pleasure as and when he demanded, but she would never allow him to please her. Never. It was her one furious and often self-tormenting cry of independence. It was the only thing she had which he could not reach. The only thing he could not inveigle out of her either by force or cunning. The only thing she could choose, and consequently did *not* choose, to give him. In the full knowledge that, as a sophisticated man with a fine appreciation of the bodies of women, it was something he wanted. Her orgasm. And whenever she felt that treacherous stirring at the pit of her stomach she had her own ways of dealing with it. Simply ordering it to go away, sometimes, driving it out by sheer effort of will. And when that failed she would just go on clenching her teeth and her muscles and wrestling with it until she had strangled it, not always quite at birth but usually soon enough; hating, at such moments, the female parts of her own self which, every now and then, eluded her control and began all their foolish glowing and vibrating, their *yielding*, which she could not tolerate.

Other women, like Marie Moon, might call it ecstasy. Perhaps, with another man, so might she. But now, although she would submit to the act itself, as many women did for one reason or another, and feel no shame, the enjoyment of it was an entirely different matter. The enjoyment which led to the need. *There* lay the degradation, as it had degraded lovely, passionate Marie Moon, who would have washed Christie Goldsborough's feet with her tears and dried them with her hair, stark naked in the middle of the square on market day had he taken it into his head to ask her.

She would never become his slave in that way, begging for his caresses like a dog as she had seen Marie do more than once, and with no better result—she'd noticed—than to bring out the cruel, cutting-edge of his humor, never far below the surface in any case. Although Marie seemed to welcome even that, taking her punishment for the sheer pleasure of offering him her forgiveness, of which he felt no need, for some unkind word or deed of his which he assuredly did not regret.

Cara forgave him nothing. She went to his bed as an adversary. And not always the same adversary either. Sometimes cool and remote as a maiden in an ivory tower far beyond any man's powers of awakening. Sometimes playful and provocative, full of teasing little tricks which led to nothing, on her part, but laughter. A woman, sometimes, who seemed to be smouldering on the brink of fulfillment, exciting him—and regrettably herself—the better to disappoint him when her abandon evaporated and became a yawn, a murmur of regret.

"There's no hurry, Adeane," he would say to her. "We can go on—all night if necessary... If you are dissatisfied."

But she came to regard it as proof of her superiority as a woman that she could indeed prolong her lovemaking for as long as she chose to do so, while he—a man—must eventually reach a climax which, no matter how pleasant, ended it. The victory, therefore, was hers. The only one she had. Nothing would make her relinquish it. And if, as often happened afterward, her stomach tightened and knotted with cramp and there seemed to be a claw of fire scraping somewhere inside her head, then—for her victory's sake—she could bear that too.

But, in other ways, she knew she had little to complain of. For the first year he had given her the shop rent-free but now she paid him, promptly every quarter, what the property was worth with no reduction even for the cottage in St. Jude's. And because she was known throughout the area as Christie Goldsborough's woman, or one of them, no one troubled her, or Odette, or Liam. No one stole from them or offered them the least annoyance. The butcher and the grocer were glad of their custom and happy to deliver. Not even the sharpest frost prevented the coalman from getting his cart to the top of St. Jude's Street to fill *their* coal-cellar. No one tampered with the washing from their lines. No one threw stones at their windows or used the passage between Odette's house and the one behind it as a privy. No one poked fun at Liam on his neatly-dressed way to the dame-school where he had made no friends but appeared to be learning his lessons. And at least he was safe with Odette in a house that had a chair and sofa to match, a square of real carpet, good blankets on his bed.

"Come, Cara," Christie Goldsborough had said to her once or twice lately. "You must know better than to disappoint me. You told me you wanted Miss Ernestine Baker's shop. Well then—since my amazing goodness has put your feet on the right path, when are you going to take it? I am waiting for the show to begin."

One day, perhaps. Not that she had any designs on Miss Baker's dismal, dark-brown shop. Simply her customers. And, in the meantime, there was the shop next door, rented—from Christie, of course—by a dingy grocer upon whose lease, when it expired, she had already set her mind. She needed space to display fabrics in the piece and finished goods as they ought to be displayed, space for new fitting-rooms and new showrooms, separate departments for millinery and trimmings and a pleasant, almost drawing-room area in which to serve tea in flowered china and temptation in the shape of fashion magazines, making shopping at Adeane's into a social event.

So much to do. So many plans. So many risks to be taken, so many pitfalls opening constantly beneath her feet. And who knew how much, or how little, *time?* Never so much that one could afford to waste it.

And now all she seemed able to do was lie in her armchair, facing that damned, overfed dog, and think about Daniel Carey.

Very well, then. Think hard. And get it over with. Was she still in love with him? More than likely. But, if so, what good could it do her? What had she to hope for, or to gain, or to give? And since the answer had always been "nothing" then could she really afford to grieve? Could she deliberately cloud her mind and weaken her resolution *now?* Or ever?

And what the devil was he doing mixed up with the Chartists—although it did not in the least surprise her—who kept on getting life sentences of hard labor and transportation instead of their vote and their secret ballot and their salaried MPs? And kept on dying in prison too, like that poor man at Northallerton a year or two ago, just before the riots, who had had a special hymn written for him and read at his graveside. "Great God, is this the patriot's doom?" Fine words, but small consolation to any woman who had loved him. *She* would not be in any way consoled by such things should she ever find herself standing, in rags, at Daniel's graveside. Or at the foot of the gallows.

She shuddered and got to her feet. Great God, indeed. She would have to occupy herself now, and quickly—at once—if she hoped to stop herself from slipping into the abysmal frame of mind which occasionally overcame her, where none of the things she had worked so hard for seemed worthwhile.

And if they lost their value, then what value had she? If they began to crumble then how could she hold herself together?

She could not.

Realizing, with some annoyance, that she was trembling she went back to her desk and sat for a moment with her head in her hands, almost wishing that Christie would send for her since that, at least, would concentrate her mind. But no. The Chartist candidate would not go away tomorrow. He would be here at least until the poll, three weeks hence; very present, very visible, at all the shouting and parading and tomfoolery which had ended, last election, with every window at the Dog and Gun and the Rose and Crown, and half the windows in Market Square, being put out. She would be better advised now to think of that, and the state of her shutters, than of the candidate.

She picked up her pencil and with a hand she refused to recognize as unsteady began to draw the Colclough bridesmaids, eight of them, one after the other, in various sizes and shapes and concepts so that when the dog, with a marked air of condescension, struggled to his feet to warn her someone was at her door, she was taken sadly unawares.

At this hour? Half past ten by the rather handsome clock on her mantelpiece. Not Christie, certainly, who never came here and would not have troubled to knock if he had. Not Odette, who would not leave Liam alone so late and who, in an emergency, would have sent Luke. Not Luke either, who would have whistled to identity himself and calm her fears.

Daniel?

She had turned so cold that her fingers were clumsy at the lock and she had to lean against the door a moment, her forehead clammy with the moisture of shock, until a low voice, muffled by woodwork and discretion, restored as much of her composure as she expected to need.

"I beg your pardon, Miss Adeane, for calling so late but I saw your lamp. And you know how it is. I've just come from the shop. And you know what she's like."

A neat, shabby woman stood there, forty years old by her appearance although Cara knew her to be less than thirty. Thin and slightly crooked from twisting her spine over worktables that were too low, red-eyed from peering at fine needlework in the dark. Exhausted. But, for the first time since Cara had known her, not entirely resigned. Madge Percy. The most experienced journeywoman Miss Ernestine Baker had left in her dingy workroom. The most talented embroideress in Frizingley, estimated Cara, after Odette, if one handled her properly. As Miss Baker, clearly, had not.

"You said I should talk things over with you, Miss Adeane, if I ever felt like making a change . . . ?"

What would it cost? Not a great deal. And it would be cheap at any price. She was no longer weary. No longer trembling. No longer entertained the slightest doubt as to her value. "Come in, my dear. Let's talk it over," she said.

12

*W*hen Luke Thackray called to see her the next morning at the convenient hour of eight o'clock—her shop being empty of customers so early, his mill being shut down for breakfast time—she was entirely restored to her chosen self, rustling to meet him in the black taffeta with touches of scarlet ribbon at the waist and neck which she had made her trademark, the weighty coils of her hair secured by jet pins.

She wore swinging drops of jet in her ears too, a strand of it around her throat, her manner conveying an impression that the artfully concealed pockets of her wide skirt would contain a number of significant things; a costly wisp of cambric handkerchief; the perfume bottle of vanity alongside the keys of absolute authority; a little velvet-bound appointments book and a gold pencil with which to write down their times and locations snuggling in perfect compatibility beside a book of "Spanish papers" with which to enhance the bloom of her discreetly painted face.

A woman who, no matter how greatly business might be pressing, could not conceal her delight either in her visitor nor in her little office-parlor where she made him welcome. Her *own* room where the plush covered armchairs drawn up to the fire *matched* each other, where the black fur rug and plum-colored carpet could only be called secondhand if one took into account that they had previously belonged to Christie Goldsborough, where the grate was heaped recklessly, open-handedly, with coal all day and the lamp had a base of real china. A wonderful room. The first she had ever lived in alone, her pleasure both in its magnificence and in seeing Luke so comfortably installed within it only giving way when, in his straightforward, no-nonsense manner, he asked her if she would take on Anna Rattrie as an apprentice.

Had he lost his reason? With any other man she would have assumed so and given a sharp reply. But this was Luke, the sanest and steadiest man she knew. The *only* man she knew whose judgment she would be prepared to trust if it disagreed with her own. The man of whom she could *almost* have declared, "If Luke says it will be all right, then it will be."

Therefore, trying hard to take the edge from her voice and make it reasonable, she said, "I don't take apprentices. Not yet. When I'm better established then I expect it will be worth my while. But just now I can't afford the time to train young girls. Or the bother. I only take experienced women."

And here they all were—her experienced women—hard at work in the room above her head. The two best seamstresses in Frizingley, Madge Percy and Odette, and three others who were reliable and competent if not precisely talented. A workroom of which anyone might be proud. Her best asset. *Her* women from whom she would squeeze the very best they had to give in full measure but of whom she would also take good care. Surely Luke must see that a *Rattrie*— and which one was Anna?—could have no part in her immaculate scheme of things?

"I wouldn't expect you to pay her," he said.

"Pay her?" She heard the sharpness in her own voice, the rasp of offended financial acumen, but could not soften it. "I should think not. If I were willing to take her she'd have to pay me. Or somebody would. At least £30 a year for the training and her food and lodging. That's what my apprenticeship cost, ten years ago, so I suppose nowadays I could get £35."

"If that's what you want, Cara, then I reckon I can manage it."

"Luke." She was shocked and something more. Grieved, it seemed. Did he think all she cared for was money? In most cases he would have been quite right. She freely admitted that. But not with him. Never with him. She had always wanted Luke to think well of her, and wanted it now with a force which both confused and weakened her.

"I wouldn't be taking a penny of your money, Luke Thackray, and you know it. I'd rather give . . ."

"Then give, Cara. That's what I'm asking."

Her generosity? But not for himself. Not to start up some enterprise or some course of study that would do *him* some good. Not to lift himself out of the trap of St. Jude's and the thankless grind of Braithwaite's mill to the decent, dignified future she could so easily envisage for him. She would give him the money for that all right. Would scrape it together one way or another and consider it a privilege and a pleasure no matter what Christie Goldsborough or Sairellen Thackray or anybody else had to say about it.

"Won't you give her a chance, Cara?"

It was not what she wanted to do for him. But, if it was what *he* wanted...?

"Why?" she said sullenly.

"Perhaps because no one else will."

Yes. That would be Luke's reason. Yet—although perhaps only for form's sake—she still resisted.

"I somehow don't think of *work* and the Rattries as going much together."

"Anna wants to work. I think she'll be reliable."

"Then why don't you take her to Braithwaite's. You're an overlooker, aren't you. Its up to you, surely, who you employ in your shed?"

"Cara," he said quietly, his voice and his smile telling her she must know better than that. "There are women at Braithwaite's whose husbands and sons have gone to prison because of Oliver Rattrie. I'm not saying they wouldn't work with Anna because they can't afford to lose their jobs. But I couldn't ask it of them. And how long do you think she'd last with them in any case?"

"Why should she do better here?"

"Because Oliver Rattrie's treason harmed no one in your workshop, while your customers would be more likely to applaud it than grumble. And Anna needs to get away from home, Cara. She's seventeen..."

"Seventeen." That's settled it. "Good Heavens, Luke, that's too old for an apprenticeship. You must know that. Of course you know it."

"I do. But she looks like a child of twelve and feels like one, at that, I shouldn't wonder. Although that didn't stop her father from trying to rape her the other night when he was a shade drunker than usual..."

"Oh. So that's it." She was neither shocked nor surprised, having heard of such things far too many times before. But, thinking of Mr. Rattrie, she was disgusted.

"Yes. That's it." Luke, shrugging his wide, thin shoulders, was not shocked either although she thought he sounded tired. "It's six months since Mrs. Rattrie died. Anna's the eldest girl. She keeps the house, such as it is, and carries the baby about on her hip like her mother used to do. When her father's drunk enough he can't tell the difference. Or so he said. To give the man his due—well, I think I believed him. Not that it makes things any easier for Anna."

"So you separated them, I suppose, and threw him in the horse trough again?"

He grinned, ruefully, without much pleasure. "Aye. So I did. Not that he came out much cleaner. Not that it's likely to stop him from trying again, either—if she stays there."

"I suppose not." Her voice was still sullen. "I expect its cheaper than paying a whore."

"I expect so. But I think Anna might just die of it. And then, of course, there's brother Oliver. No girl in St. Jude's will touch him now of her own free will, particularly since he lost his Judas money in the canal. Between the two of them what chance has she? And she's a *girl*."

He did not say "Like you, Cara," but she heard his thought distinctly enough. And, far more than that, she knew how dark the night could be in a house like the Rattries'; knew, with her own senses, the fear of any female animal as it is hunted and trapped. As Luke had known she would.

"Is she *clean*?" she muttered, still furious with him for asking this tedious, paltry service for a stranger—when she yearned to do something quite splendid for *him*.

"Oh yes. My mother has seen to that. She's been sleeping by our kitchen fire this last night or two."

As she had once taken refuge herself.

"All right." She acknowledged it. "But if she comes here she'll have to sleep under the counter or on a mattress in the workroom. There's nowhere else."

"She'll be very content with that."

"I dare say. I used to be content with it myself—once. Although it won't suit me at all if her father comes looking for her, drunk or sober."

"He won't do that, Cara. You have my word for it."

No more than his word had ever been necessary to her; for anything.

She sighed. "Sure and you'd better bring her to see me, then." And this time his grin held a whole-hearted pleasure, a frank spirit of fun which was, in itself, her reward. He had not expected her to let him down. She had not done so. His faith in her had been justified. They smiled at each other now, Cara shaking her head with her final traces of exasperation, Luke not touching her but somehow conveying to her—as he so often did—the impression of a warm handclasp, a strong shoulder.

"She's here, Cara—waiting in your backyard."

"Yes. I rather thought she might be."

Cara had made great and scornful play of her inability to distinguish one Rattrie from another but, in fact, she had no more difficulty in recognizing the girl who now came into the room as Anna than she had had in picking out the boy, apparently now employed in some indeterminate capacity around Christie Goldsborough, as her treacherous brother Oliver. Weasels, both of them, although taller than in the days when they had tampered with her water-barrels and annoyed her dog. Pale and thin and *furtive*, Oliver with his treachery, Anna perhaps only with shyness as she stood head bowed, hands folded, before Cara, looking no older than twelve as Luke had said, flat-hipped and flat-chested, her mouse-colored hair parted in the middle and scraped back by a severe hand Cara recognized as Sairellen's, her skimpy dress—probably older than the girl herself—washed and scrubbed and mangled, also by Sairellen, beyond even the memory of shape or color.

A drab from a workhouse or a charity-school, anonymous in her poverty and her humility who, having feared Cara in St. Jude's, was so truly alarmed by her now in her rustling black taffeta and all her authority that there was nothing to do but conclude the matter briskly, settling everything to Luke's satisfaction and then sending for Odette, whose hand with workhouse-drabs was lighter than her daughter's.

"Anna is joining us as an apprentice." She saw, without surprise, that it was no surprise to Odette. "So if you could just take her upstairs and get her started?"

What more did Luke want her to do than that?

"Oh—and you'd better find her something to wear, mother."

And *burn* those shapeless, Rattrie rags with that Rattrie odor still clinging to them, she thought. Although—because of Luke—she did not say so.

What else? Nothing, surely. She would feed the girl, teach her to sew, give her a few pennies to spend and a kind word or two whenever she remembered. Poor, sad little drab, scuttling timidly after Odette, more mouse than weasel until, reaching the doorway, she lifted her head for the first time, revealing huge, colorless, terrified eyes brimming over with tears as they shot a glance of naked adoration at Luke.

"That girl is in love with you," she accused him as the door closed behind her.

"I expect she thinks so." He sounded very composed about it.

"So—well—just be careful, Luke."

"Of what? If I have a reputation for being reckless, particularly with women, then it's news to me."

Yet suddenly he seemed extremely vulnerable to her, not innocent, perhaps far from that, yet likely to be used, exploited, *hurt* nevertheless—in full knowledge of that exploitation, almost by consent—because of his own refusal to deviate from his personal, simple creed of doing the best he could. A *good* man. She was unaccustomed to the breed, and her desire to give him a protection he neither sought nor particularly needed often soured her temper.

"You don't see danger, Luke."

"Of course I do."

"Then you don't take the trouble to avoid it. You won't win any friends at Braithwaite's mill by helping Anna Rattrie."

"I wouldn't want the kind of friends who'd leave a girl in that kind of trouble because of something her brother did."

"All right. So you've rescued Anna by foisting her on me. And now I suppose you'll be after starting a fund for the families of the men her brother sent to prison . . ."

"Very likely."

"And putting more of your own wages in it than you can afford . . ."

"I don't drink. I am moderate with my pipe. Allow me some pleasures."

"Who'd do it for you, Luke?"

"I expect you would, Cara."

Suddenly she was flustered, very nearly and quite irrationally furious.

"Don't be too sure. Although you'd have needed it, wouldn't you, if Oliver Rattrie had turned you in like the others? And if you hadn't been in bed with that fever his mother spread all over St. Jude's, then he *would* have turned you in, you know."

"Yes, Cara. I do know."

"And do you know what the little toad is doing now—in and out of the Fleece all day at Christie Goldsborough's elbow?"

"That's up to him, Cara."

It hurt her to speak Christie's name to Luke. It always had. Perhaps he didn't like to hear it. She couldn't tell. Yet, fired by anxiety for *him*—and to the devil with Christie—she rushed on, "Then I'll tell you what he's doing. He's creeping all over the town listening and prying and sniffing, and then running back to Goldsborough and Braithwaite and the rest with his tales of who the Chartists are and where they are and which ones need watching the most . . ."

"That's what I supposed he was doing, Cara."

He sounded so reasonable, so calm, that she could have slapped him.

"Oh yes—yes—of course you did. And that won't stop you from going to the hustings on polling day, will it, and letting everybody see just where you stand . . . ?"

"No. It certainly will not."

"Luke." Inwardly she knew that she was wringing her hands in anguish. "Why do you take so little care?" He shook his head and, once again, without any need for touch, she felt his hard, steady hand in hers.

"Nobody could call me a wild man, Cara. But I'm not a sheep either. And if safety is all you're thinking of, then sheep aren't even safe—are they?"

"No. Only the wolf is that." She believed it and could have slapped him again when she saw his grin.

"He may think so. I expect he does. But wolves get caught in traps, don't they, and starve to death in hard winters, or get shot at and bleed to death—like everything else. And where's the sense in trying to hide what I feel and what I am—even if I wanted to—when my father was Radical Jack Thackray and my mother is giving bed and board to the Chartist candidate?"

More than anything else she had wished to avoid any mention of

Daniel. She had found it hard enough to speak of him to Odette. Impossible, surely, to anyone else? Yet acknowledging the necessity, she said now with stiff lips and an ungainly, unwilling tongue, "I know. Daniel Carey. I met him once, years ago, on the boat from Ireland."

"So he said."

And when the desire to ask "Is he well? Is he happy? Is he in danger?" became a need that was *almost*—never quite—impossible to deny she endured it as one endures physical pain until it had eased, receded, had almost—never quite—gone away.

Was it even necessary to inquire? He would not be happy because the capacity for true happiness was in neither one of them. He would be well enough. As she was. *Of course* he would be in danger.

Yet at least she had succeeded in speaking his name without any visible emotion, a knack for which she grew increasingly grateful with the approach of polling-day. Not that the by-election—or any election—was of much importance to Cara when compared, for instance, with her negotiations for the Colclough wedding. Although—as she set about persuading Mrs. Maria Colclough of her ability to transform her awkward daughter Rachel into a bridal lily—her discovery that the Whig candidate had been selected, sponsored, bought, in fact, and paid for by the town's manufacturing interest, including the Colcloughs, did have the effect—so long as she remained in Maria Colclough's drawing-room—of making an ardent Whig of her.

An attitude she at once discarded, on her return to Market Square, when she found the truest of Frizingley's Tories, Lady Lark, awaiting her to be fitted for the accoutrements of several country-house visits.

The Larks, of course, were sponsoring their own candidate, along with the Covington-Pyms and the generous contribution of Mr. Adolphus Moon, who would have liked to stand for election himself had it not been for the handicap of his lovely but socially unacceptable wife. But a minor Lark cousin had been discovered, just as a minor Lark or Covington-Pym could always be found to do his duty as master of foxhounds or vicar of Far Flatley church, a gentleman who resembled Sir Felix Lark as closely as one Rattrie to another and whose wife—should she ever get there—would know exactly how to conduct herself at Westminster.

And it irked Lady Lark excessively that the desired result should even be in doubt.

"In my younger days." she said as Cara pinned her skillfully into a true blue dinner gown, "my father chose his member of parliament just as he chose his lawyer and his doctor, and that was that. One knew everyone personally, you see, who had the vote and one never dreamed of asking what they meant to do with it. One *knew*. So simple. So terribly *right*, somehow. One had the feeling that that was what the Deity intended. One knew one's leaders. *Oneself*, in fact. And there is no denying that ordinary people—most people—really like to be led. We looked after them, you see, as they knew we should. But now, Good Heavens, such chaos. All these new people and this new money which has been enfranchised. All this talk of opening our ports to cheap foreign grain which, apart from all the other foreign things which might come in with it, would absolutely ruin my brother—Lord Urlsham, my dear—who grows acres and acres of the stuff in Kent. Unthinkable. And really, although the Dallams and Braithwaites and Colcloughs have become one's friends, although one dines with them these days quite freely and so forth, one wonders—*quand même*—whether they really have enough experience of power? Without wishing to be unkind one feels bound to remember how very *new* they are and one would not wish to see them—well—*in error*."

"Make fools of ourselves, she means," said the strident Lizzie Braithwaite to Lady Lark's departing back. "Well we won't. We'll win because we work harder. And she'll lose because her blue blood has gone thin. And if she wants an occupation for all those spare nephews and cousins of hers then she'd better put them in the army—since they're fit for nothing but fancy uniforms—and send them off to conquer a few more heathen countries to provide markets for our manufactured goods. But what we both have to do is keep the Chartists down—stop them from poisoning the minds of honest workers against people like us, who are in a position to look after them."

"Certainly, madam," murmured Cara.

"Give us a living wage," said Daniel Carey from the hustings and Luke Thackray from the street. "Give us education. And opportunity. Give us the vote. And we'll look after ourselves."

"So they will," said Christie Goldsborough across his silken pillows to Cara. "Until such of them who are shrewd and ambitious—and there'll be plenty—start using the others as a ladder to get to the top of the heap for their own ends. One wonders who they'll vote for then."

"I don't care," said Cara, thinking of her shop-window which any stone—Chartist, Whig, or Tory—could just as easily splinter; remembering the drunken havoc of last polling day.

"Should you feel the need of a guard," murmured her lover, "I could hire some Irish muscle for your protection. No? Well then, if you don't care for that, take Oliver Rattrie."

She declined. Coldly. One Rattrie being more than enough—although Anna, so quiet as to be almost invisible, caused her no trouble, applying herself without much talent but with an almost painful diligence to the "apprentice pieces," the bonnet linings and trimmings, tedious hemming and tacking with which she was kept busy all day. A little shadow at night, making her bed in the workroom and mistaking it for luxury; denying, with a petrified shake of the head, that she was nervous of Cara's dog, although her face blanched with terror every time the animal approached her; ready to run errands at all times and in all weathers for Odette and Madge Percy; ready to lie down and die, supposed Cara, for Luke. Was she content with her lot? No doubt Luke would know. But little had the power to hold Cara's attention just then beyond the problem of having new, stout shutters fitted in a hurry, before polling day, and her sketches for the Colclough wedding which compared "adequately"—thought Mrs. Colclough—to Miss Baker's so far as style was concerned, but not in price.

Could Miss Adeane cut her cost, rather considerably, without in any way skimping on the quality or ornamentation of her original designs? And even then . . . ? Oh dear. Perhaps Miss Adeane *was* just a shade too young and daring, and had there not been some talk, once, about debts and lovers? And since—as every Colclough knew—there could be no smoke without fire, perhaps Miss Baker would be safer. As well as cheaper. Both safety and cost being of great importance to Mrs. Colclough's son, Uriah.

"Miss Adeane's designs are best," said Mrs. Colclough's awkward daughter, Rachel.

What was a poor mother to do?

She returned to Miss Adeane's shop on the eve of polling day accompanied by her son, the clerical Uriah, by his "angel"—not yet his fiancée—Miss Linnet Gage and by her sister-in-law, Mrs. Tristan Gage, now well recovered, it seemed, from her "accident" in December. Miss Adeane, with her flair for knowing just what was required, at once invited them all to be seated—no mean achievement in itself in such a limited space—and produced an extra cushion for Gemma's back while judgment was passed on the proposed wedding dress.

"Beautiful," said Gemma, the sketch in her hand. "Really, Mrs. Colclough, I do not believe you could do better anywhere."

"Is it not—perhaps—just a little severe?" murmured Linnet, willing the enamored but not *amorous* Uriah to remember her in the diaphanous draperies she had worn for Gemma's wedding; to think of her less as an angel and more as a bride.

And it was perhaps because he suddenly and most distressfully thought of her neither in lily-white satin nor feathered tulle but with no garments at all, *nude* and therefore, to one of his pious disposition, decidedly sinful, that he jumped to his feet and, in urgent need of distraction, began to peer out of the window, his equilibrium unmistakably disturbed.

"What is it, Uriah?" his mother, herself very easily agitated, required to know.

"Oh . . ." It would have to be something immediate and convincing. What, indeed? "Oh yes . . . Look here—"

"At *what*, Uriah?" His mother's eyes were very sharp.

At that Chartist fellow—yes, that's it—and his rabble, coming across the square. They'll be walking past your window, Miss Adeane, in a minute or two, bold as brass. If I had *my* way I'd have them pushed off the pavement, I can tell you, and straight into the gutter where they belong. Candidate, indeed! Just come over here and see him swaggering . . ."

They came.

"Why are such things allowed?" inquired Mrs. Colclough, addressing herself, it rather seemed, to God.

"What a terribly quaint little assembly," said Linnet, her high, light voice reducing the Chartist candidate and his considerable crowd of supporters—far more than either Whigs or Tories could hope to show—to a few ragged children at a charity-school party, grubby and noisy of course, ill-mannered and ill-lettered, but who probably meant no harm.

Mrs. Tristan Gage had no comment to make.

Nor had Miss Adeane, her eyes searching hastily through the crowd for Luke, her mind drawn far beyond her control to Daniel at the head of it, walking like a vagabond-king in his shabby green jacket, the same jaunty elegance in his step, the same hard, arrow-straight lines of him, the same slanting smile which, as he turned his head toward her window, caused her heart to thud so painfully that it seemed to bruise her chest.

She could see him plainly. She did not know how much, if anything, he could see of her from the street, with the Colcloughs and Gages all around her. And so she had no way of knowing whether it was for her or simply a hostile, staring group of manufacturers that he paused, swept off his hat with a flourish and made them a dancing-master's bow that sparkled with impudence.

There came a roar of pure delight from the crowd as it closed around him and carried him on.

"Such effrontery," breathed Linnet as if she had been threatened and was inviting Uriah to defend her.

"I'd have that one flogged at the cart-tail," he said darkly, "if I had *my* way."

Mrs. Colclough was speechless. Mrs. Tristan Gage too, although when Cara, badly in need of distraction, looked at her she seemed to be having some difficulty with the brooch on her lapel, an amethyst and diamond cat which had come loose and with which she was fiddling rather helplessly, thought Cara, in an attempt to pin it back.

"Please let me do that for you, Mrs. Gage."

Standing taller than Gemma, her long hands sure and steady, she removed the amethyst cat entirely, carefully disengaging its pins from Gemma's velvet collar and then, having smoothed the material down, quickly replaced it.

"Thank you, Miss Adeane. Most kind."

"Not at all. Perhaps you should have someone look at the pin, Mrs. Gage. It may be faulty."

"Yes. I suppose so. I have had it rather a long time you see."

"All the more reason, then, not to lose it."

"Oh yes ..." She sounded rather breathless, as if she had been running. "I did lose it once ..."

"Oh ... ?" Cara waited politely, without much interest, for the rest of the story, registering no particular surprise when it did not come.

"Would you care to sit down again, Mrs. Gage?" Her miscarriage, after all—Cara remembered—was only three months past and these middle-class women were brought up to be delicate. But Gemma smiled and shook her head.

"Thank you, no. We must really be going. Linnet ... ?"

"Are you not well, my love?" Linnet, at once, was at her most angelic.

"Perfectly. It is just rather late."

"So it is." Mrs. Colclough, who had not yet made up her mind about the wedding dress, was quick to see her excuse to get away. "Come, Uriah. You know I am uneasy at being outdoors after dark in these unsettled times. And it must be almost seven o'clock. Come, Rachel. Gather yourself together. I will let you know tomorrow, Miss Adeane—or thereabouts."

"Whenever it suits you best, madam."

Tomorrow? Polling day? Cara doubted it. Yet, as she sat behind her locked shutters the following afternoon, listening to the tumult at the hustings outside, she received a somewhat ungracious note to say that the wedding order was hers. Triumph. And richly deserved. She absolutely and utterly believed that. And with whom could she share it?

In order to avoid having her women molested in the street by men who had sold their votes for liquor she had closed her workroom for the day. Madge Percy, who had an "understanding" with the landlord of the Tory Rose and Crown, had gone off to decorate his premises with blue bunting and serve strong ale—paid for by the Larks and the Covington-Pyms—to such "undecided" voters as were able to stagger across the street from the free barrel supplied by the manufacturing Whigs. Odette had taken Liam in search of fresh air to Skipton. Or was it Knaresborough? Anna Rattrie had slipped away at first light to help Sairellen brew tea and serve bread and lard to the Chartists.

Even the grocer next door, who rarely emerged from his dingy shop, had been occupied since early morning supplying over-ripe fruit and dubious eggs to the persistent and well-paid gangs of hecklers who—using either Lark or Braithwaite money—could afford to pay his prices. Nor could she hope to see so much as a solitary customer either, for the simple reason that no lady's husband would allow her to risk his horses, his carriage, or her reputation, in Market Square until the hustings were taken down and the poll over.

Who could she talk to? She would have liked it to be Luke Thackray. "Luke—I've done it. I've got the Colclough order. I've taken it away from Ernestine Baker." But Luke had far more than his hands full, out there in the streets, with his justice and his freedom, which might lead him nowhere but prison. And Daniel. Whereas Christie Goldsborough, with whom she did not wish to share her glow of achievement but who would assuredly have understood it, had left town early that morning, so as not to declare his hand at the polls, she supposed; although she was to dine with him that evening when the votes would all have been cast and *somebody's* will had been done.

Only the dog remained, squat and ugly and almost reliably malicious as he came waddling across the room at her call, not in affection but to investigate what she might have to give him.

"All right, damned dog. Come here and listen. I've just got the order I wanted. The best one of my life. Isn't that wonderful? Well—isn't it?"

His two baleful, bloodshot eyes offered her no encouragement.

"Well it is, I'm telling you. The golden opportunity. And I'm going to make that gawky Colclough girl beautiful. That I am. For *my* sake, damned dog—not hers. Since *I'm* beautiful anyway. Don't you think so?"

Clearly he did not.

"Well, you should—foul brute—since I feed you better than they feed their children in St. Jude's."

He lay down with a heavy thud, expressing total indifference.

"And I took you in—didn't I?—when your master kicked you out?"

His master. And hers. Only rarely, these days, did she try to deny it. Miss Adeane. Dressmaker and Milliner. Woman of independence and authority in Market Square who, nevertheless, did not lose sight of the fragility of her position.

But had she ever been other than fragile, precariously balanced, her roots in shallow, treacherous soil that could so easily change to sand? She was accustomed to it. She had known worse. Seen worse. Could imagine much, much worse—dear God—*that* she could. And now, with the Colclough order in her hands and who knew how much more to come, surely her freedom from Christie Goldsborough—from any man—was not impossible. Why not? Holding the prospect on the tip of her tongue she savored it, finding it ambrosial. *Why not?* So many things could happen. One day she might even grow rich enough to snap her fingers at him as she snapped them now at his dog. Or—if that seemed unlikely—perhaps he might lose all *his* money. Or somebody might put a knife between his ribs. Marie Moon, perhaps. Or Ned O'Mara. Or any one of a hundred others who had no cause to wish him well.

How long could it be, in any case, before he took a fancy to somebody else? And, in the meantime, if she had to be his slave, then that—surely—was the lot of all women, one way or another, at one time or another; and if she could not break free, then she would employ a slave's weapons against him. She would cheat him whenever she could, wheedle out of him anything and everything she could get and steal the rest, which was no more than the system she had heard the Braithwaite and Colclough ladies telling each other they had always employed against their legally wedded husbands.

Why not? She was considering these possibilities with a certain relish as she let herself out of her house, making all secure behind her, and set off for St. Jude's Square, a black velvet cloak thrown over a gown of black lace with a white watered-silk sash and a white silk rose tucked between her breasts, her hair coiled high and pinned with a scattering of jet butterflies and pearl beads. A conspicuous figure to be walking alone at night, even for the few minutes which separated her from the Fleece, had she not also worn the unseen protection of its landlord. Goldsborough's woman who must be left alone.

And so she passed unmolested through streets already growling with peril.

The day had been tense and bitter and—if one believed half one heard of it—exceedingly treacherous, the very air, now, brooding like approaching thunder with tales of electors prevented from coming into town or if they were in town already, "persuaded" to leave it without casting a vote, as Christie Goldsborough had done; although Cara could think of no "persuasion" beyond a sizeable cash payment, which would have carried any weight with him. Yet, nevertheless, despite all threats to life and limb and reputation, there had been crowds in plenty, brass bands, processions, banners, both sides—landed against manufacturing—assembling their relatives and dependents and old retainers. The Larks and Covington-Pyms had appeared with an escort of tenant farmers, huntsmen, gentlemen of leisure or of letters, elderly clerics and classical scholars dug out of their rectories and cloisters and lecture-chambers; the Braithwaites with their mill-managers, their lawyers and bankers, their engineers and builders and such tradesmen who understood the value of Braithwaite and Colclough and Dallam custom.

A mustering of men who, no matter how loyal and true, could not be called numerous, the electoral register of Frizingley containing little more than a thousand names from a population of over thirty thousand; the day's results, fiercely scrawled in red paint on a dozen stone walls, informing Cara, as she passed by, that although 526 men had voted Whig and 522 had voted Tory, at least ten thousand others had flocked to the hustings to raise hands and voices for the Chartist cause.

They had not polled a single vote, of course, since none of them had money or property enough to qualify as electors—Cara heard them shouting as much as she hurried past the open door of the Beehive—but those thousands of Chartist hands raised at the hustings had surely put the fear of God into Whigs and Tories alike. What they had seen today was the will of the people, and they were legion, unstoppable, triumphant. What they had seen, came the answer in the precise accents of Far Flatley, was an unwashed, ill-informed rabble.

"Come on outside, lad," Cara heard a gruff yet humorous voice invite. "And I'll inform you."

Just let them keep away from her windows.

The crowd in St. Jude's Square was as heavy as market day and just as drunken, men in their Sunday best milling around still singing their campaign songs; Tories who had only lost by four votes, drawing wild conclusions as to what had happened to at least five of their electors; Whigs making it their business to resent the implication and throwing out taunts that they could afford to lose at least ten of theirs; Chartists insisting, with a resentment as yet slow-burning, that they and they alone had been victorious. The inns, which had stood open since early morning, still offering their welcome to everyone, unlikely to close now until early tomorrow when the last of the customers and the debris could be swept away all together. And forgotten, she supposed. Since tomorrow—thank God—would be a working day like any other, leaving the publicans richer, the gentry back on their ancestral acres, the manufacturers in their counting houses, at least a dozen of these "unstoppable," "triumphant" working men in jail.

Crossing the square she saw a man in front of her pick up a loose cobble and put it swiftly in his pocket. Entering the Fleece she noticed, lounging in the doorway, a young, visibly intoxicated gentleman, a minor Lark she thought, or possibly a distantly related Covington-Pym, swinging a dog-whip in his hand. From the Dog and Gun on the opposite corner there came a sudden uproar from which she could pick out the one word "Justice."

Yes. All very well. But what about her shop-windows? Would the man with the cobblestone in his pocket or the boy with the dog-whip, or all the rest of them with their pickax handles and their broken bottles spare a thought for *her* hard work and desperate effort for survival when they set about trying to slaughter each other? For their justice and freedom.

And it was with that thought in her mind that she walked into the Fleece, reached the stairs which would take her to Christie, turned on the bottom step to look back into the bar-room again—she had no idea what drew her—and saw Daniel.

He was, of course, at the center of a great, raucous, intensely joyful crowd of his supporters, spilling through the inn door and sweeping him along with them to show off their Candidate, their Champion, who would have been Frizingley's MP today by a majority, not of that puny, ridiculous four, but of many thousands had the people of Frizingley had the power to elect him. Next time, they were saying. Next time to victory. Leaping around him, jostling one another to get near him, pushing and shoving in a great, gaudy mass of color and *movement* which ended abruptly and finally—or so it seemed to her— as he detached himself from it, every other person in the throng freezing into a great stillness, so that it was only Daniel and herself who lived and breathed as he shouldered his way to the foot of the stairs and she stood there, waiting for him.

"Cara . . . ?" he said.

She held out her hand feebly, into thin air, not expecting him to take it, and said, "Daniel . . ." What else? Are you well? Are you happy? Are you in danger? But the crowd, of course, had not really ceased its ebb and flow for so much as a moment. Other hands were still tugging at his sleeves and clapping him on the shoulder, still yelling their praises at him and making their ungainly bids for his attention.

She could barely hear her thought, much less his whisper and then her own replying to it, just a candle-flame of sound in that coarsely blazing din, which soon faltered. And it was on his face, through the abrupt fading of his smile and the narrowing of his eyes, that she read the presence of Christie Goldsborough on the stairs behind her.

"Cara?" She experienced no difficulty whatsoever in hearing *his* voice. And without turning her head she felt him look at Daniel.

Was he in danger? Yes, assuredly—*now*—she believed he was.

"I see you are acquainted with our Chartist candidate."

"No. Not really."

So Judas had felt once, she supposed. But it was herself she was betraying, not Daniel, who, above all things, must not be looked at by Christie, must never, never, be brought to his notice. Never by her.

"How the eye deceives," he said. "One might almost have mistaken you for old friends."

"Lord—no." She was smiling very brightly. "Just a familiar face—from somewhere or other." And feeling as blind and dumb and disjointed as a marionette she picked up her skirts and continued up the stairs to enter the over-heated, often overpowering room, shrug off her cloak and make her curtsey—a most brilliantly polished marionette by now—to Christie Goldsborough's guest.

She had seen Ben Braithwaite many times before, waiting for his wife outside her shop with his showy, mettlesome roan horses. But neither of them cared to acknowledge it now.

She also knew him as the tight-fisted employer of Luke Thackray, the purchaser of Oliver Rattrie's cheap little soul, the lover who, having trifled with the affections of Linnet Gage, had jilted her for Magda Tannenbaum's dowry.

She did not acknowledge that either.

He knew her purely and simply as a superb piece of female flesh that he would have bought at auction, like his roan mares, and driven just as hard had she been available.

He knew of no reason to conceal it.

"So you are the lady who costs us all a fortune in silk and satin?"

Smiling, she gave him her hand, feeling no embarrassment when his eyes fastened instantly on the white rose nestling among the black lace between her breasts. No surprise either, since she had good reason to know—having measured and fitted her a dozen times—that his wife, from the waist up, could have been easily mistaken for a boy.

Let him look. It was easier than conversation. Not that such a man would have anything to say to a woman in any case. He would take his satisfactions in silence, she judged, frequently no doubt but rather fast, reserving his conversation for his own, superior sex as he was doing now, looking at her and talking to Christie about the election.

"So we have much to celebrate, Goldsborough. Only a four seat majority, I admit. And no doubt the Larks will make much of that. But we won. We got in. You did well for us there."

But he had not *voted* for them, had he, she thought? Nor for anyone else that she was aware of. No doubt he had prevented others from going to the hustings but he had not gone himself. He had neither converted that manufacturing majority of four into five nor reduced it to three, thus declaring himself as ally—as his birth dictated—of the Larks and Covington-Pyms.

"Happy to be of service," he murmured. She did not believe him. But Ben Braithwaite, she saw, did not care so long as he imagined that, whatever had been at issue, he had won.

"Aye. Very likely. So I'll drink another glass of this good old Sercial with you and be on my way. Wouldn't care to intrude—after all."

They drank. He clapped Christie fraternally on the shoulder, indulged himself with another lingering inspection of Cara's breasts, and went away well-satisfied.

"Sit down," said Christie, looking by no means disappointed himself. And, obediently and decoratively, she sat at his over-laden, over-magnificent table before his fire which burned too high, piled with enough logs, it seemed, to heat a baronial hall, drinking wine of a vintage she did not appreciate, served—to her greater discomfiture— by Ned O'Mara, who still hated her, she thought, when his head was clear enough.

Poor Ned. Another glass of this rich, rather heavy wine and every man would be her brother, every woman her sister. She would be able to weep for the entire human race, as Marie Moon often did. Perhaps—tonight—it would be just as well. Yet it was not until they had finished the turbot and wild duck and syllabub, until Ned had gone and Christie Goldsborough, showing her to a chair by the fire, had put a glass of brandy in her hand, that she felt pert enough to ask him, "So what can a fine Tory gentleman like yourself have to do with a manufacturing Whig like Braithwaite?"

He smiled through the smoke of a large and certainly expensive cigar.

"I can use him."

"It looked to me as if he thought he was using you."

"So much the better."

"What do you want from him?"

"Money, Cara."

Of course. She smiled at him, and shrugged. "Did you *really* help him today? To get his candidate elected?"

"He thinks so. Because it happened to suit me, of course. He knows that. And—as that four seat majority shows—he had need of me. I expect there must be at least five good men and true among my tenants who, if left to their own devices, would have voted Tory."

"But you made sure they didn't."

He inclined his head as if acknowledging a compliment. "Oh— nothing much to speak of. I merely did what any lord of any manor has always done—and will always manage to do. I instructed such of my tenants who have the vote how to use it. No more."

"You told them they'd be after losing their leases otherwise."

He looked very much amused. "My dear—there was no need to make explanations. They already knew the penalties—believe me. After all, which one of Braithwaite's mill-managers could have expected to keep his employment had he not followed the Braithwaite line?"

"And then you left town before the polling started and didn't use your own vote at all—to keep in with everybody."

The fragrant cigar smoke curling all around him, the firelight darkening him, adding bulk to a body already quite powerful enough, he stretched himself easily, lazily, into the warmth, and smiled.

"Ah yes. But—there again—where did I go? Ben Braithwaite certainly doesn't know, although Lady Lark just might. Perhaps I voted in another constituency."

"Could you?"

"Of course. The vote is attached to a man's property not to his person. I am one man. But my holdings in land etcetera may be numbered in their dozens. So I can vote anywhere and everywhere I own sufficient property to qualify, so long as I can get there on the appropriate day. An acquaintance of mine is entitled to vote fourteen times in fourteen different places and would gladly do so—if he had wings. He usually manages five."

And Luke Thackray, surely the most responsible man she knew, had no vote anywhere at all.

"So you helped the manufacturers to win Frizingley and then went off somewhere else to vote for the gentry, I expect. For your own kind."

"I did."

"Why? I thought you despised the millocracy."

"Oh my dear—so I do—with an absolute contempt which makes the pleasure of taking their money all the keener, I find."

"How?"

In certain moods he would tell her nothing. But now, relighting his cigar, one leg thrown over the arm of his leather chair, the other stretched out at ease on the bear-skin rug before the blazing hearth, his heavy body dominating that prime area of heat and comfort with the same total self-indulgence as her dog, he seemed almost amiable.

"Quite easily. There is a thing called civic pride, my dear, which *I* certainly do not feel and which you may never even have heard of.

But, nevertheless, I fully expect it to make me a fortune. Ben Braithwaite feels it, you see."

Civic pride? She looked at him blankly. No. It meant nothing to her.

"I am talking of Frizingley, my dear. Do you love it?"

What a ridiculous suggestion. This slag-heap? "No," she said. "That I do not."

"Exactly. Nor—I must confess—do I. Possibly I have a few boyhood memories which retain their charm. But the town as it stands today—" He shuddered. "One might call it the last place God ever made, except that God didn't make it. The Braithwaites and the Dallams and the Colcloughs did that, with their mills and their muckheaps and their pious cant. And they like it, my dear. After all, they've created it in their own image, so why shouldn't they? And, that being the case, the next step is bound to be civic pride. Just now all they can think of is setting themselves up as ladies and gentlemen, building themselves mansions in imitation—and poor imitation, at that—of what used to be mine. And improving their factories to astonish—well—if not the world then at least one another. But once that's done then somebody is bound to point out to them what a disgrace the rest of Frizingley looks compared to Leeds, say, or Halifax, or Bradford. *Somebody* is going to mention the magic words 'Charter of Incorporation,' which means having a proper town council with a mayor and aldermen and a real town hall to put them in. And if they have a town hall then they'll need a whole set of other public buildings to go with it. A brand-new Frizingley as a monument to the brand-new middle-classes. And if the first mayor—Ben Braithwaite, I rather think—can manage to get the railway line in, then he'll need a station, won't he, and very likely a station hotel. Or two. All—my dear—in the center of town. Which is the only flat land, and therefore the only decent building land, there is. St. Jude's Square. And Market Square. And then, of course, the hilly ground beyond would come in handy for all the increased business premises the railway would bring in."

He paused, and smiled.

"Who owns all that, Cara?"

"You do."

"I do. It may take ten years, of course. But when it happens I intend to be very certain that my relationship with My Lord Mayor will ensure me an excellent price. I shall probably go into the construction business, too."

She smiled back at him, rather palely.

"And what happens to the people who live here now?"

"My dear . . ." He flung out an arm in a gesture of surprise. "How can I possibly have a notion? Any more than my father had when he sold the manor lands. Although my father, of course, was a mad fool, as everybody knows. I am no fool, at any rate."

The heat of the fire suddenly incommoded her and getting up she crossed to the window for the simple coolness of the glass against her cheek, the hint of the March wind in the square outside. Yes. It would all happen as he had said. Ben Braithwaite would be powerful. And dignified. Christie would be rich. St. Jude's would be leveled into broad thoroughfares and civic palaces, its ant-hill population scattered and gone. Where would she be then? And Luke? And Daniel?

She had just ten years, according to Christie's reckoning, to make her fortune and win her freedom. And, contemplating it, she felt a sudden and most uncharacteristic flagging of her energies. She would be very tired by then.

He came up behind her, putting one arm around her waist and slipping the other hand casually between the black lace of her dress and her bare breasts.

"What is it, Adeane?" And she felt his breath as an intrusion, a small rape, down the back of her neck. "Are you looking for the Chartist candidate? *Do* confess. They say it eases the soul."

"I hardly know him, Christie." But, because she had shivered with sudden cold and knew he had felt it, she added quickly, "We met once on the boat from Ireland."

His broad hand had taken the whole of her breast now and began to caress it with a complete assurance which offended her, his other arm encircling her, pinning her against him so that the heat of his well-nourished, heavily scented, luxurious yet never indolent body seemed to scorch the whole length of her back.

"I think not, Cara." He put his mouth to the nape of her neck and even as he kissed it she could feel him smile. "It was, naturally, of interest to me to know whatever there was to know about all three candidates. Even the one who could hardly have expected to poll a single vote, and did not do so. His name—Cara? Come now, I *know* you can tell me."

"Daniel Carey."

There was no longer any point in pretending.

"So it is. And I have a creature about me at present called Oliver

240

Rattrie—as you know—who remembers him well. In particular he was able to recall for me a day when Mr. Carey called to say goodbye to you in that cottage of mine where your mother still lives. The walls of those cottages are lamentably thin and Oliver, who was living next door just then, has sharp ears in any case. The episode, even now, appears to excite him. Certainly he tells it with great relish. Could Oliver be in love with you too, Cara, do you suppose—as well as the candidate?"

"It was two years ago, Christie."

"Yes. And when you met again tonight, so romantically at the foot of my stairs, one could see in his face that to him it seemed like only yesterday."

The lace had parted now, leaving her breast exposed, covered only by his square, stroking hand.

"It seemed to me, Cara, that he loves you still. How does it seem to you?"

"What difference does it make?"

Once again she felt his mouth curving with laughter against her neck.

"My dear—that is entirely a matter for you to decide. You are a free woman. Nothing keeps you here—or anywhere else—but yourself. Would you like to go to him? Now?"

"You wouldn't let me."

And this time she could hear his laughter as well as feel it vibrating down her spine as he began to bite her nape and her shoulders very softly with his lips.

"Cara—Cara—my dear girl—*of course* I would let you go. How could I *really* stop you? The door is over there. You have only to walk through it. After all, the poor man may still be sitting downstairs in the tap-room, in his agony—thinking of you up here, just above him, with me. Go, my dear. If you want to. A flight of stairs will take you to him. Do you really think I would lift a hand to stop you?"

She shook her head, his breath all over her, her whole body trembling in his hands with cold and the fear of certain hurt to come. She knew what he was about to do to her. She knew, too, that she would submit to it. She hated him. And herself. Bitterly.

"So—having established your freedom of choice—what *would* I do, Cara? If you left me?"

Toss her back into the street, naked and hungry and unprotected as she had been before. As she had always been until he had given her this taste—this sip—of security and self-fulfillment to which all her instincts now clung as desperately as if she were drowning. Until, by showing her what could be hers, what her life might become, he had weakened her.

"Tell me, Cara?"

"You'd take my shop away."

"If you love the man, then that shouldn't matter. Should it?"

Her teeth were chattering, her tongue frozen somewhere and useless inside her mouth. She knew what he wanted her to say. How could she say it? Desperately she shook her head, trying to avoid the spoken words. But it did not suffice.

"Come, Cara—tell me. If you love him, then it shouldn't matter."

"No."

"So it follows, therefore, that you don't love him."

She closed her eyes.

"Cara?"

"Yes. It follows. I don't."

"In fact, what you love—purely and simply and with a love surpassing all others—is my money."

"Yes. I do."

Once again she felt his mouth smile against her skin.

"Good. Then we understand each other. And you, my dear, would be well advised to learn to understand yourself. You are here, Cara, with me, because you want to be here. Not because I force you or threaten you but because your dependence on my support has become so great that you cannot do without it. *That*—dear little Adeane—is the truth and the sum total of you. Is it, or is it not?"

"It is." She had not even whispered the words but had stated them flatly, dully, knowing them to be true. He turned her around in his arms and smiled at her.

"Very well. You pass the test. So come to bed with me now and if it should please you to close your eyes and think of the man you love—although not enough, of course, to leave my money for him—then you may feel free to do so."

Even that?

"It wouldn't trouble you, Christie? If I pretended you were somebody else while you were . . ."

"No. Why should it? The benefit would be mine, after all. Not his."

Absurdly perhaps, when he had already emptied her of illusion and of so many things she had deeply prized, it was too much.

"You'll go too far one day, Christie."

"I dare say. You are not the first to tell me so."

"But you will. You'll play your cat and mouse once too often. You'll make somebody too unhappy or too ashamed—you'll strip somebody too bare. More than they can stand."

"And what will happen then?"

"I don't know. I suppose somebody might kill you."

He laughed, ready to believe it, she thought, without the least sign of alarm.

"I suppose somebody might. But not you, Adeane. Not before I give you the deeds of that shop, at any rate. And since I don't mean to do that, then my life must be very precious to you, Cara. You need me, in fact. *Do* remember."

She would remember.

She was here, with him, because she wanted to be. He had given her leave to go and she had remained half-naked and trembling in his hands, pressed against him, turning as he turned her, moving as he wished to move her for his pleasure, no longer even struggling to be free. She needed him. She loathed him. He had held a mirror to her face and shown her a reflection she had no choice now but to acknowledge. Miss Adeane. Dressmaker and Milliner. For whom love might be one thing but money most certainly another.

It would be well to harden her heart now for she would not see Daniel again.

He would leave Frizingley now and never return.

Such indeed was his intention as he walked to the top of St. Jude's Street that night, shaking off the several dozen new-made bosom friends who would have difficulty, he knew, in remembering his face tomorrow.

He had every reason to leave. None to stay. And it was entirely by chance that, turning up his collar and hunching his shoulders against the raw March cold, he thrust a despondent hand into his pocket, his fingers encountering—remembering—a sharp, solid object which had been delivered to him earlier in the day. A woman's brooch in the shape of an amethyst cat, along with a note reminding him of the day on which he had first seen it, and wishing him good luck.

The news that Mrs. Tristan Gage had employed the Chartist candidate as master of the Dallam mill-school burst upon certain areas of Frizingley with the force of thunder and lightning.

Mrs. Ethel Lord, the brewer's wife, being of a charitable disposition and inclining to a view of "live and let live," preferred not to believe it. Mrs. Lizzie Braithwaite, whose daughter Amanda was married to Mrs. Lord's son, spoke sharp words, in Mrs. Lord's hearing, about foolish women who kept their heads in the sand, declaring herself more than ready to believe anything about Gemma Dallam, who—particularly since her refusal to marry Lizzie's son Ben—had struck her as decidedly odd. The result, undoubtedly, of a girlhood spent poring over books instead of her sewing. Thank Heavens *her* daughter, Amanda, who was placidly pregnant once again, had shown so little interest in learning to read.

Mrs. Maria Colclough muttered darkly of "possession" by evil demons about which her son Uriah—who increasingly had the look of a man wearing a hair shirt beneath his pure silk vest—appeared to know a great deal.

Lady Lark and Mrs. Audrey Covington-Pym looked down their high-bridged noses with the uncomprehending scorn they accorded to all the vulgar goings-on of the middle-classes.

"But the boy is beautiful," said Mrs. Marie Moon, although no one had asked her, considering that to be explanation, and justification, enough.

"Yes, indeed. There is a great deal in what you say," murmured Cara Adeane to each lady in turn, keeping her counsel as all shades of opinion began to be aired over the fabrics and fashion plates in her shop.

But Ben Braithwaite, it was felt, had expressed the collective view of Frizingley's gentlemen, had put the matter in its right and proper nutshell in fact, by declaring that the girl did not know what she was doing—what woman did?—and that her father, John-William Dallam, would soon put a stop to it.

He did not.

"The position was vacant and Mr. Carey is highly qualified," Gemma told him, her voice as matter-of-fact as she could make it, very mindful, on the surface, of her dignity as a matron of almost twenty-five years old—no giddy girl by anybody's reckoning—who had been given responsibilities she considered herself well able to fulfill.

"Aye, lass?" John-William, who had come from Almsmead on purpose to sort the matter out at his wife's urgent request, since she vowed she could face no one until he did, was in no doubt as to where *his* responsibilities lay. He had given his daughter the mill-school to play with exactly as he would have given her a pony cart. And now, if she seemed likely to make a fool of herself or to upset her mother, then he would take it away from her just as if the pony had turned out to be fractious or she had shown a tendency to drive too fast.

Twenty-five years old, married woman, or not.

"*Father.* The schoolmistress we had was ready to retire and she was hopeless in any case. She had been a governess for most of her life teaching "accomplishments" to young ladies and she had no conception at all of what these mill children need."

"And your Mr. Paddy O'Riley has, has he?"

She straightened her back and folded her hands together, small yet resolute, her feet, despite their diminutive size, planted as firmly on the ground as her father's, a man who was "large" mainly in spirit, in grit and determination, in endurance rather than inches, himself.

"His name is Daniel Carey. And the children's parents will not object to his politics since they are all Chartists already."

"Oh yes—and just what do you know about politics, my lass?"

As much as anybody, she thought. As much as *you*. But to say so, of course, would have been very unwise. She smiled, therefore, taking the edge from her voice, stating her case calmly, reasonably, with proper respect for his status and his seniority, not making the demand to which she felt fully entitled but making an appeal. Getting her way by stealth, in fact, as all the other women she knew did.

"Don't think I made the appointment lightly, father. I did take his political persuasion into account and it seems to me that it could even work to our advantage. You built the school, after all, at great expense and our main problem has always been getting children to attend."

"No problem," he said flatly, lighting one of the cigars his doctor had forbidden him and which Amabel's tearful pleading had banished at least from Almsmead. "How many children do you want? A hundred? Two hundred? Have a walk round the mill cottages and pick them out yourself as they take your fancy. All I have to do is say the word and every man in my employ will have his bairns on your doorstep tomorrow morning. You know that well enough."

"Yes, father." She sighed and then, in an effort to cover her exasperation, managed to look perplexed. "But I want them to come because they want to learn, not because they're sent."

"That's idealistic twaddle, lass."

"All right. Then I want to feel we have something useful to teach them. Something more likely to stimulate their interest and their intelligence than Miss Wren's deportment and those dreary jingles she has them singing about 'Waste not want not' and 'We are happy, poor and humble . . .' "

She had made a mistake and realized it at once.

"What's wrong with that?" inquired her father with a mildness which did not deceive. "If your Miss Wren has set herself to teach my employees' brats to be thrifty and to know their place then that's good enough for me. And good enough for them. Because there's nowhere for those brats to go, Gemma my lass, but the place to which God's wisdom has called them. My factory floor and St. Jude's."

"So the Larks and the Covington-Pyms used to talk, father, about men like you."

He grinned, puffing happily on his cigar since he knew she could not afford to betray him to her mother.

"Ah—so you want to fill that classroom with a dozen like me, do you? Then there *would* be a revolution." But he was rather flattered just the same—and deeply touched—that she should choose him as her model.

"Hardly a dozen, father. But if I could find one like you and give him a start, then wouldn't that be splendid? *I* think so. To me it would be immensely worthwhile."

"Aye." He patted her arm awkwardly, remembering the doctor's embarrassed reassurances, too hearty for comfort that of course she'd have another child. Well, there'd been no sign of it yet. It struck him, with the force of a premonition—and he was not a fanciful man—that there never would be. Poor Gemma. Married to decorative, shallow, feather-headed Tristan. It wasn't difficult to understand what that might mean to her. How she might need to reproduce her own kind; just as—married to Amabel—he'd always loved to catch a glimpse of himself in her.

"Aye, lass."

"And I'd have a better chance of doing that, surely, with a proper schoolmaster, a man of real education and experience than with these faded spinsters, like poor Miss Wren? I'd thought of keeping her on to teach sewing and housecraft, since obviously Mr. Carey can't do that. But as for the rest, if we are to have a school, father, then why not have a good one instead of the run-of-the-mill variety that *everybody* has? Why not pick out our own bright little boys and teach them to be bright young men who can help Mr. Ephraim Cook in the counting house one day? And how can Mr. Carey possibly corrupt them when they are constantly hearing the same thing from their own fathers? One might almost call it fighting fire with fire—if one wished to excuse oneself to Mrs. Braithwaite or Mrs. Colclough, that is."

He was instantly, predictably, belligerent. "And what has Lizzie Braithwaite to say to it?"

"That I'm misguided—and peculiar."

"She'd better not let *me* hear her, Gemma."

"Oh no. She won't. Because she thinks you agree with her. She's going around saying what an oddity I am for employing Mr. Carey but that there's nothing to worry about because you'll soon put a stop to it."

"Ah—she's saying that, is she?"

But in the end it was Linnet Gage and the Colcloughs who tipped the scales in Gemma's favor.

"Linnet, my dear, I find this situation most awkward," Uriah Colclough told her. "So much so that unless it should be speedily resolved, then—at no matter what personal sacrifice—I would feel it my Christian duty to disassociate myself... For the sake of my sister, Rachel, you understand. A bride whose innocence should not be troubled—forgive me—by the strange behavior of one among us who—well—must surely be aware of the error of her ways...?"

And Linnet, in something of a panic, knowing Uriah Colclough to have formed a highly personal relationship with a god he closely resembled, a prim and intensely shockable deity whose notions of "Christian duty" exactly matched Uriah's own, had gone at once and made a fuss to Amabel. Gemma, she insisted, must be protected from her own good nature, must be prevented, at all costs, from falling into the clutches of a scheming and, rather worse, a *common* man. And quickly too, before social ostracism overcame her. Before "everybody" in Frizingley began to snub her, to draw their skirts aside whenever she happened to pass as they did with Mrs. Marie Moon. To make of her, and of all those closest to her, a band of outcasts, no longer to be seen at the Assembly Rooms or the Hunt Ball.

Social death. Could Amabel survive it? Amabel certainly did not think so. But, in reducing her to a state of abject terror, Linnet also revealed herself a little too plainly to John-William, who, although he might be ready to give her a certain amount of pin-money and put up with her as a companion for his wife, had not the least intention of allowing her to interfere.

"Stuff and nonsense," he told his weeping Amabel. "I'll not turn against my daughter for the sake of an old maid in breeches like Uriah Colclough. Not for the sake of Miss Linnet Gage either. Because all that's bothering her is that he might not wed her. Which he won't—no matter what Gemma does."

"But John-William, Linnet and Uriah are absolutely devoted..."

"So they are," he said sourly, feeling far from well that morning. "Linnet is devoted to Linnet. And Uriah to Uriah. But they won't make a match of it. If he weds anybody at all then he'll go for money, like his father did. Like Ben Braithwaite. Like they all do. And *will.* And if Miss Linnet had her wits about her she'd settle for the curate or the doctor, before it's too late. It would be a kindness, Amabel, to tell her so. And while you're about it, you might as well mention that Gemma employed that Chartist fellow on my instructions. Well—he got me home from the moor that day, didn't he, when I had my attack? We owe him something. And I'd like to hear Lizzie Braithwaite questioning *my* judgment. Or that canting little Colclough."

Amabel, who had no experience whatsoever of being spoken to so sharply, had wept and then submitted. If her John-William said it would be all right then it would be. And she would just have to be especially kind to Linnet when the time came for Uriah Colclough to jilt her. She wondered if a little holiday somewhere in a warm, soft climate might be the best thing to distract the poor girl's mind? But Linnet, aware that her only chance of getting Uriah to the altar lay in persistence, by dragging on their relationship so long and getting it speculated about so widely that neither he nor his god could shirk the "Christian duty" of marrying her, was most anxious to give him no excuse to break free. Not only must she herself remain blameless and angelic, so must everyone around her. She perfectly understood that. And, Gemma's father having failed her, she turned at once to Gemma's husband.

"Tristan, you must learn to control your wife a little better, you know."

"Oh—is it really so desperate as all that, my darling? Just a storm in a stirrup-cup, maybe? The Larks and the Covington-Pyms aren't inclined to fret over it, I can tell you."

She smiled at him, coolly but very patiently.

"The Larks and the Covington-Pyms have different standards, Tristan. So, very possibly, do you and I. But if the Colcloughs find Gemma's behavior shocking, then I—my darling—have no choice but to be shocked by it too. Therefore I *am* shocked. Most deeply. It damages me, Tristan. Can you allow that?"

"Good Lord, no. Absolutely not."

"Then do keep your wife in order, my love. For my sake, and your own. The Chartist candidate is a very handsome man, they say."

Smiling easily, lazily, he threw an arm around her shoulders and hugged her tight.

"No fear. I don't think Gemma goes in for that sort of thing, you know."

"I do know. But 'knowing' doesn't matter, does it. It's what people are saying that counts. And until I'm Mrs. Colclough we'll just have to be above suspicion, won't we? Even Gemma. So help me now, Tristan darling—as you know I'd help you."

Of course he knew it. Dearest Linnet. Still the loveliest girl in the world. *He'd* never yet seen anybody to compare with her, at any rate. And when had she ever let him down? Never. She never would. But, when he saddled his new bay gelding and rode over from Almsmead to Frizingley Hall, his interview with Gemma came a day too late, producing nothing but a calm statement that the appointment of Mr. Daniel Carey had been sanctioned, in fact suggested in the first place, by her father.

"If you object so strongly, Tristan, then all I can tell you to do is have a word with him about it."

"Well—no. Perhaps not." Tristan knew, none better, how futile that would be. "But you know, Gemma, I do feel . . . Well, shouldn't you have talked it over with me first? I mean, at least mentioned it, and given me a chance to speak my piece . . . ?"

"Would *you* really have minded, Tristan—one way or the other?"

Her eyes looked very clear to him, not unfriendly but with a cool, *knowing* look about them which not only made him uneasy but reminded him far too much of her father.

"Dash it all, Gemma, of course I mind. You'll be getting yourself talked about. And that's one of the worst things that could happen to a woman—surely?"

She smiled at him, quite pleasantly, sitting well away from him, he'd noticed, in this strange little low-ceilinged parlor, made almost circular by its wide bay window, which her father had used as a smoking-room and her mother had called, for form's sake, his study. Gemma's study now, it seemed, with a gentleman's leather-topped, somewhat battered oak desk—a relic, he supposed, of the Goldsboroughs—placed solidly in the window, the tiny panes of glass making their colored reflections behind her.

"That's right, Tristan," and her voice, too, was cool and friendly, rather as if she were explaining a joke she didn't even expect him to understand. "A woman should never get herself talked about. That's one of the first things I ever learned. My grandmother was so proud of her obscurity that she even had them put it on her gravestone. 'Mary-Jane, beloved wife of Tom, who never drew attention to herself in any way.' But what they also taught me, Tristan dear, is the absolute obedience one owes to a father. And in the matter of the schoolmaster I am merely carrying out my father's wishes. Surely no one can blame me for that?"

Linnet, of course, could blame her—Tristan had no doubt about it—and did so, thoroughly and finally, when he rode back to Almsmead to report his total lack of success. Although she did not, of course, blame him.

"Oh dear," she said, smiling at him because she loved him and had always known he was not strong. "What a pity. Never mind, of course. Although you do realize, darling—don't you?—that, as her husband the law allows you to *compel* her—to ensure her obedience in just about anything you'd like her to do. Lucky for her you're not that kind of man."

He smiled down at her, loving her too, wishing he had the whole world to lay at her feet, but knowing his own limitations. As she knew them.

"Yes. Lucky for Gemma. Not so lucky for you, though, Linnet."

"I suppose not."

"I'm sorry. But I can't tackle that old man, my darling. And even if I had the courage to try—which I haven't—it wouldn't work. He'd out-fox me in the first five minutes flat."

"Of course." She laid her cool, narrow hand on his arm and leaned against him companionably, as light and fragrant as a drift of lavender. "Because he's a horrid old money-grubber. And you're a gentleman. But one should take into account, of course, that poor Mr. Dallam is an *old* man, and very far from well."

He chuckled and dropped a kiss on her lovely, passionless forehead, her "angel's brow" as Uriah Colclough called it although he had kissed it only with his eyes.

"That's right. Not well at all. So—it means you're ready to wait, then?"

"My darling, I see no alternative," she said and, returning to the house, wrote a note to Gemma full of tea-parties and dinner-parties and "I do hope you are coming over on Thursday to meet dear Mr. Adolphus Moon, who is bringing a musical friend to play the violin," followed by a rather longer note to Uriah Colclough in which she endeavored to suggest that it would be a "Christian duty" indeed, and one very likely to score heavy points in heaven, should he attempt her rescue from this house of the ungodly, where her chaste warnings had fallen on such stony ground.

And within a week or two the scandal of the mill-school had effectively blown over, helped not a little by Rachel Colclough's agonized midnight revelation that she was destined not for the wealthy Rochdale cotton spinner and lay preacher they had found for her but to become a nun; Frizingley finding ample diversion in the attempts of her mother—and Miss Cara Adeane—to nip her sudden vocation in the bud.

The wedding-invitations had been sent out, after all. The wedding-dress ordered. The Colcloughs had spent money visiting Rochdale during the courtship, which had involved new clothes, gifts to the fiancé's mother and sisters and a sizeable donation to the restoration fund at his chapel. And one could not allow such generosity to be thrown back in one's face by a hysterical girl's notion to enter not just a nunnery but presumably—since one did not find such establishments attached to Nonconformist chapels—the High Church of England.

Scandal indeed, particularly when it became clear how inextricably the pale-lipped, blank-eyed Rachel had confused her devotion to the Anglican Christ with one of His ministers, a golden-skinned young curate at the Parish church, the resulting Colclough horror providing enough entertainment to put Gemma Gage and her Chartist schoolmaster altogether in the shade.

Sending the amethyst cat to Daniel Carey had been the greatest act of daring in Gemma's life. The brooch, of course, was her own to do with as she pleased, a jewel of only moderate value which could have been given to a woman friend as a keepsake or to an obliging maidservant as a reward without arousing any particular comment. But to give it to a man who was not a servant implied a degree of intimacy which, irrespective of whether or not intimacy had ever taken place—since who cared for pale truth when one could have multi-colored scandal—could have seriously damaged her reputation and, at the very least, caused him embarrassment.

Unthinkable, of course. A type of recklessness to which she had never been prone. But when she had seen him in the street outside Miss Adeane's shop her hand had gone at once to the little cat with its amethyst body and sparkling diamond eyes, her mind emptying of all the fussy conventions and proprieties with which she had been taught to fill it, remembering solely and acutely the day in the manor garden when other people's wishes and values—not her own—had made her clumsy about inviting him into the house and had prevented her altogether from giving him her brooch.

He could hardly have noticed her, she supposed, on the other side of the shop window, with silver-and-ivory Linnet on one side of her, the tawny magnificence of Miss Adeane on the other, the self-righteous fury of the Colcloughs all around them. He could have seen no more than a blur of faces and would have been unlikely, she concluded with realism but with not a trace of self-pity, to pick out hers. Yet she had thought of him very deeply and very seriously all the way home, her reverie effectively removing her during the carriage drive and for the rest of the evening from the posturings of Linnet and the Colcloughs, who were coming to dine.

As they dined very frequently at the manor these days, she had reminded herself, in accordance with Amabel's policy of pushing "our two dear bashful little lovebirds" into the same nest.

"We must really do all we can to help them along," Amabel was always telling her. "Linnet is so devoted. And Uriah may look stern, sometimes, Gemma, I quite agree with you there, but not small minded. No, dear. He is merely rather shy. She will be such a good wife to him. And one can tell with half an eye that he positively worships and reveres her. She is an angel from heaven to him, Gemma. You must see that."

But what Gemma saw, that evening, was that beneath all his pious talk of angels Uriah Colclough was burning for the kind of access to Linnet's body which no one—except Uriah himself—could pretend to be other than acutely carnal. Whereas Linnet, despite the melting glances of encouragement she kept bestowing upon him and all the clever ways she had of sitting with her bare shoulders in a pool of candlelight, was not only revolted at the mere idea of his touch but, if she ever managed to become his wife, would do everything in her power, on every possible occasion, to avoid it.

What Gemma saw was hypocrisy which could lead only to misery. Lives built on little but self-deception which could so easily crumble. Was her own so very different? Self-deceptions, one upon the other like bricks building up into a cloister wall. Self-denials and petty restrictions, a multitude of rules and regulations with which to fill one's hours and days, as her mother did.

She had wished to be free of that. Had schemed her own brand of scheming in order to achieve her measure of freedom. Yet how far had she really succeeded? How firmly did the straitjacket of her childhood still crush her? Only a little over two years ago it had prevented her most effectively from making a simple gift to a man who had certainly deserved it. Just how thoroughly, she wondered— if at all—had she discarded that straitjacket now? She had gone up- stairs, written her note to Daniel Carey, unpinned her brooch and put the two together in a neatly sealed parcel. What next? Where to send it? And even if she had an address she would be unlikely to use it. She would find it as impossible, she told herself, as it had been impossible, two years ago in the manor garden, to hold out her hand, the brooch already in her palm, and say in an open, friendly, *natural* manner, "It would please me so much if you would keep this, Mr. Carey, to remember me by."

Impossible.

And then. "Martha-Ann," she had called out, summoning the sharp-eyed, clear-headed girl who kept house for her now that Mrs. Drubb had gone to Almsmead. A girl who knew on which side her bread was buttered and whose family lived in St. Jude's.

"Yes, madam?"

"I wonder if you would know how to get this little parcel to the Chartist candidate?"

"Yes, madam." There had been no hesitation, no show of surprise. No explanations either.

She had thought it wise, then, to forget the matter as best she could. Possibly the parcel would never reach him. And even if it did, then what could it mean to him? He would be unlikely to do more than write her a line. What more, in fact, did she want of him? Nothing at all. Her action may have been foolish but had had very little, when she examined it closely, to do with him. It had been for herself. A small exercise of her power to choose. Which made it quite unnecessary for her to see him. Much better not. But when he called, the day after the election, her gladness was so immediate, sprang so naturally to her, that it did not even take her by surprise.

Of course she was happy to see him. And why not? *Why not?* Therefore, with a sensation of unusual lightness, a feeling of casting off winter garments and breathing through open pores, perhaps dangerously bare skin, she told him so. Nor was there any hesitation, this time, in inviting him into her drawing-room now that everyone had returned to Almsmead, leaving her—if only in their absence—the mistress of her own words and deeds.

She was a married woman, after all, permitted to know more of life than the pressing of dried flowers in tea-table albums. He was a man still ruled by impulse whose need that morning had been to escape from the hurt of remembering Cara Adeane on the tavern stairs with Christie Goldsborough's hand on her shoulder. It had not surprised him. He knew the man by reputation and had he allowed himself to draw up a list of her possible lovers he supposed Goldsborough's name would have been on it. Braithwaite. Colclough. Lord. Goldsborough. What difference did it make which one of these substantial citizens of Frizingley possessed her, since he did not?

He would do well now to harden his heart.

He had lain awake in Luke Thackray's narrow bed for most of the night convincing himself of that. She had made her choice. And if he could not respect it, then at least—God help them both—he understood. But, as for himself, when morning came, pale gray and cold-eyed, no doubt cold-hearted, through the sparsely curtained window he watched it for what seemed a long, black time, listening to the army of clogged feet on the cobbles outside, the blaring of factory hooters calling to one another like ships in a fog-bound sea, knowing that—as so often before—he had made no choices, reached no decisions as to where he wished to go.

The election was over. He had done what he had been sent here to do. Had scored a triumph, in fact, for both the Charter and its People, or so they had all been telling him last night, although the taste of it now, in his waking mouth, bore an uncomfortable similarity to ashes. And this morning who would really care to know him? He was the Chartist candidate no longer, just a wandering Irishman with a twinkle in his eye, perhaps, but a black shadow on his soul, who felt himself to be fit for nothing else—at the moment—but to wander.

Very well. He would pack and go. He was used to that. What else had he been doing, after all, for much more than half his life? And, when all was said and done, the redoubtable Mrs. Sairellen Thackray would see no sense in burdening herself with him now.

Back to London, he supposed. Where else? To write articles about freedom and justice which would never come to pass—he was suddenly very certain—in his lifetime. Probably never. Although that was no reason to give up the fight. What else had he to do, after all?

Leave, then. It would take him no more than a few practiced minutes to get his shirts and linen and brushes together and slip away. A brisk walk across the moor to the nearest station, a train to Leeds and then ...? Wherever his fancy took him. Liverpool and then to Ireland? Or South to his desk at the *Northern Star*, which would not stay empty long if he should not hurry back to claim it? Or just any train which happened to be standing ready on the first platform he came to? He had done that before. But first he would put a note through Mrs. Adeane's door for Cara, wishing her well, asking her to forgive him, forgiving her, saying ... Christ, what did it matter? Saying anything.

And then there was that funny little brown girl who had sent him a jewel. Ought he to return it? She might be worrying herself half to death by now about what he'd do or say about it, whom he'd tell—since she hardly knew him—and it would be a kindness to put her mind at rest. For although he had long ago rejected the values of his own middle-class boyhood he still remembered them. Poor little brown girl. She'd be a social outcast, among her own kind, if he let it be known what she'd done. And since a note might all too easily fall into the wrong hands—her husband's for instance, or her father's—then it seemed only decent to go himself and reassure her that she was perfectly safe with him.

Ten minutes, he'd thought, at the most, unless her husband was at home, in which case, since the man would very likely recognize him as the Chartist candidate, he'd have to brazen it out, say he was calling to take leave of everybody in the constituency, and hope they didn't set the dogs on him.

But Gemma had been alone. As plain and sturdy as he remembered her, brown eyes, brown skin, brown hair coiled smoothly but very simply—too simply, by his reckoning—on her strong, short neck; twenty-five years old he estimated, since he was now twenty-six; and looking older—not with the brittle sophistication of Cara, but with a composure he found too matronly—too soon. Yet her welcome had been warm, its spontaneity surprising him and then giving him pleasure as he saw how it took the years away from her.

"Mr. Carey, I am *so* happy you felt able to call. And if you have any thought of returning my brooch, then I must warn you that it will offend me. And since I am sure you cannot wish to do that, then please come inside and take some refreshment."

He had followed her, her frank, pleasant manner telling him plainly that no reassurance had been needed. She had trusted him. Rightly, of course. But how had she known that? And as he sat in the long, low drawing-room full of venerable oak pieces polished alike by beeswax and antiquity, dark brown shadows falling across the stone floor between dappled pools of light, he had felt deep-rooted memories of ease and contentment stirring within him.

His mother's house had been like this, very old and dim and quiet, low rooms opening one from the other with no particular plan or purpose; stone-cool in summer, cozy nests of wood smoke and the scent of winter hyacinths in the bad weather. He had grown up—or very nearly—surrounded by scarred oak cabinets and Persian rugs the color of brick dust and varnish like these; by massive copper bowls reflecting the firelight, and small window-panes of thick, flawed, jewel-tinted glass shutting out an ancient, always slightly overgrown garden.

He was at ease here. At ease, too, with this girl—he could not think of her as a woman—who so exactly matched her surroundings. He told her so. Why not? For although he remembered this world of hers and all its petty obsessions it had no hold in him, no power to prevent him from speaking as he pleased.

Except that, every now and then, nothing pleased him.

He told her that too. She nodded sagely, with quiet understanding. And when she began to speak of her school it was the steady, sustained intelligence in her face, the quietly ardent nature of her enthusiasm, her even more quietly ardent need for personal expansion, experiment, adventure, which held his attention.

The woman, far more than the undertaking.

"Would you like to come and see it?"

Not really. He knew what "ragged-schools" looked like and did not expect this to be any different. Sore-eyed urchins slumped half-asleep on what amounted to workhouse benches, with no thought of learning but simply because it was warmer than playing, half-naked as most of them were, in the street. No different from Sunday schools, he remembered, except that Sunday-school children were required to wear boots or shoes and to wash their hands.

Could an industrial school, built to comply with reforming ideals in which the industrialists themselves did not believe, show him more than that? A few clean pinafores, perhaps, on a few little girls who might well be mothers themselves before they had learned to read. A few little lads in well-darned trousers who would be in the Dallam mill, working cumbersome and dangerous machinery before their bones were fully grown.

Yet he wanted to please her.

"*Do* come, Mr. Carey. Unless you have an urgent train to catch, that is? I have so many plans and, as a schoolmaster yourself, you must be able to advise me."

He doubted it. His own teaching experience—none of it recent—having involved the preparation of young gentlemen for public school by cramming them with large doses of Greek and Latin.

He told her that too and she smiled at him calmly, hardly listening, her mind leaping ahead as her father's always did whenever he saw something he wanted and was on the brink of working out how best to get it.

"I am not totally naive, Mr. Carey. I know that most of the children who come to school can hardly wait for the home-time bell to ring. But not all. And when one considers the tedious lessons to which they are submitted—all that dreary chanting of the alphabet without the least conception that those letters can be made into *literature*. *Poetry*. Then who can blame them? And I doubt if education for girls is taken seriously anywhere in the world. Certainly not in Frizingley. The charity-schools teach them nothing but darning and mending. The workhouse schools prepare them for domestic service. In the kind of school young ladies such as myself are likely to attend it is fine embroidery and domestic service of another fashion. Yes, yes— I know that many girls find this more than sufficient. But some do not. And since I cannot believe that intelligence of the academic variety is confined exclusively to the male sex of the upper classes—no matter what upper-class gentlemen may have to say to the contrary— then I *know* I can find quick minds to educate. Both boys and girls."

"Few upper-class gentlemen would thank you for it, Mrs. Gage."

"Ah well." And her brown eyes had suddenly looked very clear to him, sparkling with a humor that seemed almost to be impish. "If they dislike the competition—these gentlemen—they will just have to work a little harder. Won't they?"

"If you have set your mind on it, Mrs. Gage, then I do believe they will."

"It is my dream, Mr. Carey—to give these children at least a *chance*."

But when, having taken him to inspect her sore-eyed, undernourished, very sleepy little dream, she had asked him to help her convert it to reality, he had answered with a peal of incredulous laughter.

"Mrs. Gage, I am a feckless, footloose Irishman. A Catholic by birth and a Chartist revolutionary by inclination. How can you think of letting me loose on these innocent, Protestant, factory children? And even if I accepted your offer both your husband and your father would feel very much obliged to chase me out of town, for your protection."

"Mr. Carey." And once again her eyes had looked clear and very steady. "Will you make a bargain with me? If I can persuade my father—and my husband, of course—to agree to this, then will you allow me to persuade you?"

Impulse. But so had he always lived. In essence there seemed no difference between this and boarding the first train out of Leeds station. He had encountered the train here, instead, in Frizingley where as yet there was no railway track, a circumstance which would have greatly appealed to his sense of the extraordinary had it not been for Cara.

His one clear aim had been never to see her again and he knew he could not avoid her in a town which, although choked by layers of population—native, immigrant vagrant, one on top of the other—was small in area. Therefore, when Mr. John-William Dallam so astonishingly handed over to him the keys of the school and the snug two-roomed house attached to it, he steeled himself to visit her, advising her beforehand of his intention, so that when he arrived her mother was beside her and—clearly at Cara's command—did not leave them alone together for a moment throughout a scrupulously polite, exceedingly painful half hour.

"So you have turned schoolmaster again, Daniel."

"One takes what comes to hand. I don't expect it to last long."

"No. I expect not."

He saw that she was living in cramped but comfortable surroundings. Luxury, he knew, for her. He saw that she was busy. In control. Beautiful. A woman who seemed the natural extension of the girl he had met on the open deck of a boat from Ireland. *His girl*. Not his woman, of course, although the certain knowledge of that did not stop him from wanting her.

"Is the shop doing well?"

"It is. For its size. And as soon as I can get rid of the miserable old skinflint of a grocer next door it will be doing better. The moment his lease is up then out he goes, down comes the dividing wall and *I* move in."

"Yes. Very good."

"Yes. So when you are headmaster of a public school, Daniel, send your wife to me and I'll dress her like a queen."

"I doubt if any schoolmaster can afford a queen, Cara."

"No. I suppose not."

He left her, feeling bruised, exhausted, finding the schoolhouse almost a refuge although he did not plan to hide, nor even to go on asking himself why he had taken this step. He was here. He had agreed to it and had no intention of letting that brave little brown girl down. He would apply himself, therefore, to discovering those bright, quick minds she wanted, no easy task and one which gave him little pleasure, since his instincts were not scholastic, his patience by no means inexhaustible, his knowledge of working-class children below the working-age of nine even less than he had imagined.

Miss Wren, his predecessor, had done little more than hand out scraps of material to the girls and slates to the boys, setting the male sex to practising their letters, the female to hemming and tacking and stroking gathers. A realistic goal it began to seem to Daniel when his first attempts to instill into them a spirit of inquiry were met by an apathy which may well have stemmed from undernourishment and overcrowding, but which struck him as impenetrable nonetheless.

But. "I know you will succeed, Mr. Carey," Gemma Gage told him.

He doubted it. Was success of the kind she envisaged even possible with these little mites who seemed in far greater need of good beds and good dinners and a motherly woman with *time* for hugs and kisses and to delouse their heads and wipe their noses, than a man like himself with a short temper and a classics degree? And further-more, as he quickly discovered, children of that age bored him. Yet he had stated publicly and loudly, over and over, his belief in the right of every child to an education. Of what use, after all, would be the People's Charter to a people who could not read it and who, having won the right to vote and make laws, could not write them down? Education—how often had he said it?—was the best weapon a man had against exploitation, an essential ingredient of the Liberty and Equality he so prized. And so now, being faced with the raw material of humanity and the sadly tedious business of instructing it not in the glorious Rights of Man but the Alphabet, what else was there to do but get on with it as best he could?

He worked hard. Hating the routine, of course, as he'd always hated it. Deciding, more often than not, that he was wasting both time and talent. But he had done that often enough before—too often, he knew full well—and although he had no intention of staying long, never losing for a moment the sense of those trains steaming in and out of their stations, ships gliding smoothly from their moorings, he nevertheless delayed.

He owed her that. Steady, quiet-eyed, *hopeful* Mrs. Gage, the very portrait of strait-laced middle-class womanhood, whose audacity in employing him had aroused his curiosity. And, having glimpsed the beautiful husband, the stern father, the exquisite, ambitious sister-in-law, the child-mother in her background, she had also aroused his compassion. Poor little brown girl. How could she be happy with them? And if this was the only escape she could find, then he—who understood escape—would do all he could to help her.

Not much, he supposed. And not for long. But what he could.

Inevitably he saw a great deal of her. She came, quite regularly, to read aloud for a valiant hour or two from the story books of her own childhood. She came, sometimes, on cold mornings, with cans of hot soup packed in hay boxes or, when March and April had turned to a warm Spring, a dusty, stifling June and July, with baskets of oranges and lemons. Every Friday evening he spent an hour at the manor in the little circular parlor she used as a study, reporting to her on the week's progress or lack of it, acquainting her with the names and natures of any new children—coloring it all with the vivid paint-brush of his imagination, for her pleasure, when the reality seemed too pale—while she, sitting behind her battered oak desk, listened intently, never giving him orders but making suggestions, asking his advice and often reading into it innovations *he* had never thought to make; deeply and seriously interested in everything he had to say.

And whenever she invited Mr. Ephraim Cook, the mill manager, and his wife to dinner—perhaps twice a month—along with a few other academic or musical or "social reforming" guests to whom Linnet and her mother referred as "Gemma's oddities," she would include Daniel too. Delighted—as she made no secret—to have him at her table. Delighted to see him welcomed by her other friends, most of whom she had met through the Ephraim Cooks, as one of themselves. Delighted, above all—he could see it very clearly—to have this new circle of acquaintances who were exclusively her own, on no more than nodding terms with her mother and not even that with Linnet.

But they were not alone together for any appreciable length of time until an evening toward the end of August, a Friday when, coming as usual with his weekly report and looking forward to presenting it this time, since he had unearthed, at last, a boy with a talent for drawing and a girl whose mathematical memory had astonished him, he found her as usual in her little circular office. Quietly awaiting him. Accustomed to waiting. Trained for it, as all women of her class were trained to sit placidly, passively indoors, ready to make the best of whatever was brought to them from the real world outside. And because tonight his news was good—although he needed her to tell him to what use a girl pupil might put a mathematical gift—he could hardly wait to lay it at her feet with all the flourish he could contrive.

She deserved it. Not that it would amount to much in the end, he supposed. Unless the boy could be diverted from drawing trees and flowers to engines and industrial machines. Whereas the girl, who came from a desperate family in St. Jude's Passage, must certainly be destined for the mill at nine and maternity at thirteen unless Mrs. Gage should bring about some drastic alteration. Could even she, with those steady brown eyes, convince a family of half-Irish tinkers that one of their *girl*-children deserved a higher education? He would give a great deal to be present when she tried.

"You look very pleased with yourself, Mr. Carey."

He began to tell her why, noticing, not quite at once, that she was dressed to go out yet seemed in no hurry to do so.

He paused. "Am I detaining you?"

"Oh no. I was to dine at the Jacob Lords but Amanda has had her baby sooner than expected. I was already dressed when the message came. Fortunately my cook is very even-tempered and doesn't *seem* to mind getting something ready at a moment's notice."

And so engrossed did they become in their conversation, so pleasantly did the time pass, that it seemed entirely natural to them both when she invited him to take pot-luck with her in the dining-room.

"I have given cook carte-blanche, I must warn you, so it could be anything from Yorkshire puddings to Irish stew."

"Or both together?" he said. "They might blend very well. Why not?"

And because he had meant nothing by it, because it had been merely the first thing that came into his head, he did not remember, until later, that she blushed.

The table, of course, was exquisitely arranged with the crystal and silver to which Gemma had been accustomed every day of her life, the meal turning out not too badly to be mutton chops in onion sauce, cold custard tart, fruit-cake and cheese, quality and quantity filling up the spaces where imagination had been lacking. And since Daniel kept no regular meal-times, eating when the opportunity presented or simply when he happened to remember, he was able—to her evident pleasure—to do her food full justice.

"Do have a little more, Mr. Carey." She served him herself, heaping his plate with tart and cream, as anxious to nourish him as so many other women in so many other places had been. He knew the signs. His lean, dark looks, his air of hungers never really stilled, appetites never fully satisfied, had always tended—to one degree or another—to make women want to heal and nurture him. He knew—with those other women—where it had led and how it had ended. Yet, because this was the serious-minded, faintly unhappy, admirably well-intentioned, thoroughly responsible Mrs. Gage, he did not believe it could come to that.

He knew, of course, that sending him her brooch had been a gesture not lacking its element of romance. He also knew—how could he not?—that her interest in him contained its whisper of an attraction which seemed appropriate to a woman who had been reared in total ignorance of her sensuality and taught, instead, to replace it with sentiment. The feeling, he supposed, that some medieval lady in her ivory tower might harmlessly extend to a knight-errant. A kind of dalliance, no doubt. And yes, there had been times, lately, when he *had* flirted—slightly, easily, because it came naturally to him. But touching her had never crossed his mind. He did not believe it had crossed hers.

And, in that case, being perfectly willing to play any role she might allot him, knight-errant or wandering minstrel or court jester, whichever should please her best, he allowed himself to bolt his food with a schoolboy relish he knew—because the other women had told him—to be charming, relaxing readily into the atmosphere she created. The house which she had made *her* house, the warm, dim room with its unexpected pools of light scattered like green and topaz and purple jewels through those shadows of deep, polished brown. Her brown hair so neatly parted, so plainly coiled on her short neck, her shoulders looking small and square, not fragile in the least but nevertheless vulnerable above the low neck-band of a brown satin dress embroidered, here and there, with fleurs-de-lys in gold.

Her brown eyes watching him, steadily, as he watched her; a quietness falling.

"What a pretty dress," he said rashly to break that quietness, although he knew "pretty" was not the right word for it. Handsome, he supposed. Unusual, with that coppery sheen to the material, the simple, probably beautifully cut skirt and wide sash with its golden lilyflowers making her waist—now that he looked at it—seem smaller, the wide, puffed sleeves giving an almost fashionable droop—that air of vulnerability, he supposed—to her shoulders.

A dress which softened the resolute stiffness of her little body and which had a plainness he recognized as elegance.

"It suits you perfectly."

He had never paid her a compliment before yet she took it very calmly.

"Thank you. It is not at all new. Heavens—it must be the first dress Miss Adeane ever made me."

"Ah . . ." He should have thought of that. Too late now, though. She had seen the recognition in his face, heard his exclamation; although there was no reason, after all, to suppose him unacquainted with his fellow Irish. More surprising if he were not.

"Do you know Miss Adeane?"

"Yes." To lie would be to make more of it than was strictly needful. "And her family."

"Family?" Leaning an elbow on the table, her chin on her hand in a gesture of friendliness and spontaneity—almost of familiar ease—Gemma was greatly interested. "How amazing. In fact, I rather think, how *sad*. I have known Miss Adeane for something like three years now without being aware that she had a family. I always assumed her to be—well—*alone*."

Had she meant, "I assumed her to be *free of all that*," he wondered? But then, did she know the private circumstances of her own parlormaid or the dour man who drove her carriage? Probably not.

"No. She has her mother with her."

"Does she really?"

"Oh yes—a rather pretty and very tender-hearted little Frenchwoman who does exactly as her daughter says . . ."

"But that is Madame Odette, who is in the shop sometimes . . ."

"Yes. Mrs. Adeane's name is Odette." Seeing her delight in this glimpse through Cara's back door, there seemed no harm in giving her full measure.

"But how extraordinary. I had simply no idea they were mother and daughter. They are not alike."

"No." He would have to talk about Cara eventually, he supposed, to someone. Why not prove to himself now that he could do it with calm? "I suppose Miss Adeane must resemble her father, although I have never met him. He ran off to America some years ago and left the three of them stranded . . ."

"Three?"

"Yes." He had not intended to tell her this. Nor did he wish to do so now. It was simply that he felt an even stronger wish not to deceive her. And he trusted her too. "Miss Adeane has a son—about five years old."

"And her husband?"

He listed his shoulders in a brief shrug.

"Oh—I believe he may have died."

She smiled, her eyes very steady again. "And I believe you think me incapable of understanding, without recourse to my smelling-bottle, that she may never have married at all. I am hardly so naïve, Mr. Carey."

"I am very glad to hear it, Mrs. Gage."

"So Miss Adeane must have suffered hard times—unbearably so. Except that I am sure she has always somehow managed to bear it—courage being one of the first things one understands about her."

It had been the first thing he had understood about her too. Instantly. Along with the hot leap of his desire, which had never eased.

"Yes. She is very brave."

"And things are going well for her now—surely?"

"I believe so, Mrs. Gage."

"I *hope* so. I have always liked her. And admired her too. I can't pretend to understand the difficulties she has had to face. I only wish I could. But I can be very glad of her success. It cheers me, I can't tell you how much, that a woman—alone—should be capable of such a thing. Unless . . . ? She *is* alone, I am assuming . . . ?"

"I beg your pardon?"

She smiled again, frankly, the clean, open nature of her honesty taking his breath away.

"No, Mr. Carey. I beg *your* pardon, for I have asked an indiscreet question—as you have so rightly reminded me. One which your code as a gentleman may not permit you to answer. I understand that. But I know very little of Miss Adeane's world. And whereas—believe me—I am not concerned with vulgar curiosity, I have often wondered . . . ? Miss Adeane is very beautiful. Fascinating, in fact. You have confirmed, as I suspected, that she arrived here penniless and unprotected. In *my* world such a girl would have no choice but to look for a man to marry her—any man. Probably an old one, since they are usually the only kind who can afford to buy youth and beauty. In effect—in *my* world—such girls can find no solution but to sell themselves for a position in society. A roof over their heads. A little pin-money. And, even taking into account that young ladies of my sort are trained only to be decorative and idle and are actively discouraged from making themselves useful... Well—can it have been so totally different for Miss Adeane, who is capable, I am sure, of turning her clever hand to anything? Mr. Carey, is true independence really possible for a woman—in either Miss Adeane's world or mine?"

"No," he said. With clarity. And regret.

"I am so sorry," was her answer.

"Yes. So am I." He had always believed a woman's life to be unenviable. Now, through her eyes, he saw it to be frightful.

"Poor Miss Adeane," she said. "So she has a—what does one call it?—a protector? Someone rather powerful, I suppose. And rich. No, no—please don't tell me his name. In a town of this size I must surely be acquainted with him. Or with his wife. And I should not wish to start disliking him more than I may well do already. Does she care—at all—for him?"

"She would hardly confide in me, Mrs. Gage. But I am sure she does not."

"Oh dear, I *am* so sorry. It seems to have meant rather more to me than I knew—thinking of her going about her own business in her own fashion, answerable to no one. She had always seemed so free. So unfettered."

"She can have had little choice," he told her quietly. "Only between sexual submission or destitution. And with a child to think of, what choice is that? I would have done the same, in her shoes. Who would not?"

It eased his heart to say it.

"You are quite right, Mr. Carey." There was no hesitation in her at all. "It merely seems to me quite terrible that she should lack the securities and luxuries of my world, yet still be subject to the same captivities. I had thought—*at least*—that she would have had the compensation of freedom. I have never suffered hardship in my life and so I cannot judge what the fear of it might do to me. But I have been obliged, so very often, to *plan*—to make arrangements—and careful ones, in order to get myself what has amounted to a measure of fresh air to breathe. I have had to *obtain by stealth*, I suppose, instead of simply asking, or taking, or stating my intentions. And not very drastic intentions either. Just the ordinary happenings of daily life. It saddens me immeasurably that a woman like Miss Adeane must do the same."

Her small hand lay palm down on the table and, with a movement that was purely instinctive, he put his own hand over it, his touch banishing restraint between them, sending it scuttling away over the far shadows like the false creature that it was. He held her hand because it seemed right to him. She did not draw her hand away.

"I know," he said. "I believe I have always thought so. You are a captive species."

"Why, Mr. Carey?"

She was asking him to be eloquent and it was an invitation he rarely declined.

"Because we desire you, I suppose. Which makes us afraid of losing you. So we can have no peace of mind until we have put you in chains. And then—there's no denying—you can somehow manage so easily to make us feel small when we are so anxious to be big. Because those of you who do rise above the petty goals we set you become far more truly adult—it seems to me—than men ever do. A man will sacrifice himself to get his name in the history books. Quite readily. It takes a woman, I think, to sacrifice herself unseen, unsung, knowing she won't even be thanked for it because Society has cast her in the role of sacrifice. So all she's doing, according to society, is her duty."

"Yes, Mr. Carey." He had never received more ardent encouragement to go on.

"I suppose it is the same everywhere. In my country, when famine strikes, it is the women who die first because—as a matter of course—they give their food to their children. You would do that, Mrs. Gage. So would Cara Adeane. *I* might succeed in convincing myself that I had much better stay alive and get a law passed—or start a revolution. In your country—*here*—your father employs women in his weaving sheds, not men, because women will work for even less than Irish wages, just so long as they can get their children fed. He knows that. He also recognizes it, I imagine, as a kind of courage and maturity few men possess. Which is probably why—forgive me—he keeps your mother a child, so she cannot challenge him. Men have created themselves a society, Mrs. Gage, in which we force you into a position of inferiority and then despise you for being inferior. Which makes you horribly dissatisfied. And very resentful of us. We have enslaved you for our own pleasure and find very little pleasure in it at all. Because we want you to love us—God help us—and slaves don't love. They cheat and deceive and grow sly. It is a natural result of servitude. They plot against us. They 'obtain by stealth.' They become small-minded and petty and childish and lazy. They marry us for the money we have passed laws to prevent them from earning. They sit about all day on sofas with smelling-bottles. They mock us. We grow cruel and blame them for it. The fault is ours. Do you understand me?"

"I do." She had spoken her wedding vows less fervently.

"And it is wrong, Mrs. Gage. I am against all this talk of man and woman, class and creed and nation. I am against anything which divides us. We are people. Just that. Each one of us to be judged only on our merits, not by the labels society has put upon us. I was not born to live in a cage and neither were you. I believe I was born to grow. And I must fight anything which stunts me or stifles me. So must you. All of us. Perhaps we were born to free ourselves of prejudice and the obsession with saving our own souls which makes us so narrow and mealy-mouthed and petty. Perhaps we were born to save and to free one another. I would like to think so.

Swept along by the flow of his own words he squeezed her hand hard, in a spirit of whole-hearted camaraderie and, hearing the clock strike, they got up both together, their hands still joined so that inevitably he drew her very close to him and held her a moment, as he would have held any other comrade, in his arms. A declaration of spiritual unity, until he suddenly understood the soft, dove-yielding of her little body, all its stiffness gone, the look of rapturous drowning on the small brown face she lifted up to him to be kissed.

There was no doubt. None whatsoever. Every line of her body and of her drowning face spoke to him with a voice he recognized. He knew her to be helpless and overwhelmed by entirely natural forces within herself of which *he* had never been ashamed but which she, surely, did not understand. The same sweet delirium of physical desire to which he had surrendered many a time, losing his head gladly and completely, for as long as desire prevailed. Since he was a man, after all, to whom "consequences" need not matter.

He had regretted nothing. So far as he knew he had done no harm. The last thing he wanted was to harm this woman, now.

This woman, least of all.

Yet her face remained lifted toward him, small and smooth and impossibly enraptured, waiting with the hushed and almost terrifying intensity of an initiate before a shrine, for an act of revelation. Although the reality—he knew—could hardly match the expectation.

To kiss her could only be to confuse and distress her, to give a harsh jolt she would not, afterward, find welcome to her fragile world and her own uncertain place therein. Not to kiss her would be rejection.

Rejection, it seemed to him, would be the most cruel. For both of them. Therefore he kissed her, gently, hesitantly, paying homage to her womanhood rather than seeking to possess it until her lips, opening readily, made direct appeal to his body in which—being healthy and only twenty-six years old—desire could be quickly kindled.

She was young. Her scents were fresh and wholesome and delicate. She had his respect. His *liking*. Suddenly, in full awareness of her well-muscled, sturdy, resolute limbs, her well-nourished stamina and endurance, she seemed so frail in his arms that he was terrified.

He must not hurt this girl.

And therefore when the long kiss ended he said, breathlessly, rapidly, so that she might think the passion, the loss of control, the instigation, had really been his, "Please forgive me. If I have offended you . . ."

The conventional words. The polite formula. He could think of no other.

"*Can* you forgive me?"

"Oh please . . ." she whispered. "Don't say that. Please. Don't even think of it again."

That too was what women said, had been taught to say, on these occasions. Even when their hearts were overflowing, their values shaken, their senses dizzy and timidly ecstatic as hers now were. When something momentous, that would disturb and unsettle her for a long time, had overtaken her.

He had done no more than kiss a pleasant, willing girl. She had broken the most serious taboos of her class and of her conscience.

Forget it, she had told him.

Please don't think of it again.

Very likely. And it might well be that tomorrow he would find the sounds of those trains and boats more than ever enticing. He was far too honest not to admit that.

But a tame agreement to forget, never to think of it again, was far less than he owed—far less than he wanted to give—to this girl. And if he gave her nothing else then, at the very least, he could convince her that she had been truly desired, that he had kissed her in a pure, white-hot passion—as he had first kissed Cara—rather than the far more muted and complex temperature of his real reasons. Whatever they had been.

"No," he said, drawing her close to him again, making his voice unsteady and wilder, he hoped, than she had bargained for. "Don't ask me that."

"Mr. Carey . . ."

"No—no," he repeated. "I may never take the liberty again—if that's what you're telling me. But what I won't do—and don't want to do—is forget."

She awoke early the next morning and lay for a long time listening to the sounds of the manor garden, in a state of frank and considerable astonishment. She was in love with Daniel Carey and what amazed her was her happiness. Joy. Incredible joy. No shame whatsoever. No sorrow either. Not yet. Although—being somewhat less innocent than he had supposed—she knew he did not love her. And, in any case, since every possible social and legal and moral barrier separated them, then for his sake she ought also to be glad that he did not.

Nothing could come of it. Nothing real, that is, or lasting. Better then just to savor it while the taste remained so sweet. Better just to accept it naturally, passively, without resistance or recriminations. It had happened. Why reproach herself this morning when, assuredly, she had loved him yesterday, a month ago, perhaps much longer. And she had blamed herself for nothing then.

She would simply continue. Go on. Content—for the moment—just to *feel*, to gaze at the miracle without any urgent need to touch. As she would not have disturbed a closely-curled, new-born child. Thus would she walk on tiptoe for a while around her love, cradling it in silence and in secret, brushing heat and cold and noise and every speck of dust away from it with a vigilant hand. Keeping it safe from the outside world of harm. And it if turned out that it had been born to grow—or she had . . . ? If he and she might grow—in some way that gave no pain to anyone else—together?

She doubted it.

Was she even equipped, after these dry, dutiful years, to cope with so rich a flood?

Probably not.

Better then just to *continue*. To tread warily. To find a way of loving him from which only good might come. *His* good, most of all. Even if it meant giving him up.

Could she really doubt that it would come to that?

Yet she ordered her carriage later that morning and drove to Miss Adeane's shop in Market Square simply to be in the presence of someone who was acquainted with Daniel, someone whose accent resembled his, whose childhood memories were of the same green Irish meadows, someone who may even have the familiar use of his Christian name as she, as yet, did not.

Not, of course, that he could be spoken of or even hinted at. Particularly not in this crowded, well-nigh frantic room in which the whole of the Colclough wedding party appeared to be assembled, the virginal Rachel still rather more inclined to be a bride of Christ than of a Rochdale cotton spinner; Mrs. Maria Colclough with her mind still fixed firmly on the *expense*; and all eight bridesmaids including Linnet Gage, who had driven over from Almsmead to be fitted for yet another supporting role she did not wish to play and who, as the thorn in the side of Uriah Colclough's self-imposed chastity, had long since fallen out of favor with his mother.

Therefore she was not pleased to see Gemma, who was rich, married to the most beautiful man in the world—her own darling brother—and two years younger than herself. Nor was Gemma pleased to see Linnet, being at once too closely reminded of Tristan, with whom love had never been a possibility, and of her inescapable duty to Amabel, her mother.

But. "Darling," they said, "how lovely—what *luck*—to see you here."

"Will you drive back with me to Almsmead?" cooed Linnet. "Just as soon as this torment is over. Aunt Amabel would be *so* pleased. And we are having—well—Heaven knows who to lunch. Do come."

Gemma smiled, aleady caught. Already committed. And there was little of Daniel about Miss Adeane in any case as she went rustling here and there in her famous black taffeta with its touches of scarlet, smiling and murmuring soft words to her customers, issuing crisp commands to her staff, not a hair out of place, nor a nerve anywhere in her body—by the look of her—that was less than perfectly in control.

"You are having a busy morning, Miss Adeane."

Cara smiled her agreement yet managed, somehow, to signify that she had *always* time to spare for Mrs. Gage. "Yes. Very busy. But do sit down a moment, Mrs. Gage." And, in a twinkling, she had produced a small blue chair from a corner where no one could have supposed a chair to be.

"May I show you something?"

"No—no. I am just waiting for my sister-in-law. Please don't let me distract you from your fittings."

Yet, a moment later, the thin, pale girl called Anna, who never spoke above a whisper, had brought her a tray of tea and Miss Adeane's special biscuits, exceedingly fragile in their appearance but flavored most robustly with lemon or bitter chocolate or vanilla.

Highly enjoyable. As Miss Adeane intended.

And so she sat for a while, at ease, sipping her tea, turning over the pages of the *Ladies' Journal*, mildly amused by the small dramas of lace edgings and pearl beads going on around her, wondering vaguely about the possible identity of Miss Adeane's lover, completely unaware—as Miss Adeane intended *everyone* to be unaware—of the state of near emergency currently prevailing. That no matter how calmly Miss Adeane might be smiling, she had been taken considerably aback half an hour ago when, though she had wished to set this morning aside for the Colclough fittings, Mrs. Marie Moon had wandered through the door, minutes before their arrival, and was at present—one hoped—being sobered up in the back-room by Odette.

And Cara was in no doubt that, should she escape Odette's control and wander back through the shop again in the disheveled and distressed condition, Mrs. Maria Colclough might well rise up in righteous fury and take her daughter and—rather more to the point—her custom away. To Miss Ernestine Baker, in fact, who was still spitting forth her malice about Cara's extravagance and immorality and who would still have time, if only barely, to take over the Colclough order herself by piecing together her standing but morally untainted bridal frills.

Not that Mrs. Colclough could really hold Cara to blame for Marie Moon's appearance nor seriously expect her to turn so free-spending a lady away from her door. But should Mrs. Colclough, who still considered Cara's charges—indeed any charges at all—to be too high, be looking for an excuse to cancel, then here, undoubtedly, she had it. Particularly if Miss Baker, as seemed highly likely, had offered her a bargain price. A ridiculous price, where the sole profit lay in taking Cara's customer away. And since Cara could not allow that to happen, she went on smiling, the very soul of patience and good humor and lightness of heart, not a cloud in her sky. Good Heavens, what cause could *she* possibly have to worry? "No—no, Mrs. Colclough, absolutely no rush. We have all morning. All day if necessary. Please take your time." And although she had little faith in Odette's ability to restrain Marie, should restraint be needed, she nevertheless waited, with an appearance of complete calm, until Mrs. Colclough became engrossed in counting the pearl beads on her daughter's gown in case she should be paying for one less than the several hundred contracted for, before seizing her opportunity to slip away.

"I shall only be a moment."

It would have to be now.

Mrs. Colclough had reached a count of only two hundred and one and could be safely left—thought Cara—to make the count again. Rachel, the bride, appeared to be praying. Three bridesmaids were in the fitting room in charge of Madge Percy and her minion. Four more were whispering and giggling around the counter, dipping greedy fingers into the ribbon boxes. Mrs. Gage seemed lost in pleasant contemplation. Miss Linnet Gage seemed fully occupied in despising Mrs. Colclough, the woman she was hoping to make her mother-in-law. Anna Rattrie, moving like a shadow but a surprisingly effective one, was pouring tea where it seemed appropriate, modeling, at the same time, about her thin but—there again—surprisingly effective shoulders, a silk fringed shawl of the type Cara hoped to be selling in quantity throughout the autumn season.

The scene had a settled look, she calculated, likely to last an hour or more no matter how speedy they managed to be with their needles and pins. And since the mere idea of "rushing" her customers offended her deeply in any case, her best hope lay in tidying Marie up and, at the most convenient moment—when Mrs. Colclough should not be looking—whisking her into the street. Providing, of course, one could find her carriage and get it to the door. And her front door at that—damn the woman—her back door opening into a foul little yard which was blocked, at present, with builder's rubble.

And when all was said and done Marie Moon was a customer too, drunk or sober, who should not be asked to go scrambling over bricks and mortar to the back gate by the privy door.

Unthinkable. Especially since she would be more than likely to lose her way and end up in the shop again, with brick dust all over her.

The carriage, then, to begin with. Cara smiled, most encouragingly, at Mrs. Maria Colclough and then, beckoning to Anna Rattrie, sent her out to look for a landau with blue upholstery and a pair of chestnut horses. Could there be many such in Frizingley?

"You may have to go as far as the Fleece," she warned her, making it sound like nothing to make a fuss about.

"Oh, Miss Adeane..." Anna's eyes, eternally apprehensive, had grown terrified, imagining she had been asked to manage a team of horses.

"Oh Miss Adeane *nothing*, Anna." Cara had no time, just then, for anybody's terror but her own. "Just do it. There'll be a coachman, you ninny. All you have to do is tell him to come here. And if not..." because it was just possible that Marie might be driving herself, "then—well—ask your brother Oliver to help you."

Marie Moon was sitting with her elbows on Cara's table, her arms and shoulders bare, since she was still in evening dress, her hair coming down, her cloudy, short-sighted blue eyes somewhat out of focus but gazing, with the intensity of a woman baring her soul, at Odette who, speaking softly and swiftly and in French, was clearly offering her comfort.

Damn the woman. How could she—how could any woman—let herself down in this way, wandering around a town like Frizingley in the early morning dressed in the beautiful ball-gown Cara had once made her, an enchantment of white silk now shamefully soiled at the hem, dragged through the mud and the gutter as she seemed intent on dragging herself. And why? She was rich and extremely beautiful. She had the best proportioned figure Cara had ever measured. Poise and grace and her own carriage. And, in that case, why should it matter to her that petty-minded provincial bores like Maria Colclough and Lizzie Braithwaite would not invite her to their daughters' weddings? She had been an actress, hadn't she? Or perhaps just an artiste of the music-hall, the café-concert—accounts varied. But nevertheless it was a profession, an identity, a life of her own. Why didn't she just snap her fingers at Frizingley and go back to it? Damn the woman.

Why? The answer came to Cara very suddenly as she saw Marie's face, upturned to Odette, in a shaft of sunlight and understood this lovely woman to be far closer in age to her mother than to herself. And Odette had just turned forty-five. Not easy, one felt bound to admit, to return to the exhaustions and rivalries of the music-hall at that age unless one had been an outstanding success. A name not yet forgotten. And even then it might be unwise. Tiring, at any rate, to compete all over again—at that vulnerable time of life—for men and money in the market-place. Particularly if one tended to wilt easily. And to bruise easily. For Cara had now seen the swelling around one cloudy blue eye, the dark smear along the papery cheek, the red wheels turning yellow at their edges and starting to blacken along Marie's shoulders. Old wounds that were still smouldering with new, raw wounds on top of them.

"My husband beats me, madame—from time to time," said Marie Moon simply, "because he is impotent. Beating me is all he *can* do, you understand. It is the alcohol."

Odette understood. So too, with a tug of pity she did not really wish to feel, did Cara.

"How long, madame?" murmured Odette with some tenderness.

"Since we were married. He believes it to have been caused by the scandal. Therefore it is I—he says—who have castrated him. After all, who was it who inflamed him to the point of carrying me away from my lawful husband? Who tarnished his reputation so that his own sister named him unfit for the care of his children? I did. And in those flames, which *I* created, perished his manhood. So he tells me. Therefore, when his frustrations overcome him and incline him to violence, who am I to complain . . . ?"

"I suppose he tells you that too." There was no tenderness in Cara.

"He does."

"Why do you put up with it?"

"My dear." Marie spread her arms in a comedienne's wide gesture of regret, assuming, for a moment, the mask of a sad, terribly endearing clown. "One does the best one can, as *you*—my little one—should know. And after these dozen years without debts and all that weary business of finding work and keeping it, *this*—I fear—seems little enough to pay. Have you any idea how much a dancer's legs can ache—and her back—at this 'certain age' we have reached, your mother and I? Do you know how many exceedingly tired dancers there are, offering themselves from the passageways of Montmartre. Or Mayfair? Or anywhere? And one grows tired, mademoiselle. Your mother understands."

Yes. Cara was in no doubt of it. Just as she knew that Mrs. Colclough, whose narrow virtue inclined far more to punishment than pity, would not choose to understand at all.

"I am sorry, Mrs. Moon," she said stiffly.

"Sorry? Are you really, Miss Adeane? Or do you feel that I should simply pack my jewels and anything else I can carry and run? At your age perhaps I would. Oh yes. Even at mine. Last night—or perhaps it was this morning—that is what I tried to do. Or so I seem to remember. We had been—oh—*somewhere*—no matter—Adolphus and I. Drinking. His children are with us just now, which makes him agitated. And then sentimental. It gives him a tendency to weep for his lost wife and his lost virtue. So *vivid*, you see, is his imagination. Last night I wept too, I think, and was chastised as being unworthy to shed tears for such a noble lady. I seem to remember that as being the reason. Although I confess that I am easily muddled these days. It is the champagne. What else? A blow to the head? Ah well—one grows accustomed. Then I found myself in Frizingley in full daylight, with no jewels, of course, in my carriage, no money in my pockets, nothing but these very unsuitable clothes I am wearing. I went to the tavern we both frequent occasionally, Miss Adeane, but the landlord was not sympathetic. I took a stroll to clear my mind. Your door was open. Have I greatly inconvenienced you?"

"Oh no," murmured Odette.

"Yes," rapped out Cara.

Marie smiled, very sweetly.

"Then I must leave at once."

"Where will you go?"

"Why—home to my husband, of course, my dear—where else? As I always have. As a penitent, to beg his pardon. He so enjoys that, and since his remaining pleasures are few ... Do you have a back way?"

Cara shook her head.

"I see. And your shop is full of pious wolves? Then throw me to them, dearest. Don't hesitate. They will be so happy naming me slut and slattern and asking each other if they noticed the terrible state of my hair and my gown that no blame will attach to you at all. Nor to my husband. Poor man—they will say—tied to a woman like me. And so they will all fall over themselves in the rush to invite him to dinner. I am speaking seriously, Cara. He needs pity. So join with them and save yourself."

Shakily, she got to her feet, perfectly willing to trail her disgraceful gown, her disheveled head, her black eye and bruised shoulders at once past the scandalized wedding-party, who most certainly would not keep silent about it, their outraged twitterings unlikely to escape the notice of Marie's husband. Thus giving him another reason to punish her.

Sacrifice me, Marie was saying. Everybody else does.

"No," said Cara. "Mother—go and take Mrs. Colclough into the fitting room. Turn the bridesmaids out if you have to. Tell her you are not satisfied with the bodice of the dress we have made her for the wedding. Keep her there until I come. Set her to counting the buttons. And you, Marie Moon—take off that dress."

Swiftly she pulled and tugged Marie's entirely passive figure into a dress of her own that seemed quite suitable for a morning carriage drive, did up her hair as if she had been a doll, powdered her face and then, when the black eye would not succumb to cosmetic artifice, covered it by a hat with a high brim, tilted rakishly to one side—the strategic side—and a spotted veil, pulled well down.

"There. No one notices a woman's eyes," she said with professional satisfaction, "when she wears a hat like this."

"I will pay you for it, my dear."

"I sincerely hope you will. I can hardly take it back for resale, can I, when all those Colclough cousins and Miss Linnet Gage have seen it on your head."

"Linnet Gage." Marie wrinkled a fastidious nose. "*That* one offends me."

Cara shrugged. "Are you ready?"

"I am. And will you worry about me, Cara, once I am off your premises and out of your sight—causing my embarrassment and my alarm elsewhere?"

"Probably not."

She smiled. "Quite right. Nor would I give a thought to you. And yet—how strange it is ... We give all our emotions to men, do we not? And our bodies. They are all in all to us—these gentlemen. Oh yes—everything. And yet one can turn for comfort only to another woman. Or are you too young, as yet, Miss Adeane, to be philosophical?"

They walked together through the shop, the knot of bridesmaids tying and untying themselves in girlish confusion at the approach of Frizingley's acknowledged adulteress, their round, over-innocent eyes fastening avidly on her stylish blue gown, her dashing veiled hat, so that every detail could be recounted later to one's younger sisters, who would listen with relish, and to one's mamma, who would pretend not to listen at all.

Gemma Gage took absolutely no notice. Linnet Gage, being on exceedingly sympathetic terms with Mr. Adolphus Moon, looked through his wife as if she did not exist. Miss Rachel Colclough, uncertain as to whether sinners ought to be prayed for or burned at the stake, glanced around apprehensively for her mother, who would be sure to know. Anna Rattrie, slipping noiselessly forward, opened the door. A landau and a pair of chestnut horses stood in the street.

"Friday then, Miss Adeane, for the black velvet?" called out Marie Moon, negotiating the carriage-step with the help of Cara's strong arm and then collapsing into helpless giggles on her blue-upholstered silk cushions.

"Black velvet—to go with my new diamonds. Large ones, Miss Adeane—so the neck will need to be very low."

"Certainly, madam." And Cara stood, with her habitual courtesy, on the pavement, while Marie—still giggling beneath her spotted veil—was driven off.

"Miss Adeane—this will not do, you know," announced Mrs. Colclough stridently as she returned to the shop. "I must say a word to you . . ."

"Yes, madam?"

"This bodice, Miss Adeane. We settled, I believe, for three rows of braid. How is it that you have given me four?"

"I judged it to be smarter, madam. I will gladly remove the extra row, of course, if you wish, but since the price remains the same . . . ?"

Mrs. Colclough's eyes brightened, the sharp-edged brain behind them busy enough now with her favorite pastime of getting something for nothing to overlook a dozen Marie Moons.

"I merely wondered," she said, quick as a flash, "since the price remains the same—whether four would be enough? Madame Odette, come here a moment and give me your opinion. Shall it be four? Or five?"

The fitting ended, the wedding-party dispersing in several busy directions, the Dallam carriage remaining in Frizingley to collect various parcels for Amabel while Linnet rode back to Almsmead with Gemma, who had little to say beyond "Yes." "Indeed." "Really?" as Linnet aired her opinion that Mr. Adolphus Moon was a man who had a truly heavy cross to bear.

"Poor little Mr. Moon." He had been figuring rather a great deal in Linnet's conversation lately. "So amiable and obliging and so easily put upon. Although I *was* somewhat surprised at seeing Madame

Marie in town so early, it being her practice—one hears—to lie in bed all day with slices of cucumber on her eyes. Recovering, one supposes, from whatever a woman of that sort may have to recover from. I am sure I cannot imagine."

"No, Linnet. Of course not."

Only to Daniel could she have said, "The poor woman drinks. I wonder why?"

"One feels particularly for the children," said Linnet, her light voice chirping on like a pretty little bird of bright plumage, the hoarse croak of a bird of another variety hidden well beneath it. Listening now, with Daniel's ears, Gemma had never heard it so clearly.

"Children?" she said quickly, shocked and then suddenly very amused at her own conviction that if they resembled their father they would have been better drowned at birth.

That too she could have said, easily and happily, to Daniel.

"Why yes, dear—Mr. Moon's children by his first marriage. His *real* marriage, as I once heard him call it in an unguarded moment—with tears in his eyes, poor soul. He had an absolute love of a girl about fourteen and a boy a little older. Very timid and shy, although the girl will talk to me, I find, if I am very patient with her and take an extra special lot of care. And the boy *has* started to follow me about rather—hovering around me looking moonstruck as boys do at that age—*you know*. Poor things. They have that same lost little air as their father. One shudders to think what they may learn from *her* example . . ."

"His wife, you mean? Their stepmother?" She knew Daniel Carey would have said that, just as acidly.

"Oh, my dear . . ." Linnet sounded very much the older sister. Infinitely patient if slightly amused. "It is common knowledge that she *enticed* him—quite blatantly—for he is very, very rich, you know—into an entanglement which she has since given him every cause to regret. They say, in fact . . ."

"I suppose you mean *he* says?"

There was a moment of chilling silence although Gemma, in fact, was not chilled by it.

"Yes," said Linnet crisply. "I see no reason to deny that Mr. Moon confides in me. One is simply happy to be of service to one's friends. One is even proud to be accorded their trust."

What game was this? No game at all, of course, since Linnet did nothing with less than serious intent. And how ruthless she was in the pursuit of that "position in society" she craved. Her *own* establishment, rather than a dainty toe-hold in some other woman's home. Her own horses to drive, her own servants, instead of Amabel's, at her beck and call. Her own invitations to be sent out for impeccable dinners at which *she*—as the wife of any man who could pay for it— would shine. How very clever she was in her various campaigns to hunt him down—whoever he happened to be. How admirably she would fulfill her chosen role, should she ever gain it. How versatile she was. And, at the same time, how unsuccessful.

Sophisticated confidante to Mr. Moon, who was not free to bestow upon her his sugar fortunes in Martinique and Antigua even if he so desired. Woman of slow-burning fires to Mr. Ben Braithwaite, who, even now that he had married the textile fortune of Magda Tannenbaum, still cast ardent glances upon her. Would she fare any better with Uriah Colclough, who might well be content just to gaze at her beauty until it withered, scourging his body and thus purifying his soul by denying his lust for her until there should be nothing left to arouse it?

And after Uriah Colclough, who was left in Frizingley with means enough to give Linnet the life she desired? The life, indeed, which in her own view she richly deserved. Would she settle for less? Fervently Gemma hoped so. For, in marrying Tristan, she had made no allowance for having Linnet on her hands—and under her skin—for the rest of her life.

Nor could she reconcile herself to Almsmead. A handsome house, of course, so beautifully set at the bend of Colonel Covington-Pym's river, containing everything—her father kept on telling her bluntly— to make any woman happy. Her mother's house, built to ease her mother's fears of dirt and noise and riotous assembly in the city streets and into which her mother now welcomed her as rapturously as if she had not seen her these ten years.

"Oh, my darling—what joy... I knew, as soon as I opened my eyes, that something wonderful was going to happen today."

"Good Lord, mother, I have only come from Frizingley you know, not from Arabia Deserta."

But, although John-William's brows drew warningly together at Gemma's tone, Amabel did not notice it.

"I am sure I have no idea where that might be," she answered sweetly, quaintly, more of a little birthday-party girl than ever in her ribbons and curls. "I am simply determined that you shall not go back again. We shall keep you here—Tristan and I—you may be certain. Shall we not, Tristan?"

"Rather," he said cheerfully, reliably. "I should jolly well hope so." Although, as a matter of fact, he was going off to Leicestershire that afternoon to look at a horse with Felix Lark and a pack of minor Covington-Pyms, and he *did* rather hope that Gemma wouldn't want him to cancel. Unlike her—God bless her!—if she did.

"I shall stay to lunch and see you off," she said when, rather hesitantly—not wanting to upset her for the world—he reminded her; swiftly, pleasantly setting his mind at rest before giving her attention to her mother's luncheon guests.

Or were they indeed her mother's guests? Or Linnet's? Ebullient Mr. Moon and his two faded, fidgety children, a pair of tame little sparrows to their father's prancing, curly-headed peacock—all three with their eyes forever straying to Linnet—and a serious, middle-aged man, the doctor from Far Flatley, who was looking at Linnet too.

Two grown men and a puny, unhappy boy competing for her attention, which she gave like handfuls of tiny diamonds, just enough to dazzle and then make them long for more when the sparkle was scattered so daintily, so artfully, elsewhere. Her whole, diamond-sharp mind on her task of being the only woman—anywhere she happened to find herself—to be noticed and wanted. Her dear Aunt Amabel watching her with fond amazement.

"Miss Linnet—do give me your opinion—I cannot rest until I know what you think . . ."

"Miss Linnet—may I show you—ask you—tell you . . . ?" And what they were really saying was "Linnet, look at me—at *me*."

"Are we to eat today?" inquired John-William Dallam sourly. "Or next Tuesday."

The dining-room at Almsmead was high and enormous and disturbingly unreal to Gemma as she took her place at the table, a screen of thin glass, it seemed, having arisen between herself and these others—her family, her husband, their chosen friends—who now appeared, sickeningly if not perhaps suddenly, to be members of one species, she of another.

So had it always been. Now she was ready to acknowledge it, to see herself fully and finally as the cuckoo in this swansdown nest, who had never belonged here and yet had never had any choice but to remain.

She saw it clearly now. She saw, too, that her mother—bound

as securely by her father's love as a Chinese emperor might bind the feet of his concubine—had receded more than ever into childhood, her growth irrevocably stunted. (What had Daniel said? "He keeps her a child so that she cannot challenge him?" Not entirely, although the result had been the same.) She saw, somehow too plainly, how little it took to make Tristan content. A hearty luncheon. A trip to Leicestershire. The certainty of a good horse and a good meal tomorrow and most days thereafter. The company of like-minded men, "good fellows," "jolly decent chaps" and—she did not doubt it—chance-met, easily forgotten encounters with "obliging" women.

She saw that Linnet would very likely fail to find contentment anywhere.

She saw, most of all, that her father was tired, short-winded and short-tempered. Unwell.

The meal over, they took a stroll, father and daughter together, over Almsmead meadows to the quiet, shallow river, neither of them being much inclined to listen to the schemes of Mr. Adolphus Moon for parties and picnics and "rustic entertainments" for which—although the presence of his wife forbade him to offer the hospitality of his own home and gardens—he was most enthusiastically willing to pay.

"A masked ball, even. Why not?" he had been saying as John-William had taken his daughter's arm and led her outdoors. "With our dear Mrs. Dallam as a Dresden shepherdess. Yes, yes, dear lady. Who better to portray the very heart and soul of porcelain than yourself? And I know of a most highly talented theatrical designer who could whip up the costumes in a trice. You may leave it all to me. And to Miss Linnet, of course, who shall be dressed as—yes—good gracious, I see it all too clear. Diana the Huntress, my dear—or Artemis as the Greeks called her. Beautiful and eternally chaste. Forever. Beyond the reach of mortal man. Alas. Alas."

"Damned posing fellow," grunted John-William as he stumped over the fields toward the water.

"Mother seems to like him."

"Your mother likes anybody who takes the trouble to be civil to her. You know that."

She knew.

"And it's Miss Linnet who likes him—or likes what he brings here. The riff-raff he entertains from London and calls 'my artistic friends.'

The backstage gossip. The money. Always a few bottles—or a few dozen bottles—of some wine nobody but Miss Linnet has ever heard of in his carriage. Always French chocolates and hot-house flowers, which would be all very proper if the sweets didn't come in silver filagree boxes and the flowers tied up with little gold chains that Miss Linnet is wearing now around her wrists—whether she'd care to admit it or not. Always something or other he just happens to have in his possession and wants to get rid of, so that anybody kind enough to take it off his hands would be doing him a service. Trifles, he calls them. Well—damned expensive trifles, in my opinion. I don't like it, Gemma. And I don't like all the whispering and giggling she does with Felix Lark, either, and that idle tribe of cousins and God knows what else he drags around with him, trampling all over my garden, talking their damned hunting jargon and drinking my claret. She even had that scoundrel Goldsborough, from the Fleece, breathing down her neck the other day. And whether he hunts and shoots with the Larks and the Covington-Pyms and is related to half the County— as Miss Linnet pointed out to me—or not, I don't trust him. And that's that. I don't like it at all, Gemma. You'll have to watch our Miss Linnet—one day."

She chose to ignore the implications of that.

"I don't suppose Mr. Colclough would like it either, father. Let's hope he doesn't get to know."

John-William snorted his contempt.

"Makes not a ha'porth of difference, lass, whether he gets to hear of it or not. Because she'll never get him to the altar. And if his mother thought there was the least chance of it, then she'd put a stop to Linnet's game just as fast as Lizzie Braithwaite did. But she knows her Uriah. He'll go on saying his prayers another twenty years and then wed a fifteen-year-old with enough money in the bank to ease his conscience. And as for Miss Linnet she'd do well to lower her sights and settle for what she can get while she can get it. Because her looks won't last forever. There's the doctor, for instance. I keep asking him here, putting him in her way and hoping she'll see reason. A widower with a couple of hundred a year and four young children to bring up. That's the kind of husband she ought to be aiming for. Nice little practice in Far Flatley that she's quick and clever enough to help him develop. And she'd be a dab hand, I reckon—if she set her mind to it—in getting his children educated and set up in life.

With the thousand or two I might settle on her he'd be glad to have her. And good to her. She ought to think about that."

"She won't," said Gemma, feeling very certain. Suddenly quite distressed.

"I know. Which is why you'll have to watch her, lass. She'll be here—like as not—in your mother's house, twisting your mother around her little finger. Taking the place over, given half a chance, and your mother with it. When I'm gone, I mean."

"Yes, father." She saw no point in pretending that he might be immortal.

"I reckon you'll have to give up the manor and come and live here then, Gemma. Because going back to Frizingley would break your mother's heart. And I can't have that, lass. Can I?"

No. She understood that he could not. Since it was he, after all, who had put the swaddling bands on Amabel's nature, giving her those tiny lotus-feet of a Chinese concubine on which she could never stand alone. Child-wife, child-mother, who would accept each and every sacrifice easily, naturally, without understanding that a sacrifice had been made, like any babe in arms.

Her mother and Tristan she had always bargained for. Not Linnet.

But what difference did it really make? Except to strengthen her growing convictions that when women of her sort hoped for freedom all they were really doing was waiting for others to die.

It shocked her. And hurt her. She bowed her head and accepted it. So be it. It had always been so.

"I'll look after her, father."

"Good girl." He had expected no less. "Although you'll have your work cut out. I'm telling you. Because when I'm gone your husband will be legally in charge of you—and of some of the brass I leave you."

"Oh yes, father. I know."

"I dare say you do. I'm no fool, my girl. I dare say you thought it over and came to the conclusion that you could keep him on a short rein. Well—and so you could if you had nobody but *him* to deal with. It doesn't take much to keep him happy. I came to that conclusion myself, when I agreed to let you wed him. But *she* won't let go of him, mark my words, once she finds out she'll never be Mrs. Colclough or Mrs. Anything else that's grand enough to suit her. She'll be at him all the time to do things he'd never think of on his own.

To assert his rights. To take control. And you'll have to fight her tooth and nail, my lass, for control of him. And for your mother's peace of mind. There'll be no leaving him to his harmless amusements in the country—if that's what you'd planned—because they won't stay harmless, once she gets wind of her opportunities. She'll have him down at the mill, every verse end, plaguing Ephraim Cook and my lawyers and bankers for *my* money. *Your* money. Well— they'll give him a hard ride. I've seen to that. But what I can't tie up in a legal document is Miss Linnet's temper, and her spite, and all the ways she'll very likely find to upset your mother. Nor the way she can queen it over your mother, at your mother's expense. No, I can't do that. And neither can you, from Frizingley. Not if you want to make certain that it's *your* will that's done. So that's that, lass— once I'm gone."

He had no need to ask if he could rely on her. She had no need to promise what she had been bred and conditioned to perform. He squeezed her hand, those old man's tears he so detested rising, as so often now, to his angry eyes. And he *was* angry, without knowing exactly why. If only she'd been a boy. If only Amabel had been a woman. He loved them both, in the only way he knew. The only way life had taught him. Had he done well?

"So make the most of it, lass," he told her gruffly, not caring to investigate his true meaning. "While you can."

She drove back along to Frizingley, having said her friendly, affectionate goodbyes to Tristan.

"I hope the horse turns out to be a success."

"I don't really need another horse, you know," he'd offered, perfectly ready to give it up should she think him extravagant. Wondering, just a little—as he sometimes did—what he was really doing to earn his keep.

"My darling," Linnet had murmured, patting an airy ringlet, an airy flounce of her muslin dress. "Can one ever have too much—of anything?"

"If you like it," Gemma told him flatly, "then buy it."

"I say." He was, to his sister's evident amusement, rather embarrassed. "What a good sort you are, Gemma. Absolutely first-class."

She thought of him on the drive home, seeing no reason to alter her opinion that he was a "good sort" himself. A man who would prefer to do right, if it could be managed without causing too much fuss, than to do wrong. A man of charm and beauty whose body, as she stood on tiptoe to kiss his cheek, had had no greater substance for her than a beam of sunlight on summer grass. A happy, shallow man who could never be deeply harmed.

She could still smile at his easy, sunbeam shadow as she had always done. Yet no weight had ever oppressed her like the brilliant gloom of Almsmead, the slow pavane she would have to dance there of duty and devotion to the child her father would leave her. What had he said to her, the man who had so inspired her last night? And this morning? *"I was not born to live in a cage and neither were you. I believe I was born to grow. And I must fight anything which stunts me or stifles me."*

Yet how could she do that when what stifled her most were the ones she loved? At least—how could she fight for long?

What had her father said to her, speaking from unacknowledged regions of his heart and his conscience?

"Make the most of it, lass. While you can."

She walked the quarter of a mile to the school-house as she often did, finding Daniel alone, as she had known he would be at this late hour of the afternoon, correcting excercises in the empty classroom, his mood restless enough—fevered enough, it seemed to him—to pack up and leave; yet too intrigued, involved, *moved*—dear God—to make up his mind to do it.

All day he had thought of Gemma Gage. All day. Her plight overtaking him so completely that at times he had stood inside her head, inside the skin of a woman caged by her conscience. And he had not liked it. A woman of honesty and courage and worth. How could he go when she needed him? Yet that was captivity too. And if he had understood her need aright, how dare he even approach her, much less hope to fulfill it? For she was the last woman in the world he would run the risk of offending.

Yet when she came into the chalky, chilly schoolroom and stood before him in the slow-gathering summer twilight her face was calm and gentle, older in its female widsom than his own, the hands she held out to him firm and steady, although once he had taken hold of them he did not know what else to do.

Should he kiss her again? It would be no hardship.

"Daniel . . . ?" And the naked honesty in her face, her awareness of the enormity of the risk she ran, her full acceptance of it, seemed marvelous to him. Beautiful. Exciting, too.

"Gemma?" He wanted to kiss her now, wanted to know her and

learn her and discover her. To unlock her and let the riches and the sorrows, all the hopes and joys and shades and textures of her nature come spilling out. Into *his* hands. But, smiling, she freed one hand and, with a light touch, held him back.

"Daniel." Could he doubt the pleasure it gave her to speak his name. "Let me tell you that I have only a little time—to myself, I mean. Just a short while, I think, to be myself. My father is old and ill, you see. And I shall be needed—at home—quite soon. As women are. And when the need arises then I shall go. I think you will understand."

Yes. And far more. He knew now exactly what to do.

"Gemma." He said it clearly, precisely, meaning every syllable. "Shall we make love together now. As friends, who care about each other?"

The radiance in her face answered him, warming him beyond awkwardness to a point where making love to her seemed easy and natural. As if it had happened a dozen, joyful times before.

"Yes, Daniel. As dear, close friends."

It was a radiant, loving promise. And he knew that whatever promises she ever made to him she would keep. Taking her to his bed—experiencing a moment's anxiety that his sheets might not be quite fresh—he saw the truth in her, the enduring strength, undressing her slowly, carefully, with deep reverence for everything in her that he so prized. A brave and desperate woman. A little brown cob of a girl lying trustingly beneath him. Sturdy. Serious. Sweet? He put his mouth to her shoulders, tasting the smooth, amber skin. Yes, sweet and very soft around the contours of her breasts, fragrant in the cleft between them and the place where they gave way to ribs and flanks, solidly, *sweetly* curved.

Kissing her body he fell into a dream over it, feeling it move gently, confidingly beneath him, whispering to him, timidly as yet, that although not virgin, it had never been truly touched before. And *that*, above all, must be his concern, his aim, his deepest joy. *Her* pleasure. Its slow gathering from limbs his hands roused at first to hope and expectation, over which his mouth breathed and caressed and made promises into every crease of her flesh, into which his own body finally sank as an instrument of her fulfillment, seeking it out, coaxing it from her with every dreaming, gentle, dallying stroke. Arousing harmonies and playing upon them, drawing them out, until he knew her to be throbbing with his music, every note of her leaping to its first crescendo. And then he held her for a long time, kissing her cheeks and her ears with closed lips, cradling her and murmuring to her, lavishing a shower or tiny, tender caresses upon her to guard her from any hint of shame.

"You're a lovely woman, Gemma."

"Oh no." She put a hand to his lips, no shame in her anywhere that he could see. "You don't have to say that, Daniel."

"I don't have to say anything. You're a lovely woman."

"I don't think so."

And because she was not asking for compliments but stating her considered opinion he grew angry, on her behalf. And glad of it. Since he had now found something else to give her.

"You'll let me be the judge, I reckon. And I'm not talking about height and color. What's that? It fades. And one gets used to it in any case. I'm talking about *you*, Gemma. What you are. What you have inside you. And by those standards—*real* standards—you're a lovely woman."

She smiled again and trailed a hand along his spine, rejoicing in him. *Rejoicing*. He knew it. Dear God, what had he done to deserve such bounty?

"You're beautiful, Daniel," her eyes said. Very soon her lips would open, as she had opened her heart, and she would dare to speak of love.

What answer could he give her then?

 15

The Marriage between Rachel Colclough and her Rochdale cotton spinner was celebrated, with as much pomp and circumstance as seemed compatible with her brother Uriah's Christian conscience, on a clear morning in September, the bridegroom looking well satisfied with his lot, the bride somewhat pale and bemused although few people paid any attention to that, being far too busy staring at her dress, the skirt stitched in overlapping layers like the petals of a flower, a water-lily with a pearl-encrusted stem rising from its center, between two feathery, beaded waterfalls that were the sleeves.

And the whole congregation rose, it seemed, for the dress alone with a gasp of wonder, a murmur that, in another place—the Palace Theatre, for instance—would have been applause, no one sparing a second glance for Rachel's scared eyes and aching head, which were well hidden in any case by the silver lilies and roses embroidered on her veil.

The mother of the bride, Mrs. Maria Colclough herself, looked very well with far more black braiding on her cinnamon brown dress than had ever been intended. Her friend Mrs. Lizzie Braithwaite was attired as usual in purple, while her daughter, young Mrs. Amanda Lord, known affectionately as her mother's "little shadow," came in pale lavender. Mrs. Tristan Gage, usually overshadowed by her splendid husband, seemed—due no doubt to some artifice of Miss Adeane's— to have lost much of the stiffness which had always marred her figure, looking, indeed, so very well that a rumor was soon started that she might be in that special "interesting condition" again. Frizingley's ladies knowing of no other cause which could bring such a bloom to a woman's cheek, nor give her that particular air of dreamy, languorous bliss.

Mrs. Amabel Dallam, her mother, was dressed very sweetly in pale blue lace over pale blue taffeta, Mrs. Ethel Lord of the brewery in an outfit of dove gray designed, by Miss Adeane, for the express purpose of showing off a magnificent new rope of pearls. Mrs. Ben Braithwaite—who had been Miss Magda Tannenbaum—presented a startling appearance, it was generally considered—and one not likely to please her mother-in-law—in a gown of gold and orange stripes, also by Miss Adeane, an artfully placed arrangement of gold satin chrysanthemums hiding the deficiencies of her bosom, the skirt so wide that there had been trouble with the carriage. While of the eight bridesmaids in their lily-of-the-valley dresses of white tulle with pale green watered-silk sashes—made, on the strict instructions of Mrs. Maria Colclough, to a pattern which could in no way overshadow the bride—the loveliest, although also by no means the youngest, was held to be Miss Linnet Gage.

Certainly Mr. Uriah Colclough thought so, her presence behind him at the altar affecting him so profoundly that he had to be asked twice to give his sister away. Mr. Ben Braithwaite evidently thought so too—more than one person remarked on it—if the fierce glances he kept darting at her through the orange plumage of his wife's outrageous hat were anything to go by. And Mr. Adolphus Moon, that dapper, amiable little dandy, so liberal with all those fortunes his family had made in West Indies sugar and spice, seemed far more than willing, that bright, clear morning, to share all he possessed with Linnet had not the slight inconvenience of a wife prevented him.

That inconvenient wife herself, Mrs. Marie Moon, wore a dress of heavy cream lace threaded with brown velvet ribbon, a brown hat like a highwayman's with a cream feather and a topaz buckle. And, since—*naturally*—she could not be invited to the wedding, she spent the morning in the back room of Cara's shop drinking gin and talking to Odette of love, mainly as it concerned her relationship with Christie Goldsborough, the man she shared—although only, these days, from time to time—with Odette's daughter, and whose cruelty she declared to be of a more rare and exquisite variety.

"One constantly looks beneath it for signs of remorse and finds none," she told Odette, whose understanding of love was entirely different. "It is the fascination of having a purring tiger in one's hand. It is the fascination of giving everything, madame—everything and then twice as much again—with no hope of reward."

"It is the fascination of being a damn fool," said Cara from the doorway, returning from the wedding service in a stunning confection of black and white striped satin and a tall black hat with a white feather curled around the brim.

But Marie, who adored everybody past a certain level of the gin bottle, smiled at her fondly.

"Ah—but you are not in love with him, Cara."

"Neither are you. It is only passion."

"*Only*—" Marie raised a quizzical eyebrow, a quizzical jeweled hand and laughed, very merrily. "Oh, my dear—my very dear—*only* passion. Sometimes I ask myself—I wonder—what you are missing."

Cara shrugged, entirely undismayed. "I am not a lady of leisure like you, Marie, with all the time in the world to play your games. I can't afford your passion."

Nor love either. Nor anything else, in the hectic months to follow, which could distract her from the task of following through her triumph at the Colclough wedding, when Frizingley's ladies, struck by her transformation of Rachel Colclough from a droopy nun to a delicately swaying water-lily, came flocking—at last—to purchase a similar magic, a new impression, a comforting illusion.

Mrs. Magda Braithwaite, still basking in the outrageous glory of her orange stripes and feathers, appeared in the shop the next morning with a list of social engagements at which, knowing herself to be a plain woman married to a handsome husband, she wished to attract attention. Christmas was on the horizon, involving her not only in the seasonal balls in Frizingley's Assembly Rooms at the "better end" of Market Square, but in visits to the far more cosmopolitan atmosphere of Bradford, where her German cousins gave musical entertainments graced by international concert performers and where such things as cut and style and *originality* were soon noticed. Could Miss Adeane be *very* original? Black lace over orange satin with a Spanish mantilla, gold silk damask with silver embroidery as delicate as the veins of a leaf, a double-skirted carriage dress in black and yellow tartan and black velvet, a claret-colored velvet cape with a gray fur hem and hood; an Elizabethan extravaganza to wear at her Bavarian uncle's fancy-dress dance, a French farthingale with drum ruffles and an authentic stomacher with black Spanish embroidery studded with ruby beads and gold threads, if Miss Adeane could manage it?

Miss Adeane believed she could manage very well.

Mrs. Ethel Lord came the same morning in search of a velvet evening gown which might show off her pearls as well as the new "dove gray" Miss Adeane had made for the wedding, indulging herself, at the same time, by ordering a watered silk in pale ice-blue and a delicate silver gauze, both far too young for her as she wryly admitted but perfectly in keeping with the mood of extravagance which overcame her from time to time, whenever her husband's behavior gave her cause to suspect him of "getting up to no good."

"He has done *something* I shouldn't like," she told Cara, lovingly fingering her pearls. "Or why has he given me these? And since it is my birthday next month—what do you think?"

"An emerald would be nice," said Cara, bringing out an apple green brocade, "set as a pendant on a heavy gold chain, so that, with a dress of this color, with the neck cut just so . . . ?"

Mrs. Lord ordered the green brocade, a green plaid carriage-dress, a green velvet pelisse and, having run through Cara's stock of greens, a fawn silk—because she liked the look of it—and a matching shawl with a coffee-colored fringe.

Mrs. Covington-Pym, who would not condescend to enter a fitting room, ordered—or perhaps commanded—a riding-habit in dark blue with a white silk waistcoat and a ball gown in ruby velvet, requiring one side-seam to be left open so that her maid might stitch the garments upon her whenever she wore them, thus avoiding even the suspicion of a wrinkle. The Larks, with their hunt ball in mind, descended in a high-pitched flock to "honor" Miss Adeane with their custom, in exchange for which, and for the undoubted advantages to Miss Adeane in having her handiwork displayed in their historic home and parkland, they would expect a certain discount.

"I am sure we can come to some arrangement," murmured Cara very pleasantly, aware not only that Lady Lark was no Mrs. Maria Colclough when it came to arithmetic, but that she had a great many rural, North Yorkshire sisters and cousins who, being obliged to travel *somewhere* to a dressmaker, might just as well come to Frizingley.

Mrs. Amabel Dallam and Mrs. Gemma Gage ordered their entire winter wardrobes, the mother in sweet-pea shades of gauze and taffeta, the daughter in amber velvets, cinnamon and coffee browns, her manner warm if just a little absent, her body unusually passive and supple although, as Cara skillfully pinned and pleated, she could detect no telltale signs of the possible childbearing which Frizingley still supposed had given rise to the rich, dreaming quality to be detected, now and then, in Gemma's smile.

Mrs. Marie Moon bought everything which took her fancy, wore it once or twice and then gave it away to the village girls of Far Flatley, thus increasing her husband's reputation for generosity and her own for the criminal extravagance with which—it was generally held—she abused it. Certain gentlemen of the town and of the surrounding squirearchy also began to call, usually at a discreet hour of the early morning when Miss Adeane could safely be consulted alone about the purchase of silk shawls and lace-topped gloves, feathered or painted fans, perfumes in heavy glass bottles, a whole froth of *little*, expensive, pretty things which were not always seen, afterward, in the hands or around the shoulders of the lady one might have supposed.

Strange and often sophisticated faces started to put in an appearance, elegantly dressed women filling the shop with the rustling of scented skirts and unfamiliar voices, who turned out to be Tannenbaums from Bradford; ladies with double-barreled names from the North Riding who saw no reason why Miss Adeane could not "run up a couple of dresses by tomorrow morning" to be taken home after visiting the Larks; a few rather more exotic creatures, "artistic acquaintances" of the Moons from London, doing *their* bit to enlarge the glorious reputation of Adolphus Moon by choosing a whole excitement of frills and fripperies and charging them to him.

Mr. Moon came himself with his timid daughter to buy her one plain gown, one simple bonnet, one not entirely Cashmere shawl—since she was still growing—and, at the same time, to mention very discreetly to Miss Adeane that should she care to offer a selection of evening dresses to Miss Linnet Gage at a special price he would be more than glad—without Miss Gage being aware of it, of course—to pay the difference.

"You see, Miss Adeane, one can only admire a girl of breeding like that one, don't you know, making the best of things—putting a brave face on it all—as she does. A Bartram-Hynde on her father's side, without a penny of her own. Terribly sad when you think of what a name like that *ought* to entitle her to. So if she should take a fancy to this spangled gauze, for instance, then—well—if you could do her proud, eh?"

"Certainly, sir," murmured Cara, with the result that Linnet Gage acquired a dress of starry white tulle for the Far Flatley Hunt Ball while Mrs. Marie Moon—from whom her husband appeared to keep no secrets—had Cara design her a gown of the same foamy gauze only more of it, the same spangles only larger and finer which—since *naturally* she could not be invited to the ball—she wore the next morning for driving about the village delivering hampers of roast chicken and game pies and a rare selection of her husband's vintage wines to pensioned-off Lark and Covington-Pym servants who—their pensions being very small—did not care a fig for her notoriety.

"You are quite mad, you know," Cara told her when, exhibiting the shadow of another black eye beneath another spotted net veil, she brought the dress back for repairs to the hem which, in those country lanes, had been dragged rather considerably through the mire.

"Then take advantage of me, Cara—as everybody does. Miss Linnet is sure to get another new dress for my foolishness. And my husband is sure to make it up to everybody else—for the embarrassment I have caused, that is—by giving that costume ball he has been threatening them with. Which means you will have dozens of eager ladies to dress as Marie Antoinette and Good Queen Bess and the Spanish Infanta—and Miss Linnet herself as Artemis the Maiden Huntress or the Virgin Mary. Do you feel up to it?"

She did. It was what she had prayed for. A full order book. Her shop bursting at its seams, day in, day out, with women eager to order more. Her workroom throbbing and humming like an agitated hive of bees. And she closed her mind, that autumn and winter, to everything but the need to fill those orders not only on time but *splendidly*, to give value and service and to do just a little more, on each and every occasion, than had been expected, so that those women from London and Bradford and the North Riding would remember and Frizingley's women would forget—fully and forever—the dismal reign of Miss Ernestine Baker.

She placed blinkers on either side of her mind, therefore, drew a deep breath, gritted her teeth and plunged into the work in hand like a swimmer breasting a whirlpool, acquiring, as the hectic weeks went by, three separate faces. The calm, courteous Miss Adeane of the showroom and fitting rooms in her black and scarlet taffeta for whom nothing was too much trouble, who pinned and tacked and chatted, served tea and biscuits and discussed the requirements of one's figure and coloring with all the time in the world, it seemed, at her polished fingertips. A face rarely seen by the women in her workroom to whom she appeared as a sharp-eyed, briskly-spoken demon of energy, driving them on when their own energies faltered, requiring neither sleep nor sustenance herself, it seemed to them, allowing them to cut no corners, scrutinizing every piece of work as it was done and handing back anything which did not pass muster to be unpicked and started afresh as calmly as if the Hunt Ball were a month away, not the day after tomorrow, and Christmas not even in sight. And then the private face, seen only by her dog who never deigned to notice her as, having worked her women fifteen hours, seventeen hours, twenty hours sometimes at a stretch, she forced herself, through the remainder of a painful night, to do what even she could not ask of them, to put her account books in order, to redesign the complicated boning of Magda Braithwaite's Elizabethan dress, to sew with her own hands the fine seam which an exhausted Madge Percy, or even Odette sometimes, had abandoned in tears.

And if her hands were slower than theirs her mind was quicker, her nature infinitely more determined. She would not fail. No one should have cause to complain of her or anything upon which she had put her signature. And when her women had worn themselves out she would carry on. Nothing must be less than perfect. Nothing must be late. Toward Christmas she laid mattresses on her workroom floor and organized her seamstresses in shifts, sleeping or working. She served them port wine and red meat to keep them going, purchased extra lamps and candles for their comfort, dried their tears which, more often than not, she had caused herself, praised them and promised them—should her will be most meticulously done—a bonus.

She employed a decent, elderly man and a respectable-looking young one to make deliveries in her pale blue, gold-lettered boxes. She ransacked Leeds and Bradford for fancy goods, wrinkling her nose at what they offered and driving a hard bargain, encouraging them to send to Manchester and Liverpool for anything that was unusual, exotic, which might be labeled as exclusive to Miss Adeane of Frizingley. She made contact with a dealer in Whitby jet and South Sea coral and various semi-precious stones, rose quartz, agate, moonstones, tourmaline, and, by suggesting to certain ladies that "art objects" in these substances were exactly what they had been searching for for years, managed to supply them to everybody's satisfaction. And when Christie Goldsborough required her attendance she gave it, sitting cross-legged as a tailor afterward on his sumptuous bed, talking to him of prices and profit margins and how much easier her life would be if only he would evict her next-door neighbor, that feckless grocer, and lease his premises to her.

"Come, Cara. Surely you wouldn't have me put the poor man in the street? Tut, tut—how very unfeeling."

"I dare say. But all he does now is stand in the street complaining about my ladies' carriages blocking his door, and quarreling with their coachmen—which does *me* no good. Not that he ever sells anything, so why should it matter whether his entrance is blocked or not? All he knows how to do is breed mice in his corn sacks and send them round to plague me—I swear it. And the place is filthy—dropping to bits—you'll lose money on it if you're not careful. He has a daughter in Hebden Bridge. He could go there, if she'll have him. I need the space, Christie—I really do."

"So you keep on saying. His lease expires next year. We'll see."

"I want it now."

"Yes. I know you do."

"Can I get it?"

"In *my* time, Cara."

She shrugged. "Oh well—I'd have done better, I suppose, to tell you I didn't want it and let you force it upon me."

"Would I have believed you?"

She shook her head. But then, what would he believe? She knew no more about him now than she had known three Christmases ago when he had first brought her to this room and spent three festive days and nights instructing her in the vast yet somehow impersonal study of "appetites," feeding her rich food and wines, dressing her in barbaric silks from wild places, massaging heavy scented oils into her skin as she lay posing for him on the rug before his fire, moulding her body to the needs and whims and fancies of his own, eating her and drinking her, toying with her, taking whatever remained of her innocence which, in fact, had been a great deal. Far more than anyone would have supposed.

"What a savage you are, Adeane," he had told her. "You know almost nothing at all, do you, my lamb. Luckily—for you, of course—I can change that."

And so she had passed the orgy that had been Christmas Day and Boxing Day and the day after in a bemused, almost a drugged condition, knowing many things, at the end of it, about the broad-chested, thick-set, powerful body which had acquired such dominion over her, little about the man inside it.

A voluptuous education during which she had earned the lease of her shop. Three Christmases ago. And now nothing had changed except that this year she had her own money in her hands.

The week before Christmas Mrs. Ethel Lord brought her daughter-in-law Amanda to Miss Adeane's, risking a serious family crisis, since Amanda's mother, Mrs. Lizzie Braithwaite, had remained persistently faithful to Miss Baker.

"It is time this child had something decent to wear," said Mrs. Lord.

"Certainly, madam," said Miss Adeane.

"For Christmas Eve?"

"Of course."

Odette turned pale when Cara came into the workroom with the good news. Madge Percy put her head in her hands. Anna Rattrie's eyes filled silently with tears although one heard distinctly from somewhere in the room a loud, indeed almost a defiant sob.

"Isn't it *wonderful*," said Cara with no question in her voice whatsoever, issuing an undoubted threat to any who might disagree with her.

"Wonderful, Miss Adeane," they chorused.

And by eight o'clock on Christmas Eve the workroom tables were bare, the workroom floor swept clean of pins and tacking thread, every frill and flounce and feather packed into its pale blue box and carried to its destination, every one of Miss Adeane's "women" on her way home with a Christmas goose, a bottle of Madeira wine—all inveigled at cost price from Christie—and Miss Adeane's permission to rest the whole of Christmas Day and Boxing Day, after which there were two February christenings to consider, a March wedding, stock to take and replenish, and a certain amount of thought to be given to Easter-bonnet time.

Cara came out into the frosty evening air to wave them all good-bye and then, walking briskly across Market Square, bought every toy she could find that might please Liam, chocolates and crystallized fruits for Odette, offered a courteous "Compliments of the Season" to all her fellow tradesmen, including the grocer of whom she was doing her utmost to be rid, obtained a more than usually generous marrow-bone for her dog and, still in her rustling black taffeta with its scarlet bows, locked her door and collapsed across her bed.

The Christmas bells of the parish church woke her the next morning and by the time she had scrambled into a dark wool dress, the wonderful black velvet cape with its scarlet lining which she had made for herself in an off-season, and reached the top of St. Jude's with her heavily laden market-baskets, Odette and Liam had already returned from mass, held by the Irish priest on a strip of wasteland beyond St. Jude's Passage, there being no Catholic church in Nonconformist Frizingley. Even the Queen's Church of England being held, by some, to be a shade idolatrous.

The morning was clear and hushed and very strange. No factory hooters, for this one day of the year, no clattering of clogged feet on the cobbles, no gray river of bowed, shawl-wrapped heads flowing sluggishly to the mill-gates and out again, at breakfast time. An unaccustomed silence, familiar streets made alien by their emptiness as Frizingley's worker-bees, drudges and drones together, slept late—for this one blessed morning of the year—in their beds.

An odd reversal. Since it was the masters, not the men, who were abroad—on this day—so early. Ladies and gentlemen with souls as well as bodies to consider—and who had other opportunities for sleeping late in any case—who, as Cara hurried across Market Square toward St. Jude's, were proceeding solemnly to their places of worship, the Colcloughs, mother and son in the same carriage, to their chapel; Mr. and Mrs. Lord of the brewery driving a smart new landau to the parish church which—unlike the chapels—was not given to preaching against strong drink; Mrs. Lizzie Braithwaite, by no means averse to a drop of port wine herself although she did not think the workers ought to have it, going to a chapel of her own, Methodism of a different brand and in a different building to the Colcloughs.

They raised gracious hands to Cara as they drove by. So did Mrs. Magda Braithwaite, wearing her flamboyant gold and orange stripes to the parish church, having decided to be an Anglican largely because she liked the organ music and the altar cloths and because Lizzie, her mother-in-law, did not.

So did many others, to whom Cara replied with a brilliant smile, her good humor helped not a little by Christie Goldsborough's sudden decision to spend a "hunting Christmas" at Far Flatley where, she supposed, he would be standing now in the ancient village church among his kith and kin, while the vicar—a minor Lark of exceedingly high church persuasions—preached his doctrine of obedience to God in the form of one's local squire. Particularly should his name be Lark or Covington-Pym.

He would be away at least a week. Ned O'Mara no longer presented any threat to her. For the first time in her life her income exceeded her expenditure. For the first time in her life she could hold up her head and see her way forward. Perhaps—for this one day of the year—she could even allow herself, as a Christmas gift from Cara to Cara, a measure of satisfaction? Why not? Particularly when, all around her, other people were indulging themselves. Christie Goldsborough and the Larks with their old style boars' heads and punch-bowls and their ritual slaughtering of foxes, the Dallams and Braithwaites with Queen Victoria's Germanic innovations of Christmas Trees and present tables. Could she not find her own enjoyment? Surely, now, she had *some* reason? And although Liam's reception of his toys was less boisterous than she would have liked—than her own would have been at his age—she stopped herself, just in time, from saying so. From scolding him, in fact, which would have served no purpose but to distress Odette.

Let him amuse himself in his own way and if he chose to neglect the rather splendid army of tin soldiers she had brought him, and the drum, and the hobby-horse which had caused her so much trouble on the way up St. Jude's hill, then she would just have to swallow her disappointment and make the best of it. Perhaps he would turn to them later when he had finished scribbling in his picture book. Never mind. And at least there were other pleasures. The goose, for instance, the biggest and best she had been able to find, roasting in Odette's oven with a large ham beside it. The game pies and pork pies on the larder shelves. The oranges and nuts. The giant slab of plum cake. The bottles of port wine and Old Sercial. All brought here, on her instructions, by her own delivery men. The turkey it was her great joy to carry across the street as a gift to the Thackrays, although all she had received in exchange was a curt nod from Sairellen and a "Put it over there, lass."

Yet, having spent an unaccustomed night in her mother's cottage she awoke feeling restless and ill-at-ease, faintly unwell, an ache in her head, another—every now and again—in her back, the morning an empty space with no urgent tasks to fill it, giving way to an afternoon in which she made slow conversation with her son, who did not really wish to be distracted from his book, and quarreled with Odette about a letter from her father.

"I don't want to know how he is, mother."

"Cara—such bitterness—"

"That's right, mother. Bitterness. He sends you his love, but has he sent you any money?"

"My child, is that all you can say?"

"All I can think of, you mean? One tends to starve without it, I find. And what use would all this cheap affection be to you then?"

And it was a relief, as well as a pleasure, when Luke Thackray invited her to walk over Frizingley Moor with him. His presence making her feel right with herself, comfortable inside her own skin, allowing her to forget the prickling discomfort she had felt all day whenever her own son had turned his deep, uneasy eyes on her, almost, she thought, in some kind of judgment.

"What is it, Liam?"

Nothing.

He did not say so in words, only with swift, down-drooping eyelids shutting his eyes—himself—away.

"Liam . . . ?"

She had never received a reply. Nothing at all but the satisfaction of watching his soundly growing limbs, the almost unnerving sensation, sometimes, of him watching her.

How *did* he judge her? Had it meant anything, this afternoon, when, during her argument with her mother, he had suddenly but very quietly closed his book, got up and—just as quietly—crossed the room through all the Christmas debris and Cara's anger to stand beside Odette, saying nothing, doing nothing, just there, his hand sliding, once again with that strange quietness, into hers, his blank, judging eyes on Cara's face.

Had he understood the reason for her anger, or for Odette's weeping? Or, in the opinion of those troubled, troubling eyes, was Cara simply an angry person, Odette often in tears? Or, even worse, did he judge Cara, with his stark logic of childhood, as no more than the woman who made Odette cry?

Surely not. She must ask Luke about that. Or Liam.

It was a sharp afternoon of sunshine and frost, the air, as they emerged from the smoky confines of the town, striking them hard, clean blows which brought color to their cheeks and made them gasp, whipping Cara's heavy black and scarlet cloak around her ankles, invigorating her although she could see nothing much to admire but a wasteland of coarse grass in front of her, the wasteland of St. Jude's behind.

What a grim place. A dry, dusty place in which to settle. Yet she had settled here. She had done the best she could. And it meant nothing—it was foolish, even, to be distressed—when Odette shed quiet tears over those cheerful, *cruel* letters from America and Liam could hardly trouble to talk to her.

Children of that age—she supposed—were difficult to please. And Odette, after that glorious Christmas rush, must surely be tired. Perhaps she could manage without Odette at the shop for a week or two. She would try to arrange it. Perhaps—in the summer—she might even manage to send Liam and Odette away for a while—as the Colcloughs and Braithwaites might send their children—to the sea. It would mean paying three separate lots of rent, of course. The shop, Odette's cottage and whatever accommodation might be had for them at Whitby or Scarborough. Her jet and coral merchant would be sure to know. But... Yes. She would do her best, whatever it took, to achieve it.

For a while she kept pace with Luke's stride, for she was hardy and strong-winded, her legs almost as long as his, but eventually the weight of her cloak—the very symbol of her success—impeded her and she called him to a halt beside a flat rock upon which, having dusted it down with her hands, she sat.

"This is far enough, Luke."

"You're growing soft."

"Oh no I'm not."

Smiling he lit his pipe, a leisurely, steady-handed procedure, and sat down beside her, decently dressed in his brown tweed "Sunday" jacket, only a brown-checked shirt beneath it which could hardly be much protection from the cold. Yet he seemed oblivious to the weather, sitting in apparent contentment smoking his quiet pipe, his light, untroubled eyes watching the flight of a bird, a mere charcoal sketch of wings against the pink winter sky, and then turning to check a rustling in the tufted, heather-mixed grass which might be a rabbit.

"You like it up here, don't you?" she said, the accusation in her voice making him smile.

"Yes. Is there any reason why I shouldn't?"

And suddenly—she didn't really know why—because the day had let her down a little, perhaps; because she had cared more than she liked to show about Liam's silences and Odette's preoccupation with her father's letter; and because she was tired and her nerves fraying at their edges in any case, she found herself saying angrily, bitterly, "Because it's not enough for you, Luke. You could do better than this—much better ..."

302

"Cara . . ." Knowing that he was about to be reasonable, rational, she rapidly shook her head.

"Oh no—don't hush me like you always do. Just tell me what future you see for yourself—in that damn mill."

"Oh—it's not so bad . . ."

She did not believe him. "Bad? It must be hell."

"I'm used to it, Cara. You're not."

"No, thank God."

Thank Him indeed. For if she had known toil and hunger in Ireland, at least there had been no factory gates to slam shut behind her, no power-driven mill-wheels to grind her down.

"Then how can you judge?"

"Because I have eyes and ears, Luke. It's like a prison. Everybody says so. They lock you in, don't they, every morning and don't let you out again until the hooter goes?" And, having never experienced it, it seemed doubly terrible.

"Ah yes." He was smiling. "That's one way of looking at it. Another way is that they're not so much locking us in as locking the latecomers out. Othewise how could they collect the fines? It's a shilling per head for latecomers, you know, if they want to be let in at all."

"I know. And fines for other things . . ."

"Of course. All sorts of things: a shilling for being found dirty at work, and another shilling if you get caught washing yourself. And then, at Braithwaite's at least, there's a fine for whistling because old Mr. Braithwaite, who's been dead ten years, didn't like the sound of it. And another shilling to pay for opening a window. And if you fall ill you're expected to send somebody else to do your work, otherwise they'll charge you six shillings a day for the steam they reckon they've wasted on account of your machine standing idle. They don't leave anything to chance."

Nor did she, if she could help it. But—even so. It was too petty, too mean, for *him*.

"And is it part of your job to supervise all that?"

"Oh no. I'm just an overlooker, Cara—a loom-tuner. When a loom breaks down, the weaver comes running to me to put it right—and running in a panic, at that, since she's paid by how much work she can produce and a loom standing idle is taking money out of her pocket and bread out of her children's mouths. And when six of them want me at the same time I have to exercise the judgment of Solomon because whichever one I choose the other five will accuse me of favoritism, and accuse her of letting me have my evil way in a corner somewhere, on a heap of waste."

"You wouldn't do that." It was not a question and, drawing on his pipe, he smiled.

"There are those who do. And too many women feel forced to put up with it."

But this was too near her bone and she said roughly, "I know all about that. And what about you? How do you spend the rest of your time?"

"Very pleasantly."

She had expected him to say that. And she knew all about the lectures he attended at the Mechanics Institute on history and music and such things at which no fortunes could be made, and the "study group" which met every Thursday night to read and discuss works of literature and philosophy in a shed in Frizingley Park which, having been used as a cholera hospital in the last epidemic five years ago, they had been able to rent cheap. She knew about the money he sent every week to the fund to pay off Richard Oastler's debts. She knew about the visits he made on Fridays to the back room of the Dog and Gun to drink his moderate weekly allowance of ale, read the tavern's copy of the *Northern Star* and listen to itinerant Chartists—like Daniel—reporting on their cause. She understood the tolerance, the plain-spoken affection, the amused loyalty, the tough-grained respect he felt for his mother. In her better moments she felt it herself. But was it something which should go on unchanged, day in, day out, forever. Was it a future?

"It's not good enough for you, Luke—not halfway good enough."

"What isn't, Cara?"

"This—this *situation.*"

This trap of poverty into which they had both been born and from which she was slowly, by the skin of her teeth perhaps, but *surely*, lifting herself. He had it in him to do the same. She would take her oath—any oath—on that. She believed in him utterly.

"Situation?"

How maddening he could be when he didn't want to understand.

"Yes. Working for Ben Braithwaite, who isn't half the man you are . . ."

"You know him, then?"

304

"I know him. He should be working for you."

He looked amused, tolerant, unruffled, as he often did with Sairellen.

"That's not likely to happen."

"No." She was seized, as she often was, by a great resentment. "I agree—not until you start studying something more practical than Handel's Messiah and Plato's Republic—not until you let your mother stop pushing you into one lost cause after another."

There was a short silence.

"Do I have to apologize," she said, "for saying that?" He drew on his pipe again, the fragrance of the tobacco reminding her, with a sharp pang, of the nights he had come to meet her from the Fleece— before Christie. Before so many things. Reminding her that he was the last person with whom she could bear to quarrel.

"No, Cara." And the even tone of his voice immediately reassured her. "There's no need. Because you know I choose my own causes. And, for the rest, perhaps I do the best I can. Like you."

"No you don't. That's just it. You could be . . ."

"What?"

"A mill-manager, couldn't you?"

"No. I couldn't."

"Why not? You're clever enough."

She *knew* that. And, furthermore, she *was* acquainted with Ben Braithwaite, well enough to know that he desired her. And she acknowledged to herself, quite coolly, that if Luke wanted to be a mill-manager, she would do anything to help him.

He shook his head. "Well—I reckon I could do the job. But they wouldn't give it to me. Because my father was Jack Thackray. And I wouldn't take it for the same reason. And what else is there for a man like me? Be realistic, Cara. I'm not like our Chartist candidate, who can afford to play the grasshopper because he already has his education in his hands—his classics degree that can open doors in his life for him whenever he chooses. Those doors are closed to me, Cara—tight shut. You know that as well as I do. Yes, I have a good brain. I even use it, to keep it active, in the only way I can—by reading all those poets and philosophers which, as you rightly say, are unlikely to profit me financially by one penny. I went to a dame-school, Cara, where an old woman taught me the alphabet, which was about as much as she knew herself. And I was lucky to have even that much schooling, since my mother never went to school at all. And then, when I was eight years old, I went into the mill—like

---

305

everybody in this town goes into the mill—because there was nowhere else to go. And now I'm nearly thirty. Half-educated. Self-educated. A success in St. Jude's, where overlookers are men to be looked up to and kept on the right side of. Nothing in my own estimation, perhaps. Full of haphazard reading that doesn't qualify me for anything and never could. The professions are for gentlemen, Cara, you know that. And the only men who get promoted from the factory floor are those who think as Mr. Braithwaite tells them to think. I don't."

"Oh Lord . . ."

"Yes, Cara?"

"Your fancy ideals."

"I'm afraid so. I'd feel the cold without them."

She glanced at him sharply. He was warm then, it seemed, in his integrity. While she needed a velvet cloak with a double lining between herself and the weather. *Needed* it. Bitterly she drew it around her, shivering slightly, her throat, suddenly and to her intense annoyance, very tight with tears.

"I have no religion either," she said.

He smiled, enduring and immovable, his straw-colored head bare, his eyes far-sighted and kinder, sometimes, than her flesh and blood could stand.

"What does that mean, Cara?"

"I don't know—I don't know— No ideals, no religion, no politics. Oh Lord—you know what I am." Christie Goldsborough's woman, she meant. He did not. And again, at this vulnerable, fragile moment when she could least resist it, she felt that he had clasped her hand.

"Yes, Cara. I do know what you are. From the start—I knew."

"*Luke.* I want something wonderful to happen to you," she hissed at him, meaning it with all her heart yet sounding as if she were spitting venom.

He took it calmly. "Perhaps it has."

She was very cold now, struck by a chill which brought her yet another memory, of Gemma Gage's wedding morning when she had stood in the churchyard wrapped in two plush tablecloths stitched together, shivering before Christie Goldsborough and longing for nothing more—in that killing wind—than his spectacular fur-lined cloak.

She had her own cloak now, and she was no warmer.

No. If Luke meant that *she* had happened to him then it was not wonderful. No. When there was so much of her that she could neither show him nor tell him. Could he mean that? She felt her heart lurch and a great fluttering start up inside her, like wings beating through warm water.

"I want you to be happy, Luke." It was a plea. For if she could see joy in his life, then at least she would have had something. She believed it would content her.

"That's a lot to ask," he said. "I want the same for you—although perhaps I don't expect to get it. I reckon that's the difference between us. I can settle for less."

They walked back quietly, rather carefully, Luke's hand not touching her elbow but, just the same, guiding her, guarding her, first over the coarse tufts of moorland grass and then, when the town started, over the uneven cobbles. Although in fact she did not stumble, keeping pace with him, warmed by him and cleansed by him as she had always been. From the start. A little exasperated too. But that had always been present in the brew that was her affection for him. Her trust. The comfort she derived from her certain knowledge of his worth.

Had anything changed? If, now, she were to reach out and put her hand in his, what would he do? Once again she felt that strange, churning sensation of wings through water. An excitement she did not wholly welcome. She had wanted peace from Luke. Now her mind was filled with what he might want from her. And whether—or not—she could give it.

A crowd had gathered at the top of St. Jude's Street, not the usual, indifferent ebb and flow of passers-by but silent, solemn groups of women in blanket shawls and men in cloth caps, all staring in the same direction, a sure sign of something amiss. An accident? Common enough in these streets where children were left to roam untended. And in these houses with their open, unkempt fires of sticks and rough-hewn wood that sparked and splintered and could so easily set fire to a child's dress. Liam? Her heart lurched now with an entirely familiar panic. But no, for there was Odette looking troubled but not bereaved—sorry for others, thank God, not herself—standing beside a grim, bare-headed Sairellen Thackray, who seemed as impervious to the cold as her son.

"It's the Rattries," Luke said.

Of course. What else? The Rattries, or rather the end of them. A common enough sight in St. Jude's. And as she watched the landlord's men—Goldsborough's men—carrying out the few pathetic sticks of furniture into the street, roughly, since nothing was fit to sell to recover the arrears of rent, she was merely surprised that Mr. Rattrie had managed to keep a roof over his head for so long. He had had no work, that she knew of, since his wife died. Yet, since he had been continuously drunk and she was not ignorant of the price of gin, money had come from somewhere. The pittance she gave Anna, she supposed, and whatever Oliver could earn from Christie. Dutiful children then, in their fashion. Despicable father, who had spent their wages on strong drink, which meant that Christie Goldsborough, who owned both the cottage and the gin-shop in St. Jude's Passage, had had his money in any case. Once, that is, rather than twice over.

An old story. Particularly at the end of a short winter afternoon with the sky darkening and the rain coming on. And there was often high drama at evictions, sobs and swoons and hysteria, fisticuffs sometimes as husband and wife turned on each other, tooth and nail. "See now what you've done to me. If you hadn't been bone-idle, or drunk. If *you* hadn't always been pregnant." So that St. Jude's was accustomed to public agony and humiliation, skin and hair flying and, rather less often, to surprising moments of love. They had seen old couples who, clinging together like limpets, had been prised apart and taken off to the separate male and female wards in the workhouse. They had seen a young man, last winter, put out into the street with his sick wife in his arms, begging for shelter none of them could afford to give, since she had been spitting blood and everybody knew what that meant. They had seen men who had once been decent, cursing and foaming at the mouth, turned into mad dogs by frustration. And although it was not a spectacle which anybody in St. Jude's savored, it brought them out of doors as they would have come out to watch a funeral, to pay respects, to acknowledge the ease with which it could happen to any one of them, to give whatever help one could so as to be able to claim help, more easily, in one's turn.

But the Rattries came quietly, nine—or was it ten?—little weasel-children huddled together in drooping, blank-eyed silence around the soiled mattresses and broken chairs, the few gaudy fairground jugs and vases which had been their mother's treasures piled up on the cobbles, with not even a wheelbarrow, by the look of it, to carry them away in. Ten little weasels, all alike except for Anna, who had grown taller since Cara had been feeding her, and furtive, fidgety

Oliver, who ran errands and listened at keyholes for Christie Golds-borough.

And their father? Where was he?

Nobody knew. Perhaps nobody cared, except that he ought to be doing something now about getting his furniture and his children off the street instead of leaving it to Anna, who could do nothing but tremble like a broken sparrow, or the hated Oliver to whom no one in St. Jude's would extend a helping hand.

Where was he?

"Have you seen my father?" asked Oliver of the silent, somber faces around him, squaring his puny shoulders, his eyes desperate, his alert, trapped-animal senses aware not only of hostility but of the approaching dark, a taste of snow in the damp air. Unless the furniture, such as it was, could be moved it would be gone by morning, broken up and used for firewood by families every bit as desperate as his own. And, no matter what these grim, reproachful watchers might think of him, he didn't want to be the one to take his brothers and sisters to the workhouse.

Would anybody lend *him* a handcart? He didn't think so. And the landlord's men were feeling the cold and growing impatient, wanting to seal the doors and windows and get back to their ale and hot meat pies at the Fleece.

He felt the crowd closing in on him, waiting, asking him with silent accusation if he knew how easily his fleshless, half-naked brothers and sisters could freeze to death. He knew.

"Where's my father?"

"Inside." It was Anna's scared whisper that answered him. "He went back inside."

They found him, a few minutes later, hanging from the meat-hook in the cellar, the first carcass ever to be suspended there; the land-lord's men by no means pleased about it as they cut him down, since it meant delay, additional complications, a constable. Damn him. The man had always been a nuisance.

Who mourned him?

Outside, in the street, his daughter Anna fell to her knees on the wet cobbles, her thin arms around as many of his other children as they could accommodate, no idea in her reeling head but to stay there, clutching them, until such things as were about to happen had happened. Whatever they might be.

"Get those bairns off the street before they carry him out," commanded Sairellen Thackray, her loud, flat voice easily stirring the crowd of barely-shocked women who had seen and heard all this before. For whatever the man had been, and no matter how vile the treachery of his eldest son Oliver, one did not leave children in the street to perish of cold. Sairellen had no need to tell them that, although she did so, just the same.

"You'll take one, Martha-Ann, won't you? And you can make room, can't you, Mary-Ellen—Beatrice—Sophia?"

They could. For a night or two, perhaps longer, being so over-crowded in any case that it was a simple enough matter to move over the few inches it took to accommodate a stranger, who might stay among them, relatively unnoticed, forever. Or not. Who knew?

One by one the Rattrie children were led away silently by women who made no show of affection since they did not feel it, nor of pity either, which in itself brought no solutions. Stray weasels now, huge, hungry eyes swallowing their wizened, baby faces, making no protest, going where they were taken; unlikely, in this shifting, uncertain population, to see much of one another again.

The pawnbroker from St. Jude's Passage came sidling up to Oliver. "These articles of furniture are worthless, of course," he said to him. "A hard man might ask you to pay him for taking them off your hands. But, as it is, I'll take them free of charge."

Dumbly Oliver nodded his head.

The body was carried out, frail as a child's beneath a tattered sheet, and handed over to "Authority" in preparation for its pauper's grave.

The landlord's men, grumbling profusely, nailed boards across the windows, sealed the door, and went away.

The crowd dispersed.

The snow came on.

The Rattrie family was no more, only Anna still kneeling where the pawnbroker poked and pried among her mother's pathetic treasures; and Oliver. Both of them shivering with shock and with cold.

"Come inside, Anna lass, and get warm," said Sairellen. But Cara, standing by the Thackrays' doorstep, saw plainly that Anna could not move, that in her thin white face and her wraith's body through which the wind already seemed to whistle, only her huge, transparent eyes were alive, their gaze fastening on Luke as on her only hope of Heaven as he crossed the street, lifted her as carefully as a new-born child and carried her through his mother's door.

But when Oliver Rattrie attempted to follow, a stern sentinel barred the way.

"Not you, lad," said Sairellen, her face carved in granite.

He backed away, knowing why.

"It's—it's bitter cold, Mrs. Thackray," he whispered.

"Aye. No doubt the lads you sent to Northallerton jail might say the same."

She slammed the door.

"It's bitter cold," he said again, helplessly, humbly, hunching his scarecrow's shoulders, tears spilling suddenly from his eye corners.

So it was. Beneath her splendid black and scarlet cloak Cara could feel the chill, sharpened by a spasm of pity for this ugly, puny, vicious boy. And a spasm of disgust. Oliver the traitor who had sold his mates for money and then Oliver the fool who had lost every penny of it in the canal. Oliver the spy who listened at doors and windows for Christie Goldsborough. Hateful little Oliver who had been desperate and hungry and frightened every day of his life and who was shaking now with a cold she understood, until his bones rattled.

"Go across to my mother's house," she told him curtly. "She will give you a hot drink."

Ducking his head, unable to answer her, he scuttled away.

"That was kind of you, Cara." Luke's voice spoke from behind her and spinning around she fell against him as if propelled by the forces of sorrow and struggle and endless strife rising from the very cobbles of the street, feeling his arms close around her with a sense of homecoming. She had been here before. Had stood—God knew when—in this man's embrace, just so, just like this, so that when he carried her, her feet just skimming the ground, into the narrow passage between his mother's house and the next, she seemed to float on air with him, lifting her face to a kiss which did not seem strange to her and then nestling against him, the rough texture of his jacket comforting her cheek, the odor of pipe tobacco which clung to it moving her as she suddenly remembered odors of a secure and happy childhood.

Peace. Safety. Absolute trust. The stirrings of passion which—with *this* man—held no danger. So her body told her as his hard, work-stained hands touched it beneath the folds of her cloak with tenderness and integrity, her breathing in perfect tune with his as they held each other tight and fast.

Luke—and it was her body that spoke—don't let me hurt you. It was the first time she had ever felt such concern, such need to protect and cherish a grown man. Such awareness of his worth and of her own shortcomings.

"I know," he said, his mouth against her forehead. "I know." Of course. What had happened to the Rattries could still happen to her. But not while she stood in his secure embrace. Not while he kept his arms around her.

May he never release her.

There came a sharp tap on the side-scullery window, his mother's imperious hand which caused Cara to stiffen with alarm and Luke merely to smile.

"Luke," and the voice, too, was imperious. "Go fill the coal buckets. And then come inside, the pair of you. Are you daft, standing out in the weather?"

He smiled again, not yet taking his hand from Cara's shoulder, his mouth tender, his eyes amused, tolerant, steady, the pressure of his long, hard fingers telling her that if Luke said it would be all right then it would be. No other man had ever made her feel that.

"I'll get the buckets. You go inside. She won't eat you."

He went off to the backyard while she remained leaning against the wall, feeling shaken and—for a panic moment—unsteady on her feet without him there to support her. She wanted him back again. Badly. She wanted him to lift her and carry her and care for her. Yet how could she give way to it? How could she not? Oh God—had it happened to her again? Don't let me hurt him. Please let me do him no harm. This was the message her heart pounded. This time—with *this* man—her own hurt did not seem to matter.

Let me do him only good. Or nothing at all. And when she drew herself together sufficiently to go and face his mother, Oliver Rattrie was standing at the end of the passage, the narrowness of the space giving him more substance than usual, his malice spurting out of him as his tears had spurted ten minutes before.

Malice, and something more tormented and twisted than she had ever imagined.

"I saw you," he hissed at her. And suddenly her skin was crawling.

"What do you mean?" Although she knew.

"I saw you—with *him*."

How dare he? Yet daring had nothing to do with it. He had always looked at her, slyly she'd thought—longingly she now supposed—making her uncomfortable. When she had lived in that cottage next to his own he had always been *there*, under her feet, staring, watching her, listening at the wall as she almost—but never quite—made love to Daniel. Wanting her himself. And as that impotent, impossible desire of his reared up at her from his eyes and seemed to touch her—*his* dream of love turning her stomach to nausea—she pushed him aside with savage fingertips, disgust swamping even the remembrance of pity. Get away from me, foul creature—little rat—little toad—little weasel. And whether she spoke the words or not she believed he heard them as, her stomach heaving, she stepped past him into Sairellen's kitchen.

The room was warm and clean and empty, only Sairellen herself dropping vegetables in separate string nets into the cooking pot on her fire, the steam of onions and cabbage and herb dumplings making the mouth water: although Cara's had turned very dry.

"I have a word to say to you, lass."

"Yes?" She had expected it.

"So I'll say it straight out. Before Luke comes back with the coal, or Anna comes downstairs."

"All right."

"You'd do well to leave my lad alone."

Yes. On the whole—and with infinite sorrow—she tended to agree, although she did not mean to admit it. At any rate not yet, and not to Sairellen.

She sat down, flinging back her cape to show the scarlet lining and the expensive black wool dress piped in red. Bravado, she well knew it, both her energy and her confidence being at a low ebb. It had been a strange, disturbing day. She was tired.

Nevertheless.

"Is that really for you to say, Mrs. Thackray?"

"Maybe not. But I'm saying it."

"Go on then." She did not expect to be given any quarter.

"I will. Because like needs like in marriage, Cara Adeane. And I'm calling it marriage because that's what he'll be calling it, ere long, if you let him. And it won't do, lass. Like to like—mark my words. Either that or it takes one to lead and one to follow. Will you follow him? He won't follow you."

No. She knew it. Mournfully. Despairingly, almost. But she had no intention of giving in so easily. She was bound to lose him, she supposed, but that would be tomorrow. Perhaps the day after. And, until then, she was fighting still.

"He could do worse."

"Oh yes?" Clearly his mother did not think so. "And what would you do with him, lass. Set him to delivering your fancy boxes?"

She was very angry now. "Where's the shame in that?"

"No shame. But it's not work for him."

"No, it's not. So I'd set him up in something else—something he wanted . . ."

Something worthy of him. She rose to her feet in her anger and her eagerness, ready now to do battle, her energy flooding back.

"At least I wouldn't be forever pushing him into those hopeless causes of yours, Sairellen Thackray . . ."

But Sairellen's answer was quick, unruffled, and final.

"You know better than that, Cara Adeane. They're *his* causes. He gives half his income to them. Wed him and he'll want to give half of yours. Would you work your fingers to the bone, night and day, making your dresses to benefit the Chartists—or Richard Oastler's ten hours campaign?"

To benefit *Luke* she would give anything. She sat down again.

"No. And he wouldn't force me either."

"Of course he wouldn't." But Sairellen, as they both knew, was pursuing her advantage. "He believes in the rights of women as well as men. He'd let you go your way. And he'd go his. Knowing you as I know you, Cara Adeane, that wouldn't suit you. You'd try to stop him. And he wouldn't be stopped. You know it, lass—very well."

Cara looked down for a moment at her clever, agile hands, breathing hard and slowly, her head bowed not in submission but because, recognizing the truth in Sairellen's words, she was forcing herself not to believe it.

"Have I convinced you, lass?"

"No, you haven't." And she heard the stubbornness in her own voice followed, to her surprise, by Sairellen's deep, almost echoing sigh.

"Very well, Cara. Then there's something else. And maybe I didn't want to say this to you. You'll know what it is."

"No." But she did. She had even prepared herself to meet it. What she had not allowed for was how much it would hurt.

"You already belong to a man, Cara. You're Goldsborough's woman—the landlord's woman . . ."

"Sairellen . . ." Was she asking for pity? They both thought so. But Sairellen, at that precise moment, could not afford to give it.

She raised a roughened, work-swollen hand instead, commanding silence.

"Let me finish. And hear me. I don't want—*I won't have*—the attention of that man drawn here, to this house, to my lad, by you or by anybody. Do you hear me, Cara?"

"I hear." But when she looked up, intending defiance and insolence if she had to, the rough sympathy in Sairellen's face, rather than the contempt she had expected, took her off-balance to a point where she could cry out in all sincerity, "He doesn't care what I do, Sairellen. He only wants me because I'm convenient, and because other men want me. He likes that. That's all."

And thinking of those other men, Ned O'Mara, Ben Braithwaite, Oliver Rattrie—dear God—a dozen others, she shuddered.

"Sairellen—he doesn't *care*."

Sairellen sighed again. "Happen not. And it's not that I blame you, lass. Maybe, in your place, I'd have done the same—except that I've never been a handsome woman, like you, so I've had neither the chance nor the temptation. And when you've never been invited to sin then I call it foolish to take credit for virtue. So I don't judge you. But, where my lad's concerned, I can't take a risk either. You say Goldsborough doesn't care. But the whole of St. Jude's can testify to his queer temper. And how do I know—or how do you know—that he's not the same mad devil as his father? He surely looks like him."

"I don't know anything about his father."

Nor did it seem to matter. But Sairellen once again gave a deep, hollow sigh and shook her head.

"No. He'd not be likely to tell you either. I reckon he'd be glad to forget him, except that Frizingley was a smaller place in those days— much smaller—and everybody knew about Squire Goldsborough and how he'd have put chains on his poor lady if he could, for jealousy. I had a sister in service at the manor and she reckoned you could see that poor woman shrinking, day by day. From too much loving and wanting to make her all his own so that she couldn't breathe for him, or stir hand or foot without him trying to put a strait-jacket on her. I've seen her myself, sitting in her carriage, not daring to look left or right, with him beside her just looking at her—*eating* her with those pitch black eyes. Jealousy like that is a sickness. A madness. It was too much for any woman to bear."

"His son's not like that, Sairellen."

"Nor was the squire, until she came along. Just a roistering young buck like the rest of them, fond of his cards and his claret and not a maidservant safe from him if she was under thirty. Then—Well—everybody knew what he did. Not that he ever paid for it."

"What, Sairellen?" Ought she to know? Might it be a help to her, even, the next time she wanted something from Christie?

"No, *they* don't pay—the quality. They band together, close ranks, and hush everything up. One law for them, another for us. Him a Goldsborough and her a Covington-Pym. They forget that the servants have eyes and ears, and the word gets out."

"*What*, Sairellen?" Unease flickered briefly in her mind, warning her that Christie's secrets, after all, might be better left alone, but her mind looking back over a far distance, Sairellen seemed almost to be talking to her memories.

"No, he never paid. And it didn't keep him from his hunting and his shooting and his wenching, either. Nor from selling off his land, in bits and pieces, to pay for his pleasures. If he was mad with jealousy before, then he was mad with drink afterward—or guilt. Maybe that was his punishment."

Cara swallowed rather nervously, no longer certain she wished for an explanation. Perhaps it would be better not to ask. Assuredly. She would wait until the haze had gone from Sairellen's eyes and then begin to talk of something else.

"What did he do, Sairellen?" she said.

"He killed her." Abruptly Sairellen's eyes became sharp, gray chips of flint again, her voice curt, almost matter-of-fact. "They didn't call it that, of course—the Goldsboroughs and the Larks and the Covington-Pyms. But so it was. He couldn't live with how much he wanted her, my sister reckoned. So he killed her. His lady wife."

Christmas passed. And, in the following February, Richard Oastler the Factory King, Champion of the Factory Children, was released from prison, sufficient funds having been raised to pay off his debts, his arrival at Brighouse Station being attended by a crowd of several thousand supporters of as many shades of opinion. Oastler's men one and all in their various fashions. Veterans of the Ten Hours' Movement who had made the Pilgrimage to York, like Luke Thackray. Campaigners against the New Poor Law and its evil new workhouses in which the poor were imprisoned, like the radical Parson Bull of Bierley and Luke Thackray. Dedicated Chartists who sought political freedom for the working-classes, like the radical landlord of the Dog and Gun, and Luke Thackray. Men of sensitivity from all walks of life who, quite simply, recognized Oastler's humanity. Like a minor Lark or two, a few fairly distant Braithwaite cousins, men of letters and law and medicine, men of vision. Luke Thackray.

And the Chartist candidate.

Daniel spent the eve of the great day with Gemma as he spent every evening she could be at liberty. Far more of them, in fact, than he had imagined possible or—to begin with—had even wanted. Although the wanting had changed both in its degree and its quality. Quite soon, it seemed to him although so gradually, so naturally, that he could name no precise moment at which the faint flicker of relief her absences at Almsmead initially afforded him had been snuffed out like a candle by the softer, infinitely more appealing sensation of missing her.

He told her so. "I miss you, Gemma." He told her many things, whatever sprang into his mind, wasting nothing that might please her by holding it back from her. He talked to her. Teased her. Lectured her. Flirted with her. Listened to her. He desired her openly and happily with all the abundant, uncomplicated sensuality of his youth and health, all the delicacy of his imaginative razor-sharp mind. And, with regard to the days and nights they spent apart he never questioned her. Nor she him. She had been with her husband. He had taken—or not taken—such diversions as he thought fit. It did not seem to matter. She had said to him, gravely and sincerely, her small chin tilted at the pugnacious angle which so pleased and amused him, that she would have this measure of time, however short or long, for her own self. And then she would do her duty. This one measure, and no more. He understood and had made up his mind—*chosen*—to devote himself to her wholly and entirely, until the measure was full.

He did not even ask how long. Nor think of it. Whenever she was in Frizingley they were together. When her duty should recall her permanently to her mother's house and to her marriage, he knew she would tilt her chin once again to that resolute yet so vulnerable angle and tell him so. Whereupon he would resume the journey from which she had distracted him almost a year ago, would sling his bag over his shoulder, set off across the moor to Leeds and take a train, the first which seemed good to him.

Trains and roads and ships. His own life once more, so contrary to hers. A wandering man. And a motionless woman who would remain here on her lotus-feet which had been bound and crippled as securely, in their fashion, as her mother's, rooting her in this one place, this one soil which claimed her and diminished her. While he would continue rootless, swift and haphazard, settling nowhere.

But until then she held him. For if her one experience of love was to come to her through him—as seemed likely—then he wanted it, however imperfect, to be the best he had. Flawed of course and less than whole-hearted which seemed, he thought wryly, to be a fairly accurate reflection of himself, but unstinting, his admiration, his honest liking for her, his *pride*, it began to seem, in her integrity, her soundness, her worth, growing day by day.

She moved him. His life had never lacked affection but the truth was that no woman had ever loved him so generously as Gemma Gage. And, being moved, he told her that too.

"You move me, Gemma."

"Heavens—that sounds uncomfortable."

"So it is."

They smiled at one another through the dark brown shadows of the house in which they felt so perfectly at ease. A restless, reckless man held, almost calmly, almost in tranquillity, by a woman who showered him not with the material gifts it would have made him uneasy to accept, but with herself. A woman who was pure and honest even in her sensuality, who could walk naked toward him through these same dear dark brown shadows without any taint of wantonness, wanting his hands and his heart upon her in the same manner as she placed her own upon him, delicately, with a tenderness which, even in moments of deepest rapture, retained its innocence.

And her rapture in itself thrilled him by its depth and intensity, her excitement and the wonder it aroused in her generating his own, without either of them being aware of the sexual dominion she was attaining over him. He knew, simply, that he wanted her body. Opening sturdy, generous, loving arms she gave it to him and took his, loving him without shame or restraint while her time of love endured.

And here too he made certain that her measure was full.

"I want you, Gemma." He would send that message to her with his eyes whenever she visited him in his classroom, across the heads of his lethargically scribbling pupils, for the sheer pleasure of seeing the hushed, dreaming quality of her answering smile. And as soon as the children had piled up their untidy slates and gone, he would speak the words to her.

"I want you, Gemma."

"Now?"

"Absolutely now."

She would laugh her delight, take his hands. She was his, eagerly and joyfully. His friend and confidante who knew his moods and his mind, his great hopes and small achievements. His lover, rich with wisdom, who could pour herself over him like a healing balm, whenever healing was needed.

Gemma.

"Let me look at you." And, in the soft lamplight of her bedroom at the manor or by the light of his schoolhouse candle, she learned to think of herself—because he desired her—as a desirable woman. That much at least, he told himself, he had known how to give her. Not beauty as such but an illusion of beauty, a belief in her own power to attract, a confidence of movement and manner never to be found in women who considered themselves to be plain.

That much. Not enough, of course. But something to leave behind.

"Look at me, then." She did not say "Enjoy me," but it was enjoyment she offered, enjoyment he took in her smooth brown skin, her heavy breasts which were, nevertheless, so softly rounded, her strongly arched back which became supple at his touch, the brown oval of her face on the pillow surrounded by the fine brown hair which he had loosened from its prim confinement of hairpins and chignon to a disorder that had the scent of fresh lemons and the texture of silk.

Her clear brown eyes, the sharply questing intelligence behind them which, for all its keenness, did not and could not and must never know that the source of his own deepest emotions had been tapped and then scorched only once—by Cara Adeane—remaining dried up and dormant ever since. Leaving him with only the lesser capacities to like, to respect, to desire, to grow fond. Above all to grieve honestly and sincerely at his own inability to lose his head now over a woman who so thoroughly deserved it.

When their measure of time was over he would miss her, he knew that. But those trains and ships and broad highways would still retain their power to enchant him, while her memory would be no searing pain, like Cara's, but a lingering, altogether bearable, sweetness. She was the best woman he knew or would ever be likely to know. He would *enjoy* remembering her. On the night before Oastler's return to the West Riding, lying beside her in her huge, canopied bed, he realized how much he wished it could be otherwise. She deserved not only his love but his suffering and, the two going so inextricably together, he accepted, with bitterness, his inability to give her either.

"Gemma, are you awake?"

"Yes." She rarely wasted the nights they spent together in sleep, finding a rich, deep pleasure in simply lying beside him in the dark listening to the living and breathing of his body, in the cocoon of this wide, elaborate bed where Tristan had left so little impression.

She rarely thought of Tristan or, at least, not at any level which troubled her. Not now, in this time she had chosen to call her own. Although she saw him quite often, of course, usually at Almsmead, where, from the start, she had found it almost unnervingly easy to persuade him to spend his time in doing, when all was said and done, very much as he pleased.

August, the month in which her love for Daniel had first declared itself, had also brought the start of the grouse-shooting season when Tristan had asked for nothing better than the excitements of the grouse-moor Mr. Adolphus Moon had recently purchased from the Larks.

Autumn and winter had offered him partridge and pheasant; invitations to shooting parties, some of them at a fair distance, from which Gemma had had no trouble in getting herself excluded; a deer-stalking trip to a Scottish castle which had been a cheerfully bawdy, entirely masculine affair; the thrills of the Far Flatley hunt. Long days in the fresh air, striding over plowed fields with a gun, or in the saddle. Heavy hunting and shooting dinners followed by heavier nights of claret and cards and billiards with hunting and shooting gentlemen who, at this season of the year, preferred the pursuit of game-birds and foxes to the pursuit of women, so that when he did happen to stumble into her bed his embraces were rarely more than fraternal.

Yet, when he wished to make love to her she allowed him to do so, recognizing very clearly now, from her new and joyful depth of experience, how much he considered it to be his duty, accepting him no more and no less placidly than she had always done because she considered it to be her duty too. She felt no guilt. And if, occasionally, the calm and friendly manner with which she treated her husband surprised her, she had only to remind herself that she was continuing to give him everything he wanted, which had never included her passion. He had married her for this life, this ease, these sporting guns and thoroughbred horses, this carefree, mindless existence to which he seemed so perfectly suited. She had married him to gain her freedom from another man—her father—who loved her and was loved by her far more than Tristan. And, if adultery had formed no part of her original plans, her love for Daniel had no shame in it, nothing, in any shade or nuance, that had succeeded in making her feel like an adulteress.

Therefore she did not behave like one.

How foolish, she reckoned—as her father might have reckoned—to squander the treasure of her time with Daniel in self-reproach. How futile to stir up thoughts of sin and try to convince herself that she ought to believe in them when what she was doing felt so completely right. Particularly since she risked hurting no one, she believed—at any significant level—but herself. And, setting her chin at the fighting angle which so delighted Daniel, she claimed the right to take that risk, to do herself that hurt, and—should she be wounded or broken—to pick up her own pieces afterward, bind her own scars in her own fashion. As best she could. And be a trouble to no one.

There would be no cries for help. She knew her responsibilities and never, for one moment, thought of shirking them. Though the list was long. Her mother, who was entitled to her consideration. Tristan, to whom she had made promises and who was, after all, keeping his part of the bargain. Linnet, a fighter too in her way who, missing every victory by inches, was both to be pitied and to be reckoned with. Her father. Much loved. Deeply resented. Her own blood and bone.

She could save only a few precious drops from the ocean she owed to them for Daniel. Would they grudge it to her? Yes. She felt sure they would. But the knowledge only strengthened her resolve, firming the angle of her chin which was already quite firm enough as she lived the surface of her life among them, attending her mother's parties in the dark satin dresses cut so severely and skillfully for her by Miss Adeane, smiling serenely across the room at her father as he muttered darkly to Sir Felix Lark about the perfidy of the gentry in supporting cranks like Richard Oastler and his notions of factory reform; smiling, reassuringly this time, at her mother's fears that Sir Felix, who made her uncomfortable, and his mother, Lady Lark, of whom she was still in awe, might take offense and refuse to come to Almsmead again; smiling, only politely, as she chaperoned Linnet through long, tedious visits to the Colcloughs, listening with only a fraction of her mind to Uriah's sermons and Linnet's pious sighing; smiling again, in the carriage home, with some real amusement, as Linnet, instantly shedding her saintly mantle, began to scatter hints like sparkling, quite poisonous drops of rain about the outrageous behavior of Mrs. Marie Moon who, forsaking all other passions, had taken to spending her time with a certain very minor, entirely penniless Lark in a manner—as Linnet discreetly put it—likely to do "the poor boy" harm.

"Lady Lark, of course, is mortified. The young man was entrusted to her care, it seems, when he got himself sent down from Oxford. She was to do great things with him, put some backbone into him, you know—his poor mamma being much too nervous and weak . . . In the head, perhaps? With the Larks one often wonders. But now our Madame Marie has bewitched him right away. *Quite* at her feet, one hears, fed on chocolates and champagne just like her poodle. How sweet. Except that Lady Lark, as I said, is horribly put out about it. His dear mamma is having the vapors and swearing that her fledgling's life forces are being drained away. Whereas Mr. Adolphus Moon—poor soul. Naturally one's heart goes out to him. He has been obliged to return his children to their aunt, to spare them the example. And really—really—one can hardly blame him—can one?"

"For what, Linnet?"

"Why—for taking—well—the most *extreme* of measures."

"Divorce?"

"Yes." Linnet's voice sounded absent, her exquisite features sharpening and then—very rapidly—hiding beneath a mask of airy smiles. "Yes. Why not? Although divorce," she wrinkled her nose, "is so socially awkward. And costs a fortune too. Annulment would be the answer. *Annulment.*" She breathed the word almost with rapture. "I wonder what could be done about that? One would need to know ... And who would have that kind of information about her? Captain Goldsborough?"

Gemma, realizing that Linnet was talking to herself, went on smiling.

"But would you marry a divorced man, Linnet?"

Instantly the airy mask shattered, a smile of brilliant, brittle gaiety breaking through. "*Marry.* Good Heavens, Gemma. Mr. Adolphus Moon? Whatever are you thinking of? The poor little man barely reaches my elbow. And even if he stood six feet four and as beautiful as my brother, you know that my heart is given entirely—don't you?— to my saintly Uriah."

And closing one delicately veined eyelid in a wink she leaned forward, all fragrance and amusement, to whisper a few swift comments regarding the origins of Uriah's saintliness in Gemma's unusually receptive ear.

Gemma's smile deepened and remained undimmed throughout dinner at Almsmead that same evening, despite her father's scowl and his audible mutterings when he saw her mother's—or Linnet's—choice of guests. An array of lounging, staring Larks who made Amabel so uneasy. Mr. Adolphus Moon, who so embarrassed her. Captain Goldsborough, who had never owned her beautiful Almsmead as he had once owned her previous home at the manor but nevertheless behaved as if he had.

"Are these *your* friends, Amabel?" John-William Dallam wanted to know.

"Oh, darling—of course—please don't fuss ..." She was pleading with him, trying hard to convince herself that she *did*, in fact, like these people, did want them here, *could* view them as welcome guests rather than hostile and scornful invaders.

"Say the word," her husband offered, "and I'll put them all at the other side of the door."

Amabel gasped and turned pale.

"Oh—John-William ..."

Coming between them Gemma slipped an arm through theirs, drawing them together, smiling at each in turn and then at Tristan as he came hurrying downstairs, late for dinner as he always was after a full day's hunting, his uncomplicated soul moving easily, happily in its superbly healthy body as he came to kiss his wife.

She smiled now very serenely.

"Hello, Tristan. Was it a good day?"

"Splendid."

And it would be a good day tomorrow. He was leaving to hunt foxes for a week in Leicestershire. She was going home to Daniel, returning to her real life, her true identity, content to leave behind, in her mother's house, the sturdy, brown-haired, serious-minded little woman, far too busy with her own odd little occupations, her mill-school and her decaying little manor, even to realize that her husband neglected her.

"Tristan—are you off *again*?" murmured Linnet wickedly, exchanging a knowing glance with Captain Goldsborough, who could be relied on, it seemed, to share her opinion as to why the husband of such a bluestocking should spend so much time away from home. Not much of a wife, Linnet's glance implied, for a splendid, sporting, *virile* young blood like her brother. Was it any wonder that he felt the need to get off on his own—or perhaps not quite on his own—every now and again? Captain Goldsborough's pitch black eyes conveyed to her that it was no wonder to him.

"Poor Gemma," sighed Linnet.

"Gemma—if you'd rather I didn't go ...?" Tristan offered later that night, having accompanied her to bed instead of lingering in the billiard-room as he had, in fact, intended.

"Tristan—what nonsense. I want you to enjoy yourself."

She was speaking the truth.

"Well yes—" he frowned, torn as he often seemed to be between reluctance to sacrifice his own pleasures and a nagging urge to do the decent thing. Whatever it might be. "But we can't have people talking, can we? Don't want them saying that I ... Lord, you know what I mean."

Yes. She knew. And was he unfaithful to her, casually, occasionally? She thought so. She even hoped so until she understood that it did not really matter to either of them.

"Tristan. *Enjoy* yourself."

It was a command. She was the stronger. And now, on a moonlit February night, she lay with Daniel in her own bed, playing a far more honorable role, it seemed to her—albeit adulterous—than any she fulfilled at Almsmead. Sin, of course. But with love on her part. Integrity, she believed, on his.

Her measure of time.

"Gemma—are you awake?"

"Yes."

"Wouldn't you like to come with me in the morning, to meet Oastler?"

"No."

"Why not?"

"Oh—you can be sure I have my reasons." Smiling at him through the dappling moonlight, her special smile of joy in loving that could flow easily and sweetly into laughter, she looked wise and a little mysterious.

"Why then? Because he opposes your father?"

"No. Although he does oppose him, of course."

"He does. He'll stop him from keeping his engines running twenty-four hours a day and working children in relays to stay within the law."

"If he can." She smiled again. "And they'll be my engines, Daniel, you know. One day."

"I know." It made him uneasy to think of it. As it made him uneasy to think of other things. English, Protestant, mill-owning Gemma, his best and most trusted friend. As he, who despised everything she stood for, was trying to be hers.

"Is that why you won't come?"

She shook her head, the lemon-scented brown hair brushing his shoulder.

"Why then? The gossip if anyone saw you?"

"Oh no. People think me so odd already that I believe I could get away with it. What *has* the Dallam girl done now? Gone tramping across the moor with her Chartist schoolmaster. Well—I never. Poor John-William. And poor, poor Amabel."

They laughed softly, together.

"Then come. On the tramp. It's a good life."

Suddenly he saw her, striding alongside him bareheaded and gypsy-fashion, her hair loose and taking flight on the wind, her sturdy, cob-pony limbs keeping pace with his. Suddenly—fiercely—he wanted her like that.

"*Come*, Gemma. And politics be damned." Fathers and husbands too, for that matter.

She sighed. "Oh no, Daniel. Mr. Oastler's politics have nothing to do with it, don't you see. It's just—well—eight miles across the moor to Brighouse Station and eight miles back. Rough ground and a very tidy distance, when you must know quite well—Mr. Carey—that I have not been brought up to walk. Only to stroll. And only then with my carriage following discreetly behind me to pick me up if I swoon or stumble—which, with all my skirts and petticoats, is only too likely. I couldn't manage it, Daniel. You'd have to carry me. Or abandon me, which might be best, considering that I weigh rather more than a feather."

It had not occurred to him. Lotus-feet again, planted not in solid earth but in the soft pile of drawing-room carpets and carriage rugs. A spirit fit for adventure in a body conditioned to helplessness. And he understood, with some surprise, that he hated her father. Or her mother. Or whoever it was who had cushioned and cosseted and overprotected her in those velvet swaddling bands so that only her will had been allowed to grow and harden.

"Run away with me," he said, wishing it might be possible, wishing he could mean it.

"Well—not very far. And not very fast either. Only the five miles there and five miles back that one's carriage-horses can manage in a day."

Throwing back the bedcovers he studied her body intently, brooding over it, grieving over it almost, a peasant sturdiness forced into the drooping languor of a hot-house lily, good, serviceable bones designed for a strength that had never been tested, tender, unblemished knees which had knelt only on a velvet prayer stool or a silk cushion, soft, smooth things which, as his mouth brushed them, turned his sorrow and his pity for her into desire. How timeless she was. How eternal. A lake of still, deep water into which he needed now, absolutely and as if his life depended upon it, to plunge, his senses instantly and hugely aflame.

"I want you, Gemma." And she slid down to him, swathes of her like brown silk all around him, gathering him to her, giving herself and taking him, no longer a penetration on his part but a joining together, a fusion of his body with hers so that, for a few dizzy moments, there seemed no inch of skin that was entirely hers or his, no clinging-place of bone to bone, no point of contact where he could be certain that his body ended and hers began.

"Heavens," she said, her laughter sounding weak. "Good Heavens."

Breathing heavily, he sank his head into her breasts needing comfort for having loved her so mightily.

"Yes," he said.

He left her very early the next morning, slipping out like a thief before the servants were awake although he was in no doubt that the housekeeper, Martha-Ann, knew all about him. Yet a servant who gossiped lost not only her position but all hope of another and since Gemma seemed to trust the woman he supposed he must do the same. Possibly Gemma's mill-manager Mr. Ephraim Cook and his wife knew about him too. Or suspected. But it could serve no interest of theirs to betray him, considering the precarious state of health of Gemma's father and the decidedly uncommercial character of her husband. While the husband himself and his exquisite sister who had drifted into the mill-school once or twice, patted a few heads and drifted quickly out again, seemed far too busy about their own affairs to take much notice of Gemma's.

Not that he feared discovery on his own account. What could the father do to him, after all, other than warn him off or try to buy him off or have him whipped out of town? While, if the husband felt obliged to take a shot at him, he acknowledged no similar obligation to make himself a willing target. Yet discovery for Gemma would be a disaster which stirred in him an unexpected vein of guilt and caution. What would he be able to do for her then? Indeed, could anything he had in him to give her possibly compensate for the loss of her good name and her security? For the luxury she did not value because she had never felt its lack? He doubted it. And therefore, for the first time in his life, he deliberately curbed his recklessness and—for her sake—was discreet.

He cared deeply about her well being. About *her*. Yet he was not long on his way to Brighouse that raw February morning before his conscious mind had ceased to think of her at all, the road—*any* road—claiming his eager attention, the distance meaning nothing to him—

as it would have meant nothing to Cara—nor to the hardy, wiry men who fell into step beside him, coming down in droves from the hills in every direction as Brighouse drew near.

"Now then, lad—and how are you?" Some of them had recognized Frizingley's Chartist candidate, an Irishman, of course, although he could be forgiven for that in view of the risks he'd taken for the Cause.

"I'm well. And you?" He remembered none of them, these stocky, craggy Northcountrymen looking much alike to him, although it made no difference to the carefree warmth of his greeting.

"It's a grand morning."

"So it is." And he walked on with chance-met strangers who, in the space of ten minutes, had become chance-met friends, fellow way-farers, comrades in arms.

So had it always been with him.

Turning up his collar against the wind, his dark head bare, a spot-ted black and red gamekeeper's kerchief around his neck, he strode out into the cold, bright day—into a hundred such days to come—whistling these English marching songs when the words evaded him, his blood stirring, his heart light.

So would it be again.

There were ten thousand men and women and four brass bands waiting around the Station Hotel at Brighouse where Richard Oastler had spent the night to take him back in triumph to Huddersfield, which as yet had no station of its own. He was fifty-five years old and had spent three years and two months in jail for debts incurred in the service of men and women like these who, in their turn, had raised the money to pay what he owed and set him free. And now they expected a great deal—perhaps too much—of him.

He was a man of presence and dignity. A man of emotion. No man of the people, to begin with, being High Church and High Tory, a country gentleman employed as steward by Squire Thornhill of Fixby who had first lent him money and then had him locked up for debt, leaving a mainly Nonconformist, Chartist, very far from Tory popu-lation to buy him out again.

He was a man of natural authority, a man who was *noticed* by other men, a supporter of the campaign to abolish slavery in the West Indies until, one day in 1830, only fourteen years past, he had been invited to ponder the state of Yorkshire's mills. And had looked on slavery of another kind, much nearer to hand.

"Let truth speak out," he had written to the editors of the *Leeds Mercury*, who may not have greatly wished to hear. "Thousands of our fellow creatures and fellow subjects, both male and female, the miserable inhabitants of a Yorkshire town, are at this moment existing in a state of slavery more horrid than are the victims of that hellish system Colonial Slavery. The very streets are wet with the tears of innocent victims at the accursed shrine of avarice who are compelled by the thong or strap of the overlooker to hasten half-dressed to these magazines of British infantile slavery—the worsted mills in the town and neighborhood of Bradford."

Or Halifax, of course, or Huddersfield. Or Frizingley where the looms were kept turning day and night when trade was good, tended by weary women and those pitiful "factory brats" who were kept awake, toward the end of their fifteen-hour shifts, by that dreaded overlooker's thong, choking on the dust and grime they took in with their few mouthfuls of food eaten—to save time—in the loomgate, subject to appalling injuries, broken arms and thighs, torn flesh, the loss of scalps and eyes and lives when, despite the vigilance of the strap, they tumbled fast asleep into the machines.

For wages which could hardly feed a sparrow.

Oastler and his Short Time Committees declared war on all that. They would have the ten hour working day, at least for women and children which—since no millmaster could afford to keep on his engines for the men alone—meant ten hours for all.

They would have the ten hour day. Oastler and his Ten Hours' Men would raise the North for it. The Short Time Committees, the gathering crowds, the pilgrims on the march to York, chanted it:

> We will have the Ten Hours' Bill.
> That we will, that we will.
> Or the land shall ne'er be still.
> We will have the Ten Hours' Bill.
> For Oastler says we will.

What they had received, after four years of mass meetings, petitions, wild unrest and the threat of more to come, was "The Act" forbidding the employment of children under nine, and stipulating that those under thirteen might work no more than forty-eight hours a week and attend schools like Gemma's for two hours a day. A small victory instantly canceled out by the system of working children in shifts so that the working hours of men and women need not be reduced at all.

It was not enough. Both Luke Thackray and his mother, Sairellen, had stood in the rain and heard Oastler say so. And they had cheered him as loudly as they had cheered in the Castle Yard at York, continuing the struggle, at his direction, against fresh forces of oppression, the New Poor Law which by then had started to creep north, having—without too much trouble—already filled the southern half of England with large new workhouses into which the poor were herded, graded, separated into groups labeled "sick," "insane," "male," "female," and locked away in their separate categories.

Forever, in most cases, following the New Poor Law policy of making conditions in the workhouses so horrible, so shameful, that people would—it was hoped—become industrious, hard-working, give up strong drink, or starve to death, before making an application to enter.

But what the quieter agricultural populations of the South had accepted would not do for the harder, more turbulent masses of the industrial North. The North would not have it. Oastler and his Short Time Committees said it over and over, loud and clear, and the North agreed with them. Poverty was not a crime to be punished with imprisonment. Nor was it the result of laziness, inflamed sexual appetites or natural inferiority, as the Poor Law Commissioners seemed to think, but of social oppression. Luke Thackray had carried that message back to Frizingley, one sweltering August day, with Richard Oastler's blessing. And so thoroughly did the North respond that when an Assistant Poor Law Commissioner arrived in Huddersfield to meet the local Board of Guardians, the Riot Act had had to be read to save his skin from the angry crowds. No Huddersfield inn would give him room and board. Effigies of the Poor Law Officers were burned in the market place. And when a meeting of the Workhouse Board was finally held the Oastlerites broke down the door and canceled all the Board's decisions.

The North would not, and did not, have it. But the North did not keep its Factory King for much longer either, Squire Thornhill intervening at this moment to claim back the money which Oastler had long since given away to the needy, the unfortunate, the Short Time Committees, the Anti-Poor Law Campaign. Causes which no longer found favor with the Squire who had come to feel that his steward, instead of saving the world, would have been better employed in looking after his estate.

Oastler went to prison. Chartism blazed out suddenly, fiercely, and then seemed to flicker although not to fade. The world outside the prison walls moved on, perhaps only an inch or two, while Oastler remained motionless inside. And even now, as he was escorted all the way home to Huddersfield by cheering crowds and stridently triumphant brass bands, there were some—Daniel Carey among them—who wondered how he would take up his work again within the wider movement of Chartism which catered by no means exclusively for factory reform.

With the ten hour working day still to fight for, still looming large in his mind, could he really make the adjustment? Or would he remain on the fringes of the new agitation to carry out his own reforms in his own fashion, the Factory King unwilling to accept that the quickest road to his ten hour day was through the Charter?

It was the subject of much discussion later that day between Daniel and Luke Thackray who, having spotted each other in the crowd, had quenched their thirst in the same ale-house, shared a meal of pork pies and pickled onions and then, as the early winter dark began to fall, made their way, in no great hurry, back to Frizingley.

There had been speeches, declarations, pledges of loyalty brother to brother, much back-slapping and laughter, a few tears. Daniel, never averse to airing his views, particularly after a jug or two of ale and a drop of malt whisky, had stood, most of the convivial evening, leaning against a bar-counter, speaking at length on the Rights of Man as they concerned his listeners, both enthusing and amusing them with his verbal blue-prints for at least a dozen perfect societies. Luke, his pipe in his hand, had told, by request only, the tale of his pilgrimage to York and had given, to the older men, such details as he remembered of the massacre of Peterloo and his martyred father.

It had been a long day but even so, with a three hour walk over rough, uphill ground before them, they felt no need to pace themselves, leaving Huddersfield behind and striding out in the general direction of Frizingley with no apparent regard for either the dark or the cold. Neither one of them possessed an overcoat. They simply turned up their collars and went on their way, Luke taller, much more loosely put together, his legs in their Sunday-best moleskin trousers much longer, Daniel a more compact, far more flamboyant figure with his scarlet neck-cloth and his jacket of Chartist green, his hands in his pockets, whistling snatches of English marching songs and Irish ballads, still setting the world to rights, talking easily, rapidly, while Luke, drawing on his pipe, dropped no more than an occasional accurate word into the conversational pool, each one a well-aimed stone causing its share of ripples.

And having settled without the least animosity that Luke would probably support first Oastler and the localized issues of factory reform and then the Charter, Daniel the Charter alone, they talked on for the pleasure of talking, of morals and music and manners, poets and philosophers and preachers, a classically-educated and a self-educated man each with his own brand of knowledge, so intent on sharing and comparing that they were both equally startled by the figure which seemed to come upon them as if it had risen from the ground.

"I reckon you'll not be wanting me alongside you, Luke Thackray."

Daniel saw a thin, crook-shouldered lad in his early twenties, he supposed, pasty-faced and sharp featured as a rodent with his red-rimmed eyes and furtive manner, his clothing by no means shabby, a very decent broadcloth coat, in fact, when one really looked at it through the impression of unwholesomeness he somehow created. Daniel knew, at once, that he did not like him. He saw too that the stranger did not like Luke Thackray and that Luke, although fully aware of it, seemed disinclined to make a fuss.

"Why not, Oliver? If we're going in the same direction. You'll know the face of our Chartist candidate I reckon. Daniel—this is Oliver Rattrie, who used to be a neighbor of mine."

"Yes. I know Mr. Daniel Carey all right."

Unable to return the compliment Daniel said a brief "Good evening," puzzled by the degree of emotion in the young man's face.

"You'll have been to Huddersfield, Luke," he said, his thin mouth working strangely. "To see Oastler?"

"You know I have, Oliver."

Luke's voice sounded perfectly steady, so natural and matter-of-fact that Daniel could find nothing in it to cause, in this strange young Oliver, such a jittering of what looked like temper and nerves. Yet—whatever it was—the boy was shaking with it, his emaciated body in disjointed turmoil beneath his incongruously smart new jacket.

Luke had evidently noticed the jacket too.

"You're looking well, Oliver."

"I can't complain. I do the best I can, Luke."

"Aye. You'll have been to see Oastler yourself, I expect."

"I have. A fine man. And a crowd of fine men around him."

Luke drew on his pipe and then grinned suddenly, not unkindly. "Very fine, Oliver. Will you be able to remember all of their names tomorrow?"

At once Daniel understood, accepting Luke's comment as a warning to himself to guard his tongue, to say nothing in the presence of an informer—and, God knew, there were plenty of them—that might harm himself or others. Filthy little brat. Daniel glared at him, conveying contempt and then experiencing a moment of shock as Oliver Rattrie's sore, red-rimmed eyes darted at him a glance of pure and almost comically savage hate. What had *he* done to merit that? He had never seen the lad before in his life. Or, at least, had never noticed him. Was the boy half-witted as well as treacherous? Certainly he looked it, standing there with his bones rattling like a demented skeleton, his eyes spitting venom at a stranger. Unbalanced, certainly. An opinion confirmed by the manner in which, after keeping pace with them for a quarter of an hour, he suddenly broke away on a path of his own, muttering about "friends to meet" as he disappeared into the dark.

"I wonder what friends he'll find up there," said Luke calmly, his eyes on the high, stony track Oliver had taken.

"Where does it lead?"

"The main road if he climbs far enough. But if he takes to the road he'll have to walk a good few miles farther than us to get to the same place. Maybe he's scared to be on the moor alone. Aye—very likely. He could meet a lot of men tonight, coming back from Huddersfield, with no reason to wish him well."

"An informer?"

"Yes. Not a good one to begin with. He sold the names of the Plug Rioters to his master back in 1842 and nearly got himself drowned by their wives for his trouble. But he works for somebody else now who seems to have taught him his trade. I never caught a glimpse of him today and I had my eyes open."

"Would it be a bad thing if somebody *did* catch him alone on the moor?"

"Maybe not. But I couldn't do it, Daniel. Could you?"

Daniel hesitated, and then sighed. "No. I'd even like to. But when it came to it . . . No. More's the pity."

"And that's just what it is, isn't it. Pity." Luke's voice was completely without sentimentality. "A lad who's lived worse than a stray dog. Never enough to eat. Barefoot until he learned how to steal himself a pair of clogs—and then, I reckon, he'd never manage to get the right size. Verminous and lousy too, as I remember him, since the house he lived in was crawling with bedbugs and lice and a rare assortment of fleas. Everybody knew about the Rattrie brand of fleas in St. Jude's, I can tell you, so nobody would ever have anything to do with him. And St. Jude's isn't very particular. A lad has to be really dirty, really scabby and mangy and mucky to stand out in *that* neighborhood. Oliver stood out. Now he has a new coat and real leather boots, I notice, and smells of strong soap—maybe a mite too strongly. So he's come up in the world, by his standards, I reckon . . ."

"He doesn't like you, does he."

"Ah well—" Luke's wide, strong mouth smiled, just a little, its movement crinkling the fair skin at his eye corners. "No. I suppose he doesn't."

And for a moment that was all he said, his eyes seeing through the winter dark to some warm memory which evidently gave him pleasure and which—it seemed—he intended keeping to himself.

"Does he have a reason? To dislike you, I mean?" Daniel was unashamedly curious, his interest in this tall, craggy, quiet man increasing with his liking and respect. Already he considered Luke Thackray to be a friend—friendship springing up rapidly between traveling men—and one had a right, surely, to know the hearts and minds, and possibly the loves, of one's friends.

Although he was far from certain that Luke would tell him.

He did.

"Yes." He was speaking slowly, still smiling very slightly. Could it even be tenderly? "There's a reason. A girl. He certainly can't have her. But then—neither can I."

"Do you want her?"

"Oh yes." There was no hesitation. No doubt. No self-pity. "I want her all right."

"Could you get her?"

Luke hesitated again but only briefly this time. "Oliver Rattrie seems to think so," he said. "And—*yes*—I reckon I'd have a chance. But it wouldn't do. There'd be no happiness in it, you see. Not for long. Like needs like, they say. I reckon I agree."

Was that a sufficient reason? Abruptly, shockingly, the memory of Cara Adeane shot into Daniel's mind and lodged there like a poisonous, precious dart, causing him pain.

Once it had been sufficient for her.

Never quite, it seemed, for him.

"If you want her, Luke, then—for God's sake—*take* her. I know what I'm saying."

"Aye. I reckon you do."

"Take her, Luke, and worry about the rights and wrongs and the common sense of it later. I'm telling you. If you let her go you'll regret it."

"I know."

"But you'll let her go just the same."

It was neither a question nor a rebuke, simply a statement of cold, not always sweet, reason. So people left each other every day, because a career or a conscience might suffer. Because mamma or papa—or a husband—would not like it. Because it would not do. Not for long. His hands clenching into fists he was conscious of only one violent thought, thudding against his head like a hammer-blow. *Why* could he not forget her? Why—every now and again—did this desire for her come clawing its way inside him. Unbidden. Unwelcome.

The February wind was very cold and now, as the day's elation faded, he knew he was tired. The last few miles would be long.

They passed. And then, as he stood at the top of St. Jude's Street, in the place where Cara Adeane used to live, refusing Luke Thackray's invitation to step inside and sample his mother's ginger parkin and her strong tea, the shadow that was Oliver Rattrie slipped past them going down the hill toward Market Square.

How, when they had left him so far behind them, had he arrived so fast? Daniel asked the question. Luke, a shade wearily, thought Daniel, shrugged his shoulders.

"He was heading for the road to meet a friend. Maybe the friend had a carriage."

"His paymaster?"

"Very likely."

"How much harm can he do you, Luke?"

Once again the eye corners crinkled with his smile and—once again—there was a hint of weariness in his shoulders as they lifted in a shrug. The gesture not of a man who no longer cared but who had perhaps had enough.

"There were ten thousand men around Oastler today. The mill-masters can hardly sack us all."

"They can make examples of a few, though—to encourage the others."

"So they can."

"And you'd be the right man to choose, wouldn't you, with your radical connections? Your father killed at Peterloo, I mean . . ."

"Aye." Luke grinned. "And my mother giving free board and lodging to the Chartist candidate."

"I'm sorry, Luke. Will he turn you in?"

"I should think so. Me and as many of the others as he can remember. But we all knew that when we set off for Huddersfield this morning."

"If you lose your job can you get another?"

"Not in Frizingley."

"It's not the only place in the world."

"I reckon I agree with that."

They shook hands.

"It won't happen tomorrow," Luke said. "And whether it happens at all will depend on who really pulls Oliver's strings. If it's Ben Braithwaite then he might not want to lose a hard-working over-looker like me, even if it *does* come out that I'm a founder member of Frizingley's Short Time Committee. But if Oliver's master is somebody else, then my skill as a loom-tuner and my twenty-two years service at Braithwaite's mill may not cut much ice."

Twenty-two years. Daniel was horrified.

"I'm thirty," said Luke, reading the question in his face.

"And I've never stayed in one place," said Daniel, "for more than a year or two in my life."

Suddenly, and very urgently, Frizingley was beginning to seem far too familiar to Daniel, to close in around him like the cage he had spent his life avoiding.

Luke smiled and nodded his head.

"Come and talk to our Short Time Committee before you leave. We meet every Thursday night at the Dog and Gun. Come and see Oastler again too, while you can. It's going to be a fine sight watching him raise the North again. High time, I reckon."

"High time," said Daniel. But it was not of Richard Oastler or the raising of the North that he was thinking.

17

For Cara the start of the New Year of 1844 was a time of assessment, most of it pleasurable. Her order books were full and Miss Ernestine Baker's—as she knew from further desertions among Miss Baker's staff—most lamentably empty. Her reputation, both for originality and reliability, was growing, Miss Baker's foundering, among rumors—discreetly fanned by Cara herself—of that good lady's imminent retirement due to the failure of her eyesight, her nerve and her temperament.

"Selling up? Oh—no doubt it is only gossip," Cara would reply innocently to an inquiry from Mrs. Colclough or Mrs. Lord. "Although—well—she is not young, of course—it *might* be true. Oh dear—I suppose I shall have to glance at her stock as a matter of charity—although what I shall do with such a mound of parlormaid's calico and those miles of purple satin, I can't imagine."

"What a wicked girl you are," murmured Marie Moon, who came fairly often—whenever the mood took her and no one else would have her—to sip her red wine, her champagne or, at times of particular stress, her gin in Cara's back room where, always exquisitely dressed and slightly disheveled, always with a bite mark of passion or a bruise of anger somewhere about her body, she would talk of her new lover, the wild-eyed, weak-chinned young Lark whose brand of cruelty she now infinitely preferred to Christie Goldsborough's.

"It is the feeling of having a dear little Persian kitten on one's lap, purring one moment and flexing tiger-claws the next. It is the feeling of giving everything one has—everything one is. A total offering of oneself—a gift—without expectations or conditions—"

Cara nodded and smiled and did not listen, having heard the same declaration several times before, continuing—as Marie wildly enthused—with her own immaculate bookkeeping, the neat columns of figures which told her that for the first time in her life she was free from the basic, primitive and all too familiar anxiety of how to get through the winter. For *this* year, no matter how cold the wind blew, no matter how keen the frost or how deep the snow, she was *assured*, not only of the wherewithal to keep body and soul together, but of plenty. Of a surplus even so that the formerly all-absorbing matters of heat and light and food, of new boots and warm clothing and ready money to pay a doctor for Liam should he require one no longer concerned her. She knew she could have all these things. They presented no problems, had removed themselves from the persistent ache they had once occupied at the back of her mind. Now it was no longer a stark matter of enduring the winter but of enjoying it, of daring—for the first time—to look ahead with confidence and anticipation, with a fine sense of getting her teeth into this brand-new era of expansion, this local goldfield of opportunity which—according to Christie Goldsborough, and she had no reason to doubt him—would surely bring the railway, before long, to Frizingley.

Frequently, and in a state of high glee, she dreamed of it. Goods trains bringing her, at top speed, the bales of silk which reached her now so slowly, so uncertainly, on the rutted road from Leeds. Passenger trains cutting out her own tedious carriage journeys on that road to bargain with her suppliers. A station hotel alive with potential customers. Frizingley no longer hidden behind its encircling hills but open to the world, not just of commercial gentlemen seeking increased opportunities for trade but their ladies, seeking adornment, susceptible to the kind of temptation Miss Cara Adeane knew how to provide.

The station would, of necessity, be in the neighborhood of Market Square.

"You'll leave my premises alone," she had warned, pleaded, inquired of Christie, knowing the decision would be largely his, making herself very pleasant to the railway engineers who sometimes dined at his table.

"You wouldn't be wanting to knock my house down, Christie?"

"Wouldn't I?"

"No. You wouldn't. The top end of Market Square would suit a station better."

"Miss Ernestine Baker's end you mean?"

"I do. It's flatter. And far enough from St. Jude's not to trouble the passengers when they stay at the fine hotel you'll be building."

"And near enough to Miss Adeane's when they go shopping?"

"That's right. And since Miss Baker is about to retire in any case . . ."

"Who told you so?"

"Oh—it's common knowledge."

"I see. So there'd be no harm in my knocking *her* house down?"

"None at all. That's about as much as it's good for."

"I dare say. But then, *your* house may turn out a more convenient place to end the track. In which case, my dear, I do regret . . ."

But when the site was officially chosen, although it left Miss Baker's premises regrettably intact, it proved most advantageous for Cara, the station yard itself at a sufficient distance to save her the worst annoyances of steam and noise and the congestion of waiting carriages and cabs, but the accompanying hotel—in all its presumed magnificence—near enough for her shop to be seen clearly from all its front windows.

Only two issues now remained to vex her; the question of space, of extra windows of her own to display the new range of goods she spent her nights so avidly planning, extra floor-space to accommodate her new range of customers with a degree of arm-chaired, foot-stooled comfort which would induce them to linger. And the even more urgent matter of unpaid accounts.

No problem existed, of course, with the "millocracy"—all accounts sent in to the Colcloughs and Braithwaites, the Lords and Dallams, being settled promptly on their due date and in full. No problem would arise—she felt quite certain—with the "passing" railway trade to whom she envisaged the sale of ready-made goods for which credit could neither be expected nor given. But the slow and grudging manner in which Mrs. Audrey Covington-Pym paid her debts, the number of times it seemed necessary to send in one's invoice in order to attract so much as that equestrian lady's attention, had done Cara's temper no good. While Lady Lark, at present blithely ordering Easter bonnets for herself and her tribe of daughters, nieces, resident cousins, had paid not one penny as yet for the outfits they had all worn at the Colclough wedding in September.

"Have I your account?" she asked blankly when Cara, very apologetically, mentioned it, her aristocratic and painfully raised eyebrow clearly wondering why anyone should think it right to trouble *her* with such sordid matters.

"I will let you have it at once," promised Cara humbly, omitting to add that she had sent it four times already. "And for December too."

"December?" Lady Lark had never, it seemed, heard of "December." Nor could she imagine what it might have to do with her.

Cara told her. "The Christmas ball dresses, madam—for yourself and your daughter. Four velvet, four satin, one tulle with spangles, one plain tulle, two watered-silk, one silk gauze, one gold brocade. Fourteen in all . . ."

"Fourteen? Impossible." There was no doubt that Lady Lark meant exactly what she said.

"I will check my books again, madam."

"I must strongly advise you to do so. I will take that feathered bonnet with me now, Miss Adeane, if you will have it put in my carriage. And please send the cream straw not later than Tuesday. The girls will be along in a day or so for their fittings."

Smiling, Cara placed the feathered bonnet into its box and carried it herself to the waiting carriage.

"Good morning, Lady Lark."

"And to you, Miss Adeane. And please remember I must have the cream straw by Tuesday. Morning would suit me best."

"Certainly, madam."

They smiled at one another.

"Thieving bitch," muttered Cara as the vehicle lumbered away and, marching back to her office, began to write out in great detail the Lark account once again.

"And if she doesn't pay me this time then I shall send it to Sir Felix."

"My dear, he won't care." Marie Moon, still sipping her gin and gazing at her lover, sounded very much amused. "He will use it to light his cigar. What else are bills good for? Only the poor Braithwaites and Dallams feel obliged to pay them, because they are uncertain of their place in society. Or men like my husband who have to earn theirs by paying for everything. But when one is a Lark of Moorby Hall there is no need for that. One pays one's gambling debts, of course. Are they not called debts of honor, after all? But there is no honor involved in paying a tradesman—or a woman. You should know that, my love. And face up to it. As I face the sorry fact that my husband is, at present, scurrying from his lawyer to his banker to his priest—even to his member of parliament—seeking a way in which—without costing him too much—he can be rid of me."

"And you'll just sit there, won't you, Marie, and let him cast you off?"

"My dear," Marie gave her languorous always half-tipsy smile. "What else?"

"Fight him. If not, he'll leave you nothing to live on. And there'll be no little Persian kitten to console you then."

Sagely Marie Moon nodded her lovely blonde head. "Quite so. Then I must enjoy what there is to enjoy here and now—must I not?"

"Do as you like." Cara was seriously out of temper. "But I don't mean to lose fourteen dresses, I can tell you that."

Suddenly the mere thought of it brought angry tears to her eyes. It was her substance, her profit, her *right*. It was Liam's school fees, his holiday by the sea, his—and Odette's—security for that stormy day which would burst upon them, eventually, she had no doubt about it, when least expected.

"Thieving bitch," she muttered again, murder stirring inside her. "Either she pays me or I'll stop her credit and let Mrs. Braithwaite and Mrs. Colclough know why . . . How they'd love that."

"No!" Christie Goldsborough told her later that evening when she repeated her threat to him. "Grizelda Lark is my cousin and *you*— my dear—will not humiliate her."

"I won't lose fourteen dresses. Will *you* pay me?"

"Certainly not." He looked as blank and disdainful as Lady Lark herself when the debt had first been mentioned. What could such trivial, trading matters possibly have to do with either of them?

"Thank you, Christie. But you'll want your rent on time, won't you?"

"Of course."

"And when she comes to order her summer wardrobe what am I to do about that?"

"Feel honored, my dear, at her condescension. And increase your prices accordingly, for Mrs. Braithwaite and Mrs. Colclough, to cover the cost."

"Make the 'millocracy' foot the bill, in fact."

He looked faintly surprised that she had found it necessary to ask.

"But naturally, Adeane—naturally—since paying for things is what they *do*. And then, if one day Lady Lark should find it convenient to settle her account, you will have been doubly reimbursed."

But she needed her money for those fourteen dresses, now. Not for living expenses any longer, thank God, or to settle her outgoings but as a matter of pride. She wanted her money. One way or another she would have it.

"It drives me mad," she raged to Marie and Odette, "to think of that woman flaunting herself in *my* satin—*my* velvet—Where does she think I get it from? Does she think they give it away, those merchants in Leeds—as sharp as needles? *I* have to pay on delivery and no excuses—or there'd be no more. And she was here, this morning, as bold as brass, looking at the summer patterns, wanting everything doing sooner than yesterday. Thieving, condescending bitch. And her waist is an inch thicker since December, with all her Christmas puddings. *Greedy* bitch, too."

Sometimes she could hardly bear the frustration, the injustice.

"She *is* an earl's daughter," Marie Moon suggested placidly by way of comfort.

"What of it?"

"Her name adds luster, my love. Or so she imagines. So do they all. Even my little Persian kitten has a notion that he is doing me an honor by loving me—because his name is Lark. After all—what else of value does he have?"

"What will *you* have, except the clothes you stand up in if you let your husband disown you?"

Marie smiled, her blue eyes out of focus. "Oh—as for me—perhaps I was born to be destroyed. Perhaps I invite destruction. I often think so. It may be that I have been searching all my life for the *coup de grâce*. I think it is a scene I shall play to perfection."

"You'd do better to buy all the jewelry you can, on his account, and hide it away somewhere. Or get a lawyer of your own to work out a settlement for you. Or stop driving around all day with that little tom-cat of a Lark in your carriage, so that your husband's lawyer will have less evidence against you."

Marie opened her lovely eyes very wide and smiled. "Are you trying to save me, Cara? How sweet. But not very practical, my love. Not realistic. I fear I shall go the way of your fourteen dresses— And you will make the wedding gown, I dare say, for my husband's next bride, whether it is Miss Linnet Gage or some fresh little fourteen-year-old he has managed to buy from her mamma. You know that I shall not hold it against you."

Very likely. But Cara still intended to have her fourteen dresses, or their value, back again. And it was in this atmosphere of triumphs and tediums, occasional anxieties and growing satisfactions, an ever-increasing sense of going forward, of being a part and taking her share of the boom-time, the harvest-time, the burgeoning and blossoming envisaged with the coming of the railway that she heard what had befallen the Thackrays.

It happened suddenly. In April. Not the best time for disaster with the air soft and green and even the harsh landscape of Frizingley touched by the blossom-tints of the season. Suddenly. One evening she was walking on the moor with Luke talking pleasantly of nothing in particular, since there was an ocean of time before them. And then, only two mornings later, there came a tearful Anna Rattrie to tell her that Luke had been dismissed from Braithwaite's and Sairellen was to be evicted. It was true. Anna's heart was clearly breaking at the thought of it. The lodgers had already packed and gone. The lace curtains—Sairellen's pride and joy—had been taken down. The hens in the backyard had been sold to the landlord of the Dog and Gun. Would anything ever be the same again?

Leaving Odette in charge of the shop, Cara went at once to St. Jude's Street, finding Sairellen alone, impassive and hard as granite, already packing her cast iron pots and pans, her baking bowls and canisters, her rolling pins and meat skewers and flat irons into wooden boxes. A woman going about her business, unbowed, simply getting on with things as she had done all her life. A woman who kept her own counsel and did not greatly wish to be disturbed although she looked up as Cara came through the door, registering no surprise, no welcome, no particular condemnation other than a sardonic twist of the wide, strong mouth, a lifting of the heavy graying eyebrows which conveyed bluntly, "This is your doing, Cara Adeane. I told you it would be."

"I've just heard—this minute," said Cara.

"Aye. It's no secret. And you've come running all the way up St. Jude's in your fine black taffeta, have you? Very good of you, lass."

"When did it happen?"

Sairellen raised her shoulders in her heavy, always faintly scornful shrug, her back a ramrod in its stiffness and its absolute refusal of sympathy. "They never give much notice. Why should they? Luke got his marching orders from Braithwaite's last night, at the end of his shift, as you might imagine. *After* his day's work was done. Paid him off and told him not to come back again. And the landlord's men were here to see me an hour or two later to let me know as how the landlord would be obliged if I'd vacate his premises by the end of the week. Luke has been at Braithwaite's twenty-two years. We've lived here twenty-five."

"Can he do it?"

Sairellen's face assumed the expression it always wore when she considered herself to be talking to a half-wit. Of which, in her view, there were a great many.

"Goldsborough? Don't be daft, lass. My lease has expired. And even if it had another ten years to run, I'd have to leave if that was what he wanted. You're an Irishwoman, Cara. They turn your people off their potato patches, don't they, without a rag to their backs and nothing to do but dig themselves holes for shelter in the ditches. Isn't that what they do?"

Cara nodded.

"Well then, you ought to understand about evictions."

"It's not my fault, Sairellen." It was a cry from the heart which she did not expect to be heeded.

"Happen not." Again there came the heavy, disdainful shrug and then, abruptly, Sairellen's broad, scarred hand banging hard against the table, setting the iron utensils grotesquely dancing. "Happen not. But then—tell me this, Cara Adeane—who was it standing in the passage not long since, with my lad, letting him have his way, as any man will—since it's a man's place to try and a woman's to deny, did they never teach you that—and Oliver Rattrie looking on? That was you, my lass, and no mistake. And what I saw, Oliver saw—and more, I shouldn't wonder. Strikes me that he went running to Goldsborough . . ."

"Sairellen, it would make no difference." Her life, it seemed, depended on her ability to make Sairellen believe her. "Really it wouldn't. He'd laugh. He'd make fun of it . . ."

But he had not done so. He had not even mentioned it. Had found nothing to amuse him, it seemed, in the thought of her standing in an alleyway in the rain clasped in the arms of an ordinary working man. As he should have done.

Realizing that, she faltered.

"He wouldn't care, Sairellen." And now she felt a need to convince herself. "He wouldn't give a damn. He even likes it when other men look at me. It flatters him."

Look, but not touch. Desire, as men as diverse as poor gin-soaked Ned O'Mara and Ben Braithwaite himself desired her. But were not desired by her in return. Abruptly her nerve snapped and, knowing that her voice betrayed it, she muttered again, "He wouldn't care." And then repeated the words as if they had been a talisman.

She could not be, must not be, the cause of this.

"Happen not." Sairellen had drawn her own conclusions and had been given no reason as yet, it seemed, to change them. "Except that it's a mite too neat, the house and the job gone in the same night."

"What reason did they give at Braithwaite's?"

"That he was an Oastlerite—which he is. And a Chartist—which he's never kept secret. Yes—he's been to hear Oastler speak, maybe a dozen times since February. Him and ten thousand others. But there's been no trouble, no agitation, no strikes. My lad hasn't taken so much as a day off his work. So why should Ben Braithwaite single him out now, unless it was to oblige a friend? And why should I lose my lease when I've kept this house clean and decent and respectable for twenty-five years, unless it's to make sure I can't offer him a home in this town? Have a bit of sense, lass."

She had borne Sairellen's scrutiny many times before, had suffered the hard, sardonic eye, the abrasive tongue and had rushed, at once, to defend herself by *attack* as one had to do—*always*—with a granite-hard woman like this one. But now, instead of rising to her call, she felt her energy draining away as rapidly, and as dreadfully, as if it had been unplugged at its source, her heart thudding badly out of control, her eyes not focusing as they should, her body turning hot and then very cold.

"Sit down," Sairellen said sharply, "before you fall down. I've no mind to strain my back picking you up." And then, bluntly, a woman who always preferred to know the worst, the better to come to grips with it. "It's not like you to turn faint, Cara Adeane. You're not in the family way, by any mischance? Out with it, lass. Let's be knowing."

In which case—as Cara well knew—having suffered the rough side of Sairellen's tongue she would be offered all the help that was needed.

She sat down and shook her head.

"No. And it wouldn't be Luke's in any case."

She could be blunt too. And hard. She had had to be. And now, her weakness lasting only a moment—since when had she ever been able to afford more than that?—she lifted her head to meet the critical, suspicious eyes and began to fight back.

"How do you know it's Luke they want out of Frizingley, Sairellen? Couldn't it be you?"

"Could it?"

"Why not? You've made this house into a Chartist center—lodging every wandering radical who happened to be passing through. Dozens of them, Sairellen, with their pamphlets and their broadsheet ballads. If I've seen them, and heard them, then so has Oliver Rattrie. He'll have gone running to Goldsborough with that too. Won't he? Well—won't he, Sairellen?"

"You're a clever lass, Cara."

"So it might all be your fault . . ."

"It might."

"Not mine at all—not altogether."

"Happen so."

Sairellen sat down heavily at the other side of the well-scrubbed, well-bleached table, her gnarled hands resting on the wood, touching it, her sigh, when it came, very long and hollow and painful to both of them. A moment of grudging affection which could not be spoken. A certain unwilling respect. The acknowledgment, whether they liked it or not—and they did not much like it—that in many essential ways they resembled each other.

"Where will you go?"

"Nottingham. I have a brother there. And Luke thinks he can get work. The lodgers left this morning. Two of them in a hurry—being Chartist pamphleteers. We'll be gone by Friday. My brother can give us a roof for a night or two, I reckon."

"Have you any money?"

"That's a question I've been brought up neither to ask, my girl, nor to answer."

"That means you haven't, I suppose—that you've given your savings to 'the Cause.' Or one of them."

But what savings had there ever been, she wondered? When one remembered the number of traveling "politicals" who had stayed here free of charge, the coal Sairellen had used to warm them after their cold and dangerous journeyings, the ample dinners she had set down before them to stave off the near starvation of the open road. When one remembered the pittance Luke earned and how much of it he had given to Richard Oastler, to waifs and strays like Anna Rattrie: to Odette and to herself in those far-off days of near destitution when they had formed part of the multitude who needed it.

How much could possibly be left? The price of the journey to Nottingham, living expenses for the week which would be all Luke could allow himself to find work, and the week it would then take before his first wages? Little more than that. They both knew it. And so they sat face to face across the kitchen table throwing words at each other, kind words spoken tersely, sharply, to keep in its proper place—well hidden—their most grudging affinity.

"I can help you, Sairellen."

"I dare say. But it's not needed."

"Yes it is."

"Nay, lass. I'll be the judge of that. Luke's a careful man, never one for putting his money across a bar-counter. I saw to that. We've enough put by."

"Sairellen—I've done well lately . . ."

"Your sort always does."

"So take advantage of it. You helped me once."

Sairellen shook her head. "Luke helped you. I told you to take yourself off and leave him alone—which is what I'm telling you now. And if you had . . ."

"Then you'd still have been housing the Chartists and the Oastler-ites and handing out their damned pamphlets."

"So I would. And I'll have no bad language in this house, my girl—since it *is* my house, until Friday."

Three days.

Cara got to her feet.

"All right. *Be* stubborn. *Be* awkward." And then, tears welling up into her eyes she burst out, "I don't know what to say to you." She knew that the truth, if she could speak it, would be "I'll miss you. I can't imagine this place without you. I can't bear it." But it would have been unwise, of course, to say so.

"Then don't waste your words, lass. Just go about your business, look after yourself, and good luck to you. I doubt we'll be seeing you again."

"Sairellen . . ."

Sairellen shook her head.

"No, Cara."

She got up too, stiffly, as if her joints, once allowed to rest a moment, needed time and a little persuasion to get themselves started again. An old woman. Over sixty, supposed Cara, whose fighting strength—quite soon perhaps—must surely fade. How bitterly, when that day came, she would resent her own weakness. How bitterly Cara resented it now, on her behalf.

"I'll tell you this, Cara Adeane," she said. "Luke *wants* to go. He was born and bred here but now he wants to leave. Something here has started to unsettle him. Am I to blame for that?"

Dumbly, still close to tears, Cara shook her head.

"So, when he comes to say goodbye to you—as I expect he will—you'll be a good lass, won't you, and make it as easy for him as you can. No letting him think he has something to come back for—when he hasn't, Cara. No filling him up with your blarney so that I have to watch him eating his heart out instead of getting on with what he *ought* to be doing. That's how you can help him—and me—if you'd be so kind. Don't hurt him."

"I wouldn't."

Once again, for perhaps the last time Cara would see it, came the heavy, sardonic shrug.

"Left to yourself, miss, there's no telling what you'd do. But my lad has a good head on his shoulders, the Lord be thanked. He'll take himself a decent, quiet wife one of these days—the sooner the better— And you'll be all right, Cara. You'll always do well, in your fashion."

She opened the door. Cara went out into the street and walked away, hearing the door close firmly and—if Sairellen had her way—finally behind her.

She did not believe it.

For a few moments, walking down the familiar hill to St. Jude's Square she felt bereaved, dispossessed, a hungry, harassed girl again dressed in two plush tablecloths stitched together against the cold, shivering as she had shivered then despite her cashmere shawl and the pale, uncertain sunshine of April. But it was not in her nature to accept defeat, or loss, so tamely. *She would not have it.* The injustice burned her. The absence of Luke was already gnawing a void inside her that not even fourteen times fourteen dresses could hope to fill. And she had walked through the door of the Fleece, as desperate in her way as on the morning she had lost Gemma Gage's brown satin, before she realized it. She had taken no conscious decision, laid no plans. She simply knew—as she had known on that other morning—

that if Christie wanted to help her then he could. And, just as there had been a price then, she was in no doubt that there would be one now.

She would pay it. Gladly.

"He's busy," said Ned O'Mara, his unsteady bulk filling the passageway leading to the back stairs.

"Tell him I want to see him."

"What's the good o' that?" Ned was grinning drunkenly, lewdly she supposed, although anything he did had ceased to trouble her. "If he was after wanting to see you—Miss Adeane—then he'd have sent for you. And since he hasn't . . ."

"Who's with him?"

"Wouldn't you just like to know?"

"Not particularly." She had learned, quite easily in fact, to be brusque with Ned, or anyone else who stood in her way. "So either you go and tell him I'm here or stand aside and I'll go myself."

"I'm not no message boy." Ned's mouth had grown ugly, remembering, perhaps, the time when she had begged him, very prettily sometimes, for chicken legs and custard pies, for her little boy's supper, bones for her dog; and when possessing her had seemed by no means impossible.

That time was over.

"No kind of a boy at all, Ned. Not any longer."

Her voice had a cutting edge to it like a knife and, clumsy in his need to hurt her, he called out loudly, his thick voice reaching as many ears as it could, "Oliver, my lad—get yourself upstairs and tell the captain that his doxy's here abeggin' for him—can't wait much longer by the looks of her."

"Thank you," she said.

He was, in fact, alone.

"Did I say he wasn't?" muttered Ned turning sullen.

"He says you're to go up," Oliver Rattrie told her in his furtive whisper, not meeting her eye.

He was at his desk, a log fire blazing despite the mildness of the weather, going through what she recognized as building plans, drawings of hotels and banks and offices, the new Frizingley that was to make him a millionaire so that he could leave it—she hoped—and go back to Antigua or Martinique or wherever it was he had acquired his liking for constant heat.

Already the roaring fire and the firmly sealed windows, the deep reds and brown of the furnishings beneath a low ceiling, the air heavy with tobacco and the musky scent to everything he wore, lingered in every chair in which he sat, upon every pillow on which lay his head, had started to overpower her.

"What is it, Cara?"

No need to waste time on preliminaries. Indeed, she saw that it would be unwise to do so. He was busy with his plans to knock down the Frizingley he had inherited from his father and build it up again not at all to his taste but certainly to his advantage. Therefore she would do well to state her case at once.

"Christie, you have just evicted a friend of mine. I wondered why?"

"Ah yes," he smiled at her. "The fighting Mrs. Thackray. The Boadicea of St. Jude's. I was expecting you, Cara."

Once again, when she had thought the advantage of surprise to be hers, he had taken it from her, cutting the ground—which had been none too solid in any case—from beneath her feet. Opening up a pit, very likely, into which she knew she might all too easily tumble.

But if *that* was his price then she would tumble with a good heart.

She shrugged off her shawl, seriously incommoded now as she always was, by the fire. "Expecting me?" She thought it well to bide her time and allow him to tell her a little more.

"Yes. Expecting you. Ought you to be surprised?"

"Probably not." No doubt she would find out, at his good pleasure.

"You heard about the eviction—when, Cara?"

"This morning."

"Early, I imagine. And when was it served?"

"Last night."

He nodded. "Yes. Rather late, in fact. Who told you of it?"

"Anna Rattrie."

"Quite so." He sounded pleased with her, as if—at whatever game they were playing—she was making progress.

"And how do you suppose Anna Rattrie knew about it—so early this morning? Too early for her to have seen either of the Thackrays, wouldn't you imagine? So, unless she saw one of them late last night, which seems unlikely—and which you would know, in any case, since she is your apprentice and sleeps in your shop—who told her?"

She looked at him for a moment quite blankly, marveling, as so often, at the tortuous processes of his mind. And then she sighed.

"Her brother Oliver," she said.

"Precisely."

350

"And then he told you that he had told her so you knew she had told me..."

He clicked his tongue. "With rather more finesse than that, my dear. I knew at what time the information was given. Therefore—allowing our good Anna a few minutes to have her cry and you to have yours..."

"I haven't been crying."

"Your tantrum then. It suits you better. After which you walked up St. Jude's Street, had your explanation with the formidable Mrs. Thackray, reached the obvious conclusion that only I can help you, and have arrived accordingly. You should learn to play chess, Adeane. I have told you so before. With a little practice you might graduate to playing with live pieces, as I do."

"I'm too busy for games."

"Nonsense. It is all a game, Cara. I have told you that too. If one started to take it seriously one shudders to think where one might end..."

"Life, you mean? *I* take it seriously."

"Of course. So do most people. So does Ben Braithwaite, believe me—our future Lord Mayor and all those other pompous gentlemen who will be his Corporation. My greatest single advantage is that I do not. Nor do I intend to. You have something to ask me, I believe?"

An awareness of danger, the need to tread warily, filled her whole mind. For if he had planned all this in such detail then he had some specific purpose in which she—as ever—might be no more than a pawn, but would have to take care for all that. Since pawns, as she well knew—like herself and Luke—could suffer as grievously as any kings and queens or bishops.

"Mrs. Thackray has been kind to me. I wondered why you have turned her out? She has been your tenant for twenty-five years, after all."

"Oh—hardly mine, Cara. I am not so old. My father's tenant first. Then my trustee's. Then my agent's. Mine when I came back from the West Indies a matter of ten years ago. A model tenant at all times, I understand."

"Well then...?"

"The woman is a Chartist and an Oastlerite."

"What do you care for that, Christie?"

"Not a scrap."

"So...?"

The heat in the room had taken her by the throat now, parching it so that it cost her an effort to speak at all.

"So? Do you need a reason, Cara? Allow me to give you one. Mrs. Thackray is the sole tenant of a house large enough to provide me with a greater revenue than can possibly be extracted from a single tenancy. It is, therefore, far more to my advantage as a landlord to divide the house—and all other houses like it—into as many separate lettings as I can. In simple terms, my lamb, if I have the choice of one tenant at ten shillings a week for occupation of the whole house and eight tenants at two shillings each for a small part of it, then I will have the eight tenants, at sixteen shillings the lot. A clear profit of six shillings a week over your Mrs. Thackray."

"You'll let tinkers in, you mean, and vagrants, and see the house go to wrack and ruin, since they'll take no care of it."

He nodded, as if in indication that she had passed a test. "Exactly—which matters not a damn since the whole street is due to come down as soon as I can contrive it. Hence my policy of squeezing whatever profit I can get before it crumbles to its dirty knees. You know that, Cara. It is a policy I have pursued most enthusiastically at every possible opportunity. Have I not?"

Indeed he had. Yet, just the same, she found it hard to believe that the Thackray house, at the very top of St. Jude's Street, would be needed, in the foreseeable future, for any kind of redevelopment plan. Broad thoroughfares there would doubtless be, but hardly yet, hardly reaching so far from the center of town.

She shook her head.

"Do you think I am lying to you, Adeane?"

Playing with her more likely.

"You are not telling me the truth."

He laughed. "A fine point. But we are not really concerned about *Mrs.* Thackray, are we, Cara? Which means you have not been telling me the truth either. I do think you should begin."

She swallowed, her throat still painfully dry.

"Luke?"

"Yes?" His voice was as soft and coaxing as a priest in the confessional, forever pushing and persuading her to reveal more than she had intended.

"Don't draw that man's attention to my son," Sairellen had warned her, and she had paid no attention, thinking the warning unnecessary, naïve. "For all I know he may be the same mad devil as his father." She had not heeded that either. But too self-contained and self-indulgent for madness. Too proud to stoop to jealousy. Too uncaring. So had she judged him. So, indeed, she judged him still.

"Christie." And once again she swallowed, speaking slowly and carefully, weighing every word. "Luke Thackray is a millworker. An ordinary man with no money and no position, without education or breeding or anything else that could possibly matter to you."

"Have I said he does matter to me?"

He got up and came around the desk, smiling at her, his approach disconcerting her so badly that she would have taken a step away from him had she not realized the folly, standing her ground instead while he lounged against the leather desk-top, perfectly at *his* ease, it seemed, but stifling her.

"But then, Cara, you have very little education yourself and certainly no breeding. Not that you matter to me either. Do you?"

"I suppose not."

"Perhaps you hope not. But talk to me a little of Luke Thackray."

"What—?"

"Tell me, for instance, why you have come to me with this tale of Mrs. Thackray being kind to you when it is, in fact, her son for whom your heart is bleeding?"

"I . . ." Of course it was true. How could she best conceal it? "But she *has* been kind to me, Christie, she took me in—and my mother—and helped with the cottage . . ."

"He is your lover, of course."

"No."

"My information leads me to think otherwise."

His voice still had that soft, coaxing quality, that invitation to ease one's burdens by confession, to tell and be forgiven, be set free, although his mouth looked hard, his eyes so black she could hardly see them. She was in deep and very murky water, she knew that much, and once again—instead of struggling to keep afloat—she felt the draining of her energy as she had done with Sairellen, that frantic thudding of her heart, the racing pulse-beat, the rapid alternation of sickening heat and damp-palmed cold, leading on to nausea.

"What information?" It was necessary to say something and it seemed to be the question he wanted in any case.

"Why—my dear—information that this millworker—this ordinary

man—cannot keep his hands away from you—greatly, it seems, to your satisfaction. That you can neither one of you control your passion even on the most public of occasions . . ."

"Oliver Rattrie," she said.

"Of course. An observant lad, Oliver. A sensitive lad, even. It shocked him deeply, it seems, seeing you in Mrs. Thackray's passage, pressing yourself against that ordinary man—her son—"

"Christie."

"Letting him have his way with you, says Oliver."

"Stop it."

It seemed there had been a flash in her head, evaporating her fear, freeing her tongue. For this had been one of the tenderest moments of her life, one of the most precious of her memories, and she would not have him soil it. *Him*, and Oliver Rattrie.

"Stop it, Christie."

He smiled at her. And then reproachfully clicked his tongue. "Opening your cloak for him, I hear, and more besides, so he could get his workaday hands on your skin . . ."

"I told you to *stop it*."

"And really, my dear, crushing yourself against him so lewdly, Oliver thought—gorging your little self by the sound of it, up against that wall—"

She began to shriek "Stop it" she didn't know how many times, the thudding in her chest creating its echo inside her head, muffling her own voice like something heard through a sea-shell, her own violence frightening her badly.

"And with your skirts up around your middle . . ."

"No they were not—*never*—"

Never, never, would Luke have offered her such an insult. He had been comforting her, *loving* her, not treating her as a toy for his own perverse pleasure. A slattern. As this man often did.

She struck out at him wildly, not expecting to hit him, not even seeing him very clearly, locating him mainly and inaccurately by his hot odor of musk and tobacco, her hysteria soon melting, in that thick air, to a fresh nausea so that she was not even sorry when he caught her wrists and held her steady.

"So he does mean something to you—this working man?"

"Yes. He does." And, her mouth very close to his face, she threw each word against it, feeling as if she were spitting venom, wishing that she could. "He's the best man I've ever known. The very best. A *good* man. Worth a thousand of you. I'd trust him with my life."

To her astonishment he laughed and let her go.

"So that's it." Evidently he had discovered whatever it was that he wished to know. "Trust. And goodness." He sounded highly diverted, although not greatly impressed. "Really, Cara, it is just as well that I have sent him away. You could never have lived up to all that excellence, you know."

Perhaps she *did* know.

Standing away from him she pressed her hands against her temples, trying to shut off the beating sea-sounds that were making her so dizzy, her vitality ebbing fast, a great weary wave of futility and defeat—not quite of resignation—washing over her in its place.

But at least on the surface, it restored her calm.

"Christie, if you wanted to know what I felt for Luke Thackray why didn't you just *ask* me?"

"My dear," he sounded almost shocked. "What a tame little notion. And would you have told me? Did you even know yourself? Or perhaps you didn't really *want* to know. In which case—well—now you do. The poor fellow. You esteem him. You trust him. Perhaps he would have preferred a little honest passion."

She clasped her hands very tight together, amazed, in this inferno, to feel them so cold.

"Perhaps he would."

"But you had none to give him, had you, Cara? Not really. Not the kind that launches ships and moves mountains. Not the kind one couldn't live without?"

"I dare say."

"Then say a little more. Be honest with yourself, my darling. Could you really be his wife and bear his children in poverty—with no hope, ever, of any silk dresses to wear . . . ?"

"No. I couldn't."

"I think you are even a little sorry about that."

"Yes. I am. It means I know he is too good for me."

He threw back his head and laughed, most heartily.

"Oh dear—oh dear—poor Cara. You will learn to accept your own nature one of these days."

"And play games with other people's lives—like you?"

"Have I hurt you, Cara?"

"Yes."

He had done more than that. Chastened her, it seemed, torn out of her so much that had been precious and fragile and exposed it to this scorching, acrid air, ridiculed it, soiled it, and then invited her to watch it wither. While he—for his diversion—had watched her suffer.

"Have you finished with me now? Can I go?"

"Of course. And don't feel too badly. There *is* a new move afoot for a Ten Hours' Bill. Oastler *has* been making trouble. Ben Braithwaite is not the only mill-master to start weeding the Oastlerites out. What has happened to the Thackrays would probably have happened in any case."

"But you could have stopped it?"

"Oh yes."

"Why? *Really* why?"

"Because I am, by nature, possessive. I was an only child, you see. I never learned to share. What was mine *was* mine and mine only—whether I really wanted it or not. And even when I had lost interest entirely, what had been mine tended to stay mine, if only so that no one else could have it. An unpleasant trait, I admit. I have never outgrown it."

"You were never so possessive with Marie Moon or Audrey Covington-Pym."

"Of course not." He seemed surprised. "They are married women, the property of their husbands. *I* was the poacher of other men's preserves, which is an entirely different matter from having someone—however upright and worthy—poach on me."

A moment passed, prolonged and uncomfortable, in which nothing seemed able to match the astonishment and unease she was feeling. And when she could speak it was only to produce a trite little remark which rang in her own ears as totally inadequate. A foolish, childish thing to say.

"So I am to have no friends."

He smiled a cordial agreement. "Not if they happen to be personable young men who lead you to misbehave in public. You should not have done that, you know, Cara. Fortunately you managed to restrain yourself rather better with your Chartist candidate. Although it makes no difference now, of course, in his present circumstances . . ."

"What circumstances?" And, the hairs rising on the back of her neck, her spine tingling a warning, she felt the trap snap shut around her even as she spoke the words. What had he done to Daniel? What was he leading her to now? Another place of chastisement? Another whipping post? Another opportunity for him to watch her bleed?

What had he done to Daniel?

"What circumstances?"

"Well—I hardly like to mention them . . ."

"Oh yes you do."

"Particularly when it concerns a lady . . ."

"What have you done to him?"

She was playing into his hands and knew it. But what did she care for that? Because if he had hurt Daniel she would . . . She didn't know.

One day he would go too far. She had told him that. One day he would hurt somebody too much, strip somebody too bare. Had the day come now?

"I have done nothing to him, Cara—nothing at all. In fact, what could any man do but wish him well. She is a charming woman."

She had no voice to ask the name. She looked at him. Stared her question. And he answered crisply.

"Gemma Gage. They have been enjoying a most passionate, most voluptuous idyll together since August of last year. Why else did you think she braved social ostracism by employing him in her school if she was not in love with him?"

She didn't know what she felt. She held her breath and let it take her, wondering, as the first shock receded, what else he meant to take away from her. And then, surprised by her own strange calm, she said, "How do you know that, Christie?" For had there been the faintest whisper of speculation about Gemma Gage—dear God, how plain she was; how serious—then it would have reached the shop. And Cara had heard nothing, noticed nothing except, just occasion-ally, that dreaming smile which had been put down to anything but a lover. Gemma Gage was simply not that kind of woman.

"How do I know?" he said airily. "Oh—in the dirtiest and most underhand way possible. I do assure you. And quite easily. Women like Gemma Gage—who are basically honorable and decent—are never much good at the mechanics of adultery. Passion they understand but deceit is always a little beyond them. They never seem to carry it far enough. So—while dear Gemma has obviously remembered to de-ceive her husband and the rest of her family and purchased her housekeeper's silence, I suppose, with suitable presents, she appears to have forgotten the lesser members of her staff. Ladies tend to do that, I find. A little kitchen skivvy, in fact. Mrs. Gage may not even have known the girl was there. But my boy Oliver knew. He is really a most useful little beast."

"Useful?" Once again the hairs had risen on her neck. "What use could this be to you?"

"Who knows? One tends to store these things in the memory. To be used—or not—as seems appropriate. It is always of great interest, you know, to see what happens when one opens a cupboard door and all the skeletons come tumbling out."

"You mean you'd tell her husband?"

She heard the harsh note of disgust in her own voice. So did he. It made him smile.

"I doubt it. Such a dull fellow. Entirely predictable. He would take it like a gentleman. But he has a sister ..."

"I know."

"An exquisite woman of very precise ambitions and no scruples to speak of. In fact no scruples at all, I rather believe. A cousin of the Bartram-Hyndes who really should not be living on Amabel Dallam's good will like a paid companion. This little snippet of information about her brother's wife could be of assistance to her. Interesting—at any rate—to see just what she might do with it."

Cara was appalled. So horrified, indeed, that for the first time since the distant convent schools of her childhood she felt a compelling urge to cross herself.

"Christie, you mustn't do that."

"Why? Do tell me."

"Because you mustn't, that's all—or anything like it. Can't you see that it's ... It's *evil*. The devil's work." He laughed at her. "Cara, my lamb, I do believe you are afraid for my soul."

For her own, perhaps.

"Christie." And she had never pronounced his name so fervently. "Why hurt a woman like Gemma Gage? She's done nothing to you, has she? Unless—is it because she lives in your manor?"

"Good God." This time his laughter was neither mocking nor maddening but quite genuine. Almost hearty. "Most certainly not. What use have I for the place now they have surrounded it with their factories? I have nothing against Mrs. Gage whatsoever. Does that make me better or worse?"

"Worse."

"Yes. I imagined you would think so. You will simply have to put it down to my meddlesome nature. There are theories which it pleases me, from time to time, to test. And certain demonstrations I like to make. As I demonstrated to you, a moment ago, just how fragile is your affection for the excellent Mr. Thackray when set beside the so much greater love you bear to Miss Cara Adeane and her thriving little establishment in Market Square. Time well spent, I feel, although it went much as I had expected. *I* knew all along that you and he could have no real future together. Didn't you?"

She knew now.

One day he would go too far. Strip somebody too bare. She had to get away quickly, this minute, before it happened. Before she was the one.

Turning from him the fire struck her a scorching blow, a log erupting into hot, fierce sparks as she felt herself to be erupting, only barely holding herself in check as she hurried from the room and then no longer in check at all as she came upon Oliver Rattrie crouching halfway up the stairs, perhaps only stooping to pick something up or to fasten a boot-lace, although—at that volcanic moment—she had no doubt that he could only be listening, spying.

"Little toad—get out of my way."

Perhaps she only meant to push him aside.

She pushed him. Hard.

"Little rat."

He retreated before her, backward down the narrow stairs, his pale eyes bulging and watering, she thought, not defending himself, a rodent indeed—as she had always known him—hypnotized by her towering rage, her wild beauty—as he had always been hypnotized— so that when she pushed him again he fell, head over heels down the few remaining stairs, landing in a limp sprawl, his head striking the banister with a crack which, while muddling *his* senses, should have restored her to her own.

It did not.

He got up, rubbing his eyes like a child about to cry and she went on pushing him, spitting abuse at him all the way through the back door and into the stable yard, still sane enough to wonder if she had gone mad, although the suspicion did not trouble her—she didn't care—her heart thudding again, too large for her chest, a drum-beat in her head, her pulses throbbing and racing, all pity and common sense burned out of her by the violence that *had* to be released, one way or another, before it split her apart.

"Rat. Toad. Little weasel." She went on slapping him, pushing him, cuffing him, everything she had been feeling throughout the terrible morning, everything she had lost or seen besmirched, everything she had been made to fear and suffer crystallizing into hatred for Oliver Rattrie, who was not worth it, who was not even to blame for it, but who was *here*, squirming in her hands as she had been made to squirm, cringing as she had had to do. And now she was a dozen feet tall in her anger. Impossibly strong. Her body hard as iron and invincible, enraged far beyond the capacity to feel pain.

"I'll kill you, Oliver."

She had snarled the words at him several times before she realized she meant them. She was going to kill him. Stamp on him. Squash him flat like the vermin he was. She could taste his murder in her mind and on her tongue, feel it in her savage hands which had grown so powerful that he could not escape her, could do nothing but gibber like the idiot he had always been and let her drag him about, shaking him, kicking him, butting him with her knees until the horse trough blocked her way.

Good. She would drown him. Why not? It was what one did with rats, after all. Although, of course, now, when he could surely sense her madness, he would begin to fight back?

Surely?

He did not. Or not enough to stop her from getting his head into the shallow water and holding it there.

Two voices spoke to her, in her head. "Kill him," said the loudest, the strongest. And then a second voice, pleading, "Stop me. Please stop me. Somebody—please."

He struggled free choking and retching and she ducked him again.

Kill him. Get on with it. Do it and good riddance. As he's killed you a dozen times over. But who was she thinking of?

Stop me. Stop me.

For God's sake.

"Let him go, Cara."

The voice alone, speaking behind her, was enough, although the man who stood there did not touch her, the odor of musk, the sudden heat, identifying him plainly.

"That's enough. Let him go."

Thank God. Truly—from the depths of her heart—thank God.

Her hands dropped to her sides and she turned to face him, as limp and helpless now as a marionette, water all over her dress, her hair coming down. The whole of her body throbbing like an aching tooth.

Somewhere, just behind her, she sensed that Oliver had shaken himself like a dog and scurried away.

"Have I hurt him?" Nothing in the world could have forced her to look.

"Not much. He'll recover."

"Why didn't he fight me back—the little idiot."

"Oh—because he's been trying to attract your attention all his life, I suppose. And now, at least—he has had it."

She shook her head, very much as Oliver had done, but failed to clear it.

"Why did I do that? Oh God—how *could* I . . . ?" She could feel her mouth trembling, tears gushing from her eyes. "How could I?" And then, with horror, her eyes tight shut again, she whispered, "I wanted to kill him."

"No—no. No, you didn't."

But she shook her head, her whole body and soul aflame now with the single urge to confess, to lay herself down as a penitent, heap ashes upon her guilty brow and seek atonement.

"Yes I did."

"No. You were trying to kill me, through him. That's all."

"All?" She collapsed against him surprised that he even took the trouble to hold her up.

"All? Don't you mind?"

"No—since you didn't succeed. Don't worry, Adeane. I know something of these killing rages. Has it never happened to you before?"

Hiding her face against his chest, shuddering and shaking her head, recognizing not kindness in his voice but something she had never heard there before, a deep seriousness, a note almost of solemnity with which she was too dazed to grapple.

"Well then—take my word for it—it passes. The restriction in the chest, the pounding in the head. The choking fear that one's breathing will stop. Is that what you felt?"

"Yes."

"So I imagined. And now there will be exhaustion. Perhaps a little sickness. And then, in your case I suppose, anxiety about who saw it and who has heard about it and what they might be saying. Brandy helps. Shall I give you some?"

Raising her head she looked up at him, her chin still trembling, seeing at least no laughter in him, no mockery, his face intent and still. Watching her.

"You drove me to this," she said.

"Yes. I know."

"Are you sorry?"

He smiled, very slightly. "Go home now. In my carriage, if you like. I'll have somebody drive you."

Home? To Odette. But she could tell her mother none of this. To Luke? She had no mind to increase *his* burdens. To Daniel, who seemed to be in love with another woman. To Sairellen?

"Your carriage! Oh—thank you very much, sir. How kind." She was reviving.

For who had there ever been to look after her but herself? Cara Adeane from the back streets of Dublin and Edinburgh and Manchester and Paris. Miss Adeane of Market Square. Not everything she had hoped to be, but good enough.

She stood away from him drying her cheeks with the palms of her hands, raking through her disheveled hair with hard, clever fingers, plaiting the length of it rapidly into a skillfully improvised chignon and then covering it Spanish-fashion, gypsy-fashion, with a fold of her expensive cashmere shawl. And if anyone noticed the stains and splashes or the traces of manure on the skirt of her dress, then there were enough puddles and gutters and fractious horses in Frizingley to account for that.

"Oh—I wouldn't want to trouble you, Christie. I'll walk," she said.

She did not expect any further blows to fall. This, surely, was enough. She had been almost happy. Had almost dared to think that she could have, not everything, of course, but more than she had dreamed of possessing. Her work. Her measure of comfort and success. Money in the bank and—in case the bank should fail—money in the tin box she kept hidden under the floorboards where her dog slept. All that *and* loving friends. Both. Not one or the other.

But now, once again—now, when there was not a pawn-ticket in the house and she could pay her grocer and her butcher and her coal merchant no longer with a pang of pride but as a matter of course. *Now*, when her mind, freed from the basic anxieties of survival, had space and leisure to think of other things—*now*, at this vulnerable moment, she had been forced to make a brutal choice. And had chosen not to rely on the love of another frail human being, but only on herself.

She could trust no one else. She dare not take the appalling risk of giving herself. Christie had shown her that. She accepted it. Two men had loved her and she had turned away from both of them, knowing it to be for the best. Yet, just the same, she envied Gemma Gage with a heavy, gnawing agony which would not leave her. Plain, awkward, passionate Gemma and another woman, unknown to her as yet, *any* woman who might walk through the world, if only for a step or two, with Luke.

She was, therefore, taken unawares, that same evening of her attack on Oliver Rattrie, when her mother, waiting until the shop was empty, came into her office and said gently, "Cara, we have something to talk of, I think—"

"Well, of course, mother. It's understood, isn't it, that you're to be calling and seeing Sairellen on your way home. I thought you'd have gone by now. Find out what she needs, since she won't tell me. Train tickets. A baggage cart. See if there's anything she wants to leave behind that I can store for her. Any messages I can forward or deliver. There must be something."

There would have to be. Hopefully something difficult that would cost her time and energy and money, if she were ever to have her peace of mind again.

But Odette did not appear to be listening.

"No, Cara—not the Thackrays."

What else could it be then? For Heaven's sake, what else mattered? Unless Odette had heard something of Gemma Gage and Daniel? Some rumors that she would do her level best to quash. Was he in danger now from the Dallams? Did he need a warning? Cara's eyes, and her voice, instantly sharpened.

"What is it, mother?" But her mind was racing ahead, plotting a refuge for Daniel if harm threatened. A place to hide. A covered cart to escape in. With herself at the reins, if need be. And money for his journey. How much did she have, tonight, in her cash-box underneath the dog's basket? Enough she supposed. And if not, there was always the gold bracelet Christie had tossed at her last Christmas and her stock of coral and jet.

"Mother—?" It would be as well to know the worst so that she could act accordingly, for it might not be easy, at this late hour, to hire a cart.

Odette gave a quick, nervous sigh.

"I find this so very difficult. And, yes—that grieves me. Really grieves me. For what I have to tell you should not be difficult, Cara. It should be joyful. Joyful."

She saw that her mother's softly rounded chin was trembling and that she had tears in her eyes. Yet Odette cried so easily, overflowed so often with tenderness for the sorrows of near-strangers that Cara sighed too. Impatiently.

"What do you want, mother?" And the tone of her voice so plainly said "Tell me, for God's sake, and have done" that Odette shuddered.

"Good Heavens, mother—what is it?"

Could she be over-tired, or even unwell? She was at an age, after all, when women suffered the exclusive female maladies about which Cara had heard whispers, but without much interest. Did Odette need a doctor? Once again her mind flew to the cash-box in its cavity beneath the sleeping dog. She should have the very best.

"Don't worry, mother," she wanted to say. "I'll look after you. No dirty hospitals where you go in with measles and come out with cholera or the pox. A decent nurse to look after you at home, like a lady, and then I'll send you to the seaside for as long as you like, with Liam. I'll see to everything, mother. There'll be no problem about the doctor's bills. Don't fret."

"Cara—it's your father. He's here," said Odette.

She turned ice-cold and horribly still.

"Here?"

"In Leeds."

"I see."

She saw nothing, in fact, but resentment, bitterness, the sickening memory of his betrayal which always inclined her to cruelty. He was to blame for all of this. And she had loved him far too much to forgive.

Her mind went to her cash-box again.

"And how much is that going to cost me, mother? To get rid of him, I mean."

"Cara—oh my dear—"

"Don't be shy of naming his price, mother. I'll consider it money well spent."

"Yes." And there was a world of sorrow in Odette's voice. "He told me you would probably say that."

How dare he? Her hands clenching into fists she rose to her feet and glared at her mother. How dare he pass his clever, cocksure opinions as to what she might be feeling? She would let him know *that* all right, soon enough, if she ever set eyes on him. And in the meantime, *how dare he?* How dare he make assignations with Odette behind her back? How dare he come within a hundred miles of either of them, even if his life depended on it? As it probably did. Well, she would pay off his creditors—once—and send him on his way. Once. No more. For Odette.

"But he doesn't need money, Cara."

"Don't be stupid, mother."

"Cara." Odette had clasped her hands in anguish, her face blanched by her need to be understood. "He is not poor . . ."

"Mother."

Taking a deep breath, her eyes half shut like a child repeating a lesson, Odette began to speak rapidly, disjointedly, refusing, by the simple process of talking on and on, to be silenced.

"He is not poor—not rich—not yet—but comfortable. It is the bakery, you see. He finds it congenial and his sister has come to depend on him—as he expected. She is not young and, after all, they are of one blood—who else should she trust, who else should she want beside her when her health is failing, but her brother? Quite natural—surely . . . ?"

"So *he* says."

"He says that his relationship with her is a joy to both of them. Not all at once, of course, for she was understandably suspicious . . ."

"Understandably."

". . . of his intentions. And what did he know of the bakery trade? Would he settle? Of course not, she first thought . . ."

"Rightly."

"Wrongly. He settled. He worked. He learned—and quickly. As one always knew he could learn anything, if he chose to apply himself. Now he has chosen. None of this is new to me. He has told me of it, over and over, in his letters which you would not read, Cara—would not even touch . . ."

"There was no money in them, mother."

"There was hope." Odette's teeth were chattering, her twisted fingers painfully showing their knuckles. "There was a new life. There was a challenge, which he did not shirk. There was a sense of responsibility—yes, yes, the hardest lesson of all for him, I know—but he has learned that too."

"A clever schoolmistress then, my New York aunt."

"Oh no," she shook her head. "Clever, certainly. A woman much like yourself, Cara, in some ways. But I believe it was his time to learn."

"You *believe* . . ."

"I do. These things come in their season. As it says in the Bible. A time to be born. A time to die. A time to learn, also. A time to settle. A time for the spirit to mature. I believe it."

Cara made a dismissive gesture with an angry, empty hand. "Of course you believe him, mother. If he told you black was white you would believe him—because it pleases you. So tell me why he is in Leeds? For his health? Yes, very likely, since my New York aunt and half the city bailiffs will be after his blood by now—which is as much as they'll be likely to get in any case . . ."

"No, Cara . . ."

"Why then? To wheedle his way back into my good graces because *you* have told him I can afford it? To come back here and lord it over me at my expense—free board and lodging—dressed like a dandy—*my* workwomen at his beck and call stitching him fancy shirts and waistcoats—letting me earn the money for him to spend . . . ?"

"No. He has come to take me back with him, Cara."

Silence fell.

Staring through it Cara did not know how it could be broken, did not even realize she had started to laugh until she heard the ugly sound.

"Shall we talk about the Easter bonnets, mother?"

"Cara—I have agreed to go."

"Yes. I dare say. But it's not likely to happen, is it mother? Because even if he had the passage-money when he landed—which I doubt— he certainly won't have it now. It will have gone in a card game, or on a horse, or just on making himself king—for a day—in Leeds. Well—won't it, mother?"

"No, Cara." And it was the sudden absence of her mother's tears, the relaxation of those tortured hands, a new and very quiet determination in her voice which opened Cara's mind to dread.

"I have tried to tell you, Cara—to prepare you. So many, many times have I tried. He has come to fetch me because he knows I wish to go with him. It was decided between us in our letters. My darling, from the very first we have always known that if we both survived we would eventually be together again."

"No, mother."

"Yes, darling . . ."

"*No.* And how can you talk about survival when he left you here to die? Well—didn't he?"

Very slowly Odette nodded her head.

"Yes—in the sense that I would have died had you not come to me. Yes, he did. But he did not mean to hurt me, Cara. He acted rashly, unwisely. I know. But what I also know is that he acted in the only way he could. *Yes,* Cara. Please hear me out. You would not have left me here alone had you been in his place. You would have stood your ground beside me. I know that. I am grateful for it.

I love you for it. I love *him* for entirely different reasons. You are strong and steadfast and determined. He is none of those things. He is weak and often very much afraid. He has spent his whole life walking on sand with the tide coming in. And he knows he cannot swim. Occasionally the knowledge overwhelms him and he runs away. Knowing this has never seemed to be a reason for loving him less. And I do love him. My life is with him. When I saw him again in Leeds, the other day, I was my true self again. As I have not been—not at all—since he went away. And whether you choose to believe it or not he has only ever wanted one thing. You have often heard him say it. 'I'll make you a queen, Odette my darling'—in Edinburgh—or London—or Frizingley—or whatever great city had caught his fancy. Every time he believed—if only for an hour or two—that he could do it. The fact that I knew he could not has never blinded me to his sincerity. He saw me as a queen and that has always been enough. So, when he left me here to die, as you say, it was not without making provisions for me which *he* believed to be adequate. That they did not seem very adequate to me, and certainly not to you, takes nothing away from his good intentions. He left me money which I allowed to be taken away from me. I had employment which he did not foresee that I would lose. And, above all, he trusted you. He knew you would not fail me. I knew it too."

"I dare say. But what if the ship had gone down on the way from Ireland, and me with it? What then, mother?"

Incredibly Odette smiled.

"You must know him well enough, my dear, to realize that he would never think of that."

"Yes, I know him."

"Then you must also know—as I have so often tried to tell you—that he never intended our separation to be final. He simply went ahead, as he has done often enough before, to pave the way for us . . . Oh yes, Cara, for *us*, not for me alone. The Adeanes. As we were before. The four of us. Only this time he went further, the risk was greater, the time longer. The money is certain, Cara. I have letters from his sister confirming it. I have letters from his banker and his lawyer. They are intended for you, I think, rather than for me since he knows I need no assurances."

"You trust him, then, do you?"

"I love him, Cara."

"Oh splendid, mother—that answers everything—"

———

"Yes. For me, it does."

She did not want to believe her ears. She did not want to believe that her mother could do this, feel this, say this. She did not want to believe that Odette could feel so little bound to the dutiful daughter, so totally by the feckless husband. The lover.

"You are being ridiculous," she said. "At your age. You are behaving like a fifteen-year-old houseparlormaid slipping out at night to meet a chimney sweep."

"What is so wrong with that, Cara?"

"You are behaving like Marie Moon."

"Ah no—poor Marie."

"You are throwing back in my face everything I have done for you . . ."

Gravely, very sweetly, Odette looked her full in the eyes and smiled.

"But you did it for love, my darling, did you not?"

"*Yes.* So what are you saying? That love is its own reward?"

"My dearest, of course I am saying that. It is the only reward I have ever looked for . . ."

There seemed to be a slight explosion in Cara's head, a flash of light which, although clearly illuminating her mother's sincerity, gave her a stab of pain.

"Oh good," she said. "So now you'll just take yourself off without a backward glance, will you, to the man you love? Very pleasant for you, mother. Have a wonderful new life together. And whatever else you do, please don't give a thought to the man *I* loved—once. The man I met on the boat from Ireland when my father tricked me into coming here. When he lied to me and cheated me and cared not a damn about the trap he was leading me into. No, mother, don't think about that. Don't upset yourself about the man I sent away, because of you—because I couldn't abandon you like your precious husband had abandoned you—because to take what I wanted would have meant killing you . . . Or so I thought. So I didn't kill you. I killed myself instead. Yes, I did. That's how it feels to me now."

Once again her heart and her head were pounding, her breathing labored, hurting her chest as she began to pace up and down the room, down and up, while Odette stood motionless, her face pale and pitying yet very quietly, very gravely resolute.

"And I wanted Daniel Carey, mother. Make no mistake about it. No mistake. I wanted him."

She wanted him now. And her father was to blame for it. She

would never forgive him—never—for anything. She went on at great length, enumerating the occasions on which he had deceived her, listing his faults, his failures, his crimes, continuing to pace the floor, exhausting herself, making herself cough until at last—to her own relief as much as her mother's—it ended in a storm of weeping, a grand explosion which, after some initial resistance, sent her into Odette's arms to be comforted.

And then it was Odette's turn to speak quiet words, many of them meaningless except for their soothing quality, their whisper that everything would seem better tomorrow.

It did not, except that the morning brought a certain calm, no pleasant thing in itself, far too cold for comfort, but containing its measure of resignation. She had accepted, during the uneasy night, that her mother would certainly leave her. But she was by no means inclined to forgive her for it.

"So—will you be going at once or can I rely on you to finish the beading on Magda Braithwaite's Spanish bodice?"

"I would like you to come to Leeds with me and see your father."

"I think not."

"He wants to take you with us, Cara. A princess in New York. He believes he can do it. *I* believe that, at last, he can give us a comfortable life. As a family. As we were."

"Then he'll just have to come and buy me back from Christie Goldsborough, won't he—since he's so rich. And since he it was— my dear father—who sold me to Christie to begin with."

The morning wore on and became an afternoon in which Cara spoke so sharply to Madge Percy that the woman walked out in a huff, to her lover at the Rose and Crown, threatening never to return.

Let her go. Let everybody go. She didn't care. But Odette, very quietly, put on her hat and stepping over to the Rose and Crown made a sufficiency of soothing murmurs to bring Miss Percy back again."

"You will need her, Cara. She is an excellent embroideress."

"If I can manage without you—as I can—then I can manage without her."

Evening fell. The shop emptied of customers. The dog lay, growling from time to time as if he needed the practice, in his basket. Upstairs in the workroom Madge Percy, who had been promised a bonus, was at work on the Easter bonnets, assisted by a sad-eyed but nevertheless blossoming Anna Rattrie. In the back-room, across the tidy, busy desk, Cara faced her mother again.

"I shall be here, of course, mother, when you need me."

"Yes. And I know you would welcome me back with a good heart—barefoot and in rags as you are expecting me to be."

She had not said "hoping me to be" although they both understood it.

"It may well come to that," said Cara stiffly.

"It may. It is a chance I am used to taking. Will you not change your mind and see your father?"

"No." Her voice had the sound of a door slamming shut . . . "And don't encourage him to come here, either. I shall see you on your way with a full purse and a full trunk . . . Don't expect more than that."

Another night went by. Another tender pink and green morning. A clear afternoon: Cara sitting at her desk again, Odette standing before her, their arrangements almost completed. The daughter's heart no softer, the mother's very full.

"There is something else, Cara."

"Yes?"

"Liam."

"Of course. I wondered when you would spare a thought for him. He will be miserable without you. It might even make him ill."

"I am sure of it."

"So am I. When you left him with me in Ireland he grieved so much that he forgot how to speak."

Nor had he spoken overmuch since, she thought grimly. Or not to anyone but Odette.

"Yes, I remember." Odette's voice was sorrowful again and very gentle. "Which is why—my dear—it would be best . . . Cara—think carefully before you answer me . . . I want to take him with me."

Think? There was no need to think, carefully or otherwise.

"Never," she bellowed, striking her closed fist against the edge of the desk, the snarling fury in her voice a menace in itself. Although timid, gentle Odette, who so hated anger and loud noises, stood her ground.

"Cara—*think*, Cara."

"Never."

"*Cara*—you hardly know him."

"And whose fault is that?"

"Not wholly mine. You were just sixteen when he was born, with no man to look after you. A child yourself not ready to be tied down, and so I made you both my children. Be honest, Cara. Don't deny it."

"He is my son, mother."

"Indeed he is. And you love him. I have never doubted it. Sadly—and it pains me to say it—*he* has doubted it."

For a moment she could not speak. And then, in a strained whisper, she said, "You'd better stop this, you know. Really you had, mother. I'm not sure I can stand it."

But Odette—so yielding, so biddable, so easy to manage—merely shook her head.

"I think you must."

"Mother—don't push me too far."

"You must face the truth. Indeed—you know the truth. You have worked yourself half to death for him. You have gone hungry yourself so that he could eat. You have walked cold and lonely miles up and down this city begging for work to keep a roof over his head. You gave yourself to a man you did not love to pay your son's doctor's bills and his schoolmaster. To give him a future. I know that. He—as yet—does not. What he knows is me. Day by day. Imperfect as I am, but present. The center of his universe. Without you he would have starved to death. One day he will understand that. But *now*—as he is *now*—without me he will pine."

Her quiet voice ended and then, receiving no reply, began again.

"I feel the injustice of it for you, Cara. But I cannot explain you to him in any way that he will understand. Circumstances have forced you to be a father to him, and me a mother. And what he needs most, at his age and with his odd, closed little heart, is a mother. I am sorry, my love."

Was there no reward, then, for courage and endurance? Only punishment. Only this calm, steady voice she hardly recognized telling her that her strengths and her achievements were no longer required. Only her sacrifices. First her lover, and now her son.

"What would you do with him, Cara? You have no time to be with him yourself. You would have to pay some other woman—a stranger—to take care of him. Or send him away to school. And he could not stand it. He has an uneasy nature. You know that. Do you wish to do him further harm?"

She looked up quickly, staring at her mother with keen, incredulous eyes. "How hard you are, Odette Adeane." And there was wonder in her voice, for she had never sensed hardness in her mother before, nor even suspected it.

Odette smiled. "All women are fierce, I think, when it comes to defending their young. And you don't need me, Cara. As Liam does. And your father. *They* are my children. I think you know that."

Yes. And it was the blackest injustice of a black and treacherous world. How could they? How dare they? A family. As we were. The four of us. But, if not, then a family without her. The three of them. Shutting her out.

"He's my son, mother. You can't take him."

"I am not sure he will stay with you, Cara."

"Oh yes he will. He'll do as he's told. And now, if you wouldn't mind, I have my work to finish."

Luke came to say his goodbyes that evening and for half an hour was reasonable, rational, telling her how easily things might turn out for the best. And when she said abruptly, rather harshly, "Am I to blame for this?" he laughed at her.

"Lord no. If I'd stayed at home and fed my mother's chickens instead of walking the hills after Richard Oastler then I'd have been right as rain. The charges against me are true. I'm guilty, lass, and fairly proud of it. And as for the house—well, it's not the first one to go that way lately. St. Jude's is changing. For the worse, I reckon. Happen I'm ready for a change myself."

"Do you have to go so far?"

"I have to go where the work is."

She saw, with a terrible relief, an even more terrible regret, that he would not ask her to go with him. What would be the use? If only "things" had been different. But what things? In an ideal world—perhaps the one he was striving for—there would have been no barriers between them. In that world of sanity and opportunity there would have been no need for her to defend him against men like Christie Goldsborough with the surrender of her body.

Her soul too? she wondered.

Well, she did not believe in that ideal world. She believed in what she saw all about her, the dog-fight of everyday in which Goldsboroughs and Braithwaites—and Cara Adeane—would always pick themselves up again and snatch enough to settle their appetites. A black, brutal world where one struck first, if one could, and very hard, not for riches or triumphs but simply to avoid being ground into the dust.

A world where she, who understood the rules, might survive and where Luke, who understood them but would not play, might not.

He was the best man she had ever known or would ever be likely to know and now, at this moment of parting, her heart—because of Odette—felt like a stone.

"And I suppose the first thing you'll do when you get to Nottingham is join their Short Time Committee and anything else they have down there that can get you into trouble."

"I reckon so."

"And you'll never have a penny in your pocket that isn't spoken for by Justice and Freedom and Equality—instead of a pair of new boots and a decent overcoat. What good do you think it will do?"

He shrugged, the heavy movement of his wide, sparsely covered shoulders inherited from his mother, and smiled at her. Reasonable and steady and infuriating as ever.

"Maybe not much. Happen a shade more, though, than doing nothing at all."

She made an irritable exclamation and he smiled again.

"It makes sense, Cara. You wouldn't scoff at Sir Felix Lark for planting an acorn on his land, would you? He knows he'll not live long enough to see it grow into a tree. But his children might. And their children. The gentry have always understood that. Why shouldn't we? We may not get the vote soon enough to do ourselves much good. But the world doesn't end with us, does it now?"

She had always believed that it ended with herself. More than ever now, because of Odette and Liam. And, not caring to brood just then on the coming generations, she burst out, "I have to help you, Luke. If you care anything for me at all then you must let me do something."

"Yes," he said. And to what had he agreed? That she could lend him money, see to the disposal of his luggage, have him driven to Leeds station? Or that he cared for her?

She cared for him. She trusted him. What a foul slag-heap of a world, festering in its malice, hugging its filthy self in glee because it had prevented them from finding a place in which they could live in peace together.

"Cara . . ."

"Yes?"

He paused.

"Luke?"

Her voice, as she saw him waiting, trailed away into the air.

"I'm taking Anna Rattrie with me," he said.

She closed her eyes. Could she bear this? And then it came to her that she was not even surprised. Disappointed though, sadly and deeply. For *him*.

"*Taking* her?"

He sighed. "Yes. I made her my responsibility, didn't I—a long time ago. I'll marry her, of course. If that's what she wants."

"Of course she does." She had not intended to sound so brusque. "And I call that carrying your responsibilities a shade too far."

He looked at her steadily. "Yes. It would be. If that's all it was. There's more to it, Cara. There would have to be."

Yes. Anna loved him, had never loved anyone else, could not even see any other man clearly. Could Luke be happy with Anna's happiness, contented by her devotion? She supposed a great many men made do with less. And Anna, with the feeding and grooming and polishing Cara had given her, had acquired a certain fragile grace, a soft-eyed, soft-voiced charm which suddenly reminded Cara of Odette.

Would Anna—like Odette—lie down and die for the man she loved? Undoubtedly. And what remained now was to bring herself to wish them well.

"She's a lucky girl. She'll . . . *Luke*. Will it be enough for you? Pity? Oh God—I didn't mean to say that."

Her head was on his shoulder, she never knew how, her hands against his chest, the coarse material of his shirt scratching her cheek.

"I'm thirty years old," he said into her hair. "Time I was wed. My mother is in her sixties. High time she had a willing young lass to help her in the house. These are valid reasons, Cara. St. Jude's reasons. I've never pretended to myself that I could have you. So I reckon it's best, all things considered, to settle for your opposite. A girl who could never be you, rather than one who might be, but never quite. And I'm fond of Anna. Always have been. I don't want to deny it."

Very carefully he stood her away from him, handling her as gently as a child he might have lifted down to safety from some high and dangerous wall.

"I'll be on my way now. I don't need anything, lass. It's all arranged. I have some savings, believe it or not. So has my mother. And my uncle in Nottingham is a good sort. He'll put us up until we can find something to rent. You can help me best by looking after yourself."

Yes. And a little more than that. If he would take nothing from her, then she would just have to grit her teeth tomorrow and give

Anna a wedding-present beyond her wildest dreams. How much did she have tonight under her dog-basket? More than Anna had ever held in her hands before, that much was certain. And neither Luke nor Sairellen would have the heart to take it away from her.

"I'll be off," he said again. She was almost ready to welcome it. And then, just as urgently, she could not bear him to move a step.

"Don't go." At first she meant nothing more than that. Only the words she had spoken. And it was in the intensity of his glance and the response it kindled that their meaning began, slowly and in a deep hush, to change from an innocent cry for companionship to an offer of love.

She had not planned it. Nor prepared herself for it. Yet now the feeling which had arisen between them lay heavy and glowing as sunlight on dusty, midsummer air. A temptation. An enticing whisper in Cara's astonished head, telling her that she could, at least, have this much—why not? why not?—and then, if it should never happen again, at least ... *This* much. This once.

And she had never given herself to a man before. The boy who had fathered Liam had taken her by slow, eager inches, *his* desire, not hers, pushing her, coaxing her, pleading with her to go always a little farther than she had really wanted. Christie had taken her more directly. Now, bursting suddenly upon her, the thought of giving herself, of making love rather than manufacturing pleasure enraptured her.

Once. One reckless and generous experience of the physical joys she had so far refused to let her body feel. What better gift to give him? What better way to cheat Christie? A perfect mixture of ecstasy and revenge.

She swallowed hard. "Stay with me a while longer, Luke."

He swallowed rather painfully too, his craggy face flushing as she had never seen it do before, a rush of visible emotion which left him very pale. Leaving *her* tremulous and unsteady, consumed half with desire and half with a most desperate and unlooked-for awkwardness. She had never offered herself before and, because he mattered to her so deeply, so fiercely, she wanted it to be smooth and beautiful and graceful, to be whisked by some loving magic from this tense moment of facing one another contemplating the enormity of her suggestion, to the moment of its ultimate completion. The moment when she could be in his arms sighing to him that no other man had ever really possessed her—surely?—since she had allowed no other man to give her pleasure. That, should she choose to bear another child—as women should be empowered to choose—she could wish to do so only with him.

Almost—very nearly—she wanted his child. And even when she had pulled herself very sharply away from *that* abyss she could not shake off her new understanding of what carrying the child, not of accident but of proud choice, might mean.

"Stay with me, Luke."

"Aye." And then, roughly shaking his head. "Do you think so poorly of me, Cara—that I'd take you tonight and then leave you tomorrow with the consequences?"

She swallowed again, her throat very dry, her stomach already queasy.

"There'll be no consequences."

"You can't be certain."

"Oh, for God's sake . . ." and now she realized she was losing her head completely. "Stop being so noble. There'll be no consequences. Nothing has gone amiss up to now, at any rate. And I . . . All right—all right. Whore's tricks, your mother would call them. I know. And if you don't want to soil your hands on Goldsborough's whore, then yes—all right—I understand . . ."

Incredibly, in the moment before she burst into tears, his craggy face lit up with his wide grin and, reaching out for her, he lifted her to safety once again in a bear-hug which took her breath away.

"Don't try to fool me, Miss Adeane. You should know better than that." And she could feel the laughter in his chest, beneath her cheek. "You've never once thought of yourself as a whore—not really—never in your life. You don't give a damn for anything my mother, or anybody else's mother, might have to say. And as for soiling my hands, what you really think is that I ought to be thanking my lucky stars for the chance to touch you. Well—so do I. That's what I love in you, Cara."

He had spoken the magic words. And, by so doing, had pierced her to the heart.

"You said you love me."

He was still smiling. "Don't pretend you don't know it."

"What I know is that you're the best man in the world . . ."

"Aye. I dare say. But that's not the same as love, is it, lass?"

She did not know how to answer him. Was she even capable of the kind of love that threw everything to the winds, that gave all, risked all—like Anna, and Marie Moon, and her mother? Christie had said not.

"I do love you, Luke," she whispered desperately. "I do. In the way that I know—the way that I can—"

As much as she could. As much as she dared. Touching her hair and her eyelids and her cheek with his roughened, infinitely gentle fingers, he smiled at her.

"And I reckon it would be enough to be happy on, lass, if I'd ever learned to want the life you want and the things you value. It's not in me, Cara. But I want *you* to have them. That's what loving means. Wanting the very best for the woman you love. And I'm not what's best for you, Cara. That's why I'm glad to go. And why I won't come back. It's been a hard lesson and I don't want to unlearn it. Which is why . . . Well—making love to you might seem a miracle tonight but it could only bring extra heartbreak tomorrow. For me, at any rate. I reckon I'd have the devil's job getting back my peace of mind. Maybe I never would. And there's Anna."

She had been crying almost silently against him but now, remembering Anna, she gave a deep, painful shudder.

"Don't!" he said sharply, the first command he had ever given her. "Don't grieve for what shouldn't grieve you. *Listen*—I don't want you to remember me as a man who loved your body—although I do love it—because any man with eyes in his head and blood in his veins would do that. I love *you*. Splendid, sharp-edged Cara Adeane, spiky as a hedgehog on the outside with a middle as soft as a new-born swan. That's how I love you. I love your decency, Cara, and your purity, because nothing you have ever had to do with your body—and I know as much as I need to know about that—has ever soiled you. The men who exploit you that way had dirty hands to begin with and no trace of it has come off on you. I'm not dazzled by you, Cara—as some men are. I don't recall that I ever was. I *know* you and I love what I know. The first time I saw you I started smiling and I've been smiling ever since in my heart. I don't expect to stop."

He stood her away from him again, carefully as before, and taking her face between hard, lean hands, kissed her on the mouth, tasting her, drawing the heart from her and then, before emotion turned to passion, ending.

There was not the slightest doubt in her mind that he was saying goodbye.

There were a few more moments in which, the ticking of the clock getting inside her head, they spoke rapidly of luggage, wagons, trains, of taking care of oneself, of how a final break would be kinder, of brand-new beginnings. They spoke of good luck and wishing each other well.

"I must go now," he said.

This time she did not detain him, although, at the door, he kissed her again, pressing urgently against her and she against him, both of them shipwrecked for a moment and clinging to one another, half-drowning.

But they had both learned—in murky and turbulent waters—how to swim.

"God bless you," she said and made the sign of the Catholic cross over his Protestant chest, smiling through tears at the thought of how horrified Sairellen would have been to see it.

Smiling too, he caught her moving, blessing hand and kissed it.

"I've never seen you make the sign of Rome before."

"No. I dare say one reverts, in moments of stress, to one's beginnings."

And there had been a great deal of stress lately.

He kissed her strong, competent, elegant fingers once again and then sniffed them, storing their fragrance in his memory.

"There's nothing in my chapel education that I can give you in exchange for it. Except—aye—God bless you, Cara. And keep you. There's nothing in my life ever moved me more, nor ever will, than the sight of you, that bitter winter, in those two plush tablecloths. I'd have given you the shirt from my back, right gladly. And still would."

Would she have taken it? She watched him walk away across Market Square toward St. Jude's, his long, loose-limbed stride eating the distance, his head bare, the coarse straw-colored hair the last glimpse she had of him as he climbed beyond her vision, up the hill.

Soon, very soon, she would have no reason to set foot in St. Jude's again. Soon there would be no one there who knew her name.

She went back into the house and bolted the door, remembering even in extreme distress to safeguard her property. And herself. Since who else—in this black-hearted world—would do so?

In the comfortable office-parlor only the dog was present, opening a baleful eye as she sat down in her armchair beside his basket. Both of them guarding the cash-box now. She would have a drink, perhaps. Why not? But the rich, strong Madeira with which Christie kept her supplied warmed neither her body nor her heart.

Her body. So beautiful. So ardently desired. A hundred times more enticing than Gemma Gage, a thousand times more than Anna. Yet she was alone and they, most probably, were not. Nor was her mother, nor Marie Moon. All of them ready to throw away the world for love.

As twice now she had tried to do and failed.

And she did not like failure. Did not like defeat. Did not care for the speed with which both Luke and Daniel had found consolation. She did not like this hollowness she still felt in her limbs, this emptiness in her heart.

She did not like the dog, snoring and snuffling in his basket but here, at least, she could tell him so.

"Damned dog. You must be the ugliest beast in creation."

He opened one eye, glanced at her, and then closed it again with total indifference, not thinking her worth the trouble.

Yes. Without doubt the ugliest, the most ungrateful and ill-tempered and greedy, the most useless. No doubt about it.

But, smiling slightly, she realized she would make short work of anyone else who dared to say so.

August was intensely hot that year, airless and dry and exceedingly trying for a man of John-William Dallam's weight and age and disposition. A sultry, choleric month it seemed to him, full of prattling women and bored young gentlemen waiting for the start of the grouse-shooting; a permanent tea-party transferred from his wife's drawing-room to her garden where vast quantities of strawberries and cream were consumed among the roses.

And John-William Dallam did not care for eating his food out-doors. Nor, with any excessive enthusiasm, for flowers. Not at all for gossip. Not for country life in general, he had long since decided. And, most of all, he had no patience whatsoever, no respect, and not one half ounce of liking for any of his wife's guests.

Give him a good solid dining-table to get his feet under at tea-time, standing four square on best quality Axminster carpet instead of all this flimsy garden furniture set out on damp grass. Give him a counting house or a factory floor instead of these acres of roses and fuchsias and hollyhocks and God knows what—he could certainly never be bothered to learn their names—about which his wife's friends went into such raptures. Give him the Piece Hall in Frizingley, or even the tap-room of the Rose and Crown where at least men spoke a language he could understand of profit and loss, trade fluctuations, a decent prizefight or a dog-fight even, instead of all these mincing social niceties which—and he made no bones about it—set his teeth on edge.

Give him neighbors, as he'd had before, who knew that these damned Tory Corn Laws were keeping the cities poor, closing the ports to cheap foreign grain for the benefit of these Tory gentlemen, now drinking his port and his brandy every evening, so that they could go on growing it and charging what they liked for it themselves.

One night after dinner, following a day of intense heat, he took issue—despite his wife's prior warnings—with Sir Felix Lark and Colonel Covington-Pym on the matter, both these gentlemen having dined well at his expense and made rather more use than he liked of his cigars. Nor did it suit him when, the ladies having withdrawn, Sir Felix Lark took the liberty of placing his lordly feet on John-William's table, an acceptable posture, perhaps, in sporting Tory circles—John-William had seen Christie Goldsborough do the same—but not at all to the taste of a man like himself who knew the cost to a penny not only of the inlaid table-top but of removing scuff-marks from it.

He therefore felt no compunction at barking out a command to "put those feet where they belong, lad," which, his voice easily reaching his wife through the open drawing-room windows, caused her considerable alarm.

But the matter did not rest there, Sir Felix, somewhat irritated—his mother, Lady Lark, never having objected to his heels on *her* table, even when they were booted and spurred—choosing to revenge himself by referring to the vexing question of factory reform which the Tories, in retaliation for Whig proposals to abolish the Corn Laws, were currently supporting.

"You know nowt about it, lad," John-William told him.

"But, my dear fellow . . ." Sir Felix batted artful, languid eyelids, "an absolute dunce could work it out. If the manufacturers are complaining that our corn monopoly is putting up the price of bread so that their workers can't afford to buy it, then the solution is simple. Pay higher wages, old chap."

"And reduce working hours while I'm about it, I expect? Is that what you're after?"

"Why yes," Sir Felix smiled sweetly. "One would hope so. And with Richard Oastler on the loose again one hardly sees how you industrial chappies can get away with it much longer. Damned decent fellow, Richard Oastler. Met him the other day and took to him like a duck to water. One has to take one's hat off to your workers, you know, for paying his fine. One supposes he'll set about rescuing them now with a good will from—what does one call it?—oh yes—the foul captivity of the mills."

And although John-William strongly doubted whether Sir Felix had

---

382

ever laid eyes on Richard Oastler and knew for certain that he had never, in his life, set foot in either a factory or a baker's shop, he nevertheless rose to his feet, his face an alarming shade of burgundy, and spoke at length, in far more temperate language, about meddlesome, overbred young men, still wet behind the ears, who, unable to run a few mouldy ancestral acres at a profit, had the effrontery to tell *him*—who had started with nothing and was proud of it—how to conduct his large and extremely lucrative affairs.

"They'd make mincemeat of you, lad, in the Piece Hall. They'd have the shirt off your back and you'd never even notice. And as for stirring up my weavers with all this talk of shorter hours and higher wages, who's going to foot the bill? Not you, I reckon, since footing bills is not what your kind are best at. And once you've got the workers into trouble, once it gets out of hand or no longer suits your book, what you'll do then is leave them in the lurch. Aye—and they're not daft, my factory lads. They know that as soon as their wages go up you'll raise the price of your grain to suit."

Sir Felix left, after exchanging some amused whispers with Linnet Gage about the truly quaint manners of these all-too-newly rich and John-William endured a restless night, troubled by indigestion, indignation, and a tearful Amabel, who sat a full hour at his bedside grieving for her position in local society which he had surely ruined forever.

"I think we had just better pack up and leave," she told him, her lips trembling, her whole face melting into tears like a newly released Spring fountain at his reply that nothing would please him more.

He did not like this house. He did not like these people. And even when Amabel trotted off to her own room he could not rest. He had bought this place, after all, to enjoy her company, to spend easy, tranquil days with her in the Autumn of his life. He had bought it for her benefit—dammit—and his own, not to suit the good pleasure of Miss Linnet Gage and his fancy son-in-law and their even fancier friends. Well, if this was what leisure and money and aping the gentry did for decent working folk then he'd had enough. *Enough.*

He fell asleep surrounded by green meadows and aching for the dust and grime of Frizingley, for the sound of a factory hooter instead of these damned birds which woke him just as early and reminded him, with their shrill twittering, of Linnet Gage. And it was Linnet who fell foul of him the next morning, his stomach still heavy with last night's dinner, his head aching, his temper—as Linnet signified at once to Amabel with a quizzical little pout—decidedly uncertain.

The ladies were at the breakfast table when he reached it, daintily sipping and nibbling and exclaiming over the morning's correspondence, a somewhat conspicuous silence falling at his approach, since he, of course, had formed part of their discussion; Linnet assuring her dear aunt that Sir Felix was far too large of mind and great of heart to take lasting offense; Amabel wondering with visible alarm how she was ever to face Lady Lark or the formidable Mrs. Covington-Pym again.

But, her husband's arrival putting an end to her speculation, she was relieved when Linnet, who knew how to pass so smoothly from one issue, one state of mind, to another, began to talk of the latest attempts of Mr. Adolphus Moon to rid himself of his wife. For what, after all, could there be in this continuing drama of the Moons to upset her admittedly very touchy John-William? Pouring his tea, fussing a little over his toast and marmalade, she was reassured to see him open his copy of *The Times*. No, Marie Moon could mean nothing to him. Nor to anyone else, it seemed, except foolish young Gussie Lark, who had set all the other Larks so madly aflutter. And although Amabel felt a momentary unease when Linnet, in her amused treble, began to speak that provocative name, her husband appeared to take no notice.

It was, of course, a mighty scandal containing, as it did, all the essential ingredients of money and passion, a woman of ill repute, albeit of great beauty, who had snared a bemused millionaire—Oh yes, thought Linnet, Mr. Moon's revenues from cinnamon and sugar and ginger certainly allowed him to be called that—into marriage. And who now—when no one in the world could blame him for having had enough of her—would not go quietly and with dignity, of her own accord, having absolutely refused the religious retreat and the income—perfectly adequate for a penitent, surely—which had been offered her.

"Not that Mr. Moon could ever wish to be ungenerous," breathed Linnet. "But whatever he gave her he knows she would only throw it away—that it would be gone, in no time, like a puff of smoke. In which case it seems utterly pointless to give her anything very much at all. So his lawyers tell him. And, when all is said and done, he has his children to consider."

Certain more desperate wheels, therefore, would have to be set in motion.

Divorce? Well yes, Mr. Moon had certainly thought of that and it was by no means impossible, not for a man at any rate, who would be largely spared the social ostracism and the necessity of going to live abroad, incurred by divorced women. After all—and Linnet was remarkably well-versed on the subject—the divorce laws had been formulated for the express purpose of allowing certain noblemen to free themselves so that they might remarry and produce legitimate heirs to carry on their ancient names. And although Mr. Adolphus Moon was no belted earl he was undoubtedly rich enough to afford the considerable cost of divorce proceedings and the private Act of Parliament they entailed. A shade excessive, thought Linnet, for the likes of Marie Moon, but worth it—*well* worth it—if it meant that dear Mr. Moon could be at liberty.

Whether or not it was her intention to become his next wife—the third of that name—she did not say. But her dear Aunt Amabel, nevertheless, gave her a nod and a smile of understanding, for although Linnet still enjoyed her elevated position of Mr. Uriah Colclough's angel, her thirtieth birthday *was* approaching, Mr. Colclough had had plenty of time to make up his mind, and Mr. Adolphus Moon was not only rich but appeared to be most eager.

"He is such a *dear* man," murmured Linnet. "So kind and good. Indeed, it was his very goodness which led him into the clutches of that woman. Impossible, you see, for a man like him to see through her—until afterward, of course."

"Oh yes—yes—I suppose—One sees that," said Amabel, wishing these things did not make her feel so very uncomfortable.

But divorce, it seemed, was hardly *practical* at the moment, the mere mention of it and the fact that no one could promise to keep Gussie Lark's name out of it, having so distressed Lady Lark and having proved so nearly fatal to her favorite cousin, the erring Gussie's mother, that the humane and sweet-natured Mr. Moon had felt unable to proceed. One could not have the demise of a neighbor on one's conscience after all. Nor could one afford—although Linnet did not say this *quite* so plainly—to upset so powerful a woman as Lady Lark, who could, if she so desired, impose a social ban which would probably oblige Mr. Moon to leave the neighborhood.

And since he was so agreeably settled here, in such a charming house, what was to be done?

"Incarceration," murmured Linnet, speaking the word so pleasantly, making it sound such a cheerful thing, that, for a moment, Amabel did not understand her.

"Locked away," said Linnet sweetly. "For her own good, of course. In a—well, does one call them asylums? Although one has every reason to think them most comfortable. And who can doubt that the poor woman has lost her wits?"

All the evidence pointed in that direction. There was the time, for instance, when, dressed in an evening gown—an exact copy of the one Linnet had worn for the hunt ball—she had gone traipsing about all over Far Flatley embarrassing the villagers with gifts of vintage wines for which they could surely have no use. And would a sane woman run after little boys—well, hardly more than boys—in the abandoned fashion she had pursued poor Gussie who, at *his* tender age, would never have thought of it for himself? There was even a reputable body of medical opinion to the effect that the physical appetite in itself—in a woman—was a clear indication of mental instability. Not to mention her drinking, which no one could dispute. Only think of the bruises with which she was constantly covered from falling down when in her cups.

"Oh dear," murmured Amabel, not knowing what else to say. "And if she entered an—an asylum?—would that ensure Mr. Moon his divorce?"

Linnet smiled. "Regrettably not. But at least it would rescue Gussie Lark from her toils and set him on the right road to a commission in a good regiment—which I expect Mr. Moon might buy for him—and a nice little wife with some money of her own to go with it. And then, should Madame Marie be cured in a year or two, she could come out and find herself another young man who might be named in a divorce action without upsetting anyone—anyone we know, that is . . . Leaving our Mr. Moon free, at last, to find a real mother for his sweet, sad little children."

"Oh—" Amabel sounded doubtful. "I see."

Rising to his feet John-William Dallam, a mighty man in his wrath, cast his newspaper down on to the table causing a disruption among the jugs of milk and hot water and the pots of marmalade and honey which exactly suited his humor.

"So you see, do you, Amabel?" he said, his face deepening once again to that alarming red. "Well, lass, I'll tell you what *I* see. A scheming, greedy woman—sitting there, right beside you—so desperate for money and position that she'd wed me—yes, *me*—if she could just think of some way of getting rid of you."

Amabel gave a cry of pure anguish, Linnet a light titter which said, very clearly, "Tut, tut. These quaintly, newly rich." A red rag to a bull, that morning to John-William.

"Aye, lass," he told her, towering over her, his bulk a menace from which she—who had been trained to face mutinous peasants at the castle door—did not recoil. "You'd wed me. If I'd have you. Which I wouldn't. Nor will Uriah Colclough. And you'll have your just deserts, my lass, if you manage to get yourself to the altar with that frilly, frizzed-up lecher of an Adolphus Moon."

Very gracefully Linnet rose to her feet and stood, straight and stern for a moment, a noble lady who would gladly die before she would let the rabble in.

"Mr. Dallam, I cannot allow you to insult my friends . . ."

"Sit down," he bellowed, shaking off his wife's restraining hand. "*Now*. And stay there until I've done with you."

Smiling vaguely in the direction of an imaginary audience—telling them with a faint gesture that the poor man was clearly deranged and must be humored—she sat.

"Your friends," he snorted. "What friends? Adolphus Moon? The man's a degenerate, I tell you, and vicious. And what I like least about you, Miss Linnet Gage, is that you know it very well. If anybody wants locking up in a madhouse then it's *him*. Aye, so it is, and I'd take him there myself to keep him away from those two scared rabbits you seem set on being a mother to. If you can get him to commit his legal wife to an institution, that is, to oblige Lady Lark, and then cast the poor woman off with no more than a parlormaid's wages, I expect, when it's safe to let her out again."

He paused for breath, needing it.

"John-William, I implore you . . ." moaned Amabel.

"Be quiet, woman," he said. "And those bruises you tell me she gets from falling down drunk." He snorted his contempt. "The man beats her. He drags her about by the hair and takes a dog-whip to her. For his pleasure. Every villager in Far Flatley knows it, Miss Linnet Gage, and so do you. A silly little woman like my Amabel now, oh no, she doesn't know it. Because she doesn't believe that anybody she's ever met could do such a thing. It never enters her head. But you're no milk-and-water innocent, are you, my lass? You *know* what a filthy brute the man is and so long as he puts a ring on your finger and makes you the mistress of that fine house and gives you your horse and carriage, you don't care. And you'll do anything he fancies to pay for it, so long as it can be done in such a manner that nobody will ever know. Aye, lass, I've watched the pair of you, him dangling his worldly goods like a carrot in front of you, and you tempting him with your Bartram-Hynde pedigree. Whispering behind your pretty fan, in your pretty little voice, how best to strip his wife bare and put her away. I've watched you. And there's not an ounce of decency in you, Linnet Gage, nor a scrap of human feeling. You're not fit to clean my Amabel's shoes with your Bartram-Hynde connections . . ."

Scraping back his chair he walked out through the open windows and set off down the garden, away from them, unable to bear either his wife's tears or his own choking contempt for Linnet, walking fast into the heat, toward the sun, he supposed, since something was certainly dazzling him. Damn the woman. *Damn* her. Desperate she may be. In his better moments he could even pity her. Once or twice he'd even considered buying her the kind of husband she needed. Not Colclough, of course. He would have come *too* dear. But somebody with enough prestige to make her feel a success. He hadn't done it because . . . God knows. When it came to it he hadn't seen why he should. But he'd have to get rid of her now, one way or another and no mistake, although already he was dreading the scenes there would surely be with Amabel. The tears. The supplications. The *nonsense.*

Was that why he was feeling so dizzy? He was feeling sick, too, although that, he supposed, was from losing his temper last night before he'd digested his dinner, and losing it again this morning over his toast and that dreadful weak, scented tea they kept telling him was all the fashion.

But his head was really most peculiar. Was it the heat? He was still asking himself that question when he struck the ground, grunting and snorting, regaining consciousness without realizing he had lost it, just in time to see two female figures, at what seemed the end of a long tunnel, running toward him like giant moths, their wide, muslin skirts coming at him—he was sure of it—to suffocate or drown him.

Amabel. And Linnet Gage.

And there was something wrong with his face, some leaden weight dragging it sideways out of shape. Something wrong with his legs. He couldn't move, couldn't transfer the words in his racing mind to his tongue. Couldn't speak. Dear God. Couldn't make himself understood. Couldn't tell them what he wanted done. *Couldn't defend himself.*

And here was Amabel, who would always lean to the strongest will; and Linnet already inviting her to lean.

John-William Dallam, for the first time in his life, was terrified.

"Gemma," he said. "Fetch Gemma." And when they failed to translate his harrowing grunts he used what he knew might be his final strength, not caring if it killed him—the sooner the better it now seemed to him—and painfully, grotesquely, like a retarded child fighting for speech, enunciated her name. "Gemma." *"Gemma."* Until he was understood.

He had no care any longer for the welfare of his wife. He was afraid now for himself. Not of death but that his present state, not death but not life in any way he valued it, might be prolonged. The helplessness of a child without a child's acceptance of helplessness. His towering will imprisoned, buried alive, in a dead body which lay now at the mercy of women he did not trust. Amabel, who would not know what to do. And Linnet, who would do anything to gain her own advantage.

Timid, loving, ineffective, *useless* Amabel. And Linnet, her dainty hands already reaching out to take control. Of the house. Of his wife. Of *him*.

Gemma.

The doctor was in attendance when she arrived and although he attempted to prepare her she was deeply shocked by the twisted, mottled face on her father's pillow, the eyes pleading with her as her father had never pleaded with anyone, the gnarled hand on the counterpane that had her father's diamond ring on the little finger, feeble and questing, groping as if those naked, frightened eyes had been blind.

"Help me," he said. It was as much as he could say. He had held the words in his mind for what seemed to him an eternity, clinging to them with the dregs of his determination, willing her to understand.

She understood.

"Gemma, dear," Linnet had murmured on her arrival. "Such a tragedy. Your poor mother. And your father has always been so good to me. I am so distressed. I surely have no need to tell you that you may count on me, absolutely, for anything. And I am no stranger to this, you know. I nursed my mother for a long, slow time and what I have done once I can do again. I know the pitfalls. And since my life is here, in any case, it seems pointless to disrupt yours ... And Tristan's—naturally."

"Where is my mother, Linnet?"

"Oh, lying down, dearest. You may imagine the state she was in. I have given her a whisper of laudanum and I doubt if she will wake before evening. Much kinder. And I have settled with Dr. Thomas about the nurses. A clean, competent woman for the daytime and one who can be trusted not to fall asleep at night. Although, of course, it always pays to watch the level of the gin bottle. They usually have one with them."

Linnet had escorted her to her father's bedroom door very ready to go rustling in ahead, crying out, "Now then, we have a visitor," had Gemma not prevented it.

Yes. She understood.

"Are they fretting and fussing you, father? Don't worry. I'll keep them at bay."

And, seeing that his mind still actively lived, she knelt down beside him and explained in detail and with care, that she would now make the move to Almsmead that she had promised him. She would be a daughter to Amabel, a wife to Tristan, a prop to her father's old age and the guardian of his dignity. She would do what she had been conceived and conditioned to do. Her duty.

Her measure of time was over. Not full, of course. She had realized, months ago, that it could never be that. But it had run its course. And although she had known full well that the blow must fall it was no less painful when it did.

Returning to Frizingley the following afternoon to supervise the packing of her trunks and boxes, she went first to the mill-school, standing for a long while in the doorway, signifying by a gesture to Daniel that she did not wish to interrupt him. Only to watch him. Only to be here in this place where her joy had started, where she had lived, so briefly, not as John-William Dallam's daughter, but as herself.

She was saying goodbye not only to her lover but to her identity, slowly letting it slip away from her among these odors of chalk and starched pinafores and new paint, her vigil lasting so long, her face so sad and so deeply serious that long before the class was dismissed, he knew. And although he too had known that it must surely come to this he had not expected it to be today. Not yet. Not *just* now, when he had wanted to tell her—wanted to show her—wanted to find out from her . . .

Ah well.

The children left. She touched a few tousled heads in passing, the scarred top of a wooden desk, a slate, and then Daniel's hands, grasping hers in the same speaking silence in which she had first offered her love to him. And there was no thought in her mind now of taking it away.

Yet, because her instinct in love was to nurture and to cherish, she knew that she must part from him in a manner that would cause him no remorse, no unease, no awkwardness. What she wanted most of all—the only thing she now desired for herself—was to smooth the way for him so that he would have no cause to look back over a worried shoulder and ask himself whether he had done her more harm than good. She wanted his leaving to be a warm and glowing memory of time well and truly spent; no ache of guilt. It was a last gift of love to him. And when she had smiled and seen him on his way she would cope as best she could—adequately and competently, she expected—with her own hurt.

She was strong enough.

"My father has had another attack," she said. "A very serious one."

"I'm sorry."

"And so I am needed at home now, Daniel, as I told you I would be."

"When?"

"From today."

How could she speak so calmly of what, to him, had the force and horror of a sentence of imprisonment for life? He knew she felt that horror too and her courage overwhelmed him, his pity for her making him brutal.

"He will die, you know," he said roughly, thinking—for her sake—the sooner the better.

"I know. But then there is my mother."

"She will die too."

She smiled at him very gently, recognizing that what was speaking in him was hatred of her condition, not of her family.

"Oh yes, she will. But she is not yet out of her forties and—well—although she appears rather frail I think it likely that she will live to be a hundred."

She saw the sneer in his face, heard the words in his mind. "Yes. Very likely. A woman like that who battens on others, feeds on others, who never stirs herself hand or foot for herself. Child-mother. Vampire-mother would be nearer the mark."

"Don't dislike her, Daniel," she said, still calmly. "She is only as the rules of our society have made her. You remember what we have said about lotus-feet? How the Chinese ladies bind them? And once the growth has been stunted and the bones of the feet broken, then that is the end of it, Daniel. It would be the most appalling cruelty to expect a woman whose feet—or whose spirit—had been so bound, to walk."

"They bound your feet too."

"Yes," she nodded her head very quietly. "So they did. It was because they loved me. It was because they believed it was for my own good. I have to remember that."

"In your place," he said, "I'd walk away from them."

"No, you wouldn't."

"That I would. I'd tell them my life was my own and they had no right to it. They've had their own lives. They're not entitled to a double share. I'd tell them so."

"No, you wouldn't." She sounded patient, a little amused. "Because, in my place, you'd be a woman with a woman's conscience—which is a terribly weighty thing."

"Then I'd stay—and hate them for it."

"I shall try not to do that."

He never doubted, for a moment, that she would succeed.

"You are so brave," he told her, "that I can hardly stand it."

"You are no coward yourself."

He clicked his tongue. "By fits and starts. When the mood takes me. That's how my courage comes. I might tackle a lion if one happened to be running amok in Market Square. And if I happened to feel like it. But the courage of everyday, the patient courage that has to be switched on every morning and has to last all through the day—and the year—until God knows when... No. I'm not brave like that. Like you."

Suddenly Luke Thackray came into his mind. Another tough, enduring, quietly valiant soul like Gemma's. Perhaps this damp and dismal climate bred them here.

Ah well.

"I suppose it would be best for me to go away," he said.

"Yes. I am sure it would."

"When?"

"Today, if you like."

"And close the school? I can't do that. Footloose I may be, but I'll not be leaving until you have another teacher."

"Thank you," she smiled at him. "But Mrs. Ephraim Cook can take care of it. And the delay would be irksome to you, Daniel. I don't want that. Truly not. Take a train—the one that appeals to you most as soon as it appeals to you. And set off."

He took her face between his hands. "Are you dismissing me?" And he could feel the prudent tension, the careful control of her skin beneath his fingers.

"No. I am giving what one gives to the person one loves. Or what one ought to give. The thing he wants."

"Gemma . . . ?"

"You want to go. Of course you do. By your nervous fits and starts you have wanted it all the time, I think—I know—"

He pulled her toward him and held her brown, sturdy, gallant little body very tight, feeling it tremble.

"And by the same fits and starts, do you know how much I have wanted to stay? All the time?"

"Thank you."

"Don't thank me!" he shouted at her, suddenly beside himself at the idea that she might be grateful to him—*him*—when *she*—Dear God in Heaven—when she had given him so much.

"And you," she told him, standing a little away from him, her hands against his chest, perfectly understanding his trouble. "You should feel no guilt—and no regret. None. I am not asking, but insisting—I want you to take that train, Daniel, with your bag across your shoulder and I want you to feel all the excitement in journeyings and wanderings and seeing what happens next as you used to feel. Only a year ago. And if you come to a harbor and there happens to be a ship standing there that takes your fancy, then go aboard—find out what's on the other side of the ocean—experience it— Live it."

"For you?"

"For yourself, Daniel. And no guilt. Remember that. Because I think you have felt guilty sometimes, haven't you?"

He had. At times he had been consumed with it. He wished he could tell her so. But since it had concerned his inability to fall in love with her in the head-over-heels way he believed he ought to have done, as he had even wanted to do, how could he say it?

Putting the palm of one square, brown hand gently against his cheek, she said it for him.

"It would be nonsense, you know, Daniel, to worry because I love you rather more than you love me. I have never thought of it as an exercise in mathematics where both sides must turn out equal. You have loved me enough—"

He began to tell her that no amount of love could ever be enough for a woman like her, began to spill out a wild Irish flow of words to ease his soul that was aching now, with an equal soreness, both for her captivity and his inconstancy, her gilded, overcrowded loneliness and his freedom peopled with so many chance-met, easily forgotten acquaintances. Her depth and his own damnable superficiality.

Nothing in the world, at that moment, would have given him more joy than to throw himself in an abandonment of true passion at her feet.

He could not.

"Daniel," she said firmly. "You have loved me enough to make me happy. I have been happy. And since I am the only person in a position to know how I feel then you may take my word for it."

He did not answer her.

"*Daniel.* You have given me everything I asked for and much more than I expected. You have been good to me and good for me. You don't want to fail me now, do you?"

"That I do not."

"Then be big enough to accept my love for what it is. As I can accept that you—well, you like me very much, Daniel. You are fond of me. I know. But you didn't force me to love you, after all. I wanted it. I made it happen. And if, now, you won't take it then I shall have wasted my time. Which would be a pity. I love you. Take it away with you. It belongs to you, surely—since I am the only one who can give it. And I do give it, wholly and freely. How could you possibly turn it down? I wouldn't, you know—if I were you."

And through all her luminous sincerity and tenderness there still came a faint, far nuance of her pugnacious father, John-William Dallam, who would have said, "Now let's have no nonsense, lad. Take it, since it's good for you and comes free of charge."

He walked away from her, tears stinging his eyes, and then, having blinked them away, came back again.

"Gemma, should you ever need—anything."

"Yes, of course."

"I don't know where I'll be going . . ."

"It doesn't matter. I shall be here. Should *you* need anything . . ."

"No, Gemma . . ."

"Mrs. Ephraim Cook," she continued as if he had not interrupted, "would let me know. You have her address."

He nodded.

They were reaching the end of everything that could be said.

"I had better go and see to my packing," she offered, almost presenting a solution, and they walked hand in hand to the door, civilized people who had always known that this must happen and who could never have been allowed to make a life together in any case.

She did not mention his salary. She would send it by messenger later that day, the last thing she did before leaving Frizingley, so that when he saw it to be more than was due to him he would be unable to return it.

He did not mention that, having helped the wife and family of an imprisoned Chartist friend to settle their most pressing debts, he had little more than the price of a train ticket to London left in his pocket. Such a thing did not even enter his mind.

He tidied up the schoolroom when she had left it, wanting nothing more urgently now than to leave too, to put behind him what had to be abandoned—and go. He had acquired books during his occupance of the school-house which, judging too heavy to carry, he left in a conspicuous pile, hoping she would claim them. He wrote a note to Mrs. Ephraim Cook the mill-manager's wife, explaining his departure and left it, and the school-house keys, in the care of that lady's parlormaid.

He was on his way. A year and a half ago he had walked this same road to return an amethyst brooch a virtual stranger had given him. Now it was pinned underneath his lapel for luck he thought he would probably need.

He smarted from the conviction that he had failed her, felt humbled by her greatness of heart and grieved that his own had not matched it. *But* he was on his way. Across the moor to Leeds, he thought, a much longer walk than Brighouse where he could just as easily catch a train but the night was warm, the sky full of stars, a breeze just stirring. He would walk an hour or two in the mysterious, exciting dark, sleep an hour or two in a fold of the land, watch the sun come up and then walk on again, straight into the sunrise. With no one waiting for him. No one worrying. Least of all himself.

Crossing Market Square he felt his step lighten and, catching sight of a blue and gold sign announcing the business premises of Miss

Cara Adeane, he suddenly changed course, vaulted the wall which separated her backyard from its neighbor and knocked on her door. An impulse he immediately regretted when the door opened on a scene of unmistakable domestic drama, Odette Adeane, looking years older than when he had last seen her—surely only a month ago?—lying in an armchair by the hearth quietly sobbing; the boy Liam kneeling beside her, his young face strained with some ghastly emotion far too strong for him, that looked suspiciously like hate; Cara herself bristling with nervous anger, her turquoise eyes gleaming in a way which, he remembered, boded no good.

But he would not be coming back to Frizingley again. It would have to be now.

"Daniel . . ." she sounded shocked.

"Yes. I'm sorry. Is it an awkward moment?"

She shrugged. "No more than usual, these days." And letting the door slam shut like a curtain closing on the first—or final?—act of a tragedy, she came out into the yard with him, her arms folded across her chest, shivering slightly as if her body had not noticed the warm summer breeze.

"What is it?" This time she was sharp, asking him, he thought, to state his business and be done.

"Just goodbye."

The glance she darted at him seemed to hold suspicion, calculation even. "Why? Where are you going?"

He laughed. "I don't know. That answers both questions."

"Do you need any money?"

"Cara." The sudden intensity in her, the quick, almost furtive glance she cast around her own very evidently empty yard, amused and slightly embarrassed him. "I'm not on the run, if that's what you're thinking. There's nobody after me."

"Nobody? Are you sure?"

"Of course I'm sure."

"You've just got tired of being a schoolmaster, then?"

"I suppose so." He explained about John-William Dallam and Gemma's removal to Almsmead.

"So it seemed a convenient moment for me to get away too . . ."

"And you're all right?"

"Yes I am. Are you?"

She shrugged. "Splendid."

"I shouldn't think I'll be back."

"No. There's nothing here for you."

That, at least, was plain enough.

"I *have* called at the wrong time, haven't I?"

But there had never been a right one. How beautiful she was. How hard and brilliant. And *hurt*.

"Goodbye then, Cara."

She nodded her head. He hesitated and, when she continued to stand there in silence, her arms tight folded, he moved away.

"Daniel," she called after him through the dark. "Take care. Not that you ever will . . ."

He had heard her voice break on the final word, could not have answered without a similiar, tell-tale tremor and so, having need of haste now, he lengthened his stride, desperate to leave this filthy, tortured town behind him and feel real air in his lungs again, clean empty space washing all around him.

What a cruel farce life was. What a poisonous, cheating tragedy in which the pawns thrown down on the board to play—like himself and Cara and Gemma—were doomed, despite their good intentions, to hurt one another.

Let him get away now, far and fast and alone. Let him have nothing now but those chance-met companions of the road who asked little, gave little, began with a shrug and made scarcely a ripple at their ending.

That was all he wanted. It was as much as he could accommodate. Yet, before the night was over, he sat himself down, exhausted, on a flat rock somewhere on the dark moor between Frizingley and Leeds and *knew*—as he had known all along and tried not to know—that the brave and generous words spoken to him by Gemma Gage, her assurances that he had given her everything and more than she had asked for, had been compassionate lies.

She had not been content with his liking and his friendship. She *had* wanted him to love her. *Had* wanted to hear those passionate vows of devotion he had never made. *Had* wanted to believe herself—if only for a moment or two—to be the cherished cornerstone of his life.

She had denied it only so that he might leave her with a light heart.

She had given him a treasure of which he believed he would do anything to feel himself worthy.

———

Except lie to her.

Over his right shoulder the sky began to lighten with the new morning. Colder, he thought, than he had expected.

An altogether rougher journey.

Ah well.

He picked up his bag, finding it heavy, and walked on.

Some days later Cara accompanied her mother and son to Liverpool on the first step of their journey to America, returning alone to Frizingley.

Her decision had been five months in the making, bitter months she would not care to live again, during which the sight of Odette ageing beneath her eyes and the conviction that Liam hated her, had gradually worn her down.

Throughout April she had stood firm. Odette may do as she pleased but no one would take Liam from her. If Odette cared so much for her grandson then she would just have to stay in Frizingley too. Very well. In May, when Kieron Adeane, unable to neglect his business interests any longer, sailed for New York, Odette did not go with him. She became ashen-faced and hollow-eyed instead, Liam watching her closely, watching his mother, watching—one felt—his own back, his eyes growing blank and enormous, his mood alternating between an unnerving silence and astonishing bursts of viciousness. And when Cara tried to talk to him, tried to explain that she was his mother and had always taken care of him, he struggled between her hands screaming that she was wicked and cruel and he wanted Odette.

She had slapped him. He had kicked her. The injustice of it had scarred her badly.

May had been hideous. June little better except that she had begun to make tentative inquiries about her father's situation. Both Christie Goldsborough and Marie Moon had friends in New York. Yes. Her aunt's bakery existed, or rather several of them, all doing well so far as any friends of Christie's or Marie's—not being particularly well-versed in bakeries—could see.

The money was there. "Go to him if you like," she told her mother. "But Liam stays with me."

"He doesn't want to stay with you, Cara."

"He's a child. I'll tell him what he wants and he'll do as he's told."

Liam fastened himself like a limpet to Odette, screamed himself sick, sank his teeth into Cara's arm when she tried to comfort him and kept them there, worrying her like a bull-dog until his jaws were prised loose.

He was defending his grandmother, and himself, against an intruder. "You are killing your mother," Madge Percy told her, greatly daring, keeping her job only because Cara knew it was true.

She tried once again with Liam, promising him trips to the seaside, train-rides, puppies, making him accompany her on tense, silent ramblings on the moor on warm evenings until, deliberately distracting her attention, he ran away, submitting her to the torment of searching for him in the dark, passing from annoyance to a desperation in which she ran in circles, wildly praying that if only he should be not dead in a ditch, not stolen by the gypsies, she would be kind and loving and never speak a cross word to him again.

But she boxed his ears soundly when she came upon him hiding behind a rock where he could not have failed to hear her frantic cries, marching him home in a bitter fury which did not ease the next morning when he awoke in a fever and lay cowering away from her, calling for Odette.

She wrote a crisp and imperious letter, from Miss Cara Adeane of Frizingley to Miss Teresa Adeane of New York, demanding to know, should her mother and son ever find themselves under Miss Teresa's roof, the nature of the welcome to be expected there. Miss Teresa, after all, had opposed her brother's marriage and had shown no inclination to hospitality ever since. What had happened to change her mind?

To which Miss Teresa, in due course, briefly replied that in view of the valuable assistance she had lately received from her brother, his French wife and her grandson would both be welcome in her home; an invitation she did not extend to Cara, feeling, no doubt, that two brisk and imperious women named Adeane might be one too many for New York.

Cara put the letter away. And then, a week later, on a morning when she was feeling herself to be criminal and victim, martyred saint and black-hearted devil all together, she wrote again in the same brusque manner, to the effect that, should Liam be permitted to make the journey, she would hold her Aunt Teresa wholly and entirely responsible for his well-being, her father's disposition being such that she would not care to trust him with the care of her tabby-cat much less her son. She would, therefore, expect her aunt not only to supply her with regular news of him but to give her a solemn undertaking that he should be returned to her at once should her father's situation deteriorate. In fact she would like her aunt to deposit these instructions with her lawyers or bankers or whoever one employed for these matters in America, in case Miss Teresa Adeane—when the emergency arose—might be too infirm or too deceased to see to it herself.

Miss Teresa Adeane answered through her lawyer that Cara's will—in this matter if in no other—would be done.

She put that letter away too. Endured another silent moorland ramble with Liam. Watched Odette's misery flowing around her like a mourning garment, wider and denser and more intolerable every morning. *Endured.* And then could stand it no longer.

"Take him!" she said suddenly. "This is killing all of us." And then, floundering in her bitterness, losing her head. "Take him—take him— why not? You might as well, since you've taken everything else."

That was July. And having made her decision she did not care to go on living, day after day, with a festering wound. Let them leave at once. But August was already halfway done before they finally set off for Liverpool to meet Kieron Adeane who, with great gallantry in his wife's opinion and criminal extravagance in his daughter's, had crossed the Atlantic to fetch them.

No goodbyes were said. Leaving Madge Percy in charge of the shop for the day, Cara drove up St. Jude's Street in the carriage hired for the purpose, collected her mother and son, locked the door of their cottage behind her and pocketed the keys. In the yard next door where the Rattries had once swarmed and squabbled and stolen her water, a vacant woman staring listlessly at the horses, a child on her hip, a gaggle of them around her ankles. Across the street the Thackrays' house looked like a despoiled virgin. Sairellen had gone. A motley crowd of tinkers and tarts and vagrants who wanted a room not for Sairellen's meticulous twenty-five years but only for a month, a night, had taken her place. But Cara made herself far too busy with her mother's trunks to dwell on it. They were brand-new—those trunks—and crammed full with clothes, for both Odette and Liam, to cover every eventuality and every season, woollen and cotton dresses for everyday, silk dresses to cut a dash in, underwear to last a life-time, garments to fit Liam now and lengths of good quality materials to accommodate him as he grew. Everything that could be embroidered having been embroidered, everything that required one frill receiving at least two.

Just as she had done for Anna Rattrie.

She had seen to it that her mother would not arrive in New York empty-handed, as a supplicant. Yet she still could not forgive her for going, could neither relent in her outraged hurt, her most bitter sense of betrayal, nor reach out a hand to Odette no matter how hard she tried.

"Come along, then. Let's be off." She bundled them into the carriage as if they were prisoners under escort to the Assizes at York, maintaining a silence, all the way to Leeds, which began to seem natural to her for the simple reason that she had nothing more to say. There was no conversation on the train from Leeds to Liverpool either beyond the strict necessities of the journey, Liam snuggling close to Odette and keeping a wary eye on his mother in case she should suddenly snatch him away again—although the time when she might have performed such an act of desperation had long gone— Odette very hushed and pale and still, not daring as yet to be joyful. Not wishing to let Cara see how much she longed to be with her beloved husband again.

And although Cara saw and understood both her son's anxiety and her mother's timid blend of hope and happiness and sorrow, there was still nothing she wished to say to either of them. After all, Liam would not be anxious for much longer. He would soon start to smile and chatter and be at ease with the deck of a ship beneath his feet, Kieron Adeane to tell him stories and Odette to hold his hand.

They would be happy enough—both of them—once her hurt and hurtful presence no longer stood in their way. It was a straightforward story, after all. They had needed her and taken what they needed. Now they needed her no more. It was as simple and commonplace as that. And what she now wanted most of all was to get it over and done with. She was bringing them to Liverpool because she did not trust Odette to manage the journey alone. She had even agreed to take them to the rooming-house where her father would be waiting, for the same reason. She had filled Odette's purse with money and her trunks with expensive clothes. She had written further letters to her aunt's American lawyers, instructing them, very firmly, to return her son to her in case of need and explaining how the expenses of his voyage home would be met. She had written also to a friend of Marie Moon's who, being of an inquiring disposition, could be counted on—for the simple outlay of an occasional gift of cashmere or satin—to relay any gossip about the failure of the bakery trade in New York.

She had taken every possible precaution, every care. But her heart felt like a lump of granite in her chest, sharp-edged and heavy, altogether immovable. She watched her son fear her and, with that granite heart, she bore it. She saw the ease with which Odette had rejected the life for which *she*—not her mother—had made so much sacrifice. She suffered the taste of her own love and loyalty as it curdled and turned sour. Her spiky, cumbersome, unyielding heart bore all that too.

She did not even glance at Liverpool. There was the station, another hired carriage, the very decent, almost impressive house where her father had taken rooms—a bedroom and sitting-room and dining-parlor she had heard, without listening or caring—for the few days before the ship sailed again. Time, she thought grimly, to equip his wife with an outfit that would pass muster before the scrutiny of his sharp-eyed sister.

Well. There would be no need for that.

She got out of the cab and stood on the pavement, the trunks and boxes around her feet, feeling so far away from Odette—even farther from Liam—that they might already have made the crossing to New York. So be it. She would not disgrace herself now, in her own eyes, by breaking down and begging them to stay.

"Goodbye, then."

"Cara . . ." Odette's face was suddenly ghastly. "You can't leave now—like this . . . my dear child . . ."

"What is it mother?" she said unkindly. "This is the address he gave you. Are you afraid he won't be here?"

But he had seen the carriage from the window and came running to greet them, tall and healthy and handsome, wearing his new air of prosperity as jauntily as the flower in his buttonhole, so vibrant, so rejuvenated by the success which had polished him like a diamond that Odette, as he clasped her in his arms, looked faded and old.

Never mind. No doubt the magic of New York would transform her too.

"Cara," he said, holding out a hand to her, ready, should she take it, to draw her into his arms, into his life again and hold her there, reminding her that no colors had ever been brighter than the ones he painted, no air fresher or sweeter than the air one breathed with him.

"Father," she replied, without touching him.

"Come inside." She shrugged and shook her head but, in the end, as Odette began to tremble and declare she could not part from her daughter in the street, it proved easier to obey. Quicker, perhaps. And so she went with them, aware, as the trunks were carried inside, only of a vague impression of comfort and the easy manner—no surprise to her—with which her father distributed largesse to the porter and called out, in his rich, lilting voice, for tea.

"You'll need something to refresh yourselves, my darlings."

He smiled at them all, *her* smile on a face she had never forgotten, *her* sea-blue eyes with her father's agile, feckless brain behind them. *His* charm flowing now into every corner of the room, far greater, she recognized, than her own. She understood why women loved him. She had loved him herself as much as any of them. She understood, too, that he not only intended to win her over but was sure of his ability to do it; quite certain that when their ship sailed in a day or two she would be there, on the dockside, waving them a loving farewell.

Let him think so.

"Odette, my darling, why don't you take the child and show him where he'll be sleeping so that when night comes it won't be strange to him?"

He was really saying "Leave me alone with her for a while, this daughter of ours, and let's see what can be done."

Odette heard him and smiling, nodding her head slightly, she took Liam by the hand and led him, unprotesting, away.

A boy with a pointed chin and huge dark eyes, still small for his age, still fragile, still with that wild, startled look about him of a woodland fox. Her son. She did not want to look.

"Cara," her father said, "won't you take off your hat and gloves?"

"I don't think so."

"Your dignity suits you, my darling. And it does my heart good to see you so fine and beautiful."

He meant it, of course. She knew that. As he had always meant what he said at the time of saying it. The Enchanter's golden voice of her childhood, describing to her all the shimmering colors of the rainbow. *"I'll make you a princess, my darling."* Well—she had no need of his false promises, his broken rainbows. She would be a princess, ere long, of her own creation, in Market Square.

"Cara, listen to me now for a little while . . ."

But she did not wish to hear his excuses, nor submit herself to his persuasions. She wanted to hurt him, to strike a blow at him, even if it made her fingers bleed and broke her heart. If anything, that is, could shatter this knife-edged rock she still carried in her chest.

She smiled at him, unpleasantly she supposed, since it clearly startled him.

"Time presses, father, and although I'd love to hear all about it—well—we can't always have *just* what we'd like, can we now? There *is* one thing, though—before it slips my mind. You left a debt behind in Frizingley."

"Did I now?" He looked a little puzzled, a little rueful, his smile asking her would she not rather talk of wounded pride and broken hearts and how to mend them, of gilded royalty in New York's bakehouses than sordid old tales like this.

"Yes father, you left a debt. And since we may not meet again . . ."

"To Goldsborough?"

"The same."

"I understood it has been canceled."

She shook her head.

"No. Transferred to me. And I have not canceled it. Fifty pounds."

She held out her hand.

"Is this some kind of test you're setting me, my darling?" He was smiling a little sadly now, no reprimand in him, no anger. Sorrow both for her and for him. A degree of enchantment it would, in a happier time, have been hard to resist. He was telling her he loved her and had always loved her, speaking to her of belonging and being together, of living all over again the warm magic of the past. Cara, my darling daughter, heart of my heart, light of my eyes.

"Fifty pounds," she said.

He sighed and shrugged his narrow, elegant shoulders.

"Certainly. If that is what you want."

"It is."

He counted the money into her hand and, her fingers closing around it, she swept out of the room, out of the house, and then, once safely alone on the pavement, fled as far and as fast as she could, anywhere so long as it was *away* from the tortured emotions he had aroused in her, away from the memories and the shattered trust, away from the magic circle of the family, "the four of us" from which she had been cast out, or had torn herself apart; she hardly knew the difference.

Hardship was no stranger to her. Hunger and cold and debt were enemies which, having met head-on and conquered, she would not be afraid to meet again. But she had never been alone before.

She had been trained, from her earliest youth, to act not as one but as three. Not even to think of herself in isolation from the others who completed her identity. The "three of us." The handsome, clever, infinitely superior Adeanes against the world. A delusion, like everything else, it seemed to her as she walked in her blind and angry solitude through the streets of Liverpool. A game devised by her father for his own aggrandizement in which only one player—himself—could ever win. A shadow-dance, her whole life with *them*, and nothing more, false from its very beginning.

And now it had ended.

She knew him, through and through, her father. She did not know her son at all. Nor ever would. How had she come to this? At the entrance of a public garden a woman was sitting, an image of despairing Ireland, her children squatting around her, their faces as blank and beautiful as Liam's, the same damaged, offended souls looking out of their eyes as she had seen in his. They too—she could tell—had been dragged, from their birth, at the skirts of a harassed woman, absorbing through their fragile skins the adult fears she had no time at the end of her day's labors, her day's begging for bread, to explain to them. They simply knew she was afraid. As Liam had known. Fear stalking him too, never more than an inch away, the uncertain ground beneath Cara's feet, upon which she had known how to tread, becoming a quicksand to him.

And now she was childless, with fifty pounds in her hand.

For a moment she toyed with the idea of tossing the whole of it into this woman's lap. Why not? Except that a beggar-woman in rags carrying such a fortune would—in this evil-minded world—end up getting herself arrested as a thief. Or knocked on the head, in the back alley where she lived, and robbed. Prudently, knowing the ways of alleys and pawnbrokers and gin-shops, Cara gave a single gold coin—fortune enough—and walked on.

She was calm and brisk and almost painfully in control when she returned to Market Square that same evening, inspecting her premises with the eye of an eagle as Madge Percy assured her that no customers had been lost in her absence, no valuable materials damaged or gone astray, that—however surprising it may seem—there had been no fire, no flood, no treacherous journeywoman running off with her designs to Miss Ernestine Baker.

"Thank you, Madge. You can go now."

What next?

Her body ached with the raw exhaustion of her early days in Frizingley, her head racing with half-thoughts, half-truths, a whirlwind of hurts and hopes and memories far too turbulent for sleep. If she tried she knew she would be pursued all through the night by dreams of wild and twisted things which would do nothing to improve her humor tomorrow. Better, then, to sit here a while longer with a glass of Madeira, closing her mind—if she could—to everything but the sheer physical ease of a good cushion behind her back and four solid walls around her. And tomorrow, at the very least, she would not have to endure the gradual drop-by-drop torment of her mother's misery.

She emptied her glass and poured another.

What *would* she do tomorrow? What would she think about, tomorrow evening, when the shop was empty and her women gone, when she had closed her ledgers and finished off the sketches needed for the following day? What did she know *how* to do, when it came down to it, except work and worry and pile up money to safeguard the future of those to whom she had felt bound by love or duty, or both?

Well, she had made it easy for them all to leave her. No one could ever say that she had held them back. She had sent off her mother royally, with a trousseau fit for a cherished bride. She had made Anna Rattrie almost pretty. She had made Gemma Gage look handsome enough on occasions too. And what was left to think of now, with Daniel safely out of Frizingley, with Liam's cough removed to the other side of the Atlantic where she could not hear it, with Luke married and making his own way in Nottingham; and her father, who had neither earned it nor deserved it, apparently even more comfortably off in New York than she was herself in Market Square.

What a farce life was, if one had the heart to laugh at it.

She had not. She drank another glass of wine instead and, with its assistance, was beginning to feel her eyes grow heavy, the lines of her body blur into the desired state of uncaring, when she heard a carriage crossing Market Square at speed and draw up suspiciously close to her shop front. No customer, of course, at this hour. The worthy husband, though—quite possibly—of one of them who might have mistaken her pleasant, professional manner for something else? It would not be the first time. In which case she would not answer the door. Unless it should be Marie Moon, running away from her husband? Quite possibly. Poor Marie, upon whom the hounds of legal and medical opinion, of brain disorders and asylums and declarations of her unfitness to manage money were swiftly closing. Yes, she would open the door to Marie.

But, as she hurried from her office and began to move through the darkened shop, knowing her way too well to need a candle, she could see the high-perch carriage through the window and hear the loud, unmannerly knocking on the door, the smart rat-a-tat made with the knob of a cane or a riding whip, by a man who simply did not care whether he woke the whole street from its hard-earned slumbers or not.

Who would dare to reprimand him, after all, if he did?

It could only be Christie.

She drew back the bolt and stared at him.

"I am paying a call," he said, feeling it unnecessary, although he had never visited her here before, to make any further explanation than that.

"It's after midnight."

"I dare say."

He strolled past her, a landlord inspecting his property, although in the dark she knew he could see nothing beyond the vague, pale shapes of her models and hat stands. But, because it seemed unthinkable to take him by the hand and lead him through the shop to her well-lit parlor as she would have done with almost anyone else, she ran to fetch a lamp, shielding the flame with a nervous hand. What did he want from her now?

"Have you been out to dinner somewhere?" she asked.

"I have."

Ben Braithwaite's, she thought, judging him too immaculate for Sir Felix Lark's where the "gentlemen" got up to such stupid horseplay, it seemed to her, after dinner, fencing with billiard cues, making bets as to who could shin up a tree the fastest, blindfold or with one arm tied, or some such lunacy; getting up on to the roof and running steeple chases over the chimney stacks; taking no care of their clothes whatsoever. She had seen him come back from the Larks with his expensive frilled and pin-tucked shirt ripped along the shoulder and half the buttons off, his white silk waistcoat ruined by random stains which she—with her precise knowledge of the cost of silk—had identified as soot, red wine, horse grease, and blood.

But he had done nothing more rakish tonight, she noticed, than loosen his cravat a little, his white lawn shirt and silver brocade waistcoat with no mark upon them, his black opera cloak thrown back, just as it ought to be, to show the red silk lining, a heavy jeweled ring—which the Larks would have considered vulgar—on either hand. Evidence in itself that he had been dining at an industrialist's table.

"So this is where you live," he said, taking off his hat and gloves and fringed silk scarf and tossing them in the direction of her table without even a sidelong glance to see how or where they landed, his eyes skimming over her possessions in a manner which seriously offended her since—whether or not he found them meager—*she* had never lived so well.

"And drinking alone, Cara, I see. I may join you—if you have another glass."

Of course she had another glass. In fact she had two whole dozen of them. And decent crystal, at that, since she used them for serving wine—and *good* wine—to her ladies in the shop. Her indignation growing she brought one, filled it a little too full and gave it to him without a word, her eyes shooting sparks which she hoped—although it seemed unlikely—that he would notice.

This was his property, of course, she was only too well aware of it, but nothing obliged her to like him coming here, filling the only private room she had ever had with his bulky, overheated presence, his heavy scent of musk and tobacco getting everywhere, taking everything over.

Not even the dog had growled at him.

"Good God," he said, catching sight of it. "Damn me if that's not my old Caligula."

Caligula? He has always been just "Dog" to her, or "Damned Dog" more often than not, lazy, ill-tempered, disobedient, eating his head off and biting the fingers that fed him—hers—whenever he got half a chance.

But. "Here, boy," said Christie and, lumbering to his bandy legs the faithless beast, who only came to Cara's call when it suited him, trotted obligingly across the room and placed an adoring, docile muzzle in his master's hand.

"You kept him, then?"

Yes, she had kept him. And now the treacherous beast was fawning like a day-old puppy at the feet of the man who had thrown him away. Ought she really to be surprised about it? But yes. She had kept him. It had never occurred to her to do anything else.

"Tell me, Cara," roughly scratching the dog's ears, he was laughing, oddly pleased about something or other, "I know how much this breed of dog eats. And remembering that this one was always greedy—how did you manage to feed him? In your early days together, I mean?"

She smiled, rather pleased now in her turn. "Oh, *I* didn't feed him, Christie. You did. That's how I looked at it, anyway, when I was stealing meat for him from your kitchen."

His smile broadened into a grin, showing what always seemed to her to be a powerful array of teeth, a heavy contrast of color which made the skin swarthier, the teeth stronger, the mouth more full-lipped and widely-curved and self-indulgent than ever.

"I may have expected you to abandon him, you know—although I may be rather glad you didn't."

"Do you even remember giving him to me?"

"Oh yes."

"Well then . . ." For some reason he had made her feel awkward. "Here he is . . ."

"So I see. Overfed and much indulged, by the look of him. Does he pay for it by guarding you well and faithfully?"

"He does not." The glance she shot at her treacherous "Caligula" was as vicious as his own. "If you wanted to cut my throat I expect he'd let you."

"Luckily I don't."

She had no answer to that. Nor was she really certain just why she was gritting her teeth and clenching her hands in the pockets of her taffeta skirt. It was only a dog, after all. The ugliest brute in creation. Why, in God's name, should she care about it? How was it that she could hardly stop herself from crying like a fool because he had gone wagging his stubby tail so fondly to Christie? A dog. When she had lost a son and a mother and two men she could have loved— *had* loved—how could she feel betrayed by a dog?

He sent the animal away with a snap of his fingers.

"When did you get in from Liverpool?"

"Late."

"And did it go well?"

What a ridiculous question. Fiercely, losing such caution as remained to her—not much—she told him so, asking *him* how he expected a woman to feel when she had given her son away.

To which he replied with unusual, possibly deceptive, mildness that he was hardly in a position to know.

"I have no sons to part from, which is no particular grief to me, I do assure you. And for once, my dear, you can hardly blame *me* in this matter."

"Oh yes I can."

"Cara—I hardly think so. I may have had a hand in the removal of Mr. Thackray, but what advantage is there to me in getting rid of your son? Not at all the kind of thing one would care to do, in any case ..."

"Although *one* would do it, wouldn't one, just the same—if it happened to suit?"

He nodded very slightly, his eyes amused and keen, acknowledging her mockery of his aristocratic "one" to avoid the pushy, self-aggrandizing, middle-class "I" to be a sure sign that she had not only abandoned her caution but flung it to the winds.

"One might," he said pleasantly. "But it did not suit. Therefore I have done nothing against him."

"Oh yes, that you have."

"My dear—do tell me about it."

Leaning back in her best armchair, *her* dog lying at his feet, he helped himself to another glass of her wine—no, the wine, she supposed, was really his—and appeared to be settling down very comfortably to listen.

Guarding her, of course. She knew that and even welcomed it. For if she could spill out even a little of her hurt and anger then it would do something—surely—to ease the rock she still seemed to be carrying inside her chest. And no matter what she said to Christie he would not care.

"Of course I blame you. You knew I had a child but what did he ever matter? Whenever you wanted me I had to drop everything— drop him—and come running—to you and your strange games ..."

She could feel amusement rippling in him even before he answered her. "My dear, what games are these? The only ones I know seem entirely natural."

"I'm not talking about *that*," she shouted at him, refusing to call it "making love" and knowing no other acceptable description. "I'm talking about—oh, you know very well. Playing chess with live pieces—isn't that what you call it? And if you've come here now to do it again—and you're *very* good at it—to make me admit to myself that I'm a bad mother as you've made me admit other things—made me look at myself and then watched me not liking what you've made me see . . . Well—if that's what you want tonight I can save you the trouble. I *am* a bad mother. I know. I know."

"Are you?" he said quietly. "I have never thought much about it. Are you quite certain?"

"I gave my son away, didn't I?"

"Yes," he gave her a nod of encouragement. "Can you tell me why?"

"Because . . ."

"Yes?"

"Because . . ." She pressed her hands to her cheeks, suddenly aware of the tears that were cascading down them, horrified and awkward and angry in her weeping, alarmed at the extent of it and even more alarmed that she could not stop.

"Don't worry about that," he said. "You can talk and cry at the same time, I imagine. Why did you let him go?"

"Because he wanted to," she sobbed. "Because he was afraid of me. Because I never had the patience to find out why he was so quiet and odd and separate. I was tired at the end of the day, you see, when he was a baby. Twelve hours in a sweatshop making shirts like the one you're wearing now will tire anybody, won't it? Well, *you* wouldn't know, but you can take my word for it. And so I just fed him and paid the rent and sat up making shirts for him out of scraps I'd . . ."

"Stolen?" he suggested.

"Yes, from the workroom. And put off talking to him until . . . Until I had the time, dammit—which I never had. Never. There was always *something*. Things I couldn't tell a child about, could I? That's what I tell myself now. And it's excuses—excuses—that's all—just to make myself feel better, because the truth is I hardly ever thought about it. He was just there. I just expected him to love me. I loved him. At least, I loved my little boy—and that's who he was. And I wasted my time. Because he doesn't know me and he doesn't want to know me. He knows my mother, which is all right—all right—she looked after me, it seemed natural for her to be looking after him. I didn't mind. I couldn't afford to mind. We both did the best we could, my mother and I. She looked after the child and I earned the bread.

I knew he loved her. So did I. If he'd even thought of me as a kind of older sister, it would have been something. But all I was to him was an intruder. A damned nuisance. And then an enemy who kept threatening to take Odette away. To have kept him here with me would have been cruel. Once I realized that—and I tried hard enough not to—Well—that's why I sent him away."

"An act of love," he said.

"What? What was that?"

He did not repeat it. He stood up instead, poured her a glass of wine and then made her sit down beside him with instructions to drink up her good Old Sercial and dry her tears. He was being kind to her and the realization shocked and worried her so much that the effort of searching for his motives gradually restored her calm.

"I'm sorry," she said stiffly, wiping her eyes with a wisp of cambric she did not intend anyone to steal from *her* workroom.

He shrugged. "I have more confessions made to me than you might think. Are you better now?"

She nodded, watching him like a hawk.

"Then you really shouldn't reproach yourself much more, or for much longer. How old is your boy? Seven? Eight? I went away to school at that age and took no harm. And before that I rarely remember seeing my mother for more than ten minutes a day. They used to dress me up and take me downstairs at tea-time so she could have a look at me. What lady with her social and charitable obligations to fulfill could be expected to take more notice of an infant than that? It is altogether the way things are done, my dear."

"In your world, I dare say it is." Her own world being so very far removed from it that she could imagine no similarity, no point of recognition between his childhood and Liam's. Between the parties and dances and riding to hounds, the dinners and idle afternoons of gossip and flirtation which had filled his mother's hours and the hard grind of her own.

"I see little difference," he said airily, filling up her glass again. How many times was this? "Poor children go to the workhouse, rich children are sent away to school. It amounts to much the same."

Startled and scornful—since what did he know of workhouses?— she gulped her drink, coughed, and then, to ease the coughing, finished the glass. He gave her another.

"You know nothing about it," she told him. "You've never been hungry. You can't even begin to imagine what it feels like. And if you're cold sometimes then it's only because you've lived in the Tropics, not because there's ever been a lack of fur blankets and rugs. You've always had a roof over your head, and a good one. Probably never less than a choice of two or three. And if you've always been sure of those things then you don't know what hardship is."

Suddenly her contempt for him and for anyone and everyone who had never struggled and endured as she had, overwhelmed her. He saw poverty in terms of being unable to support a pack of foxhounds for a season or two and having quietly to dispose of half the family silver. She saw it in terms of boots and bread.

Sitting up in her chair and raising her head she felt her superiority swirling around her like a wrap of ermine or sable, or something, at any rate, that was a cut above the black fox lining of the cloak *he* sometimes wore.

"Oh yes, I've always had a roof, I'll grant you that," he said, not appearing to notice the trailing magnificence of her furs. "But the kind of schools attended by young gentlemen such as I was, are designed to build character, you know, not for comfort. To turn out soldiers and statesmen and colonial governors and masters of fox-hounds, not scholars. And the only way to build character, don't you know, is through deprivation. I had to wash at a stand-pipe, my dear, in the school-yard every morning, and stand in line—a long line—winter or summer, stripped and waiting my turn. One may never learn to like it, but one learns to *endure*. That's the great thing. So that if one happens to be posted to some particularly inhospitable corner of the empire there's no fear of letting the side down by asking for tubs of decadent hot water. One learns to take a flogging too without batting an eyelid, much less making a sound, although it's rather hoped one won't develop a taste for that, even if some of the masters regrettably do. And although one can lead a good life in the army there are certain aspects of it one finds wearisome, to say the least. One gets shot at occasionally, for instance, which can be a bore. So my path has not always been strewn with roses ...'"

The army? She could not imagine him taking orders from anyone, much less some heavy, pompous, elderly schoolboy like Colonel Covington-Pym whose wife, she knew, had sometimes been his mistress. Perhaps he had never been a soldier at all. Perhaps it was just a story to cover up something else. Happily, something worse? With the wine pleasantly swirling in her head she decided that he had been a smuggler, a white slaver, the captain of a convict ship to Australia. A pirate.

She told him so and, with the smile that showed his teeth, he shook his head, not at all offended. "A soldier," he said. "My grandfather— General Sir Jarvis Covington-Pym—was obliging enough to buy me a commission in what is known as a crack regiment. The uniform would have pleased you. And I had a private income, in those days, just big enough to keep a few polo ponies and hunters and pay my mess bills. Not a bad life."

"Why did you give it up, then?"

"Oh—at their request."

"You mean they threw you out?"

"I do."

How wonderful. She had, in fact, no real idea just why young officers might be dismissed from their regiments. She simply hoped that, in his case, it had been something very bad. Although if it had caused any real scandal—if he had cheated at cards, or led his men into an ambush and left them there—would he now be on such excellent terms with his extremely conventional cousin, Colonel Covington-Pym? Doubting it, her elation faded.

"I was insubordinate," he said.

"Is that all?" It was something she could have been accused of every day of her life.

"If one works at it sufficiently and regularly then it tends to be enough."

"Were you in disgrace?"

"I was."

She felt considerably pleased about that.

"And did they break your sword and cut off your medals?" She really did hope so.

He smiled. "Hardly so dramatic as that. My grandfather, after all, *was* a general. But bad enough. However—I rallied. Instead of shooting myself or drinking myself to death I went out to the West Indies and made myself some money in rum and sugar and cloves. Now that really was a good life."

"Why didn't you stay there?"

"Do you wish I had? I came back when my father died. As lord of a manor which had been sold years before and of what was left of the manor lands. Enough to make me a handsome fortune when the time is ripe. I think you really are a little better now, aren't you? There's no healer more certain, it often seems to me, than curiosity."

So that was it. "Thank you. I'm quite well now," she said almost primly and then, very suddenly, she was not. Once again—and really *very* suddenly and well nigh completely this time—her grief had come over her. And *this* time, in this pitiful, terrible, astounding moment, she could escape neither the grief nor the revelation of its source. For what she wanted now was neither her mother nor her son but her father, Kieron Adeane, the enchanter of her girlhood, the seeker of rainbows, the sower of magical seeds which blossomed unfailingly into vivid, highly scented flowers of laughter; a garden of easily scattered but never-to-be forgotten fascinations. She did not forget them. Nor did she forget the hand he had held out to her only this morning, not asking her forgiveness so much as offering to take her riding all over again on his final rainbow, to make a princess of her as he had always promised, as she had always been to him in his blithe, butterfly-textured heart.

He loved her, in his fashion, and had always done so. A light, lilting, effervescent love which, no matter how easily blown about by every passing breeze, could enchant her still.

This morning she had refused it. She would refuse it now, she supposed, should he suddenly appear before her in a puff of golden smoke, in the manner of enchanters. But, nevertheless, what she truly longed for was to be with him now, walking arm-in-arm on the deck of a great ship, sailing into adventure. The Adeanes against the world. And of those Adeanes there had always been an inner wheel, "the two of us," a handsome father and daughter, made in the same mould, casting the same glittering shadow.

Her life had lacked color since he had left it. The realization devastated her. And jumping to her feet, needing to do something, anything, whatever came first to hand, she reached for the wine bottle and found it empty.

"Have you another?" he said.

She brought it and he opened it for her and filled her glass.

"This Madeira is a potent brew," he warned her. "You should take care."

"I always do," she snapped.

"Very well. It is simply part of one's training as an officer and a gentleman to give these warnings when drinking with women. Should they be disregarded one feels entitled, of course, to take what advantage one can and no complaints in the morning. So I have been brought up to believe."

She was barely listening. Beginning to pace up and down the room, feeling caged and hounded and in the grip of a choking agitation, she could not rid herself of the image of her father, the memories of all that he had been to her until her faith in him had died and she had turned her back. And although that faith had withered far beyond recall she knew now that she would always miss it. Would never feel entirely whole or natural or safe again.

It was unfair.

"You don't understand," she said, her thoughts racing so fast that her words, unable to keep pace, seemed to be stumbling over each other. "You don't know what it's like to be part of a family. How could you—away at school and in the army—? You don't know how much I—how it was . . ."

"How was it?"

She fought against her need to tell him. No. She must stop this and at once before she had stripped herself too near the bone, shown him too much. No. Even through the wine she knew she must calm herself. Must keep what she could of her dignity and her secrets. And it was the reminder of secrets, and her urgent need to distract his attention which made her say recklessly, "Let's talk about your father, not mine. How did he happen to lose his money?"

Raising his own glass to his lips and taking a reflective sip, he appeared untroubled by the subject.

"Oh—in a thoroughly commonplace manner. He gambled. He bought the favors of expensive women. He drank."

"And your mother?" Has she not been rather more than half-drunk she would not have dared to ask. But now, her head feeling incredibly light and somewhat higher than usual on her shoulders, she did not care for the consequences. Tame and tedious things in any case. And if he chose to make any revelations she hoped they would be shocking enough, terrible enough, to fill her mind with something that was not her father. Or Liam.

He looked at her for a moment with speculation.

"Ah yes. My mother. You have evidently heard some talk about her. What is it?"

"That she died . . ."

"Quite so. But how?"

"No one seems to know." Was she running her head into a noose?

Did it really matter? And then, as he got up and came toward her, she felt a whisper—only faint as yet, but persistent—of fear.

"Shall I tell you?"

"If you want to."

He halted a yard away from her. "Come close to me, Cara," he said. "I believe one must whisper these things."

She came, against her will and her better judgment, like a rabbit to a snare, she thought angrily, biting her lip. Yet she stood there, nevertheless, and allowed him, without any protest, to put his hands around her neck, the musky heat of him absorbing her as always into his atmosphere, her senses, which had been unsteady to begin with, starting now to swim not altogether unpleasantly beyond her reach.

"It was like this," he said. "She met my father at the head of the manor stairs. He made some accusations which she denied. He put his hands around her throat to squeeze the truth from her—am I hurting you, Cara? No? Good. She continued to deny. He continued to squeeze. Don't let me get carried away by my performance, will you? Since I am his son, after all, and have his blood in me. A violent man. Always a wild look in his eye, like a horse just before it bolts. You know what I mean. My poor mother. She fell dead at his feet. So the parlormaid said, at any rate."

"Christie."

"While the cook appears to have seen things quite otherwise. He took her by the shoulders to *shake* out the truth, not squeeze it—like this—and then, when he had it and could not bear it, he picked her up and threw her over the gallery rail down into the hall. A drop quite sufficient to kill anybody. According to cook. Although there was the groom, of course, who ... Are you not enjoying this, Cara?"

"No. *You* are."

His hands slid down her arms and then, arriving at her wrists, lingered a moment and let her go.

"Then come close to me again, since you can hardly stand up on your own it seems, and I'll whisper another version into your ear. Will you come?"

She came, entering his atmosphere like crossing a threshold, a different air to breathe, a slower pulse beat, a captivity her arms were suddenly too heavy, her body too lethargic to resist. An enchanter—this man—of a different kind to her father.

An enchanter nevertheless.

"They were a turbulent pair," he said. "You may not have found her beautiful for she was very much a Covington-Pym. And since I very closely resemble him you would obviously not have thought him handsome. They were cousins and had the same nature. Passionate. Uncontrolled. Or mad, according to who is telling the story. It is the nature of both the Goldsboroughs and the Covington-Pyms. They lost their heads easily. They were both prone to the kind of killing rage which drove you, not too long ago, to attack my poor boy Oliver. But what lit the spark for my parents was jealousy. It became the essence of their life together. Monumental battles. Followed by extravagant reconciliations. They needed their jealousy. It added a spice—a dash of flavor. It occurs to me that they may have found lovemaking difficult without it. And so they manufactured it. I am ready to swear that she was never unfaithful to him either by word or deed."

"And he?"

"Oh—only casually as men are from time to time. Mainly to hurt her so she could hurt him back and they could have their orgy of reconciliation—hours, my dear, and days locked up together behind her bedroom door. A little habit which had always had the servants muttering that he might have killed her. Well—on the day she died it is quite true that they met at the head of the stairs. But what the parlormaid did not remember was that she had chased him up from the stableyard—had been lying in wait for him there, it seems, to menace him with a dressage whip which he had really been obliged, poor chap, to take away from her. Somewhat by force, one imagines. So the groom's tale that he beat her to death has *that* much foundation. Yes, he did have his hands on her throat at one stage and he did shake her. Probably because he couldn't see well enough, at the time, to slap her with any accuracy, having so much blood in his eyes. Oh—did I forget? She'd cut him rather badly, down in the stables, with her whip. One gash across the forehead and another from eye to chin. The reason for it all seems scarcely important. She had been flirting, to tease him. Or he had been flirting. Or both. She broke free and aimed a blow at him. He ducked. She stumbled. She was wearing a riding-habit with a trailing skirt. I think it likely that she caught her foot in the hem. You may remember that the stairs at the manor are steep and were uncarpeted in our day. The hall is stone-flagged and was uncarpeted too. And possibly she was frailer than she seemed. Most of us tend to be. So—he may have been responsible for her death but he most certainly did not intend it. It broke him, of course. He vowed, then and there, to kill himself in order to join her, and no doubt she would have handed him the pistol to do it with had she been able. Regrettably he chose the very slow method of drink and all that goes with it. A sad story. Of which I have given you the most accurate version possible. Since I was present, of course, down below in the hall, home from school for the holidays, hiding and watching as children in violent households tend to do."

"How old were you?"

"Fourteen."

"I'm sorry."

"For me? Make love to me, then, and heal my scars."

She stiffened and tried to pull away from him, finding his sudden change of subject coarse and offensive. For she had seen the figure of that fourteen-year-old boy very clearly, watching in the shadows, letting the storm break over his head, thinking perhaps that if this was the love of adult man for adult woman then he would be better off without it. Worrying, even, in case these same mad emotions might be lurking somewhere in him. She had been feeling sorry for that child and now, opening her eyes to the mocking, callous, entirely haughty and entirely passionless man before her she was aware only of her only folly. How could she even be sure that he had told her the truth.

"How can you talk about *that*" she said, wrinkling her nose in disgust, "when you've just been talking about your mother? And did it really scar you?" She doubted it.

"Make love to me, and see."

That again. She had been making love to him for years. She told him so. Smiling, his arms still around her, his whole body around her somehow it seemed, he shook his head. "No, Cara. You have been lying in my bed making the movements I taught you and what you hope to be the right noises. You have been satisfying my desires and very nearly killing yourself sometimes in the effort to stop me satisfying yours. And why? For whom are you saving yourself now, my love? They have all gone. You haven't realized yet, have you, that you are quite free."

She did not feel free. Crushed, perhaps. Bewildered. She felt his arms release her. "Stay close to me," he said. She stayed, the whole length of their bodies touching, a weakness and a trembling in her legs and her stomach, from the wine she supposed, her wits with their razor edges feeling as if they had been lulled half to sleep, coaxed into a deep languor where only the things of the body, the natural things that would happen as they happened, counted.

No need to think. She had reasoned too deep and too often and what good had it done her? Why not suspend those painful, busy probings of the mind and, on this strange night, allow her senses to run amok? For even though he was not the enchanter she wanted she knew there was sorcery in him, of its own somber kind, nevertheless. Why deny herself? For whom? At least it would be something.

She lifted her head and looked straight at him. "No," she said. "I have no desires." But her whole body was trembling now as he began to touch it, beginning, despite herself, to purr beneath his stroking hands like a cat basking in unexpected sunlight.

"Use me," he said, his breath in her ear. "If you think of yourself as an instrument of my pleasure then think of me as the instrument of yours. I ask you again, Cara—for whom are you saving yourself now?"

No one. He had not said "Who else wants you?" but the ugly words, having entered her mind, lodged there for a moment until the wine and the heat of his breath, the overwhelming release of her own pent-up desire, swept them away.

She had never imagined him in her bed. She had thought of Daniel there, far more often and more recently than had been good for her. Once she had thought of Luke. Never Christie. She did not think of him now. She gave herself, spreadeagled on her own narrow mattress, with a frenzy in which her mind had no part at all. From which, indeed, her thinking self stood entirely apart, shaking its head and wringing its hands no doubt, in shame and anguish, had she cared to look. She did not. During four years of varied and prolonged sexual experiences with this man she had starved her body so thoroughly of pleasure that now its avidity, its curiosity, its sheer, honest appetite came as a shock to her, leaping and pouring out in so fierce an overflow that she seemed likely, she thought, to drown. Yet she rose to the surface, entwined like seaweed all around him, clinging with every hungry inch of skin until her first orgasm crashed over her, uncoiling her and leaving her gasping.

It must be the wine.

"It's not over yet, Adeane. There's my share to think of now."

Oh *that*. She was fully acquainted with his pleasure and now, her body still quivering with the memory of her own, she simply hoped it would not take long. Yet as his rhythms quickened she felt herself joining them, clinging and coiling again, a hard little knot of desire still left inside her for him to unravel, its strands suddenly breaking loose, shooting apart, threading her whole body fiercely with joy.

"Well done, Adeane," he said. "I always knew you for a sensuous woman. Tell me—will you ever call it 'oh *that*' again?"

She slept for a while. The wine, of course. And woke in a panic, not knowing how long she had been asleep, nor what the time was, although she did not like the look of those pale gray patches behind her curtains. There was no wine in her now and here she was with a man in her bed and her women likely to arrive at any moment. Was that a factory hooter? Good God. Odette would be . . . But no. Odette would *not* be waking Liam and taking him to school, would *not* come hurrying in, a little out of breath, without knocking. No longer. Madge Percy though, who had a sharp eye and a busy tongue.

"It's half past four," he told her irritably. "What time do your women arrive, for God's sake?"

She sighed her relief. "Not until six." But her respite was short-lived.

"Your horses, Christie."

"What of them?"

"They're outside my door, aren't they, with that flashy high-perch carriage for everybody to see—and recognize . . ."

Lying on his back, his wide shoulders taking up considerably more than half the bed and all the pillows, he laughed at her.

"And we have your reputation in Market Square to think of. I know. I thought of it. My groom took them back to the Fleece as soon as you let me in. Not that I would leave them standing in harness anyway. Passion is all very well but a man must know his priorities."

"Yes. And my first priority is to see to . . ."

"Cara—*your* first priority is to see to my waking desire. Come here."

"Christie." She was horrified. "There's no time."

She had to dress, empty the ash-trays he had filled with his tell-tale cigars, get rid of the wine bottles and the glasses, get rid of every sign of him. Didn't he realize that there were no greater gossips on earth than dressmakers? And if it was seen that she had relaxed her standards and had started entertaining lovers in her business premises, then how could she expect them to keep up theirs?

She resisted him. And then did not. Her bones melted and she lay beneath him almost swooning with the intensity of her pleasure for which wine, this time, could in no way be held responsible. And then she lay there just a little while longer for the simple reason that she was warm and comfortable and did not wish to move.

She even raised a hand to his cheek and smiled as she felt the bristle.

"So—if your horses have been taken away—are you going to walk back to the Fleece in evening dress, unshaven, at this hour? With the streets full of mill-hands by now, and brewers' drays and Lord knows what else?"

"Do you suppose anybody will question me?"

She gave what she could only acknowledge to be a giggle. "No. I just hope nobody sees you coming out of my back door. You couldn't jump the back wall and leave by the grocer's, could you?"

There was a moment of possibly incredulous silence during which she did not quite like to look at him. And then, to match her giggle, he contributed a short, deep-chested laugh.

"Naturally, I *could*. Ten years ago I might have done. And speaking of grocers . . . Before it slips my mind."

"Yes?" She was instantly bolt upright and alert.

"He's going."

"When?"

"The end of the month."

"And the lease?"

"I have it in my coat pocket somewhere—unless it fell out, of course, on my way here last night."

She leaped out of bed.

"Can I get it?" She was already searching his coat. "It's *here*."

"Yes. I fully expected it would be. It won't come cheap. And, of course, I have other takers . . ."

"You promised me."

He got up and, quickly and precisely, began to dress.

"Promises have nothing to do with it. There are my terms. Study them. Go next door and make a thorough inspection. Then let me know what improvements you want to make and how you intend to go about making them. Cost it out as accurately as you can. Then let me have your figures. If they match mine within reason then we'll talk about it. Tonight, perhaps?"

She nodded, busy reading and planning and adding and subtracting already.

"Very well, Cara. So hadn't you better get dressed now, unless you can see some advantage to greeting your customers stark naked. In which case these may not be the kind of premises in which one ought to invest."

She put the document down and suddenly—could it still be the wine after all?—danced up to him and kissed him heartily and happily on the mouth. A kiss of approval, camaraderie, fun, perfect ease and equality which she could have given to Luke. Or Daniel.

Not to him.

She saw his face darken, the quick scowl as his eyebrows drew together, felt a sudden movement in him that she felt to be recoil. "Don't approach me," that movement was saying. "It is not and never can be your place to do so. *I* will approach you."

"Get dressed," he said coldly.

She did so, aware that he was watching her, no longer with speculation or desire or amusement as he had done last night but as a piece of merchandise. An enchanter no longer. A cattle-dealer, she thought, furiously fastening her tapes and buttons. And then she decided that it was just as well. She knew him much better this way.

"If you continue to do well, Adeane, I may find it possible, from time to time, to be seen with you in public."

He meant, of course, that he would find it convenient. No doubt, when it suited him, he would tell her why.

"How kind," she said.

He nodded in gracious acknowledgment.

"Nothing excessive, of course. Dinner in a Leeds hotel, or at the Moons perhaps—whoever *Mrs.* Moon might happen to be. An occasional theater. Which would mean being seen together on the train."

"Oh—you wouldn't want me to travel second class and you first?"

Like a maid, she thought, gritting her teeth and viciously dragging a comb through her hair.

"No. And please don't grit your teeth, Cara. You'll do them harm. I would expect there to be a certain amount of socializing here too, eventually, at the new station hotel."

"Oh yes—while you're negotiating the best price you can get for St. Jude's, I expect."

He showed her his own perfect teeth in the smile that never had much mirth in it. "I expect so. Obviously, I can rely on you—at need—to wear your beautiful clothes and make pleasant conversation with my dinner guests. As a successful local businesswoman you would make a perfectly acceptable hostess. Should you prove successful, that is."

Her future had been mapped out for her.

He took hold of her upper arm, by no means gently.

"You have not given me an answer."

She tried to shake off his hand and could not.

"Yes," she snapped. "Yes, of course. What else could I ever say to you but yes?"

"Whatever you please." His hand tightened and, when she began to struggle, tightened still further so that she became very still. "You may say and do just as you like, Cara. I have always told you so. And what exactly restrains you now? There is no Odette, no Liam, to hold you back or push you forward. You can't tell yourself any longer, 'I had to do it—or not do it—or give it up—for *them*.' Because it won't be true."

"I know." She was hating him again, trying very hard not to tremble.

"And do you also know that you could have gone with them yesterday? They would have been glad to take you. Your father had landed on his feet at last and is well able to give you a new life in America where no one knows your past. Oh yes, my dear, I have made inquiries of my own and you may believe that he is very comfortable. He could even get you a decent husband, perhaps, if he passed you off as a widow, to explain Liam and one or two other little irregularities. So—what keeps you here?"

"My business keeps me here."

"Does it? Perhaps. But let us be very clear on this, Adeane. You could have gone with any one of them—with Luke Thackray to Nottingham, with your father to America, with your fine Chartist friend very probably to hell. You could have sold your business and started up elsewhere. Ladies wear hats in Nottingham, one assumes? And I could not have stopped you. Yet you stayed here with me. What does that tell you?"

Truly she did not know.

He released her arm and smiled at her. "Well, we know it doesn't mean you love me, which is all to the good. I had love from Marie Moon—poor soul—and found it—well—surprising. And I don't seem to care for being surprised by women."

"No. You want to be served."

"Cara—how perceptive. But by somebody who is not servile.

Somebody who doesn't serve others. And as time passes I am growing less and less inclined to make changes. And if, for whatever reason, I give up other women I would really take it very much amiss if you . . . But you *do* understand me?"

"Yes. I understand."

"We suit each other, Cara. That is why you stayed."

She did not believe it, but if he said so, if that was what he wanted, and she had the next-door lease in her hands . . . ? What could she do? Return the lease, of course, cut her losses and take the next train for Liverpool.

"I suppose it is," she said.

He picked up his hat and gloves and gave her a light tap on the cheek.

"Cheer up, Adeane." He set the silk top hat at its correct angle. "I may not be the man you wanted, my dear. But could it be—do you think—that what I may be is the man you deserve? Is that it?"

"I expect so," she said.

John-William Dallam remained imprisoned in his body throughout a gold and copper autumn, a gray winter to follow, his reliance upon his daughter Gemma becoming absolute. He had regained limited and labored powers of speech but Gemma was the only person he could bear to talk to. He could, with assistance and effort, shuffle a few paces from his bed to a chair by the window but, whenever such adventurings were undertaken, he required the presence of his daughter to interpret his needs; to make sure that the damn fool nurses did not let him fall and then go running for the manservants to come and pick him up like a baby; to protect him, in general, from officious or sentimental women who wished to do things to him—again like a baby—which he did not want done.

And without Gemma he could not stop them.

His helplessness enraged him, so wildly sometimes as to sever entirely the fragile connection between his brain and his tongue, so that he could do nothing but produce sounds resembling the bellow of a sick and floundering bull.

He could not bear the sight of Linnet Gage. Nor, sadly, did the presence of his wife appear to soothe him. Her heart was good. His care of her had always been a source of pride to him. But now they could only upset one another. There were a great many vital things he wished to say to her. But, at the first sight of his changed and twisted appearance, the first sound of the grunts and gutteral, undeniably animal noises which had become his voice, she was too overcome with grief and terror to understand a word.

He would try again. She would hover timidly by his bed trying to smile, telling him, "Everything will be all right, my darling—I know it will." No, it would *not*. And their inability to communicate incensed and exhausted him so much that, for both their sakes, she was advised by the doctor to restrict her visits to the hour following evening medication when her husband would be already half asleep.

She could do nothing for him. She crept downstairs and wept quietly in a corner. In no one's way, she hoped. Not wishing to be a trouble. Waiting to be told what was to become of her now.

It was Gemma who told her.

"You can best be a help to father, you know, by being cheerful, mother, and not falling ill yourself."

"Cheerful? Oh, dearest, I don't think I could be that."

"Well, mother, someone will have to be. There will be a great many people calling to inquire. And if I have to be upstairs with father then I can't be downstairs in the drawing-room giving news of him."

"Oh no. Of course not."

"And you are so much better at that sort of thing, mother, than I. They will all have to be given tea, I suppose, since some of them will have taken the trouble to drive quite a distance and we can hardly leave it to Linnet. She would be only too pleased to help, of course, I know, but it hardly seems fair to ask so much of her. Particularly when it is bound to bring back the sad time she had nursing her own mother. I think we should spare Linnet as much of this as we can, don't you, mother? She may not listen to me but I think it would be a great kindness on your part to encourage her to spend as much time as she likes with her friends. We wouldn't want to spoil her chances, would we?"

"Oh no, dear—absolutely not."

"Then send her off to Lady Lark's dance next week, mother. Be firm about it. I know how devoted she is but she has her own life to lead, and I think the people who come to ask about father will really be hoping to see you."

Two birds, thought Gemma somewhat irreverently, with one stone. And indeed, during the first few weeks of her husband's illness, Amabel was kept fully occupied by the callers who drove out in a really most gratifying profusion, it seemed to her, not only from Frizingley but from all the worsted and woollen towns in its vicinity, manufacturers from Bradford, Halifax, Keighley, Huddersfield, the Spen Valley, coming to pay homage to one of their number. Men and women with whom Amabel was far more at ease than she had ever been with the gentry, though she was bound to admit that they all sent their sympathies too, accompanied by seasonal gifts of grouse and pheasant. And when the duty calls were done and her husband's condition seemed no worse—although quite bad enough, Heaven knew—she found it possible, with Gemma's encouragement, to enjoy the company of certain neighbors who, by no means smart enough for Linnet, had been previously neglected.

The vicar, for instance, a quaint and easy-mannered man to whom Amabel could confess her sense of uselessness and be infinitely reassured by his declaration that she was talking nonsense. Dr. Thomas who, rejected by Linnet, had recently married a sensible, serviceable young woman, only in her thirties, whose attitude to Amabel was almost maternal. A pair of Miss Sedleys, two pleasant spinster ladies who lived a quietly gracious life together in a creeper-clad Georgian house by the vicarage, and their friend, Mr. Dudley Stevens, an elderly gentleman who seemed almost as spinsterish as themselves although he was a widower and a retired wool merchant with a comfortable fortune.

"Is it wrong of me, Gemma dear," Amabel inquired timidly, "to invite company?"

"No, mother. It is what father would want you to do. And if you would like to go out sometimes there is really nothing against it."

But "outside" had always seemed somewhat menacing to Amabel. She much preferred the security of her own home where she knew the servants and the layout of the rooms and was less likely to be startled or taken by surprise. And, quite soon, the Misses Sedley and Mr. Dudley Stevens got into the habit of driving over to Almsmead most afternoons in his carriage to drink tranquil cups of tea, play tranquil games of cards, chat pleasantly to a much-relieved Amabel— not of the sophisticated, cosmopolitan world of Linnet and Mr. Adolphus Moon, nor the high-bred, hard-riding existence of Linnet and Sir Felix Lark, but of ordinary, everyday, *tranquil* things. The very life, in fact, envisaged by her husband when he had first purchased Almsmead.

And so it continued, Amabel in her drawing-room. Linnet out and about in the great world of Far Flatley and Frizingley. Gemma quietly, effectively, in control.

She spent most of her father's waking hours in his room, continuing to treat him as an intelligent man rather than the fractious and frightened child he was so rapidly becoming. And when she had to go out she made certain he understood where she was going and why, and when she could return.

She guarded her dignity. She knew he was afraid without her and although his fear alarmed her and broke her heart as much as his loss of authority did Amabel, she nevertheless squared her shoulders and came to terms with it. She was often tired and harassed and so very far removed from any kind of personal satisfaction that it seemed pointless even to think about it. But she was here. She had accepted her duty. And it would be foolish now and unproductive, she decided, to resent it.

No problems could be solved that way, nothing achieved. She was here. And Daniel had gone. There was a task to do and, having agreed to do it, it was in her nature—as it had always been in her father's—to do it well. She closed down, therefore, the parts of herself which were not adapted to this target matter in hand, putting them not merely in abeyance but in a suppressed and dormant condition from which she knew it would be better if they did not wake.

There was a task to do. The woman who loved Daniel Carey to the limits of her heart and soul existed, and she had no intention of denying her. But it was John-William Dallam's daughter who was needed today, this month, this *year* it seemed as Christmas approached, then passed mournfully away. Amabel Dallam's daughter who ran down to the drawing-room for five minutes every afternoon at tea-time to reassure her mother that it was not sinful, nor proof that she had ceased to love her husband, should she enjoy a game of cards and a cozy, mildly animated chat.

And she was also Tristan's wife.

He had been in Lincolnshire at the time of her father's attack, a trip she had encouraged him to take because of Daniel, and she had supposed his speedy return to be due to Linnet who, not expecting John-William to last the night, had thought it in her brother's interests to be on hand. But John-William had lived, both against his will and the expectations of his doctor, and although Linnet, on seeing this, had been glad enough to accept extended invitations to stay with Lady Lark, where she could see as much as she liked—or as much as seemed wise—of Mr. Adolphus Moon, and had even spent a week as the guest of Mrs. Colclough in Frizingley, Tristan had remained at Almsmead.

"I expect there'll be some errands to do," he said vaguely, his smile suggesting, with considerable charm, that even a man like himself, good for nothing but chasing about the countryside after a pack of hounds as John-William had often said, might have his uses at such a time.

"If you ever need the doctor in the middle of the night I reckon I could get there faster than the groom on his cob. And apart from that I'll be as good as gold. No need for cook to start worrying about wining and dining me. I'll just have something on a tray for luncheon, as you do, and grab whatever I can in the evenings. I'm a simple soul really. Linnet is always telling me so. And if I get desperate I can always drop in to see the Larks at dinner-time. They'll be sure to feed me."

How beautiful he was. It was the only word strong enough to describe him. How incredible, therefore, that he could mean so little to her, beyond a quick and solely artistic appreciation of his silver-and-ivory looks, and her thankfulness that he was indeed a simple soul, taking the pleasures of each day as they came to him, easily contented, predictable, blessedly incurious.

Without for one moment doubting his good intentions she did not expect him to stay long in a house now organized entirely for the care of a dying man. He was merely saying what he thought to be the right things and meaning them, of course, as he said them, which would not prevent him from convincing himself just as easily, as soon as he grew bored—not long, she estimated—that he was really in the way. Soon Felix Lark would be organizing a party to go off somewhere after deer or salmon. Or to those shooting-parties she had always avoided at the homes of related Larks in Lincolnshire and Leicestershire.

Tristan would find good reasons for going too. But somehow, perhaps because she no longer troubled to supply the reasons for him, he seemed content to hunt locally that year, rarely more than twice a week and to take out a companionable rather than a competitive gun with Dr. Thomas or the vicar, neither of them a match for him. While he passed the rest of his time training a new puppy in the meadow, walking in the woods, hanging rather aimlessly about, thought Gemma, unless she gave him something to do or Linnet took him off somewhere to dinner or required his escort to some local excitement like the ceremonial opening of Frizingley's railway station by a famous duke.

Ben Braithwaite and Uriah Colclough and Jacob Lord had all been presented to that duke, along with their ladies. Even Captain Goldsborough had shaken his hand—possibly not for the first time—and Linnet had certainly considered that, as a representative of the Dallams, she ought to have been invited to enjoy that ducal handclasp too. But Ben Braithwaite, who appeared to be in charge of the ceremonies—or perhaps Ben Braithwaite's skinny, sharp-eyed wife—had not looked with favor on Linnet's application. That John-William Dallam had a right to be represented was beyond question. His wife, therefore, or his daughter, would be most warmly welcome to make the duke's acquaintance on the station platform and to dine at his table afterward at the banquet for which Frizingley's Assembly Rooms had been specially redecorated. But the sister of the Dallam son-in-law did not seem—to the Ben Braithwaites—to be quite sufficient to merit the honor; nor even the son-in-law himself without his wife. And since neither Gemma nor Amabel could be persuaded to accompany her, Linnet, a vision of pale, pure elegance, had been obliged to stand in the crowd at the station—while Magda Braithwaite in one of her gaudy outfits preened herself at the ducal elbow—and to endure considerable annoyance at the banquet when she discovered that she had been seated no nearer to the ducal table—where one of her prospective husbands, Mr. Uriah Colclough, was smugly sitting—than certain local artisans, including Miss Cara Adeane.

Tristan's heart had ached for her. It made no difference to him where he sat. The whole thing was a bore in any case and there was nothing he wanted out of it. Nothing much he knew how to get for Linnet either, worse luck, so that it was a relief to him when she was finally rescued from his obscurity and integrated into the ducal party by Christie Goldsborough, of all people. The evening was nearly over by then, of course, and becoming much more informal but nevertheless, there she was, spending her last half hour drinking her champagne with a parliamentary private secretary on one side of her and a railway baron on the other, looking as if she was exactly where she *ought* to be, making the Braithwaite and Colclough women look vulgar or dowdy.

Very decent of Christie.

Yet, noticing a certain rather feline smugness in her manner on the drive home, which deepened whenever Captain Goldsborough's name was mentioned, her brother felt inclined to give her a word of warning. In so far, that is, as his easy nature permitted.

———

432

"Linnet, my darling, I don't know what you're up to and wouldn't care to ask . . ."

"No darling, don't ask," she sounded highly diverted. "With luck I may never have to tell you."

"Well, that's up to you, of course. But if you're setting your cap at Christie Goldsborough then it's not on, my darling."

"*Tristan.* How shocking. Are you trying to tell me that he's not a marrying man?"

He sighed, very patiently. "Don't tease, Linnet. I'm not up to it right now. That claret was very good tonight—I expect Christie picked it—and there was nothing else to do but indulge."

"Darling, I'm only too glad that you did." She put her light, narrow hand on his, the cool touch he had loved and trusted all his life. "Are you worried about me, Tristan? How sweet. But there's no need—not when I'm going to be Mrs. Adolphus Moon any day now, with Uriah Colclough put by just in case of need. Christie Goldsborough is useful, darling, that's all. He got me an introduction to the duke, didn't he, when Magda Braithwaite most positively didn't want me within a mile of him. Or within a mile of her precious Benjamin, which is far more likely. And Tristan—you do know, don't you, darling, that things are going to be very different now? Don't you, Tristan? I mean—when the old man dies."

But, for a while longer, he continued not to live precisely, but not to die.

He bore Christmas impatiently, grunting nothing but contempt at the wife he had so cherished when she came tripping to his bedside with gifts wrapped in silk ribbon and gold paper. Hell's flames would have suited him better so long as it meant shaking off this useless deformity of flesh and congealed blood, this grotesque burden that was his body, and be free again. At the start of the New Year he closed his eyes and opened them, thereafter, very seldom, eating little, no longer trying to communicate beyond irritable noddings and shakings of the head. He was not in pain. There was nothing the doctor could do for his body nor the vicar for his soul. Both, he would have said, being beyond redemption and strictly his own business in any case. His measure of time was over. And on a morning of high wind and blue and white March skies, he died.

Amabel was not present at his funeral, being of a generation which did not expose the grief of its widows to the public eye. But Gemma, having protected her father's pride for so long, did not wish to relinquish the task now until its true completion, for there was still his spirit, she supposed, perhaps not far away, which might take serious offense should there be too much humbug preached in the church, too much sniveling and wafting about of fine cambric handkerchiefs, too much nonsense talked about keeping his room forever intact as he had left it, or about printing his virtues in gold on white marble headstones with white marble angels clustering above them.

A plain funeral for a plain man. A polished granite cross with his name and dates. A respectful but not heartbroken congregation, a certain amount of business discussed by the Colcloughs and Braithwaites and by Mr. Ephraim Cook, his own mill-manager, as they followed him on his final journey. She knew he would have approved of that. And then those same gentlemen solemnly taking her hand, telling her how sorely he would be missed in the Piece Hall—what a sad loss—her poor mother—nobody quite like him—Good Heavens, was that really the time? They had better be getting back to Frizingley before the rain came on.

Yes. Life went on. Her life too. And now, with the great weight of her father's impotence lifted from her shoulders, now that she was free from the daily struggle against her own pity so as not to offend him by showing it, now that the demands of his death-in-life no longer devoured her energy and swallowed her time, how could she continue—as she had been doing—to avoid herself?

"Look after your mother," he had told her. A dose of laudanum, on this evening after his burial, had done that. And while Amabel slept and Tristan and Linnet took the air together in the garden, she was suddenly assailed with the force of a great wind, by the most terrible restlessness of her life.

What was it? She was worn out, of course, and had been under intense strain for so long that it would take far more than a good night's sleep to cure her. When rest had become impossible, this past month, she had simply learned to do without it, succeeding so well that she had lost the habit of rest altogether. Her body ached with fatigue yet she did not know where to lay it down nor how to convince it that its service as John-William Dallam's daughter was over.

Amabel's daughter now. And Tristan's wife. Was he talking of her now, out in the garden with his exquisite sister? She doubted it. Nor did he appear to find this empty marriage of theirs particularly unusual. Many couples, she supposed, in the sophisticated London world of his childhood, lived as much apart as they did, and were as sparing of physical contact when they did happen to be together. Arranged marriages. Marriages of convenience. But it was she who had arranged this one. And, having done so, having no one but herself to blame, she would be obliged to live with it. The marriage would continue, one way or another, and there was still that strong voice in her—her father's voice—reminding her that once one had agreed to do something, once one had taken it on, then one did one's level best with it. And she had made no effort at all with Tristan. Must she do so now? It was a long time since he had touched her. During her father's illness no doubt he had thought it unmannerly to trouble her. Now, with the illness over, would he think it equally unmannerly to keep away?

A marriage of manners. How . . . What? Tragic? Comic? No. Nothing so definite as that. And she knew it could have been much worse. She had chosen Tristan for the vague, negative qualities he still possessed and now she must make the best of him. He passed the window, his arm around Linnet's shoulder, their heads together. What were they plotting now? The final act in the sorry drama of Marie Moon perhaps, who, suddenly losing her nerve if not her wits, had tried twice now to run away from her husband, once as far as Leeds station with a bag full of jewels and then to the dressmaker, Miss Adeane, of all people, who had allowed her to stay the night in her apartment above the rather splendid new shop she had just opened. There was also a rumor that Miss Adeane had spoken sharply to Mr. Adolphus Moon the next morning when he had come to fetch his wife home, although he subsequently denied it and spent a great deal of money in her shop, presumably to make amends, the day after.

On the whole Gemma felt sorry for Marie Moon and rather hoped Miss Adeane *had* said a hard word or two to her husband. But if Linnet did succeed in marrying Adolphus Moon then at least Gemma need no longer feel responsible for her. She would be extremely rich and extremely fashionable and would never lose face by admitting her husband to be other than the jolly little man he seemed. Indeed— very possibly—she might be able to handle him. In which case, if Amabel continued to settle down so pleasantly with her country friends it might even be possible to leave her here and move back to Frizingley.

To what purpose?

The question struck her so forcefully that each word seemed to leap out at her, starkly visible on the air. What had she to do in

Frizingley now? Could she ever bear to live in the manor again, with Tristan, remembering Daniel? During her father's illness she had thought of him constantly but at a submerged level which had even seemed to give her strength. Mourning her father's slow and furious dying had obscured her own loss of love. Nothing obscured it now. She would never see him again. He had disappeared from the face of the earth, or her part of it at any rate, and she knew she would miss him acutely and constantly, until her own dying day.

Her own fault, of course, and she would have to cope with it. But suddenly, as she heard Linnet and Tristan in the hall, she knew she could not stay and listen to their chatter with this weight on her heart. And although it was not in her nature to run away from fear or trouble it struck her now, most forcefully, that she could do no other.

"Excuse me," she said, running past them in the hall, her less than sedate posture taking them both aback, "I am very tired. Please *do* excuse me. I must go to bed."

They let her go. Why not? They were more to each other, after all, she thought, than she could ever be to either. She could allow herself, then, the luxury of weeping, a task which she undertook with her usual thoroughness, sitting alone on the windowseat in her night-gown, crying until her face was blotchy and her head aching, her astonishment almost comic when her husband came into the room.

He was the last person she had expected, particularly in his brocade dressing gown, very obviously ready for bed. Hers? Had Linnet put him up to this, warning him to make sure of his wife's affection now that her father was no longer holding the purse strings? It seemed horribly likely.

"You've been crying," he said as if he could hardly believe it. "Poor old girl—you've had a rotten time, haven't you? I know. I know. Poor Gemma." And suddenly, hardly aware of how it had happened, he had picked her up and she was on the bed with him, being rocked and stroked and "kissed better" like a child.

"Poor old thing, it's been dreadful—terrible—I know. And you've been so brave and strong and wonderful. I've watched you, all the time. Don't cry, my darling, and don't be shy. Just let me—there now—Sweet Gemma. Good girl."

He was a physical man who understood only physical remedies. "I've missed you," he said. She did not believe him but made no resistance as he began easily and pleasantly to make love to her. She knew it had to be done. But at the moment of penetration she stiffened suddenly and took fright, and, entirely against her will and all her resolution, cried out with real anguish, "Oh no. No—please." It had not seemed to matter, those few times before, when she had known she would soon be with Daniel, his caresses erasing the fleeting impression that had always been Tristan. But now it was Daniel who would be erased, and she could never have him back again.

She knew a moment of sheer panic when she feared she might scream and push him away. Betraying herself. And then it subsided. "Sweet Gemma..." he went on crooning to her, the joining of their bodies taking place even as she protested. It had happened. Easily. No pain. The beginnings even of an excitement she knew to be purely physical, mechanical, her body claiming its own right to pleasure which she saw no reason to deny.

It had happened. She was a wife again. And if her husband exchanged a knowing glance with his sister the next morning she preferred to take no notice. She heard him whistling very cheerfully as he went into the garden with his dog and could not fail to be amused, after dinner, when he began to yawn excessively and declare that what he most needed was an early night. It was not love or anything like it. It was good will. *It had to be done.* It might even have succeeded had not Mr. Adolphus Moon gone to Frizingley on a particular March Wednesday to meet a legal gentleman from the London train, a specialist in the dissolution of unsatisfactory marriages who might have saved himself the trouble, Mr. Moon's problem being solved not at all in the way he had intended when a newspaper, blown by a sudden gust of wind, caused his horse to shy and Miss Linnet's prospective bridegroom to break his neck.

At the funeral she wore mourning veils down to her ankles, leaning on Uriah Colclough's arm, his angel again and his only, since who was left now but him to marry her? Although Gemma noticed that she did pause a while at the church porch with Captain Goldsborough, who whispered something to her which Gemma half-heard and then entirely discounted, since it had sounded like "Bad luck, Linnet. But cheer up—the next gust of wind might always take off our darling Magda." Could he really have said that? Of course not. Although Ben Braithwaite had certainly *looked* at Linnet a great deal, and his wife *had* been very unfair to her at the ducal banquet. And if it had been Magda Braithwaite who had fallen off her horse that windy morning would Linnet be clinging now so hard to Uriah Colclough's bony arm? Probably not. How *false* all these people were. And it was then that she heard, for the first time, "Poor Mrs. Moon. How pale she looks."

Pale indeed. And very lonely. Yesterday's adulteress, madwoman, whore, to be shunned and abandoned and stripped as bare of property and possessions as the law would allow—which was very bare indeed—transformed, by a chance gust of wind, into the wealthiest widow for many hundreds of miles around. For it was known, at once, by the way in which the legal gentleman from London—who had come all this way to get her locked up—now threw himself at her feet, that there was a valid will in her favor. Why Mr. Moon had been so very remiss no one knew or cared. And as for contesting it, one could tell by the way that lawyer fellow was dancing attendance on her, that there was no chance of that. Mr. Moon's children were provided for in any case, it seemed, by the estate of their mother, so no one need feel the slightest pang of guilt—least of all Marie—about her absolute possession of those fortunes in spices and sugar.

Lady Lark went home at once and wrote to her amorous young nephew Gussie, who had been packed off in disgrace, out of the toils of "that woman," ordering him to return to them at once.

Uriah Colclough began to talk of the forgiveness of sins, to dream, perhaps, of his own hand placed in benediction on a bent, still very lovely, and exceedingly wealthy head. And since riches were a heavy responsibility, surely poor, frail Mrs. Moon would need advice and assistance? Uriah Colclough was not the only one in Frizingley to think so.

One morning, while partaking of Madeira and lemon biscuits in the spacious, blue and gold showroom of Miss Adeane's new shop, Linnet found herself suddenly deserted by Mrs. Colclough, who sprang to her feet at Mrs. Marie Moon's arrival and hurried, all solicitude, to her side.

"My dear lady, you look quite worn out. Do come and sit a while and take a sip of wine." And the chairs had been so placed that Linnet was obliged to move aside, a "back seat" in every sense, from which she could hear the conversation of the other two, but could not participate.

It was too much for Linnet to bear. Therefore she would not bear it. She would not stay here to see Marie Moon lionized as she knew she would be, invited everywhere, praised and petted and then splendidly married for the fortune that had so nearly been her own. She did not hate Marie. She had never even thought of her as an individual. To Linnet she had been an obstacle to be removed, a barrier between herself and the life for which she was increasingly desperate. And now, having shown Marie no mercy, she expected none.

From now on her life in a Frizingley ruled by Marie Moon and Magda Braithwaite could only be one humiliation after another. A living death. A nightmare of resentment and frustration from which she must, at all costs, get away. She went for a long, lazy stroll, therefore, with her brother, her cool hand on his arm, and told him how wonderful it would be if they all packed up their trunks and boxes and went off to live happily ever after in London. Why not? Impossible, of course, when that gruff old cross-patch of a John-William had had the reins in his hands. But now . . . Well, Aunt Amabel would go where she was taken and, as it was certainly, and morally and *legally* and every other way besides, a woman's place to follow her husband, there could be no trouble about Gemma.

"And you and she seem so very cozy together now, darling. Just make her love you a little more and she'll come running after you all the way to Timbuctoo."

Tristan did not think so. For his part he did not care where they lived. But there was the mill. Did they need it, wondered Linnet? It could be of no possible interest to him and since it did not seem likely now that Gemma would have any children, why not sell it? It must be worth a great deal. Only think of the civilized life its sale could give them.

"I'm not sure it *can* be sold," said Tristan. "The old boy left a damn complicated will. *I* don't understand it."

Linnet urged him to consult the Dallam solicitor, and *try*.

Gemma was furious when she heard of it, an emotion rare in her and therefore very deep-rooted and long-lasting when it came. Did Tristan really have the power to sell her possessions? She knew the simple, legal answer to be "yes," of course he did, a married woman having no identity of her own in law, being considered one and the same person as her husband who, as her legal guardian, could do exactly as he liked with her. She had always known that. But what of the arrangements her father had made to safeguard her against it? Did they not hold good? Certainly, her solicitor, accompanied by Mr. Ephraim Cook, assured her. She had her marriage contract, settling upon her substantial sums of money which could not be touched by anyone. *Very* substantial sums. But if her husband decided to sell the mill it seemed to both gentlemen that he could probably do so. Her father had taken every precaution to ensure the profitable management of his business, but had not apparently envisaged that it might be sold without his daughter's consent. An understandable oversight, since these matters were usually done with the full agreement of the wife who, more often than not, had no decided financial opinions of her own. But in this case, both gentlemen having met Miss Linnet Gage, they believed there could be cause for concern.

Alarm even.

Returning to Almsmead, cold with anger, Gemma saw her husband throwing sticks for his dog at the end of the carriage drive and passed him by without a word. She believed her contempt for him to be total. What could he ever be but a pawn in *somebody's* game? And she knew her business was with Linnet.

She found her alone in the parlor working on a fine and perfectly useless piece of embroidery, the purpose of which was to show off the skill and delicacy of her hands.

"Linnet," she moved at once to the attack. "I believe you have been interfering in my affairs."

"I beg your pardon?"

"Yes. I think you should."

Linnet laid down her embroidery, looking both faintly perplexed and faintly amused.

"Dearest—whatever can it be? Heavens—you look so fierce. I believe you are positively scaring me half to death . . ." Her light voice trailed off on an airy note, as it often did, signifying that nothing, surely, could be bad enough to risk frown lines across one's brow and that far-from-becoming squaring of the jaw.

But John-William Dallam's sturdy, straight-souled daughter had no inclination for the dainty thrust and parry of verbal sword-play.

"I understand you wish to go to London and live on my money . . ."

"Gemma."

"To which end you want Tristan to sell my mill and have already sent him to my lawyer to discover how best to do it behind my back."

There was a short silence, broken only by the sound of breathing, Gemma's heavy and angry, Linnet's shallow as a trill of wry laughter. And then Linnet, picking up her embroidery, said sweetly, "My dear, a woman must submit herself to her husband in Christian marriage. Surely—that is what one vows to do beneath those sweet little veils and those wreaths of orange blossoms?"

"It is. To her husband, Linnet. Not to his sister."

"Oh dear. And if the brother and sister are of one mind?"

"*Your* mind, Linnet. Yes, I know that quite well. Tristan does not think of these things for himself. He is perfectly happy with his dogs and his guns and his good dinners. He has to be told what to do. By *somebody*. And in this case I am about to tell him that I will fight tooth and nail against any suggestion of selling my father's mill. He did not build it up over thirty hard years to be frittered away by you, Linnet. Or to buy you a husband either. You should have set your sights lower, as *he* told you, instead of making a fool of yourself chasing rich men . . ."

"How dare you!"

"I dare, Linnet. And I am not to blame now if you have ended up with nothing. My father refused to pay out what it would cost to make you Mrs. Colclough and so will I. And if you go on trying to get it through Tristan then I shall oppose him in every court in the land. I have the money to do so. I may not win. In fact most probably I should not. But it would all take a very long time, Linnet. Years, perhaps. And where would you live in the meantime? Not here, certainly, for my mother has the power to turn both of you out and she would not keep you here against my wishes. And what would you live on? My father settled the bulk of his *money* on me, Linnet, with adequate provision for my mother. What remains is property which has to be sold before you can spend it. And I can block that sale long enough to make it hardly worth waiting for—at *your* age—Linnet. I can also ensure that when the mill does come into your possession it will be worth only a fraction of its value today. You do not understand business, and neither does Tristan. I do. If you go on trying to rob me I shall ruin you, make no mistake about it. You will end up living on whatever Tristan has left of my dowry, which can't be much, and with your reputation in shreds. Because I shall blacken your precious character too, while I am about it."

And her anger was so great, her contempt for this woman so absolute, that she did not take heed of the sudden alertness in Linnet's white face, the air of a vixen who, with the hounds baying all around her, suddenly catches the scent—desperate perhaps, but what now has she to lose?—of salvation.

"No Gemma—I think not."

"*Linnet*—do not imagine for one moment that I shall weaken. For I shall not. Everyone's sympathy will be on my side. People don't like it, Linnet, when men marry girls like me for money and then try to make off with it the minute her father dies. Judges and the like have daughters of their own, more often than not. So do the editors of newspapers. The brand of fortune-hunter sticks, Linnet. And I really don't know with what name they would brand you."

Linnet stood up, her embroidery falling to the ground, her empty hands gracefully and easily clasped before her, her face still very white but her pale eyes alive, vibrant and glowing as Gemma had never seen them before. With malice? With hysteria? With gloating it almost seemed, although what on earth she could have to gloat about Gemma could not imagine.

"I see, Gemma. So you are condemning me to a lifetime of serving tea from other women's china, *here*, in this place of your choosing, taking scraps, in effect, from your table, among women my mother would not have allowed to cross her threshold? Suffering insult from those women. *Wasting* myself. Wasting the talents which I do—oh yes I do—possess. Ageing. Becoming an object of pity when my looks fade. Oh yes—isn't that always the way of it? Poor Miss Gage, she must have been quite pretty once. What a dire fate, my dear. What a *charming* prospect for the future."

"I think you have brought it on yourself, Linnet."

She shook her head, smiling very strangely. And then, leaning forward from the waist with the darting movement of a snake coiled to strike, she said "No, Gemma. You will not do that to me. You will do, in fact, exactly what I tell you. Oh yes, dearest. You will go to Tristan—straight away, I think, since it is worrying him rather—slip your little hand in his, gaze trustingly into his so beautiful eyes and tell him—dear Gemma—that since he has started making love to you so very sweetly and so very often, his wish has become your command. You want only to go wherever he takes you. If he wants your mill then of course he must have it. You only wish you had two or three so that you could really spoil him, *really* make it worth his while to go on giving you all those lovely kisses. *That's* what I want to hear from you, Gemma. *That's* the attitude I want to see. That's the life *you're* going to have."

She paused not for breath but for savor and then, straightening her back, said very quietly, "Otherwise I shall just have to go and tell my brother about the Chartist candidate, won't I? He was your lover for almost a year, Gemma. There would really be no point in denying it. I have all the evidence I need."

The first shock passed.

"Evidence?"

"Yes. My informant is reliable and thorough."

Hardly necessary, since, with or without evidence, Frizingley would be only too glad to believe it. And it was true in any case. Anger seeped out of her slowly, aware of its own futility. She had no defense.

Linnet smiled. "Tristan will not take it kindly, Gemma. He has his pride. He cares about gossip and scandal. As all *our* sort of people do. And he will follow *our* code. He will cast you off, Gemma, as an adulteress. Only think what that will do to your mother. And where will public sympathies be then? Not with you, dear. When he puts your mill up for sale everyone will say, 'Poor man, he is trying to rid himself of her memory.' People don't *like* unfaithful wives, Gemma. All those judges and newspaper editors you were threatening me with just now are husbands too. So—dearest—*do* confess—have I not turned the tables very nicely?"

So it seemed.

"Then hadn't you better run along, Gemma, and tell Tristan he can sell your last petticoat if he has a mind to? Scandal is always better avoided. So be a good, sweet girl and there'll be absolutely no need for me to say a word."

"Until the next time you want one thing and I want another."

"Ah well—should the occasion arise when you may seem in need of guidance I should do my duty, of course."

"Yes." Gemma sat down and, rather slowly, folded her hands. "Then you had better go and do it now, hadn't you. Your duty, I mean."

However smug she might be feeling, Linnet was too perceptive, too completely the seasoned drawing-room campaigner, to be other than instantly alert.

"Now don't be silly, Gemma. No attacks of virtue, please. They seem hardly appropriate."

But Gemma had no choice to make. Between a lifetime at Linnet's beck and call or social disgrace, what choice existed? Death, perhaps? But she did not suppose that one died so neatly.

"Gemma—I most strongly advise you to think of your mother."

Not even for her.

She shook her head.

"I shall not relent, Gemma. And once I have told Tristan he cannot be *untold*. He will *know* and there is no doubt at all that he will be incensed and humiliated and very eager for revenge . . ."

"I imagine, Linnet, that he will do very much as you say."

"Are you challenging me to turn him loose on you?"

"I am telling you," and she was speaking through tight-clenched teeth, her pugnacious jaw shaking, "that I will not consent to place myself in your power. I will not live my life according to your whims and fancies. I will not come when you call me and go where you send me—which is what would happen. I will not hand over to you my position and my property, *and* the effective control of my mother—which is what you are asking. You have not earned any of it, Linnet, and you do not deserve it either. And I will not have this threat hanging over me—most of all I will not have that."

"I am not bluffing, Gemma."

"Nor I."

"Gemma, I have nothing to lose."

"Nor I, Linnet."

It went on a while longer. It would have gone on interminably had Gemma consented to participate, which she did not, answering every one of Linnet's threats and pleadings, occasional insults, frequent attempts to shame her and terrify her with the one, terse phrase—"I will not have it."

Both women had come face to face with a future they could not tolerate and, in this mood, were dangerous to themselves as well as to each other.

"We shall see—my girl—what you will have when this is over." And, totally beside herself, having, indeed, nothing to lose but that lifetime of other women's china in Frizingley, the slow death of herself by bitterness and frustration which she could not, *would* not bear, Linnet spun around on her heel and ran out of the room to find her brother.

Had he left the house, perhaps—who knew?—she may have calmed sufficiently to reflect, to devise some other plan, even to submit. But he was still there, on the drive, working off his uncomplicated high spirits with his dog. Looking out of the window Gemma saw Linnet flying toward him, watched them come together, and then sat down again, her head slightly bowed, not in penitence but in simple waiting.

She had always known the risk she ran. She knew that Daniel himself had often feared for her. At least, thank God that he was gone. Thank God, even, that she did not know where. That she would somehow endure it, survive it, she had no doubt. She would have to. But it would be terrible. Humiliating. Vile. She closed her eyes, her stomach quaking. If Tristan would just come, would do and say whatever his Code and his sister required of him, then at least she would know the extent of the disgrace that threatened her. And, knowing it, she could come to terms with it, could learn to think of herself as others would then think of her. A fallen woman like Marie Moon, who could not be received in the homes of decent people, the hem of whose dress must not be allowed to brush one's own hem in passing. A woman to be shunned by other women and made light of—made sport of—by men.

The prospect appalled her. Sitting tight-clenched with growing panic in her mother's hushed and sheltered drawing-room—the only world she really knew—she dared not hazard even a guess as to whether she could cope with it or not. She would be free, of course, from all restraints and responsibilities, at perfect liberty to come and go as she pleased. But how far could her pampered feet really carry her, being as unaccustomed to rough going as the lotus-feet of those Chinese concubines Daniel had told her about, who could only totter a few graceful, doll-like paces before falling down? Probably not much further. With pain she remembered Daniel on the night before Brighouse, examining her feet, grieving over them almost.

She understood.

If only Tristan would come. Why was he so long? But when she tried to get up and go to the window to see if they were still there on the path she found she could not. Her bound feet would not carry her.

When enough time had passed—*his* time, she understood, no longer hers—he came, his feet loud and firm enough in the hall, his hand rattling the door-knob in the noisy way men had, pushing open the door and striding, all hale and hearty from the fresh outdoors, into the closed and suddenly airless room. Tristan. Frivolous. Shallow. Irresolute. And who now had power over her.

Lifting her head she saw that he was biting his lip as if he had not the least idea what to say. Well—it was hardly her place to help him. Let Linnet see to that.

"Oh Lord," he sounded horribly embarrassed. "I'm not going to be much good at this."

But then, was he good for anything? Staring at him she lifted a haughty, inquiring eyebrow. He had been a very long time, she thought, out there with Linnet. But not long enough, it seemed, to learn his lesson.

Let him flounder. He took a deep breath. Clearly hating every moment of it, wishing himself anywhere but here, playing the outraged husband for his sister's benefit. Was that the trouble?

"Well—there's just this, Gemma—first of all— Look here—if you really think I'm the sort of chap who'd sell off your property over your head—without so much as a by your leave— Well, if that's what you think then I'm sorry—I'm really sorry, because— Anyway—there's not the least chance of it. Dash it all, Gemma, it would be like stealing. *I* see that. And if Linnet hadn't taken such a beating lately she'd see it too. In fact—well, yes—she does see it, right enough—of course she does, its just that she's—well, desperate, Gemma. And scared stiff at the bottom of her. So there it is. I can't do it. I might even wish I could, for Linnet's sake. In fact, to tell you the honest truth, I thought I *could* do anything for her. But not this. There's no chance of it."

Had she heard him aright? But she had no time to gather her startled, incredulous wits together before he shattered them yet again.

"And as for the other thing— Well, there was no need for her to tell me about that because, the truth is— Oh Lord, I already knew, Gemma. I've known for ages."

She put the tips of her fingers to either side of her head and pressed hard, as if she needed to be sure that it was still there, and functioning, on her shoulders.

"Tristan." She could say no more than that.

"Oh I know," he said, still hating it. "I may be a bit of a fool at times and I know I'm too damned easy-going, but I'm not a complete fool, Gemma. Not by a long chalk. I'm your husband, for God's sake. I'd have had to be an oaf not to notice the change in you—after he came along. I was the first man to touch you, Gemma. I knew you didn't love me and I could tell when you started to love somebody else. So I had a look around and eventually I saw you with him— Oh, not doing anything, just standing by that school-house talking to him and *looking* at him— It told me what I needed to know. And I thought, if that's what she wants—and I could see it was—then— Well—I'd never given you anything, had I? Done plenty of taking, mind. I'd already started worrying about that. So I thought, right, I'll give her this. And that's what I did. When you told me to go off shooting and hunting, I went. And I never came back without letting you know well in advance. Never bothered you much when I *was* at home either, no more than a chap really has to, sometimes. I did my best for you, Gemma."

"Oh, Tristan," she said. "I don't know what to say to you. I just don't know. Your *best*. Oh—Good Heavens . . ." She burst into tears hovering on the brink of something she recognized with mild surprise to be hysteria. She also saw that she had embarrassed him again.

"Lord—Gemma. I knew it couldn't last. These things don't, you know."

"Don't they?"

"No." He sounded very certain. "I was just damned glad he didn't hurt you. I suppose looking after your father took your mind off it. But the thing is now— Dash it all, let's forget it, shall we?"

"Tristan—have you said all this to Linnet?"

He nodded. "Hadn't much choice, had I?"

"And was it—very bad?"

"The worst thing I've ever done in my life."

"Oh, Tristan—I am so sorry, I am really so sorry . . ."

He sat down, elbows on his knees, biting his lip again, his face stricken. "Gemma, you'll have to try and understand about Linnet. She's beautiful and clever and she wasn't born to play second fiddle. If she'd been a man she'd have made her way in the world all right— worked her way up through the ranks and no mistake. She'd have been a cabinet minister by now, or a general. But she's a woman and the only thing a woman *can* do is get married. That's right, isn't it? And she'd have been the best wife any man could have. She knows that. And when she sees other women getting what she ought to be getting— Well—she's hurt and miserable and whatever she may have done or said I love her, Gemma, there's no getting away from it, and I'll always look after her—give her what I can. I have to tell you that."

"Yes, Tristan." And how could she tell him—this simple, physical, *honorable* man—that she would do anything to ease his pain? "Tristan—I understand."

"And will you go on living with me?" He threw the question at her so much like a hurt child that the force of his bewilderment, his need to be reassured and consoled, lifted her to her feet, aware simply that she must protect him. That she must heal him, as best she could, from the wounds he had received, so gallantly, so painfully, in her defense.

"Is that what you want?"

"Yes, it is."

"Tristan, I don't know why you should. You must know that I . . ."

"No," he said. "Don't tell me about that other chap. That belongs to you. I know it must have meant a lot to you, otherwise you wouldn't have done it. You're a good woman, Gemma. If it seemed right to you, then I just reckoned it would be. So keep it. I'll never ask. That's a promise."

He was standing now just a few inches away from her, his athletic body unusually clumsy and overburdened with a weight of emotion he was not accustomed to feel. A physical man who understood only physical remedies and who had been badly scarred today. An honorable man embarrassed by his own gallantry. A knight-errant, she thought suddenly, who probably thought all his splendid chivalry to be no more than simple good manners.

A simple man who seemed to need her. What had he said to her just now? *"If it seemed right to you, then I just reckoned it would be."* So had her mother always spoken of her father. "If John-William said it would be all right, then it would be."

Could she bear so unexpected and yet, in some ways, so wonderful a burden?

Stepping forward she put her arms around him, a huge sigh of pure and utter relief escaping his body as she touched it. Was it over, then? With a bit of luck he rather thought it might be.

"Thank you, my darling," she said.

One year and a half after leaving Frizingley Daniel Carey made the crossing to Ireland as a cabin passenger on the regular steamer from Liverpool, returning eighteen sorry months later on the deck of a pig boat tight-packed with the half-naked, stupefied skeletons which were the Irish people, reduced to bone and blank-eyed terror by famine and the pestilence it brought with it.

His first journey, in the late autumn of 1845, had been a professional assignment, an investigation into certain rumors regarding the state of Ireland which had reached the radical London editor who employed him. Famine, it seemed. What else? Daniel had raised his shoulders in resignation even as the question was asked, Famine being a regular enough visitor to an undeveloped land without industry or trade, with nothing to sell but its talent—for which the going rate was never much—and no money to spend. A country without coal mines or iron foundries or factories to employ the people who, in their hungry millions, had no other way of life but the cultivation of the potato.

Ah yes, now what of the potato? his editor wanted to know. It took as little as one acre, did it not, to feed a small family for a year? Far, far less than would have been required to grow wheat and keep one's children alive on bread. Was it then *really* the case that over half the population of Ireland fed themselves entirely on the potato, fourteen pounds a day to maintain health and strength and the raising of all those beautiful children, brought up, in many cases, in total ignorance of any other food? Could it *really* be?

So much so—as Daniel remembered it—that there was no doubt, in Ireland, that a man who lost his potato-patch also lost his life, no other work and no other crop being available, so that he had little choice but to squat in some muddy ditch somewhere with his fine children about him until starvation slowly and quietly took them off. And when the potato crop was poor, or failed altogether in some regions as it sometimes did, then many died. Very many. As Daniel's own mother had died, not from lack of nourishment since his family had had money enough to buy English bread, and French wine too if it came to that, but from a stray bullet aimed, in conditions of riot, at an evicted and therefore already dying man.

Famine and Riot. They went together, in the early stages, until starvation ate away both flesh and fury and the combination became Famine and Fever.

It had happened before.

But this year? Daniel's editor had frowned and shook his head. Rumors, perhaps. Bad weather. A wet and foggy summer. But what was new or strange about that? Trouble with the potato crop in North America the year before—a blight of some kind—and now in Southern England, Belgium, France: and spreading. Bad enough, of course, in countries like these where other crops were, one supposed, fairly readily available, and the working population regarded their staff of life to be bread. But what would happen in Ireland—where bread was foreign and by no means easily obtainable outside the cities—should there be no potatoes whatsoever?

Was it even understood, in England, that for the Irish peasant, no other diet existed? That the holdings into which the land was divided were too small to permit the cultivation of other foods? That such profit as a man could make from pigs or hens or anything else was reserved strictly to pay the rent for the land without which he would starve? And that landlords, in times of distress, were far more inclined to clear their farms of an unprofitable tenant than assist him to soldier on and stay? Did the English laborer, with his wages, however sparse, paid weekly into his hand, even know that his Irish counterpart often earned no wages at all, working wholly for food and shelter, the peat he dug for fuel and the potato—the blessed, fickle potato—from his precariously rented ground?

What would happen to Ireland, then, where three million people came near to starvation in summer in any case, without the potato? And if there *was* no likelihood of failure on a massive scale, if the stories one heard of a whole year's crop, or very nearly, turning to a stinking black ooze in the ground *were* mere exaggerations, then why was it that Sir Robert Peel, the English Prime Minister, was thought to be considering the repeal of the Corn Laws to give Ireland cheap bread? And to ruin himself, of course, while he was about it, since he was the leader of the Tory Party, backed by the landed gentry who grew the grain, and had pledged, at his election, to protect it by keeping foreign grain out and the price, therefore, of English bread high. An astonishing, courageous, and generous step, one might think. For if he carried it out he might do something to ease the hardship both in Ireland and England's own industrial cities but the man himself, as a political leader, could not hope to survive. That he should be willing to sacrifice himself seemed a fair indication of the coming emergency.

Perhaps Daniel—a man who knew Ireland—would care to take a trip across the water, and see?

Not that his knowledge of his native land was, in fact, so very accurate, having left it at the age of twelve for France, where he had been taught to think of himself as a Citizen of the World. Yet his landing in Dublin that autumn and his subsequent wanderings had shown him few changes, a people cheerful in adversity as he remembered them, who did not realize, or did not choose to realize, or had not been told, their peril. A naturally optimistic people who believed that if one kept smiling, things would surely turn out for the best. As they probably would, thought the British Commissariat officer with whom Daniel soon made acquaintance, a burly, briskly spoken man who had seen long service in India, and who now, being involved in the work of famine relief, had begun by making what he liked to think of as a "thorough study" of Ireland.

No, it would not be so very terrible, in his view. Or not much more than usual. Not until April or May, that is, by which time most people would have eaten up their surplus, made a hole in their savings, taken whatever could be taken to the pawnshop; thus enabling themselves to last until August when the new potato crop would be in. While such official measures as seemed appropriate had already been set in motion. The usual things one expected from government departments. The local landlords organized into relief committees, for instance, to collect money among themselves to purchase stores of food which they could hold and then sell, at need, to distressed persons. And since these persons would be unlikely to have any money left by then with which to buy it, these same landlords were being asked to create employment for them on their estates and pay wages which could then be used not only to keep body and soul together but to pay the rent. Owing—of course—to these self-same landlords again.

A neat scheme—the Commissariat officer wondered—for making Ireland's gentry pay for the feeding of Ireland's poor? Or a vicious circle? Depending which way one looked at it, he supposed. Particularly if one took into account that the gentry themselves, although not starving, were, in many cases, a far from thrifty lot, having spent too heavily, over the generations, on fancy manor houses and thoroughbred hunters to have anything much put by.

And should this scheme—or this circle—be found too complicated in some districts, the Irish Board of Works had been instructed by Westminster to set in motion the building of roads and bridges or anything else which might come in useful and provide mass employment for the same reasons. Although most of the cost, in the long term, would fall on the landlords who were already muttering, rather loudly in some quarters, about the point of so many roads which rarely had any specific destination, so many bridges over streams quite shallow enough to be crossed by stepping stones. Should anyone want to get to the other side, in the first place.

Furthermore, as a supplement to whatever stocks of foodstuffs the landlords were presumably building up—no, he did not think anyone had actually gone around to check—the Government had also purchased, from America, a supply of Indian Corn, choosing this admittedly very alien cereal for the simple reason that no one knew anything about it, no British merchants appeared to trade in it and could not, therefore, accuse the government of poaching their business preserves. This Indian Corn to be held in depots—one of which Daniel's new friend was to be in charge of—and sold, if strictly necessary, at bargain prices only to those who could prove their hunger to be a direct result of the present crop failures, rather than a habitual condition.

Although what use the Irish people would make of this "Indian Corn," the Commissariat gentleman was uncertain. After all, had the government even considered just how many corn mills could be found in a country where only the gentry and the alien English were accustomed to eat bread? Precious few outside the cities. In isolated regions of the South and West he was prepared to take an oath that there would be none at all.

And if that "Indian Corn," floating out there in Cork harbor still waiting to be unloaded, could not be ground for bread then what good was it? And even if it could, how many of those mud cabins in the country areas he had just mentioned were fitted with ovens? None that he'd ever seen. How many of the women who lived in them knew how to bake a loaf or had ever seen one baked, or cooked anything, if it came to that, but a few potatoes in a single pot?

"Indian Corn" indeed! No doubt they knew what to do with it in the American South, or had stronger stomachs and teeth. But not in the South of Ireland.

But of one thing he was certain. Whether it could be milled and baked or not, there was nowhere near enough of it to go around. Not a mouthful apiece to be eked out even among the so-called "genuine applicants" who, in normal years, could feed themselves. And what about the three million destitute who hovered on the brink of starvation every year, no matter what the state of the potato crop? Could anyone tell him how, when the doors of his food depot finally opened, he was to distinguish among these? Easy enough to write out instructions from behind a cozy desk in London. Not so easy when it came to looking starving children in the face.

Well, thank God it was only until August, when the new crop would be in. Eight months away. Until then life would—or would not—go on.

In some respects it went on very much as usual. The potatoes rotted in the ground but the rent had to be paid nevertheless. And when it was not, eviction orders, served sometimes by the stewards of landlords who rarely set foot in Ireland and had not the least notion of what went on there, came thick and fast. On a brisk March day Daniel stood in the village of Ballinglass in County Galway and watched as a detachment of infantry turned 300 people out of their cottages and then tore the buildings down over their heads when they tried to get in again, so that the land could be used to graze the owner's cattle. Seventy-six families in all, condemned to death, eating rotten potatoes in the landlord's ditches from which—to avoid the unpleasant business of removing corpses—they were soon driven off.

In April and May Daniel saw rotten potatoes being eaten everywhere.

Famine, then. And for those who still had the strength to be angry, Riot; menacing the landlords who *would* not, or, being almost penniless themselves, *could* not give charity; menacing the landlords who evicted for a private whim or simply to clear the land of hungry men who, being already resentful, would soon be troublesome. Menacing too, in the crossfire, the landlords who gave what they had and who, by men too desperate to tell the difference, were blamed nevertheless.

Yet a feast always followed a famine. Every Irishman knew that. Thank God it would be over by August.

In June the depots of Indian Corn, which had been only grudgingly opened, began to close, men like Daniel's friend in the Commissariat already being accused, in government circles, of being too generous, of exhausting their stocks by selling to all who had money to buy, whether genuine victims of famine or simply the eternal "Irish tinker" who was always hungry. And in July—the emergency being apparently considered over—a further cargo of Indian Corn was turned away.

In August . . . ?

The Tory Government of Sir Robert Peel had fallen, brought down, predictably, on the issue of the Corn Laws. By opening the ports to cheap foreign grain he had helped Ireland and England's industrial North but had planted a dagger most maliciously in the backs of the landed gentlemen who had elected him. So, at any rate, those landed gentlemen considered as they cast him off, submitting themselves to the policies of the Whigs, for a change, whose view of Ireland seemed no clearer.

The food depots continued to close. So too did the public works which, in many places, had only just got started, the fact that the food depots had no more corn to sell presumably canceling out the laborers' need of ready cash-in-hand, which would mean a great many half-made roads and bridges and half-drained tracts of land all over Ireland.

But who cared for that when the potato plants were not only growing but flourishing, promising the glut which always followed the hunger; the fat, full time which always came after the lean.

And then, one night in August, the potato fields from Southern Cork to Northern Donegal, from the west coast of Mayo to the eastern edge of Antrim and Meath, turned black. Everywhere. Making of that green country, from corner to corner, coast to coast, a festering, putrid, rotting mess.

The stink of it remained in Daniel's nostrils the whole of that summer and ever after. That; and the shattered, sickened hopelessness of the men and women he saw kneeling in their blighted fields, mourning over the diseased earth with a despair he knew to be total. Last year, there had been a few sticks of furniture in the house, bedding and blankets, pots and pans, to be taken one at a time to sell or pawn. Last year there had been a pig, a few chickens, a goat. Even a few precious coins of real money put by. This year there was nothing.

Last year the blight had spared not much perhaps, but at least a few fields here and there, something for somebody to be going on with. This year it had taken everything; would take everybody.

The public works could be started again, of course, all those roads leading nowhere to be dug by last year's scarecrows, fast becoming this year's skeletons. But apart from several "primitive" areas west of the Shannon, there were to be no government food depots at all this time, a sizeable number of commercial gentlemen who dealt in the import of corn and flour having demanded and received of a government elected by the commercial interest that there would be no interference with private enterprise. No government supplies suddenly flooding in to undercut their prices. No large-scale government buying in overseas markets to upset the proper balance of trade. A perfectly reasonable request—surely—since once the public works got going again and men had *wages* in their pockets instead of seed-potatoes, the food trade would flourish and *everybody* would do well out of it. And since the public works—the *wages*—were only intended to last a year, until the next harvest could be got in, it was an opportunity which really could not be missed.

The men in Ireland, of course, the men on the spot—Daniel, for one, and his Commissariat friend—were horrified. But the men in London, the grandees of both the Whig and Tory parties, so far removed from hunger that they could neither imagine it nor really believe in it, responded far more naturally to men of property who had votes to elect them than to distressed peasants, who had not.

The food depots then must close, such stocks as remained to be distributed very sparsely among the worst affected areas, provided the relief committees of such areas were still able to pay for it. *Nothing*—with that precious balance of trade in mind—was to be given away. An order with which Daniel's friend found himself unable to comply, having already distributed such corn meal as he had left, with his blessings and some assistance from Daniel, an hour before—or perhaps *after*—the message reached him.

His depot was now not only closed but empty. Nor did he believe, in this black year of 1846, with poor harvests not only in the British Isles but all over Europe, making prices high and competition fierce, that it would be filled up again.

Food there would be in Ireland, of course. Rich food to suit the splendors of the Dublin social season, brought in from London and Paris with the ball gowns and the satin slippers. The balance of trade would see to that. But how many merchant princes were there in Ireland who knew how to deal in international markets and in the bulk that would be required to feed the Irish people? None that Daniel's friend knew of. Although he had encountered plenty of the small and shady dealers who were known in every Irish village as money-lenders, merciless collectors of debts, dealers in short-measure and shoddy who could charge what they liked now for a few crumbs of bread?

Did England understand? It seemed unlikely. Did anybody—particularly the gentlemen of Westminster—fully realize that unless they broke their promise to the merchants now—*at once*—and became active in those international markets there would soon be nothing edible to buy; even the detested Indian Corn having been snatched up, this meager, blighted year, to feed the peasantry of Belgium and France?

Every Commissariat officer in Ireland knew. So did Daniel. Just as they knew that the Board of Works, sinking beneath the weight of hungry laborers but unable to find more than a handful of engineers to direct them, had given no significant employment as yet, paid no significant wages, so that even if the country markets were suddenly bursting with food it would be left, very likely, to rot. Like the potato. And when the road-building did get under way would it be easy, or even possible, to keep a family alive on the fixed rate of sixpence a day, with Indian Corn already at tuppence a pound from the village traders? Provided one was paid at all, of course, the Board having failed lamentably in finding enough wages-clerks.

What was left then? Nettles, it seemed, and grass. Until that too disappeared beneath the early and bitter snowfalls of November.

It was the coldest winter Daniel could remember. In London, he heard, the Thames had frozen over. In Ireland, turning up the collar of his own only barely adequate coat, he watched skeletons in rags fight each other for employment on such roadworks as had been started and then fight the Board of Works' officials for their wages when it was realized that no one was present on the site with the authority—or ability—to measure the amount of work done. And when the men fell down and died, as they often did, he saw other skeletons that were women come rushing to pick up the shovels from dead hands and dig or break stones or anything else for that sixpence a day which might keep the souls in the wizened and swollen little bodies of their children.

He saw gangs of emaciated, bewildered predators roaming everywhere, begging for food or work or hope—anything—listlessly, aimlessly. He saw children die, and stumbled over the bodies of others on narrow, country roads, hidden like fallen sticks by the snow, or shielded by other, slightly larger bodies which he supposed had been their mothers. He saw deserted villages emptied it seemed of their population, until one found them lying on the floor of their cabins, near-naked and too weakened to stand, hardly a rag left with which to cover themselves, no fuel, a cabbage leaf perhaps, or a handful of nettles stored away somewhere like a treasure. Death in their faces. Death too in the land, which was a ruin now of weeds, undug, undrained, untended beyond any hope of next year's harvest. Even if any of them should live to see it, which seemed unlikely. Since how could they dig new trenches and plant new seed when they were too feeble, in some cases, to dispose of their dead? When it took the last of a man's fading strength to drag out the corpses of parent, wife, infant, and leave them in the snow.

Yet there *was* food in Ireland, as the Commissariat had said there would be. Every visitor from the mainland being able to see it in abundance and, returning to England, reporting in some bewilderment on the good butter and meat and plump fresh fish on view certainly in Dublin and Waterford and Cork and anywhere else an English visitor might be likely to wander. Thus confusing the opinion of mainland England where, with an economy based on cash, not kind, it was less usual for men to die of starvation face to face with plenty.

The Irish people had no money. It was as simple as that. Would private English charity step in and collect it for them, where Government and private business enterprise had failed? Or seen no advantage? As a result of messages conveyed by men like Daniel Carey and the observations of that hardy species of "reforming" English lady and gentleman, £470,000 was raised in London that winter, £2,000 of it coming from Her Majesty the Queen, for the purchase and distribution of food, clothing and fuel, Her Majesty's Government contributing a model soup-kitchen organized by the chef of London's Reform Club, Alexis Soyer, who, from a 300-gallon soup-boiler in the middle of a long room with a door at each end, could feed relays of a hundred at a time at a rate of nearly a thousand a day. And cheaply too, Mr. Soyer having created a recipe which called for only a quarter of a pound of meat to two gallons of water.

Watching the starving multitude file in at one end and out the other, a second multitude and then a third waiting to take their places, Daniel remembered others he had seen during that bitter January and February, simply sitting down, blank-eyed and vacant, in the snow, in the attitude of resignation which seemed to welcome death.

An attitude he understood. He was not well himself that day, the greasy odor of the soup curdling his stomach, his lean, pared-down body feeling the chill, his active, hunger-sharpened mind recalling too clearly the very images he wished most to forget. The new-born, still-born children eaten by rats. The cabin doors he had pushed open to find a whole family dead, for a long time he imagined, under the same blanket. The field of corpses he had helped to bury in communal graves so shallow that they would be an offense to decency, humanity and the nostrils when the thaw set in. The hollow despair. No, he was not well, although the only remedy he was ever prepared to take against the weakness of his body was to ignore it.

Famine and Riot. There had been plenty of that around those half-made roads and canals, around the houses of food profiteers, "evicting" landlords, members of local relief committees whose only crime, in some cases, was that they had failed to work miracles. Riot when it was known that, because of the new soup-kitchens which were distributing their watery brew free of charge, the public works—which had been costing, or wasting, the British taxpayer £43,000 a day to run—were to be closed down again.

Was there now to be Famine and Fever?

It had always come before, following in hunger's wake as a black night after a black day, attacking bodies already too weak to dig a grave for a much-loved child. And attacking also—being not in the least particular—the doctors and nurses and nuns who tried to take care of them, the landlords in their manors, the silk and satin ladies at the Dublin balls. Anybody. Fever in its several varieties. Typhus, the "black fever" which scorched and darkened the body with congealed blood, bringing vomiting and madness and the vile stench that no one could ever forget. And its companion the "yellow fever" when a man fried in his own sweat, his skin the color of sulphur. These two, and the "bloody flux" when a man's bowels ran out of him it seemed. A ghastly trio, stalking a ravaged population huddled obligingly together, the better to be infected, at the soup-kitchens and what remained of the roadworks or just sitting on the ground in the torpor hunger brings, taking infection with them when they got up and wandered off again to the next feeding center, the next charitable woman dispensing soup from her own farmhouse kitchen, the overflowing workhouse, the prison.

Scurvy too, which takes out the teeth and turns the legs black. And the strange "swelling disease" of hunger, huge pregnant bellies suspended below ribs and limbs that were merely bones rattling between flaps of wrinkled, graying skin. Children with the large, wizened heads of old men and the sad, uncomprehending eyes of monkeys. All that. And Daniel, in his last dispatch to London, had discovered that in the whole of Ireland only 28 hospitals had been set up to combat the expected epidemic. That in the county of Dublin there was only one public dispensary for every 7,300 people. In Mayo, with its population of over 360,000, only one public dispensary of any kind.

"Fever sheds," wooden lean-tos tacked on to the sides of workhouses, more often than not, and army tents with boarded floors were hastily erected where doctors and nuns and good-hearted women labored with the patient, grinding despair of cart-horses. Where men like Daniel, with no medical skills, moved bodies, dug graves, restrained those driven to furious insanity at least from harming others. Labored long and hard, his eyes glazed, his mind empty, although when his own sweating and burning came upon him he walked quickly away, finding death—if that was what assailed him—to be a private matter.

There were no messages to be delivered from *his* deathbed; no hands he wished to hold; no consolation to be given since he believed in nothing, trusted nothing, wanted nothing. Unless it was to be relieved of those images of human misery which had taken over his whole mind lately, become so much a part of him that death—if it meant he would see them no longer—would not be unwelcome.

He returned to his lodgings, therefore, and locked himself in, knowing no one would trouble him once the stench of typhus seeped under his door. He knew the symptoms and stages of his disease, having seen enough of it this fair, green Springtime, in the streets and fields of the plague villages, in the workhouse hospitals where the diseased and dying lay on straw packed two or three hundred into the space for twenty. He knew that he would sweat and vomit, become delirious, cry out for water which no one—he had seen to that—would bring him, cry out that he was scorching, parching, consumed by fire.

He knew that he would stink and blacken and hallucinate and probably die.

Yet, even as he nailed up his window to stop himself from jumping out into the street and running, contaminated and amok, when the delirium struck him, he was already too dazed by sickness to care. Ought he to care? Very likely. Yes, very likely. If he had strength enough in his weary arms—in his weary soul—to drag himself across to the dresser and pick up that jug of water, strength enough for any of this vague and wearisome life or death to matter. Should he not . . . ? Well—*something? Somebody?* But he could hardly remember his own name, it seemed, much less grapple with the complex names and natures of others. Far better just to lie down and die, hoping—against all the doctrines of his youth—that it would be the end, that he would never have to look again on the complicated sufferings and satisfactions of humanity, never again have to struggle with the ills he could not cure, the hopes he could not fulfill, the love he could not give. That he might never again bruise or be bruised by too close a contact with another beautiful, terrible, desirable, *fragile* human creature, either man or woman. That he might never know pity again, nor outrage, nor tenderness. That he might give no hurt and receive none. That, no longer caring, there would be no more scars.

Far better to be alone. To leave neither footprints nor shadow behind him. To be nothing, when this accursed fire had done with him, but a handful of cold ash.

He lay down and burned, in rancid oil to begin with, then in a fierce, dry flame that gutted him as completely as fire through ancient timbers. He still needed no one to share his end. But, as layer after layer of consciousness was stripped away, the woman who had shared his beginning came to him. His mother, or so he thought, until she became Gemma and then his mother again. Or his mother with Gemma's face. Gemma with his mother's. Dying for him all over again. Blood on lavender silk upholstery, the woman lying dead across him, covering his eleven-year-old body with hers. Blood seeping from the wound in her back which had shielded his head and chest. Blood on the front of Gemma's brown satin gown, from the gash he had made in her heart. Her mouth still smiling. Her brown eyes steady. Giving their lives for him over and over, and uselessly, since he was only one man and there was a multitude out there, pressing starved and diseased bodies against his window, breaking through it, knocking down the walls, wave after ghastly wave of them trampling him underfoot.

He came to his senses a day and a night later, a corpse which, to his surprise, managed to stagger to the washstand and tip the contents of the jug and bowl over his head, his shaking hands telling him by the color of their cracked and flaking skin that he had the yellow pestilence, not the black. Not typhus, which maddened before it killed, but the sweating sickness from which here, alone in his room with no other man's pestilence to re-infect him, he might recover.

If he should think it worth the trouble.

If he could just gather himself together and hold himself together long enough to get those fouled sheets off the bed and bundle them, with the nauseating mess that was his shirt and trousers, into the closet. If he could just strip this mattress and turn it over so that should he lose consciousness again, as seemed likely, he would have a clean, dry place to put himself.

How putrid and pitiful the human body was in its sickness. How loathsome a prison for the mind.

He lay down on the bare mattress, naked with a thin sheet over him and began to sweat again. Yes, that was the way of it. He remembered now. The first attack. Recovery. Relapse. Recovery. Then relapse again. He had survived the first. If he could survive this...? Unless those women who were still muttering in his ear, the same voice speaking twice over or two voices in unison, wanted his death now, in exchange for their deaths, long ago—on lavender silk upholstery—on a narrow school-house bed—his mother dragging him behind her, exposing herself to the guns—Gemma wounding herself to spare him. Both of them calm and smiling. Gemma's crisp English voice setting the thoughts of his beautiful, whimsical, Irish mother to John-William Dallam's earth-music.

"Take what I've got to offer, lad, and let's have no nonsense—since it's good for you and comes free of charge."

But he could not take it. Nothing remained in him now that was capable of taking it. The fire had burned his individuality away, and what was left was not a man who could love or desire love but an instrument of retribution. A tool. A weapon. A metamorphosis from human flesh to bloodless and therefore far more efficient steel.

He came to again, parched and drenched and shaking, and relapsed again, waking to what he judged by the light to be mid-morning, aware now of the need for sustenance without which he would probably die in any case. And he did not intend to die now. Food and drink. Easy enough, even in starving Ireland, for a man with his editor's money in his pocket. If he could just gather himself together and stay together long enough to clean and dress himself so as not to look too much the plague victim, and negotiate the stairs. If he could raise the leaden weights which seemed to be his feet high enough to step over the bundles of human rags flung down in the hall. If he could somehow dispel the vaporous, nebulous substance in which his body was afloat, go out into the decent, respectable, even affluent street and find . . . ? Friends, he thought. Refuge. Escape, dear God. He turned up the collar of his bright Chartist-green jacket and shivered, feeling ice in the warm May breeze, feeling age in his hunched shoulders which had just turned thirty years old. Since he had been living a century in every day had he not—lately?

Had he cried out for help? Very likely. As the Irish people had cried out. As they had cried out last year too and, when it had gone unheeded, had tightened their belts, learned resignation or resentment—according to nature—prayed, kept their minds on the new harvest. But this year there would be no harvest since none had been planted. This year every field was a graveyard. Pestilence stalked the land, unabated it seemed, and greedy. And this year, when the cry once again was unanswered, the people drew the remnants of themselves together, and fled.

To British North America, for those who could still scrape together the passage-money, or whose landlords, either from charity or a less admirable desire to clear the land of a destitute tenantry and start again, were ready to pay it for them. A most convenient method of disposing of widows with small children, for instance, as well as whole cargoes of the old, the infirm, the troublesome. And cheap at the price too, the cost of sending a ruined tenant off to that Bright New World being only half the expense of housing and feeding him a twelve-month in the workhouse, or having to watch him starve to death in one's ancestral ditches. Nor, having braved the hazards of the Atlantic crossing, would he be likely to return, particularly if he had made the voyage in one of those floating coffins, under-provisioned and over-crowded, which occasionally sank within sight of the Irish coast, or, if they did manage to limp into a transatlantic port, had often buried a quarter of their passengers at sea.

For they took with them not only their despair and resentment, their grief and their sense of injustice, but their fever.

Or else the plague followed them, killing 17,000 of the 100,000 who made the crossing to Canada in that one plague year of 1847; killing them at the rate of thirty a day in the quarantine sheds where they were landed; killing them in untold, faceless numbers as they staggered off, thinly-fleshed and thinly-clad, into the Arctic winter, hoping to find their way on foot to the land they all knew to be paved with gold. America. New York. Converging there from every point of the compass, on every highway or seaway, without education or any experience of cities, unskilled in any trade or craft beyond the digging of potato patches, often with little knowledge of the Queen's English, or speaking it with an accent that the Queen herself would have been unlikely to understand.

While those who were even more destitute, those for whom no landlord felt even a "coffin ship responsibility" and who could not themselves raise a brass farthing, came to England in the hold of a coal ship free of charge as living ballast, being easier for the sailors to unload than lime or pigs or shingle. Or on the open deck of a cargo boat for the price of a few shillings slipped to them by a parish priest who knew that although the English had failed to understand the oppressions regularly suffered by the Irish people, a man who succeeded in getting to the mainland would not be allowed to starve. The English workhouses serving a rich diet in comparison with their Irish counterparts, including tea, and meat every now and then, and sugar.

No emigrants these, looking for a bright new world, a Promised Land, hoping to put down roots and prosper like the ones who had gone to America. Not even family groups, in many cases, but the vagrants, the paupers, the squatters, widows with their hordes of small, half-naked children, old women, disabled old men, expecting nothing from England but a bread-ticket and a bowl of gruel. And with nothing to give in exchange but their pestilence.

In Liverpool, with its population of 250,000 native English, 300,000 starving Irish beggars landed in the first six months of the year, necessitating the swearing in of 20,000 private citizens as special constables to control not only Irish tempers but English fears as to the spread of typhus, dysentery, smallpox, cholera. A circumstance so likely, with these most unwelcome visitors herding into derelict houses, condemned as unfit for human habitation, and squatting there as many as eighty to a room, that permission was soon granted to round up all who could be caught at the docks—all those who could not run fast enough—and ship them back to Ireland again.

A sorry spectacle to Daniel, although not unexpected, as he stood on the Liverpool docks himself one June morning, having satisfied the hard eyes and probing fingers of authority, that he had money in his pocket, employment with a journal admittedly not of the kind to appeal to officers of law and order but employment nevertheless, and a relative already established in England, a Miss Cara Adeane of Frizingley who would be glad to vouch for him.

He had used her before, eight years ago, to smooth his way through Liverpool and he employed her name now without a tremor, being perfectly ready to follow it with the name of Gemma Gage should more weight be needed. Either one of them, he supposed, without any particular emotion, would agree to help him. Gemma gladly. Cara grudging him every minute it took, perhaps, but doing it just the same.

Either one of them. And, in his taut and toughened condition, still far more a tool, a weapon, an instrument than a man, it made little difference to him which one. Whichever, at any particular moment, might serve him best.

Cara or Gemma. They both lived for him now at a great distance and a long time ago. When he had conducted himself in a carefree, easy, haphazard manner which now seemed to him both unreal and unworthy. When he had suffered for such trivialities as love, personal ambition, the satisfaction of appetites and ideals which he now knew to be irrelevant luxuries.

No longer. He was a changed man. An Irishman. And no woman of the alien, uncaring English nor any Irishwoman who had absorbed and condoned their ways could deflect him now from his true purpose and identity. From the task he had undertaken.

For the government which had refused to feed Ireland had lately fallen and he had agreed to stand as the Chartist candidate for Frizingley again.

23

*H*e had been three years away from Frizingley, traveling now on the new railway line which had opened it up to Leeds and, hence, the world. Frizingley's own narrow strip of magic carpet connecting directly with all those others which sped now, at dizzying, dangerous, highly profitable speed, the length and breadth of England, reducing to a few, not too uncomfortable hours, journeys which had taken days or weeks of jolting agony; bringing traders and merchants and news from London on the day it happened; bringing travel, movement, new sights and opportunities and ideas to those who might otherwise never have left their villages. Mixing the population together. Making it possible to move large groups of men quickly, cheaply and at a moment's notice. Troops, for instance, who could arrive fresh and rested and very promptly these days, to quell the ardor of even the most isolated Chartist demonstration.

Times were changing. Expanding and contracting both together. The streets of central Frizingley, Daniel noticed, cleaner, better-lit and better-policed than they used to be, one half of Market Square dominated now by the ornate façade of the station, the other half by a tall, Grecian-columned hotel offering seventy double bedrooms, a number of suites and private apartments, a banqueting-hall, a ballroom which had so displaced the old Assembly Rooms that they had been knocked down. The site used for the construction of Frizingley's even more Grecian town hall built to the taste of the gentleman who owned not only the land but the demolition and construction companies employed in its redevelopment, Captain Christie Goldsborough. The building to be opened, sometime after the elections, by Councillor Benjamin Braithwaite, mayor of Frizingley, and skinny, flamboyant Magda, his mayoress.

Several of the old coaching inns had gone too, the Rose and Crown and the whole cobweb of narrow streets around it being replaced by a double row of spick-and-span commercial establishments, so new that their ornate stonework was as yet unblackened by the soot from the Braithwaite and Dallam factory chimneys. A bank and a firm of shipping and forwarding agents stood on the site of the Dog and Gun. The Beehive, from where the Leeds coach had left twice daily, had closed its rowdy doors for lack of custom, its business swallowed by the railway, and, after a great deal of refurbishing, had become a well-mannered commercial hotel where the Chartists—also much better-mannered and better-dressed than they used to be—had taken rooms for their candidate.

Only the Fleece remained intact, no longer the home of Captain Goldsborough, who had moved into the greater luxuries of the station hotel, but still his headquarters in a manner of speaking nevertheless, looked after by his lieutenant, Mr. Oliver Rattrie, a thin, crook-shouldered, almost painfully elegant man whom Daniel—his mind on other matters—did not remember. Although he remembered the Fleece and, behind it, the sorry raggle-taggle of St. Jude's, a thousand miles away in spirit from the pompous splendors of Market Square but, in reality, just five minutes' brisk walk between self-conscious, well-drained affluence and those decaying alleys where the sewage ran untreated in open gutters for every child to play in, every stray cat to drown in, in which every disease which squalor bred could lurk and multiply. St. Jude's, a greater pesthole than ever now that the landlord's agent, Mr. Oliver Rattrie—doubtless on the landlord's instructions—had, these three years past, carried out no repairs, no maintenance, allowing broken windows, rotting woodwork, flooded cellars, to remain in the condition they had fallen, not turning a hair when floors collapsed and ceilings caved in, concentrating—in the painstaking manner for which Mr. Rattrie was famous—on the sole purpose of laying down in precise, mathematical arrangements, as many mattresses, and therefore as many tenants, as a room would hold. From one to two dozen, on average, in the better, predominantly English houses. Far more than that when it came to the Irish, for whom straw tossed down on bare floorboards seemed sufficient and for whose benefit the demolition of certain, almost totally derelict streets had been halted so that they might squat, for a penny or two, among the wreckage.

An invasion, Daniel was at once aware, which had horrified Frizingley as much as it had Liverpool, a ragged, famished horde descending upon them, a ghastly procession so distorted by famine as to seem members of another species not quite humanity, wilder and more primitive and perhaps more colorful, close to the earth in a way industrial Frizingley had long forgotten, believers in a religion which made Frizingley, and the English in general, frankly nervous. A foreign people worshipping a foreign Pope, speaking what amounted to a foreign language, who, having long been in the habit of crossing to the mainland in dribs and drabs to beg on English roads or, by working for less than any Englishman would take, forcing the price of labor down, were now here in their terrifying hundreds and thousands. A deluge of them, a crushing burden on the poor-rates, filling the workhouses so that the English paupers could not get in, tumbling into paupers' graves for which *somebody* had to pay the bill, living and breeding and dying in horrible promiscuity in those damp cellars and the abandoned navvy-camps which ringed the town. A skeletal hand looming out of every shadow, these days, to beg. Gangs of them huddled like the droppings of a rag-and-bone merchant's cart on the *front steps of the new town hall*, crying for bread, until the constables cleared them away. Bringing nothing to Frizingley but their fleas, their vermin, their idolatry, the strange personal habits of their alien culture, and their fever.

And although no attempt had been made, as in other, smaller places, to bar their entry into the town, Frizingley did not welcome this drain on its facilities which had been sketchy enough to begin with, this blight on its hard-won respectability, the over-tipping of its scales in the direction of degradation and misery, the outbreaks of dysentery and assorted fevers which had started with the first half-naked scarecrows to stagger down the hill from Frizingley Moor.

"You can't blame the people for not liking it," Daniel heard from the priest who had come with them, a man with the build and seasoned toughness of a navvy, the carefree jauntiness of the farm-boy from Kildare he had once been, not too long ago. "Who wants plague and vermin, when all's said and done? If you had half a dozen fine, healthy children, Daniel Carey, you might not be standing here in the middle of it talking to me quite so casually yourself."

Just as well then, thought Daniel, that he had no children. No one at all, in fact, to care for at the personal level which might worry him. No reason, any longer, to fret about the weakness, the terrible frailty of one particular human body. No cause to agonize when the wind blew cold, or pest-laden, in any particular direction. All men—

all women—were the same to him now. Thank God. Thank Him most truly. For how else could he bring himself to enter Frizingley's own fever-shed, a sounder model than the one he had helped to build in Dublin, and stroll between the rows of narrow beds with a cool but merciful detachment, looking not for a loved or even a familiar face but for the mechanics of the care that was being given, the distance between the mattresses, the number of blankets, the rapidity, or lack of it, with which excrement and vomit were cleaned up. Not flinching at any odor nor at any voice raised in a plea for assistance or for mercy, since all men and women stank alike and cried out alike in fever.

Was there a future for any of them here? Father Francis thought not. Or not in this world at any rate. Little hope for himself either, he cheerfully concluded, if the epidemic lasted much longer, since he was now the sole survivor of the dozen priests who had crossed the water with him. An occupational hazard, it must be said, since one took in a man's breath, after all, with his dying confession, like the good doctors, on both sides of the water, who had been dying like flies. More's the pity.

A bad business. Although Frizingley, after the initial moment of recoil, had done what it could, realizing—with good sense, thought the good Father—that so many people could not be asked, for reasons of sanitation and economy, to drown themselves in the Irish sea. There was the workhouse, of course, although it had soon filled up with the widows and orphans, the lame and the old, who would otherwise be rounded up as vagrants and shipped back to Ireland again. The same boat-load of disease and despair sailing backward and forward, shuttling the same diseased, desperate bodies from one unwelcoming coast to the other. Often Father Francis dreamed of that. But, on the whole, Frizingley had been as charitable as could be expected. Official charity—the cold kind—in those bread-tickets and bowls of workhouse gruel. Cold private charity too, maintaining its distance, from ladies who sent blankets and cast-off clothing with the tips of their fingers. Charity of a warmer sort from some other women, like Mrs. Gage for instance, who had not only turned her school-house into a soup-kitchen but served an excellent beef and barley broth there to all-comers with her own hands.

Daniel heard her name without a tremor.

"I know Mrs. Gage," he said.

"A fine woman."

"Yes."

It was true. He knew it, remembered it, yet could not feel it. A fine woman who could still vomit and blacken with typhus as easily as any coarse-grained peasant woman from a pig boat. He spoke her name and then, as he had trained himself to do with all names, forgot it.

He occupied himself, instead, with his candidature, worked on his speeches, saw to it that his pamphlets were well distributed throughout the town, addressed meetings of his supporters, paid well-brushed, top-hatted visits to such voters who appeared undecided and also, at Father Francis's request, to the town's few prosperous Irish residents.

"I can see they don't like me crossing their thresholds," he told Daniel, "considering the den in St. Jude's they know I come from— me with my hand out begging their hard-earned money and bringing God knows what pestilence with me into their fine houses. So if you could just go knocking on those doors for me, my lad, and remind them of their origins and obligations—with that cold smile of yours, that looks like the vengeance of the Lord . . . ?"

Was his smile cold? He had not looked at it recently, had not studied any human face in detail for a very long time and did not expect to do so again. But, he went, nevertheless, to the Irish owner of the livery stables in St. Jude's Square who gave him a guinea, to a gentleman in Frizingley Moor Road whose wife had been born in Dublin and who gave him a guinea more on the promise that he would not call again; to Ned O'Mara of the Fleece, drunken and demoted now to a mere bartender subject to the overall authority of Oliver Rattrie; to one of the many pawnbrokers in St. Jude's Passage; to a spinster lady who had once been a governess to an Irish peer; and to the dressmaker and milliner, Miss Cara Adeane.

Her name, too, caused him no emotion beyond a flicker of amusement on seeing it writ so very large in ornately scrolled gold letters on the front of her shop which now occupied a whole corner of Market Square, its windows, on one side, staring boldly at the new station hotel and, on the other side, at a small public garden laid out with sculptured flower beds and young, very hopeful trees.

A doorman in pale blue livery stood ready to open the door and direct him to left or right according to his requirements, a saleswoman, also in pale blue, asking him to be seated on one of a row of spindly blue and gold chairs while she moved off very smoothly— her pace implying that one had all the time in the world to browse and spend—to find out if Miss Adeane would see him. Was he a

salesman, perhaps? The representative of some exotic foreign establishment dealing in brocades or rare satins? The woman, making her
judgment, had smiled at him encouragingly, but he had not enlightened her, simply sending in his card, the correct, deckle-edged white
square which told nothing but his name. And while he waited he
looked with a shrewd, journalist's eye at the expanse of pale blue
carpet, the air of space and ease and tranquillity, the quiet but very
distinct impression of success. The almost casual display of garments
he knew to be minor works of art, the showcase at his elbow full of
tiny, precious objects, jeweled combs, scent bottles, mother-of-pearl
boxes, embroidered gloves, a shimmering rainbow of beads and
brooches, fans and feathers and satin slippers. The arched opening,
leading, through a bead curtain, to another room and then, he thought,
another, which offered him enticing glimpses of movement and color.

"May I give you a glass of Madeira while you are waiting?" a soft
voice said, offering the wine in exquisitely cut crystal on a silver tray.
And because those who have seen famine do not refuse any kind of
sustenance he smiled at the woman—who had Cara's air and manner
and her slender, elegant figure—and took it.

"Thank you," his eyes said and then, automatically, "How pretty
you are," because that, too, was a kind of sustenance to be taken like
bread and water, whenever one could and for as long as it lasted.

"Miss Adeane will not be long," the girl murmured, so visibly
flustered and flattered by the message of his cold and wary but nevertheless still handsome eyes that it took Cara's crisply pronounced,
"Good morning, Mr. Carey. And how are you this fine morning?" to
deflate her.

"I'm very well, Miss Adeane. And yourself?"

"Never better. Would you care to step into my office?"

It was the room he remembered as the one in which she had worked
and lived and slept, her bed in one corner, her dining-table in the
other, her work-table somewhere in between, littered with sketches
and account books and ledgers; the room in which he had last seen
her mother weeping, her son glaring at her with that burdensome
hatred, much altered now and given over entirely to the purposes of
her business, a new walnut desk of impressive proportions, high-
backed leather chairs, pictures of jeweled women in Gainsborough
hats on her pale damask walls; a pale carpet covered with cloudy,
overblown roses, vases of flowers which looked expensive and out of

season; only her dog, it seemed, left over from the old days, snoring as always in his basket by her new white marble hearth.

"Sit down," she said and he sat, watching her as, her wide taffeta skirts rustling and swaying, she walked around the desk and took her own seat, a queen on her throne, attentive yet remote. And beautiful. Her skin smooth and unlined as pale amber, older only in its sophistication, the gleaming blue-black hair coiled high and intricately on top of her head, its weight giving length and grace to her neck and her broad, straight shoulders, its color deepening the astonishing aquamarine of her eyes.

How beautiful and how *hurt*, he had thought when he had last seen her, three years ago in this very place. Crisp and composed now, and cold too, as he had grown cold himself. And although he knew he had loved her and could well remember the reasons, he could not feel even a faint echo of that love again. Desire, by all means. Plenty of that. But, merely by closing his eyes, he knew he could make himself forget her. So completely, in fact, that the news of her death by typhus or hunger or by any of the other obscenities he had witnessed lately would not unduly distress him. She would be only one among many. He was safe from mourning her.

"Is it thinking you are," he said lightly, rejoicing in his freedom from caring, "of that old adage about the bad penny turning up again— and again . . . ?"

"Yes." She was still very crisp and cool and imperial. "That's just what I might have been thinking."

"Is it any wonder? You're looking beautiful, Cara. And rich."

"I don't grumble." She began to tell him why. "I took over the shop next door and then the two next door to that as they became vacant and as I could afford them. So now I have separate departments for hats, dresses, lingerie, perfumes, fancy goods. And separate saleswomen who are expert—or supposed to be—on the particular thing they sell. My workrooms are upstairs, of course, and an apartment for myself above them . . ."

A whole floor to herself, in fact, a rose-pink bedroom with lace bed-curtains and a pink marble bathtub; a sitting-room in the pale pastel shades she loved not only because they pleased her eye but because they were impractical, less than hard-wearing, and she liked it to be seen she could afford them; a dining-parlor in traditional mahogany with apple-green Chinese rugs and apple-green silk walls. A kitchen down below with a cook-housekeeper in it. A little housemaid to carry the hot water for that precious rose-pink bath up three flights of stairs.

Had he now come to tell her she was unworthy of all that? To make her *feel* unworthy by looking at her, in the way he now had beneath all his light-hearted jauntiness, of an avenging angel? A stern, celestial judge weighing and measuring her with those keen eyes, that cold smile. When his smile had once been—*nothing* like this. An enchantment. Warm and wonderful, inviting her not to contrition but to folly, as magical in its way as her father's rainbows.

What had happened to change him?

"So—as you see—I don't complain," she ended.

"I do see. If you were a man I'd be here to coax your vote out of you. I reckon this amount of property must qualify for it?"

"It does. But since women don't vote— And I'm a woman . . ."

"I see that too . . ."

Clearly, it seemed. And not liking the open appraisal of his glance, as if there had never been anything between them but *that*, she said quickly, "What are you doing here, then?"

He told her, briefly, that he had come directly from Ireland to stand once again as the Chartist candidate, information she already knew and in which her interest did not seem intense.

"Politics . . ." she murmured, the shrug of her shoulders dismissing it as a game designed by men to be played among themselves with all the noise and fuss and disregard for the convenience of others as unruly children. Men who might call themselves ministers but would have their work cut out to make the profits she made, year in, year out, from her shop. No, she had no time for children's games. Nor their fantasies.

"Politics." The word had a bitter taste in her mouth, it seemed. A sour apple of a word she could do well without.

He smiled. "I know. You never cared for it. So tell me instead— how is your mother?"

"In America," she said flatly, throwing the words at him like a challenge. "Three years now. My father is in a good way of business in New York. I sent my boy over with them. I decided the change would do him good. And so it has. He writes to me very often— about all kinds of things . . ."

She had said too much and knew it, although the reason for her anguish escaped him. Eight years ago she had refused him because she could neither separate herself from her mother nor trust him with the care of her son. Now she had sent them off to the other side of the world without any backward glance that he could see. And it meant nothing to him. No hurt, no resentment, not the least pang of jealousy that she had done, presumably for another man, the very things she had denied him.

He felt nothing at all. He almost wished he did.

"Yes—he writes and tells me about all manner of things he'd never get the chance to see here..."

She had to let him know, whether it mattered to him or not, that her contact with Liam had not been broken, that she was still present in his life, his mother, although in fact, his letters were infrequent and stilted, prompted, she knew, by Odette. Each one a thorn in her heart.

"What things?" Daniel's eyes and her own were not in focus, no longer looking in the same direction. "What is there to be seen in New York these days but the starving Irish...?"

She tossed her head in irritation, having no intention—she really didn't know why—of telling him that she had already given some money to Father Francis, and *all* the calico she had bought from Miss Ernestine Baker, in a spirit of pure malice, when that good lady had finally liquidated her stock and closed her doors. She had even thought of taking in a couple of little Irish apprentices, orphan girls straight out of the bog that nobody wanted and giving them a chance, changing her mind only when her workwomen had started muttering and losing their heads about the Irish fever. And even now, if Father Francis could pick her out a likely child, she might just get her scrubbed and deloused and into the workroom before anybody had time to complain. But, for as long as Daniel sat there, smiling and carefree on the outside, judging her like that vengeful angel of the Lord within, she knew she could not tell him so.

"There's no need to go to New York to see the starving Irish," she said, issuing another challenge. "Only to the old navvy-camp at the top of St. Jude's Hill."

"And have you been there, Cara?"

Folding her beautifully manicured hands she smiled at him. "No, I have not. And don't intend to. A fine thing for me to be going up there—to do *what*, I'd like to know?—and then coming back to start an epidemic in Market Square."

"A fine thing indeed."

"So I won't do it."

"Have I asked you?"

She was not sure of that. "What is it then, Daniel? Has Father Francis sent you round with his begging bowl?"

"So he has."

For a moment she felt relief, since money was easy enough. Very easy, these days. And then, because it always pained her to realize that the coins upon which she could now quite casually lay her hands were somehow no longer the same golden miracles as in the days when she had had to struggle hard for even one of them, she said tartly, "And if I gave you a hundred pounds how much good would it do?"

"Not much."

She was surprised he knew that.

"A thousand pounds, then?"

He smiled at her, a covering of charm light as a gauze veil over the stern, stark countenance of blind justice, naked truth, a refusal any longer to compromise.

"Oh—it might be of some help to a few of the squatters in those foul cellars at the top of St. Jude's, Cara. Those who aren't already beyond help, that is. It might patch them up a little, so they can stagger on to the next disaster. It might put a better class of tramp on the roads, that's all. There's been no shortage of private charity. A million dollars has come in from America. And even England—Perfidious Albion herself—has raised upward of five hundred thousand pounds."

"That has to go somewhere, Daniel."

He shrugged. "Indeed. But when it has to be spread so thinly one hardly notices. Private charity can never provide a real solution, Cara. Only governments can do that. This tragedy should never have been allowed to happen. There was no need for it. Government could have prevented it. Government can make sure it never happens again. Any Government, with any famine, anywhere in the world. There *is* enough of everything to go around. There always has been. Only Governments can distribute it so that no man has to sit at the roadside—any roadside—dying of hunger and staring at a side of roast beef. Only governments can create conditions—if they want to—where nobody has to starve. The fact is they don't want to. I'm in the business of changing their attitudes. Father Francis is in the business of patching up, mending and making do. Which is why it's *his* begging bowl I'm bringing you, not mine."

"And what do you want me to put in it?"

"Whatever makes *you* feel justified. Your vote, if you had one."

"So you can change the world with your People's Charter? Nobody is going to vote for you, Daniel."

He shrugged again and smiled. "Not this time, perhaps. I'll just have to keep on trying. I'm young enough."

But it was not true. The youth had gone out of him. She saw that and mourned it, her own youth having left her long ago. But, while she had retained her resilience, her sense of sap rising and renewing, there was something dry and brittle about Daniel, something so fine-drawn and tenuous, so likely to snap that she was suddenly very much afraid of him. Yet what help could she give? What help would he take from her now? Did he even trust her judgment, which to him, she supposed, must seem self-centered and commercial? Ought she, perhaps, to send him to Gemma Gage?

Not yet.

"What makes you certain," she said, "that your Chartists would keep their promises if they ever did come to power? Nobody else does. How do you know they wouldn't turn grasping and greedy, like everybody else, once they got their hands on something worth grasping? And they'd find plenty of excuses, then, for putting off all these 'better conditions' of yours and keeping everything for themselves. How do you know they wouldn't do that?"

"I don't."

"Well *I* know." She was suddenly furious. "Because that's what people do—that's what people *are*. Dog eat dog—except that dogs don't behave so badly . . ."

"No," he said very quietly. "They eat dead children on street corners—all over Ireland."

Her fist smashed down hard and angry on her desk-top. "Don't tell me that. I don't want to know that. I made sure my own child wasn't there, didn't I, and that's as much as I could do, isn't it?— He could have starved a dozen times over before any of this started, but I wouldn't have it. I saw to it that he didn't . . ."

But she had lost him just the same. Not in the small, pine coffin which had so often haunted her, his famished little body just a handful of sparrow-bones tucked away inside it, but just as finally. She knew she would never see him again. She knew he did not want to see her.

"Well, it's *safe* he is now," she said flatly, knowing she must be grateful for it. "In America."

"Do you miss him very much, Cara?"

"No." In a way it was true. Or at least, not the child who had bitten her arm and kicked her shins and cowered away from her, crying for Odette. Not him. But Liam as he might have been—ought to have been—had her life really allowed her to have a son. Had she found the way to keep his body and soul together and be a mother to him at the same time. For *that* child her arms ached sometimes: and her heart.

"No," she said, very brisk and competent again. "I don't miss him. He's well. And I'm busy. Very busy."

"Yes. I see."

She gave him the wide, dazzling, quite empty smile she reserved for her more troublesome customers, for her suppliers when they began to show signs of raising their prices, for the men she might find it convenient, from time to time, to fascinate.

"And what about you, Daniel? What are you planning for yourself?"

And once more he matched her false brilliance with his own light veil of charm, that transparent, faintly contemptuous sketch of the blithe and carefree wanderer who, for so long, had been Daniel Carey.

"Well—let's be thinking now—first I'm going to lose the election..."

"Of course."

"And then, if it's a by-election I can be finding somewhere I may have a crack at losing that too."

"I'm sure you'll succeed—at losing, I mean."

He made a slight bow. "Your confidence touches me deeply, Cara. And spurs me on."

"And then?"

"The Dawn of Enlightenment—what else? The Age of the Charter. The Sacred Ballot Box. The lion and the lamb having dinner together in your grand new hotel over there. Or, if they're not precisely sitting at the same table, then at least a little more Liberty and Equality and Fraternity for hors-d'oeuvres—a little more Justice for dessert."

"It's all nonsense, Daniel. It won't happen."

"Oh—one has to use one's life for something, Cara."

"And are you asking me to what use I put mine?" She sounded dangerous.

"No. I am not."

"Yes, you are." She stood up, regal and outraged, intending—so she thought—to dismiss him, but then, a tremor going through her, she cried out instead, "Don't do this to me, Daniel. Don't turn all this to dust and ashes for me. It's all I have. It's what I am. Don't do it."

He stood up too, straight and taut as an arrow, the veil of charm slipping away from him and, with it, some of his recently acquired years, the air of weary timelessness, the weight of experience accumulated through long Ages far beyond the normal lifespan which made him so formidable. A clamp released, if only briefly, from his spirit, leaving him not quite the man who had loved her, but a man who understood her worth.

"And if I did that, Cara, and it all fell about you in decay, I know you'd just stamp your feet for a minute or two, in all that dust and ashes, and then set about building the whole thing up again. Wouldn't you?"

She gritted her teeth. "I would."

"I know. I think you've always had that kind of courage, Cara. I had to learn it. It didn't come naturally to me."

"That's because you were never hungry enough."

"I am now."

Abruptly, like a thread snapping, the tension broke, unraveled, taking both the stern, dark angel and the brittle sophisticate with it so that, at last, it was Daniel and Cara who stood there. Smiling.

"You've always despised every one of my ambitions, Daniel Carey."

"So I have. And you've always thought me a light-minded fool, Cara Adeane."

"And so you are."

"There now. Are we back where we started?"

Not entirely. Could either of them really want that?

"Can I come and see you again?" he said, picking up his hat and gloves.

"Yes. But use the back entrance and only in working hours."

"Ah—I see," his eyes met hers, his glance easy and even roguish, hers quite blank. "So you can pass me off, at need, as a dealer in satin slippers? You have a jealous lover, do you, Miss Adeane?"

"Yes," she very crisply said.

"The same?"

"The same."

"It has been a very long time now, hasn't it?"

"Yes."

"Almost a marriage."

As near, she supposed, as she would ever come to it. More of a business association, at times, like many marriages, a matter of giving satisfaction and balancing the books. But always, even during his absences, his shadow at the back of her mind, reminding her that she had agreed to belong to him. And did belong. Financially and physically, her quick mind lapping up the shrewd commercial refinements he fed her, her body leaping to orgasm after orgasm in his arms. Money and sex. What else was Magda Braithwaite's marriage made of? Or Lady Lark's?

Or Gemma Dallam's? Quickly she closed her mind to that.

"Yes. I suppose it is."

She walked with him to the back door, no longer flimsy and unpainted like the one she had closed between him and her weeping mother on his last visit but a new very solid structure of polished oak.

"Come and see me, then—when you happen to be passing."

"I will."

He put his hand on her shoulder and they both looked at it for a moment in slight surprise as if it had somehow landed there like a moth in flight, the taffeta of her shop-gown feeling very smooth and cold to him, his touch very cold and sharp to her. She was the woman he had wanted more than any other, and never had. Could he have her now? He leaned toward her, her mouth only inches from his, the rise and fall of her breasts almost beneath his chest, the warm sweet scents of her, the silk and velvet and steel of her, that his body instantly and predictably told him he desired still.

But that had not been *all* he had wanted of her, surely? He had wanted to love her and be loved by her, to see no one but her and have her look at no one but him.

Certainly that was over.

And in what other fashion, without soiling that distant memory, could he take her now? What had he to offer her—or she him, perhaps—to compare with that?

He brushed his mouth along the line of her eyebrows, the tip of her nose, and withdrew his hand.

"Yes. I'll come to see you."

It might even be easier now, and better. They might even be friends.
"Whenever you like, so long as you remember my situation . . ."
"I'll be discreet."
"I doubt it."
He laughed. "But I will. It won't be the first time that I . . ."
His voice broke off abruptly, memory striking him. And remorse.
The same memory—of Gemma Gage—striking Cara. Although he
did not realize why she stiffened and seemed, without actually mov-
ing away, to withdraw from him.
"I suppose not." Her voice was hard. Her eyes too. "And have
you been to pay your respects to her yet, Daniel?"
"Who's that, Cara?"
"The widow."
"What widow?"
She saw that he had not heard the news and lowered her eyes, not
caring to read the change it might make in him, whatever it turned
out to be.
"Gemma Gage. Her husband died six months ago."
There was a silence. And then, in a quiet, neutral voice, he said,
"How does a man like that die?"
"Quickly, in his case . . ."
"A fall from a horse?"
She shook her head.
"You might think so. But no . . ." She folded her arms across her
chest as if suddenly feeling the cold. "It was his wife's fault, according
to his sister, who nearly lost her mind over it. *She* might have been
the widow—at the funeral— So they said."
"Cara?"
"Yes. They met an Irish family on the moor somewhere, trying to
get to Frizingley because they'd heard about Father Francis and that
there might be work here. Among the first who came. No soles to
their shoes, or no shoes at all. Everything they owned in a broken-
down handcart—which amounted to a couple of saucepans and half
a dozen children. You know the kind."
"I do."
"And Gemma Gage is tender-hearted. You'll know that too."
"Yes, Cara."
"So her husband ended up carrying two of the children into Frizingley. One on his back and the other—the one who turned out to
have the famine fever—in his arms. The little girl—and she'd be no

more than the size of a skinned rabbit—lived. And Tristan Gage died. They say his wife started her soup-kitchen in his memory."

And when he did not answer she waited a moment and then suddenly flung at him, "But whether she did or did not, the fact remains—doesn't it, Daniel—that she's free."

He did not go to see her at once as Cara might have expected. He did not even think it wise or right or honorable to see her at all. Merely polite. Yet eventually, about a fortnight later, at a moment when his election campaign was in full swing and he really had no time to spare, he walked up to the school-house, not intending to go inside but going in just the same past the line of paupers, not all of them Irish, waiting more or less patiently at the door where the girl pupils used to file in, and coming out, with soup and bread, at the door once reserved for the boys.

The odor would have overpowered him had he not been so thoroughly accustomed to it. Hot meat and onions. Unwashed humanity. Rags stained with excrement and sweat and vomit. Foul, very likely infected breath. And Gemma Gage standing at a long trestle table with Mrs. Ephraim Cook and several other women—not Linnet Gage, he noticed, and not Amabel Dallam—ladling soup into tin bowls.

Quietly he walked behind them, took a bowl and, without a word, began ladling himself so that he did not see either the exact moment she became aware of him, or her reaction. And when the soup was done and both doors closed, there were the vats and tureens and spoons to gather up and put away in the uncomplicated company of Mrs. Ephraim Cook and her stalwart, cheerful friends, before he could exchange a significant word with Gemma.

She had known, of course, that he was in Frizingley. The Chartist candidate again.

"Are you well, Daniel?"

"Yes. Very well."

Could he ask the same question of her, six months a widow? Hardly, when she would feel bound to declare herself desolate, whatever the true state of her heart. And since he had not the least idea as to what that state might be it seemed better and safer, more courteous even, to talk generally of the election, the famine and her splendid efforts to relieve its devastations in Frizingley.

"One does what one can," she said very politely, her hair escaping from her usually smooth chignon in untidy wisps, her forehead beaded with sweat, the voluminous cook's apron tied around her heavy mourning dress making her even smaller and sturdier than he remembered.

She took off the apron and put on her hat, a plain black widow's bonnet with a long veil and a funereal feather.

"I am at the manor again, Daniel—if you would care to call? This afternoon, perhaps, at three o'clock?"

She was by no means certain he would come but, nevertheless, she ordered tea and waited, finding waiting no hardship, a task indeed for which she had considerable aptitude and had undergone a most thorough training. Waiting and solitude. Although there was nothing specific now for which she waited and she had rarely found solitude irksome. Only once, in fact, when it had meant the absence of Daniel Carey to which she had long been accustomed, living with that absence, it had often seemed to her, more closely than she had lived with the presence of others. With Linnet, for instance, who certainly hated her. With her mother, who no longer tried to understand her. Even with Tristan, who had astonished her and then humbled her by his affection.

Two years and the half of another, during which he had tried hard not to burden her with his most surprising need, and she had tried just as hard not to be burdened by it. He had loved her in a way she had never expected and which she had done her best, in every way she could, to deserve. He had trusted her in a way she had sometimes found unnerving, although not always blindly, accepting her judgments with fond amusement at times and a certain wry shaking of the head, but accepting them nevertheless.

"If Gemma says it's all right, then it will be."

And so he had picked up those pitiful children, at her direction, and carried them easily, cheerfully, all the way to Frizingley, finding it no hardship, not even breathless when he put them down at Father Francis's door. Laughing and ruffling their lousy heads, she remembered, perfectly good-humored and relaxed even when one of them had been sick on the sleeve of his new jacket. And when Father Francis had come to tell them that the child, and many others in those foul camping places around St. Jude's, were sick with the famine fever, he had been even-tempered about that too, concerned because she was concerned, involving himself because she was involved in the collecting of money and food and blankets, pressuring the Poor Law Guardians on her behalf—since it was unseemly for a married woman to speak out for herself in public—that a fever-shed be built to supplement the single ward of the workhouse hospital where otherwise healthy pauper-women were being forced to give birth to their babies in the presence of pestilence.

Doing as *she* did, because if Gemma did it then it must be the decent thing.

The guilt of his death had never left her for a single moment. She had never seen this yellow sweating fever before, never realized that the human body—particularly so superb an example as Tristan's—could melt as quickly as candle-wax, youth and vigor and that silver-and-ivory beauty reduced overnight to burned out ashes. While, in the cesspits of St. Jude's, those human scarecrows with nothing on their bones to begin with but loose skin and sore patches, managed to cling on.

His end, the doctor told her, had been quick and merciful. Linnet had threatened to kill her for it. But Gemma had quietly accepted that, receiving the accusation of murder without comment and returning to sit at his bedside, enduring the questions in his stricken face, the blank, animal bewilderment in his eyes, while Linnet knelt sobbing in the doorway, dragged to the ground by her grief yet too afraid of his infection to come any closer. A madwoman at his funeral, clutching her hair and tearing at her mourning veil as if she'd been drowning.

Mad ever since, by fits and starts, it seemed to Gemma, bitter and wild-eyed and easily hysterical, a savagely pious church-hen at one moment muttering her prayers, a flaunting, prowling sophisticate the next: a bottle of brandy always hidden away in her bedroom, of which Gemma pretended to be unaware.

And although she hated Gemma she had no intention of leaving her, her presence a living accusation which Gemma bore for two reasons: because Tristan had loved his sister and would want her to be cared for, and because Linnet's spite, the trouble she caused, the gossip she spread seemed, to Tristan's wife, a fitting chastisement. Linnet was the hair-shirt Gemma wore in atonement for not having loved Tristan with the passion of which she knew herself to be capable, and for her part in his death. Linnet was her way of doing penance.

Linnet, of course, would know that Daniel had returned to Frizing-ley. And although she was safely occupied this afternoon with some function at the parish church she would know somehow or other that Gemma had invited him to the manor.

"I hear you had a visitor, dearest," she would murmur smiling across the dinner-table with her immense, cloying sweetness. And then, abruptly throwing down her napkin and her fork, upsetting something with a splash or a clatter, the hysteria would start, the clenched fists, the trembling, the shrill, hoarse cries. "How could you entertain that man in my brother's home? Not that it ever was *his* home—you saw to that."

The scalding tears. The chair scraped back, sometimes overturning. The flight upstairs, to the brandy bottle perhaps. And then, the next morning, the letters she had written all through the sleepless night applying for posts as governess, companion, pourer of tea from other women's china in farflung outposts of the empire. A whole bundle of them placed conspicuously on the hall table, which she would never send.

The scene had been played many times over and Gemma knew she would never respond to it. She would not even glance at those accusing envelopes turned face up to show her the addresses of colonels' wives in those remote Indian hill-stations where Linnet—it clearly implied—would prefer to be buried alive, hacked to death by rebellious natives, succumb herself to yellow fever, or just to boredom, rather than remain with the woman who had ruined her brother's life and besmirched his memory.

No. She could neither put a stop to Linnet's tantrums nor pander to them. She would simply put on the black woollen mourning dress and the widow's bonnet which, despite Miss Adeane's best endeavors, suited neither her figure nor her disposition and go to work in the soup-kitchen as she had worked every day since Tristan's funeral, gaining not only a very precise knowledge as to where meat and vegetables and pearl-barley might be bought in bulk at competitive prices—matters which had never entered her head before—but a new freedom from the demands of "polite society"; few of Frizingley's ladies caring to visit her, and certainly not wishing her to visit them, while she was so regularly exposed to contamination.

Her mother had written to her very nervously from Almsmead begging her, for the sake of the dear villagers of Far Flatley, to keep away while the epidemic lasted. Two of her maids had left her service preferring the risk of unemployment to what they believed to be the certainty of infection. Neither her cook nor her housekeeper would consent to touch the tin bowls and wooden spoons used for the daily soup ration. The tenants of the mill-cottages around the school-house where the famine victims gathered every morning had voiced horrified complaints to the mill manager, Mr. Ephraim Cook, that it was no longer safe for their children—who had been know to join the soup queue—to play in the streets. And there had been several unpleasant attempts to drive these infected paupers away by stone-throwing, jeering, and dogs.

It made no difference to Gemma. She continued to purchase her shin beef and her neck of mutton at the best prices, to order cabbages and turnips by the cart-load direct from the farm, sacks of oatmeal and barley wherever she could get it, to carry out the task in hand without apparently paying much attention to what anyone had to say about it. A little brown sparrow of a woman, she was well aware of it, beside Linnet's bereaved and sorrowing eagle, but a sparrow who held the keys, the purse-strings, the authority. A sparrow whose cage, at last, was open—she knew it too—although she did not fly away. Too soon for that. Much too soon to enjoy a freedom which had been won only through the deaths of the men who had cherished and chained her. Her father and her husband. And it would take her a while longer—if ever, she sometimes wondered?—to come to terms with that.

"A gentleman to see you, madam."

She did not ask the name. She simply nodded and, as he came into the room, was standing by the tea-table to greet him, her hair tidy now but very plainly done, parted in the middle and coiled low on her short neck, her small, square hands folded one around the other very quietly, her black mourning gown completely unadorned.

"Daniel, I am glad to see you."

Her calm voice said exactly and only what it meant. "Do please sit down."

She gave him tea which he drank hot and very sweet to store up energy, and wafers of bread and butter and chocolate cake which he ate without appetite for the same reason.

"Tell me," she said, "about Ireland." And he told her rapidly, fluently, concisely, finding it easier than talking of the past in which he still believed he had not given her her due, or the future, in which for him the pursuit of personal happiness no longer existed. She had loved him. Now she was free to love him again. But looking at her in her black widow's gown, her figure upright and resolute, her brown eyes clear and wise and steady, the idea of it seemed indecent. She had suffered and *overcome*, as he knew he had failed to do. She had learned resignation, tolerance, compassion from her pain while he had learned resentment. But he had always known her heart to be greater than his. He was not surprised.

"Now tell me about your electioneering and the progress of the Charter."

He told her that too, talking on at length, drinking more of her hot, sweet tea, while she listened, her neat head on one side, gravely weighing and measuring his opinions, giving him her whole attention while a summer fire burned low in her comfortable hearth, an unseen clock ticked away the minutes of that tranquil, solacing hour. A gift of time to span the gulf between the lovers who had parted and the man and woman who had met again. *Her* gift. He realized that. As all gifts had come from her to him, not in the other direction. A bridge for him to cross—or not—as best suited him. A double gift of consideration and freedom.

"I think," she said, "that you have been in poor health, Daniel—recently—have you not?"

Yes, indeed. He had had the same famine fever which had killed her husband, lying alone in a lodging-house behind a locked door and a boarded-up window. And he had lived. Could he tell her that?

He told her.

"How very brave you were, Daniel."

"Ah no. You're wrong there. I wasn't after saving mankind from my fever. I just didn't want to catch his on top of it. That's all."

"And you lay alone for days on end by the sound of it. Tristan only lasted a day and a night. One would hardly have thought it possible—remembering him."

And seeing how much pain that memory caused her, he said quickly, "It was so in Ireland, with the fever. Doctors and priests and good ladies like yourself, all untouched by famine, going down with it in their hundreds and never getting up again. While the poor, starving wretches they'd been looking after sometimes recovered."

"Yes." She had obviously thought it over very deeply. "It occurs to me that they may have been exposed to the infection before, in childhood, and thus acquired some kind of immunity. Whereas men like my husband . . ."

Men like Tristan. Rich in health and energy. A superb physique.

Good blood and bones and sound, clean muscle. Taking the world in his long, thoroughbred stride. He had simply looked at her in bewilderment, still trusting her, still believing, in his delirium, that she would know how to save him. And died.

"Tell me," said Daniel, seeing a fresh spurt of pain in her. "How is your mother?"

She smiled and, very gently and carefully, put the image of Tristan away.

"She is well. Indeed, she is planning to remarry—as soon as her period of mourning for Tristan is over, I think."

"I see."

"Do you?" Her voice told him that she did not think so. "She has made the acquaintance of a gentleman at Almsmead, who reminds her of my father."

"Would your father take that as a compliment?"

She smiled again, her eyes unmistakably twinkling. "Perhaps not. But he would wish to see her safe and settled, and Mr. Stevens is a most reliable man. A retired wool merchant with a very adequate income, who will never startle her or surprise her."

"You approve, then?"

"Oh—shall we say I understand. My mother married at sixteen, Daniel. It is the only life she knows. It is what she *is*—a married woman."

And widowhood, as a garment, had been many sizes too large for her, a child sadly parading in her mother's clothing with no John-William to tell her what to do next, until Mr. Dudley Stevens had begun to speak to her with his voice. And then with what magical, merciful ease—how quickly—had the telling phrase "If John-William says it's all right, then it will be" become "If Dudley says one should, then one really *ought* to . . ."

What a blessed relief to Amabel.

And to Gemma. Even though, once or twice, she had caught the faint muttering of a voice in her head which she recognized as her father's. "Well—I'll be damned. The woman didn't hide in a corner and pine away for me after all. Who would have thought it?"

"So there was really no need," said Daniel slowly, "for all that worry on your mother's behalf."

Bound feet, it seemed, could walk after all, in their fashion. Or had simply acquired the art of getting others to carry them.

"There is no disloyalty," Gemma said firmly. "To my father, I mean. If she had not been happy with him then she could hardly have wished to live the same life twice over. Even though I—or you—might think it unwise—*unjust*, even—to rely so heavily on another person—to make such a total demand—"

Tristan's voice again. *"If Gemma says it's all right, then it will be."* No, she had not wanted to inspire that degree of devotion in him, she could admit that now. But once it was there, offered to her with all his diffident charm, she had felt bound to value it, taking it from him with surprised yet reverent hands. Not the love she had wanted but love, nevertheless, the most precious of human emotions, the ultimate human treasure given to her by a man she had judged incapable of truly loving. Not the man she had wanted, either, but who had become the sweetest of her responsibilities.

And now those responsibilities were over, each one of them resolved in its separate fashion. The cage door indeed was open, yet the wings she had once felt beating with such vigor, such frustration, had become very still. Not weakened, she thought, but waiting to be very sure of their direction.

"Daniel," she said, "do you really believe that your Charter could have saved all those poor starving people?"

"I do." And it was Daniel Carey the visionary, the cold flame of his adherence plainly visible, who leaned toward her. "The vote would have saved them, Gemma. There is no doubt about it. One man one vote. Every man with at least *that* much of a voice, *that* much power to speak out about what he wants, or doesn't want, done to him. Democracy. And then those "poor starving people" would have had no need to beg for the government food depots to be opened. It would have been done as a matter of course—by right. Since what government could afford to offend so many voters? And it is rights that are needed, Gemma. Not charity. Not crumbs from the table but a right to share in the feast. Opportunity. Justice. Dignity. The Charter offers that. It gives the people the right to elect their own men to office, as the gentry have been doing forever, and the "millocracy" for a good few years now. Men who understand hunger. Not only what causes it but what it feels like. Such men will act against it."

"Men like you?"

He nodded.

"And if you are elected, Daniel—one day—will you keep your faith? Not everyone does."

"Not everyone has been hungry, Gemma. I had never been hungry myself until last winter. And now my appetite for justice is so keen that I don't expect ever to fill it . . ."

"Although you have made up your mind, I think, to spend the rest of your life trying?"

"Yes. That I have."

Like a knight dedicating himself to the service of a holy cause for which he would first make sacrifice of the luxuries to which no initiate of holy causes can feel entitled. The cumbersome, personal possessions of friendship and love and happiness, and then, quite possibly, his life.

She understood.

"Then I will help you in any way I can," she said, since what was love, after all, but the gift to the beloved of what he desired most? Even if it turned out not to be oneself.

"After all," and she was smiling now, "there is a limit to the good that serving soup can do. And I have a great deal of money, you know."

Horribly embarrassed, he dropped his eyes, unable, for a moment, to answer her. He knew she had not offered money personally to him, but the very mention of it was enough to make him uncomfortable. More wealth than he could probably imagine of which she, with her father and husband gone, was now in absolute control. Until she married again, that is, bestowing herself and her fortune with her upon another man. And it struck him most forcefully that, could he be considered even remotely as a marrying man—which he could not—her fortune would stand as an impassable barrier between them. Even if he loved her to distraction he knew he could never climb that mountain of riches and tell her so.

"I have a poor understanding of money," he said, in order to fill the silence.

"Oh, I know that, Daniel. Luckily I understand it very well. I have an inbred aversion to paying tuppence for something worth only a penny. Which is not meanness, you know. Just good business sense. So you need not fear I shall throw my substance to the winds."

No, he knew she would not do that. He knew too that she was smoothing his path again, as she had done on the day he left her, easing away his embarrassment, his awkwardness, offering him with all the free-flowing abundance of her generosity the riches, not of her bank balance, but of her friendship; since he had made no sign that he wanted her love.

"A moment will come," she said, "when perhaps just a little cash in hand could make an enormous difference. It would give me pleasure—when it does—if you would apply to me ..."

"Gemma ..."

"*Apply* to me," she said firmly. "Although of course I may find your application wanting."

"Very likely."

"In which case I shall reject it."

He did not think so.

She stood up and gave him her hand, signifying, he supposed, that the conversation was at an end.

"Daniel, you must not deny me my right to be of service, you know. You would take it very much amiss if I tried to deny you yours. And when the Charter comes to pass, you must also bear in mind that my right to speak out and be heard—my right to a share in that democratic feast—will be every bit as valuable as yours. I may be a woman, and of the 'despised millocracy' at that. But if we are to have justice and dignity and opportunity then it must be for *all* the people. For me and mine, as well as for you."

He could not argue with that.

Needing to make a gesture he bent his head over her hand and kissed it, only briefly, the contact disturbing him in a manner far too complex to be desire. Or even close to it. The best woman in the world. She was still that. But her world was not his and the bridge she had offered him seemed very fragile beneath his feet.

For he was booted and spurred now, a soldier, a crusader, marching on stones to battle. How could the gentle pathway of her good intentions bear the angry weight of him?

"The world has become divided for you, Daniel, hasn't it," she said, "between those who have been hungry and those who have not?"

But there was hunger of another kind. She saw, with love and sorrow, how completely he had forgotten that.

The Charter, then. Nothing else would save the Irish peasant from famine or the English laborer from exploitation in mill and mine. Nothing else would free Ireland from England's yoke and England herself from the remote grandees of the "ruling class" that governed her. It was the quickest and surest way to the human dignities of education and opportunity, a breaking down of barriers so that men of all classes might come together to use the gifts they had been given. A new society where what counted would be a man's integrity, what he had in his heart and his head rather than in his pocket. The Charter. The Vote. Freedom and Justice for all through the Ballot Box with which no grandee of any persuasion would have the power to tamper.

It would be the salvation of the world.

Ernest Jones, the Chartist poet and a godson of the Duke of Cumberland, thundered out the message from the hustings at Halifax, winning a show of thousands of eager, voteless hands and, from an electorate—in that thriving town of several hundred thousand—of little more than a thousand men, an actual and decidedly disturbing vote of 279. The Chartist candidate polled 220 at Derby. Daniel Carey, despite everything Ben Braithwaite and Christie Goldsborough could do to prevent it, walked away from Frizingley's hustings with a defiant vote of 205. Feargus O'Connor, the Chartist leader, was *elected* at Nottingham.

Elected. Had the world gone mad? Lady Lark, that ancestral Tory, and Lizzie Braithwaite, ardent champion of the Whigs, wondered both together over a pot of china tea and the summer fashion plates so obligingly offered by Miss Adeane.

Nottingham? wondered Miss Adeane herself. Had Luke Thackray been there at the hustings, raising his hand for Feargus O'Connor, letting the whole world see where he stood, and why? She supposed so. She had not heard from him. Nor had she inquired. Although the absence of news took nothing away from the vividness with which she remembered him, the sense of warmth and comfort his distant presence still gave her. She could not think or act as he did, could not conduct her life even remotely as he conducted his own. But that did not stop her from being proud of him. Yes—*proud*. So long as Luke was there, in Nottingham—which might just as well have been Timbuctoo—she knew *something* was right with the world.

"May I give you another cup of tea, Lady Lark? Mrs. Braithwaite?" she murmured, thinking, beneath her smiling sweetness, that if it should choke them and they fell dead at her feet she would not turn a hair. Provided they had first settled their bills.

The Charter, then. A bad joke in some quarters. A golden promise in others. A growing menace, perhaps?—wondered Larks and Braithwaites—not serious enough to lose sleep over but which one might be well advised to nip in the bud. After all, in Frizingley alone two hundred and five men with enough money in the bank to place them on the electoral register had voted for it. Misguided souls, of course. Intellectuals and journalists, a doctor or two, a renegade clergyman, a few wild young men who had probably done it to annoy their fathers.

Not Mr. Ephraim Cook, need it be said, the Dallam mill manager who, whatever the persuasion of that odd creature the Dallam daughter, had remained firmly within the Whig fold. Although he had had no objection to attending the dinner-party to celebrate those shocking two hundred and five votes, given by Mrs. Gemma Gage who, since she became a widow, seemed thoroughly to be losing her always somewhat peculiar head.

A very lavish dinner too, one heard. *Not*, as the victorious Whig candidate had suggested, a variation on the good lady's Irish souptureens, but quite a gala occasion with the Chartist candidate dressed up like a gentleman and making a damned impudent speech about how—considering that show of hands in his favor at the hustings—he believed himself to be Frizingley's true representative and meant to act accordingly. An easy enough matter nowadays with those trains steaming into Frizingley morning, noon and night, so that he could spend as much time in his "constituency"—the sheer audacity of the man!—as he liked.

If he could raise the money for the fare, that is; which, when one thought of Gemma Gage's weak head, seemed far more than likely.

John-William Dallam would turn over in his grave if he got the slightest whiff of it. No one had the least doubt of that. And one of the subjects much discussed that summer, in the comfortable elegance of Miss Adeane's pale blue salon, over the tea and biscuits and magazines, was the unfortunate position of Miss Linnet Gage. The poor, dear creature. One felt so sorry for her. And losing her looks too, thought Mrs. Magda Braithwaite although her husband, Benjamin—it was shrewdly observed—did not exactly rush to agree with her. Thin nowadays—dear Linnet—rather than "spiritual" and delicate. Her profile still quite appealing as she knelt by the mellow stained-glass window of the parish church where she went every morning to pray, but gaunt in full sunlight. Magda, despite her "great fondness" for Linnet, could think of no kinder word for it. And with no gentleman hovering around her now that Frizingley's marriage market had acquired *two* rich widows to play for. Fickle Mrs. Moon and foolish Mrs. Gage leaving no one for Linnet but the vicar and Captain Goldsborough who would usually come to her rescue at the few social occasions she now attended.

And while nothing could be expected of the vicar—a natural celibate, said Mrs. Marie Moon, whose judgment could be trusted on such matters—Captain Goldsborough *had* become outwardly more respectable since moving into that splendid suite of rooms at the station hotel, the preferential treatment he received there surely reflecting the number and value of his railway shares. A woman of Linnet's high pedigree and excellent breeding might be just what he needed to get back into decent society again. Although Marie Moon did not think so.

"Why do you bother with that Gage woman?" Cara asked him, irritated by the gossip which had been aired, rather deliberately she thought, in her hearing, not a few of her customers having caught glimpses of her by now with Christie in theaters and hotel lounges and reserved compartments on the London train.

"Could this be jealousy?" he inquired.

"Should it be?"

"Cara, you have developed a most annoying habit of answering one question with another. I can't think where you have learned it."

"From you, Christie. Where else. But what about Linnet Gage?"

"She interests me."

Another living chess piece? Another specimen?

"The woman is as tart as a green lemon," Cara said flatly.

"So she is." He sounded perfectly pleased to agree with her. "But that is only an excess of virginity, you know. Quite enough to turn any woman sour."

"And are you thinking of relieving her of it?"

"Oh—hardly. Ben Braithwaite seems more inclined to do that. Which is why his wife so positively dislikes her."

"Yes, I do know that, Christie."

"Then you may also know that Linnet Gage is only interested in marriage? In her view it is the only career open to a woman of her birth and breeding. It follows, therefore, that successful women must, first and foremost, be married women. And since she is clever and ambitious—as you are—she does not enjoy regarding herself as a failure. Perhaps she would have done better to open a shop."

"I hope you are encouraging her to do no such thing."

"My dear—she would be scandalized at the very suggestion." He appeared somewhat shocked, although much amused, by it himself. "A lady does not involve herself in *trade*—you should know that. She may serve soup for charity but she certainly does not *sell* it. A lady exists to adorn her husband's home and provide him with a social life designed to promote his interests. Something Linnet Gage would do with the skill and ruthlessness of a cabinet minister. As it is— without a husband—all she can do, without losing caste, is to arrange flowers in the church. And as for the gossip linking her with me, one should discount it. Only think of the scandalous things they are saying about Mrs. Gage and your Chartist friend. Do you think it can be true?"

That Daniel and Gemma were lovers again? She was by no means certain. But . . . "I expect so," she said. It seemed safer.

"Have you seen anything of him yourself, Cara?" And although his voice seemed pleasant enough, making no more than a *chance* remark in passing, her nerves drew themselves smoothly to attention nevertheless, warning her that he would already know the answer.

"Yes. He comes collecting for the famine every now and then."

"What do you give him?"

"Money, Christie."

"Yes?"

"Yes—what?" Very much against her will, and having, in fact, done nothing to which he could really object, she was suddenly defending herself. "He visits all the Irish—Father Francis sends him—"

"*All* the Irish?"

A simple question spoken without heat or anger, yet transformed by the black art of his mockery into a challenge. But a challenge to what? It did not really matter. He had not even troubled to accuse her. Her guilt was assumed. He had already tumbled her into hot water and was concerned now only to watch her sink or swim. It was a game they often played.

"Yes. O'Halloran at the livery stables. The widow Cunningham. Myself. Ned O'Mara at the Fleece..."

"Alas no. Poor Ned is no longer with us at the Fleece."

"Oh—?" Could she use this to distract him. "Why not? Where has he gone?"

"My dear—" he gave her the familiar look of surprise she often saw in Lady Lark when presented with her millinery bills. "Where *is* it that ageing and very drunken prizefighters go when they have quite outlived their usefulness and lose what one is bound to consider their very last chance of employment? Do tell me if you know, for I have not the least idea?"

"You turned him off, then?"

"I? No—no. I simply bowed to Oliver Rattrie's judgment in the matter."

"You did *what?*"

"Of course. If one places a man in a managerial position one must allow him to manage. And poor Ned could not meet Oliver's standards, it seems..."

"You mean he couldn't work with the little rat from St. Jude's you'd set up to lord it over him..."

He clicked his tongue. "Cara—my dear—must you speak so scathingly of Oliver? I find him enormously improved. And you and he have much in common. Considering his background one could even call him as great a success in his way as you are in yours. And I have a marked partiality, I confess, for hungry fighters."

"Because you've never been hungry yourself."

"There is hunger," he said, reaching out for her, "and hunger—my dear."

And in most ways, on most occasions, she believed she satisfied his appetite. Only a pawn in the games he played, she knew that, although it pleased him to dress her as a queen for his own pleasure and the pleasure of seeing other men dazzled and tempted when he chose to display her like a collector's item of sculpture, it seemed to her, or a thoroughbred horse. He had polished and faceted her like a diamond so that in the hotels and restaurants and the luxurious houses of friends—like Marie Moon—where he spent his life, she could be brilliant, could sparkle, entertain, decorate, could arouse desire which he—when it had amused him long enough—would cynically frustrate.

She was his woman. He was not her man. He took what he desired from her as and when he wanted it. She made no claims on him whatsoever, asked him no questions—knowing full well she would get no answers even if she did—took what he gave her and watched his moods carefully to assess the right moment for obtaining more. When he wanted her to be happy then she smiled. It was much easier. When he wanted the thunder and lightning of her temper then he would stimulate it. That was easy too. When he wanted her desire he had only, these days, to put his hands upon her, sometimes only to look at her with a certain narrowing of his eyes, to set the pulses of her sensuality obediently pounding.

And whenever it happened that she, herself, experienced a moment of personal triumph or exhilaration, whenever her heart was full—if only briefly—of the mischief that came from some score being settled, some customer won or wooed back into her fold, some stray beam of sunlight crossing her life, she had learned to curb her natural instinct to throw her arms around him—if he happened to be nearby—or make any other gesture of spontaneous warmth or camaraderie. She had learned, in fact—except in his bed—not to be familiar.

Yet the dinners and receptions to which he escorted her, the parties held almost continuously by Marie Moon to celebrate the miracle of her husband's demise, the trips to London and the country homes of rackety, racing peers who were his friends, were by no means distasteful to her. She had spent too much of her life enviously watching other women stepping down from their carriages not to enjoy the landau she herself now kept at O'Halloran's livery stable, not to glory in the elaborate satin dresses she now had the leisure to design for herself, in the gold bracelets on her arms, the pearls in her ears, the lace gloves on her manicured hands. A certain dryness, a well-hidden but rather hollow space somewhere inside her giving her no more trouble, she supposed, than it gave to Magda Braithwaite. Considerably less than to Linnet Gage.

She did not care to dwell too deeply on Gemma Dallam.

"So he comes collecting for the famine," murmured Christie. "Very commendable. Although it is almost over, they tell me. This year's potato has decided not to blacken, I hear, and one expects it will be adequate. Particularly now that the landlords have so obligingly thinned out the population by shipping it off—well—wherever it could manage to land. One might succeed in feeding the rest with the Indian Corn they are suddenly sending in. I have some land in Ireland myself. Did you know that? An inheritance from my grandfather, General Covington-Pym."

She was not surprised.

"And what have you done with your tenants, Christie?"

"My dear—" once again the blank look of surprise. "I have not the least notion. My agent there does very much as he pleases. And who am I to complain, so long as he sends me the agreed amount of rent. I have never set foot on the place myself."

She did not ask him if he had taken his rents for this year, and last. She did not want to know.

"So your Chartist friend will not be coming to see you again, will he, Cara, with the famine officially over and the Queen planning a state visit to Dublin to tell them so?"

She shrugged. "Why should he? He lost the election so he'll be going back to London, I suppose—or, wherever."

"Away from Mrs. Gage? Do you think so?"

"Yes, I do."

She meant it, for Daniel would not change his course now for any woman. He would walk his own way alone, until that cold flame had burned itself out in him, or consumed him. She could see that. Could Gemma Gage? Yet Daniel made several visits to Frizingley that autumn and winter, coming, he still declared, as the true representative of the working people, which amounted, after all, to ninety percent of Frizingley. And he was dining at the Ephraim Cooks with Gemma one night the following February when the news arrived of revolution in France.

Not the first, of course, and not in France alone this time either. Although no one doubted that the revolutionary French, with their great liking for turning out their kings, had triggered it off. Beginning when the French king Louis Philippe found himself running from the Paris mob without his wig—remembering, no doubt, another King Louis, not too long ago, who had lost not only his wig but his head—

and spreading with the terrifying rapidity of a spark among dry trees to similar uprisings in Austria, Hanover, Naples, Schleswig Holstein, Prussia. A whirlwind of revolt sweeping across the whole continent of Europe, against established monarchs and dukes and generals, which only Belgium and Russia, and England so far, resisted.

In Paris a new republic was proclaimed, King Louis Philippe taking refuge with that natural patron of dispossessed royalty, Queen Victoria. Would the Habsburgs fall too? It seemed likely. And the families of Hesse and Saxe-Coburg-Gotha, and Romanov with them? There were many in England who hoped so. And what of the socialist and nationalist groups in Hungary, Poland, Italy, where voices had been crying out a long time now against oppression? Would they not take this opportunity to rise, each nation against its own brand of tyranny? What of mutilated Ireland, seething like a cauldron about to spill over? What of the Charter?

Where France had led could not England follow?

The young men of Halifax certainly thought so as they marched in military formation up and down their town, openly and volubly declaring their support and whole-hearted admiration for the republican French who had overcome their enemies and established—forever, it was hoped—the power of the people.

The Chartists of Bradford—that most hot-headed and belligerent of cities—met *en masse* on Peep Green to pay homage to the revolutionary enterprise of their brothers across the Channel; among some discreet speculation as to the expected increase in the price of pikes turned out by the local blacksmith, and much singing of Chartist hymns and the Marseillaise.

In Frizingley Daniel Carey was carried shoulder-high from a torch-lit meeting on Frizingley Moor, above St. Jude's, where he had informed a crowd of grimly exultant men—quite enough of them to trouble Ben Braithwaite's peace of mind—that the time was *now. Now.* For Justice and Democracy. For the Vote. So that no man need ever go hungry again. The Charter.

In Manchester the Chartist MP for Nottingham, Feargus O'Connor, asked a crowd of thirteen thousand men to swear to him, individually, hand on heart, never to abandon the cause of the Charter until it had been won. They swore.

It was the same everywhere. Hope and excitement, as there had been in '38 and '42. Vows. Dedication. The singing of hymns and anthems by crowds that seemed to rise from the ground like dragons' teeth. The collection of signatures for a new petition to be presented to parliament that April. A petition this time which would be too enormous to be ignored. The familiar tactics of the "moral force" wing of the movement. Victory through education, persuasion, rational argument. And, in their background, the "physical force" men polishing their home-made pikes again, oiling their guns, drilling on remote moorland all over the Industrial North on moonlit nights, no matter what their "moral force" brothers might have to say about it.

The Charter. It would now not merely have to be nipped in the bud but stamped on, hard and quick. Both Braithwaites and Larks were at one on that. So was Her Majesty's Government. So was the Duke of Wellington when he fortified London that April against the invading Northern hordes, coming to present their petition to Parliament and vowing, if it should not be listened to, to declare a Republic of Lancashire and Yorkshire instead.

There were five million signatures, one heard, on that petition and a quarter of a million men to carry it in procession from Kennington Common to Westminster. Angry men, one assumed, who knew what had happened in France and who, by sheer weight of numbers,—and despite the restraint of their "moral force" brothers—might easily overtip the scales of revolution in England.

Short-sighted, thought Ben Braithwaite, General Covington-Pym, the Duke of Wellington, to deny it. Might Buckingham Palace itself fall to their republican fervor as the Tuileries Palace had fallen to the Paris mob, with Victoria gathering up her skirts and her children and running for her life as poor old Louis Philippe had had to do? The Duke of Wellington—conqueror of Napoleon—declared he did not think so but sent the Queen and her family to the Isle of Wight just the same, out of harm's way. Troops, in large numbers, were drafted into the city, 200,000 special constables issued with batons and hastily enrolled. London's bridges and her public buildings were fortified. Noble gentlemen, with houses in town, had brought up the game-keepers from their country estates, the windows of Belgravia's mansions sprouting a wicked crop of sporting guns.

The time was now.

Feargus O'Connor would march across Westminster Bridge at the head of 200,000 loyal men—one to match every special constable the Duke had enrolled—and lay the Charter at Mother Parliament's feet. A triumph for "moral force." A peaceful and bloodless *coup d'état*, if *coup d'état* there would have to be, O'Connor having requested his quarter of a million soldiers to come unarmed.

Daniel Carey went off with the Frizingley contingent as to a pilgrimage. Would Luke Thackray make the journey from Nottingham, Cara wondered? Another pilgrim? Although one, it seemed to her, who would neither burn so fiercely nor break so easily as Daniel. Who would not rush headlong into the battle as Daniel would do—very likely without a weapon—but whose carefully husbanded strength would be far more likely to last the day.

For how taut and fine-drawn Daniel had become, paying no regard to safety. Or survival. Quickly she closed her mind to that. Damn him, the hot-headed, light-minded fool. Had he even thought to take food and money, or wondered about what to do if it did not succeed? Where to take refuge, and how to get there?

But perhaps Gemma Gage had taken care of that.

"I wonder," said Christie, spending the day which was already being spoken of as the Revolutionary Tenth, very much at his ease, drinking champagne in his new, overheated apartment with Cara.

"What do you wonder?" She was not feeling her best.

"About those 200,000 men."

"What about them?"

Two of them were giving her considerably more than enough to wonder and worry about.

"Oh—simply whether Feargus O'Connor has made suitable arrangements to get them all there."

"To London?"

"Well, not precisely. To Kennington Common where they were all to have assembled at some unearthly hour this morning. *I* know where it is. So does Feargus O'Connor. As a politician and a journalist he is more than accustomed to finding his way to all kinds of places. I wonder if one can say the same for his 200,000 men? I wonder, in fact, if there are those among them who, having made firm promises to attend, now realize that they cannot raise the train fare? They will not all have had shepherds to lead them, you know, like the men of Frizingley. And none of those special constables we have heard about will be likely to give them directions. In O'Connor's place I would have taken care of that."

"I believe you."

He bowed his head slightly.

"One can only hope he has had the sense to think of it. The Duke of Wellington will be far from pleased if he has called out all those troops for nothing."

She had hardly thought beyond her anxiety for the two individuals who mattered to her, seeing Luke and Daniel and the dangers which might befall them—which almost certainly *would* in Daniel's case—rather than the upheaval which might touch them all. But now, darting a rapid glance at Christie, taking in the value of his cambric shirt and striped satin waistcoat, the glass of vintage wine in his hand, his nonchalance, his arrogance, she said, "What if it succeeds, Christie? What if there really is a revolution? I mean a real one, like they've had in France? What would happen to you then?"

"To me?" He smiled at her and raised his glass. "What would happen to *you*, Cara?"

"Nothing," she said decisively. "Why should it? I'll start making bonnets in Chartist green, that's all. I'll survive."

And if anybody threw stones at her windows, Chartist or not, she'd make short work of them.

"Exactly," he said. "So will I. Survive, I mean."

"Do you think so?"

"Oh yes."

"They had guillotines in France, you know—not too far back."

"One doesn't forget it. I imagine a great many of one's friends are remembering it very clearly today. And yes—if they set up a guillotine in Market Square—not *too* near your shop windows, of course—then I suppose we might expect to see Ben Braithwaite in the tumbrils. And Uriah Colclough. And my cousin Grizelda Lark. Not our good Mrs. Gage, though, since she would have a member of the Revolutionary Committee or whatever they chose to call themselves, to protect her. So would I."

"To protect *you*? Who, for Heaven's sake?"

"I have no idea. Somebody who would find my services sufficiently useful to keep me alive. And in good health. It is rarely the idealists who profit from revolution. In fact hardly ever at all. The Feargus O'Connors—and Daniel Careys—may be good at toppling thrones. But there is always a new crop of kings waiting nearby, you know."

"So you would turn Chartist?"

"Of course."

"I don't think anybody would believe you."

"Why not? I have been a Whig *and* a Tory for years already. And newborn regimes need experienced men. I could probably make a sizeable fortune out of this revolution, Cara. If it happened."

"But you don't think it will?"

Leaning forward he refilled her glass.

"I think there is not the slightest chance of it."

Was he inviting her to drink a toast to that? To Luke's defeat? And Daniel's? And could Daniel bear it? Luke yes. But Daniel?

"Why?" she said.

"Oh—for one thing the English are not natural revolutionaries. Far too reasonable and good-humored. And for another thing the times are changing. We have police forces now, all over the country, which were not there during that last spot of bother, six years ago, when they unplugged Ben Braithwaite's factory boiler. We have the electric telegraph to let the government know where troops are needed, and trains to put them in and get them on the spot quickly and in very large numbers. And Feargus O'Connor knows that troops *will* be brought in and that they *will* fire on the people. It happened, very recently, in Glasgow. Some trouble about the Poor Law. At least half a dozen killed that one knows of. Not counting the wounded who dragged themselves away and may well have died since. A little demonstration that Feargus O'Connor will not have forgotten."

She shivered.

"And the sentences of transportation imposed on the ringleaders were very harsh," he went calmly on. "The ringleaders being, of course, anyone they could catch. Some poor devil no one had ever heard of, that is, and about whom no one is likely to make a fuss. To discourage the rest."

Had it discouraged them? Not Daniel. Nor Luke either she imagined. But how many others?

"Poor devils?" she said. "Do you feel sorry for them, then?"

"What I feel, Cara, is a determination never to find myself in their position. Possibly you feel that too?"

Possibly. For what thought had she ever given to the ballot box? What need did she have of such things to get her way? Believing in nothing but herself and therefore suffering no disillusion. But not Daniel.

"What will happen then, Christie?" She assumed that he would know.

"Probably very little," he said. "Feargus O'Connor wishes to make a peaceful show of numbers. I doubt he will get those numbers. The 'physical force' men will keep away because he has forbidden the carrying of weapons. The affair does not promise to be rough enough for them. Some of the 'moral force' men will keep away in case it might be too rough. Which, of course, it might, since London is bristling with guns and soldiers. The rest will not make anything like 200,000. It is illegal, in any case, for more than twenty people to present a petition to the House of Commons. O'Connor is an elected member of that House and must be well aware of it. And when he sees what a poor following he has actually mustered I hardly think he will risk breaking the law. A quarter of a million men marching to Westminster might be impressive. A tenth of that number would raise little more than a laugh. The best thing to do would be to send them all home again—and hope they get there."

"And then?"

"The end of O'Connor, I rather imagine. Which would leave the field to the 'physical force' men. And that, my dear, should effectively finish Chartism off. All our soldiers and police and trains and the fact that they have almost no support among the governing classes makes it impossible for them to succeed. So you may sleep easy in your bed tonight, Cara. Or mine."

She slept hardly at all, being as anxious for news the next morning as everybody else although, standing in her pale blue and gold shop wreathed in her welcoming smiles, she could not allow herself the luxury of either laughter or tears when it began to come in.

After all, what could the Charter matter to her? Feathered bonnets and embroidered chiffons were her trade, the adornment of woman, not the rights of man, and Magda Braithwaite would certainly not forgive a moment's inattention to the fitting of her new poppy-colored silk mousseline for the sake of these Chartist tramps who had been abandoned, left in the lurch, to fend for themselves without a penny in their pockets—hoped Mrs. Braithwaite—who may well have passed an uneasy night dreaming of that guillotine in Market Square.

But what a dismal fiasco it had turned out to be, declared Miss Adeane's ladies that afternoon, sharing scraps of information as they nibbled their wafers of lemon cake and sipped their china tea. Two hundred thousand men indeed! Twenty thousand seemed nearer the mark, from what one could gather. As for those five million signatures, how many of them were forgeries? How many Chartists could even write their names, if it came to that? And it was being strongly rumored now that all sorts of impossible names had been seen on that petition, including Napoleon Bonaparte and the Duke of Wellington, seventeen times.

Cara experienced some difficulty in smiling at that.

And there had been no grand procession, of course. No march, with banners and anthems, across Westminster Bridge. The police had simply taken Feargus O'Connor aside and, perhaps even to their surprise, that ageing warrior who had been breathing fire and brimstone down everybody's neck for years, had given in, agreed to abandon his procession and deliver the petition to parliament in a cab. Which he had done, or rather in four cabs, the petition itself with those five million signatures, taking up four of them, Mr. O'Connor himself riding tamely behind. To avoid bloodshed, he'd said. And where was the petition now, if not shut away in some archive somewhere, where it could just get on with the only thing it was fit for—gathering dust?

Cara did not find that any too amusing either.

Three London trains came into Frizingley that day and, unobtrusively, Cara sent her youngest apprentice to meet each one, a sensible girl with a Chartist father who might be supposed to have reasons of her own for haunting the station. No one came. And that evening, when the shop was closed, she walked over to the station herself, no great distance, just taking the air should anyone inquire, which no one would, she supposed, Christie having gone off to celebrate the collapse of Chartism at the Braithwaites.

She was free, then, to wait and worry, standing in the cobbled yard pressed close to the wall, a shadow in her dark cloak among shadows, her ears straining for the sound of an engine, her body dry and hot with its tight anxiety. If Daniel came she had no idea what she would say to him or what help he would allow her to offer. She simply knew that he would need help of some kind, from somebody. And she was here. She cared not a fig herself for his People's Charter. But she knew how ardently Daniel himself had believed in it, knew how that cold flame of faith had gutted him, jealously absorbing him and permitting space for nothing inside him but itself. How then must he be feeling now? As she would have felt, she imagined, if, on the same day her mother and Liam had left her, she had returned from Liverpool to find her shop and all her stock in ashes, her customers already on their way to resurrect Miss Ernestine Baker.

And she was stronger, far stronger and always had been, than Daniel.

The train arrived, almost empty, most of its passengers having got down at Leeds. Nevertheless... But no. Only two thick-set commercial gentlemen, another in a clerical collar, night-travelers emerging, all strangers, from the gloom, heavy but rapid footsteps on the cobbles, a voice inquiring for a cab, the slamming of unseen doors as the train prepared to move away.

She waited a moment longer, counting the seconds it would take him to walk along the platform, pause to fasten a shoe-strap perhaps or anything else which might conceivably delay him, and then, when all those seconds had run away, stepped briskly, irritably from the shadow to find herself face to face with Gemma Gage.

A shock to both, since both had been standing breathless and motionless, believing themselves alone and invisible because that was how they had wished to be. Yet now, with an acre of dark, wet cobbles and empty railway track around them, it would have been ridiculous and highly suspicious just to nod and smile.

"Good evening, Miss Adeane. Have you come to meet the train?"

But that too was ridiculous.

"You will have friends, of course," said Gemma quietly, "among the Chartists."

"Yes. So I have." Dare she mention Daniel's name? Perhaps not.

"Mr. Daniel Carey," said Gemma softly, not even asking a question.

"Yes." Pointless to deny it. Yet, just the same, since Mrs. Gage *could* do her harm if she so desired, she added quickly, "We have been acquainted for a long time—as members of the Irish community here..."

Through the dark, Gemma smiled. "Yes. I believe you met on the crossing from Ireland eight or nine years ago."

"We did." And even then she had told him he was born to be hanged. Inwardly and violently, although it made no ripple on her polished surface, she shivered. "But it seems we will not be meeting him tonight."

"No. I think not. Miss Adeane, my carriage is over there. Allow me to drive you home."

"You are very kind, Mrs. Gage, but it is just across the square..."

"I am aware of that." Gemma's voice wondered why the distance should be important. "Nevertheless, it is late, and rather chilly. Please do get in."

The note of authority was quiet, but very evident. And Cara found herself in the Gage carriage, allowing the Gage coachman to place a cashmere rug over her knees, wondering, as she took the soft material between expert fingers, how much it cost and if it might do well, this coming winter, in the shop.

"Miss Adeane," Gemma was speaking calmly but with purpose. "We have assumed Mr. Carey to be coming from London directly into Leeds. However, if he had found it expedient to make a detour—to Brighouse, perhaps? What do you think he would do then?"

"He would walk over the moor, Mrs. Gage."

"Yes. Do you, by any chance, know the way he would be likely to take, Miss Adeane?"

Of course she did. She had taken it herself, many a time, in the old days when the only way to get wherever she wished to go, or *had* to go, had been on foot.

"Across country," she said, "and rough country. Impossible in a carriage."

"Might he be visible from the road?"

All too clearly Mrs. Gage had never walked on the moor at night, thought Cara, shaking her head. "No. It is as black as pitch out there. And treacherous. Like being in the middle of the ocean."

But Mrs. Gage had never been to sea, either.

"Would he notice a passing carriage, do you think?"

"He'd hear it. But they all sound alike, Mrs. Gage."

"Even if one stopped occasionally," said Gemma quietly, "and got down—with a lantern—to identify oneself?"

"Mrs. Gage—I don't think you should do that."

"Why not?"

Good Heavens, where had the woman been all her life? Did the world really seem so safe and one's own person so inviolable from the shelter of those close-carpeted drawing-rooms, these cashmere traveling rugs?

"Because if you start making signals with a lamp you don't know who might answer them. The moor might look empty but it's got bolt-holes all over it where men hide or dig themselves in. Hungry men still on the tramp because of the famine who aren't fussy what they do now, since they've got nothing to lose. And not all the Chartists are really Chartists, Mrs. Gage. Some of them just like causing trouble. And there are one or two ale-houses up there that are—Well, dens of thieves and dens of iniquity. If somebody dragged you into a place like that I don't know how you'd get out again."

And Daniel was probably safe and sound somewhere in London. Probably not. She shivered again.

"It's far too dangerous for you, Mrs. Gage."

The carriage came to a halt outside her shop.

"Yes. You are quite right," said Gemma. "And even if one took the risk, and he happened to be there, one would be unlikely to find him. I must agree."

What more was there to say? Cara did not, in fact, intend to say any more, yet her voice, speaking alone it seemed, asked the question nevertheless. "How much danger do you think he is in, Mrs. Gage?"

Not from moorland tramps and bandits. Surely even Mrs. Gage must realize that he was accustomed to that? But from the fear he had aroused in men like Mrs. Gage's own father and husband, whose vested interests he had appeared to threaten.

"It will have to be stamped out." She had come near to screaming from listening to Mrs. Braithwaite and Lady Lark saying that. "And now—at once—before it spreads, as it did in France."

Neither of those two good ladies had slept easily in their beds this last night or two because of men like Daniel. Obviously such men would have to pay.

"I don't know," said Gemma, her eyes on the far distance. "I was invited, this evening, to dine with Ben and Magda Braithwaite, who are behaving very much as if some kind of Bastille has been prevented from falling. My sister-in-law has gone to celebrate with them and called me naïve when I insisted that no guillotines and tumbrils and revolutionary tribunals had ever been intended. Not by any responsible Chartist, that is. But Linnet finds it more amusing to believe that my father's workers were all hovering around our gate waiting the signal to snatch our jewels and strip the clothes from our backs. A great many others seem to have been genuinely afraid of it. And while Ben Braithwaite—and the Duke of Wellington—may not have been *too* bothered about their jewelry they neither of them like the idea of one man one vote. That is the very last thing they would care to encourage. I suppose, therefore—yes. There is danger. They have managed to ridicule the Charter. So now, while people are still laughing, I expect they will do their best to crush it. Without too much fuss, perhaps, so that by the time people begin to reconsider, it will be gone."

"How?"

She made a small and yet still purposeful gesture with her carefully gloved hands.

"Earlier this month a bill was rushed through parliament—a 'gagging act' they call it—increasing the penalties for the making of 'seditious speeches.' A crime of which we have all been guilty, from time to time, I should think. Or *could* be guilty if someone particularly wanted us to be. And every Chartist who has ever opened his mouth in public could certainly be accused of it—if one wished to do so. I imagine it will be found convenient now to make those accusations."

"You mean they will be rounded up," said Cara flatly, "and sent to jail."

"I do."

Could the fine, steel thread in Daniel survive that, she wondered, without snapping? Not that she would let it happen. America, she thought. Let her father come in useful for once. If she could get Daniel on a ship then her father could arrange his reception in New York. He owed her that much. She would see to it now that he paid.

"Good night, Miss Adeane."

"Good night, Mrs. Gage. Thank you for bringing me home."

"My pleasure, Miss Adeane. I must be off now, to mine."

But as Cara stood in the shop doorway taking out her keys the carriage turned quite sharply in the empty street going off at speed not in the direction of Mrs. Gage's comfortable home but out of Market Square to St. Jude's hill and beyond it.

Cara had already planned his escape to America. But Gemma Gage had gone, with her bound feet, to fetch him in from the dark.

She did not find him, of course. Cara, haunted all through the night by dreams of Mrs. Gage making signals with her lantern on the moorland road which were answered by every nightmare species of man and beast, went herself the next morning to the manor to check on her safety, inventing a quick excuse of orders for gray and lilac half-mourning dresses when Linnet Gage came into the drawing-room.

But, although Mrs. Gage was safe enough, having encountered nothing more alarming than a rabbit, Daniel had not been there. Nor did he come the next day, or the day after. Or a week, or a month after that.

If only, prayed Cara, he would have the good sense to lie low and keep *quiet*. But now that the petition, the "moral force" tactics of peaceful persuasion had once again failed so lamentably, so tragically and comically, the "physical force" pikemen were out again, marching with green rosettes and green banners flying through the streets of Manchester, Nottingham, Halifax, Leeds, rebellious Bradford where a Chartist mob fought, with sticks and stones and desperation, against the drawn cutlasses of a squadron of dragoons who cleared the streets more effectively—one heard—except for the wounded.

It was the same everywhere. Arrests of Chartist leaders leading to riots, leading to jubilant rescues of those arrested, which led, in turn, to drawn swords, soldiers on horseback, guns. And the same arrests all over again.

In May the Irish Chartist John Mitchel was sentenced to transportation on a convict ship to Australia, his harsh treatment giving rise not to a scuttling for cover—as Cara thought it should have done—but to a new boldness, a new surge of protest, the flinging down of new challenges by men, in her opinion, who were in no position to pick them up again.

Ernest Jones, the Chartist candidate for Halifax, was arrested in June on the charge of making seditious speeches, his arrest resulting in a firm and exceedingly blunt-spoken declaration from the town of Halifax that should the same sentence of transportation be passed upon him as had been passed on John Mitchel, then the government might expect to see riot indeed. And of a most blood-curdling variety. Her Majesty's Government could take the collective word of Halifax for that.

To which the said government replied by sending for trial a further three hundred men, most of them on that convenient charge of seditious speeches which, in the opinion of Bradford and Halifax, Leeds and Frizingley, meant no more and no less than speaking one's mind.

And then, late one summer afternoon, an Irish beggar child somehow "got in" through Cara's front door, causing as much consternation among the pale blue and gold chairs where Magda Braithwaite and Maria Colclough and Linnet Gage were taking tea as if a whole family of mice had suddenly run loose around their feet.

"Good Heavens—Miss *Adeane*," Magda Braithwaite, who did not like children since she had proved unable to have any of her own, raised a wisp of scented cambric to her nose, thinking quite visibly of things she could certainly never bring herself to mention, like fleas, and scabies, and the plague.

"That child," declared Mrs. Colclough accusingly, obviously holding "the child" entirely to blame for it, "is not wearing shoes, and her skirt is so short and in such rags and tatters that—well—she is showing her knees."

"How shocking," said Linnet Gage in her amused treble. "What can she want, I wonder?"

"Miss Adeane, do give her some money," moaned Magda Braithwaite feebly, her nerves not having quite recovered from the specter of that Chartist guillotine, "and send her away. Ought she to be allowed in the center of town in any case? I must speak to my husband about it."

"Oh *do*," murmured Linnet. "Mr. Braithwaite is so—resourceful?"

"Well, of course he is," said Magda huffily, provoked beyond measure, as she often was nowadays, by Linnet's smugness, her habit of using a word—like resourceful—to which no one could possibly object but pronouncing it in such a way that one actually objected very strongly. A way, in fact, which forced Magda Braithwaite to wonder about the exact nature of her husband's friendship with Linnet. Had she, in fact, become his mistress? His wife believed she had and, in her absolute determination never to admit it, rather lost interest in the beggar child.

Not so Linnet.

"Miss Adeane—what *is* the girl saying? That is not English, surely?"

Cara, whose knowledge of the Irish language as spoken in the mud cabins of Kerry and County Clare was rusty and had never been perfect, was not entirely sure herself. Nor was she able to make her own inquiries, in that same lovely, lilting tongue, in any other way but haltingly.

"What is it?"

"He says he's up on the moor at the inn they call the Gamecock. He said not to speak his name in case somebody heard."

"Are they after him, then?"

"That they are."

She gave the child a coin, took her by the ear, and led her to the door.

"All right. This is for you. Tell him I'll come after dark."

"My word," she said, coming back into the shop, wrinkling her nose and smiling her apologies, "what a menace. That child *stank.*"

"Was it wise," asked Linnet, "to give her money?"

"Oh—probably not. But what *is* one to do, Miss Gage? She would not have gone so quietly otherwise."

"Is that what she was saying to you, Miss Adeane?"

"Yes it was. And it is not the first time I have been troubled, either. But please don't let it trouble *you*, Miss Gage. If Mr. Braithwaite could manage to stop these tinker families coming into town I should be very much obliged to him."

Linnet smiled very sweetly. "I am sure he will do all he can. He is most—effective? But I had really no idea that you spoke that very ancient language—Gaelic is it not?—so fluently."

Cara smiled too. "By no means fluently, Miss Gage. I only know enough to understand when I am being asked for sixpence."

She had betrayed nothing by her manner, she was quite sure of that. Nor did she betray anything during the rest of that suddenly tedious afternoon, showing herself perfectly ready to linger an extra half hour over samples of striped foulard with Mrs. Colclough, standing almost as long at the step of Mrs. Braithwaite's carriage discussing lace peignoirs and a suitably flamboyant costume for the Tannenbaum Christmas Ball, only six months away.

"Something which will be *noticed*, Miss Adeane. *Do* put your mind to it."

"Oh—better than that, Mrs. Braithwaite. I shall start on some sketches."

Would Linnet Gage be present at the Tannenbaum dance, dressed in white tulle? Or perhaps pale gray or lavender would now suit her better. Still pale blue elegance in the candlelight, perhaps, but growing a little too sharp for comfort around her edges. What would Magda Braithwaite do, Cara wondered, if she were to tell her just who it was who paid Linnet's millinery bills nowadays? As Mr. Adolphus Moon used to do.

But secrets of that kind were perfectly safe with her. She smiled, wished Magda Braithwaite a "good night," although she did not think there was much chance of it, and went back into the shop, making the rounds of inspection she always made, balancing the day's takings, spending the length of time she usually spent—no more, no less—in the workroom, saying the kind of things she usually said. She ate the supper her housekeeper had made her and, having been in service herself, was far more skillful than Gemma Gage had ever been in avoiding the tell-tale signs of haste or nerves or dawdling which might arouse suspicion.

A normal, peaceful, possibly rather dull evening, so cleverly portrayed that both housekeeper and housemaid would have been astonished, once they were out of the way, at the speed with which she moved the by no means obliging dog out of his basket and prised the loose floorboard up.

She did not know how closely Christie watched her, or rather employed someone else to do it. She did not, as it happened, *think* he had bribed or otherwise persuaded one of her staff but, just the same, it had become a habit to tread warily. And, in this matter of Daniel, she left nothing to chance.

Since the Revolutionary Tenth she had kept enough money in her cash box to get him to America twice over and keep him there for at least a comfortable month. She had already alerted her father to the possible arrival of someone to whom every assistance must be given. She had kept herself informed as to what ships were sailing and prepared a list of addresses in Liverpool where, at a price, fugitives might find help.

All it would take—like most things in her experience—was money. For who knew the face of Daniel Carey—and who cared—in Liverpool? All he needed was the money to buy a passage to New York, to buy silence and a little temporary loyalty along the way, and he would be free. Only here, in the neighborhood of Frizingley, did he run real danger of being recognized. Yet where else could he come for help? Except to her, or to Gemma Gage.

And she did not think it opportune to dwell too closely, just yet, on why she, and not Gemma, had been chosen.

Darkness fell and very carefully she turned down the lamps in her sitting room and lit them in her bedroom as she did every evening, so that to anyone watching in the street it would seem she was preparing for bed. She put on old boots which had seen rougher service than any she thought likely to be in the possession of Mrs. Gage, a black wool dress without petticoats to weigh her down, a black cloak with a deep concealing hood and, going downstairs without a candle, let herself out of the back door and set off in the direction of St. Jude's.

A dangerous walk, she knew that, the streets being full not only of the tinkers and beggars and ne'er-do-wells of a dozen varieties who might easily accost her but a crop of brand-new, self-important special constables, patrolling night and day since the troubles, who would no doubt be interested to know her purpose and her destination. But she had learned, in a hard and dangerous school, how to fend off the attentions of prowling, predatory men, as Gemma Gage had not. She knew how to keep herself afloat—none better—in these murky waters. She knew too that once she left the town behind anything could come out at her from the dark.

But she knew her own strength, as Daniel must surely know it. Which was why, she supposed, he had sent to her instead of Gemma. A compliment of sorts, perhaps. Perhaps not. Although it had not once occurred to her to refuse it. He had called, she was ready, and what happened afterward would just have to happen, and she would just have to do the best she could with it.

At the top of St. Jude's she left the road, plunging into the dark like a swimmer, refusing even to think about what she might encounter now or how afraid she was. After all, she had been wandering alone in dark and difficult places for most of her life, and these few easier years had not weakened her. What mattered was keeping her sense of direction and her balance on this rough and pock-marked ground, not turning her ankle on a stone or stumbling over a rabbit hole and breaking her neck. What mattered was getting there. For if she were now to turn aside, to lose courage or fail in some other way to reach him, she knew there would be no living with herself hereafter.

There had been no decision to make, no weighing of profit or loss. This was something she had to do. And in that case she felt she had better get on and do it, as quickly and competently as she could.

The Gamecock. A sinister place indeed, a rough stone shack in the middle of the dry and empty moor, a meeting place once for Luddite hammermen, all of them dead now, she supposed, some of them hanged, their places on the ale-benches taken by the Chartist drill-master and his pike-men who went through their military exercises nearby—the whole town knew it—every moonlit night.

There was an uncertain moon now, palely appearing and disap-pearing behind a veil of cloud, but she could see nothing around the inn except bare black land and sky, the building itself showing no light, appearing deserted and desolate, haunted, until she pushed open the door and saw, with shock, that the ruined hulk of a man behind the bar was Ned O'Mara.

She said nothing. Nor he. And why—she reasoned—should she be surprised to find him here. Where else could he get employment, now that Christie had dismissed him? And since only the Chartist pike-men and fugitives would be likely to drink his ale she supposed Ned had become as good a Chartist—in his own opinion—as any. Why not? She nodded in his direction and smiled. He nodded back and made a gesture which showed her Daniel leaning in the doorway of an inner room where, without any conscious memory of how she crossed the uneven, sawdust-covered floor, she joined him.

They did not touch one another.

"You look terrible," she said, "—disgraceful!"

"I expect I do." He did not sound particularly ashamed of it. "I've been walking for days. And sleeping rough."

"You haven't shaved either."

"No. I thought a beard might help."

"No you didn't. You just couldn't be bothered."

"That's right, Cara. It didn't seem important."

She supposed not, now that his terrible flame was gone. Would *she* have cared about such trivialities if they had taken away her livelihood, her skill, her final opportunity? Yes. She thought it very likely that she would.

"How bad is it, Daniel?"

"Ah well—bad enough." And without that cold, pure flame it was just a shadow of his carefree, footloose self who spoke to her, a sketch in thin and hasty charcoal. "I have been arrested once already and got away . . ."

"For what?"

"A dastardly thing. For standing up on a rock in the middle of a field and telling half a dozen extremely tired men—all of them feeling understandably a bit let down—about justice and freedom and that we ought to have it sooner rather than later—You know."

Of course she did.

"We were on our way home from London, walking back to Manchester and Leeds and such places, since Feargus O'Connor had lost interest, or nerve, or whatever—had chosen discretion instead of valour. If that's what he did. Because while he was trundling across Westminster Bridge in a cab, feeling foolish, no doubt, but not getting his feet wet, it didn't seem to strike him just how many men he was leaving stranded. They'd come to be conquering heroes, you see, and I doubt if more than one in ten had the train fare home."

"You must have had your return ticket, Daniel. I suppose you gave it away?"

He shrugged. "I suppose so. But there I was, just cheering the lads up. Justice and Freedom and not just for them, either, in my ideal world, but for everybody. Ben Braithwaite and the Duke of Wellington included. But before we can share with them they'll have to share with us. And until they do we shouldn't knuckle under. That's more or less what I said. The officer who arrested me reckoned I'd get two years for it."

"So you escaped and dashed off to another field to say it all over again?"

He smiled at her. "No, Cara. No more. I seem to be—well—a bit on the tired side just at the moment. To tell you the truth, I think it's over."

"The Charter? They'll bring it out again."

"I dare say." His eyes seemed to be looking through her into the distance. "But what I learned—you see—the other day in London, is that it probably wouldn't work. Human nature being what it is. So why bother?"

Why indeed? She had always known that. Always. But what mattered now was that he should "bother" to save himself and get away. Quickly she began to tell him what she had planned, to give him money and names, dates and times and "safe" addresses.

"And when you land in New York my father will look after you. And my mother. You know her."

"Yes. I do."

"It's a new life, Daniel. Freedom, at any rate. A new opportunity."

Was that what he wanted?

Standing only inches away from her he seemed, for a moment, hardly there at all, almost as if he had passed over a threshold of time to wear, once again, the skin of the young man who had known Odette; or forward to become somebody else. A stranger to them both.

It seemed unlikely they would meet again.

"You'd better go," she said. "The town is crawling with constables. You can't wait until daylight."

"No." He looked at her. "There was no one else I could call out to, Cara."

"All right—it's all right."

"Have I put you in danger?"

"How did you know you could trust me?"

"It never occurred to me not to."

"Well—" she gave a high, cracked laugh. "Thanks for that much, at any rate. Now just go, Daniel—go—oh—with good riddance if you like—But go."

"Yes. I'm going." But he was standing very still. "Cara—there's Gemma Gage."

"Yes? What about her?"

"Would you tell her you saw me?"

"Just that I saw you?"

"Yes." He shook his head like a dog coming out of water. "That's all. I couldn't be asking her to come here, now could I? A woman as—sheltered—as that . . . ?"

"No, Daniel. It's all right."

He smiled, shakily she thought. "So now I'll be on my way, Cara my darling, never to trouble you again."

"It's no trouble. No trouble at all," she told him, and burst into tears.

"It was a long time ago, Cara," he said.

Another world. A girl on the open deck of a cargo boat wearing a secondhand dress as a queen might wear her coronation robe, a young man taut and slender as an arrow, wearing a shabby top hat and a light heart. They embraced each other now, that girl and that young man, in a hard, fierce hug; and parted.

"Keep safe. Keep out of trouble," she said.

"I loved you, Cara."

"I loved you."

The young man had become a disillusioned crusader, spiritually sickened and physically exhausted. The girl, no matter what other skills and sophistications she had acquired along her way, had never learned to love anyone else.

The door of their inner room opened. "Ah—there you are, Mr. Carey," a voice said and, with the most extreme horror she had ever felt in her life, she found herself looking straight at Christie.

He took no notice of her. She stood pressed against the wall and watched, in a sick haze, as the room filled up with men she knew to be special constables, moving deliberately and slowly, ponderously almost, yet everywhere, their menace seeping through every crack like floodwater. Christie's men, under his command, working at his direction.

"Good evening, Ned," she heard him say, "I told you I'd be paying you a visit one of these dark nights." And she might have suspected Ned of treachery had it not been impossible to miss the snarling hatred in his face, the murderous grip of his hands on the bar counter.

Christie made a gesture and two young, burly, pink-cheeked men stepped forward and, twisting Daniel's arms behind his back with the roughness of inexperience, tied them with a cord. He did not move. Nor she. He did not turn his head to look at her. He looked at Christie, leaning against the edge of the bar, his black fur cloak falling to his ankles, a gentleman taking his arrogant, high-bred ease among low company, according no more than faint amusement to the scalding hate he was arousing in the barman behind him. Knowing quite well—she thought—how desperately Ned was longing to put a meat-cleaver into his back, yet dare not.

Not caring.

"Take him," Christie said. And she knew that was what they were doing exactly. *Taking* him. Daniel still arrow-straight and hard but growing every minute more anonymous. Not really Daniel any longer but the Prisoner. The Victim. The Sacrifice.

She couldn't bear it. And yet she made no sound, continuing to press herself against that wall until she seemed to be growing there, or simply disappearing in her helplessness. There was nothing she could do. No choice but to stand grafted to the wall as they took Daniel away. There was nothing he could do but go with them. In absolute silence. Still not looking at her. Doing nothing, in fact, but stare into the distance beyond all of them, across that threshold of time, backward or forward she couldn't tell. But in another place. Already somewhere else.

Did he think, seeing Christie, that she had betrayed him? Could he possibly think that?

Reaching the doorway Christie paused, his long fur cloak swaying around him, his eyes blank, his mouth, although it was smiling most charmingly, very hard. "Thank you, Cara. I'll make it worth your while, of course," he said.

The door closed behind him. Behind Daniel. She had never known a room so empty. A wall so thin, collapsing on her, it seemed and pushing her forward as she fell against the bar counter, toward the bulk she only barely remembered to be Ned.

"*Do* something," she shrieked and went on shrieking until he caught her by the shoulders and shook her into silence.

"All right. I bloody will." She expected nothing from him, nothing from anybody, ever again, and he had to shake her very hard this time to quell the hysteria and make her listen.

"What that bastard Goldsborough who thinks he knows everythin' don't realize is that there must be at least three dozen of the lads out there tonight, drillin' on the moor. If they can head him off . . . Aye— and gi' me ten minutes with him—"

She paid no heed to that nor to any of the other threats and re-criminations he muttered as she ran beside him over the rough ground, jarring her ankles on stones and spiky grasses but keeping on going, running headlong to anyone, anywhere, gypsies or vagabonds or thieves, who might help her. She was aware of pain without really suffering it. She had no time for that. She had several vital and most specific things to do. Get to Daniel. Set him free. Tell him she had not betrayed him. Kill Christie Goldsborough. And if Ned meant to kill him too, as seemed likely, then she would just have to make sure she got to him first.

But she had fallen some way behind when she saw the band of "physical force" men marching like a spectral battalion out of the dark, Ned falling in beside them and muttering urgently enough to make them change direction. They had agreed to go after Daniel, and she with them, desperate to keep them in view since she was completely lost by now in a night that was growing blacker and most unseasonably cold.

They were not heavily armed. Only sticks and pickaxe handles, rather than their home-made pikes, but it was enough to put the fear of death into the special constables—only young bank-clerks and solicitors' and merchants' sons after all, enrolled for the occasion—when they breasted the hill and came roaring down on them, yelling Chartist slogans and "Vive la République."

Cara had seen enough violence to know that one never took in the whole of it, that it became fragmented, split, distorted, a raucous confusion lasting an eternity and over in moments, into which she plunged headlong as she had been doing all evening, regardless of the blows and curses thudding all around her, ready to walk through anything or anyone to get to Daniel and somehow getting there, to throw herself on her knees behind him and claw, with her strong, dressmaker's fingers, at the cord about his wrists.

Urgency was all that was in her now. The "specials" were giving ground, scattering, she could see that. But there might be others. Might well be soldiers somewhere nearby in the hills, a squadron of dragoons like the one used to such lethal effect in Bradford, coming at full gallop to ride them, and then to cut them down. Hurry then. Hurry with this damnable cord some nervous young idiot had pulled so tight. She could hear Daniel breathing heavily and felt a tremor of pain in him. Well, she was hurting herself too, splitting her nails and her fingertips so that when she finally tore the knot apart there was blood on it and on Daniel's shirt cuffs, blood on her hands. Both his and hers.

"Run," she yelled at him.

"I didn't believe what he said about you," he yelled back.

What did that matter now?

"Run," she shrieked. "*Go*. I'll be all right. Run."

And when he caught hold of her hands to take her with him she wrenched them free. "No. I can't keep up with you. I'd slow you down. Go."

"Cara . . ."

"For Christ's sake . . ." Putting her bloodstained hands against his chest she pushed him as hard as she could and ran away in the opposite direction, stopping for breath only when she saw a knot of "physical force" men close in around him and disappear, all together, into the night.

They would know about the soldiers. They too would wish to move fast, not caring to go up against military sabers with their walking sticks. Having saved Daniel they would now, very naturally, set about saving themselves. Suddenly she was alone on an empty battlefield, the wind getting up, a weight of darkness falling around her until she came upon one of those hollow basins in the land walled in by high and always unexpected moorland stones, and saw, in a brief unveiling of the moon, that she had reached a killing-ground.

The moon went in again and quickly, her own life perhaps depending upon it, she stepped back into the shadow of the most distant rock and froze there, her very breathing suspended, as she watched the half-circle of men close in upon their quarry. Ned O'Mara, former champion of the bare-knuckle boxing ring, and five others, big, gnarled men, every one of them, with the long arms and wide shoulders of manual labor, the blank half-mesmerized expressions of those about to perform an act of ritual slaughter. Not Chartists, these. Just men who had been branded as troublemakers and had allowed their grievances to fester. Men who hated authority, the mill-master, the landlord, and who had cornered themselves a prime member of the species now in Christie Goldsborough.

Six of them moving very slowly toward him and Christie moving just as slowly away until his back was against the rock. The moon came out again and she saw him in what—in that dark place—seemed almost a flash of light, saw the sudden white gleam as he smiled, the white of his shirt as he threw back his cloak and shrugged it off.

"Gentlemen . . . ?" he said.

Once again she could do nothing but press herself against cold stone and wait. For murder to be done, this time, there seemed no doubt of that. Murder which reached her ears as panting, hot and animal through the gloom as he went down beneath the first hammer blows of those dozen fists, striking in unison, to be trampled into the earth by a dozen booted feet. And then their six dark, intent figures crouching over him, mangling and mauling like hounds worrying a fox, inflicting a far more leisurely and lethal damage now as systematically, almost lovingly, they reduced the great landlord of St. Jude's to a bundle of bleeding rags.

She had not the least conception of how long it lasted. Time, like her breathing, being held in suspension, put in abeyance until first one, then two of them, broke away from the circle of human sacrifice, blood-lust cooling to a point where it was no more than a common beating and they had had enough of it.

"Come on, lads." Somebody was calling to them from the brow of the hill. One of the "physical force" men, she thought, for whom violence was strictly a political, never a personal matter and who, by his tone of voice, did not approve of this. He shouted something else she did not catch. Something more urgent. And even then Ned O'Mara launched a final kick from his studded, steel-toed boot before shambling away into the night, stumbling and cursing and needing a drink now, she supposed, far more than anything else.

Christie remained very still. So did she. *"Some day you'll go too far."* How often had she told him that? *"Some day you'll strip somebody too bare."* So it had been Ned.

Releasing her breath, almost learning to breathe again, she stayed a while longer in the shadows, doubting her ability to move had she even wished to try. Which she did not. Yet—eventually—she had to acknowledge that Ned might well come back again. And if he saw her here and had enough energy left, she thought he would probably rape her. What better way, after all, to round off his revenge? Christie dead on the ground. Christie's woman used and humiliated and then left to die beside him. She knew how much that would appeal to Ned. She had better get away, then. Quickly, while she could still tell herself, with conviction, that he *was* dead and beyond any help she could give him. While she could just tiptoe away without looking, without having to reproach herself later . . . ? Could she? Damnation. Why not?

Emerging from her shelter she walked gingerly toward him, treading on eggshells, and knelt on the churned-up ground where he lay curled in what she knew to be an attempt to protect the most vital parts of himself against impossible odds, his knees drawn up to his chest, his arms around his head, trying to save his eyes and teeth and his brain at the sacrifice of his ribs.

But they had managed to kick him in the face just the same, she noticed, blood pouring—as the blood of dead men did not flow—from his nose, one cheek gashed to the bone, one eye blackened and closed, the other cheek embedded with grit, made hideous by torn and hanging strips of skin. His ribs were certainly broken. The tortured scrape of his breathing told her that. One arm too, she thought, by the awkward set of it. What else?

He was not dead. But if she left him to lie here she knew he would not last the night. For if the cold and damp failed to finish him off, and Ned O'Mara did not return, the hills were full of tramps and vagabonds who would make short work of him for the rings on his fingers and the money he would have in his pockets. Could she leave him long enough to fetch help? She thought not. Could she even be sure of finding him again, one stretch of moorland looking very much like another in the dark?

She would have her work cut out, she thought grimly, to find Frizingley itself, let alone a man huddled in the shadow of a rock. Where was it? Somewhere to the left—surely?—and then downhill? She hoped so. Dare she even risk the road? Glancing down at him she decided she would have to. He was a big, solid, well-nourished man. And heavy. Oh Lord—Dear Lord. What a farce life was. What a tragedy.

It no longer even entered her mind to leave him where he lay.

"You'll have to get up, Christie."

He was conscious and the obscenity he groaned at her made her smile.

"Yes you will. Come on. I don't care how much it hurts you. And neither do you. Because if you don't make the effort you'll die. Ned O'Mara will be back when he's had another drink or two, with his axe to grind—right in your skull, I reckon. And if *he* doesn't get you, then some tinker will come along and cut your throat as soon as look at you, for that gold medallion you wear, and your gold rings. So get up, Christie. Come on. Let's hurry up about it, shall we?"

"I'm coming," he said.

If he fainted from the pain and effort she had no idea what she would do with him, his unconscious weight being totally beyond either her physical powers or her ingenuity. But at last she had him half-sitting, half-lying on a low rock while she wrapped his cloak around him to ease his shivering and hide the blood all over his shirt front. All over the front of *her* dress too, and her sleeves, seeping through the soft fabric to stain her chest and her arms, running down her hands. Giving her a brief and disturbing sensation of familiarity.

When had this happened before? Because it *had* already happened, exactly like this. This same man. This same blood making patches of gore on her bodice; disgusting her. Although she had held on—that other time—just as she was doing now.

The same thing? When? Her head swam with a spasm of dizziness and then cleared. Of course. On the night he had put the dog in her arms. The fighting dog which had lost the fight. One ear torn off. One leg horribly mangled. The ugliest, most vicious, most ungrateful brute in the world. That was it. The night of her twentieth birthday, eight years ago. *"Happy Birthday, Miss Adeane."* And, without any warning, he had tossed her that wounded carcass which even then, as she had clutched it and held it instead of letting it fall, had snarled and tried to bite her. And had been snarling at her ever since.

"Come on," she said. "Stir yourself. You're supposed to be a hard man, aren't you? Put your arm around my shoulder—and get on your feet."

And even though she was prepared for it the weight of him crushed her, as the weight of the dog had made her gasp and stagger on that other night. But she had carried it, nonetheless, up the hill of St. Jude's, cursing and grumbling at every step, fretting about the bloodstains on her one good dress. Without the least idea what she meant to do with him when she got there.

It had simply not occurred to her to put him down.

The first steps he took now were so drunken, his breath grating so painfully through his shattered chest that, for a moment, hope left her.

But he did not intend to die.

Neither did she. And the fusion of their two wills produced, not a weapon, but a crutch adequate—if only barely—to their needs. She made no attempt to spare him pain. She had no time to discover the nature and exact location of his injuries. She simply grabbed him where she could and staggered on while her own strength lasted, her back-bone endured, her heart went on beating, her head remained steady enough to locate first the road and then which of its various twists and turns would lead her to Frizingley.

She would be quite safe, of course, to ask help of any passing carriage. None came. She stumbled on. Not thinking. Enduring. As he was doing. If he fell she knew she could not pick him up. If she turned her ankle on a stone . . . ? Thoughts. Suppositions. Useless things. If she paid any heed to them she would simply sit down and die. Of fright. Or violence. Or cold. And it was only speculation. *Reality* was the iron bar of his arm tearing a path of muscles from the nape of her neck and along her shoulders, the sound of breath rising through splintered bone, the jarring at the base of *her* spine with every slow, dragging step *he* took, the pounding and aching in her head and chest. Reality was the almost unbearable ferocity of his undamaged will, the complete absence of mercy with which it drove his wounded body on. Her will, too.

It did not occur to her to drop him.

It did not occur to him to fall.

The first sight of St. Jude's hill in the distance came to her like a mirage in the desert. She did not believe it. Yet, ten agonizing minutes more, and there it was, grimy, squalid, incredibly—if only for that one night of her life—beautiful and blessed.

"Leave me now," he said, "and run down to the Fleece."

But somebody could cut his throat here as easily as on the moor, for the same reasons.

"No. Come on."

"You are saving my life, Adeane. I wonder why?"

"I don't know."

She was speaking the truth.

Down the hill of St. Jude's where drunken and wounded men abounded they were an unremarkable couple. And it was downhill now, no more rabbit-holes and the sudden, icy plunge into a moorland stream hidden in coarse grass. Just uneven, sharp-sided cobbles, gutters running foul with sewage, indifferent passers-by who did not recognize their landlord as he hobbled and groaned and cursed his way home.

She took him in through the back door of the Fleece, knowing he would not care to be seen in the station hotel in this condition, spreading consternation among the pot-boys and barmaids who were all strangers to her now until Oliver Rattrie came hurrying down the passage, smooth and suave and painfully elegant, the strong musky scent of him—copied from Christie—mingling with the blood and mud and sweat to turn her stomach.

"My word—Good Heavens." But Oliver Rattrie, who had seen his mother die of disease and childbirth, his father hanged by suicide, his brothers and sisters carried off to the workhouse where they had died like flies, one after the other, of "workhouse fever," was not the man to be moved by a few broken bones and a little gore. Not the man to be moved by anything at all, these days, as he glided smoothly through the "administrative tasks" of rent collecting and eviction which Christie had set him. A power in St. Jude's, Mr. Oliver Rattrie. A man to be reckoned with. To whom the proper reception of his injured master, the whisking away of curious onlookers, and the calling of a doctor, were simple matters. Nor did the requirements of his master's mistress prove beyond him.

"I will have them send up hot water, Miss Adeane. And then tea—or something stronger?—by the fire. And we should all feel easier, I think, if you would permit the doctor to have a look at you, too. Such an ordeal. My goodness."

She was taken to the sitting-room—now Oliver's—which had once been Christie's; Christie himself in the room next door. Now Oliver's too, she supposed. She sat down by the fire—a fire in July? This too he had copied from Christie—took off her shoes and tried hard, because her mind had emptied now of its immediate fear and pain, to fill it only with inconsequential things. Anything that was not Daniel—where was he? how was he? Not Christie, standing in the inn door, smiling at her and killing her with his *"Thank you, Cara. I'll make it worth your while, of course."* Not Christie, bleeding all over her dress. Not that damned dog, doing the same thing, years ago.

Why did she keep on remembering that? Why should it mean so much to her? She had been a green girl then, not half so clever as she pretended. And smooth, suave Oliver with his musky African perfume and his roaring log fire had been a scabby, flea-bitten urchin playing barefoot in the St. Jude's gutters and stealing rainwater from her barrels.

And Daniel? Footloose and light of heart, fond of Justice, of course, but madly in love with Fun and Freedom. Only Christie had been the same, all those years ago. Or was it that he had not appeared to change because he allowed no one close enough to notice? Well, he had nearly died tonight, and although he hadn't pleaded with her to save him she *had* saved him nevertheless. Just like the dog. Would it make amends to the demon in him for finding her with Daniel? *His* woman with another man. Had that been it? The jewel he had polished and faceted for his own pleasure running around the moor in a plain wool dress without her petticoats, like the common trollop she used to be? But she had saved his life at the risk of her own. Her motives being uncertain, her feelings in such confusion that—oh, God dammit—she hardly knew where she was and certainly not why. There had been tremendous changes tonight. Tremendous forces. It had been one of those central pivots, those key experiences, after which things might be better or worse but never quite the same again.

Getting up she walked through into the familiar bedroom and stood by the bed.

He was lying on one side, his back toward her, one bulky shoulder visible above the heavy quilts, his head in profile on the satin pillow in evident pain, one eye bandaged over, the other closed.

"Cara . . . ?"

She thought that he made an effort to turn toward her.

"Yes?"

Reaching down she put her hand carefully, lightly, on his shoulder and bent over him, a gesture which held all the beginnings of concern, which might have become very concerned indeed had not his body suddenly stiffened beneath her touch, his one eye shooting open and glaring as balefully as ever that damnable, vicious brute of a dog had glared, first at her and then at Oliver Rattrie, who was hovering solicitously behind her.

"Get that woman out of here, Oliver," he snarled, "and see to it she doesn't come back."

26

*E*scaping from the "physical force" men who did not greatly wish to detain him in any case, Daniel lay flat on his back in a fold of the rough grassland, staring at the sky and wondering, mainly, why he had so little inclination to get up and be on his way.

He knew approximately where he was. He had enough of Cara's money in his pocket to take him anywhere else he wished to go. It seemed only right, then, for her sake, to go somewhere, since she had risked life and limb to bring it to him. He should not have involved her, of course. He knew that. Yet, finding himself at the Gamecock, penniless and on the run as she had always expected to see him, calling out to her for help—giving her the chance to say "I told you so"—had seemed natural. Not *right*, perhaps, as he had realized ten minutes after sending the tinker girl with his message. After which it had been too late.

She had not failed him. Although when Goldsborough had stood like a black peacock in the inn doorway and thanked her for turning him in, he had, for just a moment, believed her guilt. But no. Not Cara. She would never do a thing like that. And if he still had faith in her, could he not learn to have faith in himself again? Even though the time when they might have been lovers had passed so imperceptibly for him that he could remember no precise moment when his desire for her as a woman had lessened and, by some strange chemistry, had increased her value to him as a friend. What she had done for him tonight he would do tomorrow for her. He hoped she knew that.

He had been wrong about too many things. Or had wanted too much too soon. Too many grand and noble designs for which no one—including himself—seemed to be ready. And from having believed too fervently, with too whole a heart, he found it impossible now to believe in anything at all. He had dedicated his life and health and vigor to a Charter which now lay in a government office somewhere gathering dust, an object of ridicule and scandal, its undeniable truths just as undeniably tarnished by grubby-minded, grubby-handed men. As religions were often tarnished, he supposed, by those who practiced them. He understood that. Yet, since that damp squib of a Revolutionary Tenth, his understanding of human frailty had brought him no consolation. Had, indeed, only caused him to wonder if such a feeble, fickle species could be worth the trouble?

He had not wanted blood. He had wanted justice and dignity, for which he had been prepared to bleed. And all he had won was a choice between exile in an alien land, or the company of his fellow idealists, his fellow fools, in jail.

Ought he not to be making himself busy now about organizing the one and avoiding the other? Running away, in fact, instead of lying on damp grass looking up at the sky and finding it very large and very empty. Far too big for him. And far away. He had better go, then. Cara had kept faith with him. She had wanted him saved and so the least he could do was get up on his feet and go through the motions.

That was as much as he felt about it.

Leeds was over there. And then Liverpool. Then safety. With money there would be no difficulty. Cara had always said money was all it took. If safety was what he wanted? Perhaps not. But since, at the moment, there was nothing else he wanted either, he sprang up suddenly and set off at speed. While the mood lasted.

And then, as suddenly, he stopped.

What was it? He had not intended to be moved or stirred by emotion ever again. After the famine had dried him and scourged him and then remoulded him, a stranger to affluent humanity, he had judged himself incapable of it. *Wanted* to be incapable. Had he been wrong about that too? What, after all, had he achieved? Nothing and less than nothing, since, hypnotized by the vast needs of mankind *en masse* about which he could do nothing, he had deliberately turned aside from the individual needs it had been well within his power to fulfill. He could not save the people of Ireland from hunger but there were other and very human hungers which he had himself aroused and, quite knowingly, left unfed.

In Gemma—he could no longer close his mind to it—who, in exchange for his obsessions, had given him warmth and love and who could have made him happy had he allowed it. But he had set personal happiness aside, sacrificed it, like everything else, to the Charter. Thrown it away. Despised it. He knew now that he could have approached his exile with less desolation had he been able to tell himself that he had made her happy too.

At least that would have been *something* worth doing with his life.

He sat down on a rock, his chin in his hand, staring back to the smoky glimmer of light, a fair way below him, which he knew to be Frizingley. As he had sat once before, reproaching himself for the manner in which he had left her. She had been going into exile then, to the care of her sick father and her uncertain marriage, he to his freedom and his grand and glorious destiny. And she had sent him on his way with generous lies to ease his mind and lighten his heart for not grieving at the loss of her. At least not in the way she had wanted. Although she had denied that too, of course, so that he would not have to mar his grand future with any feeling of guilt or double-dealing.

She had smoothed his path, she had *loved* him, had given him the ultimate gift of true love, the thing he most wanted—his unconditional freedom. Permission, in effect, to leave her. She had told him it was "all right" that he did not love her. She had said she didn't really mind. And when he could no longer pretend to believe her he sat down on a rock like this one and damned himself for a selfish fool. He should have fallen at her feet and had the greatness of heart to lie to her. He had known it then. He still knew it. "I love you, Gemma. I love you." What would it have cost him to tell her that?

And what was love, in any case? Did it even exist beyond the fierce explosion he had felt for Cara which neither of them had really trusted or expected to last? And even that had proved false as everything else now seemed false and flimsy to him. Except Gemma. As everything had turned to dust in his hands, ashes in his mouth. Except her. As everyone else had failed and faded in his vision.

Surely he could tell her that? Surely that would be something worth doing, worth dying for. Worth living for if he could. And if not, then at least she would know of his faith in her. He could give her that.

Frizingley, of course, was full of constables but, covered by boldness and darkness, he reached the manor wall unchallenged, climbed it, waited a few moments in the shrubbery until he saw her small, sturdy shadow and then, the windows being open, walked through them straight into her drawing-room. An act of rash folly. He saw as much in her face. But at least he was here and whatever might happen next he would have the time to make his declaration, even if he had to shout it as they tied his hands again and dragged him off.

She asked no questions. She came running toward him, he opened his arms and, as she entered them, it was a homecoming, a perfect sense of being where he ought to be. Not in Frizingley, or in this house, but with her. Anywhere. He had not touched her since his return from Ireland. What a fool he had been. He had come, a starving man, to stand before the feast of her, the bounty of her, and had not even held out a hand. He touched her now, inhaled her, took the scent of her and the warmth of her into his lungs, the famished, brittle steel of him dissolving into her so that he was clamped and pierced and narrowed by it no more. The famine and the Charter had emptied him. Now he was full of her.

Could it be love after all? He asked her the question.

"I used to be so certain, Gemma. No more. I used to *know*. Now I'm just groping toward what I think—or what I hope. And that's a miracle in itself because I had no hope of anything until half an hour ago. And no belief left either. Not in myself. And not in any of my grand crusades for justice and freedom either. I'd seen what they amounted to at first hand—standing too near. I could see no truth anywhere—nothing I'd be even halfway ready to die for—Galahad lost in the storm without his Holy Grail, poor devil. Poor fool. But there's truth in you, Gemma. And hope. And goodness. I would give my life for yours and count it a privilege. Is that love? I think it must be. Don't you?"

And if not, then love must be rare and strange indeed. Little more than a lightning flash soon gone and forgotten across this deep, calm sky.

"Yes, Daniel. I think so." Love as she could understand and give it. Clear water to his parched spirit. A nurturing, healing balm.

"Yes." Her voice had grown firmer now. "It *is* love." She had made up her mind to it. And she was right, of course. She always had been. Not the love he had imagined. But he could relinquish his airspun imaginings readily now, for this warm, solid earth of her reality. He had never searched for happiness nor expected it. How odd and foolish and miraculous that, with nothing but a choice between exile or imprisonment before him, he could be so happy, and so peaceful, now.

Dear Gemma. Beloved brown cob of a girl. What could he give her? What tremendous act of love could he perform. What was it she most wanted? What ultimate, unstinting gift?

She disengaged herself gently, went to the window and looked out. "When must you leave?" she said.

He got up too and looked at her. Saw her. As she had always been. The finer half of himself.

"I don't relish the thought of prison, Gemma."

"No. Is that what it would be? Prison?"

"Yes."

"Not transportation?"

He shook his head. "No. There was too much fuss when they sent Mitchel to Australia. They won't want to stir that up again. I dare say they might ship off a few men nobody has heard of, to lessen the load. But not the candidates."

"And America?"

He sighed and smiled at her. "Yes, Gemma. It would be more comfortable to go there, wouldn't it? But exile goes on forever. If I asked you to join me would you come? When I'm established and have a roof to shelter you?"

"Of course. Gladly. And proudly. Anywhere, Daniel."

He smiled at her again. "And hide with me. No peace of mind. No friends."

"You are the only friend I need."

"You are *all* I need, Gemma."

"Darling . . ." Her gesture said "Here I am."

"And so . . ." The gift was there, in his mind, ready to be given.

"Yes?"

"I can't leave you, Gemma. Ships sink. Letters take forever to cross the ocean. I wouldn't know how you were, or where you were for weeks on end. I couldn't stand it. Not now. York prison is handier."

He saw she was crying and took her in his arms again. Another homecoming.

"When a man has something to live for he doesn't throw his life away, my darling. I've taken no great care of myself, I admit. But that's over now. If you need me, Gemma? You do need me, don't you? I surely need you."

Drying her eyes with the palms of her hands she stood away from him a moment, her face radiant and tender yet touched, nevertheless, with something of her father's sound good sense, his honest determination to have and to hold forever under his wing all those he cared for. And Gemma cared only for Daniel.

"I would go to prison in your place if I could," she told him quietly, meaning exactly what she said. A sensible arrangement, in her view, since she could bear the restraint far more patiently.

"You can't. What we have to decide now is how I am to contrive it. I can go out, of course, and get myself arrested . . ."

"*No!*" And the sharpness in her voice told him she was fully aware of his danger from men who, thinking it unlikely that the Chartists would be punished enough since the outcry concerning John Mitchel, were more than ready to take care of the matter themselves. "No, Daniel. If this is really the best way—the safest way—and it is you who must decide . . ."

"I have decided, Gemma. America is too far. And too risky. I'll serve my sentence. Two years at most, the constables were saying. And then—if you'll have me—we can be together openly—with dignity—"

"Openly?" she said, smiling.

"Why—yes—"

She stepped forward, raised herself slightly on tiptoe, and kissed him.

"Will you marry me, Daniel?" It was not a question but a formal proposal of marriage which took him aback only because it had not occurred to him.

"So you want to make an honest man of me, do you?"

"No. You are that already. I simply wished to spare you the awkwardness of proposing to me yourself. Because of my money."

"Yes, Gemma."

"So what is your answer?"

"Yes, Gemma."

Although he would never feel more united to her, more bound in every real and lasting sense than he did tonight. Nor she to him.

They told each other so. An exchange of vows they would not break, a ceremony of hearts and minds which left them pefectly united.

"Now I shall send for Ben Braithwaite," she said. "And for Uriah Colclough. And I shall not release you from my custody until they are both here."

"Why, my darling?" He did not like the sound of it but he knew she would have her reasons.

"Because one is the mayor, the other the mayor-elect, and they dislike each other. If you were ill-treated in any way while in their care each one would hold the other responsible. So they will make sure you are not ill-treated. Particularly if I declare my interest and let them know what a great fuss I can be counted on to make about it."

Seeing the pugnacious line of her chin he smiled and bending over her, kissed it. An attitude by no means shared by Messrs. Braithwaite and Colclough when they were summoned to her presence an hour later to be informed, in a manner reminding them all too strongly of the late John-William Dallam, the precise nature of everything she wanted done. By *them*. By Ben Braithwaite, who had not taken an order from anyone since his father died, a dozen years ago, and by Uriah Colclough, who took his only from God.

But John-William Dallam had always known how to get the better of them. So did his daughter.

She had in her custody the Chartist Mr. Daniel Carey which, when one bore in mind the rumors of which certainly *Mrs.* Braithwaite and *Mrs.* Colclough were only too well aware—having started most of them—concerning her interest in him, could hardly be a matter for surprise. Therefore it would be a waste of time on anyone's part to show it. What she wanted now were not promises, which could be broken, but *assurances* which—as any gentleman with his reputation in the Frizingley Piece Hall to consider might tell her—could not. Safe conduct for Mr. Carey to York came first on her list, by which she did not mean a negligent half-dozen special constables or a squadron of dragoons but a first-class train journey accompanied by either Mr. Colclough or Mr. Braithwaite, as proved convenient, so that he might arrive not as a prisoner apprehended on the run but a free man delivering *himself* to justice. And since—considering the political nature of Mr. Carey's offenses—it clearly could not be considered appropriate to hold him overnight in the squalid old building, once a cockpit, which served as Frizingley's jail, she proposed that he should be offered hospitality in the home of Mr. Ephraim Cook, also a magistrate and a special constable, and absolutely beyond reproach.

Mr. Cook was waiting, now, in her study and had expressed himself delighted to be of service to Mr. Carey, to the extent, in fact, of offering to join the expedition to York tomorrow. Mr. Cook had also offered, quite freely, to testify as to the integrity and worth of Mr. Daniel Carey's character, at his trial. Perhaps Mr. Braithwaite and Mr. Colclough, after spending a day in his company, might be inspired with a wish to do the same? She rather hoped so. And there was something in her manner, as there had always been in her father's, which advised them, rather strongly, to agree with her.

For the Dallam fortune, after all, was very sound and John-William himself had been hard and crafty and much respected. There would be favors still owing to him which his daughter looked as if she knew how to call in. The old man had been powerful. The daughter was a widow. Supposing she married the fellow? Supposing she tamed him and made a cabinet minister out of him one day? She seemed quite capable of it, by the look of her. She could afford it, too. In which case both Mr. Braithwaite and Mr. Colclough would find it most useful to have the acquaintance of Mr. Daniel Carey.

"I am sure we understand one another," Gemma said.

It was done. Restrained goodbyes were said. The four gentlemen left the house all together conversing in a most civilized manner as they got into their carriages, arranging to meet at Mr. Ephraim Cook's in the morning and then to the station as naturally as if it had been their own idea, not Gemma's.

A remarkable woman. So thought three of those gentlemen who had all, at some stage, wished to marry her. So thought the fourth, Mr. Ephraim Cook, who had not. Practical, shrewd, efficient, a woman with a man's head on her shoulders and her feet firmly on the ground.

Yet, when they had left her, she sat at her desk for a very long time, her chin on her hand, dreaming and sighing like any romantic girl, her head in the clouds, her feet skimming the air, her reverie ending only when she heard another carriage on the drive—her own—bringing Linnet home from the Braithwaites where the musical Magda had been holding a soirée with piano and violins.

She sighed and straightened her back. Quietly folded her hands.

"Good evening, Linnet." Her voice was perfectly steady.

"Good evening, Gemma." Linnet's light warble was no higher than usual. Yet a challenge had been thrown down and accepted, hostilities begun.

"You have come from the Braithwaites, I suppose?"

"Indeed yes." Linnet sat down or rather sank, most gracefully, into a moving cloud of lavender tulle frills releasing a faint, sharp scent all around her. "Yes, Gemma—the Braithwaites—and such a flutter you have put them all in . . ."

"You know, then, that Ben Braithwaite came to see me a little while ago—and why?"

"My dear—how could I fail to know?" she sounded playful,

"—when you obliged him to leave his supper, not to mention his guests, who were all absolutely agog to know what was amiss. As I was. And could hardly believe their ears, I might add, on his return . . . The whole of Frizingley is talking about it, Gemma."

Gemma smiled. "You must mean the two dozen or so who happened to be at the Braithwaites."

Linnet smiled too, tight-lipped and cold. "That *is* the whole of Frizingley, Gemma. I defended you as best I could—naturally."

"Why, Linnet? There was no need."

"Why?" She leaned forward, setting the lavender frills swaying, her face, above their fragrant softness, pinched hard with anger. "I'll tell you why. In order to defend my brother's memory."

Gemma allowed a moment to pass, not pleasantly, and then, leaning forward too, said quietly and slowly, "As I told you, Linnet, there was no need. Tristan knew far more about my relationship with Daniel Carey than you do. He did not grudge it to me then. And he would not grudge it to me now. I am very sure of that."

"Oh yes—why not? And I hope it is a comfort to you. Since my poor brother had no choice—had he?—in what he grudged or didn't grudge, or anything else? He did as you told him—always—even to picking up diseased urchins . . ."

"That will do, Linnet."

"Yes. I believe it will. Since it was *I* who told him to marry you. He would not have thought of it for himself. So, by that reckoning, it was *I* who killed him."

"If you like to think so, Linnet. Although, in fact, you think nothing of the kind. Frankly I find no profit in this conversation—which we have had several times before, in any case."

"Profit? You will have little of that, my girl, in your new marriage. If it ever takes place."

"Is that what they are saying at the Braithwaites?"

Linnet laughed and made an airy gesture, stirring her frills. "That— yes. And feeling sorry for you, of course—as one does for a woman who lets her money go to her head. And sorry for me—as one who must live with the consequences . . ."

Gemma placed her hands, palms down, on the desk-top—a gesture of her father's—her face thoughtful and alert, as if a moment of decision, long overdue, had been reached and must therefore be dealt with forthwith.

"Yes, Linnet. I think we should talk about that. There is no reason why you should go on living with me, you know, should you find it awkward or in any way unpleasant—"

"Are you throwing me out, Gemma?" There was a note of warning in her voice and a note of satisfaction, for it might well be to her advantage, at this delicate moment, to appear a victim.

"No. I am simply putting the position to you frankly. I am going to marry Daniel Carey. There is no doubt about that. You do not approve. How, then, can you possibly share a home with us?"

"What shall I do then, Gemma? Go as a governess?"

"If you wish. Although there is no need. You still have the allowance my father made you, as well as the allowance you inherited from Tristan. It is more than enough to live on . . ."

"In a small house in a quiet backwater, with a tabby cat."

"Your life is your own, Linnet. It is up to you what you make of it."

Another moment passed.

"I see. When would you like me to leave?"

"When your arrangements are completed."

"And your arrangements, Gemma?"

Gemma smiled, warm again and soft with the memory of Daniel. "I am in no rush. I have at least a year. Perhaps two. I shall take my time. Make haste slowly, I think—and surely."

She smiled again and would have liked to end there, not in harmony but not in sworn enmity either. But Linnet could not bear that softness in her, that deep and joyful glow of love remembered and certain, which had made her almost beautiful.

"How very fortunate," she said, patting her frills, "that there is no price on Mr. Carey's head. Otherwise we would have our work cut out to know which one of us should claim it. You for sending him off to York. Or me . . . ?"

"Yes Linnet . . . ?"

"Yes, Gemma." Her smile had the bite of a sword raised in elegant defiance. For what had she to lose now? What pleasure was left to her but to give hurt? "I was in Miss Adeane's shop, you see, this afternoon—oh, making no purchases myself, just encouraging dearest Magda to overspend her pin-money—when a diseased little urchin ran in—of the kind you inflicted on my brother . . . Begging for sixpence, Miss Adeane said, and in the Irish language too which none of *us* could understand. Naturally. Who does? Miss Adeane herself appeared to be having trouble with it and taking more pains—I thought—than one would have expected for sixpence. One supposes Mr. Carey, with his fine social conscience and his devotion to the common man, must understand such languages very well?"

"I believe he does."

"Yes," Linnet nodded, as if she had been complimented on her quick wits. "That occurred to me, very nearly at once. It occurred to Captain Goldsborough too when I stepped over to the hotel to ask his opinion. He was most interested. I knew he would be. He had good reason."

"Had he?"

"Oh yes." And Linnet, with a smile of malicious sweetness, waited a moment before telling her what it was. "Yes. I knew Christie would go after him because he is jealous."

Gemma looked puzzled for a moment as if she had lost the thread. Linnet supplied it.

"Jealous, my dear—jealous as all hell, I do assure you—of your precious Daniel and Miss Adeane. Now—dear Gemma—what do you think of that?"

Very little, it seemed.

"It ought to surprise you," said Linnet, rushing on. "A man like Christie. And a woman of her type and station. He has been her lover for years—not that you will have noticed it, dear Gemma, such things being so far beneath you—we all know that. No grand romance like yours, of course, with Daniel. Just the sordid, carnal variety that goes on between powerful men and women who need the money. And Christie is very carnal. Adeane was very poor. He bought her—which is just as it should be, except that—well—no matter how astonishing one may find it—and it *does* astonish me—he appears to have developed feelings for her. *Feelings.* Fancy that."

"She is very beautiful," said Gemma calmly. "And clever. Any man might care for her."

"Yes. Your Daniel for one, I believe."

"I know, Linnet—all about it. He told me."

"Good. I am delighted. So you will understand, then, why Christie should be in such a frenzy. The fascinating Miss Adeane. One can hardly credit it."

"Why not?"

"Because he is a Goldsborough," she said curtly, bitterly, "and she is a common trollop. Because he has a name and a pedigree and she has neither. Because he is a man of education and manners and she is the daughter of an Irish mountebank and a French parlormaid . . ."

"I see," said Gemma.

"Do you? He would cut out his tongue, of course, before admitting it. But I know."

"Yes. I am sure you do."

"I do. One has only to catch the tension in him when her name is mentioned. I have mentioned her name to him in order to catch it. One has only to take note of the wariness in his manner when she enters a room. I have noted it. And other things. Poor Christie. He does not like it, you see. I believe he is very much ashamed of himself. And rightly so."

"Rightly?"

"Of course. It demeans such a man, Gemma, to care for such a woman. He knows that."

Gemma smiled. So did Linnet.

"Would you like him to care for you, Linnet?" Gemma inquired, her smooth oval face and steady brown eyes wearing an expression which, in her father's case, had been known as bluntness and shrewdness; self-assurance in hers. And having asked her question she waited calmly for a reply.

"I would like him to marry me," Linnet flung at her.

"Yes. So I imagined."

"So *you* imagined? And what do you know of such things? He is very rich, these days. More so than one might think. He made money in the sugar trade which is how he became acquainted with Adolphus Moon, and he has made money here. More than enough to redeem his misdemeanors which have been many and various, I do assure you. He was sent down, for instance, from Oxford *and* dismissed by his regiment. He has kept low women of all creeds and colors quite openly and sometimes two or three at a time, like a veritable sultan. He has set himself up in dubious establishments, some of them far worse than the Fleece. He has lost caste and respectability . . ."

"And you wish to help him regain it?"

"Of course. I am a forgiving, Christian woman. Ask Uriah Colclough if I said one word to reproach him when he began to pay his court—if that is what one could call it—to Marie Moon. Ask Magda Braithwaite how patiently I bear the insult she heaps upon me. Ask your sainted mother, or Uriah Colclough's sainted mother, how very obligingly—and for *years*—I have fetched and carried their embroidery silks and smelling salts and endured their tedious conversation. And Adolphus Moon, if he were able, would have a word to say about how very forbearing and discreet I am. I am an angel, Gemma. Everyone knows it. So, naturally, I can forgive every one of Christie's trespasses. I cannot even *see* them, my dear. The dazzle of his gold quite obscures my vision. His also, it seems. For if he wishes to reclaim his position in society he needs the right wife to help him."

"Yourself?"

"Of course. My pedigree, particularly on my father's side, is a match for his."

"I see." Gemma smiled again, John-William's shrewdness and, increasingly, his authority, very clear in her eyes. "So when you went to tell Captain Goldsborough about Daniel, who were you really seeking to punish, Linnet?"

"I beg your pardon?"

"A simple enough question. Did you wish to punish the captain for preferring Miss Adeane? Or Miss Adeane for being preferred? Or me for being loved when you have never thought I deserved it?"

"Loved?" Linnet gave a harsh, croaking laugh that had anger and contempt and pain in it. "What nonsense, Gemma. Loved, indeed. The man is after your money. Like Tristan."

"No, Linnet."

"My dear—one would not expect you to admit it. Even to yourself. Not yet. But, nevertheless—my poor, rich little widow—so it is."

"If it pleases you to think so."

But nothing pleased Linnet any longer. Nothing remained to her. No faith in anyone. No hope. No joy in life.

"I loved my brother," she said suddenly. It was all she had left. All she had ever had. And, so long as he had been there to plan for and care for and fight for, it had been enough.

"He loved you too," said Gemma, quickly understanding.

"Dear God—of course he did." Linnet did not intend to be patronized. "I was everything to him. And you were . . ."

Nothing? Knowing it was not true and hating that knowledge, resenting it with all the long-stored bitterness of her heart, she swallowed and blinked rapidly, determined not to give this calm, plain little woman—half her size—the satisfaction of seeing her tears.

"My brother was the best man in the world. And as Christie Goldsborough demeans himself with Cara Adeane so are you demeaning my brother with Daniel Carey . . ."

Gemma rose to her feet, quietly.

"And you too, Linnet," she said, "with Ben Braithwaite."

It had been spoken. Linnet's exquisite, porcelain face became chalk, her light, laughing eyes blank and wild both together, a cornered and therefore a dangerous beast.

"You have been listening to his wife," she said. "And why not? You have so much in common. Poor Magda. Another plain, awkward, *passionate* woman like yourself, married for her father's money."

"I dare say. Does that excuse you?"

"*Excuse* me." Fury released itself suddenly in Linnet like a shower of sparks. "How dare you blame me? *You*—after the crimes you committed against my brother? I commit no adultery, Gemma Dallam. Ben Braithwaite—my lover—does that. As you did. I have no husband to deceive. So I am blameless. Blameless. I am his victim—and yours. He uses me—as you and your mother have done—for his convenience. As everyone does . . ."

"Are you not in love with him, then?"

Linnet made a strangled exclamation of contempt. "Love? What a fool you are. Love is for those who can afford it. Or for persons of low degree who have no thought beyond self-indulgence. If he had married me and given me the place in society I wanted—and deserved—oh yes, I would have loved him then. Dear God—how I would have loved him. No man would have had a wife more dedicated to his service. No man. He knew it. He knew—make no mistake—how clever and skillful and devoted I would have been. He even desired me. He married a rich fool. He continued to desire me. And when the time came that no one else did, I went to his bed because—yes—because I had nowhere else to go. Because it was better than nothing. Or so I thought. So I convinced myself . . ."

Pausing she seemed almost to gulp for breath and then, to her own distress and Gemma's, gave a long, shuddering sigh. "Yes. Dear Magda is quite right to be jealous and to weep her lonely nights away. I am his mistress. And I loathe it, Gemma—loathe it—loathe it—so that my skin crawls even as I am inviting him to touch me . . ."

"Linnet . . ."

"Oh no—don't stop me now. You wanted to see me shamed and brought down, I dare say—like everyone else. Why not? I would bring *you* down, Gemma, if I could. You know that. I have tried—haven't I?—often enough. With Tristan, whose affection for you was a knife forever in my back. With Daniel Carey, who might have been on his way to Liverpool by now, without seeing you, had I not interfered and delayed him. What a farce life is. Really. What a tangle. Poor Magda. And poor me. I have the man. She has the husband. We share him and he gives to each the very things we do not desire. She wants his passion. I want his position. I want to sit in his drawing-room and receive his guests. She wants to lie in his bed and suffer the indignity of his attentions, as I have to do. Except that to her they would be a pleasure. They are no pleasure to me."

She paused again, gulped once again, most painfully, for breath.

"Does he love you?" Gemma said.

"I have no idea. He made up his mind to have me. He has me. And he is generous. His demands are less burdensome, I suppose, and the material rewards greater than one might expect as a paid companion somewhere in the Punjab. So I calculated. And it saves me, if only in my own eyes and Magda's, from the brand of spinsterhood. I may be a whore, of course, but I am no longer an old maid. That matters to me."

"Will it last?"

Linnet shrugged, the fire out of her now, only its cold and bitter ashes remaining. "I shall make it my business to see that it does. I shall have to, shall I not? Since who else would have me now?"

"It may surprise you ..."

"No, Gemma. Don't talk to me of country doctors and parsons. Don't talk to me of enterprising women like Cara Adeane either. I was not bred to be a drudge in a vicarage or to open a shop, I was educated and trained to be the wife of a gentleman. Nothing else. And so ..."

"Yes?"

Tossing her silver head, setting her tulle frills swaying again, she smiled. "So I will take my share of the husband I am offered—my dear Benjamin—so ardent at the moment and so very disappointed in Magda, who seems quite unable to give him any peace or satisfaction or even children ..."

"Can you?"

"My dear—*of course*. I am the most magical mixture of peace and satisfaction any man could wish for. And as for children—Oh dear. He does so desire at least one child of his body. And although I have already turned thirty, so absolutely everybody keeps on so kindly reminding me—Who knows? Ardor cools. And I do believe Ben would always cherish the mother of his child. He might even marry her, in due course, should he find himself a widower, for the child's sake if not for the woman's. It would mean establishing me well away from Frizingley, of course. But I should not mind that. And Magda has never been very robust, you know. Do I shock you, Gemma?"

Gemma shook her head.

"Then perhaps you think me foolish—or pitiful? I assure you I am not. I shall survive, Gemma, in my fashion . . ."

"I hope so, Linnet."

"My dear—I am in no doubt at all. Will you wish me luck?"

"Indeed."

"And I will do the same—poor little Gemma—for I know of no one who will need it as much as you."

She left the room and Gemma sat down again, calm and smiling, her tranquil, competent hands immediately busy with pen and paper, her mind retaining Linnet's presence at no deeper level than the faint drift of lavender she had left on the air.

Linnet no longer worried her. Not even her mother, who would be perfectly happy as the wife of Mr. Dudley Stevens, her new husband. Only Gemma, who carried so much of him within her, truly remembering John-William. But he, too, would not grudge her this. She was busy now, and very sure of her own ability to perform each and every task—any task—she set herself. To make haste slowly, perhaps, but with the certainty not only of success but of great joy.

One step at a time. Tomorrow she would go and tell Miss Adeane what had happened to Daniel. And then there was the matter of his defense, his accommodation and treatment during his sentence, a level expanse—she rather thought—of happy, useful years to come, a whole new world of experience and experiment, of deep fulfillment, for her new-found, firm and steady feet to tread.

She had been thoroughly trained in the art of waiting. It would not be much longer now.

27

*F*rizingley had been shaken for a moment, no one denied that, but the Chartist dust soon settled, as the Luddite dust had settled years before, as it is the nature of all dust to settle, allowing life to continue very much as the Braithwaites and the Larks believed it should. A few arrests were made. Of the Chartist contingent which had set out for London one or two did not return but as these men had been known, in the first place, as discontented husbands rather than political activists, it was considered to be a private matter and left alone.

The dust was allowed to settle there too, the whole annoying episode of Chartism easily forgotten had it not been for the extraordinary insistence of Gemma Gage in paying for her own pet Chartist's defense. Shocking, of course. But, with neither father nor husband left to restrain her, she might go to the devil, or to the bankruptcy court more likely, in her own sweet way. A matter of regret to some, of high glee to others, and occasioning universal sympathy with her mother, Mrs. Amabel Dallam Stevens, who did not have sense enough, it appeared, to realize how miserable she ought to be, and with Miss Linnet Gage, who had felt obliged to quit the Dallam residence, taking refuge in a small house on the outskirts of town with a maid-of-all-work and a cat.

Poor Linnet Gage: although, indeed, she bravely kept up her spirits by spending far more on dress and adornment—it was noted—than she had ever done, appearing fresh every morning, it seemed, in some new creation from Miss Adeane's clever hands. Gossamer-fine confections of tulle and silver gauze and sprigged organdy totally unlike the flamboyant, almost Oriental tastes of Frizingley's other Queen of Fashion, the feverish and somehow hungry Magda Braithwaite, thin as a stick and restless as a hot wind, parading herself all day and every day in stridently colored satins, her gold bracelets jangling like fetters, the orange and emerald feathers in her hat as tall and unable to keep still as the lady herself.

Both Miss Gage and Mrs. Braithwaite ceding first place for elegance, of course, to Mrs. Marie Moon, the pale and lovely enchantress who had caught and held so many exceedingly willing victims in her spell. And, quite soon, *these* were the vital questions which Frizingley's upper echelon asked itself. If Marie Moon did not wish to marry again, as it seemed she did not, then to whom—when the time came—would she leave her money? To her pretty little Persian kitten Gussie Lark, or to Uriah Colclough, her spiritual adviser? Or had she, perhaps, some inconvenient relative, a sister or a child—a grandchild, even—hidden away in France? Would Miss Linnet Gage succeed, after all, in enticing Captain Goldsborough, or *someone* to the altar? Or could the hints concerning her virtue possibly be true? Could it really be that the chaotic Magda showered Linnet with invitations and drove her up and down in her carriage only because her husband forced her so to do, keeping her quiet with presents of jewelry and new pianos and—even worse—his occasional favors, like some kind of male harlot, in her bed? In which case might it not be advisable to keep a sharp lookout for any suspicious increase in Linnet's figure, although—to the chagrin of many—she seemed to be getting even more slender, Magda positively thin, while that other subject of scandal, Gemma Gage, had a bloom on her like a peach and a waistline that had not budged an inch.

Or had it? Miss Adeane would know.

"Mrs. Gage is looking very well, Miss Adeane?"

Cara nodded and smiled.

"Miss Adeane—would you not agree that Miss Linnet Gage has a frail look about her these days?"

Cara murmured that she would.

"Whereas Mrs. Magda Braithwaite seems to be burning away quite to the bone—like a stick of firewood?"

Cara agreed with that too.

She had lost weight herself, although no one appeared to notice. Why should they? She could not sleep either, nor eat very much, which seemed ironic, now that she had, all to herself, a feather bed big enough for two and could afford any delicacy she wanted. As she could afford "time" and that strange substance called "leisure," once so desirable, now so perplexing, so heavy on her hands, such a void to be somehow and very inexpertly filled.

Work and struggle were both familiar to her. She understood the fight but was uncomfortable, it seemed, with the victory, if it could be called that. And now that her business was running smoothly, her customers loyal, her competition insignificant, her workrooms and her salesrooms competently staffed, her bank balance healthy and her cash-box beneath the floorboards always full, there were many times when, quite simply, she had no idea what to do.

She had achieved not merely her goal but her wildest dreams. What next? To have more of the same in a richer measure? She could do that now with half her mind, leaving the other half far too much liberty to pester her with inconvenient questions. Why? What now? What is it worth? To whom? *For* whom? She could not even pretend that she had done all this for herself. No. Why try? It had been done to save Odette and Liam from destitution. Had she been free to choose—had her father not so casually abandoned them—she would have thrown in her lot with Daniel Carey, and lived poor no doubt but, just possibly, happy. She was free now. Free and richer than she had ever expected. And the time for loving Daniel had passed. She accepted that without pain. Just as she accepted that there had never been a time for loving Luke. Yet she was empty and lonely. Empty in the presence of everything she had always wanted to fill her, lonely in a constant, ever-clamoring crowd.

Occasionally she had tea with Gemma Gage who, no longer caring what anyone had to say of her, was placidly making arrangements to rent a house in York should Daniel be detained in the Castle prison. Occasionally she dined with O'Halloran, who kept the livery stable, or a certain railway engineer whenever he happened to be staying in Frizingley. Occasionally she took Madge Percy to the theater and supper afterward at a Leeds hotel. Once she spent three tedious days and nights at the sea. She wrote letters to her mother and her Aunt Teresa concerning the welfare of her son and wept a little, sometimes, at her aunt's refusal to allow her the satisfaction of declining to visit them by the simple process of not inviting her. She wrote letters to her son and gritted her teeth over his stilted replies. She walked on the moor with her dog, designed her dresses, cared for her face and her figure and the glossy sheen of her hair, sparkled—so long as anyone was looking—like the polished, faceted and hollow diamond Christie had made her.

She heard nothing from Luke although she had written to him several times since the Chartist troubles. She had seen Christie only in the distance, limping badly, and heard nothing from him, no message, no curt command, no word. He had let her go. Or cast her off. Her prayers, then—in his direction—had been answered. She was free of him too. Her own woman. Just as she had always wanted. Yet the sight of Oliver Rattrie in the foyer of the station hotel, raising his tall silk hat to her, his eyes no longer sore but horribly knowing, always caused her an uncomfortable pang. What could he tell her, she wondered? Had Christie replaced her? And how soon? And what did it matter? Now that she was free, why was it that she had suddenly lost all her enthusiasms and her mad urges to do this or that or the other? Now that she could do anything she pleased it seemed such a pity—such a waste—that nothing managed to please her any more. Or not enough to make a fuss about.

She was like a bird with the cage-door open and afraid to fly. How very stupid. Yet such birds did fly away eventually. Or almost always. Perhaps all she required was time to accustom herself to the astonishment of affluence and the perfect liberty of being needed by no one.

Her own woman.

"I am so very easy and comfortable now," she wrote to Odette, "I have trouble in thinking of something to want."

A great trouble. She who had wanted everything the world had to offer at least twice over. What a death it was now, what a sorry decay of the spirit, to live in this dreary realm of plenty and peace. This flat pasturage, this safe harbor, where nothing challenged her. This tame and—oh, so stuffy, paradise.

And then toward the summer's end her housekeeper came to her most apologetically at breakfast time with the information that there was a "person" at her door who would not go away. An old woman tall enough to be a Grenadier guard, with a face like dusty granite, carrying something wrapped in a blanket shawl. A formidable old woman who could not be persuaded that Miss Adeane did not receive callers at this hour of the day and who had planted herself in the doorway like a gnarled old tree which might have been growing there, immovable and distinctly malevolent, for generations.

"A Mrs. Thackray," the housekeeper said.

Throwing down her napkin and picking up her trailing taffeta skirts Cara ran downstairs as if to a lover, her pulses racing with the excitement of moorland water released from its winter confinement by the merest stirring of spring. Just one warm breeze. What more was needed? Just one breath from the past, and she was her bustling, busy self again. The nurturer, the provider, the bearer of fire and water that she had always been.

Was there news? Help to be given? Did someone need her again? Sairellen? So it was. Incredibly dusty and travel-stained as if she had come from Timbuctoo instead of Nottingham, and so old—so very old—so weary. Her craggy face hardly a woman's face any longer, stripped by grim endurance of its final femininity, Luke's face as it would be when he became an old and sorely tested man.

Luke's face. Where was he? How was it that he had allowed his mother to come here alone in that rusty old skirt and boots it would be kinder not to notice?

At least she could alter that.

She began to say many things and finish none of them. Her words, her cries of welcome, her questions overflowing now like the same moorland streams which had been her pulse-beat a moment ago. To which Sairellen listened, impassive, unimpressed, apparently uncaring. The old Sairellen—except that she was so very much older— her arms folded, her eyes sardonic and grim, her mouth unyielding, humorless, and hard. And when Cara had finished, "He told me you'd take the child," she said.

"What child? Luke's child?"

"Well of course, lass. Have a bit of sense. Who else's child do you think I'd have carried here from Nottingham?"

And pushing back the shawl she revealed a tiny, sleeping child perhaps two years old, straddling her hip and held there by the blanket, peasant fashion, as once and for dozens of miles together, Cara had carried Liam. Luke's child. A girl's face, petal-fine and soft, a flushed cheek, a curl or two of thin, fair hair. A miracle. Where was Luke? And Anna?

"Come upstairs," she said anticipating distress and not wishing to suffer it here on her doorstep for anyone to see. "Come and sit down."

"Aye, lass. I will."

They went upstairs, Sairellen sitting down heavily without a word, the child still on her lap, a stool at her scandalously ill-shod feet.

Boots which looked as if they had walked every step of the way from Nottingham.

With shock, Cara realized that they had.

"The train . . . ?" she said weakly but Sairellen, quickly understanding her meaning, waved it aside.

"I don't hold with trains."

"You mean you couldn't afford the fare."

She had forgotten—*almost*—how it felt to have no money at all, not one penny or the hope of any. Nothing. So that the only way to get to one's destination was to walk. And she had been twenty, not seventy, when such a necessity had last befallen her.

"Where is he, Sairellen?" It was time now to know. "In prison?"

"Aye. I reckon you'd call it that. A floating prison. Unless he's arrived by now. They sentenced him at the beginning of May and, since I don't rightly know where Australia is, I don't know how long it takes to get there."

Neither did Cara. The other side of the world, she supposed. Wherever that was. Very far away.

"They transported him? Like John Mitchel?"

"So they did. A Nottingham man, you see. One of Feargus O'Connor's own. The only Chartist to be elected. Luke helped him to that."

"And you're proud of him, aren't you, Sairellen."

Cara's own first instinct had been to tear her hair and beat her breast.

"Aye, lass. That I am." And there was that, in Sairellen's tone, which gave clear warning that she would do well to keep her weeping and wailing to herself.

"Did he go to London, too, with the petition?"

"Of course he did." What else? Cara was in no doubt that Sairellen would have gone herself, had she not been needed at home by the child. And Anna?

"Sairellen," she whispered urgently, "is there nothing to be done?"

Someone to bribe to get him better food and cleaner water, as Gemma was doing in her dignified, placid way for Daniel? Something? Could one really be condemned to stand helplessly by, doing nothing?

"Aye, lass." Sairellen's eyes were like stones set deep in her head. "*Wait*. That's all. Seven years. And since I haven't got seven years by anybody's reckoning I've brought you the child, like he said. Anna's gone. Dead and buried two weeks ago. She'd been ailing since the little lass was born and Luke's sentence finished her. She knew I hadn't long to last and nobody ever thought she could manage with the little lass alone. You'll have seen women die like that, I reckon, of—well—whatever it is that kills them."

"Despair," said Cara flatly.

Yes, she had seen it. Once, very nearly, in Odette. But it had not killed Cara herself. Nor Sairellen, who had spent her last penny burying Luke's wife in a proper grave—none of the dismal shoveling away designed for paupers—and then set off to walk, from Nottingham. How long? Ten days?

"When did you last eat?"

"I don't eat much, lass, at my age."

At least these were practical issues which required no more than her hand on a bell, a few orders for tea and muffins, fresh milk and new bread.

"Eat." It was done without ceremony or gratitude, as a matter of course, Sairellen eating to fuel her body as one might fuel an engine for the few miles still left inside it, while Cara stared at the sleepy child, looking for Luke and finding Anna.

"How old is she?"

"She'll be three on Christmas Day."

"She's very small."

"Aye. She takes after her mother."

"Were they happy, Sairellen?"

"I believe so. Aye—I know so. They were happy, Cara Adeane."

She smiled, poured out more tea, left the room for a further consultation with her housekeeper and, returning, found Sairellen dozing by the fireside, the child sitting placidly on the hearthrug. Dear God. She had forgotten the dog. That savage brute. That peevish monster, jealous of his private and pampered kingdom by her fire. She moved forward swiftly to throw herself between the lethal jaw and the fragile, elfin hand reaching out, with unmixed delight, to pat that most churlish of canine heads. No need. For what she heard was no crunch of tender bone but a resigned sigh from the animal, a gurgle of pleasure from the child. What she saw was the wagging of a stumpy, grudging tail, a wide smile which rendered the pale, plain face of Anna Rattrie's daughter luminous with joy.

Sairellen opened her eyes.

"I wasn't sleeping."

"No. But you soon will be."

She had told them to clear out the room at the end of the passage where she stored her fancy goods and cosmetics and prepare it for her guests. Two soft beds with feather mattresses and brand new linen, rugs on the floor and pictures on the walls, a marble wash-stand with a jug and basin in flowered china.

"Nay, lass, I've done what I set out to do," said Sairellen. "I've brought little Anna. That's what my lad wanted. So if you'll take her..."

"Of course I'll take her."

"Then I'll be on my way."

"Just where?"

"Is that any business of yours, Cara Adeane?"

"If I make it so. Because there's nowhere you can go—is there?"

Only "away," wandering off like an old cat to die in a ditch somewhere, in solitary dignity, a trouble to no one. She wouldn't have it.

She wanted to be troubled, in any case.

"You'll stay here, Sairellen Thackray."

"I reckon I'll make my own mind up about that..."

"You'll do as you're told..."

Sairellen stood up, her bones beneath their sagging, yellowing skin still tall and valiant, still capable of making short work of any little flibbertigibbet such as Cara Adeane; or dying in the attempt.

"I don't take charity," she said. "Never have. Never will. And that's that."

"You stubborn old woman," Cara yelled at her. "He told you to bring me the child because he wanted me to look after you—don't you know that? He had to give you a reason for coming, to save your stupid pride. He trusted me not to let you wander off again and I won't—dammit, Sairellen—even if I have to tie you."

Sairellen sat down again. Heavily. Gladly, perhaps.

"Don't use foul language to me, my girl," she said.

"You'll stay."

"Happen so."

"No 'happen' about it. You'll stay. And don't think of it as charity because I can easily employ you. There's always work to be done. There's—well—a hundred things."

"Aye," said Sairellen, closing her eyes. "You'll think of something if you put your mind to it. But he won't come back, you know, lass, if that's what you're hoping for . . ."

"Of course he will. He's strong enough . . ." Cara's mind leaped instantly to survival, the rigors of a convict ship and of penal servitude, men like Luke in chains, digging and tending an alien land, building roads and railways and bridges as her own people had done in England. Surely he could survive that?

Sairellen shook her head. "Strength has nothing to do with it. He'll serve his time and then he'll stay out there, wherever it is. That's what I reckon. Why shouldn't he? Anna's gone. I won't be far behind. Seven years from now he won't know the child. And if you've made a fine young lady of her, as I expect you will, she might be none too pleased to know him. So he'll leave well alone. He'll stay. A new land. A new opportunity. That's what he talked about, sometimes, before they took him. You'll never see him again, Cara Adeane. Neither will I."

But she would see his child grow up. She would have that much. That miracle. How wonderful that it was through Luke this joy had come to her. No child of her own body but a child nevertheless, coming to her now when the easy circumstances of her life would allow her to be a mother. No substitute for Liam but a girl whose wide, breathless smile was already tugging at her heart. A little doll to be cherished and protected and dressed up in lace and sprigged muslin, who would grow into a "young lady" of education and manners upon whom could be lavished every advantage—every single one—that Cara's own girlhood had lacked. Luke had given her what she most needed. Another human being to work for and care for. An opportunity to redeem the mistakes of her hectic past. He had sent her the means to start again.

"Sairellen," and she was pleading now. "Whatever ails you, there are doctors, you know. And with proper food and rest . . ."

Sairellen smiled, not unkindly, and shook her head. "Nay, lass. There's a time for everything and I've had mine. More than my share, I reckon. And more than enough. Because what have I to show for it? One son alive—if he is alive—out of thirteen. And this little scrap of a girl that he's given to you. I've outgrown my usefulness, Cara. Some women can cope with helplessness. Some even like it. Not me. Not you either."

No. She could not cope with it. Could not stand even the thought of it. Could hardly bear to see it now in this gnarled, grim-visaged woman she resembled far more than she had ever resembled pretty, patient Odette.

Outgrown her usefulness? Never. Not so long as Cara needed her.

"Sairellen," she said, hot tears in her eyes, kneeling now beside the old woman's chair like a penitent before an imperial throne, "let me look after you. *Please.*"

Sairellen sighed. "Aye, lass," she said, in the manner of one who bestows a favor. "You might as well."

Daniel Carey was sentenced that autumn to spend the following year in confinement at York castle, the leniency of his sentence occasioning no surprise in those who knew how diligently Mrs. Gemma Gage had employed the influence of her father's name and fortune on his behalf. Foolish Mrs. Gage. Daughter of a foolish mother, the eternally romantic Amabel, who would be returning from her own second honeymoon—in the south of France, of all scandalous places—in time to attend her daughter's second wedding.

On the whole Frizingley felt much inclined to wash its hands of the Dallams, seeing no point any longer in being surprised at anything they did, although Gemma's attendance at her lover's trial in the company of Miss Cara Adeane *did* give rise to a ripple—no more—of speculation.

Could Miss Adeane, perhaps, be a sister of Mr. Carey's? Mrs. Magda Braithwaite rather thought so, although Miss Linnet Gage very knowingly smiled and shook her head. Very sweet of Magda, of course, to take that view, if a little unworldly—dear Magda—but what of the little girl Miss Adeane had acquired so suddenly? A dear creature, no doubt—if one happened to care for children—in all the frills and finery with which Miss Adeane kept on smothering her. Finery, indeed, far and away greater than anyone would be likely to lavish on a child who was not a—well—a *near* relation. And who was the grim-faced and exceedingly haughty old woman one saw so often taking the air in Miss Adeane's carriage? A positive virago, one heard, who, having driven Miss Adeane's housekeeper to give her notice, had now taken charge herself, keeping Miss Adeane's maids and apprentices in better order—it must be said—than they had ever been.

But, after all, so long as Miss Adeane continued to turn out her exquisite dresses, to fulfill her commitments promptly and pleasantly and to make herself so very obliging about the face creams and powders one's husband or father forbade one to buy, one might allow her to call her private life her own.

So she called it.

The departure of her housekeeper had provided accommodation for Sairellen, a handsomely furnished room on the ground floor behind the kitchen, with two maids and a cook-daily at her command. While Cara lived upstairs with the dog and the child, the one in his habitual basket guarding her money, the other in a nursery with pink silk walls and a pink muslin bed, a wardrobe overflowing with pink frills. Although Miss Anna Elizabeth Sairellen Thackray, an elf with a mind of her own, was often to be found curled up on the drawing-room hearth-rug, her head on the dog's patiently heaving flank, her cloudy blue eyes enraptured by the pictures they could see in the fire.

A child with a wide, breathless smile and a breathless wonder at everything she saw in the happy, friendly, quite wonderful world around her. A child who gave affection freely and joyfully, finding nothing surprising about it and who chattered and gurgled with no vestige of shyness, seeing no reason why anyone should do her harm. Anna Rattrie, as she might have been, without the scars of her rat-poor, rat-infested childhood; with Luke's capacity for reflection.

Cara loved her and told her so. She loved Sairellen too, although she knew better than to mention that. It was the cornerstone of her nature to look after those she loved and now she had the means to do it. The money to supply their material needs. The time to get to know them.

Her letters to Liam and to her mother became easier, happier. She wrote to Daniel in his prison cell and, by tortuous means, in the spirit with which one might cast adrift a message in a bottle, to Luke with news of his daughter and his mother. Once, encountering Christie Goldsborough face to face in the station yard, she paused signifying her willingness to speak to him—a notable concession on her part, she considered, after the way he had treated her—although he had simply raised his hat and walked away. Still limping badly, she noticed, as he approached the sporting phaeton and the high-bred, high-tempered bay horse waiting for him in the street.

All too clearly his fractures or his severed tendons or whatever Ned O'Mara had done to his left leg had healed badly. Watching him, she'd hoped, for a savage moment, that he might miss his footing, fall and break his other leg to match. Or his neck. But he had reached the high-perched driving seat, not easily perhaps, but safely enough, leaving her to trot tamely away in her hired, livery stable landau.

And when her quarter's rent fell due she paid it disdainfully to a suave and smiling Oliver Rattrie.

She was free of Christie. It was what she had always wanted. Why was it, then, that freedom still did not seem to be living up to her expectations? Was the habit of captivity too strong in her to be shaken?

"How is the captain these days?" she suddenly inquired of Oliver, wishing she had bitten out her tongue instead.

"Planning a trip to Antigua, I believe," he replied smoothly, not looking up from his ledgers.

With whom?

"My sister-in-law is going abroad quite shortly," Gemma Gage told her a few days later, sounding most unconcerned about it. "The south of France—she says."

"How can she afford it?" Frizingley wondered.

Putting together some sketches for traveling dresses which Miss Linnet Gage had ordered, Cara realized that her mind was spitting out thoughts of a most vicious nature concerning shipwrecks in shark-infested waters, rebellious cutters of sugar-cane brandishing their knives for quite another purpose, death-watch beetles in the linen closet, snakes in the grass. Yes. That was Linnet Gage. A snake. And Christie. They would do well together, discussing their respective pedigrees and the number of dukes and earls to whom they were related, while murderous natives broke down the door.

Linnet and Christie. She was not in the least surprised about it. No more than she had been surprised by Daniel and Gemma. Anna and Luke. Odette and Kieron the Enchanter.

Nor did she care.

She had her child, and her dog. Every fine evening that smoky, gold autumn she put both in her carriage and drove them out to a point beyond Frizingley Green where there were trees and a level stretch of shallow water, leaving the landau on the road while child and dog together rustled through magic mountains of fallen leaves, each one turning to gold in Anna's inquiring yet always careful hands.

"A leaf? *Leaf?*" What riches. What marvels this world had in store. Leaf. And stone. Root. Soil. Beloved *dog*.

Cara laughed at her.

"Look, Anna. Sunset." And with the red dazzle in her eyes it was the crackling of those golden leaves underfoot, one step heavier and surer than the other, which warned her of the approach of Christie.

That, and the sudden tight vibrations in the air. The musk.

She was sitting on the wide stump of a tree, with plenty of room for two, and he sat down beside her without a word, his black fur cloak hunched around him like a storm-cloud, his mood she thought, enveloping him in another, both eyes open now and all his gleaming wolf's teeth intact, but the cheek he turned toward her still sliced from eye to chin by an angry scar.

She made no attempt to conceal her interest in it but he did not turn away.

"That cut is healing badly," she said. "It was infected, I suppose."

"Yes."

"And the leg, by the look of you. Does it give you much pain?"

"Oh yes. Constant agony. Every step a torment."

"Why walk then?" She had not heard another carriage. And he had come a long way on foot from the station hotel.

He shrugged, quite heavily, as if his shoulders felt the weight of the black, musky fur.

"My dear," he said. "A man on horseback may not limp but he doesn't come to terms with his disability either. Or learn to overcome it. And, in any case, it has the effect, I find, of tugging at female heart-strings . . ."

"Not mine!"

"I dare say."

"Did you do anything to Ned O'Mara?"

"What should I have done? He seemed to think I had done enough already."

"Yes. You went too far. I told you so."

And now there was nothing more he could do to her either. She was free and unafraid of him. Both his menace and his enchantment dimmed beyond recall. Just a man with a bad leg hunched up in his cape and feeling the cold, a suspicion of pain about him, a frown of effort between his brows telling her that he had paid dearly to get here. Her landlord to whom she owed nothing and who could claim nothing from her, any more, but her rent.

"That dog's temper was never sweet," he said. "Is the child safe with him?"

"Oh yes. He loves her."

"Indeed?" He watched them for a moment, quietly smiling. "Beauty and the Beast, then?"

"I suppose so."

"She is Anna Rattrie's daughter, is she not? Oliver Rattrie's niece?"

"Yes."

"Does that not make Oliver her next of kin?"

She had not thought of that. She thought of it now. Considered what Christie might do with it. And then turned her own, undamaged body very slightly on the tree stump toward him.

"No. She has been left in the care of her grandmother, who is living with me. And if your boy Oliver makes any attempt to claim her I shall certainly strangle him. Make sure he knows that."

There was a slight, almost strangled pause and then, in a sudden and quite strangled fashion, he laughed.

"There is no cause for alarm. He will not approach her unless I tell him. And I shall not."

"How kind."

"Yes. I think so. She is the only card I had to play and I have willingly surrendered her ..."

"Games," she said. "Games—all over again." She had had enough of that. "I don't think I want to talk to you, Christie. I don't *have* to talk to you, do I—unless I want to."

"No. Surely not."

"And it was vile of you—do you know that?—to have Oliver Rattrie turn me out of the Fleece that night."

"I know."

"So why did you do it?"

"Because I wanted you to stay—somewhat too badly."

For a moment she stared at him, incredulous, aghast.

"Oh God," she said. "Will you say something, just for once, that I can understand?"

"Yes. Have you missed me—in any way at all, Cara?"

"No. Have you missed me?"

"I should not be here otherwise. Should I?"

She smiled at him. "Then you have my leave to go away again." Had she really said that? Yes. And how she had enjoyed every syllable of it. So much so that she smiled at him again. "I'm going home now in any case."

Jumping to her two sound, elegantly-shod feet, she called the dog and the child and went blithely across the uneven ground to her carriage, still smiling.

"Won't you give a lame man a ride to town?" he said, having managed to keep up with her.

"Why should I?"

Once, a long time ago, he had driven off and left her shivering in the snow with two plush tablecloths wrapped around her. A long time ago.

"Because you think you are getting the upper hand of me and want to enjoy it."

Because she was a damned fool.

He got in beside her and snapped autocratic fingers at the dog, who went obediently under the seat at his command.

"Dog?" said Anna, who wanted the animal's head on her lap.

"No," he said pleasantly. "Little girls sit on chairs. Dogs on the floor."

Anna looked puzzled.

"Believe me. I know," he said, smiling down at the child who, to Cara's intense annoyance, lifted up her breathless, eager little face and smiled back.

Beauty and the Beast indeed.

He came with her, as if by right, into the shop and, since he *did* own the premises, she could hardly deny him. Or so she told herself as she climbed the stairs to her apartment, the dog and the man still behind her, both panting hard, the child going off to be cleaned and tidied for bed by her grandmother.

"A glass of wine?" She had noticed how the three flights of stairs had tired him but did not ask him to sit down. He sat, nevertheless.

"Brandy would suit me better."

"Certainly." Brandy it should be. And not his brandy either, but her own purchase, her own crystal goblets. She would even take a sip of it herself.

"You are looking far from well," she told him joyfully. "Rather drawn—and old—in fact . . ."

"Thank you."

"Never mind. The sunshine in Antigua will do you good. And Miss Gage will look after you."

Was it the brandy that had gone to her head? So quickly? She doubted it. Triumph, more likely. And a sparkling, tantalizing little imp of pure mischief.

"Miss Gage has nothing to do with me."

"Really?"

"Why should you think so?"

"Because she is going abroad too, and certainly can't afford to pay for it herself..."

"Not with me. She is going abroad to have Ben Braithwaite's child, I imagine. Don't you? Whereas I may not go at all. In fact, I think not..."

"Don't stay for me," she said. "Because I don't want you. And you can't force me to take you either. Can you?"

"No. I never could. I think it high time you understood that. It was always in your power to leave me."

"Yes. And now I have."

"Cara," and something in his tone cut through her growing smugness to hold her attention. "I was immensely jealous of Daniel Carey—*insanely* jealous one might even say..."

"You had good reason."

"He *was* your lover, then?"

"No. But that doesn't seem to matter. If he sent to me now for help I would do the same things all over again."

"Yes. I see. Then perhaps it is as well you will be spared the trouble—since he is to marry Gemma Gage, I understand...?"

"That he is. And I shall make her look very handsome on her wedding day. Gold satin. I have already done the sketches."

"So—could one take it, then, that your affection for Mr. Carey is..."

"None of your business, Christie."

He looked away from her and then, his hands clenching the arms of the chair, gave her a somber, haggard look.

He was in pain. She was very glad of it.

"Do you thoroughly detest me, Cara?"

"I think you have given me every reason."

"Deliberately."

"Games again, Christie."

"No. A simple need to protect oneself—*my*self..."

"Games."

"Survival, Cara. And that is what I am. A survivor. So are you. Whatever threatens me I destroy. And quickly. I strike first, and fatally if I can. You know that. You even understand the necessity."

She nodded.

"What I can use I take, Cara. What I cannot use I discard. What I found necessary to discard in my youth was a certain inconvenient inheritance from my parents—It may not be possible for a child to feel compassion for a father, or a mother. Certainly I felt none for mine. I watched the turmoil they lived in—it would have been hard to miss it—and what I felt was embarrassment. I never pitied them. I was ashamed. They may have thought themselves magnificent in their passion and their jealous rages. I thought them undignified. When my mother fell to her death down the manor stairs I believed she had brought it on herself—thrown her life away. Wastefully. When my father began to destroy himself with drink and all that goes with it, he may have thought himself a hero. I thought him a fool. I did not intend to lose either my life, or my dignity, in that sorry fashion."

He paused and gave her the same somber, haggard look which had so pleased her a moment ago.

"Do you understand any of this, Cara?"

"Of course not. How could I? I'm just an ignorant peasant from across the water. You're wasting your time, you know, talking to me."

"Very likely." He sighed and stared into the fire for a moment, finding it too small, she supposed, feeling the cold again; and thinking hard. *Scheming*—she never for a moment doubted it—although he was trying not to let it show.

"However," he said, "the only card I have left is to talk. Isn't it? I did not *like* my father. He offended me. His type still does. And when I realized that I carried a part of his nature in mine—as was inevitable— I crushed it. Thoroughly. Or else I channeled it in useful directions. In me his wild jealousy became a straightforward urge to possess for my pleasure. Not women only, but money—authority—the upper hand. And I had no need to force myself into this mould. It came quite naturally to me. I have enjoyed my life, Cara—playing my games. Self-centered perhaps—but not a fool. Safeguarding myself by associating with women like Marie Moon and Audrey Covington-Pym of whom one could hardly be jealous if one tried. And with girls like you who happened to take my fancy. Except that you took rather more, I am sorry to say . . ."

"Are you?"

"Yes. Very sorry. It was the last thing I could have wanted to happen. So I put chains on you. And—to test myself—dared you to break them."

"Why didn't you make me fall in love with you instead?"

Silence fell.

"Could I have done that?" he said.

She shrugged and smiled and, moving around the room, she began arranging and re-arranging the many small objects on her inlaid tables. Little things. Insignificant things. She had not the least intention in the world of giving him an answer.

"You would have found it uncomfortable, I think," he said. "Loving me?"

"I suppose I would."

Another silence. Much longer.

"Very well, Cara. Hear me out. What I will do is build a house for you. As fine as you like . . ."

"Here?"

"On the outskirts of town. Near enough to get to the shop early every morning, if you wanted to . . ."

"Of course I want to. And what about this apartment?"

"Give it to that formidable old woman you've taken in—with a maid to look after her. She'll keep a sharp eye on your property, all right. She likes her independence, by the look of her. So you'd be doing her a service."

"*And* salvaging your conscience for having her evicted to begin with."

"I have no conscience."

"So you say. What about the child?"

"You would have her with you—naturally. And your own child back again, if you want him."

She wanted him. "No!" she said sharply. It was too late for that. He seemed to understand.

"Very well. A home, then, Cara, and all that goes with it. I can afford most things you will be likely to ask for."

"And you would live with me, in this fine house—openly?"

He nodded. "I would."

Carefully, with great concentration, she adjusted, very slightly, the position of the clock on her mantelshelf and the candlesticks on either side of it. A delicate task, to be undertaken with care and skill, before she turned to smile at him.

"So what would I do in your fine house all day, Christie?"

He shrugged. "What is it women do . . . ?"

"Wait for their men to come home," she said flatly. "And put up with whatever mood is on them when they do. That's how it seems to me, at any rate, from the ladies who sit here every afternoon drinking my tea, fine and haughty as you please and as worried underneath as any weaving-woman from St. Jude's about what 'himself' might have to say to the size of my bills. No, thank you very kindly, Christie, but I won't be a fine lady in a fine house—begging for crumbs like a pet sparrow. It might be cake instead of bread and the bars of the cage might be gold. But a cage is a cage for all that, and I haven't a mind to it."

"What do you want then?"

He had thrown that challenge at her feet once before, with that same casual tossing of the hand. A gentleman dispensing arrogant largesse to a drab in a blue plush cloak. But she could afford to be arrogant herself now. And hard. If she chose to be.

"I want another shop," she told him. "In Bradford where the Tannenbaums and their smart friends come from. And one in Leeds . . ."

"I have no property in Bradford, Cara."

"Have you not? How very remiss. Then build some—can't you? A big corner site, three or four floors high, all in carved stone with windows as tall as I am and my name in gold letters *this* big—"

"*My* name," he said.

"What?"

"My name, Cara." He did not sound particularly pleased about it. Simply a little resigned and very determined. "Why so astonished? Should I agree to make such a sizeable investment then naturally I shall put my mark on it."

"On a shop-front?"

"Why not? So long as it is the grandest and best in the North. Goldsborough's."

"Adeane's." She too was very determined and had no resignation in her anywhere.

He smiled, slowly, with speculation and something beneath it she was, as yet, unwilling to recognize.

"Would 'Goldsborough & Adeane' suit you better?"

It would not. "*My* name," she told him through clenched teeth. *"Mine."* Already she could see it there, glittering down at her from a façade of mellow, honey-colored stone, a royal swan of a building dominating the commercial duck-pond of Bradford—Leeds—Halifax . . . *Adeane's.*

"My name," she said, prepared to fight him to the death for it.

"Very well."

Why had he given in so easily? What trickery was this? He told her.
"There *is* a solution . . ."

"Oh . . . ?"

"Make your name mine . . . as a last resort, of course. Marry me, Cara."

Had he thrown this at her too, like a challenge?

"And if I did," she threw back at him, "then I'd still call it Adeane's."

He turned his head away from her and then gave her, once more, his somber look.

"Would you now?"

"So I would."

"What else would you do, Cara? Marry me or fight me every afternoon across a boardroom table? Or both? Yours is the power to choose."

Power over *him*? Or was he using the lure of it to tempt her into yet another trap? A dazzling bait, a lilting, dancing enticement until the cage door slammed shut behind her, giving the power—as always—to him?

"Games, Christie."

"No. No games. The truth is . . ."

"Do you know what the truth is?"

"Oh yes."

The haggard eyes seemed about to tell her, the hard, tense mouth to make revelations which aroused her curiosity, as the weary line of his shoulders, the fatigue and the hint of pain in him stirred her compassion. Deliberately, she supposed. Christie the Enchanter. His sorcery more powerful and tortuous and fascinating than ever her father's. Of another order entirely. Christie. Grand Master of his Craft. And her Craft too, of course.

Could she match him now? It seemed to her that she could.

"Cara . . . ?" Once more the haggard look.

"Don't play the wounded soldier with me, Christie Goldsborough," she told him, half-furious, half-amused. "Oh no—don't come limping to me now, all out of breath and broken down, and expect to melt my heart-strings . . . Because you won't . . ."

"Will I not?"

"You will not. Because it's all nonsense, Christie. You may look lame but you don't feel it. You can still go anywhere you please and do as you please and get any woman you want . . . Well—can't you?"

"Yes." The answer came like a slap, with not the slightest doubt about it. "*That* I can."

"Then why...?"

"Because it has been a long time, Cara, since I wanted *any* woman." He paused.

"I want you, Miss Adeane." The confession did not appear to delight him.

"Oh."

"Is th t an answer?"

"I shouldn't think so."

"*Cara...*" He allowed her to see his pain again.

"What, Christie?"

"Would it be possible, do you think, Cara, to start afresh? To give ourselves another chance...?" Slowly, with the merest hint in her own heart now, of those other things she would name as and when she pleased, she smiled at him.

"It might."

"I hope so. I would like that, Cara. Very much—as it happens..."

"Would you?" She smiled at him again. "Then you had better be on your best behavior, Captain Goldsborough. Truly. If you want to have any dealings with Miss Adeane of Market Square, that is. A very particular woman she is, believe me, and not easily pleased. Not easily impressed either. Why should she be—with her wardrobes crammed full of silk dresses and her reputation for sound, honest trading from here to Manchester? A man would have to put himself out to *win* a woman like that. And think himself lucky if he succeeded. Wouldn't he now, Christie?"

He looked away from her and back again.

"Yes, Cara," he said.

How much had those two words cost him? Supposing it to be a great deal she rewarded him with a smile.

"And now I must go downstairs a moment."

"Why?"

She saw that he would find the moment long. Uneasy, perhaps. That he would listen for her returning footsteps on the stairs and worry, even, that she might not come.

How wonderful.

"Because I am a careful shopkeeper, Christie, and it is absolutely necessary at this hour to check my doors and my locks and see that everything is in order. For instance, no candles left burning in the workroom and no . . ."

"All right—all right . . ." Irritably he waved her away and, pausing in the doorway, she turned and looked at him, his legs stretched out toward the hearth, his eyes closed, the fickle dog lying in adoration at his feet, both of them wishing she would put more coal on the fire, both of them ill-tempered, over-bred and over-complicated and vulnerable in a shared need of her which did not entirely please them.

But she must go now and see to her lamps and her locks. Must go about her own business at her own pace. Leisurely, she thought. One step at a time. No need for haste. Choosing her own moments to suit her own needs. And theirs, of course: Sairellen and Anna; Liam, whose needs she had fulfilled by letting him go free; the dog and the man who would both be here, she knew, staring into the fire, when she came back.